Oswald Cray by Mrs Henry Wood

Ellen Price was born on 17th January 1814 in Worcester.

In 1836 she married Henry Wood, whose career in banking and shipping meant living in Dauphiné, in the South of France, for two decades. During their time there they had four children.

Henry's business collapsed and he and Ellen together with their four children returned to England and settled in Upper Norwood near London.

Ellen now turned to writing and with her second book 'East Lynne' enjoyed remarkable popularity. This enabled her to support her family and to maintain a literary career.

It was a career in which she would write over 30 novels including 'Danesbury House', 'Oswald Cray', 'Mrs. Halliburton's Troubles', 'The Channings' and 'The Shadow of Ashlydyat'.

Sadly, her husband, Henry died in 1866.

Ellen though continued to strive on. In 1867, she purchased the magazine 'Argosy', founded two years previously by Alexander Strahan. She was a prolific writer and wrote much of the magazine herself although she had some very respected contributors, amongst them Hesba Stretton and Christina Rossetti. Although she would gradually pare down writing for the magazine she continued to write novel after novel. Such was her talent that for a time she was, in Australia, more popular than Charles Dickens.

Apart from novels she was an excellent translator and a writer of short stories. 'Reality or Delusion?' is a staple of supernatural anthologies to this day.

Ellen Wood died of bronchitis on 10th February 1887). He estate was valued at a very considerable £36,000.

She is buried in Highgate Cemetery, London.

A monument to her in Worcester Cathedral was unveiled in 1916.

Index of Contents

OSWALD CRAY

CHAPTER I

DR DAVENAL

It was market-day at Hallingham. A moderate-sized and once beautiful town, cut up now by the ugly railroad which had chosen to take its way right through it, and to build a large station on the very spot where the Abbey Gardens used to flourish. Famous gardens once; and not so long ago the evening recreation of the townspeople, who would promenade there at sunset, whatever the time of year. Since the gardens had been seized upon for the railway purposes, a bitter feud of opinion had reigned in the place; the staid old inhabitants mourning and resenting their town's desecration; the younger welcoming the new rail, its station, and its bustle, with all their might and main, as a grateful inbreak on their monotonous life. The trains from London (distant some sixty or seventy miles) would go shrieking and whistling through the town at any hour of the day or night: and, so far, peace for Hallingham was over.

Possibly it was because the town was famous for little else, that these Abbey Gardens were so regretted. Hallingham Abbey had been renowned in the ages gone by; very little of its greatness was left to it now. The crumbling hand of time had partially destroyed the fine old building, an insignificant portion of it alone remaining: just sufficient to impart a notion of its style of architecture and the century of its erection: and this small portion had been patched and propped, and altogether altered and modernised, by way of keeping it together. It was little more than an ordinary dwelling-house now; and at the present moment was unoccupied, ready to be let to any suitable tenant who would take it. But, poor as it was in comparison with some of the modern dwellings in its vicinity, it was still in a degree bowed down to by Hallingham. There was something high-sounding in the address, "The Abbey, Hallingham," and none but a gentleman born and bred must venture to treat for it.

It stood alone: the extensive gardens in front of it; the space once occupied by the chapel behind it. All traces of the chapel building were gone now, but its mossy gravestones were imbedded in the ground still, and the spot remained as sacred as a graveyard. The Latin inscriptions on some of these stones could be yet made out: and that on one attracted as much imaginative speculation as the famed gravestone in the cloisters of Worcester Cathedral. A few Latin words only were on it, signifying "buried in misery:" no name, no date. Thoughtful natures would glance at that stone as they passed it, with an inward breath of hope—perhaps of prayer—that the misery experienced by its unhappy tenant in this world had been exchanged for a life of immortality. This graveyard was not a thoroughfare, and few cared to walk there who were absorbed in the bustle and pleasures of life; but the aged, the invalid, the mourner might be seen there on fine days, seated on its one solitary bench, and buried in solemn reflections. A short space of time, more or less, as it might happen, and they would be lying under gravestones in their turn: a short space of time, my friends, and you and I shall be equally lying there.

The broad space of the public road running along the Abbey's front divided it from the gardens, the gardens being the public property of the town. On the opposite side of these gardens, furthest from the Abbey, were the buildings of the new station and the lines upon lines of rails.

It is well to say lines upon lines of rails! Hallingham said it—said it with a groan. Not content with a simple line, or a double line of rails, sufficient for ordinary traffic, the railway authorities had made it into a "junction"—"Hallingham Junction!"—and more lines branched off from it than you would care to count. This was at the east end of the town; beyond it was the open country. Some of the lines made a sort of semicircle, cut off a corner of the town, and branched off into space. It's true it was a very shabby little corner of the town that had thus been cut off, but Hallingham did not the less resent the invasion.

Walking down to Hallingham along the broad road leading from the Abbey, its busiest part was soon gained. Let us look at it today: Tuesday. It is market-day at Hallingham, and the hot July sun streams full on the people's heads, for there's no room for the raised umbrellas, and they afford little continuous shade. It is the large, wide, open space in front of the town-hall where we have halted, and here from time immemorial the market people have sat to chaffer and change, barter and sell. Country women expose their poultry and eggs, their butter and cream cheese, and their other wares, all on this spot. No matter what the weather—in the dog-days of summer, in the sharp snow, the pitiless storm of winter— here they are every Tuesday under their sea of umbrellas, which must be put down to allow space to the jostling crowd when the market gets full. The town had been talking the last ten years of erecting a covered market-house; but it was not begun yet.

Still on, down the principal street, leaving this market-place to the left, and what was called the West-end of the town was gained. Proud Hallingham had named it West-end in imitation of London. It was nothing but a street; its name, New Street, proclaiming that it was of more recent date than some of the other parts. It was really a fine street, wide and open, with broad white pavements, and its houses were mostly private ones, their uniformity of line being broken by a detached house here and there. It was a long street, and five or six other by-streets and turnings branched off from it at right angles.

Lying back from the street at the corner of one of these turnings was a handsome white house, detached, with a fine pillared-portico entrance in its centre and a plate on the door. It was fully as conspicuous to the street as were the other houses which abutted on the pavement. A level lawn was before it, divided from the street by low light iron railings, its small light gate in the midst, opposite the entrance-door. Narrow flower-beds, filled with gay and charming flowers, skirted the lawn before the rails; on the sides, but not in front, flourished evergreens close to the railings behind the flower-beds, making a sort of screen. An inclosed garden lay at the back of the house, and beyond the garden were the stables. On the brass plate—you could read it from the street,—was inscribed "Dr. Davenal."

He was the chief surgeon of Hallingham. Why he had taken his degree—a recent accession of dignity— people were puzzled to tell. Had he cared for high-sounding titles they could have understood it; but he did not care for them: had he been a slave to example, that might have accounted for it, for this degree-taking, as you must be aware, has come into fashion of late years: had he wished to court notoriety, he might have thought that a means to bring it to him. But Hallingham knew Dr. Davenal better. He was a simple-minded man; he liked to be out of the fashion instead of in it; and whether he wrote "doctor" or "surgeon" after his name, he could not be more deservedly renowned in his locality than he already was. He was a skilful surgeon, a careful and successful operator, and his advice in purely medical cases was sought in preference to that of any physician in Hallingham. A rumour arose, untraceable to any certain source, that his son Edward, a dashing young captain of infantry, had urged the step upon him with a view to enhance his own standing with his brother officers. The son of Mr. Davenal, a country surgeon, might be thought slightingly of: the son of Dr. Davenal need not be. Be that as it might, the rumour gained some credence, but it died away again. One patient only ventured to question Dr. Davenal as to its truth, and the doctor laughed heartily in his patient's face, and said he expected handsome Ned could hold his own without reference to whether his father might be a royal physician or a parish apothecary.

Before we go on, I may tell you that you will like Dr. Davenal. He was a good man. He had his faults, as we all have; but he was a good man.

On this same hot July afternoon, there came careering down the street, in its usual quick fashion, a handsome open carriage drawn by a pair of beautiful bays. Dr. Davenal did not see why, because he was a doctor, his carriage should be a sober one, his horses tame and rusty. Truth to say, he was given to spend rather than to save. I have told you he had faults, and perhaps you will call that one. He sat in his accustomed seat, low in the carriage, his servant Roger mounted far above him. He rarely drove, himself; never when paying professional visits: a surgeon needs to keep his hands steady. Roger was a favourite servant: fourteen years he had been in his present service, and was getting fat upon it. Dr. Davenal sometimes told him jokingly that he should have to pension him off, for his weight was getting too much for the bays. The same could not be said of Dr. Davenal; he was a spare man of middle height, with a broad white forehead, dark eyes, and a careworn expression.

The carriage was bowling quickly past the market-place—Dr. Davenal's time was too precious to allow of his being driven slowly—when a woman suddenly descried it. Quitting her sitting-place in the market, she set off to run towards it, flinging up her hands in agitation, and overturning her small board of wares with the haste she made. Poor wares!—gooseberries and white and red currants displayed on cabbage leaves to attract the eager eyes and watering lips of juvenile passers-by; and common garden flowers tied up in nosegays—a halfpenny a nosegay, a halfpenny a leaf. Roger saw the movement.

"Here's Dame Hundley flying on to us, sir."

Dr. Davenal, who was very much in the habit of falling into thought, seeing and hearing nothing as he went along, raised his head, and turning it in the direction of the market, met her anxious countenance.

"Pull up, Roger," he said to his servant.

The countenance was a tearful one by the time it had reached the doctor's side; and then the woman seemed to become aware that she had done an unwarrantable thing in thus summarily arresting Dr. Davenal—not that there was anything in his face or manner to remind her of it.

"Oh, sir, I beg ten thousand pardons for making thus bold! Seeing your carriage, I started off in the moment's impulse. I've been a-fearing all the morning as I sat there, that maybe you might be out when I called, after market was over. He is no better, sir: he is worser and weaker."

"Ah!" remarked the doctor. "Couldn't he come in today?"

"I don't believe there'll ever be any more coming in again for him," was the woman's answer, as she strove to suppress her tears. "'Mother,' says he to me this morning, when I tried to get him up, 'it's o' no use trying. I—I'"—She fairly broke down.

"Does the parish doctor see him regularly?"

"He comes, sir, about every third day. He caught his eye on that bottle of physic that you wrote for and told me to get made up, and he laid hold of it and asked where I got that, and I told him I had made bold to take my poor boy in to Dr. Davenal. So then he was put up about it, and said if we was going to be grand patients of Dr. Davenal's we didn't want him. And I thought perhaps he mightn't come again. But he did: he came in last night at dusk."

"Has your son taken the physic?"

"Yes, sir. I gave him the last dose afore I come away this morning. But he's worse; he's a deal worse, sir: maybe it's these hot days that's trying him."

Dr. Davenal could have told her that he never would be anything but worse in this world; a little better, a little worse, according to the phases of the disease, and then would come the ending.

"I shall, I expect, be driving out of Hallingham your way this evening, Mrs. Hundley, and I'll call and see him. Should anything prevent it this evening, you may look for me tomorrow. I'll be sure to come."

The same good, considerate man that he had ever been, sparing no trouble, no kindness, when life or health was at stake. "I'll be sure to come!" and the woman knew that he would be sure to come. How few medical men in his position would have condescended to say to this poor woman, "I'll be sure to come!" to say it in the kind tone, with the promise in his eyes as they looked straight into here, as well as on his lips! He had fellow-practitioners in that town, their time not half taken up as his was, who would have loftily waved off poor Dame Hundley, a profitless patient in every sense, and sent her sorrow to the winds.

Roger drove quickly on down the street between the rows of gay shops, and Dr. Davenal sat thinking of that poor woman's sorrow. She was a widow, and this was her only son. Did the anticipated loss of that son strike on the chords of his own heart, and send them vibrating? He had lost a son, and under unhappy auspices. Save that woman's son he knew he could not: his death fiat had gone forth in the fell disease which had attacked him: but he might possibly, by the exertion of his skill, prolong the life by a trifle, and certainly lighten its sufferings. Mrs. Hundley had toiled for this son, and brought him up well, in her poor way, and had looked brightly forward to his helping her on in her old age: as he would have done, for he was steady, loving, and dutiful. But it was not to be: God was taking him: and the mother in her alarm and grief scarcely saw why this should be. Not at the time that affliction falls, in its first brunt, can we see or believe in the love and wisdom that are always hidden within it.

Roger pulled up at the doctor's house, set his master down, and turned his horses round into the side lane—for it could not be called a street—to drive them to the stables. Dr. Davenal went through the gate, and wound round the grass-plat to the house. As he was about to open the door with his latch-key, it was drawn open for him by his attentive indoor manservant.

You never saw so respectable a servant in all your life: a very model of a servant in looks, voice, and manner. About forty years of age, his tall, slim, active figure gave him the appearance of being a younger man. His hair, brushed smooth and flat, was of a shiny black, and his white necktie and orthodox black clothes were without a spot. But—in spite of his excessive respectability as a man and a servant—there was something in the sharp features of his white face, in the furtive black eyes, that would lose their look of slyness when flung boldly into yours, which had never been cordially liked by Dr. Davenal.

"You saw me, Neal?"

"I was in your room, sir, speaking to Mr. Cray," was the man's answer: and in his low, respectful tones, his superior accent, there was really a sound of refinement pleasant to the ear. That refinement of voice and manner that may be caught from associating with the educated; not the refinement springing from the mind where it is innate.

"Has anybody been here?"

"Lady Oswald, sir. She apologised for coming when it was not your day for receiving town-patients, but she said she particularly wished to see you. I think she scarcely believed me, sir, when I said you were out."

Dr. Davenal took his gold repeater from his pocket, where it lay loose, unattached to any chain, and glanced at it. A valuable watch: the grateful present of a rich man years ago, who believed that he owed his life, humanly speaking, to Richard Davenal's care and skill.

"Scarcely believed you! Why, she knows I am never home much before three o'clock. It wants two minutes now. Mr. Cray, if he is here, might have seen her."

"Mr. Cray has but just come, sir. I was showing him in when your carriage drove to the door. Lady Oswald said she would call again later, sir."

Two minutes more, when three o'clock should strike, and Dr. Davenal's door would be beset by patients. By country patients today; on Tuesdays he would be very busy with them, and the townspeople did not intrude unnecessarily upon him on that day; all the rest of the week-days were for them. They would come, these patients, and lay down their fee of a guinea to the surgeon, as they laid it down for a physician. Dr. Davenal would see them twice for that; sometimes more—several times more; he was not a covetous man, and he distinguished between those who could well afford to pay him, and those who could not. When these last would timidly put down the sovereign and shilling, rarely in paper, he would push it back to them. "No, you paid me last time or so; you don't owe me anything yet."

Of far and wide reputation, he had scarcely a minute in the day that he could call his own, or that was not in some way or other devoted to his profession. Chief visiting surgeon to the Hallingham Infirmary, always taking the operations there in difficult cases, part of every day had to be spent at it. Early in the morning he saw patients at home, twice a week gratuitously; at a quarter to ten he went out, and between that time and three o'clock paid his round of calls and visited the Infirmary. At three he was at home to receive patients again; at six he dined; and it very rarely happened that he had not second visits to pay afterwards. Of course this usual routine of duty was often varied; visits at a distance had to be paid, necessitating post-horses to his close carriage, if no rail conducted to the place; patients hovering between life and death must be seen oftener than once or twice in the day, perhaps in the night; and sometimes a terrible case of accident would be brought into the Infirmary, demanding the utmost skill that the most perfect operator could give. In those cases of accident it was Dr. Davenal who was sent for by the house-surgeon; none other of the visiting surgeons were so sure as he: and Dr. Davenal, though he had a whole dining-room full of patients waiting their turn to go in to him, guinea in hand, abandoned them all, and strode away to the Infirmary with his fleetest step.

The dining-room was on the left of the entrance-hall: it wan of large proportions. Opposite to it, on the right, was a much smaller apartment, called by way of distinction "Dr. Davenal's room." It was in this last the doctor saw his patients, who would go into it from the dining-room, one by one, each in his turn. The two rooms looked to the front, on either side the door, and the window in each was very large. They were not bay windows, but were divided into three compartments, all of which might be opened separately. Dwarf Venetian blinds were carried up to the first pane in both windows, for the house was not sufficiently removed from the street to prevent curious passers-by from gazing in. Behind the doctor's room was another room, opening from it, the windows of which looked on the evergreens skirting the very narrow path that ran between the side of the house and the railings bordering the lane: a path so narrow that nobody was supposed ever to go down it. This second room was Dr. Davenal's bedchamber, used by him as such ever since the death of his wife. At the back of this chamber was another apartment, partially partitioned into two, one portion being used as a butler's pantry, the other as Neal's sleeping-closet, which looked to the garden at the rear of the house.

Neal had an uncommon partiality for that pantry, and would be in it all hours of the day or night, though it was never meant that he should sit in it. It was to all intents and purposes a pantry only, and a very scantily lighted one. It had a high window of four square panes, looking dead on the evergreens, very dense just there, and on nothing else. There was a door by its side, opening on the evergreens also; and one with a slim figure—as slim as Neal's, for instance—could go out at that door if so disposed, and entwine himself along the narrow path, braving the shrubs, past the windows of Dr. Davenal's bedchamber, and emerge in front of the house. It was not at all, however, in Neal's stipulated duties to do so. Quite the contrary. When Neal entered Dr. Davenal's service, he was expressly ordered to keep that pantry door always fastened. It was impressed upon him by Miss Davenal that there was no necessity ever to unlock it: his plate was there, she observed, and light-fingered beggars frequented Hallingham, as they frequent most other places.

On the opposite side, behind the dining-room, was the prettiest apartment in the house. It was called the garden-parlour, and opened to the garden at the back by means of glass doors. The state drawing-room was above, over the hall and dining-room, and the kitchens were downstairs.

Davenal's room was scantily furnished. A shabby Kidderminster carpet, a square table, some horsehair chairs, and a writing-desk. Nothing else, except some books ranged round the walls, and a plaster bust or two. On the table, which was covered with a green-baize cloth bordered with yellow, lay some writing and blotting paper by the side of a large inkstand, and the desk was underneath the table on the carpet. It was the doctor's habit to keep the desk there; he could not have told why. If he required to open it, which was very seldom—for he never used it for writing on—he would lift it to the table and put it back when he had done with it. Some of his patients sitting at the table waiting for the doctor to come in, or enlarging on their complaints as he sat before them, had surreptitiously used it as a footstool, and the result was a considerably scratched surface of the polished mahogany; but Dr. Davenal did not move it from its abiding-place.

Tilting himself on a chair, in a fashion that threatened an overthrow backwards, with his feet on the edge of this very desk, sat a young man, carelessly humming a popular song. You heard Neal tell his master he was there—Mr. Cray. His face was a sufficiently pleasing one, its complexion fair, its eyes a light blue. It was not a remarkable face in anyway; might have been a somewhat insipid one, but for these same blue eyes that lighted it up, and a gay smile that was ever ready on it. All that Mr. Cray appeared likely to be remarkable for as yet, was a habit of pushing his hair back—rather light hair, of a shade between brown and flaxen, and he pushed it off his forehead inveterately, at all times and seasons. But what with the blue eyes, the winning smile, and a very taking voice and manner, he was beginning to win his way in Hallingham. Dr. Davenal was glad that it should be so. He had taken this young man, Marcus Cray, by the hand, had made him his partner, and he desired nothing better than that he should win his way.

But to win a way in a town is one thing; to win hearts in it is another; and Dr. Davenal was certainly not prepared to hear, as he was about to do, that Mr. Cray had gained one particular heart, and had come then to ask his, Dr. Davenal's, approbation to his having done it.

Neal threw open the door of this room for his master, bowed him in with the air of a groom of the chambers, and Mr. Cray started from his tilting position to find his feet. As they stood together his height was somewhat under the doctor's, and his only reached the middle height.

"Is it you, Mark?" said the doctor, quietly, rather surprised that he should be there at that hour of the day; for Mr. Cray's routine of duties did not lie at the house of Dr. Davenal. "Any bad report for me?"

Mr. Cray had no bad report. He entered upon a different sort of report, speaking rapidly, but not in the least agitatedly. He wanted the doctor's consent to his marriage with Miss Caroline Davenal. Perhaps it was the knowledge that they must so soon be interrupted by three o'clock and the doctor's country patients, that prompted Mr. Cray to enter upon the subject at that not over-seasonable hour. There would be less time for the doctor's objections, he may have deemed—not that Mr. Cray was one to anticipate objections to any project he set his fancy on, or to pay much attention to them if they came.

Dr. Davenal stood against the wall near the window, looking very grave in his surprise and, it may be said, vexation. He had never dreamt of this. Mr. Cray had certainly been intimate with his family; many an evening when the doctor had been out professionally, Mr. Cray had spent with them; but he had never given a thought to anything of this sort arising from it. His connection with Mr. Cray was a professional connection, and perhaps that fact had blinded his eyes and kept his thoughts from glancing to the possibility that anything different might supervene.

"You look grave, Dr. Davenal," said Mr. Cray, breaking the silence, and retaining, in a remarkable degree, his self-possession.

"Yes," replied the doctor, "for Caroline's sake. Mark, I believe I had cherished more ambitious dreams for her."

"Ambitious dreams!" repeated Mr. Cray. "She will at least occupy a position as good as yours, sir."

"As good as mine!" echoed the doctor. "But when, Mark?—when?" he added after a pause.

"In time."

"Ay—in time. There it is. How long must you wait for it?"

"We shall rub on until then, doctor. As others do."

"Mark, I do not think Caroline is one to rub on, as you call it, so smoothly as some might, unless fortune is smooth about her. Remember what your income is."

"It is two hundred a-year," said Mark, pushing his hair from his brow, and speaking with as much equanimity as though he had said two thousand. "But I thought perhaps you might be induced to increase it—for her sake."

Dr. Davenal pulled open the green Venetian blind and threw the window higher up, as if the air of the room were growing too hot for him. It was the window—or rather the compartment of it—nearest to the lane, and the doctor was fond of keeping it a little raised. Summer and winter would the passers-by see that window raised behind the green staves of the blind.

"Were I to double your income, Mark, and make it four hundred a-year—a thing which you have no right to expect me to do at present, or to ask me to do—it would still be an inadequate income for Caroline Davenal," resumed the doctor, closing the blind again, and setting his back against it. "I don't believe—it is my opinion, Mark, and I only give it you as such—that she is one to make the best of a small income, or to be happy on it."

Mr. Cray had caught up one of the doctor's pens, and stood opposite to him picking the feather-end of it off bit by bit. His attitude was a careless one, and his eyes were bent upon the pen, as if to pick those pieces off and litter the carpet were of more consequence than looking at Dr. Davenal. Mr. Cray was inclined to be easy over most things, to take life coolly, and he was characteristically easy over this.

"Four hundred a-year is not so small an income," he observed.

"That depends," said Dr. Davenal. "Incomes are large or small in comparison; in accordance with the requirements, the habits, the notions if you will, of those who have to live upon them. Caroline has enjoyed the advantages derivable from one amounting to three times four."

"She may come into that fortune yet," said Mr. Cray.

The first gleam of real displeasure shone now in the eyes of the doctor as he threw them searchingly on his partner. "Have you been counting upon that?—Is it the inducement which has called forth this proposal?"

"No," burst forth Mr. Cray, feeling vexed in his turn and speaking impulsively, as he flung the dilapidated pen back in the inkstand and drew nearer the doctor. "I declare that I never thought of the money or the suit; it did not so much as cross my mind; and were Carine never to have a penny-piece to the end of her life, it would make no difference. It is her I want; not money."

Dr. Davenal drew in his lips. "Carine!" They must have become tolerably intimate for him familiarly to call her that. "Pretty Carine" was her fond name in the household.

"It was Caroline herself who spoke of the money," resumed Mark Cray. "We were consulting together as to how far my two hundred a-year would keep us, and she remembered the Chancery suit. 'Mark,' she said, 'that fortune may come to me, and then we should have no care.' It was not I who thought of it, Dr. Davenal. And I am sure I don't count upon it: Caroline herself would be wise not to do so. Chancery suits generally absorb the oyster and leave the shell for the claimants."

"You have spoken to Caroline, then?" questioned Dr. Davenal.

Mark pushed off his hair again. "O dear yes."

"May I ask when?"

"Well—I don't know," answered Mr. Cray, after considering the point. "I have been—I have been"—

"What?" cried Dr. Davenal, surprised at the unusual hesitation, "Speak out, Mark."

"I was going to say I have been making love to her ever so long," continued Mark, with a laugh. "In fact, sir, we have understood each other for some time past; but as to the precise period that I actually spoke out to her by words, I am not sure when it was."

The contrast between the two men was observable in the silence that ensued. Dr. Davenal grave, absorbed, full of thought and care; Mr. Cray self-satisfied, looking as if neither thought nor care had ever come to him, or could come. He lightly watched the passers-by in the street, over the Venetian blind of the middle window, nodding and smiling to any acquaintances that happened to appear. Mr. Cray had made up his mind to marry Miss Caroline Davenal, and it was entirely out of his creed to suppose that any insurmountable objection could supervene.

"Mark," said Dr. Davenal, interrupting the gentleman as he was flourishing his hand to somebody, "you must be aware that circumstances render it imperative upon me to be more than commonly watchful over the interests of Caroline."

"Do you think so? But, Dr. Davenal, I would be sure to make her happy. I would spend my life in it: none would make her as happy as I."

"How do you know that?" asked Dr. Davenal.

A smile hovered on the young surgeon's lips. "Because she cares for me, sir; and for none other in the wide world."

"I had thought—I had thought that another cared for her," returned Dr. Davenal, speaking impulsively. "At least, a doubt of it has sometimes crossed me."

Mark Cray opened his eyes widely in his astonishment. "Who?" he asked.

But Dr. Davenal did not satisfy him: not that he had any particular motive for observing reticence on the point. "It is of no consequence. I must have been mistaken," was all he said.

"You will not forbid her to me, sir?" pleaded Mr. Cray.

A spasm of pain passed across the face of Dr. Davenal; the words had called up bitter recollections.

"So long as I live I shall never forbid a marriage to any over whom I hold control," he said, in a tone of subdued anguish; and Mark Cray knew where the sting had pointed, and wished in his good-nature he had not put the question. "I will urge all reflection, caution, prudence in my power to urge; but I will not forbid. Least of all have I a right to do so by Caroline."

The younger man's face lighted up. "Then you will give her to me, Dr. Davenal?"

"I give you no promise," was the doctor's answer. "I must have leisure to reflect on this; it has taken me entirely by surprise. And I must speak to Caroline. There's plenty of time. To marry yet would indeed be premature."

"Premature!" echoed Mr. Cray.

"Premature in the extreme. A man who does not know how to wait for good things, Mark, does not deserve them."

A lady, with a slow walk and pale face, turned in at the front gate. It was patient the first. Dr. Davenal made no observation; he scarcely saw her, so deeply had he plunged into thought. Mr. Cray, who stood closer to the window than a doctor expecting patients generally does stand, smiled and bowed.

"It is Mrs. Scott," he observed, as the knocker sounded. "She looks very ill today."

Attentive Neal was heard to come forth instantly from his pantry, open the door, and show the lady into the dining-room. Then he made his appearance in his master's room.

"Mrs. Scott, sir!"

Instead of the "Show her in," as Neal expected, Dr. Davenal merely nodded. Mr. Cray made a movement to depart, glancing as he did so, at the very grave face of his senior partner.

"I have vexed you, sir!"

"I feel vexed in this first moment, Mark; I can't deny it," was the candid answer. "It is not altogether that Caroline might have been expected to do better; it is not exclusively that I think her peculiarly unfitted for a making-shift life, or that with regard to her I feel my responsibility is weighty: but it is a mixture of all three."

"You consider, perhaps, I have done wrong to ask for her!"

"I consider you have done wrong to ask for her so prematurely. In your place, I think I should have waited a little while, until circumstances had been more propitious."

"And perhaps have lost Caroline!"

"Nay," said the doctor; "a girl that cannot wait, and be true while she waits, is not worth a brass button."

He quitted the room as he spoke. At the risk of keeping his patients waiting, he must find and question Caroline. His mind was not at ease.

Mr. Cray went out at the hall-door. Before Neal, who was on the alert, had shut it, a carriage drove up to the gate, and stopped with a clatter. A well-appointed close carriage, its servants in claret-coloured livery, and its claret-coloured panels bearing the insignia of England's baronetage—the bloody hand.

The footman leaped down for his orders. Mr. Cray, stepping across the lawn, in too much haste to wind round it by means of the gravel-path, held out his hand with a smile to its only inmate—a little, grey, nervous-looking woman, in an old-fashioned purple silk dress.

"How are you today, Lady Oswald?"

And Neal, with his quiet, cat-like steps, had followed in the wake of Mr. Cray, unseen by that gentleman, and stood behind him in his respectful attention: there might be some message to carry in to his master—leaving three patients, who had entered the gate together, to show themselves in alone.

CHAPTER II

LADY OSWALD'S LETTER

The room at the back, looking into the garden, on the opposite side of the passage to Neal's pantry, was the most charming apartment in all the house. Not for its grandeur; it was small and very simple indeed, compared to the grand drawing-room upstairs: not for its orderly neatness, for it was usually in a litter; a fascinating, pleasant-looking litter; and perhaps that made its charm. It was called the garden-parlour. The great drawing-room was kept sacred by its presiding mistress, to whom you will soon have the honour of an introduction: sacred, and uncomfortably tidy. Not so much as a pocket-handkerchief must be laid for an instant on one of its handsome tables, its luxurious satin sofas and ottomans; not a footstool must be drawn from its appointed place, let tired legs be hanging down with weariness; not a hand-screen must be removed from the handsomely-furnished mantelpiece, were lovely cheeks being roasted to crimson. Methodically proper, everything in its appointed spot, must that room be kept: a book put down in the wrong place was treason; a speck of dust all but warning to Jessy, the unhappy housemaid. The dining-room was tidy, too; no extraneous things were allowed there, it must be kept free for the reception of the patients: the "Times" newspaper and the newest local journal lay daily on the large mahogany table, and there the litter ended. Perhaps, therefore, it was no wonder that that other room was not always in the order it might have been.

A charming room, nevertheless, on a sunny day. Watercoloured drawings and pencil sketches in plain frames lined the delicately-papered walls, loose music was strewed near the piano and harp, books lay anywhere, pretty little ornamental trifles met the eye, and fancy-work might be seen in more places than one. The glass doors at the window, large and high, stood open to the few wide steps that led to the green lawn—a lawn particularly grateful on a sultry summer's day.

For that lawn lay in the shade; the sun in the afternoon shone full on the front of the house, and the lawn was sheltered. The scent of the roses, the syringa, the heliotrope, and other powerfully-perfumed flowers, filled the air, and butterflies and bees flitted from blossom to blossom. It was quite a contrast to the other side of the house, with its busy street, its hot pavement, its jostling traversers, and its garish sunshine. Here lay the cool shade on the mossy lawn—the quiet and the repose of the tinted flowers.

Seated on the lawn, on a garden-bench, was a young lady reading. A graceful girl of middle height, with large hazel eyes quite luminous in their brightness, a well-formed gentle face, rather pale, and brown hair that took almost a golden tinge when the sun shone through it. There was no very great beauty to boast of in the face, but it was one of those that the eye likes to rest upon—and love. A far more beautiful face was that of another young girl, who was restlessly moving amidst the side clusters of shrubs and flowers, plucking the choicest. A face whose beauty could not be denied, with its dark violet eyes, its nearly black hair, and the damask complexion all too bright: these strangely brilliant complexions do not always go with the soundest of constitutions. She was little, fairy-like, somewhat pettish and wilful in her movements. A stranger would say they were sisters, and be puzzled to tell which of the two was the elder, which the younger. There was really no likeness between them, save in the dress—that was precisely similar: a thin gauzy silken material, cool but rich, and no doubt expensive, with a good deal of delicate coloured trimming upon it, and open sleeves over white lace. Sisters they were not—only cousins.

Suddenly there was a scream from the midst of the flowers, and the young lady on the garden-bench raised her eyes to speak.

"What is it, Caroline?"

She came forth in her beauty, flinging down the flowers she had gathered, and holding out the back of her hand. A deep scratch lay right across it.

"Just look! I am always tearing myself with those wild-rose brambles!"

"Poor hand! Sit still, Carine; it is too hot for anything else today. What do you want with the flowers, that you need trouble yourself to get them?"

"I don't know what I want with them. Nothing. Picking them helped to pass away the time."

"Why are you so restless this afternoon!"

"Am I restless? One can't be always as quiet as you—read, read, read for ever."

An amused smile parted the reader's lips, bringing to view the pretty teeth, so white and regular. "I will retort in nearly your own words, Carine—am I quiet? I think not."

"Yes you are, except when the boys are at home. You are noisy enough then. I shall go and eat some fruit."

"Lend me your pencil first, Caroline."

Miss Caroline Davenal put her hand into her pocket and could not find her pencil. "I must have left it somewhere indoors," she said. "You'll see it if you look."

"I must mark a passage here."

"What will Mr. Oswald Cray say to your marking his book?"

"Mr. Oswald Cray asked me to mark anything that struck me. It is a delightful book."

Caroline Davenal went joyously down the garden, singing a snatch of a song, as she put her handkerchief over her head to guard it from the sun. The upper half of the long piece of ground was all pleasure and flowers; the lower half all usefulness, vegetables and fruit-trees. Her cousin, book in hand, went up the steps and in at the glass doors to find a pencil. She was bending over the centre table, searching for one, when Dr. Davanel entered the room.

"Is Caroline here?"

"She is in the garden, papa."

Dr. Davenal advanced to the window, and stood at it, ostensibly looking for Caroline. He could not see her; the fruit-trees in the distance had effectually hidden her, and the doctor appeared lost in thought. Presently he spoke, without looking round.

"Sara, did you know that—that—in short, have you ever observed that an attachment was arising between Mr. Cray and Caroline?"

Sara looked up, but did not at once reply. The question was one, put from a father to a daughter, that brought up the blushes on her cheeks in her maiden modesty.

"N—o," she replied, at length. But the no, in its hesitation, sounded almost as much like yes.

"My dear, I did not ask you to deceive me," was the grave answer; "I ask for the truth."

"O papa, you know—you know I would not deceive you," she replied, quite in distress. And Dr. Davenal, pained by the tone, drew her to him and kissed her cheek. He knew how good, how loving, how dutiful, was this daughter of his.

"The real truth is this, papa. Very recently, only since a day or two, a faint suspicion has arisen in my mind that it might be so. Caroline has not spoken, and I have had nothing to guide me to it, except the fact that Mr. Cray is so much here. Indeed, I do not know whether it is so or not."

"I believe I have been a little blind," observed Dr. Davenal speaking quite as much to himself as to his daughter. "The fact is, Sara, I had a notion in my head that some one else had taken a fancy to Caroline; and I suppose I could see nothing beyond it. I speak of Mr. Oswald Cray."

It was well that Dr. Davenal's eyes were fixed on the garden, or he might have wondered at the startled change in his daughter's face. It had turned of one glowing crimson. She moved again to the table, and stood there with her back to the light.

"I suppose I was mistaken; that there was nothing in it, Sara?"

"Nothing, papa, I think; nothing whatever," came the low-toned answer.

"But Mr. Oswald Cray does come here a great deal when he is at Hallingham?" pursued the doctor, as if willing to debate the question.

The crimson grew deeper. Dr. Davenal did not seem to observe that there was no answer.

"How the idea came to arise, I do not understand. Heaven knows I should be the last man in the world to scheme and plan out marriages—for Caroline or for anybody else. Such matters are best left to come about of themselves. But, Sara, I wish one thing—that it had been Mr. Oswald Cray, instead of Mark."

"Do you, papa?" with the blushing face still turned from him.

"Ay, I do. I could have trusted her to Oswald. How could she choose the other in preference to him?"

Sara lifted her face. Eager words were on her lips—to the effect that perhaps Mr. Oswald Cray might not have chosen Caroline. But they died away unspoken.

"I wish you would go and tell her I want her here, Sara."

Sara slipped by the doctor, passed over the cool lawn to the distant sunny paths, and met her cousin.

"Papa wants you, Carine."

Caroline recoiled in her self-conscious timidity. "What about?" she whispered. "Did he say what about?"

"I think," said Sara slowly, scarcely knowing whether she was doing right to speak or not, "that it is something about Mr. Cray."

For a moment Caroline made no rejoinder. She walked on and had nearly gained the lawn when she turned her head again. Sara had lingered behind.

"Sara! Sara! Did he seem angry?" she whispered.

"Not exactly angry. Vexed, I thought."

Dr. Davenal stood at the glass doors still. He put out his hand as she approached him.

"Did you want me, Uncle Richard?"

"Mr. Cray has been making an application to me concerning you. Caroline, were you cognisant of it?"

"Now, Uncle Richard! If you are going to be cross, I—I shall be so unhappy."

"When did you ever know me cross?" he gravely rejoined, and Caroline Davenal burst into tears.

"Caroline, my dear, we must put away this childishness. You are but affecting it, and this is a serious moment. I must talk to you very earnestly. Come in, Sara. It is cooler indoors than out."

Sara, who in her delicacy of feeling would have remained outside, went within the room and sat down to the table with her book. Caroline had dried her passing tears, and was stealing a glance at Dr. Davenal.

"You are angry, Uncle Richard."

"If I am, Caroline, it is for your sake; a loving anger. My chief emotion, I believe, is surprise. I never gave a thought to this; not a suspicion of it crossed me."

"I fancied you must have guessed it," was the murmured answer.

"Guessed that! No, child. But the blindness was my own, I believe. When we ourselves place one view deliberately before us, it tends to shut out others. I had got it into my head, Carine, that it was to your score we were indebted for the frequent visits of Mr. Oswald Cray."

Caroline lifted her face, and Dr. Davenal observed how genuine was the surprise depicted on it. "Uncle Richard!"

"I see. I see now, child, that the idea was void of foundation. But, Caroline," he gravely added, "I would rather it had been Oswald than Mark. All the world must respect Oswald Cray."

"I should think it was void of foundation!" indignantly returned Caroline, resenting the disparagement cast on Mark. "Why, Uncle Richard, Oswald Cray likes Sara a thousand times better than he likes me! But not with that sort of liking," she hastened to add, lest a construction should be put upon the words which most certainly she never meant to put. "General liking, I mean. Oswald Cray's heart is buried in his ambition, in his busy life; he gives little thought to aught else. Uncle Richard, I would not many Oswald Cray if he were worth his weight in gold. He would find fault with me all day long."

"Well, well; let us drop Oswald Cray, and return to the point, Caroline. If"—

"Lady Oswald, sir."

The interruption came from Neal. They had not heard him open the door, and the announcement was the first intimation of his presence. Of course all private conversation was at an end, and the doctor half groaned as he turned to Lady Oswald. She came in, her warm cashmere scarf drawn round her, and her purple gown held up gracefully on the right side, after the style of walking in the fashionable world in the days when Lady Oswald was young.

Lady Oswald was one of those imaginary invalids who give more trouble to their medical attendants than a whole score of patients with real maladies. Fussy and fidgety, she exacted constant attendance from Dr. Davenal. She paid him well; but she worried him nearly out of his life. On his leisure days, when he could really afford the visit to her, and the quarter-of-an-hour's chat spent in condoling with her upon her array of ailments and in giving her the gossip of Hallingham, he spared the time with a good grace; but in a season of pressure he did chafe at having to pay this daily visit, when dying men were waiting for him. He had been with her that morning between ten and eleven: Neal had said she called while he was out; and now here she was again! Once or twice latterly he had sent Mr. Cray in his stead, and she had not seemed to object to it. But she had come for a different object now.

"Only two minutes' conversation with you, doctor," she said, in a voice naturally feeble. "You must spare it me, though it is Tuesday afternoon, and I see your dining-room's getting full. Neal said you were here, so I came in straight, not to be confounded with the patients. Only look at this letter which was delivered to me this morning, and see what it must have been to my nerves. Parkins has been giving me red lavender ever since."

"But you know, Lady Oswald, that I object to your taking red lavender."

"What am I to do when a shock like that comes to me? Do read it, doctor."

Dr. Davenal, feeling that he had no time for letters or nerves just then, was yet compelled in good manners to accede. He opened the note, which was a very short one, and ran his eyes over the contents; once and then again; the first time he did not quite master them.

It was written to Lady Oswald by her landlord, a gentleman of the name of Low. It appeared that Mr. Low had some little time back received an intimation from the railway company that they should require to take a small portion of the grounds attached to the residence occupied by Lady Oswald, for the purpose of erecting certain sheds necessary at that bend of the line. This note was to inform her that he had given his consent, and it ended with a polite hope and belief that neither the sheds nor the process of their erection would prove any annoyance to her.

Dr. Davenal folded the letter when read. Lady Oswald looked at him. "What would you advise me to do?" she asked in a fretful tone.

"Indeed, Lady Oswald, I do not see what you can do," he thoughtfully answered, "except submit to it."

"Submit to it! submit to their erecting railway sheds in my very garden!" she ejaculated in astonishment.

"From the very first hour that I knew they were carrying that new line of rail close to your grounds, I felt sure it would prove an annoyance to you in some shape or other," observed Dr. Davenal, speaking more to himself than to Lady Oswald. "It is a great pity, but we all have to submit occasionally to these untoward things, Lady Oswald, as we go through life."

"I shall not submit to this," she resolutely returned. "They have no more right to erect sheds on my grounds, than they have to erect them upon me. I shall forbid it."

"But the power to do so does not lie with you," objected Dr. Davenal. "You are but a tenant on lease. In point of fact, I do not suppose such power lies with any one, not even with Low himself. The railway companies seem to do pretty much as they please in the kingdom. Mr. Low will be sure to get well paid, and his consent, according to the tenor of this note, is already given."

Lady Oswald pushed her grey hair nervously from her brow. "Dr. Davenal, I don't believe that the law has power so to annoy innocent people and drive them from their homes. Do you know how long I have lived in that house?"

"A great many years now. Ever since the death of Sir John."

"I have lived in it fourteen years, and I will not be driven forth at their pleasure. I expected to die in it, and I will die in it. If they attempt to touch my grounds, I shall have them warned off as trespassers, and I will keep a couple of policemen on the watch day and night."

Dr. Davenal did not then dispute the policy of the avowed plan with her, or point out its futility. In her present mood he knew it would be useless, even if he had the time, to attempt it.

"Because I am a widow woman they think that they can put upon me with impunity," she resumed; "but they will find their mistake. I have telegraphed for Mr. Oswald Cray, and expect him down by night-time."

"You have telegraphed for him?" cried Dr. Davenal.

"Of course I have. Who else is there to take my part, doctor, save him or you? That letter was delivered just after you left me this morning, and I seat to the telegraph at once. Oswald can fight them; and he has influence: they will be clever to overreach him."

Dr. Davenal opened his mouth to speak, but suppressed the impulsive words upon his tongue. To what end recall to Lady Oswald's attention the fact that Mr. Oswald Cray, as one of the engineers to the line, must necessarily be against her, if she had not the sense to remember it? He said a few words to the effect that he must go to his patients, gave Lady Oswald a half promise to see her that night, and left her to be entertained by his daughter.

"My dear, why need Miss Carine have run away from me the moment I came in?"

Sara smiled. "Not from you, Lady Oswald; I think she wanted to run from us all. And perhaps she thought your visit was only to papa."

"How is Miss Davenal?"

"Quite well. Will you see her? She is in the drawing-room."

Lady Oswald hesitated.

"My dear, of course I should be glad to see her; I wish to pay her every respect; but—you know it is so great a trial to me—with my little weak voice. However, I will go up, as I am here. Is her deafness better?"

"Not at all," was Sara's answer. "I don't suppose it ever will be better. It gets worse, we think, as she grows old."

"Grows what?" cried Lady Oswald.

Sara had quick perceptions, and she felt that the word old, as applied to her aunt, had offended Lady Oswald's ear. How changed do our ideas of age become as our own years change! To Sara Davenal, with her twenty years, her aunt, verging on fifty, was old; to Lady Oswald, who would count seventy-one her next birthday Miss Davenal seemed but as a youngish woman!

Lady Oswald stepped slowly up the wide staircase, one foot at a time. Sara followed her, and threw open the door of the handsome drawing-room. A large square room, beautiful as a show place; and to keep it beautiful was the hobby of Miss Bettina Davenal.

CHAPTER III

MISS BETTINA DAVENAL

Miss Davenal sat in her usual seat near the window, her straight figure bolt upright, her knitting needles plying fast their work, the small inlaid table at her right hand holding the open pearl basket of wool. How many stockings, socks, sleeves, and chest-protectors, were knitted by Miss Davenal in the course of the year, the poor alone could tell—for they were the recipients. Hallingham surmised that she must spend half her income upon wool. There's no doubt she was a charitable well-meaning woman at heart, but she did not always show it in her manner.

A beautiful woman in her day must have been Bettina Davenal, with her pure complexion and her classical features. But the grey eyes had a cold hard look in them now; and the nose, across the high bridge of which the delicate skin was drawn so tightly, was almost painfully thin. The name Bettina had been bestowed on her at the request of a godmother, a lady of Italian origin; not an ugly name, but somewhat long for the everyday use of English tongues, and those familiar with her occasionally shortened it into "Miss Bett," a liberty that was resented by Miss Davenal. She laboured under that troublesome defect, intense deafness, and also under the no less troublesome conviction (not unfrequently accompanying it) that she was not deaf at all. Her hair of a pale flaxen, soft and abundant still, was worn in smooth braids, and was surmounted by a rich lace head-dress, very high.

She need not have added to her height; she was tall enough without it; as was seen when she rose to receive Lady Oswald. A straight-down, thin, upright figure, without crinolines or cordings, her grey damask dress falling in wrapt folds around her as she held forth her mittened hand.

"I hope I see you better, Lady Oswald."

The tone was unnaturally high: you may have noticed that it is so sometimes in deaf people. Lady Oswald, with her weak nerves, would have put her hands to her ears had she done as she liked.

"I am not well today. I am worse than usual. I have had a most unpleasant shock, Miss Davenal; an upset."

"A what?" cried Miss Davenal, putting her hand to her ear.

"An upset."

"Bless my heart!" cried Miss Davenal; "did your carriage run away?"

"Tell her, Sara," groaned Lady Oswald. "I shall be hoarse for two days if I call out like this."

"Lady Oswald has had some unpleasant news, aunt. She has received notice that they are going to run the railway through her grounds."

Miss Davenal caught a word or so, and looked terrified. "Received notice that they are going to run a railway through her! What do you mean?"

"Not through her," said Sara, putting her lips close to the deaf ears. "Through her grounds."

"But I'd not let them," cried Miss Davenal, hearing now. "I'd not let them, Lady Oswald."

"I won't," screamed Lady Oswald at the top of her voice. "I have sent for Mr. Oswald Cray."

Miss Davenal was dubious. "What good will that do? Is it to pelt upon them? I hate those wicked railways."

"Is what to pelt upon them?"

"The clay. Didn't you say you had sent for some clay?"

"Oh dear! Sara, do make her understand."

Poor Sara had to do her best. "Not clay, Aunt Bettina; Mr. Oswald Cray."

Aunt Bettina nodded her stately head. "I like Mr. Oswald Cray. He is a favourite of mine, Lady Oswald."

"As he is of everybody's, Miss Davenal," returned Lady Oswald. "I'd have remembered him in my will but for offending the Oswald family. They are dreadfully prejudiced."

"Pinched!" echoed Miss Davenal. "Where's he pinched?"

"Prejudiced, Aunt Bettina. Lady Oswald says the Oswald family are prejudiced."

"You need not roar out in that way, Sara; I can hear, I hope. I am not so deaf as all that comes to. What's he prejudiced at?—the railway? He ought not to be, he is one of its engineers."

"Not Mr. Oswald Cray, aunt. The Oswald family. They are prejudiced against him."

"If you speak to me again in that manner, Sara I shall complain to your papa. One would think you were calling out to somebody at the top of the chimney. As if I and Lady Oswald did not know that the Oswald family are prejudiced against Oswald Cray? We don't want you to tell it us from a speaking-trumpet; we knew it before you were born. I don't think he cares for their prejudices, Lady Oswald," Miss Davenal added, turning to her.

"He would be very foolish if he did. I don't. They are prejudiced, you know, against me."

"I think the world must be coming to an end, with all these rails and stations and sheds," fretfully spoke Miss Davenal.

"The news has made me ill," said Lady Oswald, who liked nothing half so well as to speak of her own ailments. "I was getting better, as Dr. Davenal can tell you, but this will throw me back for weeks. My maid has been giving me red lavender ever since."

Miss Davenal looked at her with a puzzled stare.

"That is poison, is it not?"

"What is poison?"

"Red lead."

"I said red lavender," cried Lady Oswald. "It is very good for the spirits: a few drops taken on a lump of sugar. Red lav-en-der."

Miss Davenal resolutely shook her head. "Nasty stuff!" she cried. "Red lavender never did anybody good yet, Lady Oswald. Leave it off; leave it off."

"I don't touch it once in a month in an ordinary way," screamed Lady Oswald. "Only when anything beyond common arises to flurry me."

Miss Bettina stared at her. "What common is flooded? It is dry weather."

Lady Oswald cast a helpless look at Sara. "Flurried, Aunt Bettina," said the young lady. "Lady Oswald said when she was flurried."

Miss Bettina was not in the least grateful for the assistance. She pushed away her niece with her elbow. It was in fact next to high treason for Sara to attempt to assist Miss Davenal's deafness. "I should not allow things to flurry me, Lady Oswald. I never was flurried in my life."

"Temperaments are constituted differently," returned Lady Oswald.

"Temper!" cried Miss Davenal, as angrily as politeness would allow her, "what has temper to do with it? Who accuses me of temper?"

"Tem-per-a-ment," corrected Lady Oswald, cracking her voice. "Sara, I must go."

She rose quickly; she could not stand the interview any longer; but in spite of the misapprehensions they took leave of each other cordially. The same scene occurred every time they met: as it did whenever conversation was attempted with Miss Davenal. It cannot be denied that she heard better at times than at others, occasionally tolerably well; and hence perhaps the source, or partially so, of her own belief that her deafness was but of a slight nature. When alone with the familiar family voices, and in quiet times, she could hear; but in moments of surprise and excitement, in paying or receiving visits, the ears were nearly hopeless.

Neal attended Lady Oswald to her carriage, waiting there at the gate with its powdered coachman and footman, to the gratification of the juvenile street Arabs of Hallingham; the same ever-assiduous, superior servant, quite dignified in his respectability. Lady Oswald believed him perfection—that there was not another such servant in the world.

"Your mistress grows more distressingly deaf than ever, Neal," she remarked, as he put her dress straight in the carriage, her own footman resigning the office to him with almost the same submission that he might have resigned it to Mr. Cray, had the young surgeon been at hand to assist her in, as he had been to assist her out.

"She does, my lady. It is a great affliction. Home," loftily added Neal to the servants: and he bowed low as the carriage drove away.

CHAPTER IV

OSWALD CRAY

The house of Lady Oswald was an old-fashioned red brick mansion of moderate size, two storeys in height only, and with gable-ends. It was exceedingly comfortable inside, and was surrounded by rather extensive grounds. At the opposite end of the town to the station, it might have been thought that that vulgar innovation, the railroad, so especially obnoxious to Lady Oswald, would at least have spared it offensive contact; but that was not to be. There was no accounting for the curves and tracks taken by those lines of the junction, and one of them had gone off at a tangent to skirt the very boundary of her land.

Seated in the front drawing-room, the one chiefly used by Lady Oswald, was a woman of some forty years, attired in a neat green-coloured gown, and cap with white ribbons. This was Parkins, Lady Oswald's maid, recently promoted to be somewhat of a companion, for Lady Oswald began to dislike being much alone. A well-meaning faithful woman, with weak eyes and weak will, and given to tears on very slight occasions. Parkins had also been lately made housekeeper as well as companion, and the weekly accounts connected with that department threatened to be the bane of Parkins's life. Add them up she could not; make them come right she could not: and she could get neither mercy nor assistance from Lady Oswald, who had always been her own account-keeper, and never found any trouble in it. Two tradesmen's books were before Parkins now, and she was bending over them in despair, during her lady's absence.

"I can't as much as read the figures," she groaned; "how, then, am I to add 'em up? Last week there was an overcharge of ten shillings in this very butcher's book, and my lady found it out, and hasn't done talking to me for it yet. It isn't my fault; all folks are not born with a head for figures. And why can't tradespeople make their figures plain?"

Had she not been so absorbed by the book and its complications she might have seen the approach of a visitor. A tall and very gentlemanly man of some eight-and-twenty years, with a countenance that would have been remarkably frank and pleasing but for the expression of pride pervading it: nay, that was frank and pleasing in spite of the pride. He could not help the pride; it was innate, born with him; he did not make his own face, and the lines of pride were inherent in it. The pale features were regular, the hair dark, the eyes dark blue, and lying rather deep in the head, good and honest eyes they were, searching and truthful: and when he smiled, as he was smiling now, it made full amends for deficiencies, obliterating every trace of pride, and imparting a singular charm to the face.

His approach had been discerned by one of the maid-servants, and she had come to the hall-door and was holding it open. It was at her he had smiled, for in manner he was exceedingly affable. Perhaps the very consciousness of the pride that clung to him, and was his besetting sin, rendered him resolute that in manner at least he should not offend.

"How are you, Susan? Is Lady Oswald within?"

"No, sir, my lady's out," was the girl's reply, as she dropped a curtsey. "Parkins is in the drawing-room, sir, I think: I daresay she can tell whether my lady will be long."

He laid on the hall-table a small roll of paper or parchment that he carried, threw off a dusty light overcoat, and took up the roll again. Susan opened the drawing-room door.

"Mr. Oswald Cray."

Parkins gave a scream. Parkins was somewhat addicted to giving screams when startled or surprised. Starting up from her chair and her perplexing books, she stood staring at him, as if unable to take in the fact of his presence. Parkins believed in marvels, and thought one had been enacted then.

"Oh, sir! how did you come? You must have travelled surely on the telegraph wires?"

"Not I," answered Mr. Oswald Cray, smiling at her astonishment, but not understanding its cause. "I left London by rail this morning, Parkins."

"A telegraph message went up for you an hour or two ago, sir," continued Parkins. "My lady has had bad news, sir, and she sent for you."

"I had no message. I must have left London previously. What bad news has she had?"

"It's them railway people, sir," explained Parkins. "They have been writing a letter to my lady—leastways the landlord has—saying that they are going to take these grounds and build upon them. I haven't seen her so upset for a long while, sir. When, she got a bit better from the shock and had sent to the telegraph, she ordered the carriage, and set off to tell Dr. Davenal."

"Do you expect her to be long?" he asked, thinking that if so, he might go about some business he had to do, and come back again.

"I expect her every minute, sir; she has been gone a great deal longer than I thought she'd be away."

He walked to the window, unrolled the parchment, and began to look at it. It seemed a sort of map, drawn with ink. Parkins, who, whatever might be the companionship she was admitted to by her mistress, knew her place better than to remain in the presence of Mr. Oswald Cray, gathered up her account-book and her pen and ink, and prepared to quit the room.

"Shall I order you any refreshment, sir?" she stopped to ask.

"Not any, thank you."

She closed the door, leaving him deep in his parchment. Another minute, and the carriage was seen bowling quickly up. He went out to meet it: and Lady Oswald gave a scream as Parkins had done, and wanted to know how he had got there.

"I came down on my own account, Lady Oswald," he said, as he gave her his arm to lead her in. "My visit is a purposed one to you."

"I'm sure you are very good, Oswald! It is not often that you honour me with a visit. When you are staying in the neighbourhood for days and days, a simple call of ceremony is about all I get."

His lips parted with that peculiar smile which made his face at these moments so attractive. "When I am in the neighbourhood, Lady Oswald, business nearly overwhelms me. I have not much time to call my own."

Lady Oswald untied her bonnet, and threw herself into a chair: only the drive to Dr. Davenal's and back had tired her. Parkins came into the room to take her things, but she waved her hand sharply, impatient at the interruption. "Presently, presently,"—and Parkins left them alone again.

"Oswald, do you know what a cruel letter I have had this morning? They want to bring that wretched railway through my grounds."

"Not the railway," he said, correcting her. "They are proposing to build some sheds upon the boundaries of them."

"You know about it, then?"

"Yes; I came down to acquaint you, and I am sorry you should have heard of it from any one else first. I could have spared you one-half the alarm and annoyance it seems to have caused. Look here. This is the plan."

He spread the paper out before her. He pointed out the very small portion of the grounds, and in the remotest part of them, not in sight of the house or the parts ever walked in by herself, that was proposed to be taken: he assured her that the projected sheds were but small sheds, for barrows, trucks, and such things to stand under; that they would, in point of fact, be no annoyance to her, that she never need see or hear them. All in vain. Lady Oswald had set her mind bitterly against the innovation; she could neither be persuaded nor soothed, and she felt vexed with Mr. Oswald Cray that he should attempt it.

"It is very well for you to praise it," she resentfully said. "Your interest lies in the line, not in me. Perhaps they have bribed you to say all this."

For a single moment his face grew dark, and its haughty pride shone out quite repellently; the next he was smiling his sweet smile. None knew better than Oswald Cray how rebelliously false the tongue is apt to be in moments of irritation.

"Dear Lady Oswald, you know that it is foreign to my nature to cause needless pain. When this news reached my ears a week ago, for the plan did not originate with me, I bestirred myself to see whether it might not be relinquished; whether, in short, the sheds could not be erected on any other portion of the line. But I find that there is no other portion available so close to the station."

"There's that piece of waste ground midway between this and the station," she answered. "Why can they not take that?"

"Another station is to be made there. One for goods."

"Another station! Do they think to bring all the world to Hallingham?"

"They are bringing a great many lines of rails to it."

"But they need not disturb my possessions to make room for them!" she quickly retorted. "Surely your interest might get this spared to me!"

In vain Mr. Oswald Cray strove to convince her that on this point he had no influence whatever. Nay, he confessed to her, in his candid truth, that as one of the engineers to the line, he could only acquiesce in the expediency of that part being used for the sheds, that there was no other spot so available.

"I drew this plan out myself," he said, "partly from our charts of the line, partly from my personal recollection of your grounds. I wished to demonstrate to you how very little a portion of them is, in fact, required. Will you put on your bonnet again, Lady Oswald, and walk with me to the spot? I will show you the exact measure they intend to take."

"No, I won't," said Lady Oswald angrily. "And you ought not to turn against me, Oswald. It is the principle of the thing I go upon; the resistance that, in my opinion, should be universally made to these intrusive railways, which are cutting up the country and ruining it. If they wanted to take but one foot of my ground; if they only wanted that dry ditch that skirts it, they should never have it by my consent, and I will hold out against it to the last. Now you know."

She sat nervously unpinning her cashmere scarf, her hands trembling so that she could scarcely hold the gold pins as she took them out. Oswald Cray slowly rolled up the parchment. He had come down from town at a very busy moment, when he could ill spare the time, with the sole hope of soothing the news to her, of putting her in good humour with what must inevitably be. He had received many little kindnesses from her in his life, especially in his boyhood; and he was one to treasure up the remembrance of kindness shown, and repay it if he could.

It may seem a very trifling thing, this project of erecting a few low, trumpery sheds; as may Lady Oswald's inveterate objection to it. But it is on trifles that the great events of life turn; and, but for this project of the sheds, this not-to-be-conquered refusal, the greater portion of this story need never have been written.

CHAPTER V

RETROSPECT

Of some note in the county, though poor for their rank, were the Oswalds of Thorndyke. Thorndyke, their country seat, was situated about five miles from Hallingham, and had been generally made the constant residence of the reigning baronet. It was a fine old place; the dyke surrounding it, or dike, as you may like to spell it—from which the place no doubt had partially taken its name—was of remarkable width. It was filled up in the time of Lady Oswald's husband, the third baronet of his name; and fine pleasure-grounds might be seen now where unwholesome water had once stagnated. Possibly that water had been the remote and unsuspected cause of the dying off of so many of the house's children— as they had died in the old days.

The second baronet, Sir Oswald Oswald, lost five children in succession. Two daughters and a son alone lived to grow up: and perhaps it had been as well for the peace of Sir Oswald and his wife had those three likewise died in infancy; for pain they all brought home in one shape or other. They were self-willed and disobedient; preferring their own ways. The son wished to go into the army: his father had the greatest possible aversion to it; but he persisted, and went, in spite of remonstrance. The younger daughter, Frances, married an old man for his rank: Sir Oswald objected to it; the man's character was of startling notoriety; but Frances took her own will and married him. A few short months only, and she was back again at Thorndyke, driven to take refuge from her husband in her father's home. The elder daughter, Mary, married Mr. Cray, a gentleman of no account in comparison with the Oswalds of Thorndyke. To this the most strenuous objection of all was made by Sir Oswald and his lady—in their haughty pride they looked down with utter contempt upon Mr. Cray. Miss Oswald disputed the grounds of their objection, urging that Mr. Cray, though of no particular note, was at least of gentle blood and breeding, and though his means might be small, she deemed them sufficient. It was of no use: she could make no impression on her father and mother, she could not shake their refusal of consent, and she married Mr. Cray without it. Public opinion on the matter was divided. Some took Miss Oswald's part. She was of an age to judge for herself, being, in fact, no longer very young; and there appeared no good reason, save that he was not wealthy, for objecting to Mr. Cray. But her family—father, mother, brother, sister—bitterly resented it, and said she had disgraced them.

Mr. Cray had about eight hundred a-year, derivable from money in the funds, and he lived in the Abbey at Hallingham. The Oswalds enjoyed some three or four thousand a-year, landed property, and they lived at Thorndyke, and were baronets, and very grand. Of course there was a great difference; but some thought the difference might have been got over by Sir Oswald. Some went so far as to say that Mr. Cray, with his fine manly person and good conduct, was a better man than that shrivelled old lord who was breaking the heart of his poor wife, the younger daughter. Sir Oswald and Lady Oswald could not be brought to see it; none of the Oswalds could see it; and, take them altogether—brothers, cousins, uncles and nephews—there was a large family of them.

Mary Oswald married Mr. Cray, and he brought her home to Hallingham Abbey, and her friends never saw her after; that is, they never would recognise her. Many a Tuesday, on which day the family from Thorndyke would drive into Hallingham in their carriage and four—as was the habit with some of the county people—did they pass her without notice. They would be in the large close carriage, the old baronet and my lady, and their daughter Frances—who had no home now but theirs—opposite to them, and they would see Mrs. Cray at the Abbey windows, alone or with her husband, as the case might be, for their road took them past it, and all the greeting they gave her was a stony stare. Time went on, and there appeared a baby at her side, a pretty little fellow in long petticoats, held in his nurse's arms. That baby was named Oswald Oswald, and was the Mr. Oswald Cray whom you have seen: but the stare from the baronet's carriage was not less stony than before.

A twelvemonth more, when Oswald could just begin to run about in his pretty white frocks, and get his sturdy legs into grief, his hands into mischief, another child was born, and died. Poor Mrs. Cray died herself a few weeks afterwards. People said she had grown weak, fretting after Thorndyke, after her father and mother, lamenting their hardness, regretting her own disobedience; but people are prone to talk, and often say things for which there's not a shadow of foundation. She died without having seen her friends—unreconciled; and when Mr. Cray wrote to Sir Oswald a very proper letter, not familiar, but giving the details of her death, no answer was accorded him. Mrs. Cray, as Mary Oswald, had possessed a small income independent of her father, and this on her death passed to her little son. It was just one hundred and six pounds per year, and she made it her dying request that he should use the surname of Oswald in addition to that of Cray—should be known henceforth as Master Oswald Cray.

And it was so; and when the boy first entered a noted public school for gentlemen's sons, far away from Hallingham, and the boys saw him sign his exercises and copies "O. Oswald Cray," they asked him what the "O" was for. For his Christian name, he answered. Was not Oswald his Christian name? they wanted to know. Yes, his Christian and his surname both, he said—Oswald Oswald. It was his grandpapa's Christian and surname, Sir Oswald Oswald. Oh! was he his grandfather asked the boys. Yes; but—Oswald added in his innate love of truth—he had never been the better for him, Sir Oswald had never spoken to him in his life; there was something unpleasant between him and his papa, he did not know what. No; at that stage of the boy's age he was unconscious what the breach was, or that his dead mother had made it.

Poor Oswald Cray had not had a very happy childhood's life; he scarcely knew what was meant by the words, home-ties, home-love. He had never enjoyed them. There was a second Mrs. Cray, and a second family, and she did not like the boy Oswald, or care that he should be at home. He was but four years old when he was despatched to a far-off preparatory school, where he was to stay the holidays as well as the half-years. Now and then, about once in two years or so, he would be had home for a fortnight at Christmas, and Mr. Cray would make an occasional journey to see him.

It was at ten years old that he was removed to the public school, where the boys asked him the meaning of the "O." Before that time came, grief had penetrated to the family of Sir Oswald Oswald. His only son and heir had died in battle in India; his daughter Frances, who had never gone back to the old lord, had died at Thorndyke; and Sir Oswald and his wife were childless. Neither survived the year, and when Oswald was eleven years old, and getting to hold his own in the school, the title had devolved on the next brother, Sir John. Sir John was sixty when he came into it, and had no children. He had offended the Oswald family in the same way that Mary Oswald had offended them, by marrying a lady whose family was not as good as his own.

That lady was the present widow, Lady Oswald, now lamenting over the threatened innovation of the railway sheds. Sir John Oswald enjoyed the title for four years only, and then it lapsed to a cousin, for Sir John had no children. The cousin, Sir Philip, enjoyed it still, and lived at Thorndyke, and his eldest son would succeed him. They were proud also, those present Oswalds of Thorndyke, and never had spoken to Oswald Cray in their lives. The prejudices of old Sir Oswald had descended upon them, and Sir Philip and Lady Oswald would pass Oswald Cray, if by chance they met him, with as stony a stare as had ever greeted his poor mother.

Perhaps the only one of the whole Oswald family upon whom the prejudices had not descended was the widow of Sir John. Upon the death of her husband, when she had to leave Thorndyke, she took on lease the house at Hallingham, and had never removed from it. Her jointure was not a large one; but Sir John had bequeathed to her certain moneys absolutely, and these were at her own disposal. These moneys were also being added to yearly, for she did not spend all her income; so that it was supposed Lady Oswald would leave a pretty little sum behind her, by which somebody would benefit. There was no lack of "somebodies" to look out for it, for Lady Oswald had two nephews with large families, both of whom wanted help badly. One of these nephews, the Reverend Mr. Stephenson, was a poor curate, struggling to bring up his seven children upon one hundred a year. Lady Oswald sent him a little help now and then; but she was not fond of giving away her money.

The pride and prejudices of the family had not fallen upon her and she noticed and welcomed Oswald Cray. He was fifteen when she settled at Hallingham, and she had him to spend his first holidays with her afterwards. She had continued to notice him ever since, to invite him occasionally, and she was in her way fond of him; but it was not in the nature of Lady Oswald to feel much fondness for any one.

And yet, though not in her inmost heart cherishing the prejudices of the Oswalds, she did in a degree adopt them. She could not be independent and brave them off. Conscious that she was looked down upon herself by the Oswalds, she could not feel sufficiently free to take up her own standard of conduct, and fling those prejudices utterly to the winds. Upon tolerably good terms with Thorndyke, paying it occasional state visits, and receiving state visits from it in return, she did not openly defy all Thorndyke's prejudices. Though she acknowledged Oswald Cray as a relative, received him as an equal, there it ended, and she never, by so much as a word or a nod, recognised his father, Mr. Cray. She never had known him, and she did not enter upon the acquaintance. But in this there was nothing offensive, nothing that need have hurt the feelings of the Crays; Lady Oswald and they were strangers, and she was not bound to make their acquaintance, any more than she was that of other gentlepeople about Hallingham, moving in a sphere somewhat inferior to herself.

Mr. Cray had continued to reside at Hallingham Abbey, and to live at it in a style that his income did not justify. However the Oswalds may have despised him, he did not despise himself; neither did Hallingham. Mr. Cray of the Abbey was of note in the town; Mr. Cray was courted and looked up to; Mr. Cray went to dinner-parties, and gave them; Mr. Cray's wife was fashionable and extravagant, and so were Mr. Cray's daughters; and altogether Mr. Cray was a great man, and spent thousands where he ought to have spent hundreds.

He had four children, not counting Oswald—Marcus and three daughters—and it cost something to bring them out in the world. Marcus, changeable and vacillating by nature, fixed upon half a dozen professions or occupations for himself, before he decided upon the one he finally embraced—that of a doctor. Chance, more than anything else, caused him to decide on this at last. Altogether what with home extravagance and the cost of his children, Mr. Cray became an embarrassed man; and when he died, about two years previous to the opening of this story, a very slender support was left for his wife and daughters. His will did not even mention Oswald. Two or three hundred pounds were left to Marcus—the rest to Mrs. Cray for her life, and to go to her daughters afterwards.

Oswald had not expected any. Where a home gives no affection, it is not very likely to give money. When Oswald had come of age he found that his own income, of which his father was trustee, had no only been spent upon his education, but the principal had been very considerably drawn upon as well—in fact, it would take years to redeem it. "I was obliged to do it, Oswald," his father said. "I could not limit your educational expenses, and there was the heavy premium to pay in Parliament Street. I'd willingly have paid all cost myself; but it has not been in my power."

Oswald was not ungenerous. He grasped his father's hand and warmly thanked him, saying it was only right his own money should pay his cost when there were so many at home to educate. Ah, it was not the money he regretted. Had every sixpence of it been spent—why, it was spent—he was young and strong, with a good profession before him, and brains and hands to work it, he could make his own way in the world, and he should make it. No, it was not the money; but what Oswald had been hurt at, was the manner in which they had estranged him from his home; had kept him from the father's affection which he had yearned for. He knew that the fault had been Mrs. Cray's; that his father held him aloof only under her influence. He did not allow himself to blame his father even in his own heart; but he could not help thinking that, were he ever placed in a similar situation, he should openly love and cherish his first-born son, in spite of all the second wives in the world. Oswald had yet to learn by experience how utterly futile is that boast which we are all apt to make—that we should act so differently in other people's places. Never was there a truer aphorism than the homely saying: "Nobody knows where the shoe pinches save those who wear it."

Oswald Cray had been born proud: it might be detected in every tone of his decisive voice, in every turn of his well-set head, in every lineament of his haughty features. He could not help it. It is well to repeat this assertion, because pride is sometimes looked upon as a failing demanding heavy reproach. There it was, and he could not shake it out of him any more than he could shake out his other qualities or feelings. It was discerned in him when a little child; it was seen conspicuously in his schooldays; it reigned paramount in his early manhood. "The boy has the proud spirit of his grandfather Sir Oswald," quoth the gossips; and no doubt it was from that quarter that it had come. Only in his later days, those years between twenty and thirty when thought and experience were coming to him, did it grow less observable, for he had the good sense to endeavour to keep it in due subjection.

But it was not a bad sort of pride, after all. It was not the foolish pride of the Oswalds generally, who deemed everybody beneath them; it was rather that pride of innate rectitude which keeps its owner from doing a mean, a wrong, or a disgraceful action. It was the pride of self-esteem, of self-reliance; that feeling which says: "I must not do so and so, for I should disgrace myself—those careless-living men around me may do these things, but I am superior to it" Other young men might plunge into the world's follies; pride, if no better motive, kept Oswald Cray from them. He could not for very shame have borne a tainted conscience; he could not have shown a clear outside to the world, open and fearless, knowing that his heart was foul within.

He was not proud of his family descent from the Oswalds. Quite the contrary. He found no cause to pride himself on either the Oswalds or the Crays. So far as the Oswalds went, many a hundred times had he wished they were no connections of his. All his life he had received from them nothing but slights; and slights to a man of Oswald Cray's temperament bring the deepest mortification. He knew now how they had treated his mother; he felt to his very heart how they despised himself. If he could have changed his dead grandfather into somebody else, a little less foolish and a great deal less grand, he had been better pleased.

But this very isolation from his mother's family had tended to foster his own pride—the mortification which it induced had fostered it—just as the isolation from his own home, from his father and the second family, had contributed to render him self-reliant. It is not your home darling, bred up in fond dependence, sheltered from the world's storms as a hothouse flower, who becomes the self-reliant man, but he who is sent out early to rough it, who has nobody to care for him, or to love him, in all the wide earth.

Not a more self-reliant man lived than Oswald Cray. He was sure, under God, of himself, of his good conduct; and I think it is about the best surety that a man or woman can carry with them through life. In moments of doubt, perplexity, difficulty, whatever might be its nature, he turned to his own heart and took its counsel—and it never failed him. It was with himself he deliberated; it was his own good judgment, his right feeling, that he called to his aid. He had an honest, upright nature, was strictly honourable; a proud man, if it is the proper sort of pride, nearly always is so. His ambition was great, but not extravagant; it did not soar him aloft in flights of fancy, vain, generally speaking, as they are absurd. He was determined to rise to the summit of his profession—that of a civil engineer—but he entertained no foolish dreams beyond it. To attain to that, he would use every diligence, every effort, consistent with uprightness and honour; and dishonourable efforts Oswald Cray would have scorned to use, would have shaken them from him as he shook a summer-day's dust from his shoes.

He was connected with a firm of high repute in Parliament Street: Bracknell and Street. Oswald Cray was a partner, but his name did not appear as yet: and, as you may readily imagine, the lion's share of the profits did not fall to him. In fact, he had entered it very much as his half-brother had entered the house of Dr. Davenal—to obtain a footing. For more substantial recompense he was content to wait. Bracknell and Street were engineers to the Hallingham line, and to Oswald Cray had been entrusted its working and management.

He had said to Lady Oswald, in answer to her reproach of his not calling to see her more frequently, that his time when at Hallingham was much occupied. True, so far: but the chief and real motive which kept him from her house was a sort of sensitive feeling relating to her money. It was not that he dreaded people's saying he was looking after it: he would have scorned that kind of reproach: but he did dread lest any degree of intimacy, any pushing of himself in her way, should cause her to leave it to him. I am not sure that you will quite understand this; understand him or his feeling. None but a man of the nicest honour, who was entrenched, as it were, in his own pride, the pride of rectitude, could have felt this delicacy. He did not want Lady Oswald's money; he knew that he had no claim upon any of it, no right to it, and he would not put himself in her way more than he could help, even as a passing visitor. Gossiping Hallingham had said: "My lady would be leaving her nest-egg to Mr. Oswald Cray." The gossip had penetrated to Mr. Oswald Cray's ears, and his only notice of it was a haughty gesture of contempt: but in all probability it tended to increase his dislike to go to Lady Oswald's. During these business visits at Hallingham, he sojourned at a respectable inn of the old school, a little beyond the town and the Abbey Gardens, called the "Apple Tree," and had recently become more intimate with the family of Dr. Davenal.

Driven forth all his life from his father's home, allowed to enter it but at rare intervals, and then as a formally-invited guest, it cannot be supposed that Oswald Cray entertained any strong affection for his half-brother and sisters. Such a state of things would have been unnatural, quite in opposition to ordinary probabilities. It would be wrong to say that they disliked each other; but there was certainly no love: civil indifference may best express the feeling. Marcus, the eldest child of the second Mrs. Cray, was from three to four years younger than Oswald. It had been better that Mrs. Cray had fostered an affection between these boys, but she did just the reverse. She resented the contempt cast on her husband by the Oswalds of Thorndyke; she resented, most unreasonably, the fact that the little money of the first Mrs. Cray should have descended at once to Oswald; she even resented the child's having taken the distinguishing name: he was Oswald Cray, her son, plain Cray. How worse than foolish this was of her, how wrong, perhaps the woman might yet learn: but altogether it did excite her against Oswald; and she had kept him aloof from her own children, and encouraged those children to be jealous of him. When the boys became men, they met often, and were cordial enough with each other; but there was no feeling of brotherhood, there never could be any.

For a twelvemonth after Mr. Cray's death, Mrs. Cray remained at the Abbey, and then she left it. It was too expensive a residence for her now—its rent swallowing up half her income. She removed with her daughters to a watering-place in Wales, where, as she fractiously said, she hoped they should "get along." Marcus, who had qualified for a surgeon, became assistant to Dr. Davenal, and that gentleman at length gave him a small share in the profits. It was not a regularly-constituted firm—"Davenal and Cray"—nothing of the sort. Hallingham knew that he was admitted a partner so far as receiving a share went; and they knew that that was all.

He was liked in Hallingham, this young doctor, and Dr. Davenal had done it in kindness, to give him a standing. As the time went on, he would have no doubt a larger and larger share—some time succeed to the whole. He was considered a suitable partner for the doctor; the Crays of the Abbey had always been looked up to in the town; and young Cray's skill as a medical man was in the ascendant. Lady Oswald was getting to like him very much; she evinced a desire to patronise him, to push forward his interests; and Dr. Davenal was really in hope that she would adopt him as her attendant for everyday calls instead of himself. Mr. Cray could spare the time for these useless visits better than Dr. Davenal. He, Mr. Cray, resided in lodgings in the town, and was growing in its favour daily in a professional point of view: not that he had displayed any unusual skill, but simply that Hallingham gave him credit for possessing it, because they liked him.

There was a large family of the Davenals, as there was of the Oswalds—speaking, in both cases, of the days gone by, and comprising collateral branches. Years and years ago Surgeon Davenal's had been a noted name in Hallingham; he had a large practice, and he had several children. It is not necessary to speak of all the children. Richard (the present Dr. Davenal) was the eldest son, and had succeeded to the practice. The two other sons, Walter and John, had chosen to enter the Church, and both, when ordained, had gone out to the West Indies; one of them became chaplain to the Bishop of Barbadoes, the other obtained a church in the island. Both had married there, and Caroline Davenal was the only child of Walter, the elder of the two.

Sara was twelve years old when her cousin Caroline arrived in England, an orphan; father and mother were both dead. A poor clergyman in the West Indies, dying young, was not likely to have amassed money, and the little child, Caroline, had literally nothing. Her father wrote an appealing letter to his brother Richard, on his deathbed, and Richard Davenal was not one to reject it.

"She shall be my child henceforth, and Sara's sister," said he, in the warmth of his heart, when the letter and the child arrived at Hallingham. And so she had been.

But it was by no means so certain that Caroline Davenal would not some time be rich. A very large sum of money was pending in her mother's family, who were West Indians. It had become the subject of dispute, of litigation, and was at length thrown into that formidable court in England—Chancery. Should it be decided in one way, Caroline would derive no benefit; if in another, she would come in for several thousand pounds. The probabilities were in her favour—but Chancery, as you all know, is a capricious court, and does not hurry itself to inconvenience.

Upon the death of Dr. Davenal's wife, his sister Bettina came to reside with him, and to rule his children. He had but three—Richard, Edward, and Sara. There had been others between Edward and Sara, but they died young. Fine lads, those of Dr. Davenal, although they took to plaguing stern Miss Bettina, and aggravatingly called her "Aunt Bett." Fine young men, too, they grew up—well reared, liberally educated. Richard embraced his father's profession; for Edward a commission in the army was purchased, in accordance with his strong wish, and he was now Captain Davenal.

And Richard Davenal, the eldest son, where was he? Ah! it was a grievous story to look back upon. It had clouded the life of Dr. Davenal, and would cloud it to the end. Richard was dead, and Dr. Davenal blamed himself as the remote cause.

When Richard had completed his studies, and passed the College of Surgeons, he returned to Hallingham, and joined his father in practice, as it had been intended that he should. He grew greatly in favour: he promised to be as clever as his father: and Hallingham courted him. He was a man of attractive presence, of genial manners, and he mixed a great deal of pleasure with his life of work. Dr. Davenal spoke to him seriously and kindly. He said that too much pleasure did not agree long with work, could not agree with it, and he begged him to be more steady. Richard laughed, and said he would. A short while, and startling news reached the ears of Dr. Davenal—that Richard was thinking of marrying one who was undesirable. Richard, his fine boy, of whom he was so fond and proud, marry her! It was not against the young lady herself that so much could be urged, but against her connections. They were most objectionable. Dr. Davenal pointed out to Richard that to wed this girl would be as a blight upon his prospects, a blow to his reputation. Richard could not be brought to see it. Though not equal to themselves in position, she was respectable, he said; and her connections had nothing to do with it—he did not marry them, he married her. The feud continued: not an open feud, you understand, but an undercurrent of opposition, of coolness. Richard would not give up his project, and Dr. Davenal would not view it with anything but aversion. As to giving his consent, that Dr. Davenal never would; and Richard, hitherto dutiful, was not one to go the length of marrying in defiance.

It was at this time, or a little before it, that the dispute had arisen in Barbadoes touching the money already spoken of. Particulars of it were written to Dr. Davenal by his brother John, explaining also how Caroline's interests were involved. He, the Reverend John Davenal, said in the same letter that he was anxious to send his two little boys to Europe for their education, and was waiting to find them a fit escort; he did not care to trust them alone in the ship. As Dr. Davenal read this letter, a sudden thought darted into his mind like a flash of lightning. What if he sent out Richard? Richard could sift the details about this fortune, could, if expedient, urge Caroline's interests; he could bring back the two little boys, and—and—the chief thought of all lay behind—it might break off the engagement with the young girl here, Fanny Parrack! Quite a glow of satisfaction came over Dr. Davenal's face at the thought.

He sought a conference with his son. He told him that he wished him to take a voyage to Barbadoes; that Caroline's interests required somebody to go out; that the two little boys had no friend to bring them over. Richard hesitated. To most young men a visit to the West Indies would be a welcome distraction; but Richard Davenal seemed strangely to hold back from it—to shrink from its very mention. Did some mysterious warning of what it would bring forth for him dart unconsciously across his spirit? Or did he fear that it might in some way lead to his losing the young lady upon whom he had set his heart? It cannot be known. Certain it was, remembered, oh how remembered afterwards, that an unaccountable repugnance on Richard's part did evince itself, and it was only to the persistent urgent persuasion of Dr. Davenal that he at length yielded. He yielded, as it were, under protest, and he said he did, sacrificing his own strong wishes against it to his father's.

He set sail, and he wrote on his arrival at Barbadoes, after a fine passage; and the next letter they received, a fortnight afterwards, was not from him, but from his uncle, the clergyman. Richard had died of yellow fever.

It seemed to turn the current of Dr. Davenal's life. He blamed himself as the cause: but for his scheming—and in that moment of exaggerated feeling, of intense grief, he called it scheming—Richard, his best beloved son, would be still by his side to bless him. He had never been a scheming man, but an open and straightforward one; and never, so long as he lived, would he scheme again. In his unhappiness, he began to reproach himself for having needlessly opposed Richard's marriage—to believe that he might have done worse than in marrying Fanny Parrack. He sent for her, and he found her a pretty, modest, gentle girl, and his repentance heaped itself upon him fourfold. He informed her very kindly and considerately of the unhappy fact of Richard's death, and he told her that should any memento be found left for her amidst Richard's effects when they arrived—any letter, no matter what— it should be given to her.

But that death had changed Dr. Davenal into an old man; in the two years which had elapsed since, he had aged ten, both in looks and constitution. No wonder that a spasm of pain came over his face when Mr. Cray asked him whether he should forbid Caroline to him. You can understand his answer now: "So long as I live I shall never 'forbid' a marriage to any over whom I hold control:" and you can understand the anguish of the tone in which it was spoken.

And that ends the chapter of retrospect.

CHAPTER VI

NEAL'S CURIOSITY

They sat around the dinner-table; Dr. Davenal, Miss Bettina, Sara, and Caroline. It was an unusually silent table. Dr. Davenal could not digest the demand of Mr. Cray for Caroline; Caroline was conscious and timid; Sara scented something not altogether comfortable in the air, and did not raise her eyes from her plate; and it was one of the unusually deaf days of Miss Bettina.

Neal moved about noiselessly. Being a treasure of a servant, of course he always did move noiselessly. Quite an artistic performance was Neal's waiting; in his own person he did the waiting of three; and so tranquilly assiduous was his mode of accomplishing it so perfect indeed were Neal's ways in the household, that Miss Bettina rarely let a day pass without sounding his praise.

Strange to say, the doctor did not like him. Why it was, or how it was, he could not tell, but he had never taken heartily to Neal. So strong was the feeling, that it may almost be said he hated Neal; and yet the man fulfilled all his duties so well that there was no fault to be found with him, no excuse invented for discharging him. The doctor's last indoor man had not been anything like so efficient a servant as Neal, was not half so fine a gentleman, had ten faults where Neal did not appear to have one. But the doctor had liked him, good rough honest old Giles, had kept him for many years, and only parted with him when he got too old to work. Then Neal presented himself. Neal had once lived with Lady Oswald; he had been groom of the chambers at Thorndyke in Sir John's time, and Lady Oswald kept him for a twelvemonth after Sir John's death, and nearly cried when she parted with him; but Neal refused point-blank to go out with the carriage, and Lady Oswald did not wish to keep on three men-servants. Neal found a place in London, and they lost sight of him for some years; but he made his appearance at Lady Oswald's again one day—having come down by the new railroad to see what change it had made in the old place, and to pay his respects to my lady. My lady was gratified by the attention, and inquired what he was doing. He had left his situation, he answered, and he had some thoughts of trying for one in the country; my lady was aware, no doubt, how close and smoky London was, and he found that it had told upon his health; if he could hear of a quiet place in the country he believed he might be induced to take it, however disadvantageous it might be to him in a pecuniary point of view. Did my lady happen to know of one? My lady did happen to know of one: Dr. Davenal's, who was then parting with old Giles. She thought it would be the very place for Neal; Neal the very man for the place; and in the propensity for managing other people's business, which was as strong upon Lady Oswald as it is upon many more of us, she ordered her carriage and drove to Dr. Davenal's, and never left him until he had promised Neal the situation.

In good truth, Dr. Davenal deemed that Neal would suit him very well, provided he could bring his notions down to the place; and that, as Lady Oswald said, Neal intended to do. But to be groom of the chambers to a nobleman who kept his score or so of servants (for that was understood in the town to have been Neal's situation), and to be sole indoor manservant to a doctor, keeping three maids only besides, and the coachman in the stables, would be a wide gulf of difference. Neal, however, accepted the place, and Dr. Davenal took him on the recommendation of Lady Oswald, without referring to the nobleman in town.

But even in the very preliminary interview when the engagement was made, Dr. Davenal felt a dislike steal over him for the man. Instinct would have prompted him to say, "You will not suit me;" reason overpowered it, and whispered, "He will prove an excellent servant;" and Dr. Davenal engaged him. That was just before Richard went out to Barbadoes, and ever since then the doctor had been saying to himself how full of prejudice was his dislike, considering the excellent servant that Neal proved to be. But he could not overget the prejudice.

Neal cleared the table when the dinner was over, and placed the dessert upon it. Dr. Davenal did not care for dessert; deemed it waste of time to sit at it; waste of eating to partake of it: but Miss Bettina, who favoured most of the customs and fashions of her girlhood, would as soon have thought of dispensing with her dinner. Dr. Davenal generally withdrew with the cloth; sometimes, if not busy, he stayed a few minutes to chat with his daughter and Caroline; but calls on his time and services were made after dinner as well as before it.

On this day he did not leave his place. He sat at the foot of the large table, Miss Davenal opposite him at its head, the young ladies between them, one on each side. Interrupted by Lady Oswald in the afternoon, he had not yet spoken to Caroline; and that he was preparing to do now.

He drew his chair near to her, and began in a low tone. Sara rose soon, and quitted the room; Miss Davenal was deaf; they were, so to say, alone.

"My dear, Mr. Cray is not the man I would have preferred to choose for you. Are you aware how very small is the income he derives from his partnership with me?"

Caroline caught up the glistening damask dessert napkin, and began pulling out the threads of its fringe. "His prospects are very fair, Uncle Richard."

"Fair enough, insomuch as that he may enjoy the whole of this practice in time. But that time may be long in coming, Caroline; twenty years hence, for all we know. I shall be but seventy then, and my father at seventy was as good a man as I am now."

Her fingers pulled nervously at the fringe, and she did not raise her eyes. "I hope you will live much longer than that, Uncle Richard."

"So long as I live, Caroline, and retain my health and strength, so long shall I pursue my practice and take its largest share of profits. Mr. Cray understood that perfectly when I admitted him to a small share as a partner. I did it for his sake, to give him a standing. I had no intention of taking a partner: I wished only for an assistant; but out of regard to his prospects, to give him a footing, I say, I let him have a trifling share, suffered it to be known in Hallingham that he was made a partner of by Dr. Davenal. He has but two hundred a-year from me."

"It does not cost much to live," said Caroline. "We need not keep many servants."

Dr. Davenal paused, feeling that she was hopelessly inexperienced. "My dear, what do you suppose it costs us to live as we do?—here, in this house?"

"Ever so much," was Caroline's lucid answer.

"It costs me something like twelve hundred a-year, Caroline, and I have no house-rent to pay."

She did not answer. Miss Davenal's sharp eyes caught sight of Caroline's damaging fingers, and she called out to know what she was doing with the dessert napkin. Caroline laid it on the table beside her plate.

"I cannot afford to increase Mr. Cray's salary very much," continued Dr. Davenal. "To reduce my own style of living I do not feel inclined, and Edward draws largely upon me. Extravagant chaps are those young officers!" added the doctor, falling into abstraction. "There's not one of them, as I believe, Makes his pay suffice."

He paused. Caroline took up a biscuit and began crumbling it on her plate.

"The very utmost that I could afford to give him would be four hundred per annum," resumed Dr. Davenal "and I believe that I shall inconvenience myself to do this. But that's not it. There"—

"Oh, Uncle Richard, it is ample. Four hundred a-year! We could not spend it."

He shook his head at the impulsive interruption; at its unconscious ignorance. "Caroline, I was going to say that the mere income is not all the question. If you marry Mr. Cray, he can make no settlement upon you; more than that, he has no home, no furniture. I think he has been precipitate; inconsiderately so, few men would ask a young lady to be their wife until they had a house to take her to; or money in hand to procure one."

Caroline's eyes filled with tears. She had hard work to keep them from dropping.

"Carine," he said caressingly, "is it quite irrevocable, this attachment?"

The tears went down on the crumbled biscuit. She murmured some words which the doctor but imperfectly caught; only just sufficiently so to gather that it was irrevocable—or that at any rate the young lady thought so. He sighed.

"Listen to me, child. I should never attempt to oppose your inclinations; I should not think of forbidding any marriage that you had set your heart upon. If you have fixed on Mr. Cray, or he on you—it comes to the same—I will not set my will against it. But one thing I must urge upon you both—to wait."

"Do you dislike Mr. Cray, Uncle Richard?"

"Dislike him! no, child. Have I not made him my partner? I like him personally very much. I don't know whether he has much stability," continued the doctor, in a musing tone, as though he were debating the question with himself. "But let that pass. My objection to him for you, Caroline, is chiefly on a pecuniary score."

"I am sure we shall have enough," she answered, in a lower tone.

"If I give my consent, Carry, I shall give it under protest; and make a bargain with you at the same time."

Caroline lifted her eyes. His voice had turned to a jesting one.

"What protest?—what bargain?" she asked.

"That I give the consent in opposition to my better judgment. The bargain is, that when you find you have married imprudently and cannot make both ends meet, you don't turn round and blame me."

She bent her eyes with a smile and shook her head in answer, and began twisting the chain that lay upon her fair neck, the bracelets on her pretty arms. She wore the same rich dress that she had worn in the afternoon, as did Sara; but the high bodies had been exchanged for low ones, the custom for dinner at Dr. Davenal's.

"I will not withhold my consent. But," he added, his tone changing to the utmost seriousness, "I shall recommend you both to wait. To wait at least a year or two. You are very young, only twenty."

"I am twenty-one, Uncle Richard," she cried out. "It is Sara who is only twenty."

He smiled at the eagerness. One year seems so much to the young.

"Twenty-one, then: since last week, I believe. And Mark is three or four years older. You can well afford to wait. A year or two's time may make a wonderful difference in the position of affairs. Your share of that disputed property may have come to you, rendering a settlement upon you feasible; and Mark, if he chooses to be saving, may have got chairs and tables together. Perhaps I may increase his share at once to help him do it."

"Would you be so kind as enlighten me as to the topic of your conversation with Caroline, Dr. Davenal?"

The interruption come from Miss Bettina. Deaf as she was, it was impossible for her not to perceive that some subject of unusual moment was being discussed, and nothing annoyed her more than to fancy she was purposely kept in the dark. For the last five minutes she had sat ominously upright in her chair. Very upright she always did sit, at all times and seasons; but in moments of displeasure this stiff uprightness was unpleasantly perceptible. Dr. Davenal rose from his seat and walked towards her, bending his face a little. He had a dislike to talk to her on her very deaf days: it made him hoarse for hours afterwards.

"Caroline wants to be married, Bettina?"

Miss Bettina did catch the right words this time, but she doubted it. She had not yet learnt to look upon Caroline as aught but a child. Could the world have gone round in accordance with the ideas of Miss Bettina, nobody with any regard to propriety would have married in it until the age of thirty was past. Her cold grey eyes and her mouth gradually opened as she looked from her brother to her niece, from her niece to her brother.

"Wants to be what, did you say?"

"To be married, Aunt Bett," cried out the doctor. "It's the fashion, it seems, with the young folks nowadays! You were not in so great a hurry when you were young?"

The doctor spoke in no covert spirit of joking—as a stranger might have supposed, Miss Davenal being Miss Davenal still. Bettina Davenal had had her romance in life. In her young days, when she was not much older than Caroline, a poor curate had sought to make her his wife. She was greatly attached to him, but he was very, very poor, and prudence said, "Wait until better times shall come for him." Miss Bettina's father and mother were alive then; the latter a great invalid, and that also weighed with her, for in her duty and affection she did not like to leave her home. Ay, cold and unsympathising as she appeared to be now, Bettina Davenal had once been a warm, loving girl, an affectionate daughter. And so, by her own fiat, she waited and waited, and in her thirtieth year that poor curate, never promoted to be a richer one, had died—had died of bad air, and hard work, and poor nourishment. His duties were cast in the midst of one of our worst metropolitan localities; and they were heavy, and his stipend was small. From that time Bettina Davenal's disposition had changed; she grew cold, formal, hard: repentance, it was suspected, was ever upon her, that she had not risked the prudence and saved his life. Her own fortune added to what he earned, would at least have kept him from the ills of poverty.

"Who wants to marry her?" questioned Miss Davenal, when she could take her condemning eyes away from Caroline.

"Mark Cray."

The words seemed to mollify Miss Davenal in a slight degree, and her head relaxed a very little from its uprightness. "She might do worse, Richard. He is a good man, and I dare say he is making money. Those civil engineers get on well."

"I said Mark Cray, Aunt Bett," repeated the doctor.

"Mark! He won't do. He is only a boy. He has got neither house nor money."

"Just what I say," said the doctor. "I tell her they must wait."

"Mad! to be sure they must be mad, both of them," complaisantly acquiesced Miss Davenal.

"Wait, I said, Bettina," roared the doctor.

"You need not rave at me, Richard. I am not as deaf as a post. Who says anything about 'fate?' Fate, indeed! don't talk of fate to me. Where's your common-sense gone?"

"Wait, I said, Aunt Bett! Wa-a-a-it! I tell them they must wait."

"No," said Aunt Bett. "Better break it off."

"I don't think they will," returned the doctor.

Miss Bettina turned her eyes on Caroline. That young lady, left to herself, had pretty nearly done for the damask napkin. She dreaded but one person in the world, and that was stern Aunt Bettina. Miss Bettina rose in her slow stately fashion, and turned Caroline's drooping face towards her.

"What in the world has put it into your head to think of Mark Cray?"

"I didn't think of him before he thought of me," was poor Caroline's excuse, which, as a matter of course, Miss Davenal did not catch.

"Has it ever occurred to you to reflect, Caroline, how very serious a step is that of settlement in life?"

"We shall get along, Aunt Bettina."

"I'll not get along," exclaimed Miss Bettina, her face darkening. "I attempt to say a little word to you for your good, for your own interest, and you tell me 'to get along!' How dare you, Caroline Davenal?"

"Oh, Aunt Bettina! I said we should get along."

"I don't know that you would get along if you married Mark Cray. I don't like Mark Cray. I did not think"—

"Why don't you like him, aunt?"

"I don't know," replied Miss Bettina. "He is too light and careless. I did not think it a wise step of your uncle's to take him into partnership; but it was not my province to interfere. The Crays brought it to nothing, you know. Lived like princes for a few years, and when affairs came to be looked into on Mr. Cray's death, the money was gone."

"That was not Mark's fault," returned Caroline, indignantly. "It ought to be no reason for your disliking him, Aunt Bettina."

"It gives one prejudices, you see. He may be bringing it to the same in his own case before his life's over."

"You might as well say the same of Oswald," resentfully spoke Caroline.

"No; Oswald's different. He is worth a thousand of Mark. Don't think of Mark, Caroline. You might do so much better: better in all ways."

"I don't care to do better," was the rebellious answer. And then, half-frightened at it, repenting of its insolence, poor Caroline burst into tears. She felt very indignant at the disparagement of Mark. Fortunately for her, Miss Davenal mistook the words.

"We don't care that you should do better! Of course we care. What are you thinking of, child? Your uncle studies your interests as much as he would study Sara's."

"More!" impulsively interrupted the doctor, who was pacing the room, his hands under his coat-tails. "I might feel less scrupulous in opposing Sara's inclination."

"You hear, Caroline! The doctor opposes this inclination of yours!"

Caroline cast a look to him, a sort of helpless appeal: not only that he would not oppose it, but that he would set right Miss Davenal.

"I don't oppose it, Bettina: I don't go so far as that. I recommend them to wait. In a year or two"—

A loud knock at the hall-door startled Dr. Davenal. Knocks there were pretty frequent—loud ones too; but this was loud and long as a peal of thunder. And it startled somebody besides the doctor.

CHAPTER VII

AN INTERRUPTION

That somebody was Neal. Neal's mind was by far too composed a one to be ruffled by any sort of shock, and Neal's nerves were in first-rate order. It happened, however, that Neal was rather unpleasantly near to the front door at that moment, and the sudden sound, so sharp and long, did make him start.

When Neal removed the dinner things, he placed his plate and glasses in the pantry, and carried the tray with the other articles down to the kitchen. In going upstairs again he was called to by Watton, the upper woman-servant of the family, who was as old as Neal himself, and had lived with them for some years. She was in the apartment opening from the kitchen, a boarded room with a piece of square carpet in the middle. It was called the housekeeper's room, and was used as a sitting-room by the servants when their kitchen work was over for the day. The servants' entrance to the house was on this lower floor; steps ascending from it to the outer door in the back garden.

"Did you call me?" asked Neal, looking in.

Watton had her hands busy papering some jars of jam. She turned round at the question, displaying a sallow face with quick dark eyes, and pointed with her elbow to a note lying on the table before her.

"A note for Miss Sara, Neal. It came five minutes ago."

"Jessy might have brought it up," remarked Neal. "Letters should never be delayed below."

"Jessy has stepped out," explained Watton. "And I want to get to an end with this jam; Miss Bettina expected it was done and put away this morning."

Neal carried the note upstairs to his pantry, and there examined it. But beyond the fact that it was superscribed "Miss Sara Davenal," Neal could gather no information to gratify his curiosity. The handwriting was not familiar to him; the envelope displayed neither crest nor coat-of-arms. He held it up, but not the most scrutinising eye could detect anything through it; he gingerly tried the fastening of the envelope, but it would not come apart without violence. As he was thus engaged he heard the dining-room door open, and he peeped out of his pantry.

It was Miss Sara. She was going upstairs to the drawing-room. Neal heard her enter it; and after the lapse of a minute or two, he followed her, bearing the note on a silver waiter. She had shut herself in. Somehow that conference in the dining-room was making her nervous.

"Who brought it, Neal?" she carelessly asked, taking the note from the waiter.

"I am unable to say, miss. It came when I was waiting at dinner."

Neal retired, closed the drawing-room door, and descended to his pantry. There he began making preparations for washing his dinner glasses, rather noisy ones for Neal. He put some water into a wooden bowl, rinsed the glasses in it, and turned them down to dry. Having advanced thus far, it probably struck Neal that a trifling interlude of recreation might be acceptable.

He stole cautiously along as far as the dining-room door, and there came to a halt, bending down his head and ear. Neal could calculate his chances as well as any living spy. He could not be disturbed unawares by Miss Sara from the drawing-room or the servants from the kitchen; and his sense of hearing was so acute, partly by nature, partly by exercise, that no one could approach to open the dining-room door from the inside without his getting ample warning. Neal had not played his favourite part for long years to be discovered at last.

There he had remained, listening to anything in the dining-room there might be to hear, until aroused by that strange knock—so loud, long, and near, that it startled even him. A noiseless glide back to his pantry, a slight clatter there with spoons and forks, and Neal came forth to answer the summons, with a far fleeter foot than Neal in general allowed his stately self to put forth, for the knocker had begun again and was knocking perpetually.

"Is all the town dying!" muttered Neal.

He pulled open the door, and there burst in two fine lads, sending their ringing shout of laughter through the house, and nearly upsetting the man in their wild haste, as they sprang past him into the dining-room, and on Dr. Davenal. Sara, alarmed at the unusual noise, came running down.

"You rogues!" exclaimed the doctor. "What brings you here today?"

They were too excited to explain very lucidly. One day extra in a schoolboy's holidays, especially at the commencement, will turn young heads crazy. The usher who was to take charge of such of the boys whose homes lay this way, had received news that morning of the illness of a relative, and had to leave a day sooner: so they left also.

"Nothing loth, I'll answer for it," cried Dr. Davenal; and the boys laughed.

He placed them both before him, and looked first at one, then at the other, regarding what alteration six months had made. There was a general likeness between them, as regarded eyes, hair, and complexion, but none in features. Richard, the eldest, generally called Dick, was a good-tempered, saucy-looking boy, with a turned-up nose; Leopold had more delicate features, and seemed less strong.

"You have both grown," said the doctor; "but Leo's thin. How do your studies get on, Dick?"

"Oh—middling," acknowledged Dick, a remarkably candid lad. "Uncle Richard, I'm the best cricketer in the whole school. There's not one of the fellows can come up to me."

"The best what, Richard?" said Miss Bettina, bending her ear to the lad.

"Cricketer, Aunt Bett," repeated Richard.

"Good boy! good boy!" said Miss Bettina approvingly. "Resolve to be the best scholar always, and you will be the best. You shall have a pot of fresh jam for tea, Dick."

Dick smothered his laughter. "I am not a good scholar at all, Aunt Bett. Leo is: but he's a muff at cricket."

"Not a good scholar!" repeated Miss Bettina, catching those words correctly. "Did you not tell me you were the best scholar?"

"No. I said I was the best cricketer," responded Dick.

"Oh," said Miss Bettina, her face resuming its severity. "That will do you no good, Richard."

"Aren't you deafer than before, Aunt Bett?"

"Am I what?" asked Miss Bettina. "Darker! I never was dark yet. Not one of all the Davenal family had a skin as fair as mine. What put that fancy into your head, Master Richard?"

"I said deafer, Aunt Bett," repeated Richard. "I am sure you are just as deaf again as you were at Christmas! Uncle Richard, we had a boat-race yesterday. I was second oar."

"I don't like those boat-races," hastily interrupted Caroline.

"Girls never do," said Mr. Richard, loftily. "As if they'd like to blister their hands with the oars! Look at mine."

He extended his right hand, palm upwards, triumphant in blisters. Dr. Davenal spoke.

"I don't like boat-racing for you boys, either, Dick."

"Oh, it was prime, Uncle Richard! One of the boats tipped over, and the fellows got a ducking."

"That's just it," said Dr. Davenal. "Boats 'tip' over when you inexperienced young gentlemen least expect it. It has led to loss of life sometimes, Dick."

"Any muff can scramble out of the water, Uncle Richard. Some of us fellows can swim like an otter."

"And some can't swim at all, I suppose. What did Dr. Keen say when he heard of the boatful going over?"

Richard Davenal raised his honest, wide-open eyes to his uncle, some surprise in their depths. "It didn't get to Keen's ears, Uncle Richard! He knew nothing of the boat-race; we had it out of bounds. As if Keen wouldn't have stopped it for us, if he had known. He thought we were off to the cricket-field."

"Well, you must be a nice lot of boys!" cried Dr. Davenal, quaintly. "Does he give a prize for honour? You'd get it, Dick, if he did."

Dick laughed. "It's the same at all schools, Uncle Richard. If we let the masters into the secret of all our fun, mighty little of it should we get."

"I think they ought to be let into the fun that consists in going on the water. There's danger in that."

"Not a bit of it, Uncle Richard. It was the jolliest splash! The chief trouble was getting the dry things to put on. They had been laid up in the boxes ready to come home with us, and we had to put out no end of stratagem to get at them."

"A jolly splash, was it! Were you one of the immersed ones, Dick?"

"Not I," returned Dick, throwing back his head. "As if we second-desk fellows couldn't manage a boat better than that! Leo was."

"How many of you were drowned, Leo?"

Leo opened his eyes as wide as Dick had previously done. "Drowned, Uncle Richard! Not one. We scrambled out as easy as fun. There's no fear of our getting drowned."

"No fear at all, as it seems to me," returned the doctor. "But there's danger of it, Leo."

Leo made no reply. Perhaps he scarcely defined the distinction of the words. Dr. Davenal remained silent for a minute, lost in thought; then he sat down, and held the two lads in front of him.

"Did either of you ever observe a white house, lying back on a hill, just as you pass the next station to this—Hildon?"

"I know it," cried out Richard. "It is old Low's."

"Old Low's, if you choose to call him so, but he is not as old as I am, Master Dick. Some people in that neighbourhood called him Squire Low. He is Lady Oswald's landlord. A few years ago, boys, I was sent for to his house; that very house upon the hill. Mr. Low's mother was living with him then, and I found she was taken ill. I went for several days in succession: sometimes I saw Mr. Low's sons, three nice lads, but daring as you two are, and about your present age. One afternoon,—listen, both of you,—I had no sooner got home from Mr. Low's, than I was surprised to see one of his men riding up here at a fierce rate. The railway was not opened then. I feared old Mrs. Low might be worse, and I hastened out to the man myself. He had come galloping all the way, and he asked me to gallop back as quickly"—

"Old Mrs. Low was dead!" cried quick Dick.

"No, sir, she was not dead. She was no worse than when I left her. Mr. Low's three sons had done just what you tell me you did yesterday. They went upon the river at Hildon in a rowing-boat, and the boat upset—tipped over, as you call it; and the poor boys had not found it so easy to scramble out as you, Leo, and your comrades did. One of them was out, the man said; he thought that the other two were not. So I mounted my own horse and hastened over."

"But what did they want with you, Uncle Richard? Were there no doctors near?"

"Yes. When I got there a doctor was over the lad: but Mr. Low had confidence in me, and in his distress he sent for me. It was the youngest who was saved—James."

"What! James Low, who goes about in that hand-chair."

"The very same, Dick. From that hour he has never had the proper use of his limbs. A species of rheumatic affection—we call it so for want of a better name—is upon him perpetually. When the illness and fever that supervened upon the accident were over, and which lasted some weeks, we found his strength did not return to him, and he has remained a confirmed invalid. And that was the result of one of those tips over which you deem so harmless."

"Will he never get well?" asked Leo.

"Never, I fear."

"And the two other boys, Uncle Richard? Did they scramble out at last?"

"No, Leo. They were drowned."

Leo remained silent; Dick also. Dr. Davenal resumed.

"Yes, they were drowned. I stood in the room where the coffins rested, side by side, the day before the funeral, Mr. Low with me. He told how generally obedient his poor boys were, save in that one particular, the going upon the water. He had had some contentions with them upon the point; he had a great dislike to the water for them—a dread of their venturing on it, for the river at Hildon is dangerous, and the boys were inexperienced. But they were daring-spirited boys who could see no danger in it, and—listen, Dick!—did not believe there was any. And they thought they'd just risk it for once, and they did so; and this was the result. I shall never forget their father's sobs as he told me this over the poor cold faces in the coffins."

The young Davenals had grown sober.

"My lads, I have told you this little incident—but I think you must have heard somewhat of it before, for it is known to all Hallingham just as well as it is to me—to prove to you that there is danger connected with the water, more particularly for inexperienced boys. Where does the school get the boats?"

"We hire them," answered Dick. "There's a boat association in the place; poor men who keep boats, and hire them out to anybody who'll pay."

"They should be forbidden to hire them to schoolboys of your age. I think I shall drop a hint to Dr. Keen." Dick Davenal grew frightened. "For goodness sake don't do that, Uncle Richard! If the school knew it got to Keen through you, they'd send me and Leo to Coventry."

"I'll take care you don't get sent to Coventry through me, Dick. But I cannot let you run the liability of this danger."

"I don't think I'll go on the water again at school, Uncle Richard," said Leo, who had sat down, and was nursing his leg thoughtfully.

"I don't much think you will," said the doctor.

Leo continued to nurse his leg. Dick, who had little thought about him, had thrown his arms around Sara's waist, and was whispering to her. Both the lads loved Sara. When they had arrived little strangers from the West Indies, new to the doctor's house and its inmates, new to everything else, they had taken wonderfully to Sara, and she to them. You do not need to be told that they were the lads whom poor Richard Davenal was to have escorted over; and when they came they brought his effects with them.

CHAPTER VIII

A TACIT BARGAIN

Meanwhile Mr. Oswald Cray had dined at his rustic inn, the "Apple Tree," and was on his way to pay an evening visit at Dr. Davenal's. In passing along New Street he encountered his half-brother, turning hastily out of his lodgings.

"Were you coming in, Oswald?" asked Marcus, as they shook hands. "I heard you were down."

"Not now," replied Oswald. "I am going on to Dr. Davenal's, and I go up again by the night train. My visit here today was to Lady Oswald. We are going to take a strip of her grounds for sheds, and she does not like it."

"Not like it!" echoed Mark. "It's worse than that. You should have seen the way she was in this afternoon. It won't hurt the grounds."

"Not at all. But she cannot be brought to see that it will not. In point of fact, the sound of it is worse than the reality will be. It does sound ill, I confess,—railway-sheds upon one's grounds! I was in hopes of being the first to break the news to her: so much lies in the telling of a thing; in the impression first imparted."

"She said this afternoon that it all lay with you. That you could spare her grounds if you would."

"I wish it did lie with me: I would do my best to find another spot and spare them. The company have fixed upon the site, Low has given his concurrence, and there's no more to be said or done. I am very sorry, but it has been no doing of mine. Will you go with me to the doctor's, Mark?"

Marcus hesitated, and then said he had rather not call that evening.

"Why?" asked Oswald.

"Well—the fact is,—I don't see why I may not tell you,—I have been asking the doctor this afternoon for Caroline. He did not give me a positive answer, one way or the other; and I don't think it will look well to press a visit upon them just now."

Oswald Cray's was not a demonstrative countenance: a self-controlled man's rarely is: but certainly it exhibited marked surprise now, and he gazed at his brother inquiringly.

"You are surely not thinking of marrying?"

"Yes, I am. Why should I not think of it?"

"But what have you to marry upon? What means?"

"Oh—I must get Dr. Davenal to increase my share. By a word he dropped this afternoon when we were talking of it, I fancy he would do it: would increase it to four hundred a-year. We might manage upon that."

Oswald Cray made no immediate reply. He, the self-reliant man, would have felt both pain and shame at the very thought of marrying upon the help of others.

"You are thinking it's not enough, Oswald?"

"It might be enough for prudent people. But I don't think it would be found enough by you and Caroline Davenal. Mark, I fancy—I shall not offend you?—fancy you are not of a prudent turn."

"I don't know that I am. But any man can be prudent when there's a necessity that he should be."

"It has not always proved so."

"I see you think me a spendthrift," said Mark good-humouredly.

"Not exactly that. I think you could not live upon as small an income as some can. Dr. Davenal gives you, I believe, two hundred a-year, and you have been with him six months: my opinion is, Mark, that at the twelvemonth's end you will find the two hundred has nothing like kept you. You will be looking about for another hundred to pay debts."

"Are you so particularly saving yourself?" retorted Mark.

"That is not the question, Mark; I am not going to be married," answered Oswald, with a smile. "But I do save."

"If the doctor will give me four hundred a-year to begin with, there's no need to wait."

"You have no furniture."

"That's easily ordered," said Mark.

"Very easily indeed," laughed Oswald. "But there'll be the paying for it."

"It won't take so much. We shall not set up in a grand way. We can pay by instalments."

"A bad beginning, Mark."

Mark rather winced. "Are you going to turn against me, Oswald? To throw cold water on it?"

Oswald Cray looked very grave as he answered. Mark was not his own brother, and he could not urge him too much; but a conviction seated itself in his heart, perhaps not for the first time, that Mark had inherited their father's imprudence.

"These considerations are for you, Mark; not for me. If I speak of them to you, I do so only in your true interest. We have never been brothers, therefore I do not presume to give a brother's counsel,—you would deem I had no right to do it. Only be prudent, for your own sake and Caroline's. Good evening, if you will go back."

Neal admitted Mr. Oswald Cray, and Neal's face lighted up with the most apparent genuine pleasure at doing it. Neal was the quintessence of courteous respect to his betters, but an additional respect would show itself in his manner to Mr. Oswald Cray, from the fact possibly that he had served in the Oswald family at Thorndyke, and Mr. Oswald Cray was so near a connection of it.

Dr. Davenal was then in the garden-parlour with Sara. The noisy boys were regaling themselves with good things in the dining-room, under the presidentship of Miss Bettina. A few moments, and the doctor and Mr. Oswald Cray were deep in the discussion of the proposition that had so moved them; the doctor being the first to speak of it. Sara sat near the window, doing some light work. A fair picture she looked, in her evening dress; her cheeks somewhat flushed, her neck so fair and white, the gold chain lying on it; her pretty arms partially hidden by their white lace. Dr. Davenal stood in a musing attitude on the other side of the window, and Mr. Oswald Cray sat between them, a little back, his elbow on the centre table, his chin on his hand.

"Mark has just told me of it," he observed, in reply to Dr. Davenal. "I met him as I walked here. I was very much surprised."

"Not more surprised than I," returned the doctor.

"At least, surprised that he should have spoken to you so soon."

"What do you think of it?" asked the doctor, abruptly.

"Nay, sir, it is for you to think," was the reply of Oswald Cray, after a momentary pause.

"I know—in that sense. My opinion is, that it is exceedingly premature."

"Well—yes, I confess it appears so to me. I told Mark so. There's one thing, Dr. Davenal—some men get on all the better for marrying early."

"True: and some all the better for waiting. I like those men who have the courage and patience to wait, bearing steadily on to the right moment and working for it. I married very early in life myself, but my circumstances justified it. Where circumstances do not justify it, a man should wait. I don't mean waiting on to an unreasonable time, until the sear and yellow leaf's advancing; nothing of that: but there's a medium in all things. I am sure you would not rush into an imprudent marriage: you'd wait your time."

A smile parted Oswald Cray's lips. "I am obliged to wait, sir."

"That is, prudence obliges you?"

"Yes; that's it."

"And I make no doubt your income is a good deal larger than the present one of Mark?"

"I believe it is."

Dr. Davenal stood in silence, twirling his watch chain. "Give me your advice," he said, turning to Mr. Oswald Cray.

"Dr. Davenal, may I tell you that I would prefer not to give it? By blood Mark is my half-brother; but you know the circumstances under which we were reared—that we are, in actual fact, little more than strangers; and I feel the greatest delicacy in interfering with him in anyway. I will do him any good that I can: but I will not give advice regarding him in so momentous a step as this?"

Dr. Davenal understood the feeling, it was a perfectly proper one. "Do you think he has much stability?—enough to steer him safely through life, clear of shoals and quicksands?"

Oswald Cray's opinion was that Mark possessed none. But he was not sure: he had had so little to do with him. "Indeed, I cannot speak with certainty," was his answer. "Mark is far more of a stranger to me than he is to you. Stability sometimes comes with years only; with time and experience."

"I cannot tell you how surprised I was," resumed the doctor, after a pause. "Had Mark come and proposed to marry Bettina, I could not have been more astonished. The fact is, I had somehow got upon the wrong scent."

"The wrong scent?" exclaimed Mr. Oswald Cray, looking up.

"I don't mind telling you, considering how different, as it has turned out, was the actual state of things," said Dr. Davenal, with a laugh. "I fancied you were inclined to like Caroline?"

Mr. Oswald Cray's deep-set blue eyes were opened wider than usual in his astonishment. "What caused you to fancy that?"

"Upon my word I don't know. Looking back, I think how foolish I must have been. But you see, that idea tended to obscure my view as to Mark."

Oswald Cray rose from his seat, and stood by Dr. Davenal, looking from the window.

"Had it been so, would you have objected to me?" he asked; and in his voice, jesting though it was, there rang a sound of deep meaning.

"No, I would not," replied Dr. Davenal. "I wish it had been so. Don't talk of it; it will put me out of conceit of Mark."

Mr. Oswald Cray laughed, and stole a glance at Sara. Her cheeks were crimson; her head was bent closer to her work than it need have been.

At that moment Dr. Davenal's carriage was heard coming up the side lane, Roger's head and shoulders just visible over the garden wall. Dr. Davenal gave the man a nod as he passed, as much as to say he should be out immediately, and retreated into the room. It had broken the thread of the discourse.

"You came down in answer to Lady Oswald's message?" he observed. "She said she had sent for you."

"Not in answer to the message. I came away before it reached London: at any rate before it reached me."

"Lady Oswald's in a fine way. I suppose nothing can be done?"

"Nothing at all. It is unfortunate that her grounds abut just on that part of the line."

"She will never stop in the house."

"You see, the worst is, that she has just entered upon the third term of her lease. She took it for seven, fourteen, or twenty-one years. I am not sure, however, that Mr. Low, under the circumstances, could oppose her depart"—

"Uncle Richard, the carriage is come round to the door. How are you, Mr. Oswald Cray?"

The interruption came from the boys. Both had rushed in without any regard to noise; or rather to the avoidance of it. Mr. Oswald Cray shook hands with them, and the doctor turned to shake hands with him.

"I have to see a patient or two tonight. A poor countrywoman's son is ill, and I promised her to go over this evening if possible. Perhaps you'll be here when I return. Bettina and the girls will give you some tea."

He hurried out; and the boys after him, clamorously enough. During their holidays, Dr. Davenal could rarely get into his carriage without those two dancing attendance round it, like a bodyguard of jumping savages. Mr. Oswald Cray turned to Sara, who had risen also, and stood before her.

"Just one moment, Sara, for a single question. Did you fall into the misapprehension that I was growing attached to your cousin?"

Her manner grew shrinkingly timid; her eyelashes were never raised from her hot cheeks. It seemed that she would have spoken, for her lips parted; but there came no sound from them.

"Nay, but you must answer me," he rejoined, some agitation distinguishable in his tone. "Did you do me the injustice to suppose I had any thought of Caroline?"

"No. O no."

He drew a deep breath, as if the words relieved him, took her hand in his, and laid his other hand upon it, very seriously.

"It was well to ask: but I did not think you could so have mistaken me. Sara! I am not an imprudent man, as I fear Mark is; I could not, in justice to the woman whom I wish to make my wife, ask her to leave her home of comfort until I can surround her with one somewhat equivalent to it. I think—I hope—that another year may accomplish this. Meanwhile—you will not misunderstand me, or the motives of my silence?"

She lifted her eyes to his face to speak: they were swimming in tears: lifted them in her earnestness.

"I shall never misunderstand you, Oswald."

And Mr. Oswald Cray, for the first time in his life, bent his lips on hers to seal the tacit bargain.

CHAPTER IX

EDWARD DAVENAL

It was a charming evening in the month of October. The heat of summer was over, the cool calm autumn reign ad in all its loveliness. Never had the sun set more brilliantly than it was setting now; never did it give token of a finer day for the morrow; and that morrow was to be Caroline Davenal's wedding-day.

Persuasion and promises had proved stronger than Dr. Davenal and prudence, and he had consented to the early marriage, it may be said reluctantly. He had urged upon them the verb to wait: but neither of them appeared inclined to conjugate it; Caroline especially, strange as it may seem to have to say it, had turned a deaf ear. So the doctor had yielded, and the plans and projects for the carrying the wedding out were set on foot.

Dr. Davenal had behaved generously. He increased Mark Cray's share to four hundred a-year, and he gave them a cheque for three hundred pounds for furniture. "You must be content to have things at the beginning in a plain way, if you must be in a hurry," he said to them; "when you get on you can add costly furniture by degrees." Miss Bettina would not give anything. Not a penny-piece. "No," she said to Caroline; "you are flying in the face of wiser heads than yours, and I will not encourage it. If you don't mind, you'll come to grief."

Caroline laughed at the "coming to grief." Perhaps not without cause. Were they but commonly prudent there would be little fear of it. Four hundred a-year to begin upon, and a great deal more in prospective, was what many and many a couple beginning life might have envied. Even Dr. Davenal began to think he had been over-cautious. It might have been better to wait a year or two, but they would do well as it was, if they chose. If they chose! it all lay in that. Perhaps what made people think of imprudence in their case was, that both had been reared to enjoy a much larger income.

Those prudential fears and scruples were over, however; they belonged to the past; nobody retained them in the actual face of preparation. When Mark Cray was looking out for a house, the Abbey, yet untenanted, occurred to him. It had been his father's residence; it carried a certain weight of position with it; and he thought it would be well that it should be his. Dr. Davenal acquiesced: it was certainly rather farther from his own residence than was convenient; and it was at the opposite end of the town; but that fact might have its advantages as well as its disadvantages: and Mark took the Abbey at a yearly rental.

How busy they had been, furnishing it and getting the wedding clothes ready, they alone could tell! In this bustle, in the satisfaction of buying the new furniture, and settling it in its appointed places, the old prudent objections, I say, were lost sight of; completely forgotten. Miss Bettina thawed so far as to go down two whole days to the Abbey, and superintend; and she read Caroline lessons on domestic management and economy from morning until night.

Oswald Cray had delicately placed a fifty-pound note in his brother's hands. "Present-giving at these times seems to be the order of the day, Mark," he carelessly said. "If you and Caroline will choose something for yourselves, and save me the trouble, I shall be glad. You know more about dressing-cases and work-boxes than I do." Altogether, the Abbey,—what with the purchased furniture, and a few pretty things that went down out of Dr. Davenal's house,—was quite sufficiently well set up.

And now it was the evening preceding the wedding, and the house was in a commotion of preparation. Servants were running hither and thither; Miss Bettina, with her sharp voice and her deaf ears, was everywhere, creating no end of mistakes; the breakfast-table was being laid out; Sara was quietly helping Jessy to pack her cousin's travelling trunk; and Caroline, useless as usual, was going into ecstasies over a present which had just come in.

It was from Lady Oswald. A handsome tea and coffee-pot with their stands, sugar-basin and cream-jug, all of solid silver. Caroline ran round the house to get admirers to view it, and ran into the room of Dr. Davenal.

Neal was coming out as she entered, a waiter in his hand, therefore it was evident he had been bearing something to his master. Dr. Davenal stood before the window looking at an unopened note.

"O uncle, do come and see! It is the best present I have had: a silver tea-service. I did not expect anything like it from Lady Oswald."

"Presently, child. All in good time."

He laid down the note on the table, as he spoke, not having opened it. Caroline thought his tone and countenance were alike sad.

"Has anything vexed you, Uncle Richard?"

"A little, Carine. When one waits for the sight of a dear face, and the hours go by in expectation, hour after hour, from the opening of the day to its close, the disappointment brings a chill."

Caroline wondered. She did not understand that longing waiting yet. "Do you allude to Edward, Uncle Richard?"

Whom else should he allude to? Since Richard's death, Edward Davenal had grown dearer than ever son did to father. Dr. Davenal could willingly have laid down his life for him, and thought it no sacrifice. Ah! if these sons and daughters could but realise this precious love that is lavished on them in all its strange intensity!

"Aunt Bettina's vexed that he is not here. She says it will be putting the dinner off."

"We are too impatient, Caroline. I daresay he could not get here sooner. Here's Mark," added the doctor.

Dr. Davenal's carriage was drawing up to the gate. The doctor had despatched Mark in it that afternoon to see a country patient: he waited at home for his son. Roger looked to the house as Mr. Cray got out, wondering whether the carriage was wanted again, or whether he might drive it round to the coach-house. Dr. Davenal raised his hand by way of signal, and was hastening out.

"Won't you come and see my teapot and things, Uncle Richard?" cried Caroline, piteously.

"When I come back, Carine. The teapot can wait."

"And there's that note on the table," she said, resenting the slight on the teapot. "You have never opened it."

"That can wait too. I know what it is." The doctor walked quickly on, and Caroline followed him to the front door. Mark was coming in.

"Is the London train in, Mark?—did you notice as you came by? There's one due."

"I did not notice," replied Mark. "I don't much think it is in. I saw no bustle."

Dr. Davenal stepped into the carriage. "Turn round, Roger. The railway station."

The whistle was sounding as they drew near, and Roger whipped up his steeds. The doctor stepped on to the platform as the train dashed in. He elbowed his way amidst the crowd, trying to peer into every first-class carriage.

"Edward!"

"My dear father!"

Captain Davenal leaped lightly out—an upright, slender man, with the unmistakable look of the soldier; a dark, handsome face, and a free and ready voice.

"I have been looking for you all day, Ned."

"Not up here, surely?"

Dr. Davenal laughed. "Not likely. I just happened to come up now; so it's all right. You have some luggage, I suppose?"

"A portmanteau. My servant's here."

"Good evening, Dr. Davenal. Ah, captain! how are you?"

The salutation came from a passenger who had likewise stepped out of a first-class compartment. They turned to behold Oswald Cray.

"Why! you don't mean to say that you have come by this train?" cried Captain Davenal, in his quick manner.

"Yes I have. And you?"

"I have come by it, too. Where were our eyes, I wonder?"

"In our own compartment, I expect," said Oswald Cray. "I was at the end of the train, and did not get out during the journey."

"Neither did I. The same errand brings us, I suppose—Caroline's wedding? It's fine to be Mark Cray! You and I must wait for our honours: we can't afford these grand doings yet."

Dr. Davenal looked at his son. "If you can't afford them now Ned, when are you to afford them?"

Captain Davenal's answer was to shrug his shoulders. "There may come in a great rich ship some day," he said, with his ready laugh. "Are you going that way, Mr. Oswald Cray? We shall see you by and by."

All the pride and affection of the father shone out in Dr. Davenal's face as he passed through the town, sitting by the side of his brave son, who was in Roger's place, and drove. A hundred hats were taken off; a hundred pleased faces greeted them. The doctor remained passive, save for smiles; but Captain Davenal's gay face was turned from side to side, in answer to the salutations, and he had something else to do besides attending to his horses.

"Take care, Ned."

"All right, sir," was the young officer's careless answer. But he escaped the wheel of a meeting carriage by only half an inch; and Roger, seated behind, said to himself that the captain had not yet grown out of his randomness.

He pulled the horses up with a jerk when they arrived, leaped out, and turned to give his hand to his father. Neal had the door open, and Edward Davenal passed him with a nod and a fleet foot, for he saw his sister's face behind, bright with joyous tears. He kissed them away.

"Sara, you foolish child! Keep the tears until I go again."

"When will that be, Edward?"

"Tomorrow evening. Hush!" he whispered, checking her startled exclamation. "Let me take my own time for telling papa. I know he will be vexed."

"We thought you would stay a week at least."

"I wish I could! Leave is difficult to get at all just now, on account of—I'll tell you more later, Sara."

Miss Bettina Davenal was at hand, waiting for her greeting. In the old days of his boyhood, she and he were undisguised enemies. The boy was high-spirited and rude to her, ten times worse than poor Richard: he had been the first to call her Aunt Bett, and to persist in it, in spite of her angry displeasure. He called it her still.

"Well, Aunt Bett! You are looking younger than ever."

"Are you quite well, Nephew Edward?"

"In high feather, aunt. And mean to keep so until the wedding's over. When is yours to be, Aunt Bett?"

"Tomorrow at eleven," was Aunt Bett's unconscious answer. "And right glad I shall be when it has taken place."

The shout of laughter vexed Miss Davenal; she wondered what the mistake was. But the captain turned away, for Caroline was stealing towards them with conscious cheeks, and the new silver teapot in her hand.

"It was unkind of you not to come before, Edward," she said. "Some of my beautiful new dresses are packed up now, and you can't see them."

"I shan't die of the disappointment, Carry," was the ungallant rejoinder of the captain. "What's that you are carrying? A trophy?"

"It's a teapot. It is part of Lady Oswald's present. Her's is the best of all, and I have had so many. Come and look at them: they are laid out in the garden-room."

"So many teapots?" inquired the captain.

"Nonsense, Edward! You know I meant presents."

He drew something covertly from his pocket, and clasped it on her neck. It was a dazzling necklace. Caroline, loving ornaments excessively, was wild with delight.

"O Edward! how kind you are! I never liked you as much as I do now."

"Candid!" cried the captain: and Dr. Davenal laughed outright as he walked away to his consulting-room.

His son followed him. The doctor had taken up the note which he had left on the table, and was about to open it when something strange in its appearance struck upon his eye. He carried it to the window and looked minutely at its fastening, at the claret-coloured crest stamped in the envelope, that of the Oswald family.

"Edward," said he, "does it look to you as if this envelope had been tampered with—opened, in fact?"

Captain Davenal examined the fastening. It was quite daylight still, though less bright than before the sun went down. "There's not a doubt of it, in my opinion," he said, handing the note back to his father.

"It's very strange," exclaimed the doctor. "Do you know, it has occurred to me lately to think that two or three of my letters have been opened."

"By their appearance?"

"By their appearance. But I could not be certain how or when it was done. For aught I know, they might have been reopened by their writers before forwarding them to me. I do feel, however, sure that this one has been tampered with since it lay here. It came by the same messenger that brought Caroline's present, and Neal brought it in to me. I was deep in thought at the time, and I turned it about in my fingers, looking at it, but not opening it. I knew what its contents were—that they concerned a little matter Lady Oswald had to write to me upon—and I did not open it, but went to the station, leaving it on the table. Now I am fully certain that that appearance of reopening was not on it then."

"Who can have opened it, then?" quickly cried Captain Davenal.

"Neal."

"Neal!"

"Neal—as I suspect."

"But I thought Neal was so faithful a man—so good a servant altogether!"

"An excellent servant, though I have never liked him. And latterly I have suspected the man's truth and honesty. I don't mean his honesty in regard to goods and chattels, but in regard to his own nature. If my letters have been opened, rely upon it, it is he who has done it."

"Have you spoken to him?"

"No. I shall speak now, though."

Dr. Davenal rang the bell, and Neal appeared. So calm, so quietly unconcerned!—not in the least like a man who has just tampered with his master's letters.

"Come forward, Neal. Shut the door for a minute. When I went out just now I left this note on the table—the one you brought in to me from Lady Oswald's servant I did not open it before I went out;— but it looks to me as if it had been opened since, and closed up again."

Dr. Davenal spoke in a quiet tone. Neal, entirely unruffled, save by a slight natural surprise, stepped close up to the table, and looked first at Dr. Davenal and then at the note, which, however, the doctor did not particularly show to him.

"I should think not, sir. There has been no one here to open it."

"That it has been opened I feel certain. Who has been in the room?"

"Not any one, sir," replied Neal. "It has not been entered, so far as I know, since you left it."

There was nothing more to be said, and Dr. Davenal signed to him to go. "I could not accuse him downright," he remarked to his son; "but enough has been said to put him on his guard not to attempt such a thing again."

"He does not look like a guilty man," cried Captain Davenal. "It is next to impossible to suspect Neal of such a thing. He is too—too—I was going to say too much of a gentlemen," broke off Captain Davenal, laughing at his own words. "At any rate, too respectable. His manner betrayed nothing of guilt—nothing of cognisance of the affair. I watched him narrowly."

"True; it did not. He is an innocent man, Ned, or else a finished hypocrite. Of course I may be wrong in my suspicions: honestly to confess it, I have no cause to suspect Neal, beyond the powerful feeling in my mind that he's not to be trusted—a feeling for which I have never been able to account, although it has been upon me since the first day I engaged him."

"We do take up prejudices without knowing why," remarked Captain Davenal. "I suppose sometimes they are false ones.—Here's Neal coming in again."

"I beg your pardon, sir, for having so positively assured you that no one had been in your room," he said, addressing his master. "I remember now that Mr. Cray entered it. I did not think of it, sir, at the moment you questioned me."

"If he did, he'd not touch the letter," said Dr. Davenal.

"Certainly not, sir. But I thought it right to come and mention to you that he had been in."

Neal withdrew, and Captain Davenal looked at his father. "The man seems quite honest in the matter. I think this is an additional proof of it. Had he opened the letter himself he would not have forgotten that another person had been in the room."

Very soon Neal appeared again. This time it was to say that dinner was served. Dr. Davenal nodded to him to close the door; he and his son were deep in conversation.

Ten minutes elapsed before they came out. Miss Bettina fidgeted and grumbled, but it did not bring them; and when they did come, the doctor had a strange cloud upon his brow. Edward also, or else Sara fancied it; but he grew merry as the dinner advanced, joking and laughing with every one.

She took the opportunity of speaking to him after dinner. He went out on the lawn at the back to smoke his cigar in the starlight, and Sara stole after him. He threw his arm round her, and they paced the gravel walk.

"Were you telling papa before dinner that you should have to leave tomorrow?" she asked.

"I was telling him worse than that, my little sister."

"Worse?"

"You loving ones at home will think it so. You will, Sara. And my father—it's a blow to my father."

Sara Davenal's heart was beating against her side; a thousand improbabilities rushed into her brain. "Tell it me, Edward," she said, very calmly. Sometimes, in moments of agitation, she could be calm, almost unnaturally so, outwardly. It is frequently the case with those who feel the deepest.

"The regiment's ordered abroad."

"O Edward!"

For a few minutes neither spoke again. Sara's greatest thought was for her father. She seemed to have divined how cruelly Dr. Davenal felt the separation from his sons; Richard dead, Edward in London with his regiment. If he had to go abroad to remote countries, thousands of miles away—why, almost as good that he had died. They should feel it so.

"And that explains why I could not get a long leave," he resumed. "There's so much of preparation to be made; and we officers have to look to everything, for the men as well as for ourselves. We sail in a week or two."

They paced on in silence. Captain Davenal suddenly looked down at her, and detected tears.

"Don't grieve, child. I am but a worthless sort of brother, after all—never with you. Perhaps I shall come back a better one."

"Edward, can't you sell out?"

"Sell out!" he exclaimed, in astonishment. "Sell out because we are ordered on active service. You are a brave soldier's sister, Miss Sara Davenal!"

"Some time ago, when there was a question of the regiment's going out, you were to have exchanged into another, and remained at home, Edward. It was just after Richard's death, I remember. Can you not do that now?"

"No, I cannot. I can neither sell out nor exchange. It is impossible."

There was so much grave meaning in his tone that Sara looked up involuntarily. He laughed at her earnest face.

"O Edward! must you go!"

"There's no help for it. We go to Malta first. India—as we suppose—afterwards."

"Papa may be dead before you return."

"No, no! I trust not."

"It will be as though he had no children!" she exclaimed, almost passionately, in her love for her father, in her grief. "Richard dead; you gone: he will have none left."

"He will have you, Sara."

"I! Who am I?"

"The best of us. You have given him no grief in all your life; I and poor Dick have: plenty. It is best as it is, Sara."

She could scarcely speak for the sobs that were rising. She strove bravely to beat them down, for Sara Davenal's was an undemonstrative nature, and could not bear that its signs of emotion should be betrayed outwardly. She loved her brother greatly; even the more, as the doctor did, for the loss of Richard; and this going abroad for an indefinite period, perhaps for ever, rang in her ears as the very knell of hope. He might never return: he might go away, as Richard had, only to die.

How long they continued to pace that walk underneath the privet-hedge, which skirted and hid the narrow side path leading from the house to the stables, Sara scarcely knew. Captain Davenal spoke little; he seemed buried in thought: Sara could not speak at all; her heart was full. Rarely had the night's brilliant stars looked down on a sadness deeper felt than was that of Sara Davenal.

"You will come down again to take leave of us?" she asked, after a while.

"Of course I shall."

CHAPTER X

A TREAT FOR NEAL

Nearly four-and-twenty hours subsequent to that, Dr. Davenal was pacing the same walk side by side with Lady Oswald. The wedding was over, the guests were gone, and the house, after the state breakfast, had resumed its tranquillity. Of the guests, Lady Oswald had alone remained, with the exception of Mr. Oswald Cray. It was one of those elaborate breakfast-dinners which take hours to eat, and five o'clock had struck ere the last carriage drove from the door.

Lady Oswald asked for some tea; Miss Davenal, as great a lover of tea as herself, partook of it with her. Captain Davenal preferred a cigar, and went into the garden to smoke it: Mr. Oswald Cray accompanied him, but he never smoked. Both of them were to return to town by the seven o'clock train.

By and by, the tea over, the rest came out on the lawn to join them—Lady Oswald and Miss Davenal in their rich rustling silks, Sara in her white bridesmaid's dress. The open air of the warm, lovely evening was inexpressibly grateful after the feasting and fuss of the day, and they lingered until twilight fell on the earth. Miss Davenal went in then: but Lady Oswald wrapped her Indian cashmere shawl, worth a hundred guineas Hallingham said, more closely round her, and continued to talk to Dr. Davenal as they paced together the sidewalk.

Her chief theme was the one on which you have already heard her descant—that unwelcome project of the railway sheds. It had dropped through for a time. There had been a lull in the storm ever since it was broached in the summer. Lady Oswald complacently believed her remonstrance had found weight with the authorities of the line, to whom she had addressed a long, if not a very temperate letter: but, in point of fact, the commencement of the work had been delayed for some convenience of their own. Only on this very morning a rumour had reached Lady Oswald's ears that it was now to be set about immediately.

"I am not satisfied with Oswald," she was saying to the doctor. "Did you observe how he avoided the subject at the breakfast-table? When I told him that he might exercise his influence with the company, and prevent it if he pleased, he turned it off quietly."

"I think he did not care to defend himself publicly, or to enter upon the matter," observed the doctor. "Rely upon it, he would prevent it if he could; but his power does not extend so far."

"I know he says it does not," was the observation of Lady Oswald. "Do you think he is true?"

"True!" repeated Dr. Davenal, scarcely understanding in his surprise. "Oswald Cray true! Yes, Lady Oswald. Never man lived yet more honestly true than Oswald Cray."

He looked towards Oswald Cray as he spoke, pacing the broad middle walk with his son and Sara; at the calm good face with its earnest expression, every line, every feature speaking truth and honour; and the doctor's judgment re-echoed his words.

"Yes, Lady Oswald, he is a true man, whatever else he may be."

"I always deemed him so. But—to protest that he would help me if he could; and now to let this dreadful threat arise again!"

"But he cannot prevent its arising," returned the doctor, wishing Lady Oswald would exercise a little common-sense in the matter. "He is but a servant of the company, and must carry out their wishes."

"I don't believe it," peevishly replied Lady Oswald. "He is the engineer to the company; and it is well known that an engineer does as he pleases, and lays his own plans."

"He is one of the engineers; the junior one, it may be said. I suppose you will not forgive me, Lady Oswald, if I point out, that when your interests and the line's are at issue, as in this matter, Oswald Cray, of all others, is forced to obey the former."

"Was there ever so monstrously wicked a project formed?" asked Lady Oswald, with some agitation.

"It is very unfortunate," was the more temperate reply. "I wish they had fixed upon any grounds but yours."

"I wish they had! It will send me into my grave!"

Careless words! spoken, as such words mostly are spoken, unmeaningly. If Lady Oswald could but have known how miserably they were destined to be marked out! If Dr. Davenal had but foreseen how that marking out would affect all his after-life—change, as it were, its current, and that of one who was dear to him!

"And because that worry was not enough, I have had a second to annoy me today," resumed Lady Oswald. "Jones gave warning to leave."

"Indeed!" returned Mr. Davenal, and the tone of his voice betrayed his concern. He knew how minor vexations were made troubles of by Lady Oswald; and the parting with Jones, her steady coachman of many years, would be a trouble not much less great than this threatened building of the sheds.

"Why is Jones leaving?" he inquired.

"Because he does not know when he's well off," was the retort, spoken querulously. "The servants latterly have been all quarrelling together, I find, and Jones says he won't remain. I asked Parkins what she was good for not to stop their quarrelling, and she burst into tears in my face, and said it was not her fault. You are best off, doctor. Your servants are treasures. Look at Neal!"

"I don't know that Neal is much of a treasure," was the doctor's answer. "I'd make him over to your ladyship with all the pleasure in life. Do you feel the chill of the evening air?"

Lady Oswald looked up at the clear sky, at the evening star, just visible, and said she did not feel the chill yet.

Dr. Davenal resumed.

"I have grown to dislike Neal, Lady Oswald. In strict correctness, however, 'grown to dislike' is not the best term, for I have disliked him ever since he has been with me. He"—

"Disliked Neal!" interrupted Lady Oswald, wondering whether she might trust her ears. "You dislike Neal! Why?"

"I can scarcely tell you why. I don't think I know, myself. But I do very much dislike him; and the dislike grows upon me."

"You never mentioned this. I thought you were so satisfied with Neal."

"I have not mentioned it. I have felt a sort of repugnance to mention what would appear so unfounded a prejudice. Neal is an efficient servant, and the dislike arose to me without cause, just as instincts do. Latterly, however, I begin to doubt whether Neal is so desirable a retainer as we have deemed him."

"In what way do you doubt him!"

Dr. Davenal smiled. "A doubt has arisen to me whether he is true—as you have just said by Mr. Oswald Cray. I shall watch the man; and, now that my suspicions are awakened, detection will be more easy. Should he turn out to be what I fear—a deceitful fellow, worse than worthless—he will be sent out of my house head foremost, at a minute's warning, and get his true character. Lady Oswald, I think I could pardon anything rather than deceit."

"How angrily you speak!" breathlessly exclaimed Lady Oswald. The words recalled him to courtesy.

"I fear I did; and I ought to have remembered that he was a respected servant once of Sir John's, that it was you who recommended him to me. You will pardon my warmth, Lady Oswald. To any less close friend than yourself I should not have mentioned this. The fact is, a most unjustifiable trick was played me yesterday, and it is impossible for me to suspect anybody but Neal. I shall watch him."

"What trick was it?" asked Lady Oswald.

Dr. Davenal hesitated before he spoke. "Perhaps it would be scarcely fair to mention it, even to you, Lady Oswald. I am not certain: there's just a loophole of possibility. If I find I am wrong, I will honestly confess it to you; if the contrary, you and the world will know what a worthless scamp we have nourished in Neal."

Very agreeable words indeed! especially to Neal himself, who had the satisfaction of hearing them. Mr. Neal, with his soft tread, was gingerly pacing the narrow path behind the privet-hedge, his steps keeping level with theirs; he having strolled out to take the evening air, and to hear all that he could hear.

They were interrupted by the approach of Captain Davenal and Mr. Oswald Cray. It was getting towards the hour of their departure. Sara came up with them. The doctor laid his hand on his daughter's shoulder, and she walked by his side.

"Going? Nonsense!" said the doctor. "There's no hurry yet."

"When shall you be down again, Oswald?" asked my lady.

"I believe very shortly. I must be down—about these alterations," he had been on the point of saying, but stopped himself in time. There was no cause for bringing up the sore story oftener to her than was necessary.

"Will you promise that they shall not build those horrible sheds?"

"If it lay with me, I would willingly promise it," was his reply, "I wish you would believe me, dear Lady Oswald."

"Of course I have no claim upon you," she fretfully continued. "I know that. It is not my fault if I am unable to leave my fortune to you—what little I may have to leave. There are others who, in my opinion, have a greater claim upon me."

He seemed not to understand her. He turned his glance full upon her. "I beg your pardon. What did you say, Lady Oswald?"

"Oswald, I have never spoken distinctly to you about my money," she resumed. "I like you very much, and should have been glad to leave some to you; it is natural you should be looking out for it, but"—

Every line of his pale face was ablaze with pride as he interrupted her; his voice, calm, low, terribly stern, was ten times more impressive in its truth than one loud and angry could have been. "Allow me to set you right, Lady Oswald. I have never in my life looked for one shilling of money from you: I do not recognise, or believe in, or see any claim I can by possibility have upon it: of the whole world, the Oswalds are those upon whom I could least recognise it—from whom I would the least accept it. I pray your ladyship to understand me in the fullest sense of the words—from whom I would never accept it."

Never had he looked so like the Oswalds as he looked then. The red colour came into Sara's cheeks, and a faint sense of dread (did it come as a prophetic warning?) stole into her heart—that that pride might prove her deadliest enemy; perhaps his. Lady Oswald's mood changed, and she laughed.

"You are independent, Oswald."

"I am self-dependent," was his answer. "A fair field and no favour are all I ask. I believe I can make my way in the world far better than money could make it for me. It is what I mean to try at—and do, Heaven helping me."

"But you need not have glared at me in that way," she said, relapsing into fretfulness. "I declare I thought it was old Sir Oswald of Thorndyke come out of his grave. My nerves are not strong, and that you know."

A better feeling came over him, and he held out his hand to Lady Oswald, his atoning smile wonderfully frank and sweet. "Forgive me if anything in my speech or manner has offended you, dear Lady Oswald. But I believe you vexed me more than I have ever been vexed in my life."

"Well, well; you shall be as independent as you please," said Lady Oswald. "Let us change the subject. When do you intend to follow Mark's example and marry?"

"Not until I can afford it better than—than Mark could, I was going to say," he added, glancing at Dr. Davenal and laughing.

"You do mean to marry some time, Oswald?"

"I hope so."

The answer was spoken so fervently, that they looked at him in surprise. Sara contrived to draw behind, and began plucking one of the flowers, already closing to the night. He resumed carelessly, as if conscious that his tones had been too earnest for general ears.

"Men do marry for the most part in this good old-fashioned land of ours, and my turn may come some time. I think our time is nearly up, Davenal."

The captain took out his watch. "In a minute or two. We can walk it in ten minutes, if we put out our best speed."

As they went in, Oswald Cray looked round for Sara, and found she had not followed them. He turned back to her.

"I must say goodbye to you. Sara! you are crying!"

"O no," she answered, brushing away the rebellious tears. "It's nothing."

He took her hand and placed it within his arm, and they advanced slowly to the house. "Will you tell me what the 'nothing' is?" he asked in a low tone, which of itself was sufficient to invite confidence.

"I cannot bear to part with Edward," she answered. "Nothing has been said about it; but he brought down bad news. They are ordered to Malta; and thence, he thinks, they shall go to India. Edward said he should tell you as you went back tonight."

It was entire news to him, and he thought how greatly Dr. Davenal must feel it. Few admired that fine young officer, Edward Davenal, more than Oswald Cray. But he had no time to discuss it now, scarcely to say a word of sympathy.

"Goodbye," he whispered, as they halted on the threshold and he turned to press her hand in both of his, bending his face a little down. "Goodbye. And remember."

"Remember what?" she asked.

"That you don't belong quite to yourself now."

He hastened in, leaving Sara standing there: standing there with the significant words and their meaning beating pleasant changes on her heart Captain Davenal came springing out.

"Hush, darling, be brave!" he said, as he took the kiss from his sister's lips. "Leave all that until I come down for my real farewell."

And Sara was brave, and dried her tears, and confided in the prospect of that real farewell; little dreaming that it was destined never to be spoken.

CHAPTER XI

LADY OSWALD'S JOURNEY

Mr. Marcus Cray's marriage had taken place on a Thursday, and the time went on to the following Saturday week with little to mark it. Enough, as events were unhappily to turn out, was to mark it then. They, Marcus Cray and his wife, were expected home that evening: but it is not with them that we have just at present to do.

On this Saturday morning, Oswald Cray had come down to Hallingham on business connected with the line. In the course of the day he called on Lady Oswald, and found her in a state not easy to describe. That very morning certain men had been seen on her grounds, marking off the small portion of its boundaries intended to be taken for the sheds. Convinced that all her hopes of immunity had been but vain dreams, she had become angry, hysterical, almost violent. Oswald Cray had never seen her like this.

It was an illustration of the misery we may inflict upon ourselves, the evil spirit that will arise from self-grievance. In point of fact, these sheds, to be built on a remote and low portion of her land, could not prove any real annoyance to Lady Oswald; she would not see them from her window; she did not go, ever, near the spot. The grievance lay in her imagination; she had made it a bugbear, and there it was. In vain Oswald Cray pointed out to her that it had been the same thing with regard to the rail itself. When she first heard it was to skirt her grounds, she had been as alarmed as she was now; but when the work was complete, the trains were actually running, then Lady Oswald found (though she did not acknowledge it) how void of reason her alarm had been; had the trains been fifty miles off she could not have seen less of them. It would be so with regard to the sheds, Oswald Cray told her; he told her that even a less portion of the ground would be taken than was at first intended: he did not add that he, by his persistent efforts in her cause, had obtained this little concession, but he might have told her so with truth. He assured her that the thing could not prove an annoyance to her. All in vain. He might just as well have talked to the winds. She would not listen. Parkins sat 'n tears, administering specifics for the "nerves," and entreating my lady to be tranquil. My lady replied by saying she should never be tranquil again, and she actually abused Mr. Oswald Cray.

"Nay," said Oswald, good-humouredly, "it is your landlord you should blame, not me. He agreed to the thing instanter—the moment it was proposed to him."

Lady Oswald's cheeks were burning as she turned to Oswald. "If he had refused, instead of consented, what then? Could they have done it in spite of him?"

"It would have been done eventually, I suppose. Not just yet: the company would have had to bargain with him, perhaps to dispute the matter with him legally: and all that takes time."

"Had he persistently contended against it, the company might have grown weary; have ended by fixing upon some other spot for their sheds," she breathlessly cried, the excitement on her face deepening.

Mr. Oswald Cray hesitated. "It is possible, certainly; but"—

"I will go to him," broke in Lady Oswald. "I will go to Low this very hour."

She started from her seat, upsetting a bottle which Parkins held in her hand, almost upsetting Parkins herself in her vehemence. Mr. Oswald Cray gently restrained her.

"My dear Lady Oswald, you will do no good by going to Low now. It is too late. The thing has gone too far."

"It has not gone too far, Oswald Cray. So long as the sheds are not begun it cannot be too late. If Low did give his consent, he can retract it. The land is freehold, and freehold land cannot be seized upon lightly. Get my things, Parkins, and order the carriage." And Parkins submissively retired to obey.

"Lady Oswald, believe me," said Oswald, impressively, "Mr. Low cannot now retract his consent if he would. The agreement is signed; nay, I believe the money is paid. Your going to him will do no possible good; it can only be productive of further unpleasantness to yourself."

"Have you a motive in keeping me away from him?" asked Lady Oswald, and his brow momentarily contracted at her blind pertinacity. "Do you know that I have never once seen him upon this subject I— never once."

"No!" he said, really wondering at the omission.

"I would not go to see him; I was too angry; I contented myself with writing to him, and telling him what I thought; and then, you know, until this blessed morning, when Jones came into the house with the news that the men were measuring the land, I never thought the thing would be really done. I will go to him now, Oswald Cray, and all you can say against it will not avail with me. If you had any courtesy you would accompany me, and add your voice to mine against this unjustifiable wrong."

Courtesy was an adjunct in which Oswald Cray was not naturally deficient; in time, that day, he was. The business which brought him down was pressing, must have his full attention, and be finished so as to enable him to return to town that night. He had snatched these few minutes, while the clerks at the company's offices were at dinner, just to see Lady Oswald.

"It would give me great pleasure to escort you anywhere, Lady Oswald, but today I really cannot absent myself from Hallingham. I have my hands full. Besides," he added, a frank smile on his face, "have you forgotten how impossible it would be for me to go against the agreement made by the company with Mr. Low, by soliciting that gentleman to attempt to retract it?"

"I see," said Lady Oswald, beating her foot pettishly on the carpet; "better that I had called anybody to my aid than you. Are you cherishing resentment against me, Oswald Cray?"

Oswald Cray opened his dark blue eyes in surprise.

"Resentment?—against you, Lady Oswald! Indeed I do not understand you."

"I thought you might be remembering what I said at Dr. Davenal's the evening of your brother's wedding. I mean about the money; which I said I could not leave you," she continued in a low tone. "You took me up so sharply."

"I fear I did. I was vexed that you could so misapprehend my nature. We need not recur to the subject, Lady Oswald. Let it pass."

"I must say a word first, Oswald. I believe, with all your fiery pride, and your aptitude to take offence, that your nature is honest and true; that you would save me from annoyance if you could."

"I would indeed," he interrupted earnestly. "Even from this threatened annoyance I would doubly save you, if it were at all within my power."

"Well, I want to say just this. I have always liked you very well; you have been, in fact, a favourite of mine; and many a time it has occurred to me to wish that I could put you down in my will"—

Lady Oswald, I pray you"—

"Now do be quiet, and hear me. I consider it a duty to myself to tell you this, and I always intended to tell you before my death. I fully believe what you say; that you do not wish for my money, that you would prefer to make your own way; I say I fully believe that, Oswald. There are some men—honourable to fastidiousness, I call them—who are utterly incapable of casting a thought or a wish to the money of others: you are one, as I believe; and there's the additional bar in your case with regard to my money, that it comes from the Oswalds. I don't think you would accept money in whatever form it came to you, from the Oswald family."

"I don't think I would," replied Oswald. And he spoke the truth of his heart.

"Still, I judge it right to give you this little word of explanation," she proceeded. "I daresay, whenever my will comes to be read, that you will feel surprised at its contents; may even deem that you had more legal claim upon me than he who will chiefly inherit. I do not think so. I have left my money to please myself: he to whom it is left has the best claim upon me in my judgment. I am happy to know that he will be rewarded: and he knows it."

Oswald felt a little puzzled: the words "and he knows it" somewhat excited his curiosity. With her own family, who alone (in Oswald Cray's opinion) could be said to have claims on Lady Oswald, she held but little communication: and a conviction stole over him that she did not allude to them. He was destined (as it proved) never to forget those words; and the construction he put upon them was, that the future inheritor of the money knew he was named as the inheritor. He said nothing. It was not a subject he cared to pursue; he had neither right nor inclination to inquire as to the disposal of what Lady Oswald might leave behind her. Had he dreamt of the ill those words would work, he might have asked further particulars.

"I thought I'd say this to you some time, Oswald. Had you been less fiercely proud, and I more at liberty to dispose of what I have to leave, I should regret not remembering you. As it is, perhaps all's for the best."

That again struck upon him as strange: "I more at liberty to dispose of what I have to leave." Was she not at full and entire liberty?—if so, why was she not? The question set Oswald thinking.

But circumstances seemed inclined to prove themselves stronger than Lady Oswald's will, in regard to this visit to her landlord. Her coachman made his appearance with hindering news; one of the carriage horses had fallen lame.

"Accept it as an omen that the visit would have brought forth no good luck," said Oswald Cray, with a smile, while Jones stood, deprecating his lady's anger.

A doubt flashed across her mind for a moment whether the excuse was real, and the amazed Jones had to repeat it, and to assure his mistress that he was going "right off" for the veterinary surgeon then.

"It will not avail," said Lady Oswald. "I shall go by train. Perhaps you can tell me, Oswald Cray, at what hours the trains leave for Hildon!"

Oswald Cray said not another word of objection. To make use of the railroad, to which her dislike had been so insuperable, proved that she was indeed bent upon it. He bade her good-day and left, and encountered Dr. Davenal's carriage in the avenue. The doctor was arriving on his usual daily visit.

She was somewhat of a capricious woman, Lady Oswald. A few months before, in the summer-time, Dr. Davenal had been hoping, it may almost be said secretly plotting—but the plotting was very innocent— to get Lady Oswald to favour Mark Cray sufficiently to allow of his paying these daily visits. Since then Lady Oswald had, of her own accord, become excessively attached to Mark. That is, attached in one sense of the word. It was not the genuine esteem founded on long intimacy, the love, it may be almost said, that draws one friend to another; it was that artificial liking which suddenly arises, and has its result in praising and patronising; artificial because so shallow. In the new feeling, Lady Oswald had not only sanctioned Mark's visits to her in the place of Dr. Davenal, but she had recommended him to everybody she knew as the cleverest young surgeon in Hallingham or out of it. It had been Mark's luck speedily to cure some fancied or real ailment of Lady Oswald's in a notably short space of time, and Lady Oswald, who set it down to skill, really had taken up the notion that he had not his equal. We all know how highly-coloured for the time are these sudden estimations of a popular doctor's skill. None rejoiced more than Dr. Davenal, and he resigned Lady Oswald to Mark with inward satisfaction, and the best grace in the world. But during Mark's absence on his wedding-tour the doctor had taken again the daily visits.

Roger pulled up in the gravel drive when he saw Mr. Oswald Cray; but Oswald, who had out-stayed his time, could only shake hands with the doctor and hasten onwards. Parkins met Dr. Davenal surreptitiously as he entered: she had seen his approach, and she stole forwards on tiptoe to meet him, her tears dropping. When Lady Oswald was in her fretful moods, Parkins generally found refuge in tears.

"What's the matter now?" asked the doctor.

"The men have begun to measure the ground, and that stupid Jones came running open-mouthed to the house with the news, and my lady heard him," explained Parkins. "I'd not have told her: if people held their tongues, the sheds might be built, and up, and she never know it. I thought she'd have gone out of her mind, sir; and then Mr. Oswald Cray came in, and he talked to her. I think she's calmer now; I heard her talking quietly to Mr. Oswald Cray before he left. But she says she'll go off by rail to Mr. Low's."

"Is she in the drawing-room?"

"Yes, sir. So well, to be sure, as she was this morning!" continued Parkins, drying her tears. "I don't know when she has been in such spirits, and all because Mr. Cray was coming home tonight with his wife. The fancy she has taken for him is extraordinary: she has been counting the days off since he was away, like a schoolgirl counts them off before her holidays?"

Dr. Davenal entered. He did not attempt to reason Lady Oswald out of the visit to Mr. Low. Quite the contrary. He told her the short trip by rail would do her good: and he thought, which he did not tell her, that the interview with Mr. Low might set the affair at rest sooner than anything else would, by convincing her that there could be no appeal against the fiat, no delay in the carrying out of the work.

When Lady Oswald reached the station, it happened that Oswald Cray was there. He was emerging from one of the private rooms with some plans under his arm when he saw her. She looked scared at the bustle of the station, and was leaning helplessly on her maid's arm, uncertain where to go, what to do. Oswald hastened to her and took her on his arm. Parkins slipped behind, quite thankful to see him: she was as little used to the ways and confusion of a station as her mistress.

"Will you venture still, Lady Oswald, with all this turmoil?"

"Will you cease worrying me!" she answered, and the tone was a sharp one, for she fancied he still wished to stop her, and resented the intermeddling with her will.

Did he wish to stop her? If any such feeling was upon him, it must surely have been instinct: a prevision of what the ill-fated journey would bring forth; of the influence it would indirectly bear on his own future life.

He said no more. He led Lady Oswald at once to a first-class carriage, placed her and Parkins in it, procured their return tickets, and then leaned over the carriage-door and talked to Lady Oswald, ill as he could spare the time. No man had kinder feelings at heart than Oswald Cray, and it seemed to him scarcely courteous to leave her—for she was in a tremor still—until the train should start.

He talked to her in a gay laughing tone of indifferent subjects, and she grew more at ease. "Only think!" she suddenly exclaimed, "I may return with Mr. Cray and his wife! Dr. Davenal told me today they were expected early in the evening; and this is the way they must come. I shall be so glad when he is home!"

Oswald shook his head at her with mock seriousness. "I'd not acknowledge my faithlessness so openly, were I you, Lady Oswald. To turn off Dr. Davenal for Mark, after so many years' adhesion to him!"

"You know nothing about it, Oswald. I have not turned off Dr. Davenal. But you may depend upon one thing—that Mark is a rising man. He will make a greater name than you in the world."

"Very likely. I hope he will make a name. For myself"—

The whistle sounded, and Oswald drew away from the door. Lady Oswald put out her hand, and he shook it warmly. "Shall I see you on my return!"

"Possibly, just a glimpse," he answered. "I'll look out for you when the train comes in. Goodbye."

"But you'll wish me luck, Oswald—although you may be bound in honour to the interests of the enemy and those wretched sheds."

"I wish it you heartily and sincerely; in all ways, Lady Oswald."

His tone was hearty as his words, his clasp sincere. Lady Oswald withdrew her hand, and left him a pleasant, cordial smile as the train puffed on.

"One can't help liking him, Parkins, with all his obstinate contrariness," she cried. "I wish he had been the surgeon! Only think what a name he would have made, had he possessed his brother's talent!"

"So he would, my lady," dutifully acquiesced Parkins.

"What a good thing we are alone! Most likely he contrived it. I declare I don't dislike this," continued Lady Oswald, ranging her eyes round the well-stuffed compartment. "It is almost as private as my own carriage."

"So it is, my lady," answered Parkins. And the train went smoothly on, and in twenty minutes' time Lady Oswald was deposited safely at the Hildon station.

CHAPTER XII

WAITING FOR NEWS

Mark Cray and his wife had not indicated the precise hour of their return: "early in the evening, but not to dinner; have tea ready," had been Mrs. Cray's words to her servants in the letter received by them on Friday morning. Sara Davenal went to the Abbey about five o'clock to wait for them.

Mark and Caroline were beginning as prudently as their best friends could desire; two maid-servants only, engaged under the careful eye of Miss Bettina, comprised their household. The large heavy door of the Abbey opened to a large stone hall; on the left of this was a large sitting-room, with cross-beams in its ceiling and deep-mullioned windows, looking on to the branching lines of rails and the station in the distance; not so pleasant a view as had been the gay Abbey gardens. Indeed, with the doing away of those gardens, the pleasantest part of the Abbey as a residence, had gone. It was a rambling sort of place inside, with very little comfort. This room and the drawing-room above were the only good-sized rooms in the house; four modern rooms might have been put into that drawing-room, and what its carpeting had cost was something to be talked of. The bedchambers were pigeon-holes, the domestic offices dark closets paved with stone; in short the Abbey was a grander place in sound than it was pleasant for use. The Crays, who had lived in it so long, were party-giving people, thinking more of show than comfort; the pigeon-holes were good enough for them; the dark stone kitchens might be made the best of by the servants; the great drawing-room, larger than anybody else's in Hallingham, gladdened their hearts. It was certainly an imposing room when filled with company and lights.

Sara Davenal waited and waited in the downstairs room. She had taken off her things, and made herself at home. Her dress was of dark-blue silk, the bands of her brown hair were smooth and silken, and excitement had brought a colour to her cheeks. She had never before been parted from Caroline since the latter arrived, years ago, from the West Indies. The tea was on the table in readiness, with a cold fowl and tongue, thoughtfully ordered to be provided by Miss Davenal.

Five o'clock; half-past five; six o'clock; half-past six; seven o'clock; and still they had not come. Sara grew impatient—it is of no use to deny it—and blamed them for want of punctuality. They had not bargained for her feverish longing.

She stood at the window, looking still, as she had done since five o'clock. It had grown into night since she stood there; would have grown to dark, but for the brilliant moon that lighted the heavens. A servant came in.

"Shall I bring lights, miss?"

"Not yet. I want to watch for the train."

The maid retired. Sara waited on—waited and waited, until she felt sure that it must be half-past seven; but then she was counting time by her own impatience, not by the clock. Her eyes began to grow weary with the intense and incessant gaze at the station, and she could see a good many people standing at its entrance in the moonlight—stragglers, no doubt, waiting for the train, wondering, like herself, that it was not in, and what had become of it.

As she thus stood, there was a loud ring at the dour-bell. Sara flew into the hall in glee, thinking how stupid she must have been not to observe them crossing the bridge round by the lines; flew into the hall, and was met by her aunt.

Miss Davenal! when she had expected the bridegroom and bride! but Sara had to make the best of it, and she did so in her pleasing, graceful manner, drawing her aunt in by the hand to the dark room.

"They have not come yet, Aunt Bettina."

"Whatever's the meaning of this?" was the surprised question of Miss Davenal. "All in the dark? and where are they?"

"They have not come yet," repeated Sara. "Bring the lights," she added in a low voice to the servant.

"Not come! Where are they stopping?"

"The train is not in, Aunt Bettina."

"The what's not in?"

"The train."

"Why, what has come to it?"

Miss Bettina, all amazed, and scarcely believing the information, went hastily to the window, and looked towards the station. At that moment the other servant, Dorcas, came into the room. She was not a stranger to the family, having once lived with Miss Davenal, before that lady took up her abode with her brother. Dorcas was getting on to be middle-aged,—a sensible-looking woman, with a turned-up nose and reddish hair.

"Miss Sara," she whispered, "they are saying there's been an accident to the train."

Sara Davenal's heart seemed to stand still and then bound on again as if it would break its bounds.

"Who says it?" she gasped.

"I saw the folks standing about, and talking one to the other; so I opened my kitchen winder, and asked what was amiss, and they said the seven o'clock train was not in, that it had met with an accident. Miss Sara"—

But Miss Sara had turned from her. Silently snatching her shawl and bonnet from the sofa where she had laid them, she quitted the room, the unconscious Miss Davenal standing yet at the window. Dorcas followed her, and, by the lights that were now being carried in, she saw how white she looked.

"Miss Sara, I was about to say that it may not be true," continued Dorcas, as Sara hastily flung on her things. "I don't think it is: there'd be more uproar at the station if any news of that sort had been brought in."

"I am going over to see; I cannot remain in this suspense. Not go by myself?" she repeated, in reply to the woman's remonstrance; "nonsense, Dorcas! Everybody knows me: I am Dr. Davenal's daughter. You stay with my aunt Bettina, and be sure don't alarm her if you can help it."

Pulling the door open with her own hand, she passed under the red light of Mr. Cray's professional lamp, and hastened by the side-path and the bridge round to the station. Her face was pale, her pulses were beating. Sara Davenal had a quick imagination, and all the horrors of accidents by rail that she had ever heard seemed to rise up before her.

There was no impediment offered to her entering the station. Several persons were standing about, but they did not appear to notice her, and she passed through the room where the tickets were given, on to the platform. There she found herself in the midst of a crowd. Not a moving crowd but a waiting crowd, whose faces were mostly turned one way—that by which the expected train ought to come. Sara saw a talkative porter, and got near him, a man she knew.

"Has there been an accident?" she asked.

"Well, miss, there's nothing known for certain. It's odd where the train can be; and if anything has happened, it's odder still that the telegraph haven't brought word of it. I remember once she was half an hour late before."

"Who was?" asked Sara, bewildered.

"This here seven o'clock train. 'Twarn't nothing wrong with her then; some of them bothering excursion-trains had blocked up the line. I'd lay, miss, it's the same thing tonight. The doctor ain't gone down the line, is he?"

"No, no. I am expecting my cousin and Mr. Cray."

"It'll be all right, miss. She won't be long. We shall hear her steam directly."

Somewhat reassured, Sara turned, and was pushing her way through the throng, wishing to get clear of it, when she found herself a sort of prisoner. A gentleman had placed his arm before her, and looking up in the moonlight she discerned the features of Oswald Cray. Her heart gave a great bound of satisfaction, of love, and she almost caught at his protecting hand.

It was a curious and exciting scene. The station raising its imposing height to the night sky, so blue and beautiful; the crowd gathered there, unnaturally still in the intensity of awed expectation; the lights and bustle of the town not far away; the noiseless tread of the porters, as they moved restlessly in their suspense;—all made a painfully interesting picture in the bright moonlight.

Oswald Cray was waiting for the incoming train. It was the one he intended to depart by. He drew Sara away from the throng, and gave her his arm. Her heart was beating at the consciousness of his presence; her whole frame had thrilled at the touch of his hand.

"Is there danger, do you fear?" she whispered.

"No, I trust not. I think not. Were anything wrong, the telegraph would have brought the news. It must be some obstruction on the line."

Sara's fear faded away. She had confidence in him. If he, so experienced, the line's own engineer, saw no cause for dread, why should she? Perhaps she could not quite banish one little corner of doubt in her heart; perhaps Mr. Oswald Cray might have some slight corner of fear himself, which he did not deem it expedient to impart to her.

"Did you get frightened, Sara?" he asked, as they walked slowly to and fro in the moonlight.

"I was at the Abbey waiting for them, and Dorcas, one of their new servants, came to me with the news that people in the street were saying there had been an accident. I was very much frightened and came away; ran away, I may say," she added, smiling, "without saying anything to Aunt Bettina."

"Is she at the Abbey?"

"She has just come. She expected they had returned."

"I fear Lady Oswald is waiting for this train at Hildon," he remarked. "She will not like the delay."

"Indeed! Lady Oswald at Hildon!"

He explained to her how it was: that Lady Oswald had gone to Mr. Low's, and was not yet back. "Did you know that I called at your house this afternoon?" he asked.

"No," she said, lifting her head. "Did you call?"

"It was about five o'clock. I have been very busy all day, but I managed to get a minute. You were out, Neal said, and the doctor was out; only Miss Davenal at home, so I did not go in."

"I had come down to the Abbey," said Sara. "I thought they might arrive by an earlier train than this. Are you obliged to go back to London tonight?"

"Quite obliged, if the train shall arrive to take me. What's that?"

Some stir was discernible in the throng. Oswald Cray held his breath, listening for any sound that might indicate the approach of the train; but in the distance he could hear nothing, and the stir, caused perhaps only by the restlessness of waiting, died away. They paced on again.

"Since I saw you, Sara, I have had an offer made me of going abroad."

"To stay long?" she quickly asked. "Where to?"

"To stay a long while, had I accepted it; perhaps for life. In a pecuniary point of view the change would have been an advantageous one: it would have given me a position at once. But the climate is shocking; so I declined."

"Oh, I am glad?" she involuntarily said. "You should not run any of those risks."

"I did not hesitate on my own score. At least, I am not sure that I should have hesitated, but I really did not think of myself at all in the matter. I did not get so far. I should not like to have gone out alone, Sara: and I felt that I had no right to expose another to these chances; one whom I should then be bound to protect and cherish, so far as man's protection goes, from all ill."

He spoke in what may be called general words, in a general tone, but it was impossible for Sara to misunderstand him. Every pulse within her beat in answer, quietly as she continued to walk, calmly as her eyes rested straight before her. She knew it was his intention not to speak openly, until he could speak to some purpose: and she thought he was right.

"So I resolved to continue where I am, and plod on diligently," he continued. "Advancement, though more slow, will be sure. Do you think I did right?"

"Quite right, quite right," she murmured. And, had they been speaking without reserve to each other, she might have added, "Papa would not like me to go abroad."

A silence ensued. They paced together in that quiet spot away from the busy crowd, the silvery moonlight above, the pure passion of love's first dream filling their hearts within. No need of words: the conscious presence of each was all in all.

"Where can this train be?" exclaimed Oswald at length, breaking the charm of the silence.

Almost as the words left his lips one of the porters came hurriedly up, touching his hat as he spoke.

"There has been a mistake in the telegraph-room, sir. Leastways, some bungle. The train was telegraphed from Hildon."

A moment's startled pause on the part of Oswald Cray.

"It was told to me positively that the train had not left, Parker?"

"I know, sir; we all understood it so. But James Eales is come back now, and he says we misunderstood him; that the train was telegraphed at the proper time. There's an accident, sir, for certain; and it's between this and Hildon."

"I think there must be a mistake," murmured Oswald Cray to Sara. "Stay here quietly, away from the crowd."

Giving no further satisfaction to her fears—indeed he could not give it—he walked hastily to the small room used as the telegraph office. The news which the porter had brought to him was spreading elsewhere, and the entrance to it was blocked up with an eager throng. He began to work his way through.

"By your leave, by your leave, good people." And they drew aside so as to give room for him to pass when they saw who it was. Mr. Oswald Cray's right of authority, as being superior to that of any at the station, was known and recognised.

The telegraph clerk was a young man named James Eales. It was his duty to receive the messages, and in due course he ought to have received the one from Hildon, signifying that the expected train (called in familiar terms at Hallingham the seven o'clock train, although it came in five minutes sooner) had duly quitted Hildon. This message was due somewhere about twenty-three minutes to seven, and it came this evening as usual quite punctually. No sooner had it been received than James Eales, who wanted to absent himself for a short while on an errand to the town, asked one of the men to take his place. Other messages might be expected relating to the trains, not to speak of private messages, always liable to come; and the man took the place accordingly. As Eales was going out, the man, whose name was Williams, called after him to know whether the train was signalled. Eales thought he meant the down-train, whose signal was nearly due, and replied, "No, not yet." But in point of fact Williams had alluded to the up-train from Hildon, which had been signalled. That man was an accurate time-keeper; it wanted two or three minutes yet to the signalling of the down-train, and he would not have been likely, from this very accuracy, to inquire whether that message had come, it not being due. Eales, who did not possess the like innate accuracy, and was besides in a hurry to depart, confused the question, and took it to allude to the down-train. It is through these mistakes, which are caused half by carelessness, half by what may be almost called unavoidable misapprehension, that accidents occur. It did not lead to the accident in this case, but it has led to many a one. Williams ought to have said, "Is the up-train signalled!" Saying what he did say, "Is the train signalled?" Eales should have answered, "The up-train is signalled; not the down."

Williams sat down to the desk or bureau, the telegraph indicator being in front of him, above his head. Precisely to time the down telegraph came, a confirmation it may almost be said of the mistake. Williams noted it, and wondered what the up-train was about that its signal did not likewise come. After seven o'clock came and passed, and the up-train did not arrive, the station-master, who had been enjoying a little recreative gossip on his own score, and not attending to his duties quite as closely as he might have been, made his appearance in the telegraph office.

"Where's James Eales?" he demanded.

Williams explained. He had stepped out on an errand, and he, Williams, was taking his place. The station-master made no demur to this: Williams was as capable as Eales, and often worked the telegraph.

"Has the up-train been signalled from Hildon?"

"No, sir."

"Not been signalled!" echoed the station-master, in an accent of disbelief.

"It has not been signalled for certain," was the reply of Williams. "Eales told me the signal had not come when he left, and I am sure it has not come since."

"Where can it be?" exclaimed the station-master. "I suppose some of those monster excursion-trains are blocking up the line somewhere."

A consolatory conclusion, quite doing away with uneasiness or fear. The station-master promulgated the news that the train had not been signalled from Hildon, together with his own suggestive idea of the offending excursion-trains. He told Mr. Oswald Cray it had not been signalled, and he told others: therefore the officials were perfectly at their ease upon the point, whatever the assembled crowed might be.

It was just five-and-twenty minutes past seven when Eales returned. He had stayed longer than he intended, and he dashed into his office head foremost, catching a glimpse of the crowd on the platform, now quickly increasing.

"What do they want, that lot?" he cried to Williams. "Is anything wrong?"

"They are waiting for the up-train. It's preciously behind time tonight, and I suppose some of them are alarmed—have got friends in it, maybe."

"What up-train?" asked Eales.

"The seven o'clock up-train to London." Eales stood confounded. "Why, is that not come up? An accident must have happened."

"Not obliged to," coolly returned Williams. "It's kept back by the excursion-trains, most likely."

"There are no excursion-trains today between this and Hildon," quickly observed Eales.

"It has not got so far yet. It has not passed Hildon."

"It has passed Hildon," replied Eales. "It passed at its proper time, and was signalled up."

Williams turned and stared at Eales with all his might. "Who says it has been signalled up?"

"Who says it! Why, I say it. I got the signal as usual."

"Then how came you to tell me you hadn't had it?" asked Williams.

"I never told you so."

"You did. You'll say black's white next. It was the only question I asked you—whether the up-train had been signalled, and you replied it had not been."

"You said the down-train: you never said the up."

"I meant the up. It's not likely I should ask whether the down-train was signalled, when it wasn't near due! You have done a pretty thing!"

How long they might have continued to dispute, one seeking to lay the blame upon the other, it is impossible to say. But at that moment the station-master came in again, and the mistake was made known to him and to others. The train had left Hildon at its proper time, and therefore the delay, whatever might be its cause, lay very near to them—in the six miles of rail intervening between Hallingham and Hildon; the train must be on some spot of it.

That an accident of some nature had taken place, the most sanguine could now only believe, and a whole shower of verbal missives was hurled upon the two men, Eales and Williams, who did nothing but retort on each other. Each firmly regarded the other as being alone in fault; an impartial judge would have said they were equally culpable. Extricating himself from the confusion, Mr. Oswald Cray returned to Sara. She looked at him with questioning eyes, her heart shrinking; that hubbub in the station had reawakened her fears. He quietly placed her hand within his arm, and began to pace as before.

"I find things do not look quite so well as we fancied"—

"There has been an accident!" she interrupted. "Do not hide it from me, Oswald."

He lightly laid his other hand on hers, an assurance of his truth, "I will hide nothing from you, my dearest," and the never-yet-used term of endearment seemed to slip from him involuntarily, in the moment's need that he should soothe her. "We have not heard that there is any accident, for no tidings of any sort have come up; but the train, it seems, did leave Hildon at its usual time, and something must therefore have occurred to delay it."

A deep, sobbing sigh nearly broke from her, but she coughed it down.

"Do not meet trouble half-way," he said in a lighter tone. "It does not follow that an accident, in the popular sense of the term, must have occurred, because the train is not up. The engine may have broken down and be unable to come on, but the passengers may be as safe and well as we are. There's no doubt the engine is disabled, or it would have come on for assistance."

"Assistance for the wounded?" she quickly rejoined.

"Assistance that may be wanted in anyway. The telegraph is at work to stop all trains, and some of us are going down"—

It was the last collected word they were enabled to speak. The news had spread in the town, and the affrighted people were coming up in shoals. News, at the best, loses nothing in carrying, and the delay was magnified into a dreadful accident, with half the train killed. In the midst of it the guard of the missing train arrived, flying up the line as if for his life, and carrying a lantern.

The engine had run off the line on to the bank, and turned over. A few of the passengers were injured, but he thought not many; some of them were coming on, the field way. It had occurred about midway between the two stations, a little nearer to Hallingham than to the other. An engine was wanted to bring on the train, and it might be as well if a doctor or two went down.

This was the climax for the affrighted crowd, and those who had relatives in the train seemed to well-nigh lose their senses. A scene of inextricable confusion ensued. Some were restrained by force from jumping on the line and setting off to the scene of accident; some strove to get upon the carriage and engine about to start for it. Order was restored with great difficulty, and the carriage and engine rescued from the invaders, who then quitted the station, and set off to run to the scene, through the same fields that, as the guard said, passengers were advancing.

Two medical men, who had been hastily obtained, Mr. Oswald Cray, and sundry officials of the line, took their seats in the carriage to be conveyed to the spot. The engine had given its first puff, and was snorting off, when a loud shout arrested it.

"Stop! stop! One single moment! Here's Dr. Davenal!"

His name, for those poor wounded ones, was a tower of strength—worth all the rest of the surgical skill in Hallingham—and he was pulled into the carriage, having caught a glimpse of the white face of his daughter outside the throng. Sara, terrified and bewildered, wondering what she should do next, was suddenly pounced upon by Miss Davenal.

"You naughty girl! What is it that you are doing here?"

"O Aunt Bettina, there has been an accident to the train! Caroline and Mr. Cray are sure to be in it."

"Caroline and Mr. Cray are what?" cried out Miss Bettina.

"I fear they are in the train. There has been an accident between here and Hildon. An engine has just gone down with assistance."

"I don't want to know about engines," returned Miss Davenal, who had not understood one word in ten. "I ask what you do here alone? Caroline and Mr. Cray can come home, I suppose, without your waiting for them in this public manner. What would your papa say if he saw you?"

"Papa has seen me," replied Sara. "Papa has just come up to the station and is gone down with the engine."

"Gone down with what engine? What do you mean?"

Sara put her lips close to Miss Davenal's ear. "Papa's gone down the line with some more gentlemen, to see about the wounded."

"Wounded!" shrieked Miss Bettina. "Has there been an accident? Who's wounded? Caroline and Mr. Cray?"

"We don't know yet, aunt." And in the best way that she could, Sara strove to make the case comprehensible to her aunt. Miss Davenal understood at last, and was somewhat mollified.

"Sara, I am not very angry with you now. I might have stopped myself. An accident to the train, and the doctors gone down! O those dreadful railways!"

A little longer of suspense, and then the passengers began to arrive. After the shock and fright, it had seemed safer to many of them to walk the three miles of distance than to trust to the rail again and another engine. The path fields were dry, and it was a pleasant walk by moonlight. Miss Bettina, whose eyes were as quick as her hearing was dull, was the first to recognise Mrs. Cray amidst them.

Caroline burst into tears as they laid hold of her, and Sara's heart began to sink. But the tears were only the effect of the fright and excitement she had gone through. She could give no clear account of the accident or what it had brought forth. All she knew was that there was great banging and bumping of the carriage she was in, but it was not overturned. Two other carriages were; and the engine was lying on its side with all its steam coming out of it. She scrambled up the bank in her terror, as did most of the passengers, and came on with them.

"And Mark?" asked Sara, scarcely daring to put the question.

"Mark! He stayed to look after the wounded," was her reply. "He said he thought there was nobody seriously hurt. At any rate, there are no lives lost."

Sara's heart breathed a word of thankfulness. "Did you see Lady Oswald?" she asked. "She went to Hildon this afternoon, and Mr. Oswald Cray thought she must be in this train, returning."

"I did not see her," replied Mrs. Cray. "Lady Oswald in the train! I thought she never travelled by rail."

"She did this afternoon. One of her carriage-horses is ill. How thankful!—how thankful we must all be that it is no worse!" concluded Sara Davenal.

"Well, this is a fine ending to your wedding-jaunt!" exclaimed Miss Bettina. "What about your luggage, Caroline? Is it safe?"

"As if we gave a thought to our luggage, Aunt Bettina! When people's lives are at stake they can't think of their luggage."

"Nor care either, perhaps," sharply answered Miss Bettina, who, for a wonder, had caught the words. "It may be lying soused in the engine-water, for all you know!"

"I daresay it is," equably returned Caroline. "It was in the van next the engine." But the full report had to come up yet; and the excited crowd stopped on.

CHAPTER XIII

PAIN

Clear and distinct lay the lines of rail in the cold moonlight. It was a straight bit of line there, without curve or bend, rise or incline; and why the engine should have gone off the rails remained to be proved. It was lying on its side, the steam escaping as from a fizzing, hissing furnace; the luggage-van was overturned, and its contents were scattered; and two carriages were overturned also: a second-class, which had been next the van, a first-class which had followed it.

But now, as good Providence willed it, in that second-class carriage there had only been three passengers. The train was not a crowded one, and people don't go close to the engine as a matter of taste. Of these three passengers, two had thrown themselves flat on the floor of the carriage between the seats, and escaped without injury; the other had a broken arm and a bruised head, not of much moment. The first-class carriage was more fully occupied, and several of the passengers, though not fatally or even extensively, were seriously hurt; and of the driver and stoker, the one had saved himself by leaping from his engine, the other was flung to a distance, and lay there as he fell.

Mark Cray, as you have heard, remained to tend the wounded. The first face he distinguished in the moonlight, lying amidst the débris of the overturned first-class carriage, was that of Lady Oswald: and so completely astonished was he to see it, that he thought either his eyes or the moon must be playing him false. He and Caroline had been in a carriage almost at the back of the train, consequently he had not seen her at the Hildon station: and he had believed that Lady Oswald, of all persons, would have been the last to attempt railway travelling, so much was she averse to rails and trains in general. Groaning and moaning by her side was Parkins; and Mr. Cray could doubt no longer.

With assistance, the passengers were extricated and laid upon the bank. Their injuries were unequal; some, after the first shock, could walk and talk, some could do neither; while the first grumbled and complained of their bruises and abrasions, the last lay still, except for groaning. The only perfectly quiet one was Lady Oswald: she lay with her pale face upturned to the moonlight, her eyes closed. It was natural perhaps that Mark Cray should turn his first attention to her. A gentleman, one of the passengers, asked if she was dead.

"No," said Mark; "she has only fainted. Parkins, suppose you get up and try if you can walk. I'm sure you can't be hurt if you are able to make that noise. That engine appears not to be over steady. Take care it does not raise itself again and come puffing off this way."

Parkins, not detecting the ruse, started up with a shriek, and stood rubbing herself all over. "I think I'm killed," she cried; "I don't believe I have got a whole bone in me."

"I'll see by-and-by," said Mr. Cray. "Meanwhile come and help your lady. I want her bonnet and cap untied."

Parkins limped to the spot stiffly with many groans, but wonderfully well considering the belief she had just expressed. At the same moment some one came up with water, procured from a pond in the field, and the driver, who had just come to his legs, brought a lamp. The lamp was held to Lady Oswald's face, and some of the water poured into her mouth. Between the two she opened her eyes.

"What's the matter?" she asked. "Where am I!"

"She's all right," whispered Mr. Cray, his warm tone proving that he had not previously felt so assured of the fact. "Has anybody got a drop of brandy?" he called out to the passengers, who yet stayed at the scene.

"Goodness me! where am I?" cried Lady Oswald, with a faint shriek. "Parkins, is that you? What has happened? Didn't we get into the railway carriage?"

"But we are out of it now, my lady," cried Parkins, sobbing. "There has been an awful upset, my lady, and I don't know anything more, except that it's a mercy we are alive."

"An upset!" repeated Lady Oswald, who appeared to have no recollection whatever of the circumstances. "Is anybody hurt? Are you hurt, Parkins?"

"Every bone in me is broke, my lady, if I may judge by the feel of 'em. This comes of them sheds."

"Be quiet, Parkins," said Mr. Cray, who had succeeded in finding a wicker-cased bottle containing some brandy-and-water. "Help me to raise your lady a little."

Parkins contrived to give her help in spite of the damaged bones, but the moment Lady Oswald was touched she shrieked out terribly.

"Let me alone! let me alone! Is that Mark Cray? How kind you are to come to see after me, Mr. Cray? Did you come from Hallingham?"

"We were in the same train, Lady Oswald; I and Caroline. I am very glad that it happened to be so."

"To be sure; I begin to remember: you were to return tonight. I—I feel very faint."

Mark succeeded in getting her to drink some brandy-and-water, but she positively refused to be touched, though she said she was in no pain. He thought she was exhausted, the effect of the shock, and left her to attend to other sufferers, who perhaps wanted his aid more than Lady Oswald.

Then, after awhile, the carriage came up, bringing the help from Hallingham. Mark Cray saw Dr. Davenal with the greatest pleasure, and he took him at once towards Lady Oswald.

"Are many hurt?" inquired the doctor.

"Astonishingly few," was the reply; "and the hurts are of a very minor character, I fancy. A broken arm is about the worst."

"And what of Lady Oswald?"

"I don't think she's hurt at all: she's suffering from the shock. A little exhausted; but that's natural."

"To a woman of her age such a shock is no light thing, Mark. However, we must do the best we can for everybody."

"There has been enough groaning—if that's anything to judge by," said Mark; "groaning and complaining too."

"Glad to hear it," said the doctor. "When people can complain, the damage is not very extensive."

"Parkins, for one, keeps protesting that every bone's broken. But she ran out of the way pretty quickly when I told her the engine might start up again."

The doctor smiled, and they came up to Lady Oswald. Oswald Cray had found her out, and was sitting on the bank beside her. She spoke just a word or two to him, but seemed, as Mr. Cray had said, exhausted. Oswald Cray rose to resign his place to Dr. Davenal, and he took his brother aside.

"Is she much hurt, Mark?"

"O no," replied Mark. "It has shaken her, of course; but she has been talking as fast as I can."

He spoke with singular confidence. In the first place. Mark Cray was naturally inclined to look on the bright side of things, to feel confident himself in the absence of any palpable grounds for doing so; in the second, he did not think it at all mattered what information on the point was given to Oswald.

Reassured upon the score of Lady Oswald, Oswald quitted Mark, and went amidst the wounded. Proud man though he was accused of being, though he was, never was there a tenderer heart, a softer hand, a gentler voice for the sick and suffering, than his. All the patients appeared to have been attended to in some degree; and they were in good hands now. Oswald halted by the side of the poor stoker, a swarthy honest-faced man, who was moaning out his pain.

"What, is it you, Bigg?" he said, recognising the man. "I did not know you were back on this part of the line again."

"I on'y come on it yesterday, sir. It's just my luck."

"Where are you hurt?"

"I be scalded awful, sir. I never knew what pain was afore tonight. All my lower limbs is"—

"Take care?" shouted Oswald to a stupid fellow who was running along with a plank in his arms. "Can't you see there's a man lying here? What are you about?"

"About my work," was the rough reply, spoken in an insolent tone. It was one of the men just brought down, a workman from Hallingham station, and Oswald knew him well.

"What is that, Wells?" he quietly asked.

Wells looked round now, surprised at being addressed by name. He pretty nearly dropped his load in consternation when he recognised Mr. Oswald Cray. Full as his hands were, he managed to jerk his hat from his head.

"I beg your pardon, I'm sure, sir. I thought it was nothing but some idler obstricting of me. One does get beset with idlers at these times, asking one all sorts of questions. I shouldn't have answered that way, sir, if I'd knowed it was you."

"Go on with your work; there's no time to talk. And don't blunder along again without looking where you are going."

"One can't see well in the dark, sir."

"It's not dark; it is as light as it need be. Quite light enough for you to see your way. Do you call that bright moon nothing?"

"He'd ha' been right over my legs, but for you, sir," murmured poor Bigg, the great drops of pain standing out on his brow, black with his occupation. "I don't know how I be to bear this agony. That cursed engine"—

"Hush, Bigg," interrupted Mr. Oswald Cray.

Bigg groaned his contrition. "Heaven forgive me! I know it ain't a right word for me tonight."

"Heaven will help you to bear the pain if you will only let it," said Oswald. "There has been worse pain to bear than even yours, my poor fellow; though I know how hard it is for you now to think so."

"It may be my death-blow, sir. And what's to become o' my wife and little uns? Who'll work for 'em?"

"No, no, Bigg. I hope it is not so bad as that. I do not think it is."

"If one might count by pain, sir"—

"Bigg, I can give you a little comfort on that score," interrupted Oswald Cray. "A friend of mine was very dreadfully burnt, through his bed-clothes catching fire. Awfully burnt: I don't like, even at this distance of time, to think of it. The next day I heard of it, and went to see him. I am not a very good one to witness physical pain, and I remember how I dreaded to witness his, and the spectacle I did not doubt he presented. He was a spectacle, poor fellow—but let that pass. To my great astonishment he saluted me heartily as I went in. 'Holloa, old friend!' were his words, not only cheerfully but merrily spoken. I found that he did not suffer pain: had not felt any from the moment he was burnt. In my ignorance, I set that down as a most favourable symptom, and felt sure he would get well shortly. When I was leaving him, I met the doctor going in, and said how glad I was to find his patient so well. 'Well!' he exclaimed, 'why, what do you judge by!' And I said—by his feeling no pain. 'That's just it,' the doctor observed: 'if he only felt pain there might be a chance for him. I wish I could hear him roar out with it.' Now, Bigg," Mr. Oswald Cray added, "I am no surgeon, but I infer that the same theory must hold good in scalds as in burns: that your pain is as favourable a symptom as his want of it was unfavourable. Do not rebel at your pain again, my poor fellow; rather bear it like a man. Were I scalded or burnt, I think I should be thankful for the pain."

"He was burnt worse, may be, nor me, that there gentleman," remarked Bigg, who had listened with interest.

"Ten times worse," replied Oswald. "Yes, I may say ten times worse," he emphatically repeated. "Indeed, Bigg, I feel sure that yours is but a very slight hurt, in comparison with what it might have been: and I do not say this to you in the half-false light in which one speaks to a child to soothe it, but as one truthful man would speak to another."

"God bless you, sir. My heart was a-failing of me sadly. Did he die, that there gentleman?"

"He died at a week's end: but there had been no hope of him from the first; and there were also certain attendant circumstances in his case, apart from the injury, remarkably unfavourable. In a short while, Bigg, you'll be on your legs again, as good man as ever. I'll ask Dr. Davenal to come and have a look at you."

The name of the far-famed surgeon carried assurance in itself, and Bigg's face lighted up with eagerness. "Is Dr. Davenal here, sir?"

"Yes. I'll go and look for him."

"At the moment that Oswald spoke, Dr. Davenal had left Lady Oswald and encountered Mr. Cray. The latter, whose spirits were rather exalted that night, the effect probably of finding the injuries around him so slight, when he had looked out for all the terrible calamities that flesh is heir to, not to speak of death, stopped to speak to him of Lady Oswald. And he spoke lightly.

"Well? You don't find her hurt, doctor?"

"I'll tell you more about it tomorrow, Mark."

Dr. Davenal's tone was so very grave that Mark Cray stared. He thought—Mark Cray almost thought that there was a shade of reproof in it, meant for him.

"I am sure she has no serious hurt," he exclaimed.

"Well, Mark, I can say nothing positively yet. In the state she is, and in this place, it is not easy to ascertain: but I fear she has."

"My goodness!" cried Mark, conscious that he was but the veriest tyro beside that man of skill, of unerring practice, Richard Davenal, and feeling very little at the moment. "What is the hurt, sir?" he asked in a loud tone.

"Hold your tongue about it," said the doctor. "Time enough to proclaim it abroad when the fact has been ascertained that there is one."

Oswald Cray came up, having distinguished the doctor in the moonlight.

"I wish you'd come and look at a poor fellow, Dr. Davenal, who wants a word of cheering. A word of such from you, you know sends the spirits up. You should have seen the man's face lighten when I said you were here."

"Who is it?" asked the doctor, turning off with alacrity.

"Poor Bigg the fireman. You know him, I daresay. He is badly scalded and bruised."

"Oh, his hurts are nothing," slightingly spoke Mark Cray. "He seems one of those groaners who cry out at a touch of pain."

"Mark," said the doctor, stopping, "allow me to tender you a word of advice—do not fall into that, by some, professed to be entertained idea, that nobody can, or ought, to feel pain; or, if they feel it, that they ought not to show it. It is unnatural, untruthful; and to my mind, particularly unbecoming in a medical man. Pain to some natures is all but an impossibility to bear; it is all that can be imagined of agony; it is as if every moment of its endurance were that of death. The nervous organisation is so sensitively delicate, that even a touch of pain, as you express it, which most people would scarcely feel, would certainly not cry out over, is to them the acutest suffering. As a surgeon and anatomist you ought to know this."

"He's only a fireman," returned Mark. "Nobody expects those rough fellows to be sensitive to pain."

"Let him be a fireman or a waterman, he will feel it as I describe, be his frame thus sensitively organised," was the reply of Dr. Davenal, spoken firmly, if not sternly. "What has a man's condition in life to do with it? It won't change his physical nature. A duke, sleeping on a bed of down, nurtured in refinement and luxury, may be so constituted that pain will be a mere flea-bite to him; should he be destined to endure the worst that's known to earth, he will, so to say, hardly feel it: whereas this poor fireman, inured to hard usage, to labour and privation, may be literally almost unable to bear it. For my own part, when I have to witness this distressing sensibility to pain, perhaps have to inflict it as a surgical necessity, I suffer half as much as the patient does for I know what it is for him. Don't affect to ridicule pain again, Mark."

Mark Cray looked vexed, annoyed. But every syllable that had fallen from Dr. Davenal's lips had found its echo in the heart of Oswald Cray. If there was one quality he admired beyond all else, it was sincere open truthfulness: and to Oswald's mind there was an affectation, a want of sincerity, in the mocking expressions, the shallow opinions, so much in fashion in the present day. There had been a hollow carelessness in Mark's tone when he ridiculed the notion of the poor stoker's possessing a sensitiveness to pain, just as if the man had no right to possess it.

"Well, Bigg, and so you must get tossed in this upset!" began the doctor cheerily. "Oh! you'll do well, by the look of your face; we shall soon have you on the engine again. Let's get a sight of this grand damage. Who has got a lantern?"

It was a bad scald; a shocking scald; there was no question of it; and there was much injury by bruises; but Dr. Davenal spoke the simple truth when he assured the man that the hurts were not dangerous.

"Keep up your heart, Bigg. In an hour's time you will be in the Infirmary, properly attended to. You'll soon get over this."

"I dun know as I can live through the pain, sir," was the wailing answer.

"Ay, it's bad. But when we have got the proper remedies on, you won't feel it as you do now. Bigg, I once scalded my leg badly—at least somebody did it for me—and I remember the pain to this day; so, my poor fellow, I can tell what yours is."

"Mr. Cray said, sir, I oughtn't to feel no pain from a hurt like this, he did. It sounded hard like, for the pain is awful."

"Mr. Cray knows you would be better if you tried not to feel the pain—not to feel it so acutely. He is a doctor, you know, Bigg, and sees worse hurts than yours every day of his life."

"I'd like to ask you, sir, when I shall be well—if you can tell me. I have got a wife and children, sir; and she's sick just now, and can't work for 'em."

"We'll get you up again in three weeks," said Dr. Davenal cheerily, as he hastened away to another sufferer, groaning at a distance.

The term seemed long to the man: almost to startle him: he was thinking of his helpless wife and children.

"Three weeks!" he repeated with a moan. "Three weeks, and nobody to help 'em, and me laid down incapable!"

"Think how much worse it might be, Bigg!" said Mr. Oswald Cray, wishing to get the man to look at his misfortune in a more cheerful spirit. "Suppose Dr. Davenal had said three months?"

"Then, as good he'd said, sir, as I should never be up again."

"Do you think so? I don't. It is a long while to be confined by illness, three months, and to you it seems, no doubt, very long indeed; but it is not so much out of a man's life. I knew one who was ill for three years, and got up again. That would be worse, Bigg."

"Ay, sir, it would be. I haven't got just my right thoughts tonight, what with the pain that's racking me, and what with trouble about my wife and little 'uns."

"Don't trouble about them, Bigg," was the considerate answer. "They shall be taken care of until you can work for them again. If the company don't do it, I will."

A short while longer of confusion, of hasty clearance of the line, of soothing medical aid,—such aid as could be given in that inconvenient spot, where there was only the open bare ground for the sufferers to lie on, the moonlit sky to cover them,—and the return to Hallingham was organised. The injured were lifted into the carriages and placed as well as circumstances permitted. Lady Oswald, who shrieked out much when they raised her, was laid at full length on a pile of rugs collected from the first-class compartments, and the engine started with its load, and steamed gently onwards.

It appeared afterwards that the accident had been caused by the snapping of some part of the machinery of the engine. It was a very unusual occurrence, and could neither have been foreseen nor prevented.

The expectant crowd had not dispersed when Hallingham was reached. Nay, it had considerably increased. Even Miss Bettina Davenal retained her post, and Sara and Caroline were with her.

The invalid train—it might surely be called one in a double sense—came slowly into the station. The platform had been cleared; none were allowed upon it to obstruct the removal of the sufferers from the train to the conveyances that waited, in which they would be transported to their homes, or to the infirmary, as the case might be. But, if the platform was denied them, the excited watchers made up for the discourtesy by blocking up the road and doors outside—a motley group, picturesque enough in the fine moonlight night.

Dr. Davenal, Mr. Cray, and the other medical men were occupied in superintending the removal of their patients, but Mr. Oswald Cray found his way to Miss Davenal, and gave them the good news that the injuries were comparatively slight. A train for London was on the point of starting, and he was going by it. He contrived to obtain a few words with Sara, and she went with him on to the platform.

"I wish I could have remained over tomorrow," he observed to her. "I should like to see and hear how all these poor people get on."

"Are you sure you cannot remain?"

"I am sure that I ought not. You have heard me speak of Frank Allister Sara?"

"Often. The young Scotchman who was with you at Bracknell and Street's for so many years."

"We were articled together. He has become very ill lately; and—and the firm has not behaved quite well to him. I have no voice in that part of its economy, or it should never have been."

"What did they do?" inquired Sara.

"He has not got on as I have. Still he held a tolerably fair post in the house; but his health failed, and he had to absent himself. Mr. Street found out how ill he was, came to the conclusion that he'd be of no use to us again, and wrote him his dismissal. I thought it very hard; and he—he"—

"Yes!" said Sara, eagerly interested.

"He found it harder than he could bear. It put the finishing stroke to his illness, and I don't think he will rally. He has no relatives near, few friends; so I see him all I can, and I gave him a faithful promise to spend tomorrow with him. Time's up, and the guard's impatient, I see."

"Does the guard know you are going?"

"Yes. Don't you see him looking round for me? Fare you well, Sara. I may be down again in a day or two." He had taken her hands for a moment in both his as he stood before her.

"I trust you will get safe to town?" she whispered.

"Ay, indeed! This night has proved to us that safety lies not with ourselves. God bless you, my dearest!"

He crossed the platform and stepped into the carriage, which the guard was holding open. The next moment the train was steaming out of the station, Sara Davenal looking after it with a lingering look, a heart at rest, as that sweet word of endearment rang its echoes on her ear.

CHAPTER XIV

A WHIM OF LADY OSWALD'S

The medical body, as a whole, is differently estimated by the world. Some look down upon it, others look up to it; and their own position in the scale of society has no bearing or bias on the views of the estimators. It may be that a nobleman will bow to the worth and value of the physician, will regard him as a benefactor of mankind, exercising that calling of all others most important to the welfare of humanity; while a man very far down in the world's social ladder will despise the doctor wherever he sees him.

It is possible that each has in a degree cause for this, so far as he judges by his own experience. The one may have been brought in contact with that perfect surgeon—and there are many such—whose peculiar gifts for the calling were bestowed upon him by the Divine will; he with the lion's heart and woman's hand, whose success, born of patience, courage, judgment, experience, has become by God's blessing an assured fact. Men who have brought all the grand discoveries of earthly science to their aid and help in their study of the art; who have watched Nature day by day, and mastered her intricacies; who have, in fact, attained to that perfection in skill which induces the involuntary remark to break from us—We shall never see his fellow! Before such a man as this, as I look upon it, the world should bow. We have no benefactor like unto him. The highest honours of the land should be open to him; all that we can give of respect and admiration should be his.

But there is a reverse side to the picture. There is the man who has gone into the profession without aptitude for it, who has made it his, although positively incapable of properly learning it and exercising it. He may have acquired the right to use all the empty distinguishing letters attaching to it, and tack them after his name on all convenient occasions, inscribe them in staring characters on his very door-posts—M.D., M.R.C.S.—as many more as there may be to get; but, for all that, he is not capable of exercising the art. His whole career is one terrible mistake. He kills more patients than he cures; slaying them, drenching them to death, with that most pitiful and fatal of all weapons—ignorance. It may not be his fault, in one sense: he does his best: but he has embraced a calling for which nature did not fit him. He goes on in his career, it is true, and his poor patients suffer. More ignorant, of necessity, than he is—for in all that relates to the healing art, we are, take us as a whole, lamentably deficient—they can only blindly resign themselves to his hands, and when they find that there's no restored health for them, that they get worse rather than better, they blame the obstinacy of the malady, not the treatment. Upon his own mind, meanwhile, there rests an ever-perpetual sense of failure, irritating his temper, rendering his treatment experimental and uncertain. Some cannot see where the fault lies—have no conception that it is in their own incapacity. And if a man does see it, what then? He must go on and do his best; he must be a doctor always; it is his only means of living, and he is too old to take to another trade. Rely upon it there are more of these practitioners than the world suspects.

Such a man as the first was Dr. Davenal; such a man as the last was Mark Cray. But that Mark was so Dr. Davenal suspected not. Grave cases hitherto, during their short connection, had been treated by the doctor, and for ordinary ailments Mark did well enough. He could write a proper prescription when the liver was out of order, or bring a child through the measles; he could treat old ladies with fanciful ailments to the very acme of perfection. It is true Dr. Davenal had been once or twice rather surprised by downright wrong treatment on the part of Mark, but he had attributed it to inexperience.

When other doctors could not cure, people flew to Dr. Davenal; when there was a critical operation to be performed, involving life or death, Dr. Davenal was prayed to undertake it. His practice consequently was of wide extent; it was not confined to Hallingham and its vicinity, but extended occasionally to the confines of the county. It was not, therefore, surprising that on the morning following the accident Dr. Davenal found himself called out at an early hour to the country on a case of dangerous emergency. And the illness was at Thorndyke.

He responded at once to the call. Never a prompter man than Richard Davenal. Roger had learnt by example to be prompt also, and was ready with his carriage as soon as his master. The arrangements with regard to saving time were well organised at Dr. Davenal's. The bell, communicating from the house down the side-wall of the garden to the man's rooms near the stables was made the means of conveying different orders. If rung once, Roger was wanted indoors to receive his orders by word of mouth; if rung twice—and on those occasions they were always sharp, imperative peals—Roger knew that the carriage was wanted at once, with all the speed that he could get it round.

The calm peaceful quiet of the Sabbath morn was lying on the streets of Hallingham as the doctor was driven through them. The shops were all shut; some of the private houses were not yet opened— servants are apt to lie late on Sunday morning. As they passed the town-hall and the market-place, so void of life then, the church clocks struck eight, and the customary bells, giving token of the future services of the day, broke forth in the clear air.

"Stop at the Abbey, Roger," said the doctor, as they neared it.

The woman, Dorcas, was just opening the parlour shutters. She came to the door when she saw the carriage drawing up to it.

"I want to see your master, Dorcas. I suppose he's up."

"He is up and out, sir," was her reply. "He has been gone about five minutes."

This answer caused the doctor to pause. It should be explained that when the train of sufferers arrived at the station the previous night, Lady Oswald had elected to be accompanied to her home by Mark Cray, not by Dr. Davenal. Whether she was actuated by pure caprice; whether by a better motive—the belief that she was not hurt so much as some other of the sufferers, and that Dr. Davenal's skill would be more needed by them; or whether the recent sudden liking she had taken for Mr. Cray swayed her then, could not be told; never would be told. She seemed to be a little revived at the end of the journey, and she chose that Mark Cray should go home with her. Dr. Davenal had acquiesced, but he whispered a parting word to Mark. "If there is an injury, I suspect it will be found in the ribs, Mark. Look well to it. If you want me, I'm going on to the Infirmary, and shall be at home afterwards."

But, as it appeared, the doctor had not been wanted. At any rate, Mark Cray had not sent for him. And he had stopped now to hear, if he could, Mark's report.

An upper window opened, and Mrs. Cray, completely enveloped in a thick shawl, so that nothing could be seen of her but the tip of her nose, leaned out.

"Good-morning, Uncle Richard."

"Good-morning, my dear. I am glad to see you again. Can you come down for a minute?"

"No, I have not begun to dress. Did you want Mark? He has gone to Lady Oswald's."

"Ah, that's what I wish to ask about. Did you hear Mark say how she was?—whether there was any hurt?"

"He said there was not. But, for one thing, she kept fainting, and refused to be touched. At least, I think he said so, something of that; I was very sleepy when he got home; it was one o'clock. I am sure he said she was not hurt to speak of."

"That's all right then," said Dr. Davenal.

"You are out betimes, Uncle Richard," resumed Caroline. "Are you going far?"

"To Thorndyke. Tell your husband he must see my patients this morning; I shall not be back in time. Drive on, Roger."

"Very well," said Caroline. "Who's ill at Thorndyke?"

But Dr. Davenal's answer, if he gave one, was lost in the distance, and never reached Caroline's ear.

It was a singular coincidence—as was said by gossips afterwards—that one should be taken ill that day at Thorndyke and be in danger of death. It was not, however, one of the Oswald family, but a visitor of Sir Philip's, and it has nothing whatever to do with the story It need not have been mentioned, save to explain what took Dr. Davenal from Hallingham on that critical day.

Dr. Davenal found the patient alarmingly ill, in great need of medical help, and he had to remain at Thorndyke some hours. It was between two and three o'clock when he got back to Hallingham, and he ordered Roger to drive at once to the Infirmary.

The doctor went in and saw his patients. The poor man, Bigg, easier now than he had been the previous night, lay in a slumber: the rest were going on well. One woman had gone. An inmate of the wards for some weeks past, her case, a very painful one, had baffled all skill, all remedy; and she had gone to that better place where sickness and pain cannot enter. Dr. Davenal stood for some little time conversing with the house-surgeon, and then departed on foot to his home: he had dismissed his carriage when he entered the Infirmary.

As he was walking, he met an eager little fellow scuffling along, one who always walked very fast, with his head pushed out, as if he were in a desperate hurry. It was one of the Infirmary pupils, as they were called; young men gathering skill and experience to become in time surgeons themselves, who attended the Infirmary with their masters. This one, Julius Wild, a youth of eighteen, was more particularly attached to the service of Mr. Cray, went round the wards with him as his dresser, and suchlike. No sooner did he see Dr. Davenal than his pace increased to a run, and he came up breathless.

"Oh, if you please, sir, Mr. Cray has been looking for you everywhere"—

"I have been to Thorndyke," interrupted the doctor.

"Yes, sir, but he thought you must have come back, and he sent me to about twenty places to inquire. There's something wrong with Lady Oswald, sir, and he wants to see you about it."

"What is it that's wrong?"

"Mr. Cray didn't explain to me, sir; but he said something about an operation. She's hurt internally, sir, I think."

"Where is Mr. Cray? Do you know?"

"He is gone to your house, sir. Somebody told him, they saw your carriage going along, and Mr. Cray thought you might be at home. He"—

Dr. Davenal waited to hear no more. He made the best of his way towards home, but before he reached it he met Mark Cray.

There in the street, particulars were explained by Mr. Cray to Dr. Davenal, not altogether to the doctor's satisfaction. It appeared that Mark—very carelessly, but he excused himself on the plea of Lady Oswald's fractious refusal to be touched—had omitted to make a proper examination of her state on the previous night. The delay, though not fatal, was inexpedient, rendering the operation which must now be performed one of more difficulty than if it had been done at once; and Dr. Davenal spoke a few sharp words, the only sharp ones he had ever in his life spoken to Mark Cray.

"I told you it was my opinion there was some internal injury. You ought to have ascertained."

He turned his steps and proceeded at once and alone to the house of Lady Oswald. She was in a grievous state of suffering; and that she had not appeared so on the previous night could only be attributed to partial insensibility. Dr. Davenal examined into her hurts with his practised skill, his gentle fingers, and he imparted to her as soothingly as possible the fact that an operation was indispensable.

"Not a very grave one," he said with a smile, intended to reassure. "Nothing formidable, like the taking off of an arm or a leg."

But Lady Oswald refused her consent; as fractiously and positively as she had the previous night refused to be touched. She would have no operation performed on her, she said, putting her to torture; they must cure her without it. Some time was lost in this unsatisfactory manner, and Mark Cray arrived while the contention was going on. Dr. Davenal was at length obliged to tell her a hard truth—that unless she submitted to it, her life must fall a sacrifice.

Then there came another phase of the obstinacy. When people are lying in the critical state that was Lady Oswald, hovering between life and death, it is surely unseemly to indulge in whims, in moods of childish caprice. If ever there is a time in the career of life that truth should reign preeminent, it is then: and these wilful caprices are born of a phase of feeling that surely cannot be called truth. Lady Oswald consented to the operation, but only on the condition that Mark Cray should perform it. What foolish caprice may have prompted this it is impossible to say. Mark had been talking to her, very much as he would talk to a child to induce it to have a tooth drawn or a cut finger dressed: protesting that it "would not hurt her to speak of," that it "would be over, so to say, in no time." Dr. Davenal, more honest, held his tongue upon those points: it would not be over in "no time," and he knew that it would hurt her very much indeed. This it may have been that caused the wretched whim to arise, that Mark Cray should be the acting surgeon. And she held to it.

It was necessary that she should be allowed some repose after the state of excitement to which she had put herself, and half-past five was the hour named. Dr. Davenal and Mark appointed to be with her then.

"Mark," asked the doctor, as they walked away together, "are you sure of yourself?"

Dr. Davenal had had no experience hitherto of Mark Cray's skill as a surgeon, except in common cases. All critical operations, both at the Infirmary and in private practice, the doctor took himself. Mark looked at the doctor in surprise as he heard the question.

"Sure! Why, of course I am. It's quite a simple thing, this."

"Simple enough where the hand is experienced and sure," remarked the doctor. "Not so simple where it is not."

"Of course I have not had your experience, Dr. Davenal; but I have had quite sufficient to ensure my accomplishing this, perhaps as skilfully as you could."

Mark spoke in a resentful tone; he did not like the reflection that he thought was cast upon him by the question. Dr. Davenal said no more. He supposed Mark was sure of his hand's skill.

"I shall give her chloroform," resumed Mark.

"No!" burst forth Dr. Davenal. He could not have interrupted more impetuously had he been interposing to dash it from her lips. He believed that Lady Oswald would be a very unfit subject for chloroform; one of those few to whom it is not safe to administer it; and he explained this to Mark Cray.

Mark turned restive. Strange to say, he, who had hitherto been content to follow in the medical steps of Dr. Davenal, watching his treatment, pursuing the same, more as a pupil takes lessons of a master than as a man in practice for himself, seemed inclined to turn restive now. Did Mark Cray, because he had married the doctor's niece, had become connected with him by private ties, was now a more equal partner, fully recognised—did he deem it well to exercise that right of independence which we all love, for it is inherent in the hearts of the best of us, and to stand up for his own ways and his own will?

"I like chloroform," he said. "I consider it one of the most blessed inventions of the age."

"Undoubtedly; where it can be safely used."

"I have used it fifty times," rejoined Mark.

"I have used it fifty and fifty to that," said the doctor, good-humouredly. "But, Mark, I never used it in my life upon a doubtful subject, and I never will use it upon one."

"What do you call a doubtful subject?"

"What do I call a doubtful subject?" repeated the doctor. "You know as well as I. How many patients has chloroform killed? Upon certain natures"—

"Very few," interrupted Mark.

"Very few, as compared to the whole," acquiesced the doctor. "You may administer chloroform with perfect safety to ninety-nine patients, and you cannot to the hundredth. Upon certain natures, as I was about to observe, its effects may be fatal. And where there is this doubt, Mark, it should be acted upon."

"The cases are so rare."

"True. And the important thing for a medical man, in these cases, is to discern where chloroform may be given with safety and where it may not."

"It is impossible that he can do that with any certainty."

"Not at all," said Dr. Davenal. "I never knew my judgment fail. I believe it is a gift, this ability to distinguish the subtle difference in natures. Perhaps I may call it instinct, more than judgment, for I think it could not deceive or lead me to an erroneous decision."

"I am not sure that I understand you," said Mr. Cray. "My belief is, that I possess nothing of the sort. I think you must be talking of a species of second sight."

"Then, Mark," was the half-joking answer, "allow yourself to be guided by my 'second sight.' To speak seriously," the doctor continued, in a graver tone, "I know that there are many practitioners, clever men, who do not possess this peculiar insight into nature. It is a great gift for those who do. It can never be acquired by practice; it must be inherent"—

"I suppose you think I don't possess it," interrupted Mark.

"I don't think you do. But for one of us who possesses it, numbers don't; so it is no disparagement to you to say so. To return to the question: Lady Oswald, in my opinion, would prove an unsafe subject for chloroform."

"She will make so much of the pain."

"Better that she should make much of it—ay, and feel it—than that any risk should be run. I cannot allow chloroform to be given to Lady Oswald."

Mark Cray demurred: not outwardly, for he said not another word; but inwardly. He was of that class of men who disbelieve what they cannot see. Some of us will look into a man's face and read his character, read him for what he is, as surely and unerringly as we read the pages of a book; but others of us, who do not possess this gift, cannot believe that it exists, laugh at and ridicule the very idea of it. Just so was it with Mark Cray. That assertion of Dr. Davenal's, that some faculty or instinct within him enabled him to discern where chloroform might and might not be administered, was utterly scouted by Mark Cray. That subtle instinct into nature, that unerring, rapidly-formed judgment of a sick man's state, the mental grasping instantaneously of the disease and its remedy, Mark Cray possessed not. To the very end of his life he would never learn it. Dr. Davenal said that out of numbers of medical men only one would possess it, and he was right. How many do not possess it, and go on to their career's end unconscious of their deficiency, they themselves will never know. Mark could see no reason why Lady Oswald should not be eased of her pain by the aid of chloroform; he did not for a moment believe the doctor could; he regarded it as a crotchet, and a very foolish one. But he suffered the question to rest, and supposed he must bow to the decision of his senior partner.

"Shall I call for you, Mark?" asked the doctor, as they separated. "I shall go up in the carriage."

"O no, thank you. I'd as soon walk. You intend to be present?"

"Or course I shall be," replied the doctor. "Lady Oswald is my patient, in point of fact—not yours, Mark."

"Then I need not ask Berry. I thought of asking him to be present."

"You can do just as you please about that. If you like him to look on at you, you can have him. Twenty-five minutes after five, remember, punctual. You'll want the full daylight."

As they parted, a feeling was in Mark's heart that he would not have liked to confess to the other, and that perhaps he neither cared to encourage nor to dwell upon. He felt perfectly sure of his own skill; he was not nervous; nobody less so; and yet there was a half-reluctance in his mind to perform that operation in the presence of Dr. Davenal, the skilled and accomplished operator. Surely the reluctance could only spring from a latent doubt of whether he ought to make so sure of himself! A latent doubt; one not suffered to appear down far in the depths of his heart it lay—so deep that perhaps Mark thought it was not there at all, that it was only fancy.

He had a great deal rather have had Berry with him—that he acknowledged openly enough to himself. Surgeon Berry was a man of fair average skill, superior to Mark in experience, and he and Mark were great friends. Did Mark fear that the presence of the more finished and perfect surgeon, with his critical eye, his practised judgment, would render him nervous—as a candidate for the Civil Service examinations will break down, simply because those searching eyes are on him? No, Mark Cray feared nothing of the sort; and he could not have told, had he been pressed, why he would have preferred the absence of Dr. Davenal. He had looked on many a time at the doctor in such cases: but that was a different thing.

His thoughts were interrupted by Julius Wild. The young man accosted him to inquire if there were any orders—whether he should be wanted.

"Yes," said Mr. Cray. "Lady Oswald's case is fixed for this afternoon. You be up there with the dressings and things."

"Very well, sir," replied the young man, feeling some surprise; for he was not in the habit of attending privately with Dr. Davenal "Am I to go to Dr. Davenal's for them?"

"No. You can get them from the Infirmary."

"The Infirmary!" thought Julius Wild to himself. "Can he be going to take the operation?"—for Mr. Cray's surgical apparatus was kept at the Infirmary. He did not ask: his professional master seemed unusually silent—not to say cross.

"What time?" he inquired of Mr. Cray.

"Be at Lady Oswald's a little before half-past—"

The blank above is put intentionally, for it cannot be told with certainty what hour was really said by Mr. Cray. In the discussions upon it that ensued afterwards, Julius Wild declared in the most positive manner that it was six. "A little before half-past six." Mr. Cray asserted, with equal pertinacity, that he had said five. "A little before half-past five." Which of the two was right it was impossible to ascertain. Mark Cray said he should not be likely to make the mistake: the time, half-past five, had been just fixed upon with Dr. Davenal, had been repeated by word of mouth, and he had never thought of the hour six at all. There was plausible reason in that, certainly. On the other hand, Julius Wild was known for a clear-headed, steady, accurate young man, and he protested he could stake his life upon his correctness in this instance. He said the thought crossed his mind, when Mr. Cray named it, that half-past six would be the dusk hour; and he rather wondered within himself that it should have been chosen.

However it may have been, the misapprehension did occur between them.

When Dr. Davenal entered his own home, dinner had been over some time. It was their custom to dine early on Sunday: and the general rule was, by Dr. Davenal's wish, never to keep meals waiting for him. Neal admitted him, and then came for orders. Should he bring up the dinner?

"Not the dinner," said Dr. Davenal; "just a bit of something upon a plate. I am not hungry: I had a late breakfast at Thorndyke. Has anybody been here for me?"

"No, sir. I think Mr. Cray took your patients. He has been here"—

"I know all about that," interrupted the doctor.

He passed Neal, and went on to the garden-parlour, a favourite room of his daughter's. She was there alone, seated before the open glass doors. How peaceful it all looked! The green lawn stretching out in front, the bright hues of the autumn flowers, the calm purity of the dark blue sky lying in the stillness of the Day of Rest. Sara Davenal had that good Book upon her lap: but she was not then reading it. She had closed it in deep thought. Her sweet face was turned upwards, her eyes were filled with tears from the intensity of her gaze; it seemed that she was looking for something in the autumn sky. The extreme calm, the aspect of peace, struck forcibly on the senses of Dr. Davenal, and he remembered it in the days to come. It was the last day of peace for him; it was the last day of peace for Sara; henceforth the world was to change for both of them. Ere the morrow's sun should rise, a great care, a great trouble, would be tugging at their heartstrings; a skeleton would be there to keep; a secret, that must be hidden for very safety's sake, would have taken up its abode there.

Dr. Davenal was upon her so quickly that she could not conceal her glistening eyes. She started up to welcome him, and laid down the book. Owing to that most attentive habit of Neal's, of being on the watch and opening the door before people could get to it, she had not heard him come home.

"O papa, is it you? You have been away a long while."

"Sit down," he said, pressing her into her chair again. "What's the grief, Sara?"

"No grief, papa. I was only thinking."

"What about? The accident last night?"

"O no, not that. I hear that everybody's going on quite well. I was thinking—I was wondering—somehow I often get thinking on these things on a Sunday, when I am sitting alone, and the sky seems so calm and near," she broke off.

"Well, what were you thinking?"

"I was wondering whether they who are gone can look down and see us—see me just as I sit here looking up—whether they can read my thoughts. We seem so divided, papa; you and I and Edward left; mamma and Richard, and the two little ones who were between me and Edward, gone."

"Divided for a short while only, child."

"Yes, I know. The only one I can remember well is Richard. I am beginning to lose almost all recollection of mamma. But Richard—papa, at times I seem to see him before me now!"

Dr. Davenal turned to the window and stood with his back to Sara, looking out. She repented having spoken of her brother; somehow the words had slipped out in the fulness of her thoughts. Rising, she stole her hand into Dr. Davenal's.

"I forgot, papa," she softly whispered.

"Forgot what, my child?" he asked. "Nay, it might be just as well if we all spoke more of Richard, instead of shunning his name. Silence will not bring him back to us."

"Ah no, it will not!"

"And when once griefs can be talked of, their sting becomes less poignant. Did the post bring any letters this morning?" the doctor added, after a pause.

"Not for you, papa. There was one—how could I forget to tell you?—there was one for me from Edward."

"And what does he say?"

"He has not been able to get leave yet. At least, from the tenor of his letter, I don't much think he has asked for it. He says there's a great deal to do; that the preparations are going on very quickly; but no orders have been received yet as to the day for embarking. As soon as they are issued he will let us know."

"But he means to come down?"

"O yes. He will be sure to come, he says, though it should be to arrive by one train and return by the next. He writes in great spirits, and asks me—in a joke you know, papa—if I will pack up my boxes and go out with him."

"He—What is it, Neal! My dinner?"

"Yes, sir. It is served."

CHAPTER XV

MARK CRAY'S MISTAKE

Evening came, and Lady Oswald's house was prepared for what was going to take place. Dr. Davenal arrived rather before the time appointed, Mr. Cray five minutes after it. Mr. Cray was in a heat, and had evidently come at much speed, conscious probably that the time had expired. Lady Oswald was in her bedchamber when Mr. Cray came up, Dr. Davenal in the ante-chamber.

"Where's Wild?" exclaimed Mr. Cray, throwing his eyes round the room.

"I have not seen him," replied the doctor.

"It is very inattentive of him not to be here. I told him the hour. Have you seen her?" added Mr. Cray, in a whisper.

"Yes. She is all right. Are you ready?"

"No, I am not ready," replied Mr. Cray. "Wild is bringing up the dressings."

"I have everything with me," said Dr. Davenal "I have brought all."

In the room with Lady Oswald was her maid Parkins. And the very moment that Dr. Davenal set his eyes on Parkins's ashy pale face, he knew that she would be better out of the room than in it. He said something to the effect, but Lady Oswald evidently wished for her, and Parkins avowed her intention of being as brave as need be.

Time was being wasted. Marcus Cray, in a fidgety sort of manner, went down twice after his expected pupil. He opened the hall-door and stood there looking out for him; and he did this twice over, for no sooner did he get upstairs the first time than he went back again. Dr. Davenal could not exactly make him out. Mr. Wild was not required in anyway; and a half-doubt stole over Dr. Davenal whether Mark Cray could be wilfully prolonging the minutes, as people will put off things they do not care to enter upon, from nervousness, dislike, or other causes. And though he threw the doubt from him as an absurd improbability, he began to wish again to be the operator.

"Cray, I had better take this."

Mark fired up, and spoke out at the top of his voice. He would prefer to take it himself, Dr. Davenal permitting him.

Spoke out so loud that he was heard by Lady Oswald. She interrupted the discussion—if discussion it might be called—and settled it. "It should be only done by Mr. Cray."

"Very well," said Dr. Davenal in a low tone to his partner. "Be it so. But why do you wait, Mark?"

"I want that fellow to be here."

"He is not required. We shall have Lady Oswald get exhausted."

And Mark Cray, seeing the wisdom of the plea, made no further delay.

You will not wish to be present at this operation, or to have it details transcribed. Hallingham did not know them for many a long day. But one or two things must be mentioned.

At the very instant of its commencement, when Mark Cray was bending over Lady Oswald, there came something falling forward to the ground and brushed against him. It was brave Parkins, gone down in a fainting-fit Lady Oswald became agitated; she shrieked out, and would have risen had it been in her power. Dr. Davenal moved round, and bore the senseless Parkins from the room.

He could not throw her down outside like a log. He had to call some of the household and tell them what to do with her. Then she began to start and kick in incipient convulsions: altogether it was three or four minutes before Dr. Davenal got back to the room. It seemed to be delay after delay, as if the operation was fated not to be begun that day.

The operation however, was begun, he found. When he got back, Mark had plunged into it. Dr. Davenal stepped up to him, and stood overlooking him with his unerring eye; that eye which Mark had dreaded.

Was it in consequence of that, that Mark Cray lost—what shall we call it?—his presence of mind?—his surgical skill? A suppressed sound, half indignation, half dismay, escaped the lips of Dr. Davenal, and he pushed Mark aside with an authoritative hand and took his place. What could have taken Mark?—what ailed him? Lady Oswald was offering no opposition, for she lay perfectly still.

So still, so voiceless, that in the midst of his work it struck strangely on the senses of Dr. Davenal. He paused a moment to regard her attentively, and then glanced at Mark, one single word only escaping him.

"Chloroform?"

"Yes," said Mark. "I judged it best."

It was all that passed. Whatever Dr. Davenal may have felt, he could express neither doubt nor remonstrance then. His whole attention had to be concentrated on the work he was performing. Mark stood by and watched, saying nothing.

At length it was over; admirably performed, as all operations were performed, undertaken by Dr. Davenal. But Lady Oswald still lay without sense or motion; and they could not arouse her.

"You must have given her a great deal," observed Dr. Davenal, who was still occupied.

Which Mark Cray did not attempt to deny. "She required it. The fall of that stupid woman excited her terribly. The first lot made no impression on her: she did not seem to inhale it."

"But—good heavens? you could not have waited long enough to see. Mark Cray, this is a mistake, and an awful one."

Mark made no reply. Mark was doing all in his power to undo his work and arouse Lady Oswald. But he could not. Dr. Davenal touched his shoulder, and spoke upon a different subject.

"You told me you were sure of yourself."

Mark scarcely knew what he answered. Something to the effect that he always had been sure, until now: but his words were very indistinct.

"What incapacity came over you? What was its cause?"

It was impossible for Mark Cray to deny that incapacity had attacked him; that Lady Oswald under his hands would have been in the greatest danger. Its cause he could not account for: but that common expression, "losing all presence of mind," would best describe it as it really was, and as it had appeared to Dr. Davenal. The drops of sweat stood out on his brow now as large as peas.

"The woman's fall startled me," he attempted to say. "At such a moment it takes but little to unnerve a man."

"Then, if so, he is not fit for a surgeon," returned Dr. Davenal. "Mark Cray," he continued, gravely and firmly, but not unkindly, "you must never in my presence attempt a critical operation again. Recollect that."

Meanwhile their whole attention was being given to Lady Oswald; their best efforts exerted to arouse her from the effects of the chloroform. All in vain, all useless; it had done its work too effectually.

By degrees the horror of the conviction that she could not be aroused—never more would be aroused— came pressing upon them deeper and deeper. Mark Cray wiped his hot face, and felt that he would give all he was worth to recall that one act of his—the surreptitiously conveying the chloroform to the house, which he had himself so successfully accomplished, and regarded as a cause of self-congratulation. Why had he not attended to the experienced opinion of Dr. Davenal—that Lady Oswald was one of those upon whom chloroform was not unlikely to be fatal? That it would be fatal in this case, Mark felt as certain now as if the breath had actually passed for ever from her body. A horrible fear came over him, and he once more lost all calmness, all self-possession.

"Dr. Davenal, for the love of God, do not betray me! Do not let it go forth to the world as my wilful act— one you warned me against. It was a dreadful mistake. I shall carry it about with me in my heart for ever; but do not betray me to the world!"

He had seized the doctor's hands, and was pressing them nervously in his. His troubled face gazed imploringly upwards; his wailing tone of repentance struck sadly on the ear. Dr. Davenal did not immediately speak, and Mark Cray resumed.

"For Caroline's sake," he entreated. "If this mistake becomes known in all its unhappy details, my professional doom is sealed. Never again, so long as I live, as you and I are together, will I attempt to act on my opinion in opposition to yours. Be merciful to us, Dr. Davenal, and, for her and my sake, conceal it from the condemning world!"

And Dr. Davenal yielded. Ever merciful, ever striving to act in accordance with those great precepts of love and mercy which One came down eighteen hundred years ago to teach, he yielded to the prayer of the unhappy and agitated man before him. His own partner—Caroline's husband; no, he could not, would not, bring upon him the obloquy of the world.

"I will keep the secret, Mark Cray. Be easy. You have my promise."

The unhappy tidings were made known to the household—that their mistress could not yet be aroused from the effect of the chloroform which had been administered with a view of saving her pain; and they came flocking in. She was not dead; but she was lying still and motionless: and the means for recalling life went on. Mark Cray continued his efforts when all hope was gone, trying every means, probable and improbable, in his madness. Had a battery been at hand he would have essayed galvanism.

Alas! they might as well have sought to arouse a stone statue. Never more would there be any arousing for poor Lady Oswald in this world. Death was claiming her: uncompromising, not-to-be-denied death!

Parkins, considerably recovered from her own attack, but in a shaky and tearful state, had come into the room with the rest. Parkins seemed inclined to rebel at the state of things; to question everybody, to cast blame somewhere.

"Why should chloroform have been given to her!" she asked of Mr. Cray.

"It was given with a view to deaden the pain," was Mark's short answer.

"But, sir, the operation was all but begun, if not begun, when I—when I—fainted: and there had been no question then of giving her chloroform."

"No, and it was your fainting that did three parts of the mischief," savagely returned Mr. Cray, who felt it the greatest relief to be able to lay the blame upon somebody. "It put her into a most undesirable state of agitation. I should think you must have heard her shriek, in spite of your fainting-fit."

The words, the angry tone, completely did for Parkins, and she subsided into tears again. A few minutes, and Dr. Davenal turned from the ill-fated lady to her servants standing there.

"It is all over. She is gone."

And the doctor looked at his watch, and found that only one poor hour had elapsed since he had entered the house to perform that operation which had altogether terminated so fatally.

CHAPTER XVI

NEAL'S DISMAY

Dr. Davenal and Mr. Cray went forth together. Outside the hall-door stood Julius Wild. It now wanted twenty minutes to seven. The Infirmary pupil had arrived a quarter of an hour before, and had waited patiently ever since to be let in. He had rung the bell in vain. In the confusion and distress of the house, it had, perhaps, not been heard, certainly had not been attended to. His rings had been but gentle ones: Julius Wild knew better than to make a noise at a house when illness was inside it: and he waited patiently enough, wondering whether the servants were asleep, whether Lady Oswald was worse, and believing the doctors had not yet come.

When they came forth, he was excessively surprised, marvelling greatly at his non-admittance.

"I have been ringing this quarter of an hour," he said, by way of explanation and apology. "I can't think what the servants can have been about."

"What have you been about?" thundered Mark Cray, giving way to anger, although he had come straight from the presence of the dead.

Mr. Wild was astonished. "I say, sir, I have been waiting here. I have been here this quarter of an hour, and could not get let in."

"And, pray, what kept you? Why were you not here to time?"

"I was here to time, sir," was the deprecating answer; and the young man marvelled much what had so put out his good-tempered medical master. "You told me to be here a little before half-past six, sir, and I got here five minutes before it."

Then began that dispute which was never satisfactorily settled; each, to this very day, believing himself to be in the right. Mr. Cray held to it that he had told him half-past five; Julius Wild earnestly protested that he had said half-past six. The wrangling continued for some minutes, or rather the difference of opinion, for of course the pupil did not presume to wrangle with his superior. A few sharp words from Mark, peremptorily ordering him to hold his tongue, concluded it. The young man walked close by the two doctors, just a little behind them—for they had been walking down from Lady Oswald's all along, had not stayed for one minute at the door. He had wondered at first whether the operation had taken place, and why they should leave the house just about the time fixed for it: now that he heard of this misapprehension with regard to the hour, he supposed it was over, and that Mr. Cray's vexation arose from the fact of his not having arrived for it. But he was a young man of curiosity, fond of sociability in a general way, and of asking questions, so he thought he would ask one now, and make sure.

"Is the operation over, sir?"

"Yes," curtly answered Mark.

"Was it successful?"

"When did you ever know Dr. Davenal unsuccessful?" retorted Mr. Cray. "That was successful enough."

It never occurred to Julius Wild that the stress upon the word "that" implied, or could imply, that though the operation had been successful, something else was not. Perhaps it was half a subterfuge in Mark Cray to have said it. The young man asked no more questions. Finding himself so snubbed, he desisted, and walked behind in silence. Neither of them told the unhappy truth to him. Dr. Davenal may have been too pained, too shocked to speak; Mark Cray's conscience too suggestive. Nay, Dr. Davenal may not have seen his way clear to speak at all. If he was to conceal the culpability of Mark Cray, the less he opened his mouth upon the point, even by a word, the better.

Suddenly Mark turned round. "You are not wanted, Mr. Wild. There's nothing more tonight."

The young man took the hint at once, wished them good-evening, and walked off to the Infirmary, there to leave certain articles that he had been carrying. He observed that Dr. Davenal, usually so courteous, never answered him, never gave him the good-evening in reply to his.

The two surgeons walked on in silence. The streets were nearly deserted; and the sound of praise and prayer came upon their ears from the lighted places of worship as they passed them. The evening was a warm one, and the doors of the churches and chapels stood open. They never spoke a word, one to the other. Mark Cray felt as he had probably never felt in his life—ashamed, repentant, grieved, humble. He was guilty of the blood of a fellow-creature. He called it a "mistake." A mistake in one sense it undoubtedly was, but a wicked and a wilful one. Dr. Davenal felt it to be both: felt that the giving of the chloroform stealthily, in direct opposition to his expressed opinion, deserved a worse name; and, though he had promised not to betray Mark, he could not just yet subdue his own feelings, and speak to him in a friendly tone. Thus in silence they reached the doctor's gate.

"Goodnight," said he, turning in at it.

"Goodnight," replied Mark, continuing his way. But—and he felt it—there had been no invitation to him to enter, no pleasant look, no shake of the hand.

Neal was at the door, airing himself and watching the scanty passers-by in the dusky street, the rest of the household being at church. Dr. Davenal went into his study, and lifted his hat from his brow as if a heavy weight were there. He had no light, save what came in from the street gas-lamp.

He leaned against the window in thought. Two hours before, Lady Oswald had been, so to say, as full of life as he was, and now—dead. Killed. There was no mincing the matter to himself; she had been killed. Killed by Mark Cray.

Had he done right in undertaking to screen Mark Cray?—to keep his culpability a secret?—to suffer the world to assume his innocence. The reader may deem it a grave question: Dr. Davenal was asking it of himself. Had Mark's been purely an error in judgment; had he administered the chloroform, believing it to be the right and proper thing to do, leaving the issue with God, it had been different. But he had given it in direct opposition to an opinion of more value than his own; in, as was much to be feared, a spirit of obstinate defiance. It is true he had not intended to kill; he had probably been over-confident of the result. How Dr. Davenal condemned him he alone could tell; but—was it his, the doctor's place, to hold him forth to the condemnation of the world? No; he, the merciful man, thought it could not be. One strong point on the side of this mercy was—that the proclaiming the facts could be productive of no good result; they could not recall the mistaken act; they could not bring the unfortunate lady back to life. It might be said that it should be made known as a warning to others not to trust Mark Cray; but the very occurrence itself with its tragical end, would, if the doctor knew anything of human nature, be its own warning for Mark Cray's whole lifetime. He did not think much of the surgical failure; at least he was not dwelling on it. Probably the worst calamity had in a measure eclipsed the other in his mind. Young surgeons had turned nervous before now, as Dr. Davenal knew; and the fall of the maid Parkins might certainly have startled him. It was not that that was troubling him; he had arrested Mark's shaking hands, and replaced them with his own sure ones, and carried the matter through successfully; it was the other.

He thought it over and over, and could not bring himself to see that he had done wrong in promising to hide the facts. If he went that hour and stood in the market-place and shouted them forth to all hearers, it could not bring back the forfeited life; it could not remedy the past in the remotest degree. He thought of his dead brother, Caroline's father; he remembered the words he had sent out to him to soothe his dying bed—"The child shall be to me as a daughter." He could not, on the very threshold of her wedded life, bring obloquy on the husband of her choice, and blight his good name, his fair prospects. And so he resolved to keep the secret—to guard the fatal mistake from the knowledge of the world. Only their own two selves were privy to it; therefore Mark was perfectly safe—save for him. The administering the chloroform must be looked upon as an error in judgment, of his own as well as of Mark's: and yet scarcely an error, for perhaps nine surgeons out of ten would so have administered it to a patient under similar circumstances, and have made no exception in Lady Oswald. He, Dr. Davenal, must suffer this to be assumed, saying himself as little as was possible upon the matter to any one: in a case where the termination had been so unfortunate his reticence would be excused.

He leaned his head upon his hand in the dark twilight, and pondered over the circumstances: he could not keep his mind from dwelling upon them almost morbidly. A strange fatality seemed to have attended the affair altogether. There had beat the obstinate persistence of Lady Oswald to see her landlord, in spite of common-sense and of Mr. Oswald Cray's representation that it could not possibly serve her; there had been the sudden falling lame of the carriage horse, for which the coachman had been unable to account; and then there had been the accident to the train. Parkins had had told him a confused tale—confused through her own grief, poor woman—of their having gone by mistake, she and her mistress, to the wrong side of the station at Hildon to take the return train, and had thereby lost a train. They went, naturally enough perhaps to inexperienced travellers, to the side of the platform on which they had descended on going; and it was not until a train came up to the other side, took in the passengers waiting on that side of the platform, and went on to Hallingham, that they discovered their mistake. But for that, they would have been at Hallingham safe and sound when the accident happened to the late train. Then there was the fact of Mark Cray's having been in the train, of his having been the first to see Lady Oswald. When brought afterwards to the home terminus, she had said, "Mr. Cray will go home with me:" and later she had insisted on his taking the operation. He himself had been called out to Thorndyke, had been kept there while the long hours of the best part of the day had flitted away: had he not been called out, why the operation would, beyond all question, have been performed in the morning, probably by himself, for he should have seen her early and detected its need. There was the absence of the pupil, Julius Wild, through what appeared an unaccountable mistake: had that pupil been present, to him would have fallen the task of getting Parkins from the room, and the chloroform could not have been administered. A curious chapter of accidents—or what are called such—and Dr. Davenal lost himself in the chain of thought. "O merciful Father, forgive him! forgive him this night's work!" he murmured. "And mayst Thou have taken that poor woman to her rest!"

A great light and Neal's smooth voice broke upon Dr. Davenal. "Shall I get you anything, sir? Tea, or"—

"I don't want anything, I don't want the gas lighted," interrupted Dr. Davenal, starting from his chair. "Wait until you are called."

Neal, after a moment's stare, shot back again. It was not so much the sharp words, more imperative than any commonly used by his master, but the wailing tone of pain in which they were spoken, that struck Neal: nay, it almost seemed as if his entrance had brought a sort of terror to the doctor.

It was not terror. Neal was mistaken. But Dr. Davenal had been so completely buried in thoughts, not altogether of this world, that the abrupt interruption, with its commonplace excuse, had seemed to him singularly inopportune, causing him to wave away abruptly the man and his words.

He sat on in the dark again, and Neal took his place at the front door, and stood there looking out. Not a soul was in the house save himself and his master; and it may have seemed a more cheering way of passing the evening, to Neal, than to be shut up indoors.

It grew darker. Neal strolled along by the skirting shrubs of the garden, and took his stand at the front gate, ready to exchange courtesies with the people who would soon be going home from church or chapel. The moon did not give much light yet, but the night promised to be as clear and bright as the previous one had been.

"Holloa!" cried Neal, as a man he knew came up quickly. "You are in a hurry tonight."

"I have been out on business, Mr. Neal," replied the man, who was in fact an assistant to a carpenter and undertaker. "Our work can't always wait for the Sabbath to go by before it is seen to."

"Is anybody dead?" asked Neal.

"Lady Oswald. The message came down to us best part of an hour ago; so I've been up there."

It has been observed that Neal was too well trained a gentleman both in manners and nerves to express much surprise, but this answer caused him the very greatest shock. He was so startled as to take refuge in disbelief.

"Lady Oswald, did you say? But she's not dead!"

"But she is," replied the man. "I ought to know. I've just come from her."

"Why, what has she died of? They said the railway accident had not materially hurt her."

"She haven't died of the accident. She have died of that—that—what-you-call-it—as is give to folks to take the pain out of 'em."

Neal did not understand. "To take the pain out of them?" he repeated, looking questioningly at the speaker.

"That stuff that have come into fashion of late years. The doctors will give it you while you have a tooth took out, if you'll let 'em."

"Do you mean chloroform?"

"That's it. I never can remember the name. But I'd rather call it poison, for my part—killing folks dead off without a warning."

"Who gave it to Lady Oswald?"

"Your master," replied the man, lowering his voice to a whisper as he glanced at the windows of the house. "The servants was in the room with me up there, and they told me about it. There was something to be done to my lady—some bones to be set, I believe—and the doctors went this afternoon, and they give her this stuff, and it killed her. I wonder Parliament don't make a law again its use, for my part."

"I am sorry to hear this," exclaimed Neal. "My lady was very friendly to me."

"Ay. The servants be cut up like anything. And enough to make 'em! It's a shocking thing. The lady's maid says she can't think why they should have give her the stuff, for Mr. Cray himself told her, when he was there in the afternoon, that what they had to do wouldn't hurt my lady no more than a flea-bite. Anyway, she's dead. But I can't stop here, I must get along back with the measure. Goodnight, Mr. Neal."

"Goodnight," replied Neal.

He leaned on the gate, watching the man hurrying onwards with his fleet steps, and thinking over what he had heard. Perhaps it is not too much to say that Mr. Neal would have preferred to hear of the death of any other person in Hallingham than of Lady Oswald's. Lady Oswald had been a great friend to him, and it had been Neal's intention to put her friendliness to the test in a very short period of time. Neal was a subtle schemer, and he had been perfecting a plan by which at one bold stroke Lady Oswald's mind should be disabused of that suspicion against himself imparted to her by Dr. Davenal the day of

Miss Caroline's marriage, to which he had been an unsuspected listener, and by which he should also be effectually served. Neal had begun to feel that his tenure in his present situation was no longer sure, and he intended by the help of Lady Oswald to secure to himself a situation of a different nature.

Now this grand scheme was destroyed. As the rising waves dash away the "houses" built by children on the sands at the sea-shore, so this château en Espagne of Neal's was dashed down by the death of Lady Oswald. If Neal's cold and selfish heart could like any one, it had liked her. She had kept up friendly relations with Neal, as a former retainer of Sir John and Thorndyke; had shown more consideration to Neal than to her own servants—had treated him in fact as superior to her servants. When Neal waited on her at her residence to pay his respects, as he did occasionally, she would ring the bell on his departure and say sharply, "Show Mr. Neal out"—as much as to remind her household that he had not been a common servant at Thorndyke: he was groom of the chambers. She had also been liberal in her presents to Neal. Altogether, Neal in his discomfiture felt very much, as though her ladyship's death was a grievance personally inflicted on himself.

Jessy the housemaid was the first of the servants to return. The moment she entered, Neal took his hat and went up to Lady Oswald's with a view of learning particulars. The news had been so sudden, so unexpected, that some faint feeling or hope almost seemed to be in the man's mind that he should find it untrue.

He found it too true. He was allowed to see Lady Oswald, and he listened to the details given by the servants, gathering them into his mind to be turned over and examined afterwards. Parkins spoke with him privately. She was very bitter against the chloroform: she said to him that she should always look upon the administering it as an underhand trick not to be understood. There was no question of chloroform when she was in the room, and that was up to the very last moment; there was no chloroform present that she saw, and the doctors must have got it concealed in their pockets and produced it when her back was turned. She didn't blame Mr. Cray; she was certain it was not Mr. Cray; for he had told her privately in the afternoon that the operation would be a mere nothing, a flea-bite— and she could only wonder at Dr. Davenal's not having exercised more caution. One of the servants downstairs had had some experience in chloroform, she added, and her opinion was, that an over-quantity must have been given: that Dr. Davenal had mistook the dose, and given too much. At any rate, if ever there was a murdered woman, it was her mistress.

Parkins's eyes were alight when she said this, and Parkins's cheeks aflame. Her grief for the loss of her mistress was merging into anger at its cause. Like Neal, she was beginning to consider it as a personal grievance inflicted on herself, and to resent it as such. Self-interest sways the best of us more or less: and Parkins felt that through this she had lost a better place than she should ever find again. Neal asked her a few questions on his own score, and hurried away with the information he had garnered.

He hastened home with the utmost speed that his legs would carry him. He had a reason—at least he thought he might have one in future—for not wishing it known at home that he had paid that visit to Lady Oswald's. The late returners from church were but in the streets when he went back, slowly pacing along in the lovely autumn night. He whisked in just in time to admit the ladies.

"Is papa in, Neal?"

"Yes," answered Neal, haphazard, for he was of course not positive upon the point. "I fancy he is in his room, Miss Sara."

Sara knocked at the consulting-room door and entered. As she went forward, Neal contrived to obtain a passing view of the interior. It was still in darkness, and Dr. Davenal was leaning his back against the window-frame his arms folded, his head bowed, as one will stand when under the weight of care.

"It looks just as though he had purposely killed her," was Neal's comment to himself.

Not that Neal thought it then. No, no. But Neal was in a state of terrible vexation and disappointment; in that precise mood when it is a vast relief to vent one's trouble upon anybody.

"How sad you look, papa!" cried Sara, as she noted his depressed attitude. "And you are all in the dark!"

Dr. Davenal aroused himself, put his hand on his daughter, and turned round to face the street. At that moment the death-bell rang out.

Accustomed now to the darkness of the room—not that it was entirely dark, for the doctor had thrown open the Venetian blind, and the gas-lamp cast in its rays brightly—Sara could see how sad and clouded was his face. The death-bell was striking out its quick sharp strokes.

"Do you know who the bell is tolling for, papa? I never heard it ring out so late as this."

"I expect it is tolling for Lady Oswald."

"Papa! For Lady Oswald?" She quite shrieked as she said it in her startled surprise.

"She is dead, child," he said, his subdued voice a contrast to hers.

"O papa! Was it the operation? Did she die under it?"

"Yes—in one sense. The operation was successfully accomplished, but—chloroform was exhibited, and she never rallied from it."

Sara stood still, her heart beating. It seemed that a hundred regrets were crowding upon her, a hundred questions. "O papa, why did you administer chloroform?" she exclaimed, scarcely knowing what she said.

For a single moment the temptation came over Dr. Davenal to tell his daughter the truth, and he had unclosed his lips to speak; but he checked himself in time. Sara was trustworthy—he knew that; but it was impossible to answer for chance or inadvertent words, even from her; and for Mark's sake it might be better to leave her in equal ignorance with the rest of the world.

"My dear," he said—and the words to her ear sounded strangely solemn—"I have striven to do the best always for my patients, under God. Had I been able to save Lady Oswald's life, I would have saved it."

"O yes yes, papa, I know that. We all know it. Did she die quite suddenly? Was she sensible of her state?"

"People who die under the influence of chloroform seldom know anything after inhaling it. She did not. Sara, it is a painful subject; I would rather not speak of it. I feel it greatly—greatly."

She quitted him and went upstairs to take off her things. When she came down again Dr. Davenal was in the dining-room, and the tray, as was usual when they dined early, was on the table with some slight refreshment.

"Not anything for me," said the doctor to his sister. "I cannot eat tonight."

He did not sit down: he was pacing the carpet with thoughtful, measured tread. Neal stole a glance at him from under the corner of his eyes.

"Shall I light the gas in your study, sir, tonight?"

"No. Yes, you may light one burner," the doctor added after a moment's pause.

"What's the matter, Richard?" asked Miss Davenal. "You seem cut up. Have you had a hard day's work today?"

"Pretty well," called out the doctor.

"Do you know who it is that's dead? Very queer that the passing-bell should toll out at night!"

"You can tell your aunt, Sara," the doctor quietly said, as he stepped to the door of the room, and vanished.

"Well, I'm sure!" angrily cried Miss Davenal. "My brother is polite tonight. He might have answered me."

Sara pushed from her the piece of cake she had been trying to eat, and went close to her aunt, speaking in her slowest and most distinct tones.

"Don't you see that papa has had a great shock—a blow, Aunt Bettina? Lady Oswald is dead."

Poor Miss Davenal, never very quick at comprehending, confused the information together in the most helpless manner. "What do you say? Lady Oswald has had a blow? Who's dead?"

"Aunt, aunt, you will understand me if you won't be impatient. Lady Oswald is dead. And I say it is a great blow to papa. I can see that it is."

Miss Davenal heard now, and looked perfectly scared. "Lady Oswald dead! It cannot be, Sara."

"She had to undergo some operation in consequence of the accident, and papa gave her chloroform, hoping of course to lighten the pain, and she never rallied from it."

Miss Davenal seized Sara's hands in her dismay. Her senses were sharpened and she had heard perfectly; her face had turned white. Neal, who had come in, looked at her as he stood near the door, and wondered whether she was going to faint.

"Sara, I don't like that chloroform. I have told the doctor so, often and often. They should never try it upon me. Who gave it her?"

"Papa," replied Sara, never dreaming but she was correct in saying so. "Aunt Bettina, he gave it her for the best."

"Best! of course he gave it for the best—nobody disputes that. But I don't like it: I never did like it. Chloroform is come into fashion now—an improvement on the old state of things, they call it, as they call the railways—and I don't deny that it spares pain; but I do not like it."

By and by Sara went to the consulting-room. The doctor was pacing it uneasily.

"I have come to say goodnight, papa."

"You are going to bed early, is it ten o'clock?"

"Yes, I think it is past ten. Goodnight, dear papa. I hope you will be better in the morning."

"I have felt nothing like it since the death of Richard. Goodnight, my child."

It was not so much the death in itself that was affecting Dr. Davenal, as the appalling reflection that it had been, in a manner, wilfully caused. The knowledge weighed on his heart like a stone.

CHAPTER XVII

THE NIGHT VISITOR TO DR DAVENAL

The bedchamber of Sara Davenal was over the doctor's study, on the opposite side of the landing to the drawing-room. It was not a large room, but longer than it was wide, and the bed was placed at the far end of the room—the back. The chamber behind it was larger, and occupied by Miss Davenal. The room opposite Miss Davenal's, and behind the drawing-room, had been the bedchamber of Dr. Davenal in his wife's lifetime; since her death it had been kept as a spare room for chance visitors.

Sara did not begin to undress immediately upon entering the room. She put out the light, and sat down at the open window to indulge in a little quiet thought: it was rather a habit of hers to do so when the night was fine and she came up early. She liked to sit there and think of many things, to glance up at the clear sky in the bright moonlight. With all her practical good sense—and she had her full portion of it—she was of a somewhat dreamy, imaginative temperament; and since Richard's death she had grown to think more of that other home to which he was gone, the same to which we are all hastening, than it is perhaps usual for girls of Sara's age to think of it. As she had said to Dr. Davenal in the afternoon, she would wonder whether Richard and her lost mother—whom she but imperfectly remembered—could look down upon her: she was fond of fancying that they were looking down upon her: and she would lose herself in a maze of visionary imaginings.

Not on this night, however, did her thoughts turn to Richard. They were full of Lady Oswald and her unhappy death. That this fatal chloroform had been administered for the best, in accordance with Dr.

Davenal's experienced judgment, Sara assumed as a matter of course; she never so much as thought of casting a doubt to it: but she knew enough of him to be sure that the fatal termination would cause him to repent of having given it—to blame himself bitterly, and she felt for him to the very depth of her heart. An uncomfortable sensation, as if her father had been guilty of some deliberate wrong, was pervading her, and she could not shake it off.

It should be observed that although Sara sat close to the open window, she was not liable to be seen by the passers-by in the street, did any cast their eyes that way. A small stand or ledge had been constructed round the window (a bay window, as was the one answering to it on the other side, the drawing-room), and this was filled with pots in flower. Geraniums of many species, fuchsias, heliotropes, heaths, wild thyme, the fine flowering cactus, and many others, raised their heads proudly, and formed a screen behind which Sara was securely sheltered from observation, and also from the rays of the gas-lamp at the gate, which otherwise would have lighted her up. So that, although she could see out perfectly well, sitting as she now was, she could not be seen. If she chose to stand at the window and lean out, her head was above the flowers; but at the same time they entirely prevented her from seeing anything immediately below her window. The ground for a yard or two beyond Dr. Davenal's study window was as completely hidden from her as though it had been a hundred miles off; and it is necessary to mention this. The bedroom above Sara's, occupied by Watton the upper maid, had a flat window, and its view underneath was in like manner obstructed by the extending bow and the plants in it of Sara's. These flowers at Miss Sara Davenal's window were quite the admiration of the pedestrian portion of Hallingham, and many a one would halt at the front railings to take a passing gaze at them. They were really beautiful, and Sara took a pride in them and liked to tend them.

She liked to inhale their sweet perfume, as she was doing now, sweeter and stronger in the night air than in the garish day. Perhaps the heliotrope was of all the most powerful scent: and somehow that heliotrope had become associated in her mind with Mr. Oswald Cray. She could not have told why or wherefore; she had never attempted to analyse the cause: she only knew that when she approached that window, and the perfume of the heliotrope was wafted to her senses, the image of Oswald Cray was, in like manner, by some mysterious instinct, wafted to her mind.

Perhaps it did not require any extraneous aid to bring him to her memory. He was already too securely seated there. For the last twelvemonth, since Oswald Cray had become intimate at their house, her love for him had been gradually growing into being: that subtle understanding, never to be explained or accounted for, which draws together two human hearts, and only those two, the one for the other, of all the whole world, life finding life, had arisen between them. Oswald Cray had never spoken or hinted at his feelings until the time when Dr. Davenal honestly avowed to him that he had fancied he cared for Caroline: that had brought forth the one word—and it was little more—to Sara. But she had known it just as surely as though he had spoken out all along.

Save for that shrinking reticence which would fain hide the secret, as the modest snowdrop hides its head, and which must always accompany the feeling if it be genuine, there was nothing to be ashamed of in this love. It is true that it had become entwined with every fibre of her heart, was a part and parcel of her very being. It would perhaps have been impossible—at least, it would have been very improbable—for Sara Davenal, with her right feeling, her powers of discernment, which she possessed in a high degree, and her sound good sense, to fall in love with an unworthy man. She could not have met with a more worthy one than Oswald Cray. He had his faults—ay, who has not?—but they were faults of what may be called a high order; not mean, drivelling, scandalising faults, that abound in the world. Each was suited and suitable to the other, in taste, in position, in moral goodness: and their love had been given for aye; beyond the power of circumstances or time to change. They might never be more to each than they were now. Untoward fate might separate them; the world's bitter tongues, expediency, the poison of misunderstanding; any one of these separating causes might part them; Sara's unbending principle, Oswald's wrong-headed pride—it was impossible to foretell: but of one thing both might rest assured, that unto their dying day that love could never be wholly extinguished in either heart, so as to give place to another.

Somehow the thoughts of Sara Davenal had wandered from the painful subject of Lady Oswald to this brighter one: wandered unwittingly, against her will. She would not have chosen to dwell upon her love that sad night, or on the one sweet word of Oswald when he last parted from her: but there it was, sounding in her ears and her heart: and she lost herself in one of the sweetest reveries that ever maiden pictured of the future.

Suddenly she was aroused from it. Not by any thought of poor Lady Oswald, or of her father's sorrow, or of the minutes that were hurrying on, or that it was time she prepared for bed; but by the sight of some one coming in at the front gate. It was nothing unusual for that gate to be invaded at night, by messengers summoning Dr. Davenal to some urgent bed of sickness. But this intruder had something peculiar about him, or about his movements, which attracted her eye.

He was a tall man, wearing a cap and a grey Scotch plaid scarf. The cap, which had a peak to it, appeared to be tied down over his ears, and the scarf was worn in a droll fashion, one at least that Sara had never seen in Hallingham. It was put lengthways over the shoulders, as a lady puts on a scarf; it came down to the waist behind, and was held very much up to the neck in front. Sara naturally looked at the man, looked keenly with a view of distinguishing his features. In her sympathy with the sick, she thought to learn, by him, who was ill that night and wanted her father. But she was unable to do this, and the first thought that struck upon her as curious was, that a man should be so completely wrapped up on that genial night. The next curious thing that struck her was—the man's movements.

He had come up to the gate with very quick steps—as messengers from the sick often did come—opened it, and gave a sort of dart or spring to his right, which brought him under the shade of the laurels and hid him from the moonlight. There he stopped, reconnoitring the house, so far as could be seen, but really it required a quick eye to distinguish him at all from the dark shrubs. That was not precisely the way in which night applicants came to Dr. Davenal's house; and Sara, very much astonished, rose quietly from her seat, to see the better.

He came on at last, creeping close to the shrubs, stooping under their shade, until he gained Dr. Davenal's window. With all Sara's endeavours to look, she there lost sight of him, because he was beneath, but she heard a gentle tapping at the window. Not the quick imperative noise of one in haste, demanding instant attention, but a covert, stealthy tapping, which seemed afraid of being heard. More and more astonished, Sara leaned out further; but she could not lean far enough to see.

The window was opened instantly; therefore it was to be supposed that Dr. Davenal had not retired from the room; that his light had probably guided the stranger to apply at the window, instead of at the door. The first sound, after the opening of the window, was a warning hush-sh-sh-sh! but whether it came from the applicant or from her father she could not tell. A short colloquy followed, only a word or two in the most covert tones, and then Dr. Davenal went to the front door and admitted the visitor. Sara sat down overwhelmed with amazement.

Somebody else was overwhelmed with amazement unfortunately—or perhaps the better word for him would be curiosity—and that was Mr. Neal. Neal had been a witness to it all. When it struck half-past ten—and this mysterious visit occurred some five minutes subsequent to that time—Dr. Davenal had opened his study door, called to Neal, and told him to put the gas out. Which was equivalent to telling him to go to bed: the putting out of the gas being the last service usually required of Neal. Neal came forward and did as he was bid—he put out the hall-lamp and any other burners that might be alight, with the exception of the one in the doctor's study. Dr. Davenal always took that upon himself, and he put out the burner as he spoke to Neal, and lighted his candle for bed, no gas being laid on in the bedrooms. Neal then went downstairs and turned the gas off at the main; so the house was safe.

But Neal, as a matter of taste was not fond of retiring early. And when he came up again, and had shut himself into his pantry, instead of passing into his sleeping-room he blew out his candle, opened the door on the side, and, dexterously avoiding contact with the shrubs, he stole to the front. There he stood, amidst the shrubs, near the doctor's window, with a view possibly of giving himself a little fresh air.

He glanced at the window; the half-shutters were not drawn up, a thing the doctor did himself the very last thing, and he could see the wax candle on the table through the Venetian blinds. The upper shutters of the window were closed; Neal always closed those when he lighted the gas; but his orders were to leave the lower ones open. It was a fancy of the doctor's the being able to take a look out at the street until the last, if he chose to do so. The upper shutters being closed did not prevent the window being opened at will. It is as well to give these details, for this was an eventful night in the existence of Dr. Davenal: and of others besides.

Neal could see the candle, and he could see his master. Dr. Davenal was seated at the table, his head leaning on his hand. Whether he was reading, or whether he had merely bent his head in thought, Neal could not discern, but he thought he had never in his life seen a countenance so troubled.

There was nothing in all that, however, to afford particular gratification to Neal's curiosity, and he drew cautiously away from the window, and turned his attention on the street. It was necessary to be cautious, for the least stir of the shrubs would have been heard by Dr. Davenal on that still night; sitting as he did with the window a little open, his custom until he retired. Neal stood watching the passers-by. Stay; watching for any passers-by; but he had not seen one yet. Sunday evening hours were early at Hallingham, and people were mostly indoors and abed. Now, in point of fact, Neal had no particular motive in stealing out and standing there; he was not expecting any one or anything; but he had a habit of peering about him a great deal more than most people have, and Neal rarely went finally to rest without coming out to take a general glance round, and see anything there might be to see.

Little did Neal anticipate the reward his curiosity was to receive this night. He was taking a last look previous to retreating, thinking it rather slow work standing there with nothing to see, not even a passing passenger on that quiet Sunday night, when the man who had so surprised Sara Davenal darted in at the gate. Neal strained his eyes in a vain attempt to discover who it was, and backed into safe quarters.

He heard the covert tapping at the window; he heard the warning hush when the doctor opened it, and he could not say for certain, any more than Sara could, which of the two it was who had given that warning hush; and then after a short whispering, the purport of which he was entirely unable to make out, the doctor's tones were a little raised:

"I will open the door for you."

The stranger made his way to the front door. Neal, in the swift, unerring, covert manner which practice had rendered facile, stole back to his pantry with incredible speed, and was in time to peep out of it, and to see the visitor admitted.

But he gained nothing by his movement. The hall was in the dark: Dr. Davenal had not brought his candle out, and Neal could not see more than the very faintest outline of their forms. They passed into the room in silence, and Neal heard the door closed quietly and cautiously; another minute and the bolt was slipped. He took off his shoes and stole on tiptoe in his stockings to the door, and put his ear to it.

No, not a word could he hear. That door was a sound door, a close-fitting one: Neal had tried it before in his life, and obtained no more result than he was obtaining now. He made his way back through the pantry to the window again, and there Neal could have groaned in impotent rage had he dared, for Dr. Davenal had shut it.

But he had not closed the shutters. Neal, if it was any good to him, could still get a glimpse in through the upright staves of the green dwarf blinds. It was but a glimpse, for they were turned all but close together, the one stave nearly lying on the other, and it did not afford him satisfaction, for he could see neither Dr. Davenal nor his visitor, who were seated at the side of the room close together where the angle of view obtainable by Neal would not reach them. A very faint hum of voices penetrated his ear, and he was not sure whether that was not fancy. Their conversation was being carried on in the lowest tones.

Unsatisfactory as was this result as a whole, Neal waited with patience. Such men as Neal are always patient The clock struck eleven, and the clock struck half-past eleven, and Neal was still there.

Then there occurred a change. Dr. Davenal rose from his seat and began pacing the room. His whole face was working with agitation. Neal caught a sight of it occasionally as he paced, and was struck by the troubled expression, nay, by the dread that pervaded it. Neal had long ago made up his mind as to the purport of the visit—that it was in some way connected with the catastrophe of the evening, the death of Lady Oswald.

Suddenly Neal was startled. His nose was uncommonly close to the window, and the window was abruptly raised; raised without the slightest warning some half-dozen inches. Neal believed his nose was off.

When he came to himself, which he really did not for a few minutes, some words in a wailing tone were issuing from the lips of Dr. Davenal. "Silence must be purchased at any price; at any price. If it takes the whole of my fortune, I must purchase silence." Neal pricked up his ears.

Dr. Davenal was walking still; the visitor, whoever he might be, never moved from his seat. It was only when the doctor came near the window that Neal caught an occasional word. "Yes, Lady Oswald herself. She wished it," were the next words he heard, and then there was another temporary lull.

"I am aware of that. Murder? yes, the world would look upon it as such. I felt certain that Lady Oswald was one to whom chloroform, if administered, would prove fatal. Heaven help me! What have I done that the trials of this day should fall upon my head?"

Dr. Davenal was standing at the window as he said this, had halted there with his voice close to Neal's face, and Neal's hair stood on end as he heard it. From that moment the man believed—fully believed in his inmost heart—that his master had purposely destroyed Lady Oswald. Perhaps the belief, judging from these disconnected and certainly ominous words, was excusable.

For a short while Neal heard no more. His master had halted opposite the stranger and was talking fast, but nothing came to Neal but a confused sound. Then he advanced again.

"I tell you it shall be done. If it costs every penny piece that I have saved, this horrible secret must be bought up—if money will buy it. I shall never know another happy moment: I shall live as with a sword of disgrace hanging over me, ever expecting it to fall."

Some murmured words came from the stranger, and Neal stretched his ear to its utmost tension. Whether in doing so he made the least noise, touched the window, rustled the shrubs, he could not tell, but Dr. Davenal turned and shut the window down as swiftly and suddenly as he had put it up.

So, hearing was cut off. But Neal could see still—just a glimpse. He saw Dr. Davenal go out of the room with the candle and bring back a plate of biscuits and a decanter of wine. He knew he must have gone to the dining-room sideboard for them. A wish crossed Neal's mind to go indoors, make the excuse that he had heard his master stirring, and dash into the study on the pretence of inquiring if he could do anything. But he did not dare. Neal would have given a whole year's wages to get one good look at the visitor. Presently all sight was cut off. Barely had Dr. Davenal put down the decanter and biscuits than he turned to the window and pulled up the shutters.

It was a checkmate for Neal. He went in and stood just outside his pantry, hesitating whether to go close to the room door or not. A good thing he did not, for Dr. Davenal came out almost immediately, and went upstairs to his daughter's room.

Neal heard him knock at it very softly; he heard him ask in a whisper whether she was in bed yet. That she was not in bed the immediate opening of the door proved.

Dr. Davenal went in and closed the door. Neal could hear the murmur of his voice, as if he were explaining something to his daughter, and then they came down together, treading softly, not to arouse the house. Neal could see that she was fully dressed, in the same silk she had worn in the day. They went in, and the door was closed, and the bolt slipped as before.

Ten minutes, and Sara came out again alone. Neal could tell who it was by the rustling of the silk, but there was no light. She returned upstairs to her room, but not before Neal thought he had caught the sound of a sob.

The next to come forth was the visitor, without a candle still. Dr. Davenal opened the hall door and let him out. Neal, with his quick movements, glided round to his post of observation in the front garden, and was just in time to see him go through the gate, the cap drawn over his face, and the grey woollen scarf muffled around him.

CHAPTER XVIII

AFTER THE VISITOR'S DEPARTURE

If ever the signs of misery, of despair, of terror, were depicted on a human face, they were on Dr. Davenal's as he sat that night in his study. He was as a man who has received some great shock; a shock that strikes a species of paralysis alike to the heart and to the frame. His arms hung down listlessly, his head was bent, his fixed eyes had a wild anxious look, most foreign to the usually calm orbs of the composed surgeon. An hour and a quarter had he thus sat since the departure of that midnight visitor who had brought with him so much apparent mystery, so much woe, and the house clock was striking one. The sound did not arouse Dr. Davenal; he sat on with his face of terrified despair.

The wax taper, unheeded, unlooked at, stood on a side-table where it had been accidentally put. It had burnt nearly to the socket, and it now began to spurt and gutter with a great light; the signs of its end. That awoke Dr. Davenal from his reverie. The prospect of being left in the dark was not a convenient one; and he tore a bit of paper from a journal lying near and essayed to light the gas, completely forgetting that it had been turned off at the main.

Finding his mistake, he stood a moment with his hand to his temples, as if endeavouring to collect thought, and then opened the door of his bedroom. Candles always stood there on the mantelpiece ready for lighting, and he brought one forward and succeeded in catching a light for it from the dying taper.

This had the effect of effectually arousing him. He looked at his watch, and then held the candle to a book-shelf, whence he selected a local railway guide, and sat down to the table to consult it.

"Nothing until the morning!" he exclaimed in a tone that might have been one of vexation but for its deeper pain. "Stay, though! Yes, there is. There's the train that passes here at 3.20 for Merton: and I should find a train on from thence. Then I must go by it: there's no time to be lost, once the morrow has dawned, if this unhappy business is to be suppressed. Twenty minutes past three; and now it is one; I can lie down for an hour and a half."

He went at once into his bedroom, took off his coat, and lay down on the outside of the bed. There was no fear of his oversleeping himself; sleep for a troubled mind in its first shock, troubled as was Dr. Davenal's, is out of the question.

Rest also seemed to be. He could not lie. He tossed and turned on the uneasy counterpane, and finally sprang off it with a wail of agony, and took to pacing the room. Neal, who was regaling his ear at the chamber door, could hear every footfall of the slippers, every groan of the distressed heart. Never more, never more in this world, would the heart of Richard Davenal lose its care.

Neal was not in the habit, with all his ferreting propensities, of sitting up at night to pursue them; but this night was an exceptional one. To say that Neal had been astonished, confounded at what had taken place, at the knowledge he believed he had acquired, would be saying little, in comparison with its effect upon his mind. He did not love his master; he did not like him; it may not be going too far to say that he hated him; for Neal's instinct had taught him that his master partially saw through him, partially suspected him to be the villain that he was; but to believe him capable of deliberately destroying one of his patients, was in truth almost too great a stretch for even Neal. Until that night, Neal could not have believed him capable of any wrong act: he gave him credit, for he could not help doing so, for his honour and his virtues, while he disliked him: but he did in truth now believe that Dr. Davenal had wilfully killed Lady Oswald. That is, that he had given her the chloroform deliberately, knowing it would probably take her life.

The faintest possible doubt of this had been first caught from the words of Parkins. Not real doubt, but a sort of angry feeling of the extreme imprudence of the doctor in having given it: Neal no more believed then that Dr. Davenal had done it, or was capable of doing it, than he could have believed the most monstrous improbability in the world. Still the idea had been admitted: and when that strange visitor was with his master afterwards, and Neal heard, with his own ears, the suspicious words that fell, he could put upon them but one interpretation—that, incredible as it seemed, his master was guilty, and not unintentionally, of the death of Lady Oswald. Neal hoped to arrive at the why and the wherefore, and he thought nothing of sitting up the night to do it: if by that means he might gain any satisfactory solution. Neal, it must be confessed, was utterly stunned with the affair, with the belief; and could hot see or understand yet with any clearness: like a man who is struck violently on the head, and looks around him in stupid helpless maze, as if he had a dead wall before him. A shock to the head and a shock to the mind will bear for the passing moment the same apparent result.

Dr. Davenal paced his room, his two rooms in fact, for the door was open between them, and he passed from one to the other in his restless wanderings, his mental agony. Soon after two he began to wash and dress himself; that is, he changed some of his clothes, and poured out a wash-hand basin of cold water and splashed his face with it. He put on a pair of boots; he searched for his gloves; he looked out an overcoat; and then he stood for a few minutes and thought.

Lifting the writing-desk from underneath the table, where you may remember it was kept, he unlocked it, and was for some little time examining certain papers it contained. Some of these he put in his pocket, and then he locked the desk and replaced it. Next he sat down to write a note; just a line or two.

It was getting on past the half-hour then. He opened the door and went forth from his room. Neal, who had heard him coming, peeped from his pantry and saw him turn to the stairs, the candle in one hand, a note held in the other. Neal cautiously stole forward a step or two, and looked and listened.

He was downstairs again instantly; he had only gone to the first floor, and had not opened any door, or Neal must have heard it: had not, in fact, been long enough to open one. The note was gone from his hand, and Neal wondered where he had left it.

He went into the study, and came out without the light, an overcoat on, and his hat in his hand. The moonlight shone in now through the fan-light over the front door, and Neal could see so much. He appeared to be coming towards the pantry; Neal silently closed the door and slipped the noiseless bolt. Neal took very good care to keep his own locks and bolts well oiled.

Dr. Davenal essayed to open the pantry-door and found it fastened. He shook it, knocked at it, not over gently. Neal, too great a diplomatist to be taken at a loss, flung off his coat, waistcoat, and slippers, threw back his braces, rumpled his hair, and opened the door to his master with the air of a man just aroused from his bed.

"Why do you sleep with the door locked, Neal?"—and the question was put in an imperative tone.

"I—it is but very rare that I do, sir. I must have shot the bolt last night without thinking of it."

"I won't have it done. Nobody shall sleep in my house with a locked door. It is a dangerous habit. Were a fire to take place, and the sleeper a heavy one, he might not be aroused in time. Don't do it again. Neal," he continued, changing his tone, "I am summoned out farther away than usual. I don't care to disturb Miss Davenal—you can tell them tomorrow morning. I shall not be home all day."

"Have you to go far, sir?" inquired Neal.

"Yes. I don't expect to be home all day, I tell you, and that's why I bid you inform them. Nobody is to sit up for me tomorrow night; I may be detained longer. Tell Miss Davenal so."

"Very well, sir," replied Neal. "Is the carriage ready for you?"

Neal put this cunningly. He felt sure his master was not going in the carriage.

"I don't require the carriage. That's all, Neal; you can go to bed again. I was obliged to disturb you."

Dr. Davenal turned, walked straight to the front door, and let himself out at it, closing it securely after him. Neal waited a moment, rearranged his attire a little, and then stepped also to the front door and drew the heavy bolt across it. No danger now of his master's coming in with his latch-key to pounce upon him.

Neal got a light, went into the study, and took a leisurely survey. He was scarcely rewarded. There was nothing whatever about, more than on other mornings: no signs remained of the stranger's visit, not a trace that could betray any disturbance on the part of Dr. Davenal. The sherry and biscuits were put up: Neal walked across to the dining-room and found them in the sideboard, just as he had left them on the previous night. The glass, used, stood on it. Neal solaced himself with some of the sherry, and went back to the study.

The old cloth was undisturbed on the table, the blotting-book and inkstand lying on it. Neal looked through the book, but received no satisfaction. He examined the pens, and saw that in one the ink was not yet dry. In the bedroom the clothes which his master had taken off lay about; Mr. Neal en passant visited the pockets and found them empty; and the bed was pressed on the outside, but had not been slept in. That curious visit in the night might have been a dream, for all there was left to tell of it.

"But there's that note yet," thought Neal. "What did he take it upstairs for, and where did he leave it?"

Stealing up the stairs in his stockinged feet, shading the light in his hand, Neal came to the vestibule, and looked on the table. He looked on the stand which held a beautiful statue in marble, he looked up even at the frames of the pictures; he looked everywhere. But there was no letter.

"I'm positive he did not stop long enough to open a door!" ejaculated Neal, rather at a nonplus.

A bright thought struck him. He bent down, shading still the light with his hand, and peered under Miss Sara Davenal's door. And then came Neal's reward. He saw the corner of something white quite close to him, not pushed entirely beyond the door. Dr. Davenal, not to disturb his daughter, had pushed his letter to her in that way.

Neal took out his penknife, and, with its help, by dint of perseverance and ingenuity, succeeded in drawing back the note, which he stole downstairs with, and into his own chamber. A little more ingenuity with the penknife, and the envelope, not yet fully dry, came open. Neal had obtained an insight into some secrets in his life, but never one so weighty as this, never one had touched on that ugly word "murder" which was running through Neal's mind: and his usually impassive face grew streaked with scarlet in excitement.

"My Dear Child,

"Business connected with this most unhappy secret obliges me to go out for a day, perhaps two. I shall leave a message with Neal. Do not appear to know anything when he delivers it: hear it as though you were a stranger to everything. Don't talk of my absence to any one if you can help it. People will conclude I have gone to see some patient at a distance, as will your aunt: it is not necessary to undeceive them.

R. D."

There was not so very much to be made out of that, and the scarlet streaks faded again from Neal's disappointed face. "This most unhappy secret," he repeated over twice, as if the words bore some euphonious sound. Whatever it might be, the secret, it was evident that Miss Sara Davenal had been made cognisant of it; and Neal rather rejoiced in the pill it must be for her, for he liked his young mistress not one whit better than he liked his master. He read the note again, refastened it in the envelope, stole upstairs to push it under the door, and then retired to his late bed.

CHAPTER XIX

COMMOTION

Meanwhile Dr. Davenal was walking along the streets of the town, lying so calm, so still in the moonlight. Not with any hurried tread; rather with a slow one. In his restlessness of mind, he had come out sooner than he need have come; but bodily action is a relief to mental anguish.

"Goodnight, doctor! or rather morning—for that's what it is."

The salutation came from one of the general practitioners of the town, a hard-worked apothecary, whose business took him abroad a good deal at night. He was hastening up a side street, near the town-hall, and Dr. Davenal had not observed him.

"Ah, is it you, Smithson? A fine night, is it not?"

"All nights are pretty near the same to me," returned Mr. Smithson. "I see too much of them. I wish folks would be so accommodating as to choose the day to be ill in. I don't know who'd be one of us. It's not often that we see you abroad at night, though, doctor?"

"Not often. We can't help it sometimes, you know. Goodnight."

They were bound different ways. The doctor had walked on his, when Mr. Smithson came running back.

"Dr. Davenal, what is the truth about Lady Oswald? I hear she's dead."

"She is—unhappily."

"And the report going about is, that she died from the effects of chloroform! Could not rally after inhaling it."

"Ah, it's a sad thing," replied the doctor; "a grievous thing. There's the dark side in these new discoveries of our practice: sacrificing the few while blessing the many. Goodnight, I say. I can't stop."

"It's true, then, that it was the chloroform?"

"Yes, it's true." Dr. Davenal increased his pace: he was in no mood for questioning, and this in particular was painful to him. A short while, and he stood before the Abbey, looking up at its windows. He was sorry to disturb Mark, but he deemed it was necessary, and he rang the night bell.

A new bell which Mark Cray had caused to be placed in the house since he took it, and which rang himself up, not his household. Dr. Davenal waited, but the ring was unanswered, and he rang again, with the like result.

A third summons brought Mark to the window, which he threw up, half-asleep still. "If that's the way you are going to let your night applicants ring, Mark Cray, almost as good not put up the bell."

Mark Cray could scarcely believe his eyes when he saw who was the speaker. "I was in a heavy sleep," he answered. "Did you ring more than once?"

A heavy sleep! Truly Dr. Davenal marvelled at the words. He marvelled that sleep could have visited Mark Cray that night, after his share in its fatal work.

"What is the matter?" asked Mark. "Am I wanted?"

"It is I who want you," said the doctor. "I must say a word to you if you'll come down. I am called out of town."

Mark attired himself sufficiently to descend, which he did in a state of wonder. He had never received a night visit from Dr. Davenal; it was quite out of the usual order of things, and he would about as soon have expected to see a live kangaroo wait upon him. He opened the front door, and they stepped into the large parlour.

"Who is ill?" inquired Mark. "Are you called out far?"

"I am going out on a little private business of my own. The train for Merton will be through presently, and I shall take it. If"—

"Why did you not tell me last night?" interrupted Mark.

"Because I did not then know I should have to go. You must take my patients for me. What I wished particularly to say to you was about the inquest. They can't call it for tomorrow—that is, today—Monday; but I think they are sure to hold it on Tuesday. If I am not back"—

"What inquest?" interrupted Mark, wonderingly.

"The inquest on Lady Oswald."

"My goodness! Do you think they'll get up an inquest over her?"

"Of course they will. What are you dreaming of? The remote cause of her death was the accident to the train. I am not quite sure of being back. I expect to be home on Tuesday morning early; but it is possible I may be detained a little longer. If I am not back, Mark, you will be the only witness—at least the only one who can speak to the facts of the death. Let me advise you to say as little as possible. Volunteer no information; answer their questions briefly; and don't get into a long-winded narration, as you are apt to do, otherwise you may betray yourself. You will not mistake me;" Dr. Davenal added. "I have always been open, truthful, candid as the day; and if I so speak now it is in your interest. I was thinking this over a great deal last evening after I left you, and I see that it is essential for your good name in your profession that the facts of the case should not be made known. Do not suppose I advise you to a direct deviation from the truth; nothing of the sort. 'Chloroform was exhibited with a view to lessen her sufferings, and she never rallied from it,' is all you need say. Similar cases are unhappily not unknown; I fear not very uncommon; and the coroner will not be likely to exact minute particulars, or inquire whether you gave it her, or whether I did. He will assume that we acted in concert."

Mark Cray nodded. He was nervously and incessantly pushing back his hair.

"I know how fond you are of talking," resumed Dr. Davenal, "therefore I deemed it well to give you this caution. To tell you the truth, I had rather not be at the inquest, and shall not be sorry if I can't get back."

"Are you going away on purpose?" suddenly asked Mark, who was much given to leap to conclusions.

"Certainly not. I am going on an important matter of my own. Look here, Mark Cray: one good turn deserves another. It will be concluded in the town that I am called to a patient at a long distance: as I have been before, you know, and detained out two or three days. People will be sure to think it now, and there's no necessity to undeceive them. You will oblige me in this. I don't want the town to concern itself with my private affairs: let people think I am with a patient. They don't know to the contrary at home."

"I shan't say anything to the contrary," said Mark. "Let people think what they will; they are a set of busybodies at the best."

Dr. Davenal departed. And Mr. Cray went back to his room, sleepy still, but wondering in the midst of it what could have called away the doctor suddenly to a distance. No letter could have arrived in the middle of the night, Mark argued: and a suspicion crossed his mind that he was, in spite of his denial, going away to avoid the inquest.

The doctor walked over to the station, there to await the train. He had given this caution, as to Mark's testimony at the inquest, entirely in his good feeling towards him, his solicitude for his welfare. For himself, he did hope he should not be back for it. Inconvenient questions might be asked, and he did not relish the idea of standing up and avowing that he had so far helped on Lady Oswald's death as to have joined in giving her the chloroform; he could not avow it without testifying to a deliberate falsehood: yet he must do it, or betray Mark Cray. But he had a matter of greater importance to think of than the inquest: a matter that was weighing down his heart with its dread. Of all the passengers that train contained, soon to be whirling on its way to Merton, not one had the sickening care to battle with that was distracting the flourishing and envied physician.

The first to enter the breakfast-room that morning at his residence was his sister. The meal was always laid in the dining-room. Miss Davenal wore her usual morning costume, a gown of that once fashionable but nearly obsolete material called nankin—or nankeen, as some spell it. It was not made up fashionably, but in the old scant style, and it made Miss Davenal's tall spare form look taller and sparer. She wore it for breakfast only, generally dressing for the day as soon as the meal was over. Sara followed, in a flowing dress of delicate sprigged muslin, and she took her seat at once at the breakfast-table.

"Is your papa out of his room yet, do you know?"

"I have not seen him," replied Sara, a faint red tinging her pale face at the half-evasive answer. Very pale she looked: ominously pale. Had Miss Bettina been gifted with preternatural penetration, she might have detected that some great dread was upon her.

But Miss Bettina was on that morning especially self-occupied. On the previous Saturday Dr. Davenal had told her that certain country friends were coming into Hallingham on that day, Monday, and he should invite them to dinner; or else that he had invited them: in her deafness she did not catch which. She had replied by asking him what he would have for dinner, and he said they would settle all that on Monday morning. Monday morning was now come; and Miss Bettina, a punctilious housekeeper, choosing to have everything in order and to treat visitors liberally, was on the fidget to make the arrangements, and waited impatiently for Dr. Davenal Watton, a fidget also in the domestic department, liking at any rate to get her orders in time, had come in with Miss Davenal.

Miss Davenal rang the bell: an intimation to Neal that they were ready for the coffee. She turned to the table, and the first thing that struck her sharp eyes in its arrangements was, that only two breakfast cups were on it.

"What is Neal thinking of this morning?" she exclaimed.

"I don't fancy my master is stirring yet," observed Watton. "I have not heard him."

"Nonsense!" returned her mistress. "When did you ever know your master not stirring at eight o'clock?"

"Not often, ma'am, it's true," was Watton's answer. "But it might happen. I know he was disturbed in the night."

Sara glanced up with a half-frightened glance. She dropped her head again, and began making scores on the cloth with her silver fork.

"It was the oddest thing," began Watton—and she was speaking in the low clear tones which made every word distinct to Miss Davenal. "Last night I was undressing with the blind up, without a candle, for the moon was light as day, when I saw a man turn in at the gate, and I said to myself, 'Here comes somebody bothering for master!' He made a spring to the side, and crouched himself amid the laurels that skirt the rails by the lane, and stopped there looking at the house. 'Very strange!' I said to myself again; 'that's not the way sick folk's messengers come in.' After a minute he walked on, brushing close to the shrubs, afraid I suppose of being seen, and I heard him tap at the window of the doctor's consulting-room. Ma'am, if ever I thought of a robber in my life, I thought of one then, and if it hadn't been for my presence of mind, I should have rose the house with my screams"—

"Be silent, Watton!" sharply interrupted Miss Davenal. "Look there! You are frightening her to death."

She had extended her finger, pointing at Sara. Sara, her face more like death than life, in its ghastly whiteness, was gazing at Watton, her eyes strained, her lips apart, as one under the influence of some great terror. Was she afraid of what might be coming? It looked so.

"There's nothing to be alarmed at, Miss Sara"—

"Don't tell it; don't tell it," gasped Sara, putting up her hands. "It does frighten me."

"But indeed there is nothing to be frightened at, as you'll hear, Miss Sara," persisted the woman. "It's a fact that I was a little frightened myself; one does hear of housebreakers getting into houses in so strange a manner; and I went out of my room and leaned over the banisters and listened. It was all right, for I heard the doctor open the hall door and take the man into his consulting-room, and shut himself in with him. How long the man stopped, and who he was, I can't tell; he did not go away while I was awake—but, ma'am, that's how I know my master was disturbed in the night."

"Watton!"—and as Sara spoke her cheeks became crimson, her voice imperative,—"do you deem it lies in your service here to watch the movements of your master, and to comment upon them afterwards?"

The moment the words had left her lips she felt how unwise they were; but she had so spoken in her perplexity, her soreness of heart. Watton turned her eyes on her young mistress in sheer amazement.

"Watch my master's movements! Why, Miss Sara, you can't think I'd do such a thing. I watched to—if I may so express it—protect my master; to protect the house, lest harm should be meant it. Decent folk don't come in at night as that man came in."

Neal had entered, and was disposing his eatables on the table. Miss Davenal drew his attention to the shortness of the cups.

"It is quite right; ma'am. The doctor went out in the middle of the night; at least about two in the morning; and he charged me to tell you he should not be at home all day; perhaps not all night. Nobody is to sit up for him."

"Where's he gone?" asked Miss Bettina.

Neal could not tell. His master had said he was going to a distance. But Miss Bettina could not make it out at all, and she asked question upon question. How had he gone?—the carriage was not out. Walked away on foot, and said he was going to a distance, and might not be home for a day and a night? It was the most mysterious, extraordinary proceeding she ever heard of. "Did you see or hear anything of a strange man coming in in the night?" she asked of Neal.

"No, ma'am," replied Neal, with his usual impassability. "I see my master's bed has not been slept in; and he has taken an overcoat with him."

Sara lifted her burning face. It was as one stricken with fever.

"Let it rest; let it rest, Aunt Bettina! Wait until papa is home, and ask particulars of him. If patients require him at a distance, it is his duty to go to them."

The last words were spoken defiantly; not at her aunt, but at the servants. She felt on the very verge of desperation. What disastrous consequences might not this proclamation of the night's work bring forth!

"Let it rest!" retorted Miss Bettina. "Yes, that is what you young and careless ones would like to do. Look at my position! The responsible mistress of this house, and left at an uncertainty whether people are coming to dinner or whether they are not. Your papa must have gone clean out of his wits to go off and not leave word."

"You can fix upon a dinner as well as papa can, Aunt Bettina."

"Fix upon a dinner! It's not that. It is the not knowing whether there's to be a dinner fixed upon; whether people are invited, or not, to eat it."

When Miss Davenal was put out about domestic arrangements, it took a great deal to put her in again. Neal and Watton were questioned and cross-questioned as to the events of the night, and breakfast was got over in a commotion. Sara shivered with a nameless fear, and wondered whether that dreadful secret might not become known.

A secret which bore for Sara Davenal all the more terror from the fact that she was but imperfectly acquainted with its nature. Dr. Davenal had seen fit for certain reasons to call her down to his room, and she had there seen the ominous visitor: but the particulars had been kept from her. That there existed a secret, and a terrible one, which might burst at any hour over their heads, bringing with it disgrace as well as misery, she had been obliged to learn; but its precise nature she was not told; was not allowed, it may be said, to guess at. Dr. Davenal so far spared her. He spared her from the best of motives, forgetting that suspense is, of all human pain, the worst to bear.

With the exception of what that little note told her, which she saw lying inside her door when she rose in the morning, she knew nothing of the motives of her father's journey; where he had gone, or why he had gone. She only knew it was imperative that that night's visit to the house should remain a secret, uncommented upon, unglanced at. And now the servants knew of it—had seen the stranger come in—might talk about it indoors and out! No wonder that Sara Davenal shivered!—that she grew sick at heart!

CHAPTER XX

GOING DOWN TO THE FUNERAL

The commotion in the town rose that morning to its height: it equalled the commotion at Miss Davenal's breakfast-table. But not from the same exciting cause. The one was led to by the curious absence of Dr. Davenal; the other had its source in the death of Lady Oswald.

She had lived so long amongst them—had been, so to say, the head of the social and visiting community of Hallingham! A great lady once, the Lady Oswald of Thorndyke. Had she died in the common course of nature, after weeks or months of illness, it would still have created a stir; but to have died from the inhaling of chloroform consequent upon the railway accident, did cause very great and unwonted excitement. People were shocked at her death: they mourned for the somewhat eccentric old lady who had been seen driven through their streets in her close carriage for years; but they never cast so much as a shadow of reproach towards the doctors who might be said to be, however unwittingly, the authors of it. They railed at the chloroform, calling it uncertain, dangerous stuff; but not the slightest reflection was thrown on the judgment which had caused her to inhale it.

Mark Cray was beset with questions and remarks, especially from his medical brethren in the town. In Dr. Davenal's absence, people flew to him for particulars. He remembered the doctor's caution, and said as little as possible. It was an unpleasant subject to speak of, he observed to them—they could understand that. But the curious questioners only understood it partially, and rather wondered why Mr. Cray should be so chary of his information.

The inquest took place on the Tuesday, as Dr. Davenal had surmised it would. It was held quite as a matter of course—not with a view to elicit the cause of death; that was already known—simply because the law rendered an inquest obligatory.

The doctor was not back for it, and Mr. Cray was the principal witness. The operation had been most satisfactorily performed by Dr. Davenal, he testified, but Lady Oswald did not rally from the effects of the chloroform. They had tried every means to arouse her without result. The coroner presumed the chloroform had been administered with all due caution: he felt persuaded it would be by so experienced a surgeon as Dr. Davenal. Certainly, was the answer of Mark Cray. It was given her with the best of motives: to spare her acute suffering: and no one could more bitterly regret the result than they did. It was impossible to foresee, he continued, that this great blessing—yes, he must still call it so—to suffering humanity, which had spared anguish to thousands, perhaps he might say had spared lives, would have an opposite effect upon Lady Oswald, and bring death to her instead of relief. He had never for one moment in his own judgment doubted the expediency of giving it to her: were the thing to come over again (the result being hidden from him) he should do the same.

Not a word that Mark Cray said but had its weight, and was appreciated. The death was regarded as a pure misfortune, a sort of accident that could not be prevented by poor human foresight, and for which blame was attachable to no one. And the verdict was in accordance with this.

The only one on whom the facts were yet destined to make an unpleasant and not satisfactory impression was Mr. Oswald Cray The first intimation of Lady Oswald's death reached him through the "Times" newspaper. As junior in the firm, he lived in the house in Parliament Street, the senior partners preferring residences out of town. The chief part of the house was devoted to their business purposes, and Mr. Oswald Cray had but two or three rooms for his private use. On the Thursday morning, the "Times" was brought to him as usual while he was at breakfast. It was folded with the supplement outside, the deaths uppermost; and on putting it aside to open the more important parts his eye caught the word Oswald.

He looked further: and nothing could exceed his surprise. He gazed at the announcement with a feeling of disbelief, almost as though he was in a dream: "At her residence in Hallingham, Susan Hannah Lady Oswald, aged seventy-one, widow of Sir John Oswald Thorndyke."

The date of her death, probably by an oversight, had not been put in, and Oswald Cray was left to conjecture it. Certainly he did not suppose it had occurred so far back as on the previous Sunday, the day after he left Hallingham.

What had killed her? The accident? He had been given to understand that night that she was not materially injured: he now supposed she must have been. Why had nobody written to acquaint him? He would have been glad to see her for a final farewell; would have thought nothing of his time and trouble in going down for it. Mark might have written: he could not remember having corresponded with Mark in all his life, half-brothers though they were; but still Mark might have gone out of his way to drop him a line now. Parkins might have written; in fact he considered it was Parkins' duty to have written, and he should tell her so: and Dr. Davenal might have written. Of the three mentioned, Oswald Cray would soonest have expected the doctor to write, and the omission struck him as being somewhat singular.

The post brought news. Amidst the mass of letters that came for the firm was one to himself, He saw the Hallingham postmark, and opened it at once.

A look of blank disappointment, mingled with surprise, settled on his face as he read. It was not from Dr. Davenal, from Mark Cray, or from Parkins; it gave him no details, any more than if he had been the greatest stranger to Lady Oswald. It was a formal intimation from the undertaker that her late ladyship's funeral would take place on Friday at eleven o'clock, and requesting his attendance at it, if convenient.

"Her funeral tomorrow!" ejaculated Oswald. "Then she must have died almost immediately. Perhaps the very night I came up. Why couldn't somebody write?"

He arranged business matters so as to go down that afternoon, and arrived at Hallingham between six and seven o'clock. Giving his portmanteau to a porter, he went on to his usual place of sojourn, the "Apple Tree." It was near to the terminus, a little beyond the town, one of the quiet country inns now nearly obsolete. An old-fashioned, plain, roomy house, whose swinging sign-board stood out before its door, and whose productive garden of vegetables and fruit stretched out behind it. No fashionable person would look at it twice. Oswald Cray had been recommended to it long ago as his place of sojourn in Hallingham, where his stay seldom lasted more than two days: and he had found himself so comfortable, so quiet, so entirely at home, that he would not have exchanged it for the grandest hotel in Hallingham, had the said hotel graciously intimated that it would receive him for nothing.

The host, whose name was John Hamos, came forward to receive him; a respectable, worthy man, with a portly person and red face, who might be seen occasionally in a white apron washing up glasses, and who waited on his guests himself. He and Oswald were the best of friends.

"Good-evening, sir. My wife said you'd be down tonight or in the morning. We were sure you'd attend the burying. A sad thing, sir, is it not?"

"It is a very sad thing, John," returned Oswald; "I seem as if I could not believe it. It was only this morning that I received the tidings. What did she die of? The accident to the train?"

"No, sir, she didn't die of that. Leastways, that was not the immediate cause of death, though of course it must be said to have led to it. She died from the effects of chloroform."

"Died from—what did you say?" asked Oswald, staring at the man.

"From chloroform, sir."

"From chloroform!" he repeated, "I don't understand."

And he looked as if he did not. As if it were impossible to take in the words or their sense. John Hamos continued.

"It seems, sir, that on the Sunday it was discovered that her ladyship had sustained some internal injury—to the ribs, I believe, or near-abouts—and she had to submit to an operation. Chloroform was given her while it was performed, and she never rallied from it."

"Who gave her the chloroform?"

"Dr. Davenal"

"Dr. Davenal!" echoed Mr. Oswald Cray, and his accent of astonishment was so great, so unmistakable, that the landlord looked at him in surprise. "Why, he—he—"

"What, sir?"

Oswald had brought his words to a sudden stand-still. His face was one picture of doubt, of bewilderment.

"It could not have been Dr. Davenal."

"Yes it was, sir," repeated John Hamos. "Who else would be likely to undertake the operation but him? He and Mr. Cray were together, but it was the doctor who performed it. As of course it would be."

"But he did not give the chloroform?"

"Why, yes he did, sir. He gave it for the best. As was said afterwards at the inquest, they could not possibly foresee that what saved pain and was a blessing to thousands, would prove fatal to her ladyship."

"Who said that at the inquest? Dr. Davenal?"

"Mr. Cray, sir. The doctor wasn't present at the inquest; he was away from the town. He went away in the night, somebody said, just after the death: was fetched out to some patient at a distance, and didn't get back here till—Wednesday morning, I think it was."

"And she never rallied from the chloroform?"

"Never at all, sir. She died under it."

Oswald Cray said no more. He went up to the bedroom that he always used, there to wash off some of the travelling dust. But instead of proceeding at once to do so, he stood in thought with folded arms and bent brow, John Hamos's information respecting the chloroform troubling his brain.

Why should it trouble him? Could not he believe, as others did, that it was given in all due hope and confidence, according to the best judgment of the surgeons? No, he could not believe it, so far as regarded the chief surgeon, Dr. Davenal: and the reason was this.

On the night of the accident, when Dr. Davenal jumped into the carriage that was about to proceed to the scene, he jumped into a seat by the side of Oswald Cray. They entered into conversation, and the topic of it was, not unnaturally, accidents in general. It led to the subject of chloroform, and Dr. Davenal expressed his opinion upon that new-fashioned aid to science just as freely as he afterwards expressed it to Mark Cray.

How strange are the incidents, the small events that shape the course of human destiny. But for that accidental conversation—and may it not be called accidental?—half the trouble that is about to be related never would have taken place. And the cruel shadow, that was waiting to spread its wings over the days of more than one wayfarer on the path of life, would have found no spot to darken with its evil.

Dr. Davenal spoke his opinion freely to Oswald Cray with regard to chloroform. He did not deny its great boon, sparing pain to many whose sufferings would otherwise be almost intolerable; but he said that there were some few to whom he would as soon give poison as chloroform, for the one would be just as fatal as the other. And he instanced Lady Oswald.

The unfortunate fact of Lady Oswald being in the disabled train to which they were hastening, possibly one of its wounded, no doubt suggested her name to Dr. Davenal as his example. There were other people whom he attended—a slight few—to whom he deemed chloroform would be as pernicious as to Lady Oswald: but she was in question, as it were, that night, and he cited her. There must have been some fatality in it.

"She is one, if I am any judge, who could not bear it; who would be almost certain not to survive its effects," were the words he used to Oswald. "I would as soon give Lady Oswald a dose of poison as suffer her to come near chloroform."

The words, spoken to Oswald only, not to the other inmates of the carriage who were busy talking on their own score, had not made any particular impression upon him at the time, but they returned to his memory now with awakened force. He asked himself what it could mean. Dr. Davenal had distinctly told him, or equivalent to it, that the inhaling of chloroform would be as poison to Lady Oswald; he was now assured by John Hamos that, not four-and-twenty hours subsequent to that conversation, he, Dr. Davenal, had himself administered chloroform to her. And the result was death. Death—as Dr. Davenal had expressed his firm conviction it would be.

Mr. Oswald Cray could only come to the conclusion that there must be some mistake in the statement of the facts to him. It was impossible to arrive at any other conclusion. That there was no mistake on his own part, as to the opinion expressed to him by the doctor, he knew; he recalled the very words in which it was spoken; spoken deliberately and elaborately; not a mere allusion or sentence. About that there was no doubt; but he felt that a mistake must lie somewhere. The chloroform could not have been given by Dr. Davenal; perhaps he had not even been present at the operation.

He quitted the "Apple Tree," and bent his steps to Lady Oswald's. Parkins came to him in a burst of grief. Parkins was—it has been said so before—genuinely grieved at her lady's death, and it showed itself chiefly by breaking into a shower of tears with every fresh person she saw. One of the first questions put to her by Mr. Oswald Cray was as to her not having written to inform him of the death. He wished to know why she had not.

"I don't know why, sir," she sobbed, "except that I have been bewildered ever since it happened. I have been as one out of my mind, sir, with the shock and the grief. I'm sure I beg your pardon for the neglect, but it never so much as struck me till yesterday, when the undertaker was here about the funeral. He asked who was to be invited to it, and then it came into my mind that you ought to have been wrote to, but I said perhaps Mr. Cray had done it."

"Well, sit down while you talk, Parkins," he said in a kind tone. "I can understand that you have been very much shocked by it. Are any of Lady Oswald's relatives here?"

"There's that nephew of hers, sir, the parson; the poor gentleman that she'd send a little money to sometimes. He heard of it accidental, he says, and came off at once with his brother. They got here this morning. Very nice people, both of them, sir, but they seem poor. They think no doubt that my lady's money is left to them, as I daresay it is. She—"

"I wish to ask you a question or two about the death, Parkins," he interrupted in a pointed manner. None could check undue topics with more dignity than he. "When was it discovered that Lady Oswald was seriously injured?"

"Not until the Sunday, sir. When Mr. Cray came home with her here on the return from Hildon, he wanted to examine into her state, but she was very obstinate, and persisted in saying she'd not be touched that night; that she wasn't hurt. I fancy Dr. Davenal thought it was wrong of Mr. Cray not to have insisted upon it—but Mr. Cray himself did not think there was any grave injury: he told me so then. The next morning I thought they'd both be here, Dr. Davenal and Mr. Cray; but Mr. Cray came alone, the doctor it appeared had been sent for to Thorndyke—"

"To Thorndyke?" involuntarily interrupted Oswald.

"Yes, sir, somebody was ill there. However, he, the doctor, was back and up here in the afternoon. He had seen Mr. Cray, and he came to examine into her state for himself: for it had been discovered then that she was worse injured than they thought. At first my lady said she'd not submit to the operation, which Mr. Cray had already told her must take place; but Dr. Davenal talked to her, and she consented, and they fixed half-past five in the afternoon. Have you heard how she died, sir?" broke off Parkins abruptly.

"I have heard since I got here this evening that she died from the effects of chloroform."

"And so she did, sir. And it's a thing that I shall never understand to my dying day."

Parkins spoke the last words with a vehemence that superseded the sobs. Mr. Oswald Cray thought he did not understand it either; but he did not say so.

"In what way don t you understand it?" he asked quietly.

"How it was they came to give her the chloroform. I am quite certain, sir, that up to the very moment that the operation was ready to be begun, there was no thought of chloroform. It was not as much as mentioned, and if any chloroform had been in the room amidst the preparations, I must have seen it."

"Were you present during the operation?"

"I was to have been present, sir; but at the last moment I fainted dead off, and had to be taken from the room. We knew no more, any of us, till it was all over. Then we were called to by the gentlemen, and told what was the matter: that my lady was sinking under the influence of the chloroform they had administered, and could not be rallied from it. And, a few minutes after, she died."

Oswald Cray remained for some moments silent. "Was it Dr. Davenal who administered it?" he resumed.

"No doubt it was, sir; they were together. It was Dr. Davenal who performed the operation. My lady said nobody should do it but Mr. Cray, and it was settled that it should be done by him; but I suppose they thought at last it would be better to entrust it to the doctor. Anyway, it was he who performed it."

"What did Dr. Davenal—did Dr. Davenal say anything about the chloroform afterwards, or why they had used it?"

"He didn't say much, sir. He said what had been done was done for the best: but he seemed dreadfully cut up. And so did Mr. Cray. The strangest thing to me is, why they used chloroform, when I saw no signs of their attempting to use it."

"But they must have had it with them?"

"Well, of course they must, sir. It was not produced, though, while I was there. They said my lady grew agitated—it was Mr. Cray said that—that my falling down helped to agitate her; but it will take a great deal to make me believe there was any need for them to use chloroform. It has cost a good lady her life; I know that. She had her little tempers and her fidgety ways, poor dear lady, but she was one of the best of mistresses. It's just as if they had done it to kill her."

Did the words grate on the ear of Oswald Cray?—as though they bore all too significant a meaning. Not yet; not quite yet. This testimony of the maid's had confirmed beyond doubt that Dr. Davenal had been the chief and acting surgeon: how then reconcile that fact with the opinion expressed to him not many hours before the death? He could not tell; he could not think; he could not account for it by any reasoning of any sort, subtle or simple. He was as one in a mazy dream, seeing nothing distinctly.

When he quitted the house, he turned again and bent his steps to the Abbey. Possibly he deemed Mark could solve his difficulties. Mark was not in, however, when he got there, only Caroline.

Mrs. Cray was in the large drawing-room. She and the tea-table, at which she sat waiting for Mark, looked quite lost in its space. The thought struck Oswald as he entered. It had been the home of his early childhood, the scene of occasional visits since that period, but Oswald always thought that room larger and larger every time he entered it. It was at its window that he, a baby in arms, had been held by the side of his mother, when the grand people from Thorndyke in their carriage and four, her father and mother, would drive past and cast up their faces of stone. He had been too young to know anything then, but afterwards, when he could begin to understand, these stories of the passing by of Sir Oswald Oswald were impressed upon him by his nurse. They remained amidst his most vivid recollections. But that he knew it was impossible to have been so—for his mother had died when he was too young, and there was no more standing there after her death to watch for Sir Oswald—he could have affirmed now that he remembered those times in all their full detail: the steady pace of the fine horses, the bedizened carriage—in those days it was the fashion to have carriages bedizened—the servants in their claret liveries, the impassive faces of Sir Oswald and his lady. The fact was, it had all been described so often and minutely to the young child Oswald, that it remained on his memory as a thing seen, not heard.

Mrs. Cray, gay in attire, wearied in countenance, was quite alone. She wore a low evening dress of blue silk, with lace and fringes and trimmings; and blue ribbons in her hair. Rather more dress than is necessary for a quiet evening at home; but she was young and pretty and a bride, and—very fond of finery in any shape. Her weary face lighted up with smiles as she saw Oswald and rose to greet him: very, very pretty did she look then.

"I am so glad to see you! I had grown tired, waiting for Mark. He went out the moment he had swallowed his dinner—before he had swallowed it, I think—and he is not in yet. Shall I tell you a secret, Oswald?"

"Yes, if you please."

"I am quite disappointed. I shan't at all like being a doctor's wife."

Her dark blue eyes were dancing with smiles as she spoke. Oswald smiled too—at the joke.

"It is true, Mr. Oswald Cray. I don't speak against my own dear Mark: I'd not part with him: but I do wish he was not a doctor. You don't know how little I see of him. He is in just at meals, and not always to them."

Oswald smiled still. "You had lived in a doctor's house, Mrs. Cray, and knew the routine of it."

"My uncle's house was not like this. Who can compare the great Dr. Davenal at the top of the tree, waiting at home for his patients to come to him, to poor Mark Cray at the bottom, just beginning to climb it? It's not the same thing, Mr. Oswald Cray. Mark has to be out, here and there and everywhere. At the Infirmary, dancing attendance on interminable rows of beds one hour; in some obscure corner of the town another, setting somebody's leg, or watching a case of fever. Mark says it won't go on quite as bad as it has begun. This has been an unusually busy week with him, owing to the doctor's absence. He left home on Sunday night, and was not back until Wednesday. A great portion of Sunday also the doctor passed at Thorndyke."

"His patient must have been very ill to keep him away from Sunday until Wednesday," remarked Oswald.

"To tell you the truth," said Caroline, dropping her voice in a manner that sounded rather mysterious, "we don't think he was with a patient. We can't quite make out why he went or where he went. He came here in the middle of the night and rang up Mark. It was the night subsequent to Lady Oswald's death—oh, Oswald! was not her death a shocking thing?"

"Very," was the answer, gravely spoken.

"When Mark came home that Sunday evening and told me Lady Oswald was dead, I cannot describe to you how I felt. At first I could not believe it; and then I went—I went into hysterics. It was very foolish of course, for hysterics do no good, but I could not help it. You have come down to attend the funeral tomorrow, I suppose?"

"Yes."

"Well—I was telling you about my uncle. He came here in the middle of the night and rang up Mark, who went down to him. When Mark came upstairs again, he said Dr. Davenal was going away on some private errand which he had made a sort of secret of to Mark. I fancy Mark was only half-awake and did not hear him clearly; all he understood was, that the doctor was going somewhere by train unexpectedly; and Mark was to let it be assumed in the town that he was visiting a patient at a distance. Mark declared that he believed the doctor was only absenting himself to avoid attending the coroner's inquest."

"Why should Mark think that?—Why should Dr. Davenal wish to avoid attending it?" reiterated Oswald, strangely interested, he scarcely knew why.

"I cannot tell you. I fancy the admission slipped from Mark inadvertently, for he would not say a syllable more. The next day, Monday, I saw Sara. I asked her point-blank where my uncle had gone, remarking that there seemed to be some little mystery connected with it, and she turned as white as the grave and whispered to me not to talk so, to hold my tongue for the love of Heaven. You'll take some tea, won't you; Oswald? I shall be so glad of an excuse for making it."

Oswald, almost mechanically, said he would take some, and she rang the bell for the urn. He began to think all this strange and more strange; to ask himself: what it tended to. Dr. Davenal had gone away to avoid the inquest?—and his daughter when spoken to upon the subject had turned as white as the grave? What did it mean?

"Do you know the particulars of Lady Oswald's death?" he inquired as he stirred his tea.

"Yes. Don't you! She died from chloroform. They deemed it necessary to give it her, and she never rallied from it."

"Who gave it to her? Which of them?"

"Which of them?" repeated Caroline, lifting her eyes, thinking no doubt the question a superfluous one. "They were both present; they would act in concert one with the other. If you mean to cast blame on them, Oswald, I should say you must cast it conjointly. But they acted for the best."

"I do not cast blame on them," he answered. "I don't understand the affair sufficiently yet to cast blame anywhere. It is a riddle to me."

"What is a riddle?"

"How Dr.—how they came to use chloroform at all."

"Why, it is in almost universal use now!" exclaimed Mrs. Cray, surprised at the remark. "There is no riddle in that."

Oswald did not press it. In his opinion there was a riddle; one he began to think would not be easy of solution. He finished his tea in silence. By and by Mrs. Cray resumed.

"Mark seems not to like to talk of it. I asked him a great many questions, as was natural, but he put me off, saying I should be falling into hysterics again. I told him that was nonsense, now the shock was over; but he would not talk of it, seemed quite to wince when I pressed it. It was not a pleasant subject for him, he said. And of course it is not: and still less so for my uncle, whose authority sways Mark. However good their intentions were, it did kill her."

"Will Mark be long, do you suppose?" inquired Oswald, breaking another long pause.

"As if I could tell, Oswald! I have been expecting him every minute this hour past. When I grumble at Mark for staying out so, he tells me I must blame his patients. Nay, but you are not going yet?" she added, as he rose. "Mark is sure to be in soon."

"I cannot well stay longer now," he answered. "I shall see Mark in the morning. I suppose he attends the funeral?"

"Of course he will. They will both attend it. I wish you would not hurry away!"

He repeated his apology, and Caroline rang the bell. In point of fact he wanted to call on Dr. Davenal.

Scarcely had the servant closed the door on Mr. Oswald Cray than he met his brother. Mark was coming along at a quick pace.

"Oswald, is it you? Have you been to the Abbey?"

"I have been taking tea with your wife, and waiting for you. She is nearly out of patience. Mark!" he continued, passing his arm within his brother's and leading him a few steps away while he talked, "what a shocking thing this is about Lady Oswald!"

"Ay, it is that. So unexpected. Won't you come in?"

"Not again tonight. I want to know, Mark, how it was that chloroform was given to her!"

"If we had not deemed it for the best, we should not have given it," was Mark's answer.

"But—surely Dr. Davenal did not deem it would be for the best?"

Mark turned and looked at him: a quick, sharp glance. "What do you know about it?" he asked.

"I? I know nothing about it: I want to know," replied Oswald, thinking the remark strange. "I wish you would give me the full particulars, Mark. I cannot understand—I have a reason for not being able to understand—why chloroform should have been given to Lady Oswald—"

"We use chloroform very much now," interrupted Mark.

"Why it should have been given to Lady Oswald," went on Oswald, with pointed emphasis.

"It was given to her as it is given to others—to deaden pain."

"Who performed the operation?"

"The doctor."

There was a pause. When Oswald Cray broke it his voice was low, his manner hesitating. "Mark, will you pardon me if I ask you a peculiar question?—Do you believe from your very heart that when Dr. Davenal administered that chloroform to Lady Oswald he did think it would be for the best?"

Hesitating as Oswald's manner had been. Mark's was worse. He grew on a sudden flushed and embarrassed.

"Won't you answer me, Mark?"

"I—yes—of course we thought it would be for the best."

"I asked, did he think it?"

Mark plunged into an untruth. Somewhat afraid of Oswald at the best of times, conscious that he was of a far higher standard in moral and intellectual excellence than himself, he desired to stand well with him, to enjoy his good opinion; and perhaps there was not a single man in Hallingham to whom Mark would not have preferred his unhappy mistake in all its wilfulness to become known than to his brother. They were also playing at cross-purposes: Oswald was seeking to learn how far Dr. Davenal had been to blame. Mark believed it was his own share of blame that was sought to be arrived at.

"Yes, he thought it. Dr. Davenal would not use chloroform, or anything else, unless he believed it would be beneficial," rapidly went on Mark. "I never knew a man more successful in his treatment in a general way than he." But for all the apparent readiness of the words, they bore a certain evasion to Oswald's ears.

"Tell me the truth, Mark; tell it me frankly," he rejoined. "Is there not some—some secret—I don't know what else to call it—connected with this business? Something wrong about it!"

For a moment Mark Cray had to deliberate. He was driven at bay by the straightforward questions of his brother. And his brother saw the hesitation.

"Oswald, it is of no use to press me upon this matter. You will readily conceive how sore a one it is to myself and to Dr. Davenal. Had it been some poor rubbishing patient who had died through it, that poor stoker at the Infirmary for instance, it would not have been of so much account: but"—

"Be silent, Mark!" burst from Oswald with a flash of anger. "I will not listen to such doctrine. The lives of the poor are every whit as valuable as are the lives of the rich. You did not learn that from Dr. Davenal."

"What I meant was, that there'd not be half the public fuss," said Mark, looking little, and doing his best to explain away the impression given by his words. "I'm sure there has been enough fuss in the town since her death was known, but I have not heard of one single person in it casting blame on us. Why should you seek to cast it? Errors in judgment are committed now and then in medical practice, just as they are in everything else and there's no help for it; they happen to the very best of us. If we could see the end of a thing at the beginning it would be different: but we can't. Could its effects on Lady Oswald have been anticipated, we'd have seen chloroform in the sea before it should have been given her. It was done for the best."

"You think, then, that Dr. Davenal believed the giving it her would be for the best?" persisted Oswald, after listening patiently to the excited answer.

Again came the perceptible hesitation in the manner of Mark; again the flush of embarrassment rose to his cheek. Oswald noted it.

"I am quite sure that all the doctor ever did for Lady Oswald he did for the best," and Mark Cray plucked up courage and spirit as he said it: "that night as well as other nights which had gone before it I cannot think what you are driving at, Oswald."

Oswald Cray determined to "drive" no more. He believed it would be useless, so far as Mark was concerned. He could not quite make him out: but he believed it would be useless. That there was something concealed, something not quite open, he saw; Mark's manner alone would have told him that: and he came rapidly to the conclusion that Mark had been cognisant also of his partner's opinion of chloroform as connected with Lady Oswald, and could not tell why he had tried it upon her, but did suppose, in spite of the face of affairs, that he had done it for the best. All Mark's embarrassment, his evasion, his crusty unwillingness to speak frankly, Oswald set down to an anxiety to screen Dr. Davenal from the reproach of imprudence. One more remark he did make. It arose to his mind as he was about to depart, and he spoke it on the spur of the thought.

"I understand you fancy that Dr. Davenal absented himself from Hallingham to avoid attending the coroner's inquest."

"Where on earth did you hear that?" shouted Mark, with a stare of surprise.

"Your wife mentioned it to me just now."

Mark Cray waxed wroth. "What idiots women are! The very best of them! I shan't be able to think my own thoughts next. Caroline knows I did not wish that repeated: it slipped from me without reflection."

"It is quite safe with me, Mark. She looks upon me, I suppose, as one of yourselves. But why should Dr. Davenal have wished not to attend the inquest?"

"Oh, for nothing, only he thought they'd be putting all sorts of questions," carelessly replied Mark. "It was a disagreeable thing altogether, and one of us was quite enough to attend. But, mind you, Oswald, I don't really suppose he went for that: I make no doubt he had business out."

"Well, goodnight, Mark."

"Goodnight. I wish you had come in."

Mark Cray stepped on to his house, and let himself in with his latch-key, thinking how much better the world would go on if women had not been endowed with tongues, and wondering excessively what possessed Oswald to be taking up the death of Lady Oswald and putting these mysterious questions upon it.

CHAPTER XXI

THE INTERVIEW WITH THE DOCTOR

Dr. Davenal was alone in his study, pacing the carpet with heavy steps and a face that seemed to have all the care of the world marked on it, when Mr. Oswald Cray was shown in. Oswald could not avoid being struck with that expression of care; he had never seen the like upon the countenance of Dr. Davenal.

Turning his head, he looked at Oswald for the space of a minute as if not recognising him. He was too deeply buried in his own thoughts immediately to awake from them to everyday life.

"Good-evening, Dr. Davenal."

He took Oswald's outstretched hand, and was himself again. Oswald sat down and the doctor too. But after a few words, he rose, apparently in restlessness, and began to pace the room as before.

"Are you in any grief, doctor?"

"Well—yes I am," was the reply. "Or perhaps I should rather say in vexation, for that is chiefly it. We have had a line from Edward by the day post, and he expresses a doubt whether he shall be able to get down to say farewell. These young soldiers grow careless of home ties, Mr. Oswald Cray."

"Not soldiers in particular, do they, sir? It is a reproach that can be cast upon many others who live in the world."

"And get enslaved by it. True."

"I did not mean altogether that, Dr. Davenal. When does your son sail?"

"On Sunday morning, he says. He does not positively say he is not coming down, only gives a hint that he fears he cannot. What did I do with the letter?" continued the doctor, looking round. "I brought it in with me after dinner. Oh, there it is," he added, seeing it on a side table, and giving it to Oswald. "You can read what he says. Sara won't mind. It is written for us all as well as for her, I expect Edward was never a voluminous correspondent; his letters are generally pro bono publico."

Oswald saw it was addressed to Miss Sara Davenal, and began to read it. It was dated the previous evening.

"My Darling Sister,—"

We are in all the bustle and hurry of the start. Orders have come at last, and we embark from Southampton on Sunday morning. I hope I shall get down to you to say goodbye. I am not unmindful of my promise to do so, and will do all I can to keep it; poor Dick used to tell me that I knew how to break promises better than I knew how to make them, but it shall not be my fault if you have to east that on me as a last reproach. To absent one's-self, even for an hour, is a difficult task now, but I will manage it, if possible. We have been worked off our heads and legs for the last few days.

"Love to all. I suppose Carry is fairly installed at the Abbey; wish her all good luck for me.—Ever yours, in much haste,

"E. F. Davenal."

"You see," said the doctor, halting and pointing to the letter, "he emphasises the word 'hope.' 'I hope I shall get down.' That very fact is sufficient to tell me that he knows he shall not get down, and these lines have been sent as a sort of preparation for the final disappointment. And he is going out for years! But I won't blame him; perhaps it is an impossibility to him to get away. He should have remained longer when he came down for the wedding—have made it his farewell visit. I said so then."

Dr. Davenal began his walk to and fro again,—a very slow, thoughtful walk. Oswald folded the letter and laid it on the table.

"I have ever loved my children—I was going to say passionately, Mr. Oswald Cray. I believe few parents can love as I have loved. I have made—I have made sacrifices for them which the world little reeks of, and anything like ingratitude touches me to the heart's core. But in the midst of it I am the first to find excuses for them, and I say that Edward may not be at all to blame in this."

"I think it very likely that he is quite unable to get away, however much he may wish it," observed Oswald.

"I think so too. I say I don't blame him. Only one feels these things."

There ensued a silence. A feeling of dislike had come over Oswald (and he could not trace it to any particular cause) to enter upon the subject of Lady Oswald. But he was not one to give way to these fanciful phases of feeling which appear to arise without rhyme or reason, and he was about to speak when the doctor forestalled him.

"Lady Oswald's death has brought you down, I presume?"

"Yes. I was in ignorance of it until this morning, when a formal invitation to attend the funeral reached me from the undertaker. I had just read the announcement of the death in the 'Times.' How shocked I was, I cannot well express to you."

"It has shocked us all."

"Of course its reaching me in that abrupt manner, in the public column of deaths, did not tend to lessen the shock. I rather wonder you did not drop me a line yourself, Dr. Davenal."

"I was away afterwards. Called out to a distance, I did not get back for a day or two. Did Mark not write?"

"Nobody wrote. Neither Mark nor Parkins; nor anybody else. As to Mark, he is careless as the wind; and Parkins excuses herself on the plea of having been so bewildered. I can readily believe her. Dr. Davenal, she died, as I am given to understand, from the effects of chloroform!"

"We thought, on the night of the accident, you know, that she was not seriously injured," said Dr. Davenal. "At least, Mark thought it: I had my doubts: but I left him to see to her at her own desire. Unfortunately I was called out early on Sunday morning. I was wanted at Thorndyke: and when I got back the injury had been ascertained, and an operation found necessary. It was under that operation she died."

"But the operation was performed successfully?"

"Quite so."

"And what she died of was the inhaling of the chloroform?"

"It was."

"But—I cannot understand why chloroform should have been given to her?" deliberately proceeded Oswald.

"It was given to her," was all the reply he obtained.

"But—pardon me for recalling it to you, Dr. Davenal—do you remember the very decided opinion you expressed to me, when we were going down to the scene of accident, against giving chloroform to Lady Oswald? We were speaking of its opposite effects upon different natures, and you cited Lady Oswald as one to whom, in your opinion, it might prove dangerous. You stated that, so far as you believed, it would be neither better nor worse to her than poison."

Oswald waited for a reply, but the doctor made none. He was pacing the small room with his measured tread, his hands in his pockets, his eyes bent on the carpet.

"Have you any objection to explain to me this apparent contradiction? It is impossible to believe that one, whose opinion of chloroform in relation to her was so fatal, would in a few hours cause her to inhale it."

Dr. Davenal stopped in his walk and confronted Oswald.

"Have you seen Mark since you came down?"

"Yes."

"And what does he say?"

"Well, I don't fancy he understands it much better than I do. He reiterates that it was given her for the best. In his opinion it may have been. But it surely could not have been in yours, Dr. Davenal."

Dr. Davenal turned from Oswald to his pacing again. A strong temptation was upon him to tell Oswald the truth. O that he had! that he had!

There were few people in the world whom he esteemed as he esteemed Oswald Cray. There was no one else in the world to whom he had expressed this opinion of the unfitness of Lady Oswald as a subject for chloroform, and the wish to explain, to exonerate himself, arose forcibly within him. The next moment he asked himself why Mark Cray himself had not spoken. As he had not, it seemed to Dr. Davenal that it would be a breach of friendship, of partnership, for him to speak. Oswald was connected, too, with Lady Oswald, and might take up the matter warmly. No, he felt in his ever-considerate heart that he could not betray Mark, could not set one brother against the other. And he put the temptation from him.

Oswald watched him as he walked, wondering at the silence. A silence which the doctor evidently did not feel inclined to break.

"Do you remember expressing this opinion to me, Dr. Davenal?"

"Yes, I believe I did so express it."

"And yet you acted in diametrical opposition to it immediately afterwards, and caused Lady Oswald to inhale chloroform? Will you forgive me for again asking how it could have been?"

"The very best of us are led into error sometimes," replied Dr. Davenal.

"Why, that is one of the remarks Mark has just made to me in connection with this case! I cannot recognise it as applying to it. You spoke so firmly, so positively, that I should have believed there was no room for error to creep in. I feel that there is something to be explained, Dr. Davenal."

Dr. Davenal wheeled round in his walk and confronted Oswald.

"There are circumstances connected with this case, Mr. Oswald Cray, which I cannot explain to the world; which I cannot explain even to you; although I would rather tell them to you than to any one. Let it suffice to know that I could not save Lady Oswald. It was not in my power."

"But you could have saved—you could have helped giving her the chloroform?" returned Oswald, wonderingly.

A slight pause. "Will you oblige me by asking no further questions on the subject—by allowing it to drop, to me and to others? Believe me, I have no selfish motive in pressing this. No one living can regret more than I the fatal result to Lady Oswald; perhaps nobody regrets it so keenly. Could I have saved her, no care, no skill, no labour, should have been spared. But I could not. I can only ask you to be satisfied with this meagre assurance, Mr. Oswald Cray and to believe me when I state that I have private reasons for declining to pursue the topic."

"And—pardon me—one more question: To what am I to attribute her death in my own mind? Or rather this giving of the chloroform?"

"You must look upon it as an error in judgment. It was such."

It was impossible for Oswald Cray, as a gentleman, to press further the matter. Dr. Davenal was an old man compared with him; one of high reputation, skill, position. He could not understand it, but he could only bow to the request—nay, to the demand—and let the subject sink into silence. An awkward pause ensued. The doctor had not resumed his promenade, but stood under the gas-lamp, twirling a quill pen in his fingers which he had taken up.

"How are the other sufferers from the accident getting on?" inquired Oswald, when the silence was beginning to be heard.

"Oh, quite well. Poor Bigg the fireman is nearly the only one of them left in the Infirmary, and he will soon be out of it. The rest came off mostly with a few cuts and bruises. There's a summons for me, I suppose."

The doctor alluded to a knock at the hall-door. Neal came in.

"Mr. Wheatley, sir. He wishes to know if you can spare him ten minutes."

"Yes," replied the doctor, and Oswald rose.

"Will you walk upstairs and see them?"

"Not tonight, thank you."

"I won't press you," said the doctor. "Sara is cut up about this news from Edward, terribly disappointed; and Aunt Bett is as cross as two sticks. She is fond of Edward, with all her ungraciousness to him, and she looks upon this hint of not coming down as a slight to herself. In manner she was always ungracious to the boys, from some idea I believe that it tended to keep them in order. But she loved them at heart. Goodnight."

Dr. Davenal clasped his hand with a warm pressure, warmer than usual; Oswald could not but feel it, and he went out perfectly mystified.

Neal stepped on to open the front gate. Neal was always remarkably courteous and deferent to Mr. Oswald Cray. Oswald, who had only seen the best side of Neal, and never suspected there was a reverse one, looked upon him as a man to be respected, a faithful old retainer of the Oswald family. Lady Oswald had sung his praises times out of number in Oswald's ear, and she once told Oswald to try for Neal should he ever require a servant about his person, for he would find Neal a man of fidelity, worth his weight in gold. Oswald believed her. He believed Neal to be faithful and true; one whom doubt could not touch.

"This death of your late mistress is a very sad thing, Neal."

"O sir! I can't express to you how I have felt it. I'm sure I can say that my lady was a true friend to me, the only one I had left."

"No, no, Neal. Not the only one. You may count a friend in me—if only in respect to the regard you were, I know, held in by Lady Oswald."

"Thank you, sir, greatly;" and honest Neal's eyes swam in tears as he turned them to Mr. Oswald Cray under the light of his master's professional gas-lamp. "Sir," he added, swaying forward the gate and dropping his voice as he approached nearer to Oswald, "how came that poison, that chloroform, to be given to her?"

"I cannot tell; I cannot understand," replied Oswald, speaking upon impulse, not upon reflection.

"Sir, if I might dare to say a word"—and Neal glanced round with caution on all sides as he spoke—"I'd ask whether it was given in fairness?"

"What do you mean, Neal?"

"There's not a person in the world I'd venture to whisper such a thing to, sir, except yourself; but I doubt whether it was given in fairness. I have a reason for doubting it, sir; a particular reason. It makes me sick, sir, to think that there was some unfair play brought to work, and that it took her life."

"Unfair play on the part of whom?" asked Oswald.

"I am not sure that I dare say, sir, even to you. And it might be looked upon as—as—fancy on my part. One thing is certain, sir, that but for that chloroform being given to her, she'd be alive now."

"Dr. Davenal and Mr. Cray gave the chloroform, Neal," observed Mr. Oswald Cray, in a somewhat distant tone—for it was not to Neal he would admit any doubt, scarcely condescend to hear any, of the judgment of the surgeons. "They know better about such things than we do."

"Yes, sir," answered Neal, as drily as he dared. "Mr. Cray, I am sure, did his best, but he has not had the judgment and experience of my master. Anyway, it seems it was the chloroform that killed her."

"As it has killed others before her—when administered in all deliberate judgment by surgeons of as high repute and practice as Dr. Davenal. The issues of life and death are not even in a doctor's hands, Neal. Goodnight."

"Goodnight to you, sir."

Oswald Cray walked slowly towards his temporary home, the "Apple Tree," half bewildered with the conjectural views opened out to him, and not the least with that last hint of Neal's. He could not get over that giving of the chloroform by Dr. Davenal in the very teeth of his expressed opinion against it. He had supposed, when he first heard of the cause of death, that this contradiction would be explained away: but, instead of that it was more unexplainable than before. There was Mark's confused manner, his covert attempts to avoid inquiry; there was Dr. Davenal's positive denial to satisfy it; there was the man Neal's curious hint. Oswald Cray felt as one in a maze, trying to get at something which eluded his grasp.

How the imagination runs riot, how utterly unamenable it is to the rules and regulations of sober control, we most of us know.

Oswald found his mind balancing the question, "Did Richard Davenal give that chloroform in his calm deliberate senses, believing that it might take her life? If so, where was the motive?" Men don't do such things in these days without a motive; the greatest criminal must have that. Oswald Cray could see none. There was no motive, or shadow of motive, for Dr. Davenal's wishing for the death of Lady Oswald. Quite the contrary; it was his interest—if so worldly a plea may be brought into proximity with these solemn thoughts—to keep her in life. Of all his patients, she perhaps was the most profitable, paying him a good sum yearly. Then—with the want of motive, those dark doubts, born of his imagination, fell to the ground, and he had the good sense to see that they did.

They fell to the ground. And Oswald Cray, as he awoke with a start, and shook himself clear of them, pinched his arms to see whether he was awake. Surely only in his sleep could doubts such as those have arisen of Dr. Davenal!

CHAPTER XXII

THE WILL

Sara Davenal in her sick restlessness was early in the breakfast-room. The disappointment touching her brother was weighing down her heart. Since the arrival of the unsatisfactory note the previous evening, she had felt a conviction similar to Dr. Davenal's, that Edward would not come. Neither had spoken of it to the other; great griefs cannot be talked of; and to Sara this was a grief inexpressible. It seemed that she would give half her remaining years of life for only one five minutes' interview with him.

If he came at all he would come today, Friday; and she got up, hoping against hope; saying to herself aloud, in contradiction to the fear lying upon her heart, and which she would not glance at, "He will be sure to come; he will never embark on that long voyage without first coming. He will remember Richard's fate." For the time being, the eager anxiety to see him almost seemed to deaden that other trouble which lay within her—the trouble that had taken possession of her on the Sunday night, never again to quit its tenement.

"Is the post in?" asked Dr. Davenal, as he entered the breakfast-room.

"No, it is not made," sharply replied Miss Davenal from her presiding place at the table. "Neal has but this minute brought in the urn. I am making it quickly as I can."

"I asked whether the post was in, Bettina. Because, if Edward is not coming, I should think there'd be a letter from him."

Sara looked up eagerly. "Don't you hope he will come, papa? Don't you think he will?"

"Well, Sara, after his letter of last night, my hopes upon the point are not very strong."

"O papa! I want to see him! I must see him before he sails."

"Hush, child!" She had spoken in a distressed tone, and her small white hands were trembling. "Agitating yourself will not bring him."

By and by the letters came in: two. Neal handed one to his master, the other to Sara. Both bore the same handwriting—Captain Davenal's. Sara, in her bitter disappointment, let hers lie by her plate untouched, but the doctor opened his.

Miss Bettina looked up. "Is he coming, Richard?"

"No. He says he can't come. That it is an impossibility."

"What else does he say?"

Dr. Davenal folded his letter and put it in his pocket, to read at his leisure. "Ask Sara what he says," was his answer, "All the gossip is in hers."

"And this is what he calls affection!" exclaimed Miss Bettina. "To leave his native land, his home, without a farewell! That's gratitude! Richard Davenal, were I you, he should carry out my displeasure with him."

"I don't know," said the doctor, his voice sadly subdued. "Send out displeasure with one whom we may never see again! No, Bettina. And it may be as he says—that he is unable to come."

He was looking straight before him as he spoke it, in a far-off, dreamy gaze. His thoughts had flown to one who had gone out under a sort of displeasure, gone out but for a short time—and had never come home again.

The hour for the funeral approached, and the doctor in his black attire stepped into his close carriage to be conveyed to the residence of Lady Oswald. He found all the mourners assembled, for he was late, with the exception of Mark Cray. Sir Philip Oswald and his eldest son; Oswald Cray; the Reverend Mr. Stephenson and his brother Mr. Joseph Stephenson. All were there, now the doctor had come, except Mark. The funeral was to be at the church at eleven.

The time went on. The hearse and mourning coaches stood before the door, the horses restless. It was close upon eleven.

"For whom do we wait?" inquired Sir Philip Oswald.

"For Mr. Cray, Sir Philip," answered the undertaker, who was gliding about, handing gloves and fixing hatbands.

"Mr. Cray?" repeated Sir Philip, as though he did not understand who Mr. Cray was.

"Lady Oswald's late medical attendant, Sir Philip, in conjunction with Dr. Davenal."

"Oh—ah—yes," said Sir Philip. He was very friendly with Dr. Davenal, exceedingly so; and condescended not to ignore Mr. Cray as the doctor's partner. It was the first time that Oswald had ever been in a room with Sir Philip. Sir Philip had bowed to him coldly enough upon his entrance, but the son, Henry Oswald, went up to him and held out his hand in a cordial manner. Oswald, haughtily self-possessed, stood before Sir Philip with his impassive face, looking more of a gentleman than the baronet did.

The clock struck eleven. "I suppose Mr. Cray is coming?" remarked Sir Philip.

He looked at Dr. Davenal. The doctor supposed he was coming as a matter of course: he believed he was coming. He had not seen Mr. Cray that morning.

It was suggested by the undertaker that they should proceed. Mr. Cray, he observed, would possibly join them at the church; he might have been kept back unexpectedly.

So the funeral started. All that remained of poor Lady Oswald was carried out of her house, never more to return to it. Not a week ago yet, on that past Saturday morning, she had gone forth in health and strength, and now—there! What a lessen it told of the uncertainty of life!

The funeral made its way through lines of curious gazers to the church. Mark Cray was not there, and the service was performed without him. At its conclusion the gentlemen returned to the house.

A lawyer from a neighbouring town, Lady Oswald's legal adviser, was there with the will, and they were invited to enter and hear the will read.

"It cannot concern me," remarked Sir Philip. Nevertheless he went in.

"And I am sure it cannot concern me," added Oswald.

The clergyman, Mr. Stephenson, looked up with a crimson hectic on his cheek. It was next to impossible to mistake his eager glance—betraying the hope within him, sure and steadfast, that it did concern him. In point of fact he and that gentleman by his side, his brother, had the chief right to any money she might have left. It may be said the sole right. How they needed it their threadbare clothes and sunken cheeks betrayed. Gentlemen born, they had to keep up an appearance before the world; at least, they strove to keep it. But they were weary with the struggle. The brother was of no particular profession. He had been reared for the church and could never get to college, and he contrived to make a living—that is, he contrived not to starve—by writing articles for any paper or periodical that could be persuaded into taking them. Each was of good repute in the world, bearing up manfully and doing the best he could do with his lot, sanguinely hoping, humbly trusting, that time would better it. They each had a large family, and indulged the vain and wild hope of bringing up their sons as gentlemen, as they themselves had been brought up. Not as gentlemen in the matter of abstaining from labour; that would have been foolish; but they hoped to bring them up educated men, capable of doing their duty in any walk of life they might be called to. How they had looked forward to the prospect of some time possessing this money of Lady Oswald's, their hearts alone knew. If ever the excuse for cherishing such a wish could be pleaded, it surely might be by them.

"I suppose these people, the Stephensons, will chiefly inherit what she has left," whispered the baronet's son confidentially to Oswald Cray. "Perhaps you know? You have seen a good deal of Lady Oswald, I believe."

"I don't at all know how her affairs are left," was the reply of Oswald Cray.

"I should think they will inherit," continued Mr. Oswald. "Shouldn't you?"

"I should think—yes—I—should think they will. Being her only relatives, they have undoubtedly the greatest right to do so."

Why did Oswald Cray hesitate in his answer?—he so generally decisive of speech. Because in the very moment that the acquiescence was leaving his lips there flashed over his mind the words spoken to him by Lady Oswald the previous Saturday. He had not understood those words at the time, did not understand them now: but if he could interpret them at all, they certainly did not point to her nephews, the brothers Stephenson. He remembered them well: at least, their substance. "When my will comes to be read, you may feel surprised at its contents. You may deem that you had more legal claim upon me than he who will inherit: I do not think so. He to whom my money is left has most claim in my judgment: I am happy to know that he will be rewarded, and he knows it."

Not a week ago! not a week ago that she had said it. How little did Oswald foresee that he should so soon be called upon to hear that will read!

But still the words did not seem to point to either of her nephews, with whom she had not lived on any terms of friendship, and Oswald began to feel a little curious as to the inheritor.

They were waiting for the lawyer, who had not yet come into the room. He might be getting the will. His name was Wedderburn, a stout man with a pimpled face. Sir Philip Oswald had a pimpled face too; but he was not stout; he was as thin and as tall as a lath.

Dr. Davenal took out his watch. He found it later than he thought, and turned to Sir Philip.

"I cannot remain longer," he said. "I have a consultation at half-past twelve, and must not miss it. I am not wanted here: there's nothing for me to stay for: so I'll wish you good-morning."

"For that matter, I don't see that any of us are wanted," responded Sir Philip. "I'm sure I am not. Good-morning, doctor."

Nodding his salutation to the room generally, the doctor went out. Soon afterwards Mr. Wedderburn made his appearance, the will in his hand, which he prepared to read. Clearing his voice, he threw his eyes round the room, as if to see that his audience were ready. The absence of one appeared then to strike him, and he pushed his spectacles to the top of his brow and gazed again.

"Where's Dr. Davenal?"

"He is gone," replied Sir Philip Oswald.

"Gone!" repeated the lawyer, in consternation. "Why—he—Dr. Davenal should have stopped, of all people."

"He said he had a consultation. What does it signify?"

"Well, Sir Philip, he—at any rate, I suppose there's no help for it now. It must be read without him."

Not one present but looked at the lawyer with surprise, not one but thought him a strangely punctilious man to suppose Dr. Davenal's presence, as Lady Oswald's medical man and attendant at her funeral, was in any degree essential to the reading of Lady Oswald's will. They soon learned the cause.

First of all, the will bequeathed a few legacies. Very small ones. Twenty pounds to each of her servants; forty pounds and all her clothes to Parkins; fifty pounds each to her nephews John and Joseph Stephenson, with the furniture of her house to be divided between them "amicably;" a beautiful diamond ring and a little plate to Oswald Oswald Cray; the rest of the plate, by far the most valuable portion, to Sir Philip Oswald of Thorndyke; and another diamond ring to Dr. Richard Davenal. So far, so good: but now came the disposal of the bulk of her money. It was bequeathed, the whole of it, to Dr. Davenal, "my faithful friend and medical attendant for so many years."

The will was remarkably short, taking but a few minutes in the reading; and at its conclusion Mr. Wedderburn laid it open on the table that anybody might look at it who chose.

It would be difficult to say which of the countenances around him exhibited the greatest surprise. The lawyer's voice died away in a deep silence. It was broken by the clergyman, the Reverend John Stephenson.

"It is not just! It is not just!"

The wailing tone, not of passion or anger but of meek despair, struck upon them all, and told how bitter was the disappointment. Every heart in the room echoed the cry, the lawyer's probably excepted.

Lawyers, as a whole, don't think much of justice. This one took out his snuffbox and inhaled a pinch with equanimity.

"I am ready to answer questions, should any gentleman wish to put them. It was Lady Oswald's desire that I should. When this will was made she said to me, 'Some of them will be for making a fuss, Wedderburn; you can explain my motives if they care to hear them.' Those motives lay in this; her ladyship knew her health and comfort to have been so materially benefited of late years by the skill and kindness of Dr. Davenal, that she considered it her duty in gratitude to reward him."

"Nevertheless it is not just," murmured the poor clergyman again. "Dr. Davenal does not want the money as we want it."

Oswald Cray awoke as from a dream. He took a step forward and addressed the lawyer. "Did Dr. Davenal know that the money was left to him?"

"I am unable to say, sir. Lady Oswald may have told him, or she may not. He did not know it from me."

Oswald Cray said no more. He leaned against the window, half-hidden by the curtain, and plunged into thought.

"Well, I must say I am surprised," remarked Sir Philip. "Not but that Lady Oswald had a perfect right to do as she pleased with her money, and she might have signalled out a less worthy man as inheritor. How much is the amount, Mr. Wedderburn? Do you know?"

"Somewhere between six and seven thousand pounds, I believe, Sir Philip. It would have been considerably more, but that her ladyship, a few years ago, was persuaded by an evil counsellor to sell out a large sum from the funds and invest elsewhere, for the sake of better interest."

"And she lost it?"

"Every shilling," replied the lawyer, with satisfaction: for it was done without his concurrence. "She would have had double the money to leave behind her but for that."

"Ah!" Sir Philip spoke the monosyllable shortly, and dropped the point. Not so very long ago he had been seduced to invest money in some grand and very plausible scheme—one of those to be heard of daily, promising a fortune in twelve months at the most—and he had burnt his fingers. The topic, consequently, was not palatable to his ears.

"Ask him how long this will has been made, John," whispered the literary man to his brother. Of a retiring timid nature himself, he rarely spoke but when he was obliged, and he shrank from putting the question. The clergyman obeyed, and the lawyer pointed to the date of the will.

"Only in April last. Lady Oswald was fond of making wills. Some people are so. I have made her, I should think, half-a-dozen, if I have made one."

"And the bulk of the money was always left to Dr. Davenal?"

"O dear no. It never was left to him until this last was made."

"Was I—were we—was it ever left to us?" asked the poor clergyman, tremblingly.

"Yes it was," replied Mr. Wedderburn. "I don't see why I should not avow it. It can't make any difference, one way or the other. In the first will she ever made after Sir John's death it was left to you. And in the last will preceding this, it was again left to you. Once it was left"—the lawyer looked towards the window—"to Mr. Oswald Cray."

Oswald gave his shoulders a haughty shrug. "I should never have accepted the legacy," he said in a distinct, deliberate tone. "I had no claim whatever to Lady Oswald's money, and should not have taken it."

Henry Oswald laughed; a pleasant, cordial laugh, as he turned to Oswald. "You don't know, Mr. Oswald Cray. We are all so ready to be chivalrous in theory: but when it comes to practice—the best of us are apt to fall off."

"True," quietly remarked Oswald: but he did not pursue the theme.

There was nothing more to be said or done then. Of what profit to remain talking of the wills that had been, while the present one was before them and must be put in force? Sir Philip made the first move; he went out, taking a formal leave; Henry Oswald with a more cordial one. Oswald Cray was the next to leave. He shook hands with the brothers, and spoke a few kind words of sympathy for their disappointment.

"It is the disappointment of a life," replied the clergyman in a low tone. "Our struggle has been continued long; and we had—there's no denying it—looked forward to this. It is a hard trial when relatives find themselves passed over for strangers."

"It is, it is;" said Oswald Cray. "I could wish Lady Oswald had been more mindful of legitimate claims."

As he was going out, Parkins waylaid him in her new mourning. "There will be a dinner ready at five o'clock, sir. Would you be pleased to stay for it?"

"Not today," replied Oswald.

CHAPTER XXIII

NEAL'S VISIT

Causing the sweeping crape to be taken from his hat, for he preferred to depart on foot, Oswald Cray proceeded through the town to the house of his brother. Just as he reached the door Mark rode up on horseback and leaped off with a hasty spring, throwing his bridle to the man who waited.

"Of course I am too late!" he exclaimed.

"Of course you are, by pretty near two hours. How did it happen, Mark?"

"Well—I—can hardly tell how it happened," was the answer of Mark. "I had a patient to see in the country—more than one, in fact—and I thought I could do it all first and be back in time. But I suppose I must have stayed later than I purposed, for before I was ready to return I found it was half-past eleven, and the funeral no doubt over. And then I did not hurry myself."

They were walking across the hall to the dining-room as he said this. Caroline was seated at the table, her workbox before her, doing some embroidery. She flung the work down, rose, and confronted her husband.

"Mark, why did you do this? You went into the country to avoid the funeral!"

"I—I did what?" exclaimed Mark. "Nonsense, Carrie! Why should I wish to avoid the funeral? I have attended plenty of funerals in my time."

Oswald turned quickly and looked at Mark. It was not the accusation of Mrs. Cray that had aroused his attention—that went for nothing; but something peculiar in Mark's tone as he answered it. To Oswald's ears it spoke of evasion. He could not see his face. It was bent, and he was slapping his dusty boots with his riding-whip.

"But why DID you go into the country?" pursued Caroline. "It was half-past ten when you were here, and I warned you then it was getting time to dress. When I saw your horse brought to the door and you gallop off on him, I could not believe my eyes."

"Well, I mistook the time, that's the fact. I am very sorry for it, but it can't be helped now. Of course I should like to have attended and paid her my last respects, poor lady. Not but that I daresay there were enough without me. I was not missed."

"But you were missed," said Oswald, "and waited for too. It threw us pretty nearly half-an-hour behindhand. I should not like to keep a funeral waiting myself, Mark."

"Who was there?" asked Mark.

"The two relatives of Lady Oswald, Sir Philip and his son, Dr. Davenal and myself."

"Davenal was there, then. But of course he would be. Then he served to do duty for me and himself. And so Sir Philip came?"

"I should be surprised had he not come."

"Should you? He is a cranky sort of gentleman: an Oswald all over. You are another of them, Oswald. I wonder if you'll get cranky in your old age."

"Don't listen to him, Oswald," interposed Mrs. Cray. "He seems 'cranky' himself this morning."

Mark laughed good-humouredly, and tossed a late China rose to Caroline which he had brought home in his button-hole. "Did you hear the will read, Oswald?" he asked.

"Yes."

"Short and sweet!" cried Mark, alluding to the monosyllable, which it must be confessed was given in a curt, displeased tone, as if its speaker were himself displeased. "I think it is you who are cranky, Oswald."

Oswald smiled. "A thought was causing me vexation, Mark."

"Vexation at me?"

"Oh, no."

"Well, and who comes in for the money? The Stephensons?"

"No. The Stephensons come in for a very poor portion. It is left to Dr. Davenal."

"To Dr. Davenal!" echoed Mark in his astonishment. "No!"

"The bulk of the money is bequeathed to him. All of it, in fact, with the exception of a few trifling legacies. The Stephensons have fifty pounds each and the furniture."

Caroline had dropped her embroidery again and was gazing at Oswald, apparently unable to take in the news. "Are you telling us this for a joke?" she asked.

"The money is left to Dr. Davenal, Mrs. Cray," repeated Oswald, and certainly there was no sound of joking in his tone. "It surprised us all."

"What a lucky man!" exclaimed Mark. "I wonder if he had any prevision of this yesterday? We were speaking of money, he and I. It was about that field behind the doctor's stables, the one he has so long wanted to buy. The owner's dead, and it is for sale at last. I observed to the doctor that I supposed he'd secure it at once, but he said he should not buy it at all; he had had a heavy loss, and could not afford it—"

"It is not true, Mark!" interrupted his wife.

"It is true, Caroline. But don't you go and repeat it again. He said, moreover, he had great need himself of a thousand or two, and did not know where to turn to for it. Mind you, I believe he was betrayed, as it were, out of the avowal, I had been saying so much about the field: for he brought himself suddenly up as though recollection had come to him, and said, 'Don't talk of this, Mark!'"

And Mark's long tongue had talked of it! Oswald Cray listened to its every word.

"If he could but have foreseen then that this money had dropped to him! And yet—I should think he must have known it from Lady Oswald; or partially known it. How much is it, Oswald?"

"Six or seven thousand pounds. It would have been a great deal more but for certain losses. Wedderburn said she was persuaded to embark money in some speculation; and it failed."

"How stupid of her!" exclaimed free Mark. "I wonder, now whether the doctor did know of this! If he did he'd keep his own counsel. Did he appear surprised, Oswald?"

"He was not there. He left before the will was read, saying he had to attend a consultation."

"Well, so he had," said Mark; "I happen to know that much. It was for half-past twelve."

So far, then, Dr. Davenal had spoken truth. A doubt had been crossing Oswald's mind, amidst many other curious doubts, whether Dr. Davenal had made the excuse to get away, and so avoid hearing the will read, and himself named chief legatee.

He remained some time with Mark and his wife. They asked him to stay for dinner, but he declined. He had ordered a chop to be ready at the "Apple Tree," and was going back to London early in the evening—by that seven o'clock train you have before heard of.

"Had you any particular motive for absenting yourself from Lady Oswald's funeral!" he asked of Mark, as the latter accompanied him to the street-door on his departure.

"Not I," answered Mark, with the most apparent readiness. "It was very bungling of me to mistake the time. Not that I like attending funerals as a matter of taste: I don't know who does. Good-afternoon, Oswald. You must give us a longer visit when you are down next."

He stood at the Abbey door, watching his brother wind round the branching rails, for Oswald was taking the station on his way to his inn. Very cleverly, in Mark's own opinion, had he parried the questions of his purposed absence. His absence was purposed. With that chloroform on his conscience he did not care to attend the funeral of Lady Oswald.

And the afternoon went on.

It was growing dusk, was turned half-past six, and Oswald Cray was beginning to think it time to make ready for his departure. He had not stirred from the chair where he ate his dinner, though the meal was over long ago; had not called for lights; had, in fact, waved John Hamos away when he would have appeared with them. His whole range of thought was absorbed by one topic—his doubts of Dr. Davenal.

Yes, it is of no use to deny it; it had come to that with Oswald Cray—doubts. Doubts he scarcely knew of what, or to what extent; he scarcely knew where these doubts or his own thoughts were carrying him. On the previous night he had for a few moments given the reins to imagination; had allowed himself to suppose, for argument's sake only, that Dr. Davenal had given that chloroform knowing or fancying it might prove fatal, and he had gone so far as to ask what, then, could be his motive. There was no motive; Oswald glanced on each side of him to every point, and could discover no motive whatever, or appearance of motive. Therefore he had thrust the doubts from him, as wanting foundation.

But had the revelations of this day supplied the link that was wanting Had they not supplied it? The death of Lady Oswald brought a fortune to Dr. Davenal.

Almost hating himself for pursuing these thoughts, or rather for the obligation to pursue them, for they would haunt him, and he could not help himself, Oswald Cray sat on in the fading light. Ha said to himself, how absurd, nay how wicked it was of him, and yet he could not shake them off. The more he strove to do so, the more he brought reason to his aid, telling him that Dr. Davenal was a good and honourable and upright man, as he had always believed, the less would reason hold the mastery. Imagination was all too present in its most vivid colouring, and it was chaining him to its will.

What were the simple facts? asked reason. Dr. Davenal had caused Lady Oswald to inhale chloroform, having only some hours previously avowed to Oswald his belief that she was a most unfit subject for it, was one of those few to whom the drug proves fatal. It did prove fatal. There had next been some equivocation on the part of Mark, when questioned about it, and there had been the positive refusal of Dr. Davenal to afford any explanation. Next, there had been the discovery of the day—that Dr. Davenal was the inheritor. Well, it might all be explained away, reason said; it was certainly not enough to attribute to Dr. Davenal the worst social crime contained in the decalogue. But the more Oswald Cray dwelt on this view, or tried to dwell upon it, the more persistently rose up imagination, torturing and twisting facts, and bending them as it pleased.

There had been that hint of Neal's too! Oswald Cray honestly believed that Neal was one of those servants incapable of speaking ill for ill's sake; and he could not help wondering what he meant. Neal was not an ignorant man, likely to be deceived, to take up fancies: he was of superior intelligence, quite an educated man for his class of life. If—

Oswald's thoughts were interrupted by the entrance of his landlord. "I don't want lights, John; I told you I did not. I shall be going directly."

"It is not lights, sir. Mr. Neal, Dr. Davenal's servant, is asking to see you."

"Neal! Let him come in."

Neal came forward into the dusky room. He was the bearer of a note from his master. Oswald had a light brought in then, and opened it. It was written in pencil.

"My Dear Mr. Oswald Cray,—

"I very much wish to see you if you can spare me an hour. I thought perhaps you would have dropped in this lonely day and taken a knife and fork with us. Will you come down this evening?—Ever sincerely yours,

Richard Davenal."

"Neal, will you tell Dr. Davenal—he is expecting me, I find?"

"I think so, sir. He said to me before dinner that he thought you might be coming in. When he found you did not, and they were sitting down to table, he wrote this in pencil, and bade me call one of the maids to wait, while I brought it up to you."

"Tell the doctor that I am quite unable to come down. I have to return to London by the seven o'clock train."

"Very well, sir."

Neal was leaving the room, but Mr. Oswald Cray stopped him. He had taken a sudden resolution, and he spoke on the spur of the moment, without reflection. The perplexity of his mind may be his excuse.

"Neal, have you any objection to tell me what you meant last night by hinting that Lady Oswald had not come fairly by her death?"

Neal paused. He was a man of caution; he liked to calculate his words and his ways before entering on them. Neal would certainly speak if he dared. He was in a very bitter mood, for the day's doings had not pleased him. The news had reached him that her ladyship's money had been all left to Dr. Davenal; that he, Neal, was not so much as named in the will. And Neal had looked forward as confidently as had the Reverend Mr. Stephenson to the hope of some little remembrance being left to him. In his terrible anger, it seemed to him that the one enemy to prevent it had been the great inheritor, Dr. Davenal.

"Sir, if I speak, would you give me your promise first, to hold what I say sacred to yourself; to let it go no further? I know, sir, it is not the place of a servant to ask this confidence of a gentleman, but I should be afraid to speak without it."

"I will give it you," said Mr. Oswald Cray. "You may rely upon me."

And Neal knew that if there was one man more than another on the face of the earth who would never forfeit his word, upon whom implicit trust might be placed, it was Oswald Cray. Neal set himself to his task. First of all opening the door to make sure they were entirely alone, he dropped his voice to a safe whisper, and described what he had seen and heard on the Sunday night. It was certainly a startling narration, and as Oswald Cray listened to it in that darkened room,—for the one candle, now placed on a side-table behind, only served to throw out the shadows,—listened to the hushed tones, the unexplainable words, a curious feeling of dread began to creep over him. Neal, you may be very sure, did not disclose anything that could bear against himself; he contrived to come out well in it. He was standing outside for a moment before going to bed, hoping the air would remove the sad headache which had suddenly seized him upon hearing of the death of his late lady, when he saw the man come in in the extraordinary manner he had just described. Believing him to be nothing less than a housebreaker (and Watton, who had seen the man from her room upstairs, had come to the same conclusion), or an evil character of some sort, getting in plausibly on false pretences to work harm to Dr. Davenal, he had gone to the window to look in out of anxiety for his master's safety, and there had heard what he had stated, for the window was thrown open. He could not see the visitor, who was seated in the shade: he only heard sufficient to tell him that the business he had come on was Lady Oswald's death; and he heard Dr. Davenal acknowledge that it was murder, and that it must be hushed up at any price, even if it cost him his fortune. He, Neal, described the utterly prostrate condition of his master that night; both before and after the interview with the visitor, he was like one who has some dreadful secret upon the mind, some heavy guilt; Neal had thought so before ever the man, whoever he might have been, entered the house.

Will it be forgiven to Oswald Cray if in that brief confused moment he believed the worst—believed all that Neal said to him? His mind was in a chaos of perplexity, almost, it may be said, of terror. Nothing was clear. He could not analyse, he could not reason: Neal's words, and the doings of the night which the man was describing, seemed to dance before his mind in confused forms, ever changing, as do the bits of coloured glass in a kaleidoscope. Neal continued to speak, but he did not hear him distinctly now;

the words reached his senses certainly, but more as if he were in a mazy dream. He heard the man reiterate that, wherever it was his master had gone to that night, remaining away until the Wednesday it was connected with the death of Lady Oswald; he heard him say that, whatever the mystery and the guilt, Miss Sara Davenal had been made the confidant of it by her father, he, Neal, supposed front some imperative motive which he did not pretend to understand. Oswald heard like one in a dream, the words partially glancing off his mind even as they were spoken, only to be recalled afterwards with redoubled force.

In the midst of it he suddenly looked at his watch, suspecting—as he found—that he had barely time to catch the train.

And he went out in a sort of blind confusion, his brain echoing the words of Dr. Davenal, only too accurately remembered and repeated by Neal. "Murder? Yes, the world would look upon it as such. I felt certain that Lady Oswald was one to whom chloroform, if administered, would prove fatal."

CHAPTER XXIV

DR DAVENAL'S "FOLLY"

It was startling news to go forth to Hallingham—one of the nine days' wonders read of in social history. Lady Oswald had bequeathed her fortune to her physician, Dr. Davenal! Such things had been known before in the world's experiences, but Hallingham made as much of the fact as if that were the first time it had ever been enacted.

Upon none did the news fall with more complete astonishment than upon the doctor himself. Lady Oswald had more than once in the past few months mysteriously hinted to him that he would be rewarded some time for his care and attention to her; and it must be supposed that she had these hints in her mind when she said to Mr. Oswald Cray that "he" (the named inheritor of her money) knew that he would be rewarded. Upon Dr. Davenal the hints had never made any impression. Of a nature the very reverse of covetous, simple-minded, single-hearted, it never so much as crossed his imagination that she would be leaving her money to him. He would have been the first to repudiate it; to point out to her the injustice of the act.

It is surely not necessary to premise that you, my intelligent and enlightened readers, cannot have fallen into the mistake made by Neal, or drawn that respected domestic's very absurd, though perhaps to a fanciful and prejudiced mind not unnatural deduction, that the night-visit to Dr. Davenal had reference to Lady Oswald's death. Being in the secret of who really did administer that fatal dose of chloroform to Lady Oswald, you will not connect it with Dr. Davenal's trouble. A heavy secret, involving disgrace, much misery, perhaps ruin, had indeed fallen that night on Dr. Davenal, but it was entirely unconnected with the death of Lady Oswald. The words which Neal had heard—and he heard them correctly—would have borne to his mind a very different interpretation had he been enabled to hear the whole—what had preceded them and what followed them. But he did not.

Yes, this unhappy secret, this great misfortune, had nothing to do with Lady Oswald. Far from Dr. Davenal's having caused her to inhale an extra dose of chloroform as an experiment, on the strength that it might prove fatal, and so enable him to drop at once into that very desirable legacy named in her will, and which supposition, I am sure you will agree with me in thinking, belongs rather to the world of idealic wonders than of real life, the doctor had not the faintest suspicion that he should inherit a shilling. When the news was conveyed to him he could not believe it to be true,—did not believe it for some little time.

It was Mr. Wedderburn who carried it to him. When the lawyer's business was over at Lady Oswald's, he proceeded to Dr. Davenal's, and found him just come home from the consultation, to attend which he had hurried away before the reading of the will. Mr. Wedderburn told him the news.

"Left to me?" exclaimed the doctor. "Her money left to me! Nonsense!"

"It is indeed," affirmed Mr. Wedderburn. "After the legacies are paid you take everything—you are residuary legatee."

"You are joking," said the doctor. "What have I to do with the money? I have no right to it."

With some difficulty Dr. Davenal was convinced that he, and he alone, was named the inheritor. It did not give him pleasure. Quite the contrary; he saw in it only a good deal of trouble and law business, which he much disliked at all times to engage in.

Richard Davenal was one of those thoroughly conscientious men—and there are a few such in the world—who could not be content to enjoy money to which another has more right. It was a creed of his—it is not altogether an obsolete one—that money so enjoyed could not bring pleasure in the spending, or good in the end. Lady Oswald had legitimate relations, who had looked for the money, who needed the money, needed it with a far deeper need than Dr. Davenal, and who possessed a claim to it, so far as relationship could give it them. Even as the conviction slowly arose to him that the news was true that he had been made the inheritor, so there arose another conviction, or rather a resolution, with it,—that he would never accept the money, that it should go over to its legitimate owners, no matter what trouble it involved. A resolution from which he never swerved.

Never. Not even in the moment when a tempter's voice arose within him, whispering how well this legacy would serve to replace that great sum, the savings of years, which he had been obliged to part with only that very week. Partly to satisfy a debt of which until then he had known nothing, had he parted with it; partly as hush-money, to keep down that terrible secret whispered to him on the Sunday night. The thought certainly did arise—that it almost seemed as if this money had been sent to him to replace it; but he did not allow it to obtain weight. It would have been simply impossible for Dr. Davenal to act against his conscience.

"I shall refuse the legacy," he remarked to Mr. Wedderburn. "I have no right to it."

"What did you say?" asked the lawyer, believing he did not properly catch the words.

"I shall not accept this money. It is none of mine. It ought to be none of mine. It must go to Lady Oswald's relatives."

"But it is yours, Dr. Davenal. It is bequeathed to you in the will."

"I don't care for the will. I should not care for ten wills, if I had no right to the money they bequeathed me. I have no right to this, and I will not touch a farthing of it."

Mr. Wedderburn's surprise could only expend itself in one long stare. In all his lawyerly experience he had never come across an announcement so savouring of chivalry. The legatees he had had the pleasure of doing business with were only too eager to grasp their good fortune, and if any little inconvenient pricks of conscience were so ill-mannered as to arise, they were speedily despatched back again by the very legal thought—If I do take it I but obey the will.

"There never was such a thing heard of as the refusing of a fortune legally bequeathed," cried the lawyer.

"I daresay there has been, many a time. If not, this will be a precedent."

"You'll be so laughed at," persisted Mr. Wedderburn. "You'll be set down—I'm afraid people will be for setting you down as a lunatic."

"Let them," said the doctor. "They shan't confine me as one without my own certificate. Mr. Wedderburn," he continued in a graver tone, "I am serious in this refusal. I feel that I have no right whatever to this money of Lady Oswald's. She has paid me liberally for my services—"

"If you only knew how many thousands inherit money daily who have no right to it," interrupted Mr. Wedderburn.

"Doubtless they do. I was going to observe that it is not so much my having no right to it, that would cause me to decline, as the fact that others exist who have a right. I—"

"But the will gives you a right," interposed the lawyer, unable to get over his surprise.

"A legal right, I am aware it does. But not a just one. No, I will not accept this legacy."

"What will you do about it, then?"

The doctor was silent for a minute. "I should wish the money to be appropriated just as though there had been no Dr. Davenal in existence. You say this will was made but about six months ago. It must have superseded another will, I presume?"

"It may be said that it superseded several," was the reply. "Lady Oswald was constantly making wills. She had made some half-dozen before this last one."

"And each one disposing of her property differently?" quickly asked the doctor.

"Yea, or nearly so. Twice she bequeathed it to her nephews, the Stephensons. Once it was left to Mr. Oswald Cray; once to charities; once to Sir Philip Oswald. She has been exceedingly capricious."

"All the more reason why I should not take it now," warmly cried Dr. Davenal. "She must have left it to me in a moment of caprice; and had she lived a few months longer this will would have been revoked as the rest have been. Mr. Wedderburn, were I capable of acting upon it, of taking the money, I should lose all self-respect for ever. I could not, as a responsible being, responsible to One who sees and judges all I do, be guilty of so crying an injustice."

Mr. Wedderburn suppressed a shrug of the shoulders. He could only look at these affairs with a lawyer's eye and a lawyer's reasoning. Dr. Davenal resumed—

"What was the tenor of the will which this last one supersede? Do you recollect?"

"Perfectly. We hold the draft of it still. It was as nearly as possible a counterpart of the present one, excepting as relates to your share in this and that of the brothers Stephenson. In that last will they took your place. The furniture was bequeathed to them, as in this, and also the bulk of the property."

"My name not being mentioned in it?"

"Yes, it was. The diamond ring bequeathed to you now was bequeathed then. Nothing more to you."

"Then that's all right. Now, Mr. Wedderburn, listen to me. That diamond ring I will accept with pleasure, as a reminiscence of my poor friend and patient; but I will accept nothing else. Will you be so kind as to destroy this last will, and let the other be acted upon? I am scaring you, I see. If that cannot legally be done, I must let the money come to me, but only in transit for the rightful owners, the Reverend Mr. Stephenson and his brother, and I'll make them a present of it. You will manage this for me. Being at home in law details, you know of course what may and what may not be done. All I beg of you is to effect this, carrying it out in the simplest manner, and in the quickest possible time."

Mr. Wedderburn drew a long face. He had no more cause to wish the money to go to Dr. Davenal than to the clergyman and his brother, but it was altogether so unusual a mode of proceeding, would be so very unprofessional a transaction, that he regarded it as an innovation hardly to be tolerated, a sort of scandal on all recognised notions in the legal world, of which Mr. Wedderburn himself was little better than a machine.

"I cannot undertake it without your giving me instructions in writing, Dr. Davenal," he said glumpily. "I'd not stir a peg in it without."

"You shall have them in full."

"Well, sir, you know best, but the time may come when your children will not thank you for this. It is folly, Dr. Davenal, and nothing less."

"I hope my children will never question any act of mine. I am doing this for the best."

Nevertheless, as Dr. Davenal spoke, there was some pain in his tone. The lawyer detected it, and thought he was coming round. He would not speak immediately, but let the feeling work its way.

"It is a large sum to relinquish," the lawyer presently said; "to throw out of one's hand as if it were so much worthless sand."

"What is the sum?—what has she left?" asked Dr. Davenal, the remark reminding him that he was as yet in ignorance.

"I expect, when all the legacies and other expenses are paid, there will be little over six thousand pounds. There ought to have been double. Lady Oswald lost a large sum a few years ago, quite as much as that. She put it into some prosperous-looking bubble, and it burst. Women should never dabble in business. They are safe to get their fingers burnt."

"Men have burnt theirs sometimes," was the answer of Dr. Davenal, spoken significantly. "Six thousand pounds! I should have thought her worth much more. Well, Mr. Wedderburn, you will carry out my instructions."

"Of course, if you order me. Will you be so kind as to write those instructions to me at your convenience, posting them from this town to my house. I am going back home at once."

"Won't you see Mr. Stephenson and his brother first, and impart to them the fact that I shall not take the money?"

"No," said the lawyer, "I want to go home by the next train. I wish, Dr. Davenal, you would allow me to give you just one word of advice."

"You can give it me," said Dr. Davenal. "I don't promise to take it."

"It might be the better for you if you would," was the reply. "My advice is, say nothing to the Stephensons, or to any one else, today. This is a very strange resolution that you have expressed, and I beg you to sleep upon it. A night's rest may serve to change your mind."

The lawyer departed. It was close upon the hour for Dr. Davenal to receive his indoor patients, and he could not go out then. He went to look for his daughter, and found her in the garden parlour with her aunt. It was not often that Miss Bettina troubled that room—she had been wont to tell Sara and Caroline that its litter set her teeth on edge.

They began to talk to him of the funeral. It was natural they should do so. In a country place these somewhat unusual occurrences of everyday life are made much of. Miss Bettina was curious.

"Were the people from Thorndyke there?" she asked.

"Sir Philip and his eldest son."

"And Oswald Cray?"

"Of course. He came down on purpose."

"My goodness! And so they met! How did they behave, Richard?"

"Just as the rest of us behaved. Did you suppose they'd start a quarrel?"

"I was sure of it. I knew they would never meet without starting one. Nothing less could come of Oswald Cray's proud spirit and the manner they have treated him."

"At sea as usual, Bettina. Do you think they'd quarrel there?—on that solemn occasion? Oswald Cray and Sir Philip are proud enough, both of them; but they are gentlemen—you forget that, Bettina. I think Oswald Cray is about the least likely man to quarrel that I know, whether with Sir Philip or with anybody else. Your proud man washes his hands of people whom he despises; but he does not quarrel with them."

How singularly true were the words in regard to Oswald Cray! It was as though Dr. Davenal had worn in that moment the gift of prevision; "Your proud man washes his hands of people whom he despises."

"And how is her money left?" continued Miss Bettina. "To the Stephensons?"

"No, she has not made a just will. It is left to—to a stranger. A stranger in blood."

"Indeed! To whom? I hope you have been remembered with some little token Richard?"

"To be sure I have been. You know those two splendid diamond rings of hers: I have one, Oswald Cray the other. And that's all he has got, by the way, except a silver coffee-pot, or so. Sara, come with me into the garden, I wish to have a little chat with you."

"You have not told me who the stranger is," shrieked out Miss Bettina.

"I'll tell you by-and-by," called back the doctor.

"I did not think it likely she would leave anything to Oswald Cray, papa," Sara remarked, as they paced the garden path.

"I think I should, had I been in her place. A matter of five hundred pounds, or so, would have helped him on wonderfully. However, there was no obligation, and it is a question whether Oswald would have accepted it."

"You said it was not a just will, papa?"

"I could have gone further than that, Sara, and stigmatised it as a very unjust one. Those poor Stephensons, who have been expecting this money—who had a right to expect it—are cut off with a paltry fifty pounds each and the furniture."

"O papa! And are they not very poor?"

"So poor, that I believe honestly they have not always bread to eat; that is, what people, born as they were, designate as bread; proper food. They carry the signs of it in their countenances."

"And for Lady Oswald to have left her money away from them! To whom has she left it?"

"To one who has no right to it, who never expected it."

"I suppose you mean Sir Philip?"

"No, it is not left to him. But now, give me your opinion, Sara. Let us for argument's sake put ourselves in the position of this fortunate legatee. Suppose—suppose, my dear it were left to you: this money to which you have no claim, no right—to which others have a claim, how should you feel?"

"I should feel uncomfortable," replied Sara. "I should feel that I was enriched at the expense of the Stephensons; I am sure that I should feel almost as though I had committed a fraud. Papa," she added more eagerly, the idea occurring to her, "I should like to give the money back to them."

"That is the very argument I have been using myself. Wedderburn, Lady Oswald's lawyer, has been here, talking of the matter, and I told him that were I the man to whom it was left, I should give it back, every shilling of it, to the channel where it ought at once to have gone—the brothers Stephenson. Wedderburn did not agree with me: he brought forward the argument that the man's children might reproach him afterwards. What do you think?"

"I think, papa, that were I the man you speak of, I should act upon my own judgment, and give it back without reference to the opinion of my children."

"That is precisely what he has resolved to do. Sara, the money is left to me."

Sara Davenal, taken completely by surprise, halted in her walk and looked at the Doctor, not knowing how to believe him.

"It is true, Sara. I find I am the favoured legatee of Lady Oswald: knowing at the same time that I have no more right to be so than have those espalier rose-trees at your side. I have resolved to refuse the money; to repudiate the will altogether, so far as my share in it goes; and to suffer a previous will to be acted upon, which gives the money to the Stephensons. I trust my children will not hereafter turn round and reproach me."

"O papa!"

She spoke the words now almost reproachfully, in reproach that he could ever think it.

"Yes, I shall do it, Sara. And yet," he added, his voice insensibly sinking to a whisper, "I have heavy need for money just now, and the help these thousands would be to me no one but myself knows."

Sara was silent. A shiver passed over her face at the allusion. She did not dare reply to it. The subject was too painful; and, besides, she was kept partially in the dark.

"But I cannot tamper with my conscience," resumed Dr. Davenal. "Were I to take this money, it would only lie like a weight upon it for my whole future life. I believe—and, Sara, I wish you to believe it and treasure it as an assured truth—that money appropriated by ourselves, which in point of right, of justice, belongs to others, never comes home to us with a blessing. However safely the law may give it us and the world deem our claim to it legitimate, if we deprive others of it, whose it is by every moral and—may I say it?—divine right, that money will not bless us or our children. Sara, I speak this from the experience of an observant life."

"I am sure you are right, papa," she murmured. "Do not keep this money."

"I shall not. But, Sara,"—and Dr. Davenal stopped in his walk, and his voice grew solemn in its tone as he laid his hand upon her—"things have changed with me. I cannot now foresee the future. I thought I was laying up a competency for my children; not a great one, it is true, but one that would have kept them above the extreme frowns of the world. This I have had to fling away—my hard-earned savings. It may be that I shall now have to leave you, my cherished daughter, to the world's mercy; perhaps—I know not—compelled to work for your living in it. Should this come to pass, you will not cast back a reflection on your dead father, and reproach him for a rejection of these thousands."

The tears were streaming down her cheeks. Her pleading hand, her loving look, was his first answer. "You could not keep the money, papa. It would not be right in God's sight. Do not hesitate."

"I have not hesitated, Sara. My mind has been made up from the first. But I preferred to speak to you."

Neal came forward to summon Dr. Davenal. His patients were waiting for him. Sara turned to rejoin her aunt.

"You can tell her about this legacy to me, Sara; it will be the talk of the town before the day's out. And explain to her why I decline it."

The afternoon drew to its close. Dr. Davenal, engaged with a succession of patients, scarcely noticed its elapse. A wish was running through his mind to see Mr. Oswald Cray, and he hoped he would be calling. When dinner-time came and he had not come, that note, previously mentioned, was pencilled, and Neal despatched with it.

The man brought the message back in due course "Mr. Oswald Cray was unable to call upon the doctor, as he was departing for London." Dr. Davenal was disappointed; he had wished to explain to Oswald Cray his intentions respecting the money; he considered it due to him, Oswald, to do so.

How is it that there are times when an idea, without any apparent cause to lead to it, any reason to justify it, takes sudden possession of the mind? Even as Neal spoke, such an idea seated itself in Dr. Davenal's. He fancied that Oswald Cray was in some way not pleased at the disposition of Lady Oswald's property, as regarded Dr. Davenal; was in a degree, more or less, resenting it. It only made the doctor doubly desirous of seeing him.

But there was no chance of it at present, Oswald Cray having left Hallingham. Dr. Davenal put on his hat and went out to take a walk as far as Lady Oswald's.

He found the Rev. Mr. Stephenson alone. His brother had departed. The clergyman received him somewhat awkwardly. He had been brooding over his disappointment all by himself; had been thinking what a crying wrong it was that the money should be left to the flourishing and wealthy physician, Dr. Davenal, who put as many guineas into his pocket daily as would keep him and his family in their humble way for months. He was casting his anxious thoughts to the future, wondering how his children were to be educated, foreseeing nothing but embarrassment and struggle to the very end of his life; and I am not sure that his heart at that moment towards that one man was not full of envy, hatred, malice, and all uncharitableness. Ministers of the gospel are but human, swayed at times by evil passions, just as we are.

But, being in this frame of mind, it a little confused the reverend gentleman to see the object of his envy standing before him. Dr. Davenal drew forward a seat.

"I daresay, Mr. Stephenson, if the truth were known, you were at this very moment bestowing upon me plenty of hard names."

It was so exceedingly like what Mr. Stephenson had been doing, that all the reply he could make was a confused stammer. Dr. Davenal, who, for the interview, appeared to have put away from the surface his hidden care, resumed in a frank, free tone—

"I have no right to the money, have I? It ought to have gone to you and your brother?"

"Well, sir—perhaps you had been led to expect it by Lady Oswald," was the clergyman's answer. Of a timid and refined nature, he could not, to Dr. Davenal's face, express his sense of the wrong. With Dr. Davenal before him, cordial and open, he began to think the wrong less. That is, that it was not so much the doctor's fault as he had been angrily deeming.

"No, she never led me to expect anything of the sort; and you cannot be more surprised than I am at its being left to me," said the doctor. "When Mr. Wedderburn came to me with the news, I could not believe him. However, it appears to be the fact."

"Yes," meekly rejoined the clergyman; "it is."

"And I have now come to inform you, that I shall not take the money, Mr. Stephenson. Not a stiver of it. The will, so far as it concerns me, may be regarded as a dead letter, for all practical use. I have desired Mr. Wedderburn to transfer the money to you and your brother; and if this may not legally be, if I must, despite myself, accept the money, I only take it to restore it to you. You will not be too proud to accept it from me?"

Was he listening to fact?—or was he in a dream? The words, to the minister's ear, did not savour of reality. His pale face grew moist with emotion, his trembling hands entwined their thin fingers together. He did not dare to ask, Was it real? lest the answer should dissolve the spell, and prove it but illusion.

"I could not accept of this great sum to the prejudice of others who have a right to it," resumed Dr. Davenal. "I should fear its proving something like ill-gotten gains, that bring evil with them, instead of good. The money shall be yours and your brother's, Mr. Stephenson, just as surely as though it had been left to you by Lady Oswald. The diamond ring I shall keep and value, but not a shilling of the money. I thought I would come up and tell you this."

The tears were welling into that poor gentleman's eyes, as he rose and clasped the hand of Dr. Davenal. "If you could see what I have suffered; if you could only imagine the struggle life has been to me, you would know what I feel at this moment. Heaven send its blessings on your generosity!"

The doctor quitted him. He had found a heavy heart, he left a glad one. He quitted him and went forth into the stillness of the autumn night.

He glanced towards the bright stars as he walked along, thinking of the future. And a prayer went up from his heart to the throne of heaven—that, if it was God's will, his children might not feel hereafter the sacrifice he had made—that God would bless them and be merciful to them when he should be gone. The last few days had been sufficient to teach Dr. Davenal, had he never known it before, in how great need the apparently safest amongst us stand of this ever-loving mercy.

CHAPTER XXV

COMPANY FOR MR OSWALD CRAY

For some days subsequent to the interview with Neal, and that valuable servant's startling communication, Mr. Oswald Cray remained in what may be called a sea of confusion. The unhappy circumstances attendant on Lady Oswald's death never left his mind, the strange suspicions first arising naturally, as they did arise, and then augmented by Neal's disclosure, seemed to be ever waging hot war within him, for they were entirely antagonistic to sober reason, to his life-long experience of Dr. Davenal.

It cannot be denied that Oswald Cray, calm of temperament though he was, sound of judgment, did fall into the snare that the web of events had woven around him; and, in the midnight watches, when things wear to our senses a weird, ghost-like hue, the disagreeable word murder suggested itself to him oftener than he would have cared to confess in broad matter-of-fact daylight. But as the days went on his senses came to him. Reason reasserted her empire, and he flung the dark doubt from him, as unworthy of himself and the present enlightened age. It was impossible to connect such a crime with Dr. Davenal.

But still, though he shook off the worst view, he could not shake off the circumstances and their suspicion. Perhaps it was next to impossible, knowing what he did know of the doctor's sentiments as to chloroform, hearing, as he had heard, Neal's account of the words spoken at the midnight interview, that he should shake them off. They turned and twisted themselves about in his mind in spite of his will; he would have given much to get rid of them, but he could not. Now taking one phase, now another, now looking dark, now light, there they were, like so many phantoms, ever springing up from different corners of his mind, and putting legitimate thoughts out of it. Up and in bed, at work or at rest, were those conflicting arguments ever dancing attendance on him, until, from sheer perplexity, his brain would seem to lose its subtle powers, and grow dull from very weariness. But the worst aspect of the affair gradually lost its impression, and reason drove away the high colours of imagination.

The conclusion to which he at length came, and in which he finally settled down, was that Dr. Davenal had been in a partial degree guilty. He could not think that he had given that chloroform to Lady Oswald with the deliberate view of taking her life, as some of our worst criminals have taken lives: but he did believe there was some hidden culpability attached to it. Could it have been given in forgetfulness?—or by way of experiment?—or carelessly? Oswald Cray asked himself those questions ten times in a day. No, no, reason answered; Dr. Davenal was not a man to forget, or to experimentalise, or to do things carelessly. And then, with the answer, rose the one dark, awful doubt again, tormenting him not less with its shadows than with its preposterous absurdity.

What clung to his mind more than all the rest was, that he could see no solution, or chance of solution, to the question of why chloroform was administered, why even it was taken to the house. Had Dr. Davenal frankly answered him when questioned, "I thought, in spite of my conversation with you, that chloroform might be ventured upon with safety, that it would ease her sufferings, and was absolutely necessary to calm her state of excitement," why he could have had no more to say, however lamenting the fatal effects. But Dr. Davenal had answered nothing of the kind. On the contrary, he had been mysterious over it, and at length flatly refused to satisfy him at all. So far as Oswald Cray could see, there was no other solution, then or ever, that could be arrived at, save that the chloroform had been administered wilfully and deliberately. If so, then with what view had Dr. Davenal—

At this point Oswald Cray always pulled his thoughts up, or strove to do so, and plunged desperately into another phase of the affair as if he would run away from dangerous ground. Once he caught himself wondering whether, if the doctor had been deliberately guilty, it lay in his duty—his, Oswald Cray's—to bring him to account for it. No living being save himself, so far as he trusted, had been cognisant of Dr. Davenal's strong opinion of chloroform as applied to Lady Oswald. Ought he, then, not only in the obligation which lies upon all honest men to bring crime to light, but as a connection of Lady Oswald's, ought he to be the Nemesis, and denounce—

With a quicker beating of the heart, with a burning flush upon his brow, Oswald Cray started from the train of thought. Into what strange gulf was it carrying him? Ah, not though it had been his fate to see the crime committed, and to know that it was a crime, would he be the one to bring it home to Richard Davenal! The man whom he had so respected; the father of her who possessed his best love, and who would possess it, in spite of his efforts to withdraw it, for all time? No; not against him could his hand be raised in judgment.

In spite of his efforts to withdraw his love? Had it come to that with Oswald Cray? Indeed it had. He could not fathom the affair, it remained to him utterly incomprehensible, but that Dr. Davenal was in some way or other compromised by it, terribly compromised, seemed as plain as the sun at noonday. And Mr. Oswald Cray, in his haughty spirit, his besetting pride, decided that he could no longer be on terms of friendship with him, and that Sara Davenal must be no wife of his.

What it cost him to come to this resolution of casting her adrift, none save Heaven knew. The struggle remained on his memory for years afterwards as the sorest pain life had ever brought him. It was the bitter turning-point which too many of us have to arrive at, and pass; the dividing link which dashes away the sunny meads, the flowery paths of life's young romance, and sends us stumbling and shivering down the stony road of reality. None knew, none ever would know, what that struggle was to Oswald Cray.

Not a struggle as to the course he should pursue—the breaking off intimacy with her: never for a single moment did he hesitate in that. The struggle lay with his feelings, with his own heart, where she was entwined with its every fibre, part and parcel of its very self. He strove to put her out thence, and she would not be put out. There she remained, and he was conscious that there she would remain for many a dreary year to come.

But for his overweening pride, how different things might have been! He was too just a man to include Sara in the doctor's—dare he say it?—crime. Although Neal had said that Miss Sara Davenal had been made cognisant of it, Oswald did not visit upon her one iota of blame. She was no more responsible for the doctor's acts than he was, neither could she help them. No, he did not cast a shadow of reproach upon her; she had done nothing to forfeit his love; but she was her father's daughter, and therefore no fit wife for him. One whose pride was less in the ascendant than Mr. Oswald Cray's, whose self-esteem was less sensitively fastidious, might have acted upon this consciousness of her immunity from blame, and set himself to see whether there was not a way out of the dilemma rather than have given her up, off-hand, at the very first onset. He might have gone in his candour to Dr. Davenal and said, "I love your daughter; I had wished to make her my wife; tell me confidentially, is there a reason why I, an honourable man, should not?" Not so Mr. Oswald Cray and his haughty pride. Without a single moment of hesitation he shook himself free from all future contact with the daughter of Dr. Davenal, just as he was trying to shake her from his heart. Never more, never more, might he look forward to the life of happiness he had been wont to picture.

It was a cruel struggle, cruel to him; and the red flush of shame mantled on his brow as he thought of the binding words he had spoken to her, and the dishonour that must accrue to him in breaking them. There was not a man on the face of the earth whose sense of honour was more keen than Oswald Cray's, who was less capable of wilfully doing aught to tarnish it; and yet that tarnishing was thrust upon him. Anyway, it seemed that a great stain must fall upon it. To take one to be his wife whose father was a suspected man would be a blot indeed; and to slip through the words he had spoken, never more to take notice of her or them, was scarcely less so. He felt it keenly; he, the man of unblemished conduct, and, it may be said, of unblemished heart.

But still he did not for a moment hesitate. Great as the pain was to himself, little as she, in her innocence, deserved that the slight should be inflicted on her, he never wavered in that which he knew must be. The only question that arose to him was, how it should be best done. Should he speak to her?—or should he gradually drop all intimacy and let the fact become known to her in that way? Which would be the kinder course? That the separation would be productive of the utmost pain to her as to him, that she loved him with all the fervour of a first and pure attachment, he knew; and he felt for her to his very heart's core. He hated himself for having to inflict this pain, and he heartily wished, as things had turned out, that he had never yielded to the pleasure of becoming intimate at Dr. Davenal's. Well, which should be his course? Oswald Cray sat over his fire one cold evening after business was over, and deliberated upon it. Some weeks had gone on then. He leaned his elbow on the arm of his chair, and bent his cheek on his hand, and gazed abstractedly on the blaze. He shrank from the very idea of speaking to her. No formal engagement existed between them: it had been implied more than spoken; and he would be scarcely justified in say to her, "I cannot marry you now," considering that he had never in so many words asked her to marry him at all. She might regard it as a gratuitous insult.

But, putting that aside, he did not see his way clear to speak to her. What reason could he give for his withdrawal He could not set it down to his own caprice; and he could not—no, he could not—put forth to her the plea of her father's misdoing. He began to think it might be better to maintain silence, and so let the past and its words die away. If—

He was aroused from his train of thought by the entrance of a woman—a woman in a black bonnet, and sleeves turned up to the elbow, with a rather crusty expression of face. This was Mrs. Benn the housekeeper, cleaner, cook of the house. It did not lie in Mrs. Benn's province to wait on Mr. Oswald Cray, or she would probably have attired herself more in accordance with her duty. It lay in her husband's, and he had been sent out this evening by Mr. Oswald Cray on business connected with the firm. On cleaning days—and they occurred twice in the week—Mrs. Benn was wont to descend in, the morning in the black bonnet, and keep it on until she went to bed. It was not worn as bonnets are worn usually; the crown behind and the brim before; but was perched right on the top of her head, brim downwards and Mrs. Benn was under a firm persuasion that this kept her hair and her cap free from the dust she was wont to raise in sweeping. She was about forty, but looked, fifty, and her face had got a patch of black-lead upon it, and a nail had torn a rent in her check apron.

"Wouldn't you like the things taken away, sir?" she asked in a tone as crusty as her look. "I'm waiting to wash 'em up."

This recalled Oswald Cray's notice to the fact that the remains of his dinner were yet upon the table. He believed he had rung for them to be taken away when he turned to the fire; and there he had sat with his back to them since, never noticing that nobody had come to do it. It was now a little past seven, and Mrs. Benn had grown angry and indignant at the waiting.

"I declare I thought they had gone away," he said. "I suppose the bell did not ring. I am sure I touched it."

"No bell have rung at all," returned Mrs. Benn resentfully. "I stood down there with my hands afore me till the clock had gone seven, and then I thought I'd come up and see what was keeping 'em. You haven't ate much this evening, sir," she added, looking at the dish of steak and the potatoes. "I don't think you have eat much lately. Don't you feel well?"

"Well! I am very well," he replied carelessly, rising from his chair and stretching himself. "Is Benn not back yet?"

"No, he is not back," she returned, her tone becoming rather an explosive one, boding no good for the absent Mr. Benn. "He don't seem to hurry himself, he don't, though he knows if he didn't get back I should have to come up here: and very fit I be on my cleaning days to appear before a gentleman."

"Is it necessary to clean in a bonnet?" asked Oswald quietly.

"It's necessary to clean in something, sir, to protect one's head from the fluff and stuff that collects. One would wonder where it comes from, all in a week. I used to tie a apron over my cap, but it was always coming off, or else blowing its corners into the way of one's eyes."

Oswald laughed. He remembered the apron era, and the guy Mrs. Benn looked. For twelve years had she and her husband been the servants of that house. Formerly Mr. Bracknell, an old bachelor, had lived in it, and Benn and his wife waited on him, as they now did on Mr. Oswald Cray.

"Would you like tea this evening, sir?" she inquired. For sometimes Oswald took tea and sometimes he did not.

"Yes; if you bring it up directly. I am going out."

She went away with her tray of things. Down the first flight of stairs, past the offices, and down again to the kitchen. The ground floor of this house in Parliament Street was occupied by the offices of the firm, and partially so the floors above. Oswald Cray had two or three rooms for his own use; his sitting-room, not a very large one, being on the first floor.

His train of thought had been broken by the woman, and he did not recall it. He stepped into an adjoining apartment, lighted a shaded lamp, sat down, and began examining a drawing of some complicated plans. Pencil in hand, he was deep in the various mysteries pertaining to engineering, when he heard Mrs. Benn and the tea-tray. He finished marking off certain lines and strokes on a blank sheet of paper—which he did after a queer fashion, his eyes fixed on the drawing, and his fingers only appearing to guide the pencil—before he went in.

He had not hurried himself, and the tea must be getting cold. Mrs. Benn was in the habit of making it downstairs, so that he had no trouble. It was by no means a handsome tea equipage—party belonging, in fact, to Mrs. Benn herself. The black teapot had a chipped spout, and the black milk-jug had a fray on its handle, and the china tea-cup was cracked across. Oswald's china tea-service had been handsome once—or rather Mr. Bracknell's, for it was to that gentleman the things in the house belonged; but Mrs. Benn had what she herself called a "heavy hand at breakage," and two or three cups and saucers were all that remained. Oswald determined to buy himself a decent tea-set, but somehow he never thought of it, and the elegant equipage came up still.

He poured himself out a cup, stirred it, and then went for the sheet of paper on which he had been making the strokes and scrawls. Mrs. Benn knew her master well. He had said he was going out, but he was just as likely to remain over these strokes all the evening as to go out; perhaps, even, in forgetfulness keep her tea-things up until ten o'clock, or until she went for them. Oswald Cray was one whose heart was in his profession, and work was more pleasant to him than idleness.

He was busy still over this paper, neglecting his tea, when Mrs. Benn came in again. He thought she had come very soon for her tea-tray tonight. But she had not come for that.

"Here's company now, sir! A young lady wants to see you."

"A young lady!" repeated Oswald. "To see me?"

"Well, I suppose she's a young lady—from what one can see of her through her black veil; but she come to my kitchen bell only, when the knocker was a-staring her right in the face," returned Mrs. Benn. "She asked for you, sir. I said, was it any message I could take up, but she says she wants to speak to you herself."

"You can show her up."

Mrs. Benn accomplished this process in a summary manner. Going down the stairs to the hall, where she had left the applicant, she briefly said to her, "You can go up. First door you come to that's open"—and then left the lady to find her way. Had her husband, Benn, been at home, he would have asked her what she meant by introducing a visitor in that fashion to Mr. Oswald Cray; and he would probably have got for answer a sharp order to mind his own business. In point of fact, Mrs. Benn, on those two dark interludes of her weekly existence, cleaning days, had neither time nor temper to waste on superfluous ceremony.

Oswald Cray had bent over his paper again, attaching little importance to the advent of the visitor; he supposed it might be some messenger from one or other of the clerks. The footfall on the stairs was soft and light; Oswald's back was to the door, and his lines and marks were absorbing his attention.

"Mr. Oswald Cray?"

It was a sweet and pleasant and sensible voice, with a Scotch accent very perceptible to English ears. It was the voice of a lady, and Oswald Cray started up hastily, pencil in hand.

A short, slight, very young-looking woman, with a fair face and blue eyes, stood before him. Strictly speaking, there was no beauty whatever in the face, but it was so fair, so frank, so honest, with its steady good sense and its calm blue eyes, that Oswald Cray warmed to it at once. She was dressed plainly in black, and she threw back her crape veil to speak—as most sensible women like to do. To Oswald's eyes, seeing her by that light, she looked about one or two and twenty, as she had to Mrs. Benn: her light complexion, her small features, and her slight figure were all of that type that remain young a long while. In his surprise he did not for the moment speak, and she repeated the words, not as a question this time—

"You are Mr. Oswald Cray."

"That is my name," he answered, recovering his equanimity. "May I—"

"I come to you from my brother, Frank Allister," she interrupted. "I am Jane Allister."

She pronounced the name "Jean" as she had in fact been christened, but it generally gets corrupted into Jane by English ears and English tongues. Oswald so interpreted it. His whole face lighted up with a smile of welcome; it may be said of recognition. He had heard so much of this good sister from his friend Frank Allister.

"I am so glad you have come to him!" he warmly exclaimed, taking her hand. "Frank has almost pined for you: but he did not expect you yet. I seem to know you quite well: he has talked to me of you so much."

"Thank you; I'll take it," she said, in answer to the chair he offered. "And I will take off my fur," she added, unwinding a boa from her neck, and untying her bonnet-strings. "Your room feels very warm to one coming in from the keen air outside."

There was something in her frank manners that struck most pleasingly on the mind of Oswald. She sat there as confidingly in his room as though he had been her brother: a good, modest, single-minded woman, whom even a bad man could not do otherwise than respect.

"Yes, I came before Frank expected me;" she said. "I did not think I could have come so soon; but my friends kindly released me. You know my situation—why I could not come to him before."

"I know that you are"—Oswald hesitated for a moment, and then went bravely on. Before that clear eye of plain good sense there was no need to mince the matter, and pretend ignorance.

"I know that you are companion-attendant to a lady. And that you could not leave her."

"I have been companion and maid to her all in one," said Miss Allister. "When I and Frank had to go out into the world and do the best we could for ourselves, I was obliged to look out for what I was most fitted for. Our dead mother's brother offered to help Frank, and he paid the premium with him to this house, and assisted him otherwise, and I was very glad it should be so—"

"You mean Mr. Brown?" interrupted Oswald.

"Yes. He lived in London. My mother was English born and reared. He was a good friend to us so long as he lived. It was necessary that I should go out; and a situation offered in a lady's family, Mrs. Graham. She wanted some one who would be her companion, sit with her, read to her, some one well reared, of whom she might make an equal, but who would at the same time act as maid; and I took it. But perhaps you have heard all this from Frank?"

"No, not these past details. Though he has talked of you very much. He has told me"—Oswald broke into a frank smile as he said it—"that his sister Jane was worth her weight in gold."

"I should be sorry to think that most sisters are not worth as much as I am," she gravely answered. "I have but done my duty, so far as I could do it, and the worst of us ought to do no less. When Frank found I acted as maid to Mrs. Graham he was very much put out, and wanted me to give up the situation and seek a different one. But I laughed at him for a proud boy, and I have stayed on until now. What am I the worse for it? I dressed her, and served her, and when of late years she got ill and helpless, I nursed and fed her. I had become so useful to her—I must say, so indispensable—that when news reached me of Frank's illness, I could not quit her to come to him. I tried to see which way my duty lay; to leave her for my sick brother, or to leave my brother to strangers, and stay with my dying and helpless friend and mistress, Every week we expected would be her last; she has been slowly dying for these three months; and I felt that it would be wrong to abandon her. That, you see, is why I could not come to Frank."

"Is she dead?" asked Oswald.

"O yes. This mourning that I am wearing is for her. And as soon as it was possible after the funeral I came away. We had a long and bad passage, two days, and I did not reach Frank until three o'clock this afternoon."

"You should have come by land," observed Oswald.

"Nay, but that would have cost more," she simply answered. "And I know that Frank was better, so as to be in no vital hurry for my presence. I have come to you, sir, this evening, to ask your opinion of his state. Will you be so kind as to give it me?"

"First of all will you permit me to invite you to take a cup of tea?" replied Oswald, turning round to look at the tray, which was on the opposite side of the table, next the door.

"No, I thank you," she replied, "I gave Frank his tea before I came out, and took some with him. But will you let me pour out a cup for you? I saw that I interrupted you."

Before Oswald could decline, she had taken her gloves off, and was round at the tray, putting it in order. That a bachelor had been doing the honours of the ceremony was only too apparent. The teapot was stuck on the side of the tray, spout forwards; the milk-jug was not on the tray at all, but ever so far away on the table. Jane Allister had put all this to rights in a twinkling, and was pouring the slop of cold tea out of his tea-cup into the basin.

"Not for me," said Oswald, feeling as if he had known her for years. "You are very kind, but I have taken all I wish."

"Nay, not kind at all," she said, looking at him with some surprise. "I'd have been glad to do it for you."

Oswald had risen, and she came back from the tea-tray, and stood by him on the hearth-rug. Her bonnet still untied, her gloves off, her face and attitude full of repose, she looked like one in her own home.

"You'll tell me freely what you think of Frank?"

There was not the slightest shade of doubt in her voice; she evidently expected that he would tell it her; tell it her freely, as she asked for it. She stood with her fair face raised, her candid blue eyes thrown full up to his.

Oswald drew her chair forward for her, and took his own, pausing before he spoke. In good truth, he scarcely now knew what was his opinion of Frank Allister. It was one of those cases where the patient seems at death's door, and then, to the surprise of all, the disease takes a sudden turn, and appears to be almost gone. In the previous month, October, Oswald Cray had believed that a few days must see the end of Frank Allister; this, the close of November, he was apparently getting well all one way.

"I do not quite know how to answer you," Oswald began. "Five or six weeks ago Frank was so ill that I did not think there remained the least chance for him, but he has changed in a wonderful manner. But for the deceitfulness that is so characteristic of the disease, I should believe him to be getting well. Remembering that, I can only look upon it as a false improvement."

Jane Allister paused. "I suppose there is no doubt that his symptoms are those of consumption?"

"None."

"And consumption, if it does come on, is rarely if ever cured. Do you think it is?"

"Very rarely, I fear."

"But again, I have known patients who have displayed every symptom of consumption, have suffered much, and who have eventually got strong and hearty, and continued so."

"That is true," he assented. "There have been such instances. I wish I could satisfy you better, but indeed I do not know what to think. Mr. Bracknell asked me a day or two ago how Allister was getting on, and I answered as I answer you—that I really could not tell him."

"When I reached my brother's today and saw how well he appeared to be, so different from what I had expected to find him, I could not help expressing my surprise," said Miss Allister. "Frank gaily told me that his illness and its supposed danger had been all a mistake, and he had taken a new lease of life. I did not know what to think, what to believe; and I determined to come here and ask your opinion. I could not, you know, ask you before him."

"And I cannot give you a decisive one," repeated Oswald. "I can only hope that this improvement may go on to a complete restoration: and I should think it, but for the treacherous nature of the disease. Frank does certainly appear wonderfully strong and well. Even the doctor cannot say that it will not end in recovery."

"Frank wrote me word that you had caused him to see one of the great London physicians, and that the opinion was unfavourable. But that was when he was at the worst. You have been truly kind to him, Mr. Oswald Cray, and when I came here tonight I felt that I was coming to a friend."

"I should like to be your friend always," returned Oswald, in an unusual impulse. "I seem to have been so a long while, Frank has talked to me so much of you."

"Do you come to see him daily?"

"Not daily; but as often as I can. It is some distance from here."

"It is a long way. But I got misdirected.

"You surely did not walk?" exclaimed Oswald.

"To be sure I walked. How else should I come?"

"There are conveyances—cabs and omnibuses."

"But they cost money," she answered, with that frank, open plainness, which, in her, seemed so great a charm. "I am not come away to England devoid of means, but they will find plenty of outlets in necessary things, without being spent in superfluities. Anyway, they must be made to last both for me and Frank, until I can leave him and go out again. I'd not speak of these things to you, Mr. Oswald Cray, but that you must know all the particulars of our position."

She had risen as she spoke, and was now tying her bonnet-strings. Oswald picked up a glove which she dropped.

"And now I'll wish you goodnight," she continued, putting her hand frankly into his. "And I'd like to thank you with all my heart for what you have done for Frank; for the good friend you have been to him. You have brought to him help and comfort when there was nobody else in the world to bring it. I shall always thank you in my heart, Mr. Oswald Cray."

Oswald laughed the words off, and attended her downstairs, catching up his hat as he went through the hall. Mrs. Benn and her black bonnet came up the kitchen stairs.

"Goodnight," repeated Jane Allister.

"I am going with you," said Oswald.

She resisted the suggestion at first, saying she could find her way back quite well; but Oswald quietly carried his point.

He closed the door behind him, and offered his arm. She took it at once, thanking him in a staid old-fashioned manner. Mrs. Benn drew the door open and looked after them.

"Arm-in-arm!" ejaculated that lady. "And he bending of his head down to her to talk! Who on earth can she be?—coming after him to his house—and stopping up there in the parlour—and keeping up of the tea-things! It looks uncommon like as if he had took on a sweetheart. Only—So it's you at last, is it, Joe Benn! And what do you mean by stopping out like this?"

The concluding sentences were addressed to a respectable-looking man who approached the door. It was Joseph Benn, her husband, and the faithful servant of the firm.

"I couldn't make more haste," he quietly answered.

"Not make more haste! Don't tell me. Mr. Oswald Cray expected you were home an hour ago."

"Mr. Oswald Cray will be quite satisfied that I have not wasted my time when I tell him where I've been. Is he upstairs?"

"No, he is not," she sharply answered. "Satisfied, indeed! Yes, he looked satisfied when he saw me going up to wait upon him in this guise, and to show in his company? And me waiting a good mortal hour for his dinner-things, which he forgot was up which couldn't have happened if you'd been at your post to wait at table. You go and stop out again at his dinner-time, Joe Benn."

Joe Benn made no rejoinder; experience had taught him that it was best not. He passed her, and she shut the door with a bang.

CHAPTER XXVI

MORE INSTILLED DOUBT

The air was keen and frosty, and the flags of the streets were white and clean—not a common feature in November—as they walked forth. Oswald could but admire this straightforward Scotch girl, with her open speech and her plain good sense. She was so young in appearance that he could only think of her as a girl, though she had herself reminded him that she was older than Frank. This, as he knew, must bring her to a year or two past thirty: and in steadiness of manner and solid independence she was two-and-forty.

Reared in her Highland home, in every comfort for the earlier years of her life, she had since had to buffet with the world. Her mother, a widow since Frank was two years old, had enjoyed a good income, but it died with her. The uncle in London took Frank, who was then a youth; and Jane had to seek a situation. It was not easy to find. For a governess she was not qualified, so many of what are called accomplishments are essential nowadays, and Jane Allister had not learnt them. She had received a good education, but a strictly plain one.

Waiting and waiting! No situation offered itself; and when she heard of Mrs. Graham's she was well-nigh wearied out with the worst of all weariness—that of long-continued disappointment, of hope deferred. But for that weariness she might not have accepted a place where she was to be personal attendant as well as companion. She took it, determined to do her duty in it, to make the very best of it; and when her brother Frank wrote to her in a commotion from his distant home in London, where he was then with Bracknell and Street, she began by making the very best of it to him, gaily and lightly. Frank had the letter yet, in which she had jokingly called him—as she had just related to Mr. Oswald Cray—a proud boy, and recommended him to "bring down" his notions. Frank Allister had never been reconciled to it yet. Jane had grown to like it; and she had remained there all these years, conscientiously doing her duty.

"Have you lost a friend lately?" she inquired, in allusion to the crape band on Oswald's hat.

"Yes," he briefly answered, wincing at the question, could Jane Allister have seen it. All that past time of Lady Oswald's death, and the events attending it, caused an inward shiver whenever they were brought to his mind.

"It is a grievous thing to lose relatives when they are dear to us," remarked Jane. "There is an expression in your countenance at times that tells me you have some source of sorrow."

Whatever the expression she had noticed on his countenance, she would have seen a very marked one now, had they been, as before, face to face near a table-lamp. The old haughty pride came into it, and his brow flushed blood-red. Oswald Cray was one of the very last to tolerate that his secret feelings should be observed or commented upon. As she spoke it seemed to him as if the pain at his heart was read, his hopeless love for Sara Davenal laid bare.

"You are drawing a wrong inference, Miss Allister," he coldly said. "The friend I lost was neither near nor very dear to me. She was an old lady; a connection of my mother's family—Lady Oswald."

Jane marked the changed tone. She concluded the loss was one of pain to him, though he did not choose to say so, and she gathered her deductions that he was a man of great reticence of feeling. That he was a brave man and a good man, one in every way worthy of trust, of esteem, she knew from Frank long ago.

"Why, Neal! Is it you?"

Mr. Oswald Cray came to an abrupt halt in his surprise. Turning out of the door of a house that they were passing, so quickly as nearly to brush against him, was Dr. Davenal's manservant. Neal did not appear in the least taken to. He touched his hat and stood still with just the same equanimity that he would have done had he been waiting there for the passing of Mr. Oswald Cray.

"What has brought you to London, Neal? You have surely not left Dr. Davenal?"

"O no, sir, I have not left. A brother of mine, sir, has returned to England after an absence from it of many years, and a little property of ours, that couldn't be touched while he was away, is now being divided. I spoke to Dr. Davenal, and he gave me leave to come."

"Have you been up long?"

"Only three days, sir."

"Are they all well at Hallingham?"

"Quite well, sir. Mr. Cray hurt his arm as he was getting out of the doctor's carriage, and it was bound up for a week. But it is better."

"How did he manage that?"

"I don't think he knew, sir. His foot slipped as he was stepping out, and he swung round in some way, keeping hold of the carriage with his hand bent behind. It was rather a bad sprain."

"Miss Davenal is quite well?"

"Yes, sir. Miss Sara has had a cold lately, and is looking ill. The captain went abroad, sir, without coming to Hallingham, and they all felt it much."

Oswald bade the man goodnight, and walked on. He did not care, in his fastidious sensitiveness, to hear the looks of Sara Davenal commented on. If she did look ill, was it for his, Oswald's, sake!—or was she haunted with that unhappy secret which Neal had once so darkly hinted at?

Neal stood within the shade of the house looking after Mr. Oswald Cray, or rather after the young lady leaning on his arm. Neal was very curious as to this young lady, for young she looked in Neal's eyes. While apparently his whole attention was absorbed by his conversation with Mr. Oswald Cray, he had been studying the face turned to him; a fair and sensible face, as Mr. Neal could read, though less good-looking than Miss Sara Davenal's. What with Neal's legitimate observation and his illegitimate ferreting habits, he had contrived to arrive at a very ingenious conjecture of the tacit relations which had existed between Mr. Oswald Cray and Dr. Davenal's daughter; and Neal had of late been entertaining a rather shrew guess that Mr. Oswald Cray intended those relations to cease. He judged by the fact that the gentleman had never once, since Lady Oswald's funeral, been inside the doctor's doors. A formal call and a left card during one of his visits to Hallingham, had comprised all the notice taken. Tolerably safe appearances these, from which Neal drew his conclusions; and it perhaps may be pardoned one of Neal's conclusion-drawing mind, that he asked himself whether this young lady had superseded Miss Sara.

"It looks uncommonly like it," he repeated to himself, as his gaze followed them in the distance. "I should like to be certain, and to know who she is. She looks like a lady—and he'd not take up with anybody that was not one. Suppose I just see where they go? I have nothing particular on my hands this evening."

Gingerly treading the streets, as one who knows he is bent upon some surreptitious expedition is apt to tread them, Neal stepped along, keeping Mr. Oswald Cray and his companion sufficiently in view not to lose them. After a sufficiently long walk, they entered a house on the confines of Chelsea, bordering upon Brompton; the middle one of a row of moderate-sized houses, with small gardens before the doors. Neal saw Mr. Oswald Cray knock; and a young servant-maid admitted them.

But this left Neal as wise as before. He could see the house, could read the name of the Terrace, "Bangalore Terrace," in large black letters at either end; but this did not tell the name of the lady, or who she was; and Bangalore Terrace, though sufficiently respectable-looking, was certainly not the class of terrace to which it might be expected Mr. Oswald Cray would go for a wife.

Neal might have remained in his ignorance until now but for a fortunate accident. He was taking a last look at the house ere he turned away, at the light which shone behind the blinds of the first-floor windows, when the same servant who had opened the door came running out, her bonnet just perched on her head, its strings flying, and a jug and latch-key in her hand. As she passed Neal, the unsecured bonnet flew off, and Neal gallantly picked it up.

"I'm sure I'm much obliged to you, sir," she said, civilly. "Nasty tilting things these new-fangled bonnets be! One doesn't know whether to fix 'em atop of the back hair or under it."

"Can you tell me where a Miss—Miss—It is very unfortunate," broke off Neal in a tone of vexation. "I am in search of a young lady on a little matter of business, and I have forgotten her number. I think she lives at number five, but I am not sure."

"Number five's our house," said the girl, falling readily into the trap. "There ain't no young lady living there. There's three young ladies at number six, sir; perhaps its one o' them."

"No young lady living at number five!" repeated Neal

"No, there isn't. There's only my missis, and me, and two sons, and the gentleman what's ill on the first-floor. But perhaps you mean the sick gentleman's sister?" she added, the thought striking her. "She came to our house today, after a long journey all the way from Scotland, and she's going to stop with him."

Neal hardly thought this could apply. The young lady did not look as though she had just come off a long journey. "I don't know," said he. "What is her name!"

"Her name's the same as her brother's—Allister. If you'd been here two minutes sooner, sir, you might have seen her, for she's just come in with Mr. Oswald Cray. He's a gentleman who comes to see Mr. Allister."

"Allister!" The name was conclusive without the other testimony. Neal had once heard Mr. Oswald Cray describe his friend Allister's symptoms to Dr. Davenal. This fair girl with the pleasant face was Miss Allister, then!

"Ah, it's not the same," said he cautiously. "I must come down by daylight and look out. Goodnight, young woman; I am sorry to have detained you," he said as he walked away.

"Miss Allister!" repeated Neal to himself. "And so the brother's not dead yet I remember Mr. Oswald Cray saying he could not live a week, and that's three months ago."

Frank Allister was sitting between the fire and the table, reading by the light of the lamp, when they entered. He was slight and short, with a fair skin like his sister's, and a long thin neck. The room was very small, as the drawing-rooms (as they are called) in these unpretending suburban houses mostly are. What with the smallness of the room and the heavy closeness of the Brompton air, Jane Allister had felt stifled ever since she arrived that day. Frank, without rising from his seat, turned round and held his thin white fingers towards Oswald Cray, who grasped them.

"Jane, where have you been? I fancied you went out for but a few minutes' walk."

"I thought I would go as far as Mr. Oswald Cray's, Frank, and thank him for his attention to you," was her answer. "He has been so kind as to walk back with me."

"But how did you find your way?" cried Frank, wonderingly.

"I inquired. But I suppose I was stupid at understanding, for I went out of my way. What a busy place London is! I should get bewildered if I lived in it long."

Oswald Cray laughed. "It would be just the contrary, Miss Allister. The longer you lived in it the less bewildered you would be."

"Ah, yes," she answered; "use reconciles us to most things."

She had laid her bonnet and black shawl on a chair, and was going noiselessly from one part of the room to another, putting in order things that Frank had disturbed since her departure. He had wanted a particular book, and to get it had displaced two whole shelves of the cheffonier. The coal-box stood in the middle of the room, and a fancy china inkstand, the centre ornament of the cheffonier, lay on a chair. But the room, in its present general neatness and order, looked different from anything Oswald had ever seen it. Sometimes there had not been, as the saying runs, a place to sit upon. Frank ill, perhaps careless, had paid little heed to how his room went, and his landlady and his landlady's young maid had not much bestirred themselves in the matter. When Jane arrived she had taken in all the discomfort at the first glance, and did not sit down until it was remedied. Frank's bedchamber was at the back, opening from it, and there was a small room—a closet, in fact—at the bend of the stairs, which was to be Jane's.

Oswald followed her with his eyes, as she moved about in her simple usefulness. Perhaps he wished that he had such a sister to make his home a prettier place than it was made by Mrs. Benn. She was very small in figure, and the folds of her soft black dress scarcely added to its fulness. Her light hair was carried rather low on the cheeks, and twisted into a coil on her neck behind. Without her outdoor things she looked, if anything, younger than she did in them.

"And so you went to Mr. Oswald Cray's, inquiring your way!" cried Frank. "I say, young lady, that's not the fashion of doing things in London."

"May be not," answered Jane. "I daresay I and London shall not agree in our notions of fashion. Have you taken your milk, Frank!"

"I should think so. It was smoked again."

"Smoked!" cried Jane, turning round and looking at him.

"It generally is smoked," continued Frank. "I think their saucepans downstairs must be constructed on the plan of letting the smoke in."

Jane said no more. She inwardly resolved that neither Frank's milk nor anything else that he took should be smoked in future.

"Why don't you sit down, Oswald. Are you afraid of Jane?"

"Not very much," Oswald answered, looking round at her with a smile. "The fact is, Frank, I have some work to do at home tonight, and must get back."

"Plans to go over?"

"That and other things."

"I shall soon be well enough to come out again and go to work," resumed Frank Allister; and his confident tone proved how firm was his belief in his own words. "Will Bracknell and Street take me on again?"

"I think you will soon be out if you go on improving at this rate," answered Oswald, ignoring the last portion of Frank's words. "You look better this evening than you have looked yet."

"Oh, I am all right. But of course I look better, now Jane's here. Nearly the first thing she did was to part and brush my hair, and make me put on a clean collar. Only fancy her coming upon me today without warning! When the girl came up to say there was a lady at the door in a cab for Mr. Allister, I thought of anybody rather than Jane."

Oswald Cray wished them goodnight, and walked leisurely home. He really had some work to do, but he could have remained longer with them, only that he thought they might prefer to be alone on this the first evening of the sister's arrival. They had been apart for so many years.

Oswald let himself in with his latch-key. It must be supposed that Mrs. Benn heard him; for she came running up the kitchen stairs, and held put something to him under the light of the hall lamp. It appeared to be a piece of narrow black ribbon, about a third of a yard in length.

"When I had got the tea-tray down in the kitchen, sir, I found this a-hanging to it. I suppose the young lady that was with you upstairs left it here."

There was little doubt that Jane had left it. A wrist-ribbon probably, inadvertently untied in pulling off her glove. Oswald looked at the woman—at her crusty face, where the pert curiosity induced by the visit was not yet subdued. A curiosity he judged it well to satisfy.

"Did you know who that lady was, Mrs. Benn?"

"No, sir."

"It was poor Mr. Allister's sister. She has come all the way from Scotland to nurse him." The crustiness disappeared; the face lighted up with a better feeling. Mr. Allister had been a favourite of Mrs. Benn's, and if she could be sorry for anybody's illness, she was sorry for his.

"Mr. Allister's sister! If I had but known it, sir! What a pleasant-speaking young lady she is." Following his wife up the kitchen stairs, had come Benn. He waited until this colloquy was over, and then began to speak on his own account.

"A gentleman is waiting for you in your sitting-room, sir."

"Who is it?" asked Oswald.

"I think he's a stranger, sir. I don't remember to have seen him before."

Oswald proceeded upstairs. Standing at the side of the room, facing the door as he opened it, his gloves on and his hat in his hand, was Neal. And so much like a gentleman did he really look that Mr. Joseph Benn's mistake was a perfectly natural one.

"I have taken the liberty of intruding upon you, sir, and of asking to wait until you returned, to inquire whether I can convey anything for you to Hallingham. You had hardly left me, sir, in the street, when I remembered how very remiss it was in me not to ask you. Unless I have a letter from the doctor tomorrow morning, according me a day or two's more grace, which I have written for, I shall leave tomorrow evening. If I can do anything there for you, sir, or be of use to you in anyway, you may command me."

"Thank you, Neal; there's nothing I want done. I expect to go down myself next week. Come to the fire and warm yourself this cold night. Sit down."

Neal came forward nearer the fire; but he did not avail himself of the invitation to sit. Oswald inquired if he would like some refreshment, but he declined.

"Have they heard from Captain Davenal yet, do you know?" Oswald asked.

"I think not, sir. I believe they were expecting letters from Malta when I left."

"I wish he could have gone down for a short while. I am sure the doctor felt it."

"There's no doubt he did, sir, very much," returned Neal, with warm sympathy in his low, respectful tone. "I grieve to say, sir, that the doctor appears to be very much changed. He is more like one suffering from some inward painful illness than anything else."

"Of body or of mind?" involuntarily asked Oswald, speaking on the moment's impulse. And however he may have regretted the question, he could not recall it.

"I should say of mind, sir. Since the night of—of Lady Oswald's death, he has been a changed man."

Mr. Oswald Cray made no answer whatever to the allusion; he evidently declined to enter upon that unsatisfactory topic. Neal resumed.

"There are going to be changes in our house, sir; it is to be conducted with more regard to economy. Watton is to leave, and I am not sure but I am also. Miss Davenal does not wish any changes to be made, but the doctor says it is necessary."

"On the score of economy?"

"Yes, sir, on the score of economy. I heard him talking of it to Miss Sara; he said if the present rate of expense was to go on, together with the heavy sum that must now go from him yearly as hush-money, he should not keep his head above water. Miss Davenal, who does not understand why any retrenchment should be made, opposes it entirely."

Every fibre in Oswald Cray's heart resented the words—he could not bear that such should be spoken out boldly to him, no matter what their truth might be. Neal's innocent eyes noticed the sudden flush upon his face.

"I think you must be mistaken, Neal. Hush-money! Dr. Davenal would scarcely use the term to his daughter."

"Not that precise term, perhaps, sir, but certainly something equivalent to it. There is a rumour in the town, sir, that he intends to resign to the relatives the legacy left to him by my lady, or part of it."

"Indeed?"

"People have talked a great deal, I fancy, sir, and it has reached the doctor's ears. Perhaps, sir, if I may venture to say it to you, he may be afraid to keep it. The injustice of the bequest might lead to some investigation which—which would be inconvenient to Dr. Davenal."

"Neal, I'd rather not enter upon these topics," said Oswald, in a clear, resolute tone. "Things which appear dubious to us may be explainable by Dr. Davenal. At any rate, it is neither your business nor mine."

And by those firm words Neal knew that Mr. Oswald Cray had, so to say, washed his hands of the affair, and did not mean to take it up in anyway. Neal's hopes had tended to the contrary, and it was a little checkmate.

"I thought I would presume to ask you, sir, whether you might not be soon requiring a personal attendant," he resumed, sliding easily out of his disappointment, and giving no token of it, "Should I be leaving the doctor, it would afford me greater pleasure to serve you, sir, than any one else, now my late lady's gone."

Oswald laughed—he could not help it. "A valet for me, Neal! No, that would never do under present circumstances. You will be at no fault for a good place, rely upon it, should you leave Dr. Davenal. The good places will be only too glad to contend for you."

Neal did not dispute the assertion. What his precise motive might have been for wishing to serve Mr. Oswald Cray, when he could no doubt dispose of himself so much more advantageously, was best known to himself. He made his adieu in his usual quiet and respectful fashion, and took his departure, leaving Oswald Cray to the reminiscences of the interview. Oswald sat over the fire as oblivious of the work he had to do as he had been of the dinner-things earlier in the evening. Will it be believed that the hint dropped by Neal—that Dr. Davenal might be giving up the money because he dared not risk the danger of any investigation—was grating unpleasantly on the brain of Oswald? To do Neal justice so far, he himself fully believed that such was the motive of Dr. Davenal, and he had spoken for once with an earnest truthfulness that is never without its weight.

It was unfortunate that this aspect of the affair should have been the first given to Oswald Cray. Had he simply heard that Dr. Davenal was declining the bequest in his generous consideration for the

Stephensons, it might perhaps have shaken his doubts of that other dark story, since the only motive the doctor could possibly have had throughout (as Oswald's mind had argued), was the acquirement of the money. But if he was declining the money through fear, it only served to make these doubts the greater. It was most unfortunate, I say, that this aspect of the affair should have been imparted to him; for we all know how little, how very little, will serve to strengthen suspicions once aroused.

He sat on with his unhappy thoughts far into the night, the image of Sara Davenal ever before him. Never had his love for her been more ardently tender, never had the cruelty of their obligatory separation been so keenly present to his soul.

CHAPTER XXVII

AN INCLEMENT AFTERNOON

December came in with a drizzling rain, which lasted a day or two. A cold, bleak, windy rain, rendering outdoor life miserable. As Sara Davenal sat at her chamber window, looking into the street, the shivering and uncomfortable appearance presented by the few passers-by might have excited her compassion.

But it did not. Truth to say, Sara Davenal had too much need of compassion herself just now to waste it upon street passengers. The greatest blight that can possibly fall upon the inward life of a woman had fallen upon hers. Oswald Cray was faithless. She knew not how, she knew not why; she only judged by his conduct that it must be so. He had been two or three times to Hallingham, and had shunned her; had shunned them altogether. There could be no better proof. One of the visits he had remained three days; therefore he had not want of time to plead as his excuse. He had called at the door, inquired for Miss Davenal, and upon Neal's answering that Miss Davenal was out, he had handed in cards. For Sara he had not asked at all, and he had not been near the house since.

Sara could do nothing. She could only accept this change in him and bear it in silence. Had she been asked to pin her faith on the truth and honour of any living man, she would have pinned it on Oswald Cray's. Not because she loved him, not because it was to her his allegiance was certainly due, but because she believed him to be, of all others, the very soul of chivalrous integrity. But that he had changed to her there could not be a shadow of doubt: his conduct proved it. He had silently broken off all relations with her, and given no token of what his motive could be.

That some cause, just or unjust, had led to it, she yet did him the justice to believe; he was the last man so to act from caprice, or from a totally unworthy motive. And she knew he had loved her. In vain she asked herself what this cause could be; but there were moments when a doubt of whether the terrible secret, which had been imparted that past night to Dr. Davenal, could have become known to Oswald Cray. If so—why, then, in his high honour, his sensitive pride, he had perhaps decided that she was no fit wife for him. And Sara could not say that he had so decided unjustifiably. Whatever the cause, they were separated.

They were separated. And the sunshine of her life was over. Oh, the bitter anguish that it cost! There is no pain, no anguish, that this world and its many troubles can bring, like unto it—the finding one false, upon whom love, in all the freshness of its first feeling, has been lavished. The bright green of life's verdure is gone; the rich blue has faded from the wintry sky.

Sara said nothing, but the doctor spoke openly of the strange conduct of Mr. Oswald Cray.

"I know nothing that can have offended him," he observed; "unless he has chosen to take umbrage at the money's having been left to me."

"Nonsense," said Miss Davenal; "it's not that. Mr. Oswald Cray did not want the money for himself; would not, it is said, have accepted it. It is not that."

And "It is not that," echoed Sarah Davenal's heart.

"What else is it, then?" said the doctor. "Nobody in this house has done anything to offend him. You have not, I suppose, Sara,"—suddenly turning upon her, as a faint doubt flashed into his mind, never before admitted to it.

The question brought to her she knew not what of emotion. She answered it with an outward appearance of calmness, save for the burning red that dyed her face.

"Nothing, papa. The last time I spoke to Mr. Oswald Cray was the night of the accident. We parted quite good friends—as we always had parted."

And the sweet words whispered by Oswald rose up before her as she spoke. What a contrast! that time and this!

"Just so," replied the doctor. "There has been nothing whatever to cause this coolness on his part, except the business of the money. Well, as I give it back to the family, perhaps my gentleman will come round. Rely upon it, that pride of his has been touched in some manner or other?"

But the weeks had gone on, and December was in, and the gentleman had not "come round" yet. Sara Davenal sat at her bedroom window, all her shivering misery only too palpably present to her, as she watched the cold rain falling on the wet streets, in the gloomy twilight of the afternoon.

She saw Roger bring the carriage round. She saw her father go out from the house and step into it. It was the open carriage, but the head was up, and Roger and his master were sheltered from the rain. It was not the usual hour of Dr. Davenal's going out, but the bad day had kept patients from calling on him, and a message had just been delivered saying that a lady whom he attended, Mrs. Scott, was worse.

Sara heard the house clock strike four, and the lamps were already lighted in the streets. Night was coming on earlier than usual. The gleaming of the pools of water in the rays of the gas lamps did not tend to add to the cheerfulness of the scene; and Sara, with a shiver that she could not suppress, quitted her room and went downstairs.

The blaze and warmth of the dining-room, as seen through the open door, was a welcome sight. She went in, and knelt down before the fire on the hearth-rug, and laid her aching head for shelter against the side of the marble mantelpiece, and stayed there until disturbed by the entrance of Miss Davenal.

"Neal's come home," announced Miss Davenal.

"Is he?" apathetically answered Sara.

"I saw him go by with his portmanteau. What are you down there for, Sara, roasting your face? Have you no regard for your complexion?"

"I am not roasting it, aunt. My face is quite in the shade."

"But you are roasting it. What's the use of telling me that? Had I allowed the fire to burn my face at your age, do you suppose I should have retained any delicacy of akin? Get up from the fire."

Sara rose wearily. She sat down in a chair opposite to the one her aunt had taken, and let her hands fall listlessly in her lap.

"Have any patients been here this afternoon?"

"I think not, Aunt Bettina. I suppose it was too wet for them to come out."

"Have you been drawing?"

"Not this gloomy day. I like a good light for it."

"It strikes me you have become very idle lately, Miss Sara Davenal! Do you think that time was bestowed upon us to be wasted?"

A faint blush rose to Sara's cheek. In these, the early days of her bitter sorrow, she feared she had been idle. What with the shock brought upon her by that ominous secret, and the cruel pain caused by the falsity of Oswald Cray, her tribulation had been well-nigh greater than she could bear.

"Ring the bell," said Miss Davenal.

Sara rose from her chair and rang it. It was answered by Jessy.

"Tell Neal I shall be glad to see him."

Neal appeared in answer to the summons. His London journey had been prolonged by the permission of the doctor, and he had but now returned. In he came, just the same as usual, his white necktie spotless, his black clothes without a crease.

"So you are back, Neal?" said Miss Davenal. "I am very glad to see you. And pray have you arranged all your business satisfactorily?—secured your share of the money?"

"Entirely so, thank you, ma'am," replied Neal, advancing nearer to his mistress that he might be heard. "I am pleased to find all well at home, ma'am."

"You have been away longer than you intended to be, Neal."

"Yes, ma'am. I wrote to my master stating why it was necessary that I should, if possible, prolong my stay, and he kindly permitted it. I saw Mr. Oswald Cray, ma'am, while I was in London," Neal added as a gratuitous piece of information.

"You did what?" asked Miss Davenal, while Sara turned and stood with her back to them, looking at the fire.

"I saw Mr. Oswald Cray, ma'am."

"Oh, indeed. And where did you see him?"

"I met him one night in London, ma'am. He was walking with a young lady."

"Saw him walking at night with a young lady?" repeated Miss Bettina, in rather a snappish tone; for as a general rule she did not approve of young ladies and gentlemen walking together, especially at night.

"She seemed a very nice young lady, ma'am, young and pretty," continued Neal, who was getting a little exasperated at the face at Miss Sara Davenal being hidden from his view. "I believe it was Miss Allister, the sister of a gentleman with whom Mr. Oswald Cray is very intimate."

"Well, I am glad you are back, Neal," concluded Miss Davenal. "Things have gone all at sixes and sevens without you."

Neal retired. And Sara, in her still attitude before the fire, repeated the words over and over again to her beating heart. A lady young and pretty! walking with him in the evening hours—the sister of the friend with whom he was so intimate! She laid her hand upon her bosom, if that might still the tumult within, in all the sickness of incipient jealousy. Until that moment Sara Davenal had never known how she had clung to hope in her heart of hearts. While saying to herself, He is lost to me for ever, this undercurrent of hope had been ever ready to breathe a whisper that the cloud might some time be cleared up, that he might return. Now the scales were rudely torn from her eyes, and reason suggested that his slighting treatment of her might proceed from a different cause than any she had ever glanced at.

"What was it Neal said, Sara? That the pretty lady walking with Oswald Cray was somebody's sister?"

Sara turned in her pain to answer her aunt. "Mr. Allister's sister, he said."

"Who's Mr. Allister?"

"A sick gentleman who used to be at Bracknell and Street's. I remember that night of the railway accident Mr. Oswald Cray was obliged to return to town because he had promised to spend—to spend the Sunday with him."

An idea darting into her brain had caused her to hesitate. Had Oswald Cray's anxiety to return to town been prompted by the wish to be with the sister as well as the brother? Sara felt her brow turn moist and cold.

"Young and pretty!" repeated Miss Davenal. "Who knows but they may be engaged? Ah! it's Caroline who should have had Oswald Cray."

Meanwhile Dr. Davenal had been driven to the house of Mrs. Scott. It was not very far from his own home, about two streets only. Time had been, and not so far back, when Dr. Davenal would not have thought of ordering his carriage for so short a distance, would have braved the inclemencies of the weather, the drifting rain, the cutting wind, and walked it. But the doctor had been growing ill both in body and mind; since the night of that fatal revelation, whatever it may have been, he seemed to have become in feelings like an old man, needing all the care and help of one. As he had looked from his window that afternoon, a sort of shudder at the outdoor weather came over him; a feeling as if he could not and ought not to venture out in it. And he told Roger to bring round the carriage.

He stepped out of the carriage and entered Mrs. Scott's, leaving Roger snugly ensconced under the shelter of the head and the horses steaming in the rain. But when the doctor reached his patient's bed, he found her so considerably and alarmingly worse that he could not yet think of leaving her. She was a great and real sufferer; not as poor Lady Oswald had been, an imaginary one; and in the last week or two her symptoms had assumed a dangerous character. The doctor thought of Roger and his horses, and went down.

"I shall not be ready to come home this hour, Roger. Better go back and put the horses up. You can come for me at five." So Roger, nothing loth, turned his horses round and went home. And Dr. Davenal, with another shudder, and a very perceptible one, hastened indoors from the beating rain.

"What's the matter with me this afternoon?" he asked, half angry that any such sort of sensation should come over him.

Is the body at times more sensitive to outward influences than it is at others, rendering it susceptible to take any ill that may be abroad? Is it more liable to cold, to fever, to other ailments? Or can it be that the mind has so great an influence over the body that the very fact of dreading these ills predisposes us to take them? If ever Dr. Davenal sensibly shrank from an encounter with the outdoor weather, it was on that afternoon. He could not remember so to have shrunk from it in all his life.

Mrs. Scott's room was hot. The fire was large, every breath of air excluded, and two large gas-burners flamed away, adding to the heat. As Dr. Davenal sat there he became first at ease in the genial warmth, then hot, and subsequently as moist as though he were breathing the atmosphere of a baker's oven. He had had many a battle with this same Mrs. Scott over the heated rooms she loved to indulge in, but he had not conquered yet.

It was not much above half-past four when the doctor was beckoned out of the room. He was wanted downstairs. There stood Julius Wild, and Mr. Julius Wild was in as white a heat with running as Dr. Davenal was with that pernicious atmosphere above.

"I have been about everywhere, sir, trying to find you," he began out of breath. "At last I bethought myself of asking your coachman at the stables if he knew, and he said you were at Mrs. Scott's. You are wanted in the accident-ward, sir, as quick as you can get there."

"What has come in?" inquired Dr. Davenal.

"A young man fell on his head from the very top of that scaffolding in High Street, sir. It is a dreadful case, and the house-surgeon does not think he can be saved, even with the operation. The top of the head is crushed in. Mr. Berry and Dr. Ford and some more are there, but they wish for you." Dr. Davenal did not delay a moment. In a case of real necessity he threw aside all thought of precaution for himself. If human skill could save the life of this poor young man, he knew that his could, and he knew that perhaps his was the only hand in Hallingham which could successfully carry through the critical and delicate operation he suspected must be performed.

He had no greatcoat with him, and he started off at once with Julius Wild, heated as he was. The rain beat against him in a torrent, for it poured now; the wind whirled itself in eddies about his person. No umbrella could live in it; one which the doctor had borrowed from the hall of Mrs. Scott was turned inside out ere he had taken many steps.

"A rough night, sir," remarked the young embryo surgeon, as he kept by his side.

"It is that," said Dr. Davenal.

Away they splashed through the muddy pools in the streets. It was quite dark now, with the unusually gloomy evening, and the gas lamps only served to mislead their eyesight in the haste they had to make. There could be no waiting to pick the way. The Infirmary was at a considerable distance from Mrs. Scott's, and ere they reached it the cold had struck to one of them. The one was not Julius Wild.

When they came in view of the Infirmary, Julius Wild ran forward to give notice that the doctor was approaching. Two or three of the medical men were in the great hall looking out for him; Mark Cray was one of them. The news of the accident had travelled in the town, and the surgeons attached to the Infirmary were collecting there.

"We began to despair of you," cried Dr. Ford, "and there's no time to be lost. I was just recommending Mr. Cray to be the one to officiate." Dr. Davenal turned his eye with an eagle glance on Mark Cray ere the words had well left Dr. Ford's lips. The look, the warning conveyed in it, was involuntary. Had Mark actually acceded to the recommendation, the look could scarcely have been sterner. Mark coloured under it, and his thoughts went back to Lady Oswald. Never, in Dr. Davenal's presence, must he attempt to try his skill again.

CHAPTER XXVIII

THE LAST MEETING

The night's work told on Dr. Davenal. The soaking rain, the chilling wind, had struck inward the perspiration which Mrs. Scott's heated room had induced. On the next day he was visibly ill. Sara noticed it, and begged him not to go out.

"Not go out, child? I must go out."

"But you are not in a state for it. I am sure you are very ill."

"I caught cold last night; that's what it is. It will go off in a day or two."

"Yes if you will lie by and nurse yourself. Not if you go out to make it worse."

"I have never lain by in all my life, Sara. A doctor has no time for it. What would become of my patients?"

He went out to his carriage, then waiting for him. The close carriage. Bright as the day was—for the weather had changed—it was the close carriage that had been ordered round by the doctor.

"Is master ill, I wonder?" thought Roger, when he found it was only to pay the daily round of near visits.

As the doctor went out at the gate it happened that Oswald Cray was passing. And Mr. Oswald Cray quite started when he saw Dr. Davenal, the change in him was so great.

It was impossible for either of them to pass the other, had they so wished it, without being guilty of absolute rudeness, and they stopped simultaneously.

"You are ill, Dr. Davenal?" exclaimed Oswald, speaking impulsively.

"Middling. I have got a cold hanging about me. We have had some bad weather here."

It cannot be denied that Dr. Davenal's tone and manner betrayed a coldness never yet offered to Oswald Cray. Generous man though he was by nature, as little prone to take offence as most people, he did think that Oswald Cray's slighting conduct had been unjustifiable, and he could not help showing his sense of it.

They stood a moment in silence, Oswald marking the ravages illness or something else had made on the doctor's face and form. His figure was drooping now, his face was careworn; but the sickness looked to be of mind more than of body. Unfortunately those miserable suspicions instilled into Oswald Cray's brain arose now with redoubled force, and a question suggested itself—could anything save remorse change a man as he had changed, in the short space of time?

"You are a stranger now, Mr. Oswald Cray. What has kept you from us?"

"The last time I called you were all out," he answered, somewhat evasively.

"And you could not call again! As you please, of course," continued the doctor, as Oswald's feet, took a somewhat repellant turn, and the Oswald pride became rather too conspicuous. "I had wished to say a word or two to you with regard to the will made by Lady Oswald; but perhaps you do not care to hear it."

"Anything that you, or I, or any one else can say, will not alter the will, Dr. Davenal. And it does not in the least concern me."

"But I think you are resenting it in your heart, for all that."

Ah, what cross-purposes they were at! Oswald had not resented that; and all his fiery pride rose up to boiling heat at being accused of it. He had deemed that to make Dr. Davenal the inheritor was unjust to the nephews of Lady Oswald, and he had felt for them; but he had not resented it, even at heart. He spoke the literal truth when he said it was a matter that did not concern him. If the heavy cloud of misapprehension between them could but have cleared itself away!

"Will you be kind enough to understand me once for all, Dr. Davenal?" he haughtily said. "Lady Oswald's money, either before her death or after it, never was, nor could be, any concern of mine. I do not claim a right to give so much as an opinion upon her acts in regard to it; in fact I have no such right. Had she chosen to fling the money into the sea, to benefit nobody, she might have done so, for any wish of mine upon the point. I felt a passing sorrow for the Stephensons when I saw their disappointment, but I did not permit myself to judge so far as to say that Lady Oswald had done wrong. It was no affair of mine," he emphatically added, "and I did not make it one."

In spite of his impressive denial, Dr. Davenal did not believe him. Whence, else, the haughty resentment that shone forth from every line of his features? Whence, else, his studied absence from the house, his altogether slighting conduct? Dr. Davenal made one more effort at concession, at subduing his unfounded prejudices.

"I can assure you I resented the will—if I may so say it. I resented it for the Stephensons' sake, and felt myself a pitiful usurper. Nothing would have induced me to accept that money, Mr. Oswald Cray; and steps are being taken to refund it, every shilling, to the Stephensons."

"Ah," remarked Oswald, "I heard something of that. Had it been willed to me I should have done the same."

He held himself rigidly erect as he said it. There was no unbending of the hard brow, there was no faint smile to break the haughty curve of the lip. That poisonous hint dropped by Neal—that the money was about to be restored through fear—was uncomfortably present to Oswald then. Dr. Davenal saw that the resentment, whatever its cause, was immovable, and he stepped into his carriage without shaking hands.

"Good-morning to you, Mr. Oswald Cray."

And then the reaction set in in Oswald Cray's mind, and he began to blush for his discourtesy. The careworn face, the feeble form, haunted him throughout the day, and he began to ask himself, what if all his premises were wrong—if appearances and Neal's tale had been deceitful—if he had done the doctor grievous ill in his heart I It was but the reaction, I say, the repentance arising from his own haughty discourtesy, which he felt had been more offensively palpable than it need have been; but it clung to him for hours, haunting him in all the business that he had to transact.

It was somewhat strange that just when this new feeling was upon him he should encounter Sara Davenal. They met in a lonely place—the once-famed graveyard at the back of the Abbey.

His business for the day over, Oswald Cray was going to pay a visit to Mark and his wife. He was nearer the back of the Abbey than the front, and, ignoring ceremony, intended to enter by the small grated door, a relic of the old Abbey, which divided the graveyard from one of the long Abbey passages. In passing the tombstone already mentioned, Oswald turned his eyes down upon it: in the bright moonlight—for never had the moon been brighter—he could almost trace the letters: the next moment a noise in front attracted his attention—the closing of the grated door. There stood Sara Davenal. She had stayed with Mrs. Cray later than she intended, and was hastening home to dinner: in leaving the Abbey by this back entrance a few minutes of the road were saved.

They met face to face. Sara's heart stood still, and her countenance changed from white to red with emotion. And Oswald?—all the love that he had been endeavouring to suppress returned in its deepest force.

Ah, it is of no use! Try as we may, we cannot evade the laws of nature; we cannot bend them to our own will. In spite of the previous resolutions of weeks to forget her, Oswald Cray stood there knowing that he loved her above everything on earth.

"How are you, Sara?"

He put out his hand to her in all calm self-possession; he spoke the salutation with quiet equanimity; but as Sara looked in his face she knew that his agitation was not in reality less than hers. She said a few confused words in explanation of her being there at that hour, and alone. On calling that afternoon she had found Caroline not well, and had stayed with her to the last moment, as Mark was in the country.

Then for a whole minute there was a silence. Perhaps neither could speak. Sara put an end to it by turning towards the gate.

"You will let me see you home, as you are alone?"

"No, thank you," she answered. "There is nothing to hurt me. It is as light as day."

He did not press it. He seemed half-paralysed with indecision. Sara wished him good night, and he responded to it, and once more shook hands, all mechanically.

But as she was going through the gate, she turned to speak, a question having occurred to her. One moment longer, and he had arrested her progress.

"There are two or three books at our house belonging to you," she said. "What is to be done with them? Shall they be sent to the Apple Tree?"

He caught her hands; he drew her from the gate into the bright moonlight. He could not let her go without a word of explanation; the cruelty of visiting upon her her father's sin was very present to him then.

"Are we to part thus for ever, Sara?"

Surely that question was cruel! It was not she who had instituted the parting; it was himself. She did not so much as know its cause.

"May we not meet once in a way, as friends?" he continued. "I dare not ask for more now."

That he loved her still was all too evident. And Sara took courage to gasp forth a question. In these moments of agitation the cold conventionalities of the world are sometimes set aside.

"What has been the matter? How have we offended you?"

"You have not offended me," he answered, his agitation almost irrepressible. "I love you more than I ever did; this one moment of meeting has proved it to me. I could lay down my life for you, Sara; I could sacrifice all, save honour, for you. And you? You have not changed?—you love me still?"

"Yes," she gasped, unable to deny the truth, too miserable to care to suppress it.

"And yet we must part! we must go forth on our separate paths, striving to forget. But when our lives shall end, Sara, we shall neither of us have loved another as we love now."

Her very heart seemed to shiver; the fiat was all too plainly expressed. But she stood there quietly, waiting for more, her hand in his.

"I would have forfeited half my future life, I would have given all its benefits to be able to call you mine. The blow upon me has been very bitter."

"What blow?" she murmured.

"I cannot tell it you," he cried, after a struggle. "Not to you can I speak of it."

"But you must," she rejoined, the words breaking from her in her agony. "You have said too much, or too little."

"I have—Heaven help me! Can you not guess what it is that has caused this?"

"N—o," she faltered. But even as the word left her lips there rose up before her the secret of that dreadful night—with the suspicion that Oswald had in some unaccountable manner become cognisant of it.

"I loved you as I believe man never yet loved, Sara; I looked forward to years of happiness with you; I expected you to be my wife. And—and—I cannot go on!" he broke off. "I cannot speak of this to you."

The tears were rolling down her pale face. "You must not leave me in suspense, Oswald. It may be better for us both that you should speak out freely."

Yes, it might be better for them both; at any rate he felt that no choice was left to him now. He drew nearer to her and lowered his voice to a whisper.

"Is there no—Heaven pardon me for speaking the word to you, Sara!—disgraceful secret attaching now to—to your family? One which would render it impossible for a man of honour to—"

He would not say more; he had said enough; and he felt the words to his heart's core. Whatever pain they may have brought to her, they inflicted tenfold more upon him. With a low cry, she flung her hands before her face.

"Is it so, Sara?"

"It is. How did you hear of it?"

"The whisper came to me. Some people might—might—call it murder."

"No, no!" she broke forth in her pain. "It surely was not so bad as that. They kept the details from me, Oswald; but it could not have been so bad as that."

The words fell on his heart like an ice-bolt. Unconsciously to himself he had been hoping that she might disprove the tale. For that purpose he had whispered to her of the worst: but it seemed that she could not deny it. It was quite enough, and he quitted the subject abruptly.

"God bless you, my darling, for ever and for ever," he said, taking her hands in his. "I do not respect or love you less; but I cannot—I cannot—you know what I would say. It is a cruel fate upon me, as upon you; and for the present, for both our sakes, it may be better that our paths in life should lie apart. After awhile we may meet again, as friends, and continue to be such throughout life."

The tears had dried on her face, as it was lifted in the moonlight, its expression one living agony. But there was no resentment in it; on the contrary, she fully justified him. Her hands lingered in his with a farewell pressure, and she strove to re-echo the blessing he had given.

They parted, each going a different way. Oswald Cray, in no mood for the Abbey now, struck off towards the "Apple Tree;" Sara, drawing her veil over her face, went on to her home.

And so the dream was over. The dream which she had long been unconsciously cherishing of what a meeting between them might bring about, was over; and Sara Davenal had been rudely awakened to stern reality.

CHAPTER XXIX

A SPECIAL FAVOUR FOR NEAL

The whole night subsequent to the meeting in the Abbey graveyard with Oswald Cray, did Sara lie awake, striving to battle with her pain. It was very sore to bear. She knew now the cause of his absenting himself; and she knew that they were lost to each other for ever. It is the worst pain that a woman can be called upon to endure; no subsequent tribulation in life can equal its keen anguish.

Ten times in the night she prayed for help—for strength to support, and live, through her mind's trouble. She did not pray that it might be taken from her; that was hopeless; she knew that weeks and months must elapse before even the first brunt would lose its force; that years must roll on before tranquillity could come.

She did not blame Oswald Cray. She believed that that unhappy secret, of the precise nature of which she was yet in ignorance, had become known to him: how, she could not conjecture. Perhaps he knew it in all its terrible details—and that these were terrible, she doubted less now than ever. Were they not— ay, she fully believed it?—shortening her father's life? What had been that awful word spoken by Oswald Cray?—though she could not believe it to be so bad as that. But she knew that it was something to bring disgrace and danger in its train; and she fully justified Oswald Cray in the step he had taken. Still she thought that he should have come to her in the first onset and plainly said, "Such and such a thing has come to my knowledge, and therefore we must part." He had not done this; he had left her for weeks to the slow torture of suspense—and yet that very suspense was more tolerable than the certainty now arrived at. Oh, the dull dead pain that lay on her heart!—never for a long, long while to be lifted from it.

She strove to reason calmly with herself; she essayed to mark out what her future course should be. She knew that there was nothing at present but to bear her burden and hide it from the world's eye; but she would do her duty all the same, Heaven helping her, in all the relations of life; she would strive nobly to take her full part in life's battle, whatever the inward struggle.

There is no doubt that in that night of tribulation she looked at the future in its very darkest aspect. It was well perhaps, that it should be so, for the horizon might clear a little as she went on. That Mr. Oswald Cray would in time marry, she had no right to doubt—a word or two of his had almost seemed to hint at it: man forgets more easily than woman.

Towards morning she dropped into a heavy sleep, and had slept longer than usual. This caused her to be late in dressing, and brought upon her the reproof of punctual Miss Bettina. She looked at herself in the glass ere she went down; at her pale face, her heavy eyelids; hoping, trusting they would escape observation. What a happy thing it is that others cannot read our faces as we read them! Miss Bettina was at the head of the breakfast-table. She was suffering from a cold; but, ill or well, she was sure to be at her post and Dr. Davenal stood at the fire, his elbow on the mantelpiece, his forehead leaning on his hand.

Sara went up to him, and he seemed to rouse himself from a reverie as he kissed her. She noticed how ill he looked.

"Papa, I am sure you are worse!"

"I don't feel very well, child."

"If you would but stay at home for a day or two and nurse yourself!"

"Ah! I have not time. There's a great deal of sickness about, and my patients must not be neglected."

"Mark Cray can attend to them."

"To the light cases he could. Not the serious ones; I wouldn't trust them to him."

"Not trust them to him?" echoed Sara.

The surprised tone of the question aroused Dr. Davenal; he had spoken out too heedlessly his real thoughts. "People dangerously ill have naturally more confidence in me than in a young man," he said, by way of doing away with the impression his avowal might make.

They took their places at the breakfast-table, neither of then able to eat; the doctor from sickness of body, for he was really ill, Sara from sickness of mind.

"Aunt Bettina, I tell papa he ought not to go out today."

"Not going out today?" repeated Miss Bettina. "Why not? What's he going to do, then?"

"I say he ought not to go out. He is not well enough."

Miss Bettina heard this time. She raised her eyes and gazed at the doctor. It was impossible not to see that he did look ill.

"What's the matter with you, Richard?"

"It is only my cold," said the doctor. "It has settled here," touching his chest.

"That's just where mine is settling," grimly returned Aunt Bettina.

"Papa's eating nothing," said Sara.

"As if I could eat, with the skin off my throat and chest!" retorted Miss Bettina, mistaking the words, as usual. "It seems that nobody's eating this morning; you are not: we might as well not have had the breakfast laid. Toast was made to be eaten, Miss Sara Davenal, not to be wastefully crumbled into bits on the plate. I suppose you have not got a cold?"

Sara began to pick up the crumbs and the pieces, and to swallow them as she best could. Anything to escape particular observation.

"I wonder how Mrs. Cray is this morning?" she presently observed, having ransacked her brains for a subject to speak upon. Miss Bettina heard all awry.

"Oswald Cray! Why should you wonder how he is? Is he ill?"

"I said Mrs. Cray, aunt;" and she would have given much to hide the sharp bright blush that the other name brought to her face. "I told you last evening Caroline was not well. I think you always mistake what I say."

"No, I don't mistake. But you have got into a habit of speaking most indistinctly. My belief is, you did say Oswald Cray. He is in town," fiercely added Miss Bettina, as if the fact strengthened her proposition.

"Yes, he is in town," assented Sara, for her aunt was staring so very fixedly at her that she felt herself obliged to say something. "At least he was in town yesterday."

"Where did you see him, Sara?" asked the doctor.

"I met him as I was leaving the Abbey last evening, papa," she replied, not daring to look up as she said it.

"I met him yesterday also," observed Dr. Davenal. "He was passing the gate here just its I was about to step into the carriage. He is a puzzle to me."

Miss Bettina bent her ear. "What's a puzzle to you, doctor?"

"Oswald Cray is. I had the very highest opinion of that man. I could have answered for his being the soul of honour, one entirely above the petty prejudices of the world in ordinary. But he has lost caste in my eyes: has gone down nearly cent per cent."

"It's his pride that's in fault," cried Miss Bettina. "He's the proudest man living, old Sir Philip of Thorndyke excepted."

"What has his pride to do with it?" returned the doctor. "I should say rather his selfishness. He has chosen to take umbrage at Lady Oswald's having left her money to me; and very foolish it was of her, poor thing, to do it! But why he should visit his displeasure—"

"He has not taken umbrage at that, papa," interrupted Sara.

"Yes, he has," said Dr. Davenal. "I spoke to him yesterday of the will, and he declined in the most abrupt manner to hear anything of the matter. His tone in its haughty coldness was half-insulting. Why he should have taken it up so cavalierly, I cannot conceive."

Sara remained silent. She did not again dare to dissent, lest Dr. Davenal should question her more closely. Better let it rest at that; far better let it be thought that Mr. Oswald Cray had taken umbrage at the disposal of the property, than that the real truth should be known.

"I suppose Oswald Cray felt hurt at not being left executor to the will," sagely remarked Miss Bettina. "As to the money, I never will believe that he, with his independent spirit, wanted that."

"He wants his independent spirit shaken out of him, if it is to show itself in this offensive manner," was the doctor's severe remark. "What did he say to you, Sara?"

"Say—?" she stammered, the remembrance of what had really been said between them occurring startlingly to her.

Dr. Davenal noted the hesitating words, he noted the crimsoned cheeks; and a doubt which had once before risen up within him, rose again now. But he let it pass in silence.

"Does he intend to come here again, Sara?" asked Miss Bettina.

"I don't know, aunt," was poor Sara's answer. "I suppose he will come again some time."

And in good truth she did suppose he would come again "some time," when the pain of their separation should have worn away.

Sara quitted her seat as she spoke, throwing down a fork with the movement, and hastened to the window.

"What's the matter?" exclaimed Miss Bettina.

"It is the postman, aunt."

"The postman!" echoed Miss Bettina, sharply, wondering what possessed her niece that morning. "If it is the postman, you need not fly from the breakfast-table in that way, upsetting the things. Do you call that manners?"

"O papa," cried Sara, turning round, unmindful of the reproof in her flush of excitement, "I do think here are letters from Edward! Some foreign mail must be in, for the man has an unusual number of letters in his hand, and some of them look like foreign ones."

She turned from the window, and stood gazing at the room door. But no letters appeared. The postman went out again with his quick step, and Sara, feeling grievously disappointed, returned slowly to her seat.

"Is he gone?" presently asked the doctor.

"O yes, papa. He is half-way down the street by this time. He came, I suppose, for one of the servants."

"He didn't ring."

"No. He seemed to go straight to your consulting-room window. Perhaps Neal is there, putting the room to rights."

But Dr. Davenal did not rest so easily satisfied. He opened the door and called down the passage in an imperative voice.

"Neal! Are there no letters?"

Neal came gliding into the room from his pantry, two letters in his hand.

"Why did you not bring them in at once?" somewhat sternly asked the doctor as he took them, certain past suspicions regarding Neal and such missives arising forcibly to his mind.

"I was looking for my waiter, sir: I have mislaid it somewhere. Oh, I left it here, I see."

The silver waiter was on a side-table; not at all where it ought to be; as if it had been put down heedlessly and forgotten. Neal caught it up and retired. It might have been as he said—that the delay was caused by looking for it, and by that only; and Dr. Davenal, more inclined to be charitable than suspicious, thought no more of the matter.

In the keen disappointment which had come over him, he nearly lost sight of other things. Neither of the two letters was from his son; and he had so fully expected to hear from him by the present mail.

Sara's heart was beating. "Are they not from Edward, papa?"

The doctor shook his head as he laid the letters down. "They are both from Dick, I expect His holiday letters." The two letters were respectively addressed to Miss Davenal, and Miss Sara Davenal. The address to Miss Davenal bore evident marks of care in the writing; it was a clear, regular hand, though easily recognisable as a schoolboy's. The address to Sara was a scrawl scarcely legible. Upon opening the letter, hers, Sara found it beautifully written. Until she came to its close she had no suspicion but that it was really written to herself; she supposed it to be a sort of general holiday letter.

"My dear and respected Aunt and Relatives—

As the joyful epoch of Christmas approaches, marking the close of another half-year, we feel how valuable is that time which the best of us are only inclined to regard too lightly. Yet I hope it will be found that I have not wholly wasted the share of it bestowed on me, but have used it to the best of my power and abilities. When you witness the progress made in each branch of my various studies, to which I have earnestly and assiduously devoted my days and hours, I trust that you will find cause to deem I have been no thoughtless pupil, but have done my best to merit your favour and the approbation of my masters. In Greek especially—which Dr. Keen saw fit to promote me to at Midsummer—I flatter myself you will be satisfied with my advancement: it is a delightful study.

"Deeply sensible of the inestimable value of the talents entrusted to me, anxious that not one of them should lie fallow through fault of mine, it has been my constant and earnest endeavour to improve them, so that they may be turned to profitable use in the after-business of life. By industry, by perseverance, and by unflagging attention I have striven to progress, and I may say that it is with regret I part with my beloved studies, even for a temporary period.

"I am desired to present Dr. Keen's compliments to you and my uncle, and to convey to you the intelligence that our winter recess will commence on the 16th of this month, on which day I and Leopold shall hope to return to Hallingham, and to meet you in good health. Leopold regrets sensibly that he will not be able this year to write you his vacation letter: it is a great disappointment to him. He has had a fester on the thumb of his right hand; it is getting better, but still painful. He begs to offer his affectionate duty to yourself, my uncle, Sara, and Mrs. Cray. And trusting you will accept the same from me,

"I am, my dear Aunt,

"Your most sincere and respectful Nephew,

"Richard John Davenal.

"Miss Davenal."

A smile stole across Sara's features at the wording of the letter, so unlike Dick, and she turned over the envelope.

"Yes, 'Miss Sara Davenal!' Dick has made a mistake in the address. It is written to you, Aunt Bettina?"

But Miss Bettina's eyes were glued to her own letter, which she hell open before her. Her lips had drawn themselves in ominously.

"Is it the holiday letter, Sara?" asked the doctor.

"Yes, papa: Richard's. But it is not written to me."

Dr. Davenal took up the letter. Its writing, almost as beautiful as copper-plate, was as easily read as a book: Master Richard must have taken the greatest pains with it. Miss Davenal's was not so easily read, for it seemed to have been dashed off with a skewer. She threw it on the table in considerable temper when she came to its end, and laid her hand solemnly upon it.

"Dr. Davenal, if you do not return this letter instantly to Dr. Keen, I shall. It is a disgrace to have come out of any respectable school."

"Who is it from?" questioned the doctor in surprise.

"Who is it from?—from that wicked nephew of yours—Dick. And you to encourage him!" she added, directing her severe glance at Sara. "It is meant, I suppose, for you." In point of fact, Master Dick Davenal had misdirected his letters, sending his holiday letter to Sara, and one intended exclusively for Sara's eyes to his aunt. Dr. Davenal, in some curiosity, drew towards him the offending letter.

"Dear Old Girl,

"We come home the end of next week hurray! old Keen was for keeping us till the week after and shouldn't we have turned rusty but its all fixed now, the 16th is the joyful day and on the 15th we mean to have a bonfire out of bounds and shouldnt we like to burn up all our books in it you cant think how sick we are of them. Jopper says hed give all Ime sure I would, I hate learning and that's the truth and I havent tried to get on a bit for I know its of no use trying, Greak's horrid, and our greak master is an awful stick and keeps us to it till we feel fit to bufett him its the most hateful bothering languidge you can imagine and I shall never master a line of it and if it werent for cribs I should get a caneing everyday, latin was bad enougff, but greak caps it. We all got into a row which I'll tell you about when I come home and we had our Wensday and saturday holidays stoped for three weeks, it was all threw the writing master a shokking sneek who comes four days a week and found out something and took and told Keen but we have served him out, we have had some good games this half taking things together and if we could berry our books and never do another lesson Keens house wouldnt be so bad, Leo and some more of us were trying to wrench open farmer Clupps stable to get at his poney when he ran a rusty nale into his thumb, old clupp was off to a cattle fair by rail and we knew hed be none the wiser if we exercised the poney up and down the common, and a jolly time of it I can tell you we had only we couldnt find the sadle, well leos thum got bad and he hasnt been abel to write for ever so long and hes uncomon glad of it now for it saves him his holiday letter, had to write mine five times over before it did and I nearly flung it in the fire before Keens face, I never was so sick of anything in my life, its going to aunt Bett this time Keen said it went to uncle Richard at midsummer, good buy till next week darling Sara love to Carry and mind you get a jolly lot of mince pies ready for us.

"Dick Davenal.

"p. s. hows old Betts deafness, its so cold we hope all the ponds will be froze to ice tomorrow."

Dr. Davenal burst into a fit of laughter. The contrast between the genuine letter of the boy and the formal one dictated by the master was so rich. Miss Davenal's brow wore its heaviest frown: the letter was bad enough altogether, but the insult to herself, the "old Bett," could not be forgiven.

"I'll have this letter sent back, Dr. Davenal."

"Tush, Bettina! Send it back, indeed! We were schoolboys and schoolgirls ourselves once. Why, what's this?—here's the postman coming in again! He must have omitted to leave all the letters." It was even so. The postman by inadvertence had carried away a letter addressed to the house, and had now come back with it.

But that mistake was a great piece of good luck for Neal; and in truth its occurring on this morning was a singular coincidence. You will agree with me in saying that it was quite a different sort of luck from any deserved by Neal. Poor Dick Davenal's "sneek" of a writing-master could not stand for honours beside the real sneak, Neal.

Neal had not been at Dr. Davenal's window when the postman came in the first time, as Sara had surmised; Neal was standing in his favourite corner outside, amid the shrubs, having a mind to give himself an airing. It was to this corner the postman had gone, and he delivered three letters into his hands. Neal carried them to his pantry and proceeded to examine the outside with his usual curiosity. Two of them were those he subsequently carried into the breakfast-room; on the third he saw the foreign postmark, and recognised the handwriting of Captain Davenal. And, as Neal turned this about in his hand, he became aware of a curious fact—that it was open. The envelope was not fastened down. The captain's seal was upon it in wax, but it did not serve to fasten it. Whether that young officer, who was given to carelessness, had sealed it in this insecure manner, or whether it had come open in the transit, was of no consequence: it was certainly not closed now.

The temptation proved too strong for Mr. Neal. It happened that he had a motive, a particular motive, apart from his ordinary curiosity, for wishing to see the contents of this letter. He had chanced to overhear a few words spoken between the doctor and his daughter some days previously—words which Neal could, as he expressed himself, make neither top nor tail of; but they referred to Captain Davenal, and created the strongest possible wish in Neal's mind to take a peep at the first letter that should arrive from the gallant officer. Neal had not seen his way to do this at all clear; but it appeared now that fortune had graciously dropped the means into his hands. And the temptation was too strong to be resisted.

Hastily reasoning within himself (the best of us are too prone to reason on our own side of the question, ignoring the other) that in all probability the breakfast-room had not seen or heard the postman, as the man had kept on his side the garden, and had not rung the door-bell, Neal risked it, and carefully drew the letter from the envelope.

A small thin note, addressed to Miss Sara Davenal, dropped out of it. Neal was too busy to pick it up; his eyes were feasting on the opening words of Captain Davenal's letter to his father.

"Neal, are there no letters?"

The interrupting voice was the doctor's: and Neal, in an awful fluster, popped the open letter and the thin one under a dish-cover. There was no help for it; he might not delay; he dared not take the letter in open. So he carried in the other two in his hand, having looked in vain for his customary waiter.

It passed off well enough. Neal returned to the pantry, and finished the perusal of the captain's letter. Then he refolded it, placed the note, which he had not opened, inside as before, and amended the fastening with a modicum of sealing-wax, dropped artistically underneath the old seal.

He was at his wit's end how to convey the letter to the doctor, so that no suspicion might rest upon himself. Suppress it he dare not, for the postman could have testified to its delivery when inquiries were made. He was coming to the conclusion that the best way would be to put it amidst the shrubs, as if he or the postman had dropped it, and let somebody find it and convey it to Dr. Davenal, when the postman's knock at the hall door aroused him.

"I don't know how I came to overlook this," said the man, handing in a letter. "It had got slipped among the others somehow, and I didn't find it till I was ever so far down the street." If ever Neal believed in the descent of special favours from the clouds, he believed in it then. The letter brought back by the postman was directed to Watton. Neal carried it to his panty, deposited the other upon his silver waiter, and took it to the breakfast-room.

"How's this?" cried the doctor.

"The letter-man carried it away with him, sir, by some mistake, he says," answered Neal with a steady tongue and unflinching eye.

"Stupid fellow!" cried the doctor. But he spoke in a good-natured tone. None, save he, knew how welcome a sight was the handwriting of his son.

And when Neal carried down the breakfast-things he coolly told Watton there was a letter for her lying in his pantry, which had come by the morning post.

"You might have brought it down," was Watton's answer.

"So I might," civilly remarked Neal. "I laid it there and forgot it."

CHAPTER XXX

THE DOCTOR'S BIRTHDAY

The dead of the winter passed. That is, Christmas was turned, and January had come in, and was drawing to a close.

Dr. Davenal's state of health was beginning to attract attention. It cannot be said that absolute fears were excited, but people said to each other and to him that he ought to take more care. Especial care of himself he certainly did not take, and he seemed to take cold upon cold. It must not be thought that Dr. Davenal was recklessly neglectful, supinely careless. It was not that at all. But he was one of the many who seemed to have an assured trust in their own constitution; almost believing their state of good health immutable. Other folks are liable to ailments, but they have no fear of themselves. This is sometimes notably the case with those who have never experienced illness, who have passed an active life with neither an ache nor a pain.

As had Dr. Davenal. Of a naturally good constitution, temperate in his habits, taking a good deal of exercise one way or another, his mind always occupied, he did not know what it was to have a day's illness. The great blow which had fallen upon him in the death of his son told upon his mind more than upon his body. If it had bent his shoulders and left lines of care upon his face, it had not made him ill. It was reserved for the later calamity to do that—that terrible secret whose particulars none save the doctor knew. That had nearly prostrated him—it had re-acted on the body; and when the cold fastened on him the day he had to hasten from Mrs. Scott's hot room to the Infirmary, it laid hold of him for ever.

He could not shake it off. Miss Davenal told him somewhat crossly that he kept catching cold upon cold; but the doctor himself knew that it was that first cold hanging about him. He apprehended no real danger: he did not pay much attention to it. Had he possessed a mind at rest, he might have thought more of the body's ailments, but with that great burden of despair—and, in truth, it was little else—weighing him down, what in comparison was any sickness of body? As to lying by, he never so much as gave it a thought. So long as he could go about, he would go about. He thought of others before himself; he was one who strove hard to do his duty in the sight of God; and he would have deemed it little else than a sin selfishly to stop indoors to nurse himself, when there might be fellow-creatures dying for the want of his aid. It was very easy to say other doctors might attend for him; we all know how valuable in illness is the presence of the physician we trust; and none in Hallingham was trusted as was Dr. Davenal.

And so, with his aching mind and his aching body, he went about his work. It is just possible that a fortnight or so's rest might have saved him but he did not take it. He went about his work as usual—nay, with more than his wonted activity, for it was a season of much sickness at Hallingham, as it was that winter in many other places. He bore on, never flagging; but he grew weaker day by day, and everybody remarked how poorly the doctor was looking. No fears for his state were aroused indoors. Sara attributed all she saw amiss in him to the burden of that great secret, of which she had had only partial cognisance; and Miss Davenal felt cross with him.

For Bettina Davenal suspected neither illness of body nor illness of mind. How should she connect the latter with the prosperous physician? She knew that he had been grieved at the going abroad of his son Edward, a grief in which she by no means joined, deeming that a little roughing it out in the world would be found of wholesome benefit to the indulged son and brave captain; and she rather despised the doctor for regretting him. He was silent, and thin, and worn; he had no appetite; his spirits seemed gone; she saw all this, but never supposed it was caused by anything but the departure of his son.

His not eating was made the worst grievance of by Miss Bettina. Once before, in an unusual season of sickness, the doctor had—not, perhaps, lost his appetite, but allowed himself no time for his meals. Miss Bettina believed that this was a similar case; that his patients were absorbing his appetite and his energies; and she gave him a good sound lecturing, as she might have given to Dick. Get what she would for the table, plain food or dainties, it seemed all one to the doctor: he would taste, perhaps, to please her, but he could not eat.

"I can't help it," he said to her one day. "I suppose I am worse than you think."

For the truth, or rather a suspicion of it, had at length dawned on Dr. Davenal—that he was more seriously ill than he had allowed himself to imagine. Unfavourable symptoms connected with his chest and lungs had forced themselves upon his notice on that very morning, and he asked himself what they meant, and what they boded. Had he neglected himself too long?

It was the 24th of January, a notable day in the doctor's household, for it was his birthday, and was always kept amongst themselves. Dick and Leo made the day a plea for the extension of their holidays.

The school generally reopened about a week earlier, but of course, as they told their uncle, they could not go back with his birthday so near: they must stay to wish him many happy returns of it. Miss Davenal saw no reason in the plea, and was severe when the doctor allowed it—as he always did; she would never keep boys at home a single hour after the school opened. But with Uncle Richard to back them, Dick and Leo did not care for Aunt Bettina.

Yes, it was on this morning that Dr. Davenal awoke to the serious state of his own health. If what he suspected was true, he feared he should not be long in this world.

He said nothing. He went out as usual in his close carriage, which he had latterly used, and forgot not a single call. But he said to himself that perhaps in a few days, when he should have brought through, if Heaven willed, one or two patients who were lying in extreme danger, he might make arrangements for stopping at home and nursing himself.

On this same day the doctor again saw Oswald Cray. He had occasion to give some directions to Mark, missed seeing him at the Infirmary, and told Roger to drive to the Abbey. Upon entering, he found not Mark but Oswald. Oswald, it appeared, had just called, and was waiting for Mrs. Cray to come down. Mark was out.

Dr. Davenal cherished no resentment. He deemed that Oswald Cray had behaved to him badly, but he had never been of a retaliating spirit, and least of all was he inclined to it now.

The doctor pressed Oswald Cray's hand cordially as he shook it. The thought flashed over him that he would make one more effort towards a reconciliation. A few moments given to commonplace salutations, and then he spoke.

"This is my birthday, Mr. Oswald Cray. Mark and Caroline are coming to dine with us: will you join them?"

"You are very kind. But I must go up to London by the seven train."

Not a word of "wishing" he could come, or regret that he could not. The doctor noticed that; he noticed also that his tone was more polite than warm. But he did not yet give him up.

"It may be the last birthday I shall see. We shall be glad to welcome you."

"I hope you will see many yet; but I am obliged to return to town. Thank you all the same."

Coldly courteous still! Dr. Davenal, who would not wait, as Mark was out, again offered his hand in parting.

"Some estrangement has come between us which I do not understand, Mr. Oswald Cray. Remember what I say, should this be the last time we speak together, that it is you who have to answer for it, not I."

"One word, Dr. Davenal," for the doctor was turning away to regain his carriage. "Believe at least this much, that none can regret the estrangement more than I regret it."

"Is it explainable?"

"Not by me," replied Oswald, somewhat of his old hauteur coming upon him. He honestly believed in his heart that Dr. Davenal, in saying these few words, was but acting a part.

"Fare you well," said the doctor as he went out.

"Farewell," repeated Oswald. And they were the last words ever spoken between them.

It was a social family dinner that evening at Dr. Davenal's, and for some of its partakers a right merry one. Mark Cray and his wife were merry as heart could wish, the two boys boisterously so, Miss Davenal gracious. Sara was quiet, the doctor was ill, and a gentleman whom the doctor had invited after Oswald Cray declined, was grieving over the alteration so conspicuously visible in Dr. Davenal.

This was the Rev. John Stephenson. He was at Hallingham on business, had called that afternoon on Dr. Davenal, and the doctor had pressed him to stay dinner.

When the cloth was removed, and Mr. Stephenson had said grace, and Dick and Leo were up to their eyes in nuts and oranges, Mark Cray stood in his place and made a natty little speech. Mark was fond of making speeches they were a great deal more to his taste than surgical operations. His present effort lasted five minutes, and wound up with wishing the doctor many happy returns of the day.

"Hurrah!" shouted Dick. "Uncle Richard, I hope you'll have a hundred birthdays yet!"

"And plenty of good things for you to eat as they come round, eh, Dick?" rejoined the doctor with a smile.

"Oh, of course," cried Dick, his eyes sparkling. "It always does come in the Christmas holidays, you know."

The doctor slightly rose from his chair, leaning with both hands on the table. His manner was subdued, his voice inexpressibly gentle and loving.

"My dear friends, I thank you for your kindness; I thank you from my very heart. I am not well, and you must accept these few words in answer to Mark's more elaborate speech. It may be the last time I shall be here to receive your good wishes or to thank you for them. May God bless you!"—and he raised his hands slowly and solemnly—"May God bless and love you all when I shall be gone!"

The words took them utterly by surprise. Sara bent her head, and pressed her hands upon her bosom as if to press down the sudden sobs that seemed as if they would choke her; Dick and Leo stared; Miss Bettina complacently nodded her acknowledgments, she knew not why, for she had failed to hear; and Caroline looked up in wonder. Mark Cray was the first to speak.

"Do you feel ill, sir?"

"Not particularly; not much more so than I have felt lately. I don't think I am very well, Mark."

"You are overworked, sir. You must take some rest"

"Rest may be nearer for me than we think, Mark."

"O papa, don't!" wailed Sara. "Don't speak so, unless you would break my heart!"

Her emotion had become uncontrollable, and the anguish had spoken out. Never until that moment had the prospect of losing her father been brought palpably before Sara, and it was more than she well knew how to bear. In spite of her natural reticence of feeling, of the presence of a stranger, she quite shook with her hysterical sobs.

Miss Davenal was frightened, and somewhat indignant: she bent her head forward. "What on earth's the matter with Sara?"

"Hush, Aunt Bettina," called out Mrs. Cray. "Don't scold her. Uncle Richard has been talking gloomily. He says he is ill."

"Ill! of course he is ill," retorted Miss Bettina, who had contrived to hear. "He won't eat. He is out and about with his patients from morning till night, and then comes in too tired to eat anything. He has not swallowed a couple of ounces of meat all the last week. What can he expect but to be ill? But there's no cause for Sara to burst into a violent fit of crying over it. Will you be so kind as to excuse it, sir?" she added, in her stately courtesy, to the clergyman who was sitting at her right hand.

He bowed. A man who has known long-continued adversity can feel for sorrow, and his heart was aching for the grief of the child, and for the serious change he saw in the father, his benefactor. Mark turned to Miss Davenal.

"It is just what I say, Miss Bettina, that the doctor is overworked. He wants a week or two's rest."

"And what are you good for if you can't contrive that he should have it?" was her answer. "I think you might see his patients for him."

"So I could," answered Mark. "Only he won't let me."

Sara's emotion was subsiding: she sat very still now, her head a little bent, as if ashamed of having betrayed it; the tears dried upon her cheeks, but an uncontrollable sob broke from her now and then. Dr. Davenal had taken her hand under the table, for she sat next to him, and was holding it in his.

"You foolish child!" he fondly whispered.

"Papa, if—if anything were to happen to you—if you were to go and leave me here alone, I should die," was the answer, uttered passionately.

"Hush, hush! My darling, you and I are alike in the hands of a loving God."

She laid her fingers again upon her bosom. How violently it was beating, how difficult it was to still its throbs of pain, she alone knew.

"I met that gentleman this afternoon, the connection of Lady Oswald's whom I saw for the first time the day of the funeral," spoke up the clergyman, breaking the silence which had fallen upon the room. "Mr. Oswald Cray."

"I met him, too," said the doctor. "It was at your house, Mark. I asked him to come here today, but he declined."

"He is gone back to town, I think," said Mark.

"He said he was going."

"Did you ask him to dine here, Uncle Richard?" cried Leo.

"I did, my boy."

"And wouldn't he!" rejoined Mark.

"No, he wouldn't. And, mind, I think he wouldn't; although Ac declined upon the plea of having to get back to town."

"My! what a stupid duff he was!" exclaimed Richard. "Did he know there was going to be a turkey and plum-pudding?"

"I didn't tell him that, Dick. My impression is, that he never means to enter our house again," the doctor added in a low tone to his daughter.

"But why?" exclaimed Caroline, who sat on the other side the doctor, and caught the words. "There must be something extraordinary at the bottom of all this."

"Never mind going into it now, Carine," whispered the doctor. "His grievance is connected with Lady Oswald's will, but we need not say so before Mr. Stephenson."

Sara looked up hastily, impulsive words rising to her lips; but she recollected herself, and bent her head again in silence. Not even to her father dared she to say that his conclusion was a mistaken one.

"Uncle Richard, now that I look at you, it does appear to me that you are changed for the worse," remarked Mrs. Cray. "You must nurse yourself, as Mark says. Hallingham would not understand your being ill, you know."

"True," laughed the doctor.

Caroline Cray, seeing her uncle daily, or nearly so, had not perceived the great change which had been gradually going on in him. But to Mr. Stephenson, who had not met him since the time of Lady Oswald's death, it was all too palpable; as it had been that day to Oswald Cray.

"We must not forget the captain today, doctor," spoke up Mark. "Have you heard from him again?"

"O yes."

"How does he like his Maltese quarters?"

"I am not sure that he has said. It is not of much consequence whether he liked them or not. The regiment was ordered on to India."

"To India!"

"Yes." It was impossible not to note the sad tone in which the monosyllable was spoken. Dr. Davenal had begun to know that he and his son should never again meet on earth: the son whom he so loved!

Somehow, what with one thing and another, that birthday evening was a sadder one than they had been accustomed to spend. Mark Cray, as he walked home with his wife afterwards, remarked that it was "slow." But nobody dreamt of anything like fear for the doctor, save his daughter and the Reverend Mr. Stephenson.

"I can never be sufficiently grateful to you, sir," murmured the clergyman, as he was leaving. "Neither can my brother. You have done for us what I believe no other man living would have done. May Heaven reward you, and restore you to health and strength!"

"I did but my duty," answered the doctor. "The money belonged to you, not to me. I am only glad there were no vexatious legal obstacles brought up to obstruct the transfer. I shall always be glad to see you, remember, when you come to Hallingham."

Mr. Stephenson thanked him. But as he went out, the impression was strong upon his mind that the doctor himself would not long be in Hallingham.

And Sara? What must it have been for her! Her mind was one chaos of tumultuous emotion. She seemed to have accepted the fear as a certainty, to have been obliged to accept it. Oh, what would save him?—could not the whole faculty restore his precious life? She passed another night of anguish, like unto the one she had passed nearly two months before, after parting with Oswald Cray in the Abbey graveyard—like it, but more apprehensively painful; and she wondered how she got through it.

With the morning, things did not wear so intensely gloomy an aspect. The broad daylight, the avocations and bustle of daily life, are an antidote to gloom, and the worst prospect loses some of its darkness then. Sara tried to reason with herself that he could not have become so ill on a sudden as to be past recovery, she tried to say that it was foolish even to think it.

But her mind could not be at rest, her state of suspense was intolerable, and before entering the breakfast-room she knocked at her father's study-door, and entered. Dr. Davenal was closing the Bible.

"What is it, my dear?"

"O papa"—and the words came forth with a burst of pent-up anguish—"I cannot live in this suspense. What did you mean last night? What is it that is the matter with you?"

"I scarcely know, Sara. Only that I feel ill."

"But—you—cannot—be going to die?"

"Hush, my child! You must not agitate yourself in this way. Die? Well, no, I hope not," he added, quite in a joking manner. "I feel ten per cent better this morning than I did yesterday."

"Do you!" she eagerly cried. "But—what you said last night?—"

"Last night I felt gloomy—oppressed. Serious thoughts do intrude themselves sometimes on one's birthday. And I was really ill yesterday. I feel quite a different man today."

Her fears were growing wonderfully calmer. "You are sure, papa?"

"Sure of what? That I am better?—I am sure I feel so. I shall be all right, child, I hope."

"Won't you have advice, papa?" she imploringly said.

"Advice? That's a compliment to myself, young lady. Hallingham would tell you that there's no advice better than Dr. Davenal's own."

"But, papa—I mean different advice. I thought of the clever London doctors. You must have them down to see you."

"Some of the clever London doctors would be glad of the countryman Richard Davenal's advice. Seriously speaking, my dear, though I say it in all modesty, I don't believe there's a man in Europe more skilful than myself."

"But they might suggest remedies that you would not think of. O papa! if there's a necessity, do summon them."

"Be assured of one thing, Sara, and set your mind at rest. Should the necessity arise, I will not fail to seek any one or anything that I think may help me. My life has not of late been a happy one, but I am not quite tired of it; I wish I may live long, not only for your sake, but for—for other interests. There's a double necessity for it now."

"And you will not go out today, papa?"

"Today I must. I have not made arrangements to the contrary. But I do mean to give myself a rest, perhaps beginning with tomorrow. I feel a great deal better today—quite another man."

How the words lightened her heart! Dr. Davenal really did feel much better, and the saddened spirit, the almost ominous feeling, which had clung to him the night before, had vanished. But he spoke more lightly of his illness than he would have done had he not seen how it was affecting her.

Dick came drumming at the door, and then pushed it open with a bang.

"Breakfast's waiting, Uncle Richard. And Aunt Bett—Why! are you there?" broke off the young gentleman as his eyes fell upon Sara. "I'm afraid you'll catch it. Aunt Bett thinks you are not down, and it's ten minutes past eight."

"Are you ready for school, Dick?" asked his uncle. "Elated at the prospect of returning?"

Dick pulled a long face. The two boys were going back that day. A sore trial to Dick, who it must be confessed, had been born with an innate antipathy to books.

"You'll have us home at Easter, Uncle Richard?" he pleaded in a piteous tone.

"Not if I know it, Dick. Holidays twice a-year were thought quite enough in my schooldays, and I see no reason for their not being thought enough now."

"Half the boys go home at Easter—and stop a fortnight: bemoaned Dick.

"Very likely. If half the boys have friends who prefer play to work for them, I'm only glad the other half set a better example. Dicky, boy, you'll enjoy your Midsummer holidays all the more keenly for having none at Easter."

The doctor caught hold of the boy and wound his arm affectionately round him as they proceeded across the hall to the breakfast-room. Miss Davenal greeted Sara with one of her severest aspects, but before she could begin her lecture, Mark Cray had burst in upon them.

"Have you heard the news?" he exclaimed, in a state of excitement never yet witnessed in easy Mark Cray. "Doctor, have you had letters yet?"

"What news? What letters?" asked the doctor.

"Caroline has got her money."

"Caroline got her money?" repeated Dr. Davenal, understanding no better than the rest did.

"The Chancery case is decided," explained Mark. "Judgment was given yesterday, and it is in their favour. She'll get the money directly now."

"How do you know this, Mark?"

"It is in the evening papers—reported in full. I call for my letters sometimes if I am passing the post-office, and I did so this morning and got this paper. White, the lawyer, sent it, I expect, and we shall no doubt hear by this evening's post."

"Well, Mark, I am very glad. Justice lay on Caroline's side; therefore it is right that she should have it. You must settle it upon her as soon as you touch the money."

"Oh, of course," said Mark.

CHAPTER XXXI

BAD NEWS FOR HALLINGHAM

"I say, Neal, what sort of a place is St. Paul's Churchyard?"

The questioner was Watton. She sat in the servants' room near the window, against which the rain was pattering, some household sewing in her hand. Neal, who had entered to get a glass he wanted was rather taken with surprise, but he was not one to show it in his manner.

"Did you never see it?" he asked.

"I saw it in a picture once. I couldn't see it elseways; I've never been to London?"

"It is a large space of land with houses round it and the cathedral in the middle," explained Neal, who seemed always ready to oblige his fellow-servants, especially Watton. "It's a thoroughfare, you know; the road from Ludgate Hill to Cheapside winds round on each side the cathedral, between it and the houses."

"Is it very noisy?"

"Pretty well for that. But the London people don't seem to care for noise. I expect they are so used to it that they don't hear it."

"The houses round St. Paul's are warehouses, aren't they?"

"Warehouses and shops. The shops are mostly on one side and the warehouses on the other."

"Do you know a place called Cannon Street?"

"I should think I do! It leads down from St. Paul's to King William Street. Why do you ask?"

"Well," said Watton slowly, as if she mere deliberating something in her mind, "I am not sure but I am going to live there."

"To live in St. Paul's Churchyard?" repeated Neal.

"I have had a place offered me there, and it seems to me to be a very eligible one," said Watton. "It's to go as housekeeper in a house of business; some large wholesale place, by what I can understand. I should have two or three servants under me, and twenty-five pounds a-year. It seems good, doesn't it?"

"Capital," assented Neal. "Is it in St. Paul's Churchyard?"

"It's either in St. Paul's Churchyard or Cannon Street. She isn't quite sure which, she says. Anyway, it's close to St. Paul's."

"Who's 'she'?" questioned Neal.

"My sister. Her husband is in this establishment, a traveller, or something of that. He has got on well: he was only day assistant in a shop when she married him, fifteen years ago, and now he gets two or three hundred a year. When Miss Bettina told me I should have to leave, I wrote to my sister and asked her to look out for me, and she has sent me word of this."

"But can she get the place for you?" inquired Neal, who was prompt at weighing probabilities and improbabilities in his mind.

"It is in this way. The present housekeeper has been there a good while, and is much respected by the masters, and they have asked her to look out for somebody to take her place. My sister's intimate with her, and has spoken to her about me."

"Why is she going to leave, herself?" questioned Neal, liking to come to the bottom of everything.

Watton laughed. "She is going to begin life on her own score: she's about to be married. I think it's rather venturesome those middle-aged persons marrying: I wouldn't, I know."

"Wait until you are asked," returned Neal, not over gallantly.

"I have been asked more than once in my life," said Watton. "But I didn't see my way clear. It's all a venture. A good many risk it, and a few don't. I'd rather be one of the few. My goodness! how it rains!"

"When do you leave here?"

"When I get a comfortable place. Miss Bettina said I was not to hurry. It isn't as if I were leaving for any fault, or to make room for another. She doesn't like my leaving at all, you know."

Neal nodded. "I heard her grumbling to the doctor, like anything, about it. She talks loud, and one can't shut one's ears at will."

"She need not grumble to the doctor. It is not his fault. He spoke to me himself, saying how sorry he was to part with me, but he could not help it. 'He had had a severe loss of money,' he said, which rendered it necessary that he should alter the rate of his expenditure. I wonder," added Watton, musingly, "how he came to lose it?"

Neal coughed. "Perhaps some bank broke."

"Perhaps it did," answered Watton. "They are ticklish things, those banks. I say, Neal, there's the doctor's bell."

Neal heard the bell for himself, and quitted the room to answer it. Watton got up, put down her work, shook a few threads from her gown, opened a drawer and took out a letter.

She was going upstairs to Miss Bettina to show her the letter she had received, and to ask her advice upon the situation mentioned in it. She felt very much inclined to try for it; only she felt a shrinking doubt of London. Many persons do who have lived to middle age in the country.

Neal entered the room in answer to the ring. The doctor had been out that morning, but returned earlier than usual, for it was not much past twelve. It was the day subsequent to the departure for school of Dick and Leo.

"What a poor fire you have got here, Neal!" said the doctor. "Bring a few sticks and pile the coal on. I feel chilly."

"I hope you have not taken a fresh cold, sir," respectfully observed Neal, as he stirred up the fire preparatory to getting the sticks.

Whether Neal was right or not as to the fresh cold, certain it was, that before night unfavourable symptoms began to manifest themselves in Dr. Davenal. And they increased rapidly.

A few hours and the news went forth to the town—Dr. Davenal was in danger. The consternation it excited cannot well be described—and if described would scarcely be believed. Numbers upon numbers in that town looked upon Dr. Davenal in the light of a public benefactor: they honestly believed that his death would be one of the greatest calamities that could befall them; they believed that, if he went, nobody else could bring them through danger, should it come upon them.

They hastened to the door with their anxious inquiries; they saw the medical men of Hallingham pouring in. What was the matter with him? they eagerly asked. How was he seized?

It was inflammation of the chest, or lungs, or both, they were told. It was in fact an increase of the cold which had been so long hanging upon him, and which he had neglected. Oh, only a cold! they repeated carelessly as they listened—what a mercy that it was nothing worse! And they went away reassured.

A day or two, and there came down a physician from London in answer to a telegraphic dispatch. A day or two more and an ominous whisper went forth to the town—that hope was over. The saddened inhabitants paced to and fro, collected in groups about the door, and glanced up at the doctor's windows, fearing if perchance the blind should have been drawn since they last looked. They watched the medical men glide in and out; they saw a lawyer go in with a bustling step, and came to the conclusion that he went to make the will. Altogether Hallingham was in a fever of excitement.

But there occurred a change; contrary to even the most sanguine expectation a change seemed to take place for the better. Dr. Davenal rallied. The most painful symptoms left him, and some of those around him said he was getting well.

One evening at dusk Neal was observed to come out of the house with a quick movement and hasten up the street. As usual he was instantly surrounded, waylaid by anxious inquirers.

Yes, it was perfectly true, Neal answered, his master was so much better as to surprise all who saw him. The change took place early that morning, and he had been mending ever since. He was well enough to sit up: was sitting up then.

Then there was a hope that he'd recover? the questioners rejoined, scarcely daring to speak the joyful words.

O yes, there seemed every hope of it now. Mr. Cray, who had just gone out, remarked to him, Neal, that he looked upon his master as cured. But Neal couldn't stop to talk more with them then, he said; he was hastening to the chemist's for a draught which the doctor himself had sent him for.

Neal got the draught, imparted the news of the doctor's wonderful improvement to the crowd collecting at the chemist's, for no end of gossipers pressed into the shop when they saw Neal there—retraced the streets with his soft tread, and arrived at home. Entering the consulting-room, where the fire in the grate was getting low, he passed on to his master's bedchamber. Quite a bright chamber for an invalid's. The fire was blazing in the grate, and a handsome lamp, shining through the ornamental pink shade that covered its globe, stood on the small round table. The bed was at the far end of the room in a corner, and Dr. Davenal sat in an easy chair near the fire. He was dressed, all but his coat; in place of that he wore a warm quilted dressing-gown of soft rich silk; one of those rarely handsome dressing-gowns that seem made to be looked at, not to be worn.

He did not appear very ill. Wan and worn certainly, but not so ill as might have been expected. His breath and voice were the worst: both were painfully weak. The table had been drawn close to him, and he was writing at it. A tolerably long letter it looked like, covering three sides of large note-paper. Perhaps if the truth had been declared, he had got up purposely to write this letter.

Sara sat on the other side the fireplace, ready to wait upon him. How she had borne the agony of the last few days and been calm, she did not know, she never would know: it was one of the sharp lessons learnt from life's necessities. "You may be with him," the physician in London bad said to her, "provided you can maintain composure in his presence. The witnessing of a child's grief is sometimes the worst agony that the dying have to bear. I cannot sanction your being in the room unless you can promise to be calm."

"I will promise it," replied Sara in a low tone; but that one expression "the dying" had turned her whole heart to sickness.

Yes, it was one of the lessons that must be learnt in the stern school of life—the maintaining a composed exterior when the heart is breaking. That she was given to reticence of feeling by nature, was of service to Sara Davenal then. But surely the trials that had latterly fallen upon her were very bitter; the battle just now was sharp and keen.

She sat there in her soft dress of violet merino, so quiet and unobtrusive in the sick-room, with its little white lace collar and the narrow lace cuffs turned up on the bands of the sleeves at the wrist. The first day of his illness she had on a silk dress rustling against the chairs and tables, and she had the good sense to go and change it. The chair she sat in was an elbow one, and her hot cheek rested on her fingers as she strove to drive back the inward question that would intrude itself, whether this improvement was for good, or only a fallacious one. She sat perfectly still, her eyes following the motion of his feeble fingers, and it was thus that Neal interrupted them.

"The draught, sir," he said, laying it on the table.

"Set a wine-glass by it," said the doctor. "That will do."

So slowly and feebly! The voice seemed to come from deep down in his chest, and not to be the doctor's voice at all; Neal put the wine-glass as desired, and quitted the room; and the doctor wrote on.

Only for a minute or two: the letter was drawing to a close. Dr. Davenal pressed it with the blotting-paper, read it to himself slowly, and then folded it and put it in an envelope. In all this, his fingers seemed scarcely able to perform their office. He fastened it down, and wrote on the outside his son's name. Then he looked at Sara, touching the letter with his finger.

"My dear, when the next mail goes out, should you have occasion to write of me, let this be enclosed."

"To write of you, papa?" she repeated in a faltering tone. But she need not have asked the question—its meaning had only too surely penetrated to her.

"Should the worst have happened."

"Oh, but—papa—you are getting better!"

She checked the wailing tone; she remembered how necessary, as she had been warned, was calmness in that room; she remembered her promise to maintain it. She pressed her hands upon her bosom and remained still.

"I will take that draught now, Sara, if you will pour it out."

She rose from her seat, undid the paper, poured the contents of the small bottle into the glass, and handed it to him. The doctor drank it, and gave her back the glass with a smile.

"Not one of those clever fellows thought of ordering me this; yet it's the best thing for anybody suffering as I am. Ah! they have got something to learn yet. I don't know how they'll get on without me?"

"Papa, you may get well yet!" she interrupted; anti she could not prevent the anguished sound with which the words were spoken.

He turned and looked at her; he seemed to have fallen into a momentary reverie. But he made no direct answer.

"Can you draw the table away, Sara? I don't want it so close now. Gently; take care of the lamp."

"Where shall I put this, papa?" she asked, referring to the letter.

"In my desk in the next room. You'll know where to find it in case of need. My keys are here, on the mantelpiece."

She stopped to ask one question which seemed to be wrung from her in her pain. "Is it to go all the same if you get better, papa?"

"No. Not if I get better."

Passing into the other room, which was lighted only by the fire, she drew the desk from underneath the table, knelt down, unlocked it, and put in the letter. It was addressed: "For my son, Edward Davenal." Sara was locking the desk again, when some one entered the room and came round the table to where she knelt.

"My goodness! are you saying your prayers?"

Wrapped in silks and ermine, her lovely face peeping out from a charming pink bonnet, was Mrs. Cray. The doctor had expressed a wish to Mark Cray that afternoon that Caroline would come to him, and Mark had delivered the message when he got home.

"Mark says Uncle Richard wants to see me," she explained, "so I thought I'd run down at once. I can't stop; Berry and another friend or two are going to dine with us. I am so delighted to hear of the improvement in Uncle Richard! Mark says the danger is quite over."

"If I could but be sure it was!" was Sara's answer.

"There you are, with your doubts and fears! Never was anybody like you, Sara. Don't I tell you Mark says it is? Yes, I'll take my cloak off for the few minutes that I stop."

She threw off her bonnet, and let the cloak slip from her shoulders, displaying her evening attire, for she had dressed before she came out: a silk, so light as to look almost white, that stood on end with richness and rustled as she walked; the dazzling necklace, given by Captain Davenal, on her white neck; a dewdropped pink rose in her gleaming hair.

Utterly unaccordant looked she with the chamber of the dying, as she stepped into the other room. Dr. Davenal's eyes were fixed on her for a moment in simple wonder, as if he saw a vision. Then he recognised her, and held out his hand, a glad look pervading his countenance.

"Well, Uncle Richard! I am so rejoiced that you are getting better. You'll come and dance at our housewarming yet."

"Are you going to hold one?" asked the doctor, as he held her hand in his, and gazed up at her beauty.

"Mark and I are thinking of it. We can do everything, you know, now that that money's coming to me."

"Ah," said the doctor, "it's about that money I want to talk to you. Sit down, Caroline. How smart you are, my dear!"

"Nay, I think it's you who are smart uncle," she returned with a gay laugh. "So it has come into use at last!"

Caroline touched the dressing-gown as she spoke. There had always been a joke about this dressing-gown. A patient of the doctor's, as fanciful as Lady Oswald and nearly as old, had made it with her own hands and sent it to him. It had remained unused. For one thing, the doctor was too plain in his habits and too busy a man to require a dressing-gown at all; for another he had looked upon the garment as extravagantly fine.

"Yes," said he, in answer to Caroline's remark, "I have found it useful today. It is very warm and comfortable. Caroline, I have been talking again to Mark about the money."

"Well, uncle?"

"I don't know that it is well. Mark does not appear inclined to make me any promise that it shall be settled upon you when it comes. I urged it upon him very strongly this afternoon, and he answered me in his light careless manner, 'Of course. O yes doctor, I'll remember;' but he did not give a specific promise; whether by accident or design, I cannot say. So I told him to send you down to me."

"Yes, uncle," she said, thinking more of the weakness of the voice to which she was listening, than of the import of the words.

"This money must be settled upon you, Caroline, the instant that you touch it. It is essential that a married woman should, if possible, have some settlement. If I recover, I shall take care that this is so settled, but—"

"If you recover!" she interrupted. "Why, Uncle Richard, you are getting well as fast as you can. Mark says so. You are sitting up!"

"True; I am sitting up; and I could not have sat up two or three days ago. Still, I am not sure about the getting well."

"But Mark says so; he says you are," reiterated Caroline.

"And Mark's opinion, as a medical man, must be infallible, you think?" rejoined the doctor, with a momentary look in his face that Caroline did not understand. "At any rate, my dear, it is well to remember all contingencies. 'Hope for the best, and prepare for the worst,' was one of your grandpapa Davenal's favourite maxims. You must have the money settled upon you—"

"But, Uncle Richard, are you quite sure that it would be for the best?" she interposed. "If the money is settled in that way, it would be all tied up, and do us no good after all."

"You would enjoy the interest."

"That's not over much," said Caroline slightingly. "I and Mark have been planning a hundred things that we might do with the money. Refurnish the Abbey splendidly for one."

"You and Mark are a couple of simpletons," retorted the doctor, regaining momentarily his energy of voice. But the effort was too much, and he lay panting for several minutes afterwards. Caroline sat gazing at him, her finger unconsciously raised to her neck, playing with the gleaming toy there. Which should she trust to, these signs of illness, or Mark's opinion?

"Caroline, I insist that the money be settled upon you. Were you and Mark to waste it in nonsense, it would be nothing less than a fraud upon your West Indian relatives from whom it is derived. You may tell Mark so from me. That money, Carine, secured to you, would at least keep the wolf from coming quite in, should he ever approach your door."

Caroline sat aghast, wondering whether the doctor had lost his senses. "The wolf at the door for us, Uncle Richard. As if that could ever be."

"Ah, Carine, I have lived to know that there is no permanent certainty in the brightest lot," he answered with a sigh. "My dear, more experience has been forced upon me in the past year or two than I had learned in the whole course of my previous life. Understand me once for all, this money must be secured to you."

"Very well, Uncle Richard," she answered with ready acquiescence. "It shall be so, as you seem so much to wish it. I'll tell Mark all you say."

A few minutes longer, and Caroline rose. Dr. Davenal was surprised that she should be going again so very soon, and looked inquiringly at her. "Can't you stay a little longer, Caroline?"

"I wish I could; but I shall hardly get back to dinner, and we expect some friends today. Goodnight, Uncle Richard."

He drew her face down to his, murmuring his farewell. Little did Caroline Cray think it would be his last.

Sara went out with her cousin, and saw her depart with the servant who had waited for her. When she returned to the chamber, the doctor was in deep thought.

"I think you must bring the table near to me again, Sara," he said. "There's another word or two I should like to write."

"Yes, papa. Do you want Edward's letter?"

"No, no; it's not to him. There. Dip the pen in the ink for me."

It was a tacit confession of weakness that she did not like to hear; and she saw that even in the short space of time that had elapsed since he wrote before his strength had visibly declined. He was scarcely able to guide the pen.

"That will do," when he had traced a few lines. "Sara, should you have occasion to send this, enclose it in a note from yourself, explaining my state when I penned it; that I was almost past writing. Will you remember?"

"Yes, papa," she answered, her heart beating painfully at the words.

"Fold it for me."

Honourable in all her thoughts and actions, Sara folded the note with the writing turned from her. It is just possible some children might have been sufficiently actuated by curiosity to glance at least at the name at the commencement of the note. Not so Sara Davenal. She placed it in an envelope and fastened it down.

"I think I can direct it, Sara. Just the name."

She gave him the pen, and he traced the name in uneven, doubtful letters. Sara noted it with surprise, and perhaps her pulses quickened. "O. Oswald Cray, Esquire."

"Put it in my desk with Edward's, my dear. If you have occasion to send the one, you will the other." As she unlocked the desk again her tears were raining down fast. In all that her father was saying and doing there seemed to be a foreshadowing in his own mind of his approaching death. She quitted the room for a few minutes that her emotion might spend itself, and in the interval Miss Davenal entered. The soft rustling of Miss Bettina's sweeping silks aroused the doctor, who had fallen into a dose. She went up and took his hand.

"Richard, how are you tonight?"

"I hardly know. Middling."

"Sara is fancying you are not so well."

"Is she?"

"But she always was given to fancies, you know. Is it right that you should sit up so long the first time of leaving your bed?"

"Yes, I like the change. I was tired of bed. Sit down, Bettina. There are one or two things I want to say to you."

"Are you finding yourself worse?"

"Bettina, I have not been better."

"The doctors have thought you so," she said, after a pause.

"Ay, but I know more of my own state than they can tell me. When the suffering and its signs passed, they leaped to the conclusion that the disease had left me. In a measure, so it has, but they should have remembered in how many of such cases the apparent improvement is all deceit, the forerunner of the end."

Bettina Davenal fully understood the words and what they implied. But she was not a demonstrative woman, and the rubbing together of her white and somewhat bony hands was the sole sign of the inward aching heart.

"And I am thankful for the improvement," added the doctor. "It is not all who are permitted this freedom from pain in their dying hours."

"O Richard! is there no hope?"

"I fear not," he gravely answered. "I am accustomed to impress upon my patients the great truth that while there is life there is hope, and I should be worse than a heathen to ignore it in my own case. But, all I can say is, I cannot trust to it."

She had laid one of her hands upon the folds of the dressing-gown, and the doctor could feel the twitching of the fingers. He had asked her to sit down, but she preferred to stand. Close to him, with her head bent, she could hear his low words without much misapprehension, so deliberately were they spoken between the panting breath.

"Bettina, I don't go to my grave as I thought I should have gone, providing for my children. I have been obliged to sacrifice all I had put by. It was not a great deal, it's true, for I am but what's called a middle-aged man, and my expenses have been high. Could I have foreseen my early death, I should have lived at half the rate. And this sacrifice will not die with me. The house—I daresay I shall shock you, Bettina—is mortgaged; not, however, to its full value. I have directed in my will that it shall be sold; and the residue, after the mortgage is paid—can you hear me?" he broke off to ask.

"Every word."

"The residue and the proceeds of the furniture, and those two small cottages of mine, and other effects which will be likewise sold, will make a fair sum. There's money owing to me in the town, too. Altogether I expect there will not be much less than three thousand pounds—"

"Richard!" shrieked out Miss Bettina, in her emotion. "Three thousand! I thought you were worth ten at least."

"No, it was not so much as that altogether. I had four or five thousand put by. Never mind: I say I have had to sacrifice it. I feel how imprudent I have been, now that it is too late."

"To what have you had to sacrifice it?"

The doctor paused before he replied. "A sudden claim came upon me of which I knew nothing: a claim for thousands. No, Bettina, I know what you wish to say—believe me, I could not resist it: to pay it was obligatory. The worst is, I could not pay it all: and the sum which the property will realise will have to be applied to liquidate it."

"But you can tell me what the claim was for?"

"No, I cannot. It is not altogether my secret, Bettina, and you must not inquire into it. I need not have mentioned it at all to you, but for speaking of Sara. My poor children must suffer. Edward has his day, and he will have to make it suffice: Sara has nothing. Bettina, you will give her a home?"

"There's no necessity for you to ask it," was Bettina Davenal's answer. But she spoke crossly; for the want of confidence in not intrusting to her the nature of this secret was hurting her feelings bitterly. "Should anything happen to you, Sara will naturally find a home with me—if she can put up with its plainness. I shall make her as welcome, and consider it as obligatory on me to do so, as though she were my own child."

The doctor lay back for a moment in his chair, panting. His fingers clasped themselves over hers in token of thanks.

"Richard, surely you might place more confidence in me! If you have been called upon to pay this money in consequence of—of any bygone trouble or debt contracted in your youth—and I conclude it must be something of that sort—do you suppose I cannot be true and keep your counsel? I know what follies the young plunge into!"

"Follies? Crimes, rather!" And the words broke from Dr. Davenal with a groan which told of the deepest mental anguish. It pained even the dull ear that was bent to it.

"Bettina, I say that you must not ask me. If it concerned myself alone you should know as much as I do, but I could not tell you without betraying another; and—and there might be danger. Let it rest. Better for you that it should do so, for it would disturb your peace as it has disturbed mine."

"It's a dreadful sum," said Miss Bettina.

"It is that. And my poor children must be left beggars. I have enjoined Mark Cray to pay three hundred pounds yearly to Sara for five years, out of the proceeds of the practice. He can well afford to do it: and if you will give her a home, this had better be invested for her, Bettina."

"Of course. But what's three hundred for five years? You might make better terms with Mark Cray than that."

"Mark has promised faithfully to do it. I have been talking with him this afternoon about that and other things. I asked him what sum he would feel inclined to pay to Sara out of the business, and for what term. He said he thought he could give three hundred a-year, and would continue it for five years."

"Considering all things, it is not a very generous offer," persisted Miss Bettina. "Had your life been spared, Mark could not have expected to step into the whole of the practice these twenty years."

"It is very fair, I think, Bettina. Mark must acquire experience, remember, must work his way up to the public confidence, before people trust him as they have trusted me. He will not have his rooms filled daily with patients at a guinea a head. This has come upon me suddenly, or all things might have been managed differently. I think it would be a good plan for Mark to leave the Abbey for this house; I have told him so; but he will be the best judge of that." Miss Bettina quitted her stooping posture by the doctor and sat down, revolving all that had been said. She sat slowly rubbing her hands the one over the other, as was her habit when anything troubled her.

"I cannot realise it," she said, in a half whisper, "Richard, I cannot realise it. Surely you are not going from us!"

"I am but going to those who have preceded me, Bettina," he answered. "My wife, and Richard, and others, who have gone on before, are waiting for me, and I in my turn shall wait for you. This fretting life is over. How poor!—how poor!"—he added more emphatically, as he clasped his hands—"do even its best interests now seem beside eternity!"

CHAPTER XXXII

LAST HOURS

The lamp was placed on a chest of drawers behind the chair of Dr. Davenal. It was getting on for ten o'clock. Quite time, as had been suggested to him, that he should be in bed; but he appeared unwilling to move. He felt easy, he said: and therefore he stayed on.

The flickering light of the fire, now burning with a dull red heat, now bursting up into a blaze, threw its rays upon the chamber—destined, ere that night should close, to be a chamber of death, although they, the watchers, as yet suspected it not. The light fell upon the simple bed at the far corner, destitute of hangings—for the doctor was a foe to curtains—upon the dwarf cabinet beside it, whose lower shelves enclosed a few choice books, upon the drawers, upon the dressing-table at the farther window, and upon the open space at this end where the fire was. The light fell on the doctor as he lay back in the gaudy dressing-gown, on the chair-pillow, one hand hanging down listlessly, the other fondly resting on the soft brown hair of his daughter.

She sat on a footstool by his side, nestled close to him. Her head bowed down, for she had much ado to conceal and subdue her emotion, her hands clasped and laid upon his knee. The dread fear that he was dying rested on her heart; had come to it, as it seemed, by intuition. Not a word yet of this ominous dread had been spoken between them; each seemed to shrink from the task. But Sara strove to gather courage and strength, so that in his presence she might at least not give way.

The doctor stretched out his disengaged hand and pointed to a china cup that stood on the table. Sara rose and brought it to him, and he took a few spoonfuls of the refreshment it contained.

"Is not the fire getting low, my dear?" he asked, with a slight shiver.

She rose and stirred it, brought forward the coal-box and put on fresh coal, and then took the hearth-brush and swept the bars and the hearth, making things comfortable.

"Do you feel cold, papa?"

"I think so," he answered, with another shiver.

"I am sure you would be better in bed. Shall I call Neal?"

"Not yet. Come and sit down again." She took her place, nestling to him as before, and he fondly stroked her head with his feeble hand. It seemed to her that the hand grew feebler with every change, every fresh movement.

"I have a few things to say to you, my dear, and I had better say them now. I should not like to go to sleep with them unspoken."

Did he mean the sleep of death? Sara trembled inwardly: she hoped that she should retain sufficient strength, no matter at what cost to her feelings, not to tremble outwardly.

"It was necessary that I should make a fresh will," he began after a pause. "In the old will—"

"O papa! surely you are not going from me!"

Utterly unnerved, the words had broken from her in her misery. Dr. Davenal resumed in a tender, reasoning accent.

"I must have you brave, darling; just for a short while. Won't you try and be so? You see I have only you to speak to, Edward being away. My strength may not last very long."

She understood him: that his strength might not hold out if she hindered him by giving way to emotion. The precious time! not much of it might be left to them. With a mighty effort of will, with an anguished sigh to Heaven for help, Sara Davenal outwardly grew still and calm.

"Tell me all you have to tell, papa. I will try and be to you what Edward would have been."

"In the old will, made subsequent to the death of Richard, the chief part of what I had to leave was divided equally between you and Edward. Caroline—but it matters not to speak of her. In this new will, made now since this illness, all I die possessed of is bequeathed to you."

"To me!" she echoed, the injustice of the thing striking on her mind in the first blush of the words.

"Do you think, after what has happened, that Edward could have any right to it?"

She was silent. The doctor lay still for a few moments to gather breath. His voice was so weak that she could barely catch some of the words.

"When Edward brought that ill upon us, which has gone well-nigh to kill me—which I believe in a measure has killed me, in so far as that it rendered my state of mind and body such that I have been unable to fight against what might otherwise have proved but a slight disorder—when he brought it upon us, I say, I had only one way open to me—to sacrifice my property and save him. All fathers might not have done it, though most would: but I believe few fathers love their children as I have loved mine. But to save him, I had not only to sacrifice my property, but also in a measure to sacrifice you."

"Papa," she said, lifting her head, "I wish I might ask you something."

"Well—do so."

"If you would but trust me more entirely. When Edward came that night and you called me down, I learnt he was in some dangerous trouble; but I learnt no further. Since then nothing but fears have haunted me."

"And have they not haunted me?" echoed the doctor in a strange tone of pain. "The night stands out in my memory like a frightful dream. Think what it was. When I was lingering in that front room there, full of the trouble brought to me by the death of Lady Oswald, not yet cold, there came a tapping at the window, and I looked out and saw Edward. Edward, my son!—disguised, as may almost be said, for he did not care to be recognised in Hallingham; and in truth recognition might have been dangerous. 'Let me in quietly, father,' he said, 'I am in danger.' Sara, were I to live to be an old man, could not forget the effect those words had upon me. I was unnerved that evening: the recent death of Lady Oswald and—and—its unhappy circumstances were as vividly before me as though it was being enacted then, and I was unnerved to a degree not usual. He wore a cap on his head, and a plaid scarf very much up about his neck, in fact just as any gentleman might travel, but I had not been accustomed to see Edward so dressed. His voice, too, was hushed to a warning tone. 'Let me in quietly, father. I am in danger.' In the first confused moment I declare I thought of some threatened danger in the street—that some wild animal was running loose: strange ideas do occur to one in these sudden moments. I let him in, and he began hurriedly to tell me that he did not want his visit to be known, for he was absent from quarters without leave; nay, in defiance of leave, which had been denied to him as inconvenient to be granted in the hurried period of the regiment's departure. But he was compelled to see me, he continued, and—then—he told me all."

"Told you what, papa?" she whispered, when the doctor's moan of reminiscence had died away.

"Of the awful position into which his folly had plunged him. Of the crime that he had committed, and which, if not hushed up, bought up, one may say, would in a few days find him out. Sara, Sara! men have been hung for that same crime in days not so long gone by."

He, the unhappy father, stopped to wipe from his face the dews that had gathered there. It was an awful tale for a father to tell; it was more awful for him to have heard it. Sara shivered: she did not dare to interrupt by a single word.

"My gallant son, of whom I had been so proud! Youth's follies had been his in plenty; vanity, extravagance, expenditure, bringing debt in their train, which I had satisfied, more than once, over and above the handsome allowance I made him: But crime, never. Sara, when that night was over, I felt that I would rather die than live it over again, with its sudden lifting of the curtain to pain and shame."

"Papa, if—"

"Hush, child! Let me finish this part while I can speak. He confessed all in its fullest extent. The ice once broken he told the whole. Indeed, he had no choice but to tell it, for it was only by knowing it entirely that I could help him. Had he concealed the half of it he might as well have concealed all: and he might have stood at his country's bar to answer for his crime." Sara gave a great cry. Terrible as her vague doubts had been, pointing sometimes to the very darkest sin that is comprised in the decalogue, the one which Oswald Cray had even dared to whisper in her ear, it was so much worse to hear those doubts confirmed.

"At his country's bar?"

"Child, yes. Don't I tell you what the punishment would have been for it not many years ago? What could I do but save him? Had it been necessary to part with every stick and stone I possessed in the world, I must have parted with them—anything, everything, so as to save him. I told him what I would do; that I would start before morning light—for speed was necessary—and get to London and stop the danger. On his part he had to go back by the train that passes through here at midnight, and so be at quarters by the morrow, that his absence might not be known. Before he went he begged to see you. I think that he then—Sara, I think it now, and have for some little time—that he then had made up his mind not to come down again: or else he fancied that he should not be able to come. However that may have been, he begged to see you; and I, seeing I must confess no reason for it, called you down. And the rest you know."

"I don't know one thing," she whispered. "Papa, I don't know what it was—the crime."

"And better that you should not," he answered with a vehemence surprising in his weak state. "I would not have adverted to it at all, but for what I have to explain to you. Listen, Sara, for there are directions that I must give you now."

Pausing, he held his hand up for an instant as if to bespeak her attention, and then resumed.

"I shall startle you if I say that the money I was called upon to find was no less than eight thousand pounds. Ah! you may well lift your head, child! And this imprudent, sinful man was your brother and my son, and Heaven only knows how dearly I love him still! Five thousand of it I paid at once, and the rest I arranged to pay later, at different periods. This very Christmas, I have paid another five hundred, leaving two thousand five hundred yet to pay. I have directed that whatever I die possessed of shall be sold, and the money paid over to you, my daughter, Sara Davenal: The terms of the will may excite curiosity; people will marvel why I did not appoint trustees; and you, my darling, must be content to let them marvel. The residue, after my debts are paid, will be, as I judge, about three thousand pounds. And of this, Sara, two thousand five hundred must be given to these people, who hold Edward's safety in their hands."

Again she was startled. "Do they hold it still?"

"They do. They hold his—I may almost say life—in their hands. Once they are paid, the danger will have passed. You will make no unnecessary delay?"

"No," she said with a shudder. "The very hour the money is in my hands it shall be paid to them."

"In my desk, in the private compartment, you will find a sealed paper addressed to yourself. It contains full directions how you must accomplish this, and who the parties are. I thought it well to write this down for you, that there might be no mistake or forgetfulness. Inside this paper you will find a letter addressed to these people, and that I wish you to post with your own hands—with your own hands—within four-and-twenty hours after my death. Do you clearly understand?"

"Yes, she clearly understood, she answered; answered from the depths of her quivering heart.

"And I think that is all, so far as that unhappy business is concerned. Oh, my child, my child! if I could but have left you better off!"

"Papa, don't grieve for that!" she said in the midst of her choking sobs. "I shall do very well."

"You will have your home with your aunt. And Mark Cray is to pay you a certain sum for five years, which must be invested for you. Bettina will take care of you: but she is not of a cheering temper. If I could but have left you in a happier home!"

Looking forward, she felt that all homes would be pretty much alike to her with her load of grief and care. Surely the sorrows of life had fallen upon her early!

"I began to think, just about the time of Caroline's marriage, or a little before it, that Oswald Cray was growing to like you very much," resumed Dr. Davenal. "But it may have been only my own fancy. I was mistaken with regard to him once before; perhaps also was again?"

She sat silent, her head down, the fingers of her hands nervously entwining themselves one within the other.

"You don't answer me, Sara. It may be the last time I shall ask you anything."

"It is all over, papa," she said, lifting her streaming eyes. "Then there was! What has ended it?"

Ought she to tell him? Could she tell him? Would it be right or wise to do so—to increase the sense of ill, wrought by her unhappy brother, already lying with so bitter a weight, in spite of his love, on Dr. Davenal's spirit! No, she thought she ought not. Her sense of right as well as her reticence of feeling shrunk from the task.

"Child, have you no answer for me?"

"Something—unpleasant—arose between us," she said, in a faltering whisper. "And so we parted. It was neither his fault nor mine; it—it was the fault of circumstances."

"Ah!" said the doctor, "a foolish quarrel. But I had thought both of you superior to it. Should the cloud ever pass away, and he wish to make you his wife, remember that you have my full and free approbation—that my blessing would go with it. In spite of his pride and his caprice, I like Oswald Cray."

"It never will pass away," she interrupted, almost with vehemence. "It is a thing impossible. We have bidden adieu to all that for ever."

"Well, you know best. I only say, if it should be. Is it this that has kept him from the house?"

"Yes. O papa, when you were blaming him for taking foolish and unjust offence against Lady Oswald's will, I wish you could have known what a mistake it was."

"And, Sara, I have urged on Caroline, as you heard me, that that money should be secured to herself," he continued, passing to a different subject. "I have spoken to your aunt; I have written of it to Oswald Cray—for that is the purport of my note to him. My dear, do you reiterate the same to them by word of mouth; and say that I urged it again with my dying breath. I don't know why the necessity for this should cling to my mind so strongly," he continued in a dreamy tone. "Unless it is because I dreamt a night or two ago that Mark had run through all his means, and Caroline was lying in some strange place, ill, and in grievous poverty. It was a vivid dream; and is as present to me now as it was when I dreamt it."

Sara pressed her hands upon her face. The effort to sustain her calmness was getting beyond her strength.

"Say that I urged it again with my dying breath! And give my love to the two little boys, Sara. Tell them that Uncle Richard would have sent for them to take a last farewell, had death not come upon him so suddenly. But there's no time; and tell them we shall meet again in that far-off land, when their toils and mine shall be alike over. Charge them to be ever working on for it."

She could not contain herself longer. Her very heart was breaking. And she turned with choking sobs, and hid her face upon his breast.

"Don't, my darling! Don't grieve hopelessly. It is God's will to take me, and therefore we should not sorrow as those without hope. I have tried of late to live very near Him, to resign myself to Him in all things. My life had become one long weary trouble, Sara—perhaps he is taking me from it in love."

"O papa! But I shall be left!"

"Ah, child, but you are young; life for you is only in its morning, and though clouds have gathered overhead, they may clear away again, leaving only brightness behind them. Think what it has been for me! To wake from troubled sleep in a night of pain to the dread that ere the day closed the name of my only remaining son might be in the mouths of men—a felon! Child, no wonder that I am dying."

Sara could not speak. She lifted her arm and let it fall across him. Dr. Davenal laid his hand lovingly on the bowed head.

"Yes, I am resigned to die. I would have lived on longer if I could; but that is denied me, and God has reconciled me to the decree. When you shall come to be as old as I am, Sara, you will have learnt how full of mercy are the darkest troubles, if we will but open our eyes to look for it."

Sara Davenal, in her keen distress, could not see where the mercy lay for her. To lose her father seemed to be the very consummation of all earthly misery. How many more of us have so felt when stern death was taking one we loved better than life!

"I am so glad I gave that money of Lady Oswald's back to the rightful owners!" he resumed, after a pause. "It has brought its comfort to me now. I am glad, too, that I have lived to see them in possession of it; that no vexatious delays were made to intervene. Had it not been settled before I died, there's no knowing what might have arisen. Sara, remember that our past acts find us out on our dying bed. Whether they have been good or evil, they come home to us then."

His voice had grown so faint that it was more by guessing than by hearing that she understood the words. Presently she looked up and saw that his eyes were closed; but his lips were in motion, and she thought he was praying. She began to wish he would get into bed, but when she attempted to move, his hand tightened around her.

"No: stay where you are. God bless you! God bless you always, my child!"

She remained on as before, her cheek resting on the dressing-gown. Presently Miss Bettina came in.

"It is the most wrong thing for you to sit up like this, Richard!" she was beginning, when she caught sight of his closed eyes. "Is he asleep, Sara? How could you let him go to sleep in his chair at this hour He ought—What's the matter?"

Miss Bettina—calm, cold, impassive Miss Bettina—broke off with a shriek as she spoke the last words. She went closer to him and touched his forehead.

Sara rose; and a bewildering look of hopeless terror took possession of her own face as she saw that white one lying there. Richard Davenal had passed to his rest.

CHAPTER XXXIII

SORROW

To describe the sorrow, the consternation that fell on all Hallingham in the loss of Dr. Davenal, would be a fruitless task. People could not believe that he was really dead. It had been asserted that the danger was past, and he was getting better rapidly. They looked at each other in a bewildered sort of way, and asked what he had died of? Of a neglected cold, was the answer of those who knew best, or supposed they knew—the medical body of Hallingham. And indeed there was little doubt that they were correct: the immediate malady which had deprived the town of that valuable life was a very simple thing—a cold, neglected at the onset.

Sara Davenal was stunned: stunned with the weight of the calamity, with the grief it brought. And yet it probably fell upon her with less startling intensity than it would have done had she been in the full suntide of prosperity. She had been recently living in nothing but sorrow. The grief and terror brought to her by that night's unhappy secret (which you now know was connected with her brother), had been succeeded by the withdrawal of the friendship—to call it by a light name—of Oswald Cray. She had believed that the world could bring no other calamity that could add to her misery: she had not thought of that most grievous one—a father's death.

In all pain there must be a reaction: the very violence of the first grief induces it; and it came sooner to Sara Davenal than it does to most sufferers. Or, it may be, that the grave, the real nature of the grief brought its own effects. Had it been simple mourning alone, the natural sorrow for the loss of a good and loving father, she might have gone on weeping for months: but there was behind it that heritage of terror on her brother's account, there was the consciousness that with her the heavy secret was left, and the completion of its purchase. The blinding tears ceased, the lively grief settled down into one long, inward, dull agony; and ere many days went over, she had become, in manner, almost unnaturally cold and calm. "How well his daughter bears it," the town said, when it had an opportunity of seeing her. In her subdued manner, her still face, her low measured tones which never trembled, they read only serene resignation. Ah! how few of us think to remember in everyday life that it is the silent grief that does its work within.

She was obliged so soon to set about her responsibilities. Dr. Davenal's request to her had been to post a certain letter that she would find in his desk within four-and-twenty hours of his decease: to post it herself. On the afternoon of the day following the death, she carried the desk to her own room and examined it. There was the letter to Edward, there was the letter to Oswald Cray; both were lying where she had placed them; and there was the packet addressed to herself. The letter it enclosed was directed "Mr. Alfred King, care of Messrs. Jones and Green, Essex Street, Strand, London." The directions to herself were very clear. As soon as the money was realised she was to write and appoint an interview with Mr. Alfred King, and pay over to him the two thousand five hundred pounds upon his delivering up to her certain papers, copies of which were enclosed. This interview might take place at Hallingham if Mr. Alfred King would journey to it: if he declined, she would be under the necessity of going to London and meeting him at Messrs. Jones and Green's. But on no account was she to pay the money by deputy or by letter, because it was essential that she should examine the papers that would be delivered to her, and see that they tallied with the copies written down. Mr. Alfred King would then have to sign a receipt, which the doctor had written and sealed up, and which, he added, she had better not unseal until the moment came for signing it. The receipt and one or two of the papers she was afterwards to re-seal and keep until the return of Edward Davenal. If Edward died abroad, then they were to be burnt.

Sara re-locked the desk; and still she could not form any very definite idea of what Edward's crime had been. The letter to Mr. Alfred King and the letter to Oswald Cray she kept out, for they must be posted ere the day should close. She went out herself at dusk and posted them; whatever duty lay before her, she felt that she must go about it, shrinking from none. Girl though she was in years, she was beginning to feel old in sorrow: no teacher is like unto it. There are woes that bring more experience to the heart in the first night of their falling than will half a lifetime of smooth years.

It was through the letter sent to him that Oswald Cray first learnt the death of Dr. Davenal. He was seated at his breakfast-table in Parliament Street, eyes and thoughts buried in the "Times," when Benn came in with the letters, a whole stack of them, and laid them down by his side. There Oswald let them lie: and it was only in gathering them up later to take down and open in his business-room, that his eye fell on one in particular, rather a large envelope, with a black border and a black seal. He knew the writing well, and a flush of emotion rose to his face as he opened it. Two notes were enclosed.

"My Dear Mr. Oswald Cray,

"I do not knot, whether I shall be the first to tell you of the death of my dear father. He died last night, about ten o'clock. An hour or two previously he penned the enclosed note to you; and he bade me add a few lines when I forwarded it, to explain that when he attempted it he was almost past writing. But that he made this an especial request, I would not have troubled you with anything from myself: indeed I am scarcely capable of writing coherently today, for my grief is very, great.

"Believe me very sincerely yours,

"Sara Davenal."

The first rapid gathering-in of the general sense over, he leaned his elbow on the table and read the words deliberately. It was just the note that her good sense would prompt her to write, under the altered relations between them. He felt that it was—but he had not witnessed her hesitation and the doubt whether she should not rather address him formally than as a friend. If those dandy clerks in the rooms below, if those grave gentlemen with whom he would be brought in contact during the day, had but seen him press those two words, "Sara Davenal," to his lips! He, the reserved, self-possessed man of business, he of the cold, proud spirit! he kissed the name as fervently as any schoolboy kisses that in his first love-letter.

And then he recollected himself; and as his wits, which had certainly gone wool-gathering, came back to him, another flush dyed his face far deeper than the last had dyed it; a flush of shame that he should have been betrayed into the folly. Besides, that was not the way to help him to forget her; as it was imperative on him that he should forget.

He took up the note of the doctor. And he could scarcely believe that that weak, scrawling writing was traced by the once bold, clear hand of Dr. Davenal. It ran as follows:—

"My Dear Friend,—I call you so in spite of the coolness that has come between us. I would that all should be friends with me in my dying hour.

"The expected money, as you probably know, is at last to come to Caroline. I shall not be spared to urge its settlement upon herself, but do you urge it. As soon as it shall be paid over, let Mark secure it to Caroline absolutely, so that she and her children may have something to fall back upon in case of need. They are both young, both thoughtless, and, if left to themselves in the matter, will be almost sure to waste the money, so that it would do no real good to either. If Mark—I cannot write more: sight is failing.

"Fare you well, My Friend,

"R. D."

And he was dead! For a few moments, Oswald forgot all his doubts and fears of the man, and leaped back in memory to the time when he had respected him more than anybody in the world. Had he died with that weight of guilt upon him? How weighty was it? how far did it extend? It seemed strange that he should so soon have followed Lady Oswald. Had remorse hastened his death? But, in spite of these thoughts, which Oswald called not up willingly, he did feel a deep sense of regret, of sorrow for Dr. Davenal, and wished that his life might have been spared to him.

It was incumbent on him to answer the other note, and he sat down to his writing-table and drew a sheet of paper towards him, and began:

"My Dear—"

There he stopped. How should he address her? My dear Miss Davenal?—or My dear Sara? The one seemed too formal, considering how long he had called her Sara, considering that the present moment of deep sorrow should make all her friends especially tender to her. But yet—My dear Sara—better perhaps that he should not. So he finally began:

"My Dear Miss Davenal,

"I do indeed heartily sympathise with you in your great affliction. I wish for your sake and his that the doctor's life had been spared. You do not give me any particulars—and I could not at such a moment expect them—but I fear his death must have been sudden. Will you allow me to exercise the privilege of a friend, in begging you to endeavour to bear up as bravely as it is possible for you to do, in these first keen moments of grief. When next at Hallingham I will, with your permission, call on you and Miss Davenal, and express to you in person my heartfelt sympathy. Meanwhile believe me now and always your truly sincere friend,

"O. Oswald Cray.

"Miss Sara Davenal."

"Of course Mark must settle it upon her!" he said to himself as he glanced again at the contents of the doctor's note to him. "It is not to be supposed he would do otherwise. However, I'll mention it when I go next to Hallingham."

And, gathering the papers together, he locked them in his private desk, and went down to enter on his day's work, carrying the rest of the letters in his hand.

On the day subsequent to the interment of Dr. Davenal, Sara told her aunt she should go and see the two little boys. It had been her wish that they should be sent for to attend the funeral, but Miss Davenal objected: they were over young, she considered. Sara was too really miserable to care about it: of what little moment do trifles seem when the mind is ill at ease!

Miss Davenal again objected to her visit. In fact, had lookers-on been gifted with prevision, they might have seen that the opinions and course of herself and niece would be henceforth somewhat antagonistic to each other. She objected to Sara's proposed visit, recommending her to defer it for a week or two.

"But, aunt, I want to see them," urged Sara. "I know how grieved they have been: though Dick is random and light-headed, he has a most tender heart. And papa gave me a dying message to deliver to them."

"I say that it is too soon to go," repeated Miss Davenal. "A pretty thing for you to be seen gadding about out of doors the very day after your poor papa is taken from the house."

"O aunt! Gadding! I—" for a moment she struggled with her tears: the thought of the terrible weight of sorrow she must carry out with her wherever she went presented such a contrast to the word. At home or out, she was ever living in her breaking heart: and it appeared of little consequence what the world might say. She believed it was her duty to see the boys as soon as possible, and she had fully resolved that her duty, in all ways, should be performed to the uttermost, Heaven helping her.

"I must go, aunt," she said; "I think I am doing right."

She walked in her deep mourning, with her crape veil over her face, to the station. One of the porters got her ticket for her and saw her into the carriage. Whether by the good-feeling of the man or not, she did not know, but no one else was put into the same compartment. She felt quite grateful to the man, as the train steamed on, and, she lay back on the well-padded seat.

The train was express, and she reached the station where she was to descend in less than an hour and a half. Dr. Keen's house was very near. To gain its front entrance she had to pass the large playground. The boys were out for their midday play, and Dick Davenal's roving eye caught sight of her. He climbed over the railings, in spite of rules, and burst into tears as he laid hold of her. Sara had pictured the two boys in apple-pie order in their new mourning, quiet and subdued; but here they were in their ordinary clothes, dirty and dusty, and Dick had a woeful rent in one knee.

"O Sara! is it all true? Is he really dead and buried? Couldn't he cure himself?"

She subdued her own emotion—it was only in accordance with the line she had laid down for herself. She kissed the boy in the face of the sea of eyes peering through the rails, and held him near as they advanced to the house. Leo, less daring than Dick, had gone round by the gate, and Sara drew him on her other side as he came running up.

She sat down in the room to which she was shown, holding the sobbing boys to her. As she had said to her aunt, Dick had a tender heart, and his sobs were loud and passionate. Leo cried with him. She waited to let their emotion have vent, holding their hands, bending now and again her face against theirs.

"Couldn't he be cured, Sara?"

"No, dears, he could not be cured. It was God's will to take him."

"Why didn't you have us home? Why didn't you let us say goodbye to him?"

"There was no time. We thought he was getting better, and it was only quite at the very last we knew he was dying. He did not forget you and Leo, Dick. He bade me tell you—they were his own words—that Uncle Richard would have sent for you to take a last farewell, but that death came upon him too suddenly. He bade me tell you that you will meet him in that far-off land where your toils and his will be alike over; and—listen, children!—he charged you to be ever working on for it."

Their sobs came forth again. Leo was the first to speak. "Have you written to Barbadoes to tell papa?"

"Aunt Bettina has. See, dears, here are two silver pencil-cases; they were both your Uncle Richard's. The one has his crest on it; the other his initials, R D. I thought you would like to have some little remembrance of him, and I brought them. Which will you choose, Dick? You are the eldest." Dick took the pencils in his hand and decided on the largest, the one that bore the initials. The stone was a beautiful one, a sapphire.

"Is it real, Sara?"

"O yes. This is the best for you, as the initials would not stand for Leo. The other stone is real, too, Leo; opal. Try and not lose them."

"I'll never lose mine," avowed Dick. Leo only shook his head in answer, as he put the momento in his pocket.

The gifts had created a diversion, and the tears began to dry upon their faces; schoolboys' tears are not very deep. Sara spoke of their mourning, inquiring why it was not on.

"We wore it yesterday," said Dick. "And we had holiday, we two, and stopped in Mrs. Keen's parlour instead of going into school. But the housekeeper told us to put our other clothes on this morning; she said if we wore our black suit every day, it would be done for in a week."

Not unlikely—by the specimen of the present suit Mr. Dick wore. Sara pointed to the rent in the knee.

"I know," said Dick, looking carelessly down at it. "I did it only just before I saw you, wrestling with a fellow. He says he's stronger than I am, but he isn't, so we were trying which was best man. All in good part, you know. I say, Sara, shall we come home for the holidays now, as we used to?"

"My dears, I don't know yet much about the future. It will be Aunt Bettina's home now. I think she will be sure to have you as usual."

"Why won't it be your home?" cried Dick, quickly.

"I shall live with Aunt Bettina. It will not be the same home for either of us—not the same house, I mean. I think—I don't know yet, but I think it likely Mr. Cray and Caroline will come to it. Perhaps Aunt Bettina will go to one of her own houses."

"Why can't you and Aunt Bettina stop in that?"

"It is too large for us. And the things are going to be sold?"

"The things going to be sold!" repeated Dick, lifting his eyes and voice in amazement "Papa has so directed in his will. You know—at least I dare say you have heard—that Aunt Bettina has a great deal of very nice furniture which has been lying by in a warehouse ever since she came to live with us. I can't tell you yet how things will be settled."

"I say, Sara, how slow and quiet you speak! And how pale you are!"

Sara swallowed down a lump in her throat. "Papa was all I had left to me, Dick. Leo, my dear, you are quiet and pale, too!"

"I say, Sara—never mind Leo, he's all right—have you got a great fortune left you? The boys here were saying you'd have such a lot: you and the captain between you."

"The boys were mistaken, Dick. Papa has not died rich. He died something else, Dick—a good man. That is better than dying rich."

"If he wasn't rich, why did he give back that money that Lady Oswald left him?"

"O Dick! Do you know that the remembrance of having given back that money was one of his consolations in dying. Dick, dear, he hoped you would work on always for that better world. But the acquiring money wrongfully, or the keeping it unjustly, would not, I think, help you on your road to it."

They were interrupted by the entrance of Mrs. Keen, a kind, motherly woman. She insisted on Sara's taking off her bonnet and partaking of some refreshment. Sara yielded: choosing bread-and-butter and a cup of coffee. And Mrs. Keen and Dick and Leo afterwards walked with her back to the station.

CHAPTER XXXIV

WORK FOR THE FUTURE

The clocks were striking four when Sara Davenal was walking through the streets of Hallingham on her return. She stepped along rapidly, her crape veil over her face, and was molested by none with greetings or condolences: but she stopped of her own accord on meeting the poor market-woman, Mrs. Hundley. The woman, her face broken by sorrow, flung up her hands before Sara could speak.

"To think that he should have been the first to go!—before my poor boy, whose life, as may be said, he had been keeping in him! The one a-dying for months past, the other a hale gentleman as seemed to have health in him for a lifetime. Oh, miss! what will the sick do without him?"

"How is your son?" was all Sara's answer.

"He has come nearly to his last, miss. Another week'll see the end. When the news come out to us that the good Dr. Davenal was gone, we couldn't believe it: and my boy, he says, 'Mother, it can't be; it can't never be.' And he set on and sobbed like a child."

In spite of her efforts the tears overflowed Sara's eyes. To have it thus brought palpably before her was more than she could bear with equanimity. "Papa is better off," was all she murmured.

"Ay, he's better off: if ever a man had done his best in this world, miss, it was him. But who'll be found to take his place?"

With the full sense of the last question echoing on her ear, Sara continued her way. At the top of the lane contiguous to their residence was Roger, standing in disconsolate idleness. With the death of his master Roger's occupation was gone.

Sara spoke a kind word to him in passing, and met Mr. Wheatley coming out at the gate, her father's close friend of many years. A surgeon once, but retired from the profession now. He it was who was named the sole executor to the doctor's will.

The will, which was causing surprise to the curious in Hallingham, had been made in the doctor's recent illness. It directed that all property he died possessed of should be sold, and the money realised be paid at once to his daughter. Everything was left to her. In the previous will, destroyed to make room for this, Edward Davenal's name had been associated with Mr. Wheatley's: in this Mr. Wheatley was left sole executor; in fact, Edward's name was not so much as mentioned in it.

"Have you been calling on my aunt, Mr. Wheatley?"

"No, my visit was to you," he answered, as he turned indoors with her.

"I have been to see Dick and Leo," she explained. "My aunt thought I ought not to go out so soon; that people might remark upon it. But I am glad I went, poor boys!"

"People remark upon it!" echoed Mr. Wheatley. "I should like to hear them. What is there to remark upon in that? Miss Sara, I have gone through life just doing the thing I pleased according to my own notions of right, without reference to what other folks might think, and I have found it answer. You do the same, and never fear."

She led the way into the dining-room and closed the door. She understood he wished to speak with her. The fire was burning itself out to an empty room, Miss Davenal being upstairs. Ah, how changed the house was only in the short week or two! It would never more be alive with the tread of patients coming to consult Dr. Davenal; never more be cheered with his voice echoing through the corridors. The dwelling's occupation, like Roger's, had gone.

Mr. Wheatley sat down in the chair that had once been the doctor's, and Sara untied her bonnet-strings, and took a seat near him. The fresh newspapers, not unfolded, lay on the table as of yore: the whilom readers of them, the waiting sick, had ceased their visits for ever.

"Now, Miss Sara, I'm left sole executor to this will, as you heard read out yesterday," he began. "It states—I daresay you noted it—that things were to be disposed of with all convenient dispatch. Did you observe that clause?"

"Yes."

"Very good. Besides that, in the last interview I held with my poor friend—it was the afternoon of the day he died, as you may remember—he enjoined the same thing upon me; no delay. There was a necessity, he said, for your being put in possession of the money as soon as possible." Sara had no ready answer at hand. She believed there might be that necessity, but did not like to acknowledge it. She took off her bonnet, and laid it beside her on the table, as if at a loss for something to do.

"Now I don't want to inquire into reasons and motives," went on Mr. Wheatley. "I'd rather not inquire into them or hear them; what your father did not see fit to tell me, I'd prefer that nobody else should tell me. I am sure of one thing: that he kept it from me either cut of necessity or to spare me pain. That things had not gone very straight with him, he told me; and that, coupled with the curious will, leaving everything to you without the protection of trustees or else, does of course force me to see that there's something behind the scenes. But while I admit so much, I repeat that I do not speculate upon what it may be, even in my own mind; nor do I wish to do so. One question I must ask you—were you in your father's confidence?"

"Yes. At least, if not quite entirely, sufficiently so to carry out all his directions and wishes. But, indeed, I may say I was in his confidence," she added with less hesitation. "He talked to me a great deal the night of his death."

"And you will be at no loss what to do with the money that shall be realised."

"None."

"That's all straight, then, and I know how to set to work. My dear, it was necessary that I should just say so far, for it would not have been well for us to work at cross-purposes, and I am sure you do not misunderstand me. There's something behind which is no more your secret than it is mine; it was the doctor's; and we need not further allude to it. I'll carry out his will, and you'll carry out his wishes afterwards: he hinted to me that the money would have an ulterior destination. Any suggestion you may have to make to me, you will now do with more ease than if you had supposed I was under the impression that the money was only going to you. Don't you think it was better that I should speak?"

"Indeed it was, and I thank you."

"Well, now to business. As I understand it, there's a necessity, perhaps an imperative one—in fact, the doctor told me so, for immediate action. The first consideration then is, when shall you be prepared to leave the house? Measures will be taken to put it up for sale, and there's not the least doubt of its finding a ready purchaser, for it's one of the best houses in Hallingham, and in its best part. That will be easy. The next thing will be the sale of the effects. Of course the sooner you leave the house, the sooner they can be sold." It quite wrung her heart to hear him speak of all this in the dry tone of a man of business. She did what she could to bring her mind to bear it equably, heedless of the pain.

"It depends upon my aunt, Mr. Wheatley. So far as I am concerned I could be out in a few days; but she will have her home to fix upon. I had better speak to her. Papa said, when he was dying, that he thought Mark Cray ought to leave the Abbey and come here."

"Mark Cray! Well, he has the most right to do so: he was your father's partner. I never thought of him. Of course he will; he'll not let it slip through his fingers. The mere taking this house would be a certain practice for any one. Mark Cray has his practice ready cut and dried to his hand, but he'll not let the house go by him."

"Mr. Cray has just furnished the Abbey."

"But perhaps he—however, it will be well that somebody should see him, and ascertain what his wishes may be. It is a pity but he had money: he might purchase the house. By the way, there's that Chancery money come or coming to his wife."

Sara shook her head. "That money is to be settled upon her. It was one of papa's last injunctions."

"Well; and how can that be better done than by buying freehold property, such as this? It will be the very thing for them, I should say. Let them buy this house and settle it upon her; it will be a capital investment. As to the furniture, if they don't care to buy that, it must be sold. Suppose you ask Miss Davenal when she shall be ready to vacate it; and meanwhile I'll see Mr. Cray."

He was a man of prompt action, this old friend of Dr. Davenal's, and he rose as he spoke, shook hands with Sara, and bustled out so hastily that even attentive Neal did not catch him up in time to close the hall-door behind him. Sara supposed he was going then and there to Mark Cray's.

She took her bonnet in her hand and went slowly up the stairs. It was not a pleasant task, this question that she had to put to her aunt, and she was glad of the little delay of even turning first into her own room to take her things off after her journey. Since the reading of the will yesterday Miss Davenal had been in one of her most chilling moods. She had asked an explanation of Sara what was the meaning of all this, what Dr. Davenal's secret was, and where the money had gone to. Sara could only evasively put her off; one of the charges enjoined on his daughter by the doctor had been—not to place Edward in the power of his aunt.

It was not that Dr. Davenal feared the loyalty and good faith of his sister; but he knew how bitterly she would judge Edward, and he was willing to spare blame even to his guilty son. It is possible, also, that he deemed the secret safest left to Sara alone. Whatever his motive, he had said to her: "I charge you, keep it from your aunt Bettina;" and Sara had accepted the charge, and meant to act upon it. But Dr. Davenal might never have left it, had he foreseen the unpleasantness it entailed on Sara.

Very curious, very cross, very deaf was Bettina Davenal, as she sat in the drawing-room at her usual occupation, knitting. Her clinging mourning robes made her figure appear thinner and taller; and that, as you are aware, need not have been. She had seen from the window Sara come in, and she now thought she heard her footfall on the stairs; and her neck was thrown more upright than ever, and her lips were ominously compressed. It was this general displeasure which had chiefly caused the objection she made to Sara's visiting the boys. Sara had gone, defying her; at least, she looked upon it in that light. Was she about to defy her in all things?

She just looked up when Sara entered the room, and then dropped her eyelids again, never speaking. Sara stood near the window, her bead shaded by the half-drawn blind.

"Well, I have been, aunt."

"Been?" grunted Miss Bettina. "Not anywhere. Where do you suppose I have been? I know propriety better than to be seen streaming abroad today."

Sara drew a chair to the little table on which lay her aunt's pearl basket of wool, and sat down close to her. Her pale refined face was ominously severe, and Sara's heart seemed to faint at her task. Not at this one particular task before her, but at the heavy task altogether that her life had become. It was not by fainting, however, that she would get through it, neither was it the line of action she had carved out for herself.

"I observed that I had been to see the boys, Aunt Bettina. They both send their love to you."

"I daresay they do. Especially that impudent Dick."

"Mrs. Keen also desired to be remembered," continued Sara.

"You can send back my thanks for the honour," ironically spoke Miss Davenal. "The last time she was at Hallingham she passed our house without calling."

"She spoke of it today, Aunt Bettina. She nodded to you at the window, she said, and pointed towards the station: she wished you to understand that she was pressed for time."

Aunt Bettina made no answer. She was knitting vehemently. Apparently Sara was not getting on very well.

"Mr. Wheatley has been here, aunt."

"You need not tell it me. He has been dodging in and out like a dog in a fair. Anybody but he might have respected the quiet of the house on the very day after its poor master had been taken from it. He came in and went out again, and then came in again—with you. As he had come, he might have been polite enough to ask for me. Neal said he wanted you. Early times, I think, to begin showing people you are the house's mistress!"

It was not a promising commencement. Sara could only apply herself to her task in all deprecating meekness.

"Aunt Bettina, he came to speak about the future. I daresay he thought you would not like to be intruded upon today, for he wished me to talk things over with you. He was asking when we—you—when we should be ready to vacate the house."

"To do what?" she repeated shrilly. But she heard very well, Sara was close to her and speaking in low clear tones.

"When we shall be ready to leave the house?"

"Had he not better turn us out of it today?" was the retort of the angry lady. "How dare he show this indecent haste?"

"Oh, aunt! You know it is only in accordance with papa's will that he has to do it. You heard it read. You read it to yourself afterwards."

"Yes, I did read it to myself afterwards: I could not believe that my brother Richard would have made such a will, and I chose to satisfy myself by reading it. Everything to be sold, indeed; as if we were so many bankrupts? Hold your tongue, Sara! Do you think I don't grieve for the loss of the best brother that ever stepped! But there are matters a-gate that I don't understand."

"There's a necessity for the things being sold, Aunt Bettina."

"He told me so before he died: you need not repeat it to me. Where's the money to be paid to?"

"And therefore Mr. Wheatley is desirous that there should be no unnecessary delay," Sara continued, a faint colour tinging her cheek at the consciousness of evading her aunt's question. "He does not ask us to go out at once, Aunt Bettina: he only wishes to know when we shall be ready to go out."

"Then tell him from me that I will be no hindrance," retorted Miss Bettina, her temper rising. "Tomorrow—the next day—the day after—any day he pleases, now, or in a month to come. I can get a lodging at an hour's notice."

"Aunt, why are you so angry with me?"

The burst came from her in her pain and vexation. She could not help feeling how unjust it was to cast this anger upon her; how little she had done to deserve it Miss Bettina knitted on more fiercely, declining an answer.

"It is not my fault, aunt. If you knew—if you knew what I have to bear!"

"It is your fault, Sara Davenal. What I complain of is your fault. You are keeping this secret from me. I don't complain that they are going to sell the chairs and tables: Richard has willed it so, and there's no help for it: but I don't like to be kept in the dark as to the reason, or where the money is to go. Why don't you tell it me?"

It was a painful position for Sara. She had always been dutiful and submissive to her aunt: far more so than her brothers or Caroline had been.

"Aunt Bettina, I cannot tell you. I wish I could."

"Do you mean to imply that you do not know it."

"No, I don't mean that. I do know it. At least, I know it partially. Papa did not tell me quite all."

Miss Bettina's usually placid chest was heaving with indignation. "And why could he not tell me, instead of you! I think I am more fit to be the depositary of a disgraceful secret than you are, a child! And I expect it is a disgraceful one."

Ah, how disgraceful Sara knew only too well. She sat in silence, not daring to acknowledge it, not knowing what to answer.

"Once for all—will you confide it to me?"

Sara believed, as it had come to this, that it would be better if she could confide it to her; but the injunction of Dr. Davenal was a bar; and that she felt it her duty religiously to obey. In her deep love for her father she would not cast the onus of refusal upon him, preferring to let it rest on herself.

"Believe me, aunt, I cannot tell you. I am very sorry; I wish I did not know it myself. It—it was papa's secret, and I must not tell it."

In the twitching of her hands Miss Bettina contrived to throw down the ball of wool. Sara picked it up, glad of the little interlude.

"Aunt Bettina, we could not have stayed on in this large house."

"Did I say we could?" asked Miss Bettina. "Not now, when all your money's gone in ducks and drakes."

"Papa—papa could not help the money going," she returned, her heart swelling in the eager wish to defend him. "He could not help it, Aunt Bettina."

"I am not saying that he could. I am not casting reproach on him. It is not to be supposed, had he been able to help it, that he would have let it go. How touchy you are!"

A silence, and then Sara began. She mentioned what Mr. Wheatley had said, that the house might be a good investment for the money of Caroline; and Miss Bettina, not at all a bad woman of business, was struck with the suggestion. She sat revolving it in silence, apparently only intent on her knitting. She supposed it could be so settled on Mark's wife, but she did not understand much of what the law might be. The thought struck her that this ought to be seen about at once.

"Mr. Wheatley thinks it would be so much better if these things could be taken too by whoever succeeds to the house," proceeded Sara. "So as to avoid a public auction."

Now that was one of the sore points troubling Miss Davenal—the prospect of selling the things by public auction. She had a most inveterate hatred to any such step, looking upon all sales of furniture, no matter what the cause of sale, as a humiliation. Hence the motive which had induced her to warehouse her handsome furniture instead of selling it, when, years ago, she gave up housekeeping to take up her abode at Dr. Davenal's.

"Others knew that, before Mr. Wheatley," she said ungraciously. "A public auction in this house! I would not stop in the town to see it. Has old Wheatley spoken to Mark!"

"It struck me he was going to Mark's when he left here," replied Sara. "I am not sure."

Miss Davenal grunted as she went on with her knitting. She herself always liked to be "sure:" so far as her deafness allowed her. Turning to glance at the timepiece, she crossed the room and opened the door. There stood Neal.

Neal at his eaves-dropping, of course. And the black robes of his mistress were so soft, her footfall so noiseless on the rich carpet, that Neal's ear for once failed him. But he was not one to allow himself to be caught. He had the coal-box in his hand, and was apparently stooping to pick up a bit of coal that had fallen on the ground. Miss Davenal would as soon have suspected herself capable of listening at doors, as that estimable servant Neal.

"Let the dinner be on the table to the moment, Neal," were her orders. "And I shall want you to attend me abroad afterwards."

"Are you going out, Aunt Bettina?" Sara ventured to inquire.

"Yes, I am," was the sharp answer. "But not until the shades of night shall be upon the streets."

Sara understood the covert reproach. Her aunt's manners towards her had settled into a cold, chilling reserve. Sara wondered if they would ever thaw again.

Miss Davenal made her dinner deliberately: she never hurried over anything: and went out afterwards on foot, attended by Neal. Sara judged that she was going to the Abbey, but she did not dare to ask. She, Sara, went to the drawing-room, from old custom; shivering as she stepped up the wide staircase: not from cold, but from the loneliness that seemed to pervade the house. She had not got over that sense of strange nameless dread which the presence of the dead imparts and leaves behind it. The drawing-room was lighted as usual: no alteration had been made in the habits of the house; but as Sara glanced round its space, a nervous superstition began to creep over her. Perhaps the bravest of us have at times experienced such. A moment after, Watton appeared showing in a visitor: Mr. Oswald Cray.

Every pulse of her body stood still, and then bounded onwards; every thrill of her heart went out to him in a joyous greeting. In this dreadful sorrow and sadness he had but been growing all the dearer.

He was still in deep mourning for Lady Oswald. He looked taller, finer, more noble than of yore, or she fancied it, as he bent a little to her and took her hand, and kept it. He saw the quiver of the slight frame; he saw the red rose that dyed the pale cheeks with blushes, and Mr. Oswald Cray knew that he was not forgotten by her, any more than she was by him. But he knew also that both of them had only one thing to do—to bury these feelings now, to condemn them to oblivion for the future. The daughter of Dr. Davenal dead could be no more a wife for him, Oswald Cray, than the daughter of Dr. Davenal living, and most certainly he was the last man to be betrayed into forgetting that uncompromising fact.

The rose-blush faded away, and he saw how weak and worn was her cheek; young, fragile, almost childish she looked in her evening dress of black, the jet chain on her white shoulders. Insensibly his voice assumed a tenderness rarely used to her, as he apologised for calling at that hour: but he was only passing through the town and would leave it again that night. "I see how it is;" he cried, "you are suffering more than is good for you."

But for the very greatest effort, the tears she had believed to have put under permanent control would have dropped then. A moment's pause for calmness, and she remembered that her hand was lying in his, withdrew it, and sat down quietly in a chair, pointing to one for him. But the forced calmness brought a sickness to her heart, a pallor to her aching brow.

"How shall I tell you of my sympathy in your deep sorrow? I cannot express it; but you will believe me when I say that I feel it almost as you can do. It is indeed a trying time for you; a grief which has come to you all too early."

"Yes," she gently answered, swallowing the lump that kept rising in her throat. "I have a good deal to bear."

"There is only one comfort to be felt at these times—and that the mourner can but rarely feel," he said, drawing his chair near to her. "It lies in the knowledge, the recollection, that Time, the great healer, will bind up the sorest wounds."

"It can never bind up mine," she said, speaking in the moment's impulse. "But you are very kind; you are very kind to try to cheer me."

"I wish I could cheer you, I wish I could remove every sorrow under which you suffer! No one living would be a truer friend to you than I should like to be. How is Miss Davenal?" he continued, possibly fancying he might be saying too much, or at least that a construction he never intended might appear to belong to his words. "Watton said she was out. I suppose, in point of fact, she will not see me tonight. I know what war I wage with etiquette in being here so soon, and at this hour, and Miss Davenal is a close observer of it. Will you forgive me?"

"Indeed I am glad to see you," said Sara, simply. "I am doubly glad, for I feel almost ashamed to confess I was getting too nervous to be alone. My aunt is out; she went to the Abbey as soon as dinner was over. I am glad to see you thus early," she added, "because I have a word to say to you from—from papa."

"Yes," said Oswald, lifting his head with slight eagerness, an unusual thing for him to do.

"In the letter he wrote to you, and which I sent—the letter you received," she continued, looking at him and pausing.

"Yes?"

"He spoke of Mrs. Cray's money in it, as he told me. He wished you to interest yourself and see that it was settled upon her. When he wrote that letter he was almost past exertion, and had to conclude it abruptly, not having said so much as he wished to say. Therefore he enjoined me to urge it upon you from him. He thought—I believe he thought that Mark Cray was inclined to be careless, and that the money might be wasted unless some one interfered. That was all."

"I shall speak to Mark. Most certainly I will urge the settlement of the money on his wife, should there be occasion for it; but I imagine Mark will naturally so settle it without any urging. It is quite incumbent on him to do so, both as a matter of prudence and that it is his wife's money, not his."

"I don't think Mark has much notion of prudence," she rejoined.

"I don't think he has, in a general way. But the most careless would surely act in accordance with its dictates in a case like this. I am going to tie Abbey presently."

"I fancy that papa thought—or wished—that you would be one of the trustees, should trustees be required."

"I should have no objection," said Oswald, after a pause. "But—to go to another subject, if you can bear me to touch upon it—was not Dr. Davenal's death sudden at the last?"

"Quite at the last it was. He had some days of dangerous illness, and he rallied from it, as we all supposed. It was thought he was out of danger, and he sat up: he sat up for several hours—and died."

She spoke the words quietly, almost as she might have told of the death of one not related to her, her hands clasped on her lap, her face a little bent, her eyelids drooping. But Oswald Cray saw that it was the calmness that proceeds from that stern schooling of the heart which can only be enforced by those heavy-laden with hopeless pain.

"He died sitting up?"

"Yes. It was getting late, but he would not return to bed. He had been talking to me about many things; I was on a low seat, my head leaning against him. He died with his arm round me."

"What a trial! What a shock it must have been!"

"I had no idea he was dead. He ceased talking, and I remained quiet, not to disturb him. My aunt Bettina came in, and saw what had happened."

He scarcely knew what to say in answer. All comments at such a time are so grievously inadequate. He murmured some words of pity for the fate of Dr. Davenal, of compassion for her.

"It is Hallingham that deserves, perhaps, most of real pity," she resumed, speaking in this matter-of-fact way that she might succeed in retaining her composure. "I do not know who will replace my father: no one, I fear, for a long while. If you knew how he is mourned—"

She stopped, perhaps at a loss for words.

"Did he suffer much?" asked Mr. Oswald Cray.

"He suffered here"—touching her chest—"but the pain ceased the last day or two, and the breathing got better. He had a great deal of pain of mind—as—perhaps—you—know. He was quite resigned to die: he said God was taking him to a better home."

Still at cross-purposes. Sara's hesitating avowal pointed to a different cause of mental pain from that assumed by Oswald Cray.

"Yes," he at length said, abstractedly, for neither spoke for a few minutes, "it is a loss to Hallingham. This will be sad news to write to your brother."

"It is already written. The mail has been gone a day or two. O yes! it will be grievous news for Edward."

The last two words were spoken in a tone of intense pain. She checked it, and began talking of her aunt, of Caroline, of anything; almost as if she doubted herself. She told him she had been out that day to see the two little boys. At length he rose to leave.

"Will you not stay and take some tea? I do not suppose my aunt will be long."

He declined. He seemed to have grown more cold and formal. Until he took her hand in leaving, and then the tender tone of voice, the pleasant look of the eye shone out again.

"May Heaven be with you, Miss Davenal!—and render your future days happier than they can be just now. Fare you well! I hope to hear good news of you from time to time."

Which was of course equivalent to saying that he should not be a visitor. She had not expected that he would be. He turned back ere he gained the door.

"If I can be of service to you at any time or in anyway, I hope you will not hesitate to command me. Nothing would give me so much gratification as the being of use to you, should need arise."

It was very polite, it was very kind, and at the same time very formal. Perhaps the strangest part throughout the interview to Sara's ears was that when he had called her "Miss Davenal," for it presented so great a contrast to the past: the past which was at an end for ever.

He went out, shown through the hall by Jessy, and leaving his card on the standing waiter for Miss Davenal. All en règle. And Sara in the large drawing-room, so dreary now, remained on in her pain, alone.

CHAPTER XXXV

MARK'S NEW PLANS

In the dining-room at the Abbey, in her black robes, sat Mrs. Cray at the head of her table, her elbow resting on it, and a pouting expression on her pretty face. Mark was at the foot, gobbling down his dinner with what haste he could. He had been detained so long beyond the dinner hour that Mrs. Cray in despair had eaten hers; and when Mark at length entered he found a cold face and a cold cutlet. Mrs. Cray was beginning to tire of the irregularity.

"I can't help it, Carine," he said, looking at her in a pause of his eating. "My work has been nearly doubled, you know, since the doctor died."

"But it's very tiresome, Mark!"

"It is. I am nearly sick of it."

"It is not doubled, your work."

"Well, no; one speaks at random. Some of the doctor's older patients have left me: they think, I suppose, I am not sufficiently experienced. But I have a great deal to do just now; more, in fact, than I can attend to properly."

Mark resumed his gobbling, and his wife watched him, her lips a little relaxing. Caroline Cray was one of those who must have all things go smoothly; she could not bear to be put out, even is trifles.

"Mr. Wheatley has been here, Mark," she presently said.

"What did he want?"

"Well, he wanted to see you. Something about the selling of my uncle's house."

"He is losing no time," observed Mark, acrimony in his tone. "I wonder he didn't begin about it yesterday when we were there, hearing the will read. But what have I do with it?"

"He wants us to take the house—to buy it, I think."

"I daresay he does," retorted Mark, after a pause of surprise. "Where's the money to come from?"

"There's that money of mine. He said it would be a good investment."

"Did he! I wonder what business it is of his! Carine, my dear, you and I are quite capable of managing our own affairs, without being dictated to."

"Of course we are!" answered Carine, rather firing at the absent Mr. Wheatley, as this new view was presented to her.

Mark said no more just then. He finished his dinner, and had the things taken away. Then, instead of sitting down to his wine, his usual custom, he stood up on the hearth-rug, as though he were cold—or restless. Mark Cray had been reared to extravagance in a petted home, and looked for his wine daily, as surely as any old alderman looks for it. Oswald Cray, reared without a home, and to schoolboy fare, adhered still, in a general way, to the water to which he had been trained. Oswald's plan was the most profitable, so far as the pocket was concerned, and the health too.

"I say, Carine, I want to go to London for a day."

"To London?" echoed Carine, turning her chair to the fire, and facing Mark.

"There's the grandest opening: there's the grandest opening for a fortune to be made there. And—Carine—I think I shall quit Hallingham." Mrs. Cray's violet eyes extended themselves in the extreme of wonder. She sat staring at him.

"Caroline, I hate the profession, and how I came ever to be such a fool as to go into it I cannot understand," said Mark, throwing himself on a chair as he plunged into confidence. "So long as the doctor lived I could not well say anything about it; I did not see my way clear to do so. But things have altered now, and I think I shall give up the medical life."

"But—good gracious, Mark!—I can't understand," exclaimed Caroline, in her bewilderment. "If you give up your profession, you give up our means of living. We can't starve."

"Starve!" laughed Mark. "Can't you trust me better than that? Look here, Caroline; let us come to figures. I don't suppose I should clear at first above eight hundred a-year, or so, by the practice—"

"O, Mark!"

"Well, say a thousand for argument's sake. Let us assume that I net it clear. It's a nice income, no doubt, but I shall make three times that, if I go into the thing in London."

Caroline, half doubting, half eager, all bewildered, sat waiting to hear more.

"There's a splendid opportunity offered me if I give up the medical profession and embark altogether in a new line of life. I—you have heard me speak of my old chum Barker, have you not?" he broke off to ask.

"Barker?" she repeated. "Yes, I think I remember the name. He got into some dreadful trouble, did he not, and was sent to prison?"

"Sent to prison! how you speak of things! All that's over and done with. His friends were wretched screws, doing him out of money that ought to have come to him, and the consequence was that Barker got into the Queen's Bench. Half the gentlemen of England have been there some time in their lives," added Mark, loftily, as if he were just then deeming the thing an honour. "Well, Caroline, that was over long ago, and Barker has now the most magnificent prospect before him that one can well imagine; he will be making his thousands and thousands a-year."

"How is he going to make it?" asked Caroline.

"And he has offered me a share in it," continued Mark, too eager to attend to irreverent questions. "He is one who knows how to stand by an old friend. Thousands a-year, it will be."

"But, Mark, I ask you how he is going to make it?"

"It is connected with mines and pumping, and all that sort of thing," lucidly explained Mark.

"Mines and pumping!"

"Caroline, dear, you cannot be expected to understand these things. Enormous fortunes are being made at them," continued Mark, in a rapture. "Some of the mines yield fifty thousand pounds profit the first year of working. I declare when I first heard of Barker's prospects I was fit to eat my fingers off, feeling that I was tied down to be a paltry pitiful country surgeon. Folks go ahead nowadays, Caroline. And, as Barker has generously come forward with the offer that I should join him, I think I ought to accept it in justice to you. My share the first year would be about three thousand, he computes."

"But, Mark, do you mean to say that Mr. Barker has offered you three thousand a-year for nothing? I don't comprehend it at all."

"Not for nothing. I should give my services, and I should have to advance a certain sum at the onset. Talk about an investment for your money, Caroline, what investment would be equal to this?"

The words startled her for the moment. "I promised poor Uncle Richard that the money should be settled upon me, Mark. He said he urged it as much for your sake as mine."

"Of course," said Mark, with acquiescent suavity. "Where there's nothing better to do with money it always ought to be so settled. But only look at this opening! Were your uncle Richard in life, he would be the first to advise the investment of the money in it. Such chances don't happen every day. Caroline, I can't and I won't humdrum on here, buried alive and worked to death, when I may take my place in the London world, a wealthy man, looked up to by society. In your interest, I will not."

"Are the mines in London?" asked Caroline.

"Good gracious, no! But the office is, where all the money transactions are carried on."

"And it is quite a sure thing, Mark?"

"It's as sure as the Bank of England. It wants a little capital to set it going, that's all. And that capital can be supplied by your money, Caroline, if you will agree to it. Hundreds of people would jump at the chance."

An utter tyro in business matters, in the ways of a needy world, imbued with unbounded faith in her husband, Caroline Cray took all in with eager and credulous ears. Little more than a child, she could be as easily persuaded as one, and she became as anxious to realise the good luck as Mark.

"Yes, I should think it is what my uncle would advise were he alive," she said. "And where should we live, Mark?"

"We'd live at the West End, Carine; somewhere about Hyde Park. You should have your open and close carriages, and your saddle-horses and servants—everything as it ought to be. No end of good things may be enjoyed with three thousand a-year."

"Would it stop at three thousand, Mark?" she questioned, with sparkling eyes.

"I don't expect it would stop at twenty," coolly asserted Mark. "How far it would really go on to, I'm afraid to guess. In saying three thousand, I have taken quite the minimum of the first year's profits."

"O Mark! don't let it escape you. Write tonight and secure it. How do you know but Barker may be giving it to somebody else?"

She was growing more eager than he. In her inexperience, she knew nothing of those miserable calamities—failure, deceit, fruition deferred. Not that her husband was purposely deceiving her; he fully believed in the good luck he spoke of. Mark Cray's was one of those sanguine roving natures which see an immediate fortune in every new scheme brought to them—if it be only wild enough.

"How long have you known of this, Mark!"

"Oh, a month or two. But, as you see, I would not stir in it. I should like to run up to town for a day to meet Barker; and, on my return, we'd set about the arrangements for leaving. There will be no more lonely dinners for you, Carine, once we are away from here. I shall not have to be beating about, all hours and weathers, from one patient's door to another, or dancing attendance on that precious Infirmary, knowing that you are sitting at home waiting for me, and the meal getting cold."

"O Mark, how delightful it will be! And perhaps you would never have risen into note, as my uncle did."

"No, I never should. Dr. Davenal's heart was in his profession, mine—"

Mark Cray stopped abruptly. The avowal upon his lips had been, "mine recoils from it."

It was even so. He did literally recoil from his chosen profession. Unstable in all his ways, Mark had become heartily sick of the routine of a surgeon's life. And since the affair of Lady Oswald a conviction had been gradually taking possession of him that he was entirely unfitted for it; nay, that he was incompetent To betray his incompetency, would be to lose caste for ever in the medical world of Hallingham.

Mark Cray rose from his chair again, and stood on the rug as before, pushing back his hair from his brow incessantly in the restlessness that was upon him. He was always restless when he thought of that past night; or of the certainty that he might at any time be called upon to perform again what he had failed in then. It was not altogether his skill he doubted, for Mark Cray was a vain and self-sufficient man; but he felt that the very-present consciousness of having broken down before would induce a nervousness that might cause him to break down again. Had it been practicable, Mark Cray would have taken flight from Hallingham and the medical world that very hour, and hid himself away from it for ever.

"It has become hateful to me, Carine!"

The words burst from him in the fulness of his thoughts. Both had been silent for some minutes, and they sounded quite startling in their vehemence. Mrs. Cray looked up at him.

"What do you mean, Mark? What has? The getting your meals so irregularly?"

"Yes;" said Mark, evasively. He did not choose to say that it was his profession which had become hateful to him, lest Mrs. Cray might inquire too closely why.

And, besides all this, had Mark been ever so successful in his practice, the vista opened to him of unlimited wealth (and he really so regarded it) might have turned a steadier head than his. His friend Barker had been Mark's "chum" (you are indebted to Mark for the epithet) at Guy's Hospital, and the intimacy had lasted longer than such formed intimacies generally do last. Mr. Barker was of the same stamp as Mark—hence, perhaps, the duration of the friendship; he had practised as a surgeon for a year or two, and then found it "too slow," and had tried his hand at something else. He had been trying his hand at something else and something else ever since, and somehow the things had dropped through one after the other with various degrees of failure, one degree of which had been to land Mr. Barker within the friendly walls of a debtor's prison. But he had come on his legs again; such men generally do;

and he was now in high feather as the promoter of a grand mining company. It was this he had invited Mark to embark in; he wrote him the most glowing accounts of the fabulous sums of money to be realised at it; he believed in them himself; he was, I have said, exactly the same sort of man as Mark.

One little drawback had recently presented itself to Barker: a want of ready money. Mark, in his eagerness, offered the sum coming to his wife from the Chancery suit; they were expecting it to be paid over daily; and Mr. Barker was in raptures, and painted his pictures of the future in colours gorgeous as those of a Claude Lorraine. Caroline might have felt a little startled had she known Mark had already promised the money without so much as consulting her. But Mark had chosen to take his own time to consult her, and Mark was doing it now. Perhaps he had felt it might be more decent to let poor Dr. Davenal be put under the ground before he spoke of applying the money in a way so diametrically opposed to his last wishes.

He drew a letter from his pocket, one received that morning, and read out its glowing promises. Mr. Barker was evidently fervent in his belief of the future. Caroline listened as in a joyous dream. The imaginary scene then dancing before her eyes of their future greatness rivalled any of the scenes of fairyland.

"You see," said Mark, "Barker—who's that?"

The entrance of a visitor into the hall had caused the interruption. Caroline bent her ear to listen.

"It is Aunt Bettina!" she exclaimed. "I am sure it is her voice, Mark. Whatever brings her here tonight?"

Mark crunched the letter into his pocket again. "Mind, Caroline, not a word of this to her!" he exclaimed, laying his hand on his wife as she was rising. "It is not quite ready to be talked of yet." Miss Davenal entered at once upon the subject which had brought her—their quitting the Abbey for the other house. Mark understood she had come, as it were, officially; to fix time and place and means; and he had no resource but to tell her that he did not intend to enter upon it; did not intend to embark Caroline's money in any such purpose; did not, in fact, intend to remain in Hallingham.

There ensued a battle: it was nothing else. What with Miss Davenal's indignation and what with Miss Davenal's deafness, the wordy war that supervened could be called little else. Caroline sat pretty quiet at first, taking her husband's side now and then.

"You tell me you are going to leave Hallingham, and you won't tell me where you are going, or what you are going to do, Mark Cray!" reiterated Miss Davenal.

"I'll tell you more about it when I know more myself."

"But you can tell me what it is; you can tell me where it is. Is it at one of the London hospitals?"

"It is in London," was Mark's answer, allowing the hospital to be assumed.

"Then Mark Cray you are very wicked. And you"—turning to Caroline—"are foolish to uphold him in it. How can you think of giving up such a practice as this?"

"I am tired of Hallingham," avowed Mark with blunt truth, for he was getting vexed.

"You are—what?" cried Miss Davenal, not catching the words.

"Sick and tired of Hallingham. And I don't care who knows it."

Miss Davenal looked at him with some curiosity. "Is he gone out of his senses, Caroline?"

"I am tired of Hallingham, too, aunt," said Caroline, audaciously. "I want to live in London."

"And the long and the short of it is, that we mean to live in London, Miss Bettina," avowed Mark. "There. I don't care that my talents should be buried in a poking country place any longer."

She looked from one to the other of them; she could not take it in. Sharp anger was rendering her ears somewhat more open than usual.

"Buried!—a poking country place! And what of the twelve or fifteen hundred a-year practice that you would lightly throw away, Mark Cray?"

"Oh, I shall do better than that in London. I have got a post offered me worth double that."

She paused a few moments. "And what; are you to give for it?"

"Never mind that," said Mark.

"Yes, never mind that," rejoined Miss Bettina in a tone of bitter sarcasm. "When it comes to details, you can take refuge in 'never mind.' Do you suppose such posts are given away for nothing, Mark Cray? Who has been befooling you?"

"But it will not be given for nothing," cried Caroline, betrayed to the injudicious avowal by the partizanship of her husband. "The money that is coining to me will be devoted to it."

This was the climax. Miss Bettina Davenal was very wroth; wroth however, more in sorrow than in anger. In vain she strove to sift the affair to the bottom; Mark baffled her questions, baffled her indignant curiosity, and—it must be confessed—his wife helped him.

She—Miss Bettina—turned away in the midst of the storm. She took up her black gloves, the only article of attire that she had removed, and drew them on her trembling hands. In the shaking of the hands alone did Bettina Davenal ever betray emotion: those firm, white, rather bony hands, usually so still and self-possessed.

"Marcus Cray, as surely as that you are standing now before me, you will rue this work if you carry it out. When that day shall come, I beg you—I beg you, Caroline—to remember that I warned you of it."

She passed out without another word, and stalked down the lighted street, uncomfortably upright, Neal behind her with his ginger tread.

CHAPTER XXXVI

IS MARK IN HIS SENSES?

Midway between the Abbey and her own home—it was in the corner just before coining to the market-place—Miss Davenal encountered Mr. Oswald Cray.

"Is Mark in his senses?" was her abrupt greeting to him, as he lifted his hat.

"What is the matter with him?—What is he doing?" asked Oswald, all in wonder.

Miss Davenal paused. Either she did not hear the question or she took time to recover herself to reply to it. Her face was very pale, her cold grey eyes glittered like steel in the lamplight.

"My poor brother has died young, and left this valuable practice in Mark's hands. There are not many like unto it. The house is ready to be offered to him: altogether, the career spreading out before him is a fine one. And he is talking of throwing it up. He is going to fling it from him as a child flings a pebble away into the sea. He says he shall quit Hallingham."

"Quit Hallingham!" repeated Oswald Cray, the last words of what she said alone making their full impression on him in his bewildered surprise. "Mark says he shall quit Hallingham?"

"He has some wild-goose scheme in his head of setting up in practice in London," said Miss Davenal, speaking in accordance with the notion she had erroneously assumed. "It is something he is about to purchase. He is going to purchase it with that money of Caroline's. But he has as surely lost his senses as that we are here."

"I cannot understand it," said Oswald. "No man in his senses would abandon such a practice as this."

"Just so. But I tell you he is not in his senses: he cannot be. I do not understand it any more than you. Perhaps you will see him?"

"I will. I am going there now. I have been calling at your house, Miss Davenal. Now that I have met you, will you let me express my deep sympathy in your sorrow for the loss you have sustained."

"Thank you, sir. It has been the greatest blow I could have experienced, and if I have not shown it much outwardly—for it is not in my nature to show such—it has done its work on my heart There are few men who could not have been spared in Hallingham, whether to the town or to his family, better than Dr. Davenal."

"It is frequently the case," said Oswald, half abstractedly, "that those whom we think we could the least spare, are taken. Fare you well, Miss Davenal." Oswald Cray strode on to the Abbey, the strange news puzzling him much. He did not take Mark at a disadvantage, as Miss Davenal had done. When he entered, Mark was all cool and easy, having had time to collect his wits and resolve on his course of action. That course was, not to open his lips about the scheme on hand to any other living mortal until it was ripe and ready to be acted upon. Miss Davenal's communication to Oswald rendered this somewhat difficult, but Mark did not stand on an evasion or two.

He was exceedingly surprised to see Oswald, not knowing that he was at Hallingham, and Caroline gave a little scream when he came in, in her pretty and somewhat affected manner. Oswald explained that he had not come from London, but from another part of the country, and had alighted at Hallingham for two or three hours only as he passed through it. He then entered upon the strange news just communicated to him.

But Mark had his answer to it ready at hand. He talked in a mocking tone about "busybodies," he ridiculed Miss Davenal's deafness, saying that she generally heard things "double:" altogether, he contrived to blind Oswald, to convince him that the whole thing was a fable; or, rather, a mistake, partly arising from Miss Davenal's infirmity, partly from a desire on his own part to "chaff" her for her interference. How Mark Cray reconciled this to his sense of honour, let him answer.

And Oswald, perfectly truthful himself, never doubted his half-brother. But he did not wholly quit the topic. He spoke of the few words written to him by Dr. Davenal when he was dying, and their purport— that he, Oswald, should urge the settlement of Mrs. Cray's own money upon her. Though of course, Oswald added, there was no necessity for him to do so: Mark would naturally see for himself that it was the only thing to be done with it.

Of course he saw it, testily answered Mark, who was growing cross.

"I cannot think how Miss Davenal could have misunderstood you as she did," proceeded Oswald. "She actually said that this money of Mrs. Cray's was to be applied to the purchase of the new thing in London in which you were proposing to embark."

"Did she!" returned Mark, in a tone that one impudent schoolboy retorts upon another. "I do wonder, Oswald, that you should listen to the rubbish picked up by a deaf woman!"

"The wonder is, how she could pick it up," returned Oswald. "But I am heartily glad it is not so. Miss Davenal assumed that you must be out of your senses, Mark," he added, a smile crossing his lips: "I fear I must have arrived at the same conclusion had you really been entertaining the notion of quitting Hallingham and throwing up such a practice as this."

"I wish to goodness people would mind their own business!" exclaimed Mark, who was losing his good manners in his vexation. The communication to his wife of his new scheme had been so smoothly accomplished, that the sudden interruption of Miss Davenal and now of Oswald Cray seemed all too like a checkmate; and Mark felt as a stag driven to bay. "I am old enough to regulate my own affairs without Miss Davenal," he continued, "and I want none of her interference."

Oswald did not speak.

"And, what's more, I won't stand it," resumed Mark; "either from her or from any one. There! And, Oswald, I hope you will excuse my saying it although you are my elder brother and may deem you have a right to dictate to me."

"The right to advise as a friend only, Mark," was the reply, somewhat pointedly spoken. "Never to dictate."

Mark growled.

"With Dr. Davenal's valuable practice before you, Mark, it may appear to you quite a superfluous precaution to secure the money to your wife and children," persisted Oswald. "But the chances and changes of life are so great, overwhelming families when least expected, that it behoves us all to guard those we love against them, as far as we have the power."

"Do you suppose I should not do the best for my wife that I can do?" asked Mark. "She knows I would. Be at ease, Oswald," he added in an easy tone, of which Oswald detected not the banter, "when Caroline's money shall be paid over, I'll send you notice of it. Talking of money, don't you think the doctor made a strange will?"

"I have not heard anything about his will," replied Oswald. "He has died very well off, I suppose?"

"We don't think that he has died well off," interposed Caroline. "I and Mark can't quite make it out, and they do not treat us with much confidence in the matter. Whatever there is, is left to Sara."

"To Sara?"

"Every stick and stone," returned Caroline, her cheeks assuming that lovely colour that excitement was apt to bring to them, and which, to a practised eye, might have suggested a suspicion of something not sound in the constitution. "All the property he died possessed of is to be sold, even to the household furniture; and the money realised from it goes to Sara."

"And the son—Captain Davenal?"

"There's nothing left to him; not a penny-piece. His name is not so much as mentioned in the will."

Oswald looked as though he could not believe it. He had thought that, of all men, Dr. Davenal would have been incapable of making an unjust will.

"Look here, Oswald," interrupted Mark, speaking in that half-whispered tone that is so suggestive of mystery, "there's something under all this that we can't fathom. Caroline overheard some words dropped by Miss Davenal to the effect that Sara was left dependent upon her, quite entirely dependent—"

"But how can that be?" interrupted Oswald. "Have you not just said that the whole property is willed to her?"

"True: but Miss Davenal did say it. It is all queer together," concluded Mark. "Why should he have willed it all to Sara, excluding Edward?—And why should Miss Davenal assert, as she did, that Sara would be penniless, and must have a home with herself? I am sure I and Caroline don't want their confidence," continued Mark, in a tone of resentment that was sufficient to betray he did want it. "But I say it's a queer will altogether. Nothing left to Edward, when it's well known the doctor loved him as the apple of his eye! Every sixpence that can be realised by the sales is to go to Sara; to be paid into her hands absolutely, without the security of trustees, or guardian, or anything. But as to his having died the wealthy man that he was thought to be, it is quite a mistake. So far as we can make out, there was no money laid by at all."

Oswald did not care to pursue the theme. The disposal of Dr. Davenal's property was nothing to him; and if he could not help a suspicion crossing his mind as to how the laid-by gains of years had been spent, it was certainly not his intention to enlighten his brother Marcus. Neal had hinted at hush-money months ago, and the hint was haunting Oswald now.

"Was it not a sudden death at the last?" exclaimed Caroline.

"Very," said Oswald, "It must have been a sad shock for you all. I am sure your cousin feels it much."

"Sara? Well, I don't know. I don't think she feels it more than I do. She seems as still and calm as a statue. She never shed a tear yesterday when the will was being read: and I am sure she listened to it. I never heard a word for my sobs."

But for the melancholy subject, Oswald would have smiled at Caroline's faith in her own depth of grief. She had yet to learn the signs of real sorrow.

"She is not demonstrative, I think," he observed, alluding to Sara.

"She never was," returned Caroline: "and therefore I argue that there can be no real feeling. I have gone into hysterics ten times since the death, only thinking of it, as Mark knows; and I question if anybody has so much as seen Sara cry. I said to her yesterday, 'How collected you are! how you seem to think of everything for the future!' 'Yes,' she answered in a dreamy sort of way, 'I have got work to do; I have got work to do.' I don't know why it should be," continued Mrs. Cray, after a pause, "but in the last few mouths Sara seems to have altered so much; to have turned grave before her time. It is as though all her youth had gone out of her."

Oswald rose: he believed his mission had been accomplished—that there was no doubt of Mark's investing his wife's money for her benefit, in accordance with the doctor's wishes. They pressed him to remain and take some tea, but he declined: he was returning to town that night. His last words to his half-brother proved how completely he was astray.

"Mark, it would be only kind of you to set Miss Davenal right. I am sure the misapprehension was causing her serious pain."

"I'll attend to her," rejoined Mark, with a careless laugh, as he went with him to the hall-door. "Goodnight, Oswald. A safe journey to you!"

Mark returned to his wife. He had not quite liked to use that deliberate deceit to Oswald Cray in her presence. But Mark was ingenious in sophistries, in that kind of logic which tends to "make the worse appear the better reason," and Caroline put full faith in him as she listened to his half-apology, half-explanation.

"It would never have done to enlighten him," observed Mark. "What I have said, I said for your sake, Carine. Oswald is one who would rather let a man plod on for years on bread and cheese, than see him make a dash and raise himself at once to independence. He's a slow-going coach himself, and thinks everybody else ought to be!"

And, propping his back against the side of the mantelpiece, Mark Cray enlarged upon all the grandeur and glory of the prospect opening to him, painting its future scenes in colours so brilliant that his wife lost herself in a trance of admiration, and wished it could all be realised with the morning light.

PART THE SECOND

CHAPTER XXXVII

ENTERING ON A NEW HOME

For once London was bright. A glorious spring day late in March had gladdened the spirits of the metropolitan world, dreary with the fogs and rains of the passing winter, and as the street passengers looked up at the clear blue sky, the shining sun, they said to each other that the day was a foretaste of summer.

The sun drew to its setting, and its red rays fell on the terminus of the Great Western Railway at Paddington; on all the bustle and confusion of a train just in. Amidst the various vehicles driving out of the station with their freight, was a cab, containing two ladies dressed in deep mourning, one of whom, the elder, had not recovered from the pushing about to which she had been subjected in the confusion of arrival, and was protesting that she should not recover it, and that there ought to be arrangements made to protect lady travellers from such. On the box beside the driver was a—was he a gentleman, or was he a servant? If the latter, he was certainly a most superior one in looks, but the idle people standing about and casting their eyes up to the passing cabs were taking him no doubt for the former. The luggage piled up on the top of the cab and on the front seat of the inside, seemed to say that these travellers had come from a distance.

In point of fact they had come from Hallingham, for they were no other than Miss Davenal and her niece, and the gentleman on the box was Neal. Miss Davenal kept up her chorus of complaint. It had begun with the discomforts attendant on the arrival of a large train at the terminus, and it would be continued, there was little doubt, for ever and a day; for though Miss Bettina had come to London by her own free decision, she had come sorely against her will.

"Jostling! pushing! hustling! roaring! It is a shame that ladies should be subjected to such. Why don't they manage things better?"

"But, Aunt Bettina, you need not have been in the bustle. If you had but seated yourself in the cab, as Neal suggested, and allowed him to see after the luggage—"

"Hold your tongue, Sara. What was one pair of eyes to look after all the luggage we have got? I chose to see to it as well as Neal; and I say that the way you get pushed about is shameful. My firm belief is, we have lost at least ten of the smaller packages."

"No, no, aunt, they are all here; I counted them as they were brought to the cab."

"Yes, that's about all you are good for!—counting the cabs! I'd spend my moments to a little more purpose. Good heavens! we shall be run down! If this is London. I wish I had never heard of it."

The cab threaded its way amidst the crowded streets and its inmates' terrors—for Sara was little less timid than her aunt—until it drew up before a small house in Pimlico; small as compared with their house at home. Miss Davenal looked up at it and gave a groan; and Neal opened the cab door.

"Is this the place, Neal? It is dreadfully small."

"I think you will find it convenient, ma'am. It is better inside than out."

Better inside than out! It was new and fresh and pleasant-looking; but to poor Miss Davenal it appeared, as she had said, dreadfully small. Sara seemed less disagreeably impressed. She had not anticipated great things; and it was of very little consequence to her where she lived now. In reality, it was rather a nice house, of moderate size; but Miss Davenal was estimating it by comparison—as we all estimate things.

She turned herself about in the small passage in dismay. A door on the left led into the parlour, the room they would use for dining; about four such could have been put into the dining-room at Hallingham. The staircase would scarcely admit of two abreast; and in front of it, at the top, was the drawing-room, a light, cheerful apartment, with one large window. The furniture in these rooms was Miss Davenal's, and it crowded them inconveniently.

Dorcas, she who had lived at the Abbey with Mrs. Cray, stood there with a smiling face to receive them; and the landlady, a humble sort of person, in a green stuff gown, who had the pleasure of residing in the back kitchen and sleeping in some obscure attic, came forward also. The greater portion of the house had been taken unfurnished for Miss Davenal.

"About the bedrooms Dorcas?" inquired Miss Davenal, in a half-frightened tone. "Which is mine?"

"Which you please to choose, ma'am," was Dorcas's answer. "The two best chambers are the one behind the drawing-room, and the one over the drawing-room."

The room over the drawing-room was the largest and best, but Miss Davenal did not like so many stairs, and resigned it to Sara. She, Miss Davenal, turned herself about in the small back room as she had done in the passage; her own spacious chamber at home was all too present to her, and she wondered whether she should ever become reconciled to this.

Had any one told her a few short months before—nay, a few short weeks—that she should ever take up her abode in London, she had rejected the very idea as absurd, almost an impossibility. Yet here she was! come to it of her own decision, of her own accord, but in one sense terribly against her will.

Marcus Cray had carried out his plans. To the intense astonishment of Hallingham he had rejected the valuable practice which had become his by the death of Dr. Davenal, and his mode of relinquishing it had been a most foolish one. Whether he feared the remonstrances of his brother, the reproaches of Miss Davenal, or the interference of other friends of his wife, certain it is that Mark, in disposing of the practice, had gone unwisely to work. A practice such as Dr. Davenal's, if placed properly in the market, would have brought forth a host of men eager to be the purchasers and to offer a fair and just sum for it. But of this Mark Cray allowed no chance. He privately negotiated with a friend of his, a Mr. Berry, and sold him the goodwill for little more than an old song.

In vain Miss Davenal said cutting things to Mark; in vain Oswald Cray, when the real truth reached him, came hastening down from London, in doubt whether Mark had not really gone mad. They could not undo the contract. It was signed and sealed, and Mr. Berry had paid over the purchase-money.

Then Mark spoke out upon the subject of his London prospects; he enlarged upon their brilliancy until Miss Davenal herself was for the moment dazzled. She urged on Mark the justice of his resigning to Dr. Davenal's daughter part of this purchase-money; Mark evaded it. His agreement with Dr. Davenal, he said, was to pay to his daughter three hundred pounds per annum for five years; and provided he did pay it, it could be of no consequence whether he made it by doctoring or by other means: he should fulfil his bargain, and that was enough.

Mark had had it all his own way. The money expected by his wife had been paid over to him, and he kept it. It was a great deal less than was expected, for Chancery had secured its own slice out of the pie; but it was rather more than four thousand pounds. Mark was deaf to all suggestions, all entreaties; he completely ignored the last wishes of Dr. Davenal; turned round on Oswald, and flatly told him it was no business of his; and carried the money to London in his pocket, when he and Caroline quitted Hallingham.

They quitted it in haste and hurry, long before things were ripe and ready for them in London, Mark remarking to his wife that the sooner they were out of that hornet's nest the better—by which term he probably distinguished Miss Davenal and a few others who had considered themselves privileged to interfere, so far as remonstrance went. Caroline more than seconded all his wishes, all he did; Mark had imbued her with his own rose-coloured views of the future, and she was eager to enter on its brightness.

The next to look out for a home was Miss Bettina Davenal. Affairs of the sales and else had not been carried out so quickly and readily as Mr. Wheatley in his inexperience had anticipated, and there had been no immediate hurry for the house to be vacated. A surgeon in the town was in treaty for it, and the furniture would have to be sold by auction. Sara wondered that her aunt did not fix upon a residence, and she feared all would be scuffle and bustle when they came to leave.

But Miss Davenal had been fixing upon one in her own mind; at least, upon the locality for one—and that was London. Never, willingly, did Bettina Davenal forego a duty, however unpalatable it might be, and she did believe it to be her duty to follow the fortunes of Caroline, and not abandon her entirely to the mercy of her imprudent, thoughtless husband. To quit Hallingham, the home of her whole life, would be a cruel trial; but she thought she ought to do so. And she bestowed a few bitter words upon the absent Mark for inducing the necessity.

Miss Bettina set about her plans. If there was one quality she was distinguishable for, above all others, it was obstinacy. Obstinate she was at all times, but in the cause of right or duty she could be unflinchingly so. Watton, their former upper-maid, was established in her new situation as housekeeper in the house of business in St. Paul's Churchyard, and Miss Davenal wrote to her and requested her to look out for a house or for a portion of one, and let her know about it. Mr. and Mrs. Cray had taken a house in Grosvenor Place, facing the Green Park, and Miss Davenal wished to be as near to them as her pocket would allow.

Watton attended to her commission. She thought that part of a handsome house would be more suitable to Miss Davenal's former position than the whole of an inferior one, and she did her best. Miss Davenal found it, as you have just seen, anything but handsome; but she had little notion of the prices asked in London, and she had limited Watton as to the house-rent she was to offer. Neal was sent up to London with the furniture, which had been warehoused for so many years; and when he returned to Hallingham Dorcas took his place in London. Discharged by Mrs. Cray, who had not chosen to take country servants with her, she had been re-engaged by Miss Davenal, whose modest household was henceforth to comprise only Dorcas and Neal. Miss Davenal would not part with Neal if she could help it; but she had been surprised at the man's ready agreement to stay in so reduced an establishment.

And so, before things were quite in readiness for them, Miss Davenal and Sara had come up. The furniture in the house at Hallingham was being prepared for public sale, and they hastened away, not to witness the desecration. How coldly and chilly this new home struck upon both, now that they had really entered upon it, they alone could tell. Neither slept through that first night, and they arose in the morning alike unrefreshed.

Breakfast over, Sara stood at the window. In their immediate situation all the houses were private ones, but from a proximate corner she could see the bustle of the highroad and the omnibuses passing up and down. The day was bright, as the previous one had been, giving to London its best aspect, and all the world was astir.

"And now for Mark Cray and Caroline," said Miss Bettina.

It had been Miss Davenal's pleasure that Mark Cray and his wife should be kept in ignorance of this emigration of hers to London. Neal, during his brief sojourn there, and Dorcas afterwards, had been enjoined to keep strictly clear of the vicinity of their house. Having no motive to disobey, they had complied with the orders; and Mr. and Mrs. Cray were yet in total ignorance that their relatives were so near.

She put on her things and went out, Neal, as usual in attendance. Neal was well acquainted with the geography of the place, and piloted his mistress to the house in a few minutes' time: a handsome house, with stone steps and pillars before the door. Miss Davenal gazed at it with drawn-in lips.

"It cannot be this, Neal."

"Yes, ma'am, it is. Shall I ring?"

Miss Davenal pushed forward and rang herself, an imperative peal. What right had they, she was mentally asking, to venture on so expensive a house as this must be? A footman flung open the door.

"Does Mr. Cray live here?"

"Yes," said the footman with a lofty air: as of course it was incumbent as him to put on to anybody so dead to good manners as to call at that early hour. "What might your business be?"

None could put down insolence more effectually than Bettina Davenal. She gave the man a look, and swept past him.

"Show me to your mistress, man."

And somehow the man was subdued to do as he was bid, and to ask quite humbly, "What name, ma'am?"

"Miss Davenal."

He opened the door of a room on the right, and Miss Davenal, never more haughty, never more stately, stepped into it. She saw it was of good proportions, she saw it was elegantly furnished; and Caroline, in a flutter of black ribbons on her pretty morning toilette, was sitting toying with a late breakfast.

She started up with a scream. Believing that the lady before her was safe at Hallingham, perhaps the scream was excusable.

"Aunt! Is it really you? Whatever brings you in London?"

Miss Bettina neglected the question to survey the room again. She had surveyed the hall as she came in; she caught a glimpse of another room at the back: all fitted up fit for a duke and duchess.

"Where's Mark Cray?" she cried.

"Mark has been gone out ages ago, aunt. He is deep in business now. The operations have begun."

"Who took this house?" grimly asked Miss Bettina.

"I and Mark."

"And what did the furniture cost?"

"Oh, I don't know. I don't think Mark has had the bills in yet. Why, aunt?"

"Why!" returned the indignant lady, in a blaze of anger. "You and your husband are one of two things, Caroline; swindlers or idiots. If you think that strong language, I cannot help it."

"Aunt Bettina!" echoed the startled girl, "what are you saying?"

"The truth," solemnly replied Miss Bettina.

CHAPTER XXXVIII

HOPE DEFERRED

Some weeks went on. The beautiful summer weather had come, and the June sun was upon the streets.

Sara Davenal stood at her chamber window looking out on the dusty road. Not in reality seeing it; for the trouble and perplexity at her heart had not lessened, and she had fallen into that habit of gazing outwards in deep thought, noticing nothing. The same habit had characterised Dr. Davenal; but at his daughter's age he had never known any weight of care. For years and years his path had been a smooth one—little else than sunshine. She gazed outwards on the dusty road, on the white pavement, glistening again with its heat, but saw nothing. A looker-on would have said she was an idle girl, standing there to take note of her neighbours' and the street's doings: of the tradespeople calling at the opposite houses, of the servant girls flirting with them as they gave their orders: of the water-cart splashing past the corner along the public highway, but neglecting this quiet nook: of everything, in short, there was to see and be seen. How mistaken that looker-on was he could never know. Poor Sara Davenal might have been the sole living object on a broad desert plain, for all she saw of the moving panorama around her.

"Hope deferred maketh the heart sick!" When that proverb of the wise king of Israel comes practically home to our hearts in all its stern reality, we have learnt one of the many bitter lessons of life. Perhaps few have realised it more intensely than Sara Davenal had latterly been obliged to realise it. From March to April, from April to May, from May to June, week by week, and morning by morning, she had been waiting for something that never came.

A very short while to wait for anything some of you may be thinking; not much more than two months at the most, for it is only the beginning of the blooming summer month, and they had come to London late in March. But—I believe I said the same a chapter or two ago—a space of time is long or short according as we estimate it. Two months' space may pass lightly over us as a fleeting summer's day; or it may drag its slow length along, every minute of it marking its flight upon our sick and weary hearts, with enough of agony crowded into it to make it seem a lifetime.

Sara and Miss Bettina had come up in March, and the things at Hallingham were to be sold within a few days of their departure; and in a few days after that Sara had expected the money would be paid over to her. In her inexperience, she did not sufficiently allow for delays: yet had she been ever so experienced she would not have supposed the delay would extend itself to this. It is not of much moment to inquire into the precise cause of this delay: it is sufficient to know that it did occur; and it gave as yet no signs that it would be speedily ended.

Sara had expected the money early in April. It did not come. "It will be up next week," she said to herself. But the next week came and did not bring it, and she wrote to Mr. Wheatley. He hoped to realise in a day or two was his somewhat incautious answer; but in truth he himself, not being a man of business, anticipated no vexatious delay. It was an unfortunate answer for Sara, for from that date she began to look for the money daily; and you have not yet to learn what impatience this daily waiting and expecting works in the human heart. When one morning's post passed over and did not bring it or news of it, Sara counted on it for the morrow. And the morrows came and went, on and on; and Sara wrote and wrote, until she grew sick with the procrastination and the disappointment. She had waited for this money so anxiously that it had become with her a feverish longing; something like that strange disease, mal du pays, as it is called, which attacks the poor Swiss, exiled from their native land. Not for the sake of the money itself was she so troubled—you know that; but from the fear of what the evil delay might bring. In reply to the letter she had forwarded to Mr. Alfred King, on the death of Dr. Davenal, that unknown gentleman, whoever he might be, had replied in a short note and a very illegible handwriting (abounding in flourishes), that he was sorry to hear of the doctor's death, but counted on the fulfilment of the obligations without vexatious delay. This was addressed to Min Sara Davenal, and reached her safely at Hallingham.

Poor Sara, in her inexperience, in her dread of what this man might have in his power touching her brother, feared he might deem two or three weeks only a "vexatious delay:" and when the two or three weeks went on, and two or three weeks to those, and two or three weeks again, then it was that the dread within her grew into a living agony. Who Mr. Alfred King might be she knew not. On that night when she had been called down to Dr. Davenal's study and found her brother there, she had gathered from some words dropped by the doctor, in his very imperfect explanation to her, that some one else had been almost equally culpable with her brother: but who this other was, whether gentleman or swindler, whether male or female, she had no means of knowing. She did not suppose it to be Mr. Alfred King: she rather surmised that whoever it was must have gone away, as Edward had. Now and then she would wonder whether this Mr. Alfred King could be connected with the police: but that was hardly likely. Altogether, her ideas of Mr. Alfred King were extremely vague; still she could not help dreading the man, and never thought of him without a shiver.

She did not know what to do: whether to remain passive, or to write and explain that the money was coming, and apologise for the temporary delay. She felt an aversion to write, and she could not tell whether it might do harm or good. And so she did nothing; and the time had gone on, as you have heard, to June.

Sara stood at the window gazing into space, when her attention was awakened to outward things by seeing the postman turn into the street with a fleet step. Could it be the morning postman? Yes, it must be, for the second delivery did not take place until eleven, and it was now half-past nine. Something had rendered him later than usual.

She threw up the window listlessly. So many, many mornings had she watched for the post to bring this news from Hallingham, and been disappointed, that a reaction had come, and she now looked only for disappointment. You will understand this. The postman was dodging from one side of the road to the other with that unnecessary waste of time and walking (as it seems to the uninitiated) which must help to make postmen's legs so weary. He was at the opposite house now, superseding the butcher boy in the good graces of the maid-servant, with whom he stayed a rather unnecessary while to talk; and now he came striding over. Sara leaned her head further out and saw him make for their gate.

And her pulses suddenly quickened. Even from that height she could discern—or fancied she could discern—that the letter was from Mr. Wheatley. That gentleman always used large blue envelopes, and it was certainly one such that the man had singled out from his bundle of letters. Had it come at last? Had the joyful news of the money come?

She closed the window and ran swiftly down the stairs and met Neal turning from the door with the letter. That official was probably not at all obliged to her for demanding the letter from him so summarily. But he had no resource but to give it up.

It was from Mr. Wheatley, and Sara carried it to her room, a bright flush of hope on her cheeks, an eager trembling on her happy fingers. Mr. Wheatley did not like letter-writing, and she knew quite well that he would not have written uselessly. Opening the envelope she found it a blank; a blank entirely: nothing even written inside it: it had but enclosed a letter for herself which had apparently been sent to Hallingham. O the bitter, bitter disappointment! there was not a line, there was not a word from Mr. Wheatley.

A conviction arose that she had seen the other handwriting before. Whose was it?—it seemed to be made up of flourishes. Mr. Alfred King's! Her heart stood still in its fear, and seemed as if it would never go on again:—

"Essex Street, June 1st.

"Madam,

"I am sorry to have to give you notice that unless the money owing to me, and which I have been vainly expecting these several weeks, is immediately paid, I shall be under the necessity of taking public steps in the matter; and they might not prove agreeable to Captain Davenal.

"I am, Madam,

"Your obedient servant,

"Alfred King.

"Miss Sara Davenal."

So the first faint realisation of the haunting shadow of the past weeks had come! Sara sat with the letter in her hand. She asked herself what was to be done?—and she wished now, in a fit of vain repentance, that she had written long ago to Mr. Alfred King, as it had been in her mind to do.

She must write now. She must write a note of regret and apology, telling him the exact truth—that the sale of the different effects at Hallingham and the realisation of the proceeds had taken more time than was anticipated, but that she expected the money daily—and beg of him to wait. In her feverish impatience it seemed as if every moment that elapsed until this explanation should be delivered to Mr. Alfred King was fraught with danger, and she hastened to the room below, the drawing-room.

Her desk was there. It was generally kept in her own chamber, but she had had it down the previous evening. Neal was quitting the room as she entered: he had been putting it in order for the day. Miss Davenal was in the parlour below, where she generally remained an hour or two after breakfast.

The letter—Mr. Alfred King's letter—was spread open before Sara, and she sat pen in hand deliberating how she should answer it, when her aunt's voice startled her. It sounded on the stairs. Was she coming up? Sara hastily placed the open letter in the desk, closed and locked it, and opened the drawing-room door. But in her flurry she left the key in the desk.

Miss Davenal was standing on the mat at the foot of the stairs "Can't you hear me call?" she asked.

"I did hear, aunt. What is it?"

"Then you ought to have heard!" was the retort of Miss Davenal, at cross-purposes as usual. "You are not turning deaf, I suppose?"

"What is it, aunt?" repeated Sara, going half-way down the stairs.

Instead of answering, Miss Davenal turned and went into the breakfast-room again. Sara could only follow her. Her aunt's manners had never relaxed to her from the sternness assumed at the time of Dr. Davenal's death: cold and severe she had remained ever since; but she looked unusually cold and severe now.

"Shut the door," said Miss Davenal.

Sara hesitated for a moment, more in mind than action, and then she obeyed. She had left her desk, and wanted to get back to it.

"Hold this," said Miss Davenal.

She had taken her seat in her own chair, and was cutting out some articles of linen clothing that looked as long as the room. Her income was a very moderate one now, and she did a good deal of sewing instead of putting it out. Sara took the stuff in her hand, and held it while her aunt cut: an interminable proceeding to an impatient helpmate, for Miss Davenal cut only about an inch at a time, and then drew a short thread and cut again.

"Won't it tear?" asked Sara.

"It will wear. Did you ever know me buy linen that wouldn't wear? I have too good an eye for linen to buy what won't wear."

"I asked, aunt, if it would not tear."

"Tear!" repeated Miss Davenal, offended at the word—at the ignorance it betrayed. "No, it will not tear; and I should think there's hardly a parish school child in the kingdom but would know that, without asking."

Sara, rebuked, held her part in silence. Presently Miss Davenal lifted her eyes and looked her full in the face.

"Who was that letter from this morning?"

"It was a private letter, aunt."

"A what?" snapped Miss Davenal.

Sara let fall the work, and stood fearlessly before Miss Davenal. The most gentle spirit can be aroused at times. "The letter was from a gentleman, aunt. It was a private letter to myself. Surely I am not so much of a child that I may not be trusted to receive one?"

"A pri-vate let-ter!—A gentleman!" was the amazed reiteration of Miss Bettina. "What do you say?"

Sara stood quite still for a moment, while the faint flush that was called up died away on her cheeks, and then she bent close to her aunt's ear, her low voice unmistakably clear and distinct.

"Aunt Bettina, you knew there was some unhappy business that papa was obliged to meet—and bear—just before he died. The letter I have received this morning bears reference to it. It is from a Mr. King, but I don't know him. I should be thankful if you would not force me to these explanations: they are very painful."

Miss Bettina picked up the work and drew at a thread until it broke. "Who is Mr. King?" she asked.

"I do not indeed know. I never saw him in my life. He had to write to me just a word about the business, and I must answer him. In telling you this much, Aunt Bettina, I have told all I can tell. Pray, for papa's sake, do not ask me further."

"Well, this is a pretty state of things for the enlightened nineteenth century!" grunted Miss Bettina. "We have read of conspiracies and Rye-House plots, and all the rest of it: this seems a plot, I think! Have you nothing more to say?"

"No, aunt," was the low, firm answer.

"Then you may go," said Miss Bettina, twitching the work out of Sara's hand. "I can do this myself."

And Sara knew that no amount of entreaty would induce her aunt to admit of help in her cutting after that. She went upstairs, and met Neal coming out of the drawing-room.

"I thought you had finished the room, Neal," she said, a sudden fear stealing over her as she remembered that her desk was left with the key in it.

"So I had, Miss. I came up now for this vase. My mistress said it was to be washed."

He went downstairs carrying it: a valuable vase of Sèvres porcelain, never intrusted to the hands of anybody but Neal. It had belonged to poor Richard—was presented to him just before he went out on his unfortunate voyage. Sara walked to her desk; it stood on the centre table. What with vases and other ornaments, and superfluous articles of furniture, the room was somewhat inconveniently full. It was a good-sized room, too; nearly square, the window facing you as you entered it, and the fireplace on the right. Opposite the fireplace was a beautiful inlaid cabinet with a plate-glass back: it had never cost less than forty pounds: but Miss Bettina had not spared money when she bought her furniture years ago. Look at the girandoles on the walls!—at the costly carpet, soft as velvet! Opposite the window stood Sara's piano, a fine instrument, the gift of her loving father on her eighteenth birthday. Altogether the room was an elegant one, but Miss Bettina could not have reconciled herself to any other. The parlour below was a nice room also, with its handsome sideboard and its glittering mirrors: but it was smaller than the drawing-room.

Sara stood for a moment before her desk: it looked exactly as she left it. She turned the key and raised the lid, and saw that had anybody else done the same Mr. Alfred King's letter was lying face upwards, and might have been read without the slightest trouble in an instant of time. Had Neal seen the letter? Would he be likely to do such a thing as raise her desk surreptitiously? Many a servant would be in a room with an unlocked desk times and again, and never attempt to peer inside it. Was it probable that Neal had any propensity for prying into affairs that did not concern him? It all lay in that.

Vexed with herself for having allowed the chance to any one, Sara carried her desk to her chamber, and sat down and wrote her note there. But she could not get the thought quite so readily out of her head: it was most inexpedient that Neal, or any one else, should see that letter of Mr. Alfred King's. There occurred to her mind something her brother Edward had once told her—about a doubt of Dr. Davenal's—as to whether Neal had not opened a note of Lady Oswald's. Suddenly she thought of the doctor's desk. If that had been opened In an impulse of fear he put the key into the lock.

It would not turn. Something was the matter with the lock. Had it been tampered with? Sara's face grew hot.

Turning and twisting and pulling, but all gently, she worked the key about in the lock. No, it would not open it. In the previous summer's holidays a certain cupboard in Watton's room downstairs declined to be opened in just the same way, and when inquiries came to be made, Master Dick Davenal boldly avowed that, wanting some jam one day, he had opened it with another cupboard key, and so had spoiled the lock. Had this lock been put out of order in the same way? The proper key to it was always about herself.

A locksmith had to be brought in to the desk. He speedily opened it and put the lock to rights. "It was only a ward bent," he said. Sara inquired whether he thought it had been done through a strange key being put into the lock, but she did not get much satisfaction. "Like enough it might," he said, but "sometimes them wards got out of order with their own key."

"It seems quite a common lock," remarked Sara, as she paid him.

"Laws, yes! A'most any key might open that."

"What was the matter with the desk?" questioned Miss Bettina, who met the man in the passage as he was going away.

"I don't know, aunt. It would not open: such a thing has never happened to it before. Do you remember last midsummer holidays Dick spoiled Watton's cupboard through undoing it with a false key? The man says it may have been the same case here." And Neal, who was standing immediately opposite his young mistress, and met her eye as she spoke heard the words with unruffled composure; not so much as a shade of change disturbing the equanimity of his impassive countenance.

CHAPTER XXXIX

AN UNPLEASANT VISIT

"Set me down at Essex Street."

The request, proffered in a sweet and timid yoke, was made by a young lady who had just taken her place in an omnibus. The conductor's gracious response was to shut the door with a desperate bang, and call out "hi" to the driver, as a signal that he might go on.

The young lady was too pretty not to be stared at; but the crape veil, pertaining to her handsome mourning, was not raised from before her face, as she took her seat with that quiet self-possession which rarely forsakes the gentlewoman.

You will be at no loss to guess that it was Sara Davenal. The expedition she was bound upon was one that nothing save obligation could have forced upon her—a visit to Mr. Alfred King. Her note to that gentleman had brought forth another letter from him. It was to the effect that he could not wait longer for the money without the utmost inconvenience, but he would do himself the honour of calling upon her at eleven o'clock the following morning, to discuss the matter in person. A most unsatisfactory, dismaying communication to Sara. To receive him in her Aunt Bettina's house was out of all question; for that estimable lady would undoubtedly have insisted upon making a third at the interview. To have the secret brought home to her very hearth would be too fortunate an opportunity to miss acquainting herself with its nature and details, even though she had to draw the information from Mr. Alfred King. Sara saw what must be done, however she might dislike it; and she wrote a hasty note to the gentleman, saying that it would not be convenient to receive him in her own house, but she would instead wait upon him in Essex Street. Hence her unwonted omnibus journey.

The omnibus dashed along on its road. It was full, and therefore there was no loitering. Leaving Pimlico behind it, it passed Charing Cross and gained the Strand. There it stopped for somebody to get out, and Sara looked up at an exclamation made by the passenger seated immediately opposite to her next the door, a lady apparently but little older than herself: a quiet, steady, self-possessed girl with a pleasing face and fair hair.

The passing of a gentleman on the payment, close up to which the omnibus was drawn, had apparently caused the exclamation to escape her. His eyes in the same moment caught the fair face bent towards him from the door, and he approached. A bright smile greeted him, and he took her hand and kept it as they spoke together.

"You, Jane!" he exclaimed, and the voice, subdued though it was, bore a laughing sound. "It is about the last place I should have expected to see you in. I thought you and omnibuses were decided foes."

"But I am going a long way this morning; too far to walk," she answered. "We have had a letter from—"

She bent her face lower, and the words became indistinct. The gentleman resumed.

"And you are going to inquire about it? Well, Jane, don't be in a hurry. I'll tell you why another time. Inquire particulars if you like, but fix nothing. The fact is, I have something else in view."

"Of course we'd not fix anything without consulting you," she answered in her pleasant Scotch accent. "When will you be coming?"

"Tonight most likely. Goodbye, Jane. Take care of yourself."

He released her hand which he had been holding all the while, the conductor gave the door a bang, and the omnibus dashed on. Sara had turned white as death. A variety of emotions that she would not have cared to analyse were at conflict within her—for the voice was the voice of Oswald Cray.

And he had gone away, not seeing her. For that she was on some accounts thankful. He might have been as much surprised to see her in an omnibus—perhaps more so—as he was the young lady opposite; and least of all to Oswald Cray could Sara have explained the errand on which she was bent. She stole a glance at the girl's interesting face: a good and sensible face one that might well win the regard even of Oswald Cray; and that baneful plant, jealousy, which perhaps had taken root in her heart before, suddenly shot forth its sharp tendrils into every corner. What right had she, Sara Davenal, to indulge any such passion?—had she not parted from Oswald Cray for ever?

"Did you not ask to be put down at Essex Street?"

The question aroused her from her pain. It came from the same young lady opposite, and Sara looked up with a start.

"Yes;" she answered.

"Then we must have passed it, for this that we are going through is Temple Bar, and I know Essex Street is before we come to that. This young lady told you to set her down at Essex Street," she added to the conductor. And the man stopped the omnibus without offering the slightest apology.

"Thank you," said Sara to her courteously. And she walked away with the pleasant voice ringing in her ear: and the conviction within her that it must be Jane Allister.

She walked slowly down Essex Street, looking out for the offices of Messrs. Jones and Green, and soon found them. It was a large and dusty-looking house, on the right-hand side of the street, and was apparently let out to different occupants, as there were various names on the door. The top one was "Mr. Carberry:" it was simply written in black letters on the door-post; the second was on a great brass plate, nearly as large as the post itself, "Jones and Green:" and there was another brass plate, which had on it "Messrs. Knollys, Solicitors to the Great Chwddyn Mining Company."

Sara stood still as the last words caught her eye, arrested by surprise. It was not the unpronounceable name that drew her attention; but the fact that this Great Chwddyn scheme was the very one in which Mark Cray had embarked; the El Dorado of his friend Barker; the source of Mark's present flourishing prosperity and of his future greatness.

She felt sure it was the same name, though nobody ever wrote it twice alike; and whether this, or any other, might be the correct way of spelling it, the Messrs. Knollys themselves could not have told. Mark Cray and Barker, finding the word rather difficult to the tongue, had got into the habit of calling it the "Great Wheal Bang Company," as being readier than the other: "Wheal Bang" being some technical term connected with the mine; though whether applicable to any particular stratum of its ore, or to the works, or to the mine generally, or to anything else, Sara had never yet clearly understood. "The Great Wheal Bang Mining Company" was the familiar term in Mark's mouth, and in that of others interested in the mine: so prone we are to catch up phrases: and "The Great Wheal Bang" was certainly better for English tongues than the Great Chwddyn, with its variety of spelling in uninitiated hands. For once that Sara had heard the difficult name she had heard the easier one a hundred times; nevertheless, now that her eyes fell upon it, she knew it to be that, and no other.

The fact in itself was not of moment to her, but thought is quick; and the thought that darted across Sara's mind was, that if Messrs. Knollys were the solicitors to this rich and important company, there might possibly be a chance of Mark Cray's or of his friend Barker's calling in at these offices at any moment, in which case they might see her. And that would not be at all convenient.

But there was no help for it. She could but go in; and the chance only added another drop to the cup of pain. Most painful was it to Sara, from more causes than one, to come thus publicly to these places of business: and to come as may be almost said, in secret; not daring to speak of her real errand.

With her crape veil drawn more closely over her face she stepped into the passage. A door on the left bore the words "Messrs. Knollys;" and Sara was looking around her when a young man with a paper in his hand came hastily out of it.

"Did you want Knollys's office?" he asked, in a civil tone, noting her look of indecision.

"I want Messrs. Jones and Green's."

"Upstairs, first floor." Sara thanked him, and passed through the inner entrance, which stood open, and ascended the stairs. In great white letters on the door facing her at the top, she read, "Office: Jones and Green." She knocked at the door, and a middle-aged man in a seedy suit of black opened it.

"I wish to see Mr. Alfred King," she said. "Is he here?"

"Mr. Alfred King?" repeated the man. "He is not here now, and I don't know—Stay, I'll inquire."

Leaving her standing there, he retreated, and she heard a remote colloquy carried on in an undertone. Then he came back again.

"Mr. King won't be here until twelve o'clock."

"I had an appointment with him at eleven," said Sara, wondering whether there could be any mistake.

"Perhaps so," said the man. "But he dropped us a line this morning to say he could not get here until twelve. I daresay if you come then you can see him."

He shut the door, and Sara went downstairs again. What should she do with herself this long hour—for it was not quite eleven yet. Suddenly she bethought herself that she would go to see Watton. St. Paul's Churchyard, as Watton had told then—for she had paid Miss Davenal and Sara two or three visits since their arrival in London—was in a line with Temple Bar.

Sara walked quickly through the crowded streets. Once she stopped to look in at an attractive shop, but somebody came jostling against her, she thought purposely, and she did not stop again. She easily found the house of business where Watton now was, and its private door. Watton came forward all in surprise, and took her into a plain comfortable sitting-room, which was her own, she said. Sara inquired if she liked the situation any better: for at first Watton had not liked it.

"Well, yes, miss; I think I do," was the woman's answer. "Use and time soften most things. There's a great deal of responsibility on me, and enough work also. What I can't get reconciled to is the dust and the noise. As to the dust and dirt, I'd never have believed in it without seeing it. Being in mourning for my late master I have not worn white caps yet, and don't believe I ever can wear them: I'm sure I might put on three a-week and not be clean. Sometimes I wash my hands four times in a morning."

"Then think what it is for my aunt Bettina, with her delicate hands and her delicate lace," returned Sara. "I suppose the dirt is not quite so bad with us as it is here; but it seems as if nothing could be worse, and my aunt makes it a perpetual grievance. Shall you remain here, Watton?"

"I have made up my mind to try it for a twelvemonth, Miss Sara," was the answer. "It's too good a situation to be given up lightly; and it shall have a fair trial. I miss my country life; I miss the green fields and the gossiping neighbours at Hallingham: oftentimes I wake from a dream, thinking I'm there, and then I am fit to cry with the disappointment. I fear the pleasant old times have gone away from me for ever."

"They go away from us all, Watton," was the murmured answer, "never to return again."

"You will send the two young gentlemen to see me, Miss Sara," said Watton, as she was showing her out. "Perhaps they'd honour me by drinking tea here in the course of their holidays. My evenings are my own. Master Dick should eat as much jam as he'd like. I'd get in half-a-dozen pots assorted."

Sara could not forbear a smile: Dick would have gone to the other end of the kingdom for half-a-dozen pots of assorted jam: but it changed to gravity as she turned to Watton.

"Watton, do you know I have been so great a coward as not to ask my aunt decisively whether she intends to have them up for the holidays. I very much fear she does not; and therefore I shrink from asking, lest the fear should be made a certainty."

"Poor boys!" ejaculated Watton. "Well, of course it's all very different from what it was. Ah, Miss Sara! there are too many will find cause to miss the good Dr. Davenal!"

With the rebellious sorrow, called up by the words, rising in her heart, Sara walked along the hot and bustling streets again. It was a little past twelve when she reached Essex Street, and in going up the stair she happened to turn her head, and saw, stepping quickly in at the outer door, Oswald Cray. She hoped he had not seen her; she thought he had not; and she hastened on, her pulses beating. What strange coincidence could have brought him there?

Mr. Alfred King had arrived. Sara was shown through a busy room into a smaller one, long and narrow, apparently partitioned off from a third room, which she did not see. The room contained a couple of chairs, a table-desk, and a slender, dandy sort of gentleman; nothing more. He was leaning against the table, doing something to his nails with a penknife, an eye-glass in his eye, and a black moustache with rings at its ends curling on his lip.

"Mr. Alfred King?" she said interrogatively, for there had been no introduction.

Mr. Alfred King bowed. He removed his hat, which he had been wearing, shut up the penknife with a flourish of his thin white hands, courteously stepped forward, and was altogether the gentleman again.

"Miss Sara Davenal, I presume?"

How Sara entered on her task she never knew. Its nature made her feel sadly confused and diffident, as if all self-possession had gone out of her. Whatever her brother's crime might have been, she assumed that the gentleman before her had cognisance of it; and it rendered her miserably conscious in that first moment. Very much embarrassed, and aware that she was so, she apologised for the delay in the payment of the money, stated that she expected it daily, and begged of Mr. King to be kind enough to wait a little longer. Just what she had stated in her letter: in fact she had nothing else to urge.

"I am exceedingly sorry to put you to the inconvenience of coming here, Miss Davenal," he said, in a courteous but drawling tone. "It is reversing the appropriate order of things. I should have been better pleased to wait upon you."

"But I could not make it convenient to receive you," replied Sara. "The truth is," she added in her candour, "that my aunt, Miss Davenal, with whom I live, was not made cognisant of this business; and it was my father's, Dr. Davenal's, wish that she should not be."

"Ah—I see," observed Mr. Alfred King, in the same drawling tone that spoke so unpleasantly of affectation, of something not true in his nature. "Still I feel horribly annoyed at causing you the trouble of coming here, Miss Davenal."

"Will you be so kind as to tell me the object of the interview?" she said. "For what purpose did you wish to see me?"

"Ah, yes, to be sure. The fact is, Miss Davenal, some positive understanding must be come to as to the precise time when the money will be paid. You cannot imagine the inconvenience to which the delay has put me: and, but for the respect I once bore Captain Davenal, I would not have remained so passive as I have done."

There was a pointed stress on the word "once" that recalled the blush into Sara's cheeks, the dread to her heart. She murmured a hope that the money would be realised and paid to him ere the lapse of many days.

"You see, Miss Davenal, had the money no ulterior destination it would not be of so much consequence," he resumed. "Were it due to myself only I would wait with the greatest pleasure, no matter at what inconvenience; but that is not the case, it is these other parties who will not be pacified. Do you comprehend me, Miss Davenal?"

"Yes, I think so," said Sara, faintly, beginning to fear the affair was more complicated than she had thought. "Who are the parties?"

Mr. Alfred King ran his white hand and its showy ring right through his black hair. "Well—I would tell you if I could, Miss Davenal: in anything that concerns myself only, you may command me as you please: but the fact is, I am not at liberty to mention the names of those parties even to you."

There was a pause, and Sara's manner for the moment grew haughtily distant She liked his words less and less. But she recollected herself: she subdued her proud spirit. Was not Edward in his power?

"These parties have been angry at the delay," he resumed, breaking the silence that had ensued. "They have badgered the life nearly out of me over it: excuse the term, Miss Davenal, it but expresses the fact.

I assure you I have had a most difficult task to keep them from proceeding to extremities. And, in short, they won't be put off longer."

"From extremities?" she repeated, the one ominous word alone catching her ear.

Mr. Alfred King looked at her, not speaking. His gaze seemed to ask her how much she knew. She did not respond to it.

"Were this unfortunate matter made public, nothing could save Captain Davenal," he resumed, in a low tone. "He is now in India, in apparent safety, but—in short, it would only be a question of time, two or three months or so. Men are brought from the ends of the world now to answer for—for crime."

Subdued as was his voice Sara looked around in terror. That partition, if nothing more than a partition, was probably a shallow one, allowing sound to pass beyond it.

"Be at ease," he said, detecting her fear, "we are quite alone."

"Do you know Captain Davenal?" she asked.

"Very well indeed. He and I were at one time sworn friends, constantly together. Until this unhappy affair arose to part us."

Perhaps she would have liked to ask the particulars that she did not know. But her whole heart revolted from it; it would have seemed like acknowledging Edward's crime.

"You see his being in India is only a temporary safeguard, and these parties who hold his safety in their hands might bring him home if they chose. It is only in compliance with my urgent entreaties that they have kept passive so long. But the delay is extending itself beyond all reason, and they—in short, Miss Davenal, they will not wait longer."

"But what can I do?" she urged in her helplessness. "I admit that the delay is vexatious—Heaven knows I have felt it so," she added, with a burst of feeling that would not be suppressed—"but the money is there; it will very shortly be forthcoming, and then it will be paid."

"Yes, I have pointed out all this to them;" he said, flicking a speck of dirt off his coat. "I—I suppose there is no foreign delay or obstruction, beyond the delay caused by realising the different monies?"

His sudden penetrating glance at her, the hidden earnestness of his tone, told Sara that this was a question of importance to him. It was nearly the only point throughout the interview which had not borne to her ear and eye a vague and indefinite idea of something untruthful: untruthful in himself, his voice, and his words. Possibly he had sought the personal interview with the sole view of ascertaining this solitary fact. An impression that it was so passed rapidly through her mind.

"Let me thoroughly understand you;" she said, following her own thoughts rather than his words. "Tell me without reserve exactly what it is you wish to know, and I will answer you to the best of my power. There is no other cause for the delay, except that the monies have not been realised so quickly as they ought to have been; no other cause whatever. Were you thinking that there was?"

"I?" and again the false drawling tone grated harshly on her ear. "Not I, I assure you, Miss Davenal. Those parties of whom I spoke hinted to me that with all this delay it looked as if there were no intention to pay the money. Of course, I knew that it was nothing of the sort; that the money must be paid."

"The very day that the money reaches me it will be paid to you, according to the instructions of my father, Dr. Davenal," she said, impressively. "I beg you to believe this; and to convey the assurance of it to them."

"I will do so. How much longer do you suppose the delay will extend? Can you fix any definite date for the payment?"

"I wish I could. But you see it does not rest with me. A very, very short period now will, I believe, see it settled."

Mr. Alfred King mused. "I will inform them of what you say, Miss Davenal, and I do trust the period may be a short one. If protracted, I cannot answer for it that they would remain passive."

"They must be cruel men to wish to harm Captain Davenal!"

"No," he answered. "Had they been cruel men they would not have consented not to harm him. It is not that, Miss Davenal; it is the money itself that is wanted; and the delay vexes them."

She was feeling desperate, and she ventured on a bold step. "In their own interest, then, they must be cautious not to harm him. Were they to do so they would lose the money."

"Why?"

"Because I would never pay it."

Mr. Alfred King glanced at her in surprise. All her timid hesitation of manner was gone, the expression of her face had changed to resolute bravery. "I do not pretend to entire acquaintance with the details of this unhappy business, but I understand so much, Mr. King—that this money purchases my brother's safety," she continued. "If that be imperilled, the bargain would be forfeited, and the money retained. The payment or non-payment of this money rests solely with me; and I should not keep faith with the other parties if they did not keep theirs with my dead father."

"There will be no question of their not keeping faith, provided they get their rights, Miss Davenal."

"And their rights—if you mean the money—they shall have; I trust speedily. I shall be only too glad to get the matter over."

"I'm sure I shall be," returned Mr. Kino in a tone that was certainly a hearty one. "It will be well for all parties; very well for Captain Davenal."

Sara turned to the door. Mr. Alfred King took up his hat for the purpose of attending her outside.

"I am glad that you have allowed me this interview, Miss Davenal. It will be so much more satisfactory to these gentlemen now that I have seen you. Dr. Davenal's death, occurring as it did, was most unfortunate. By the way, did he not leave some papers behind him?"

"There are papers in my possession relating to this affair," she answered. "I know what to do with them when the proper time shall come."

"Ah, yes, of course; doubtless," came the untrue words in their untrue tone. "Then I may rely on the very speedy receipt of this money, Miss Davenal?"

"You may rely upon having it immediately that it is paid to me. That is all, I presume, sir?"

Mr. Alfred King could not say that it was not all. He gallantly offered his arm to pilot her through the busy office of Messrs. Jones and Green; but Miss Sara Davenal, with a gesture far more expressive of haughty pride than of gratitude, declined the honour. The interview was leaving a disagreeable impression on her mind, apart from its natural unpleasantness; and perhaps it was unreasonable of her, but she had taken an unconquerable dislike to Mr. Alfred King.

The stairs seemed more busy than the lawyer's room. Men, some of them rather rough-looking ones, were passing up and down. Mr. Alfred King drawled an anathema on the tenant of the second floor, Mr. Carberry. Mr. Carberry had only recently taken the rooms, and he appeared to have no ostensible occupation, save the receiving of a great many visitors and an occasional telegram. The visitors were supposed to be mostly in the sporting line; and during the holding of distant races the passages and door would be besieged by an eager and noisy crowd:—as was the case on this day.

"Three times have we had them scattered by the police," exclaimed Mr. Alfred King, unmistakably in earnest now. "And that pest Carberry—or whatever the fellow's name may be—can't be got rid of for nearly a twelvemonth to come! Knollys's have threatened to indict the landlord for a nuisance; Jones and Green have given conditional warning to quit; and it's all of no use. The landlord went to Carberry with tears in his eyes, and told him he'd be the ruin of his house, that he'd forgive every farthing of rent, already owing, if he'd go; but Carberry coolly said he had taken it for a twelvemonth, and he should stop his twelvemonth. Miss Davenal, you cannot! Allow me!"

For Sara had come face to face with this crowd at the street-door, and commenced a struggle with them, they not being polite enough to give way in the least. Mr. Alfred King seized her arm forcibly with a view of helping her, when she was as forcibly separated from him by an authoritative hand, and found herself on the arm of Mr. Oswald Cray, his face ablaze with haughty anger, as he turned it on Mr. Alfred King.

"Thank you, sir," he said, all the pride of the Oswalds concentrating itself in him then. "This lady is under my charge."

And Mr. Alfred King, with a somewhat subdued manner, as if he had received a check that he did not care to resist, made as polite a bow to Sara as the crowd allowed him, and disappeared from view.

Clear of the assemblage, Sara would have withdrawn her arm, but Oswald Cray held it too tightly. A moment, and he turned his face upon her, ablaze still.

"What do you do with that man? He is not a fit acquaintance for you."

At first she could not answer. Not so much from the suddenness of the whole thing and the emotion it had brought to her, as because she did not know what explanation to give.

"In going into Knollys's office just now I thought I saw you making your way up the stairs," he resumed. "I said to myself that it could not be; but I was unable to get the impression from my mind, and I waited. One of Knollys's clerks said that the young lady gone up had inquired for Alfred King. What can have taken you to him?"

He was growing somewhat less vehement. It had been a moment to convince him that the love which he had safely deemed he was subduing remained with him still in all its force. To rescue her from the undesirable companionship of Mr. Alfred King, from contact with the unhallowed crowd of gambling men, he would have parted with his life.

"I was compelled to go," she murmured "I could not help myself."

"Compelled to go up those stairs? Compelled to pay that man a visit?"

"Yes, I was. It was as distasteful to me as it could be, but I had no resource. I went there on business which no one but myself could transact. Thank you for your protection, Mr. Oswald. Cray."

She withdrew her arm now, and there was no opposition to it. Reason was resuming her seat in Oswald's mind, and he felt angry with himself for his excess of demonstration. All things considered, it had been scarcely wise.

"It is not at all a place for a young lady to go to," he resumed, as he walked by her side, and his manner became cold even to restraint. "The Knollys' are sufficiently respectable, but as much cannot be said for the tenants of the upper part of the house. You must not go to it again."

Once again she knew she should have to go to it, but she fervently hoped that would close the matter. She wished she could tell him the nature of the business that took her there. Parted though they were, she did care to stand well in the estimation of Oswald Cray; she esteemed him still beyond any one on earth.

"I never saw Mr. Alfred King until this morning; he is no acquaintance of mine, or ever likely to be. But he tells me he was once an intimate friend of my brother Edward's."

Oswald Cray's haughty lip took an additional curl. "He may have been looked upon as a respectable man once; but he lost himself. He is not a desirable acquaintance for you."

"I could not help myself," she answered, her cheeks glowing. "It was necessary that I should see him, and the interview could not be delegated to another."

He made no reply: only continued by her side. Not until her house was nearly reached did he leave her. Then he stopped and held out his hand; but he had scarcely spoken a word to her all the way.

"Thank you for your kindness," said Sara. "But I am very sorry you should have troubled yourself to come with me. It must have broken your day greatly."

"Never mind; I shall catch it up," he answered, looking at his watch.. "I do not like to see you in these London streets alone. I cannot forget that Dr. Davenal was once my dear friend, and that you are his daughter."

CHAPTER XL

A FLOURISHING COMPANY

The Great Wheal Bang Mining Company had its offices in a commodious and irreproachable quarter of the city. If I give the familiar name Wheal Bang, instead of the difficult one Chwddyn, which can only be spelt from copy, letter by letter, and perhaps wrongly then, it is to save myself and my readers trouble. Not being Welsh, they might find a difficulty in arriving at the accurate pronunciation, just as I do at the spelling. The promoter of the Great Wheal Bang Mining Company, Mr. Barker, occupied sumptuous apartments in Piccadilly; and his copartner in the scheme, as Mark Cray was to all intents and purposes now, flourished in his mansion in Grosvenor Place.

The offices were undeniable in their appointments. Situation, width of staircase, size of rooms, decorations, furniture, attendants; all were of the first water. People who play with the money of others do not in general go to work sparingly; and speculative public schemes necessarily entail a large outlay. These schemes, springing up now and again in London, to the beguilement of the unwary—one in about every ten of which may succeed in the end—have been so well described by abler pens than mine, that I might hesitate even to touch upon them, were it not that the story cannot conveniently get on without my doing so, and that I have a true tale to tell. How many hearts have been made to ache from the misery entailed by these uncertain ventures, ushered in with so much pomp and flourish, so full a promise of prosperity; and how many heads unable to bear the weight of the final ruin, have been laid low in the grave, God alone will ever know. They have ruined thousands in body; they have ruined some in soul; and the public is not yet tired of them, and perhaps will not be to the end of time.

If you never had the chance of going to bed at night a poor man, and waking up in the morning with a larger fortune than could be counted, you might have it now. You had only to enter largely into the Great Wheal Bang Company, become the successful possessor of a number of its shares, and the thing was accomplished. For the world was running after it, and some of the applicants were successful in their request for allotments, and some were unsuccessful; and these last went away with a face as long as the Wheal Bang's own prospectus, growling out a prophecy of all manner of ill-fortune for it. Their grapes were sour. The shares were up in the market to a fabulous premium, and a man might take half a dozen into Capel Court, and come out of it with his pockets stuffed full of gold.

Mark Cray's money had effected wonders, or rather his wife's; for hers it was. A great many of these magnificent projects are nipped ignobly in the bud through want of a little ready money to set them fairly going. But for Mrs. Cray's thousands, Mr. Barker's mine of gold might never have been heard of by the world, and Mr. Barker's name had not attained to its enviable preeminence. These thousands did it all. They got up the company, they set the mine a-working, they paid for the costly offices, they dazzled the eyes of the public, they gave earnest of present wealth, they seemed to assure future success.

Certainly, if any mine had ever a fair prospect of realising a golden fruition, it appeared to be the Great Wheal Bang. The working of it had begun most promisingly, and every success was fairly looked for. In calling it a gold mine just now, you of course understood that I was speaking metaphorically; for gold mines are not yet common among us, even in Wales. This very valuable mine (as it could but turn out to be) was not rich in gold, but in lead; and, as we all know, the one is speedily converted into the other. The previous autumn, in consequence of some trifling difficulty in London, Mr. Barker found it convenient to enter on a temporary sojourn at a distance; and he penetrated to a remote district of South Wales. While there, with the good luck which that gentleman believed he was born to and should some time realise, a vein of lead was discovered of a most promising nature. He contrived to secure a large interest in it, and undertook to get up a company for the working of it.

How he would have accomplished this, or whether he ever would have accomplished it, is doubtful, had he not found a coadjutor in Mark Cray, and an aid in Mark's money. Mark resigned the control of the money to him, and Mr. Barker did not spare it. No earthly adjunct was wanting to ensure the success of the scheme, provided the mine only realised its present promises.

Has anybody who may happen to read this ever assisted in getting a newly-discovered mine into working order? If so, he may remember the money it cost. How it ran out of the hands like water that is poured through a broad-necked funnel, disappearing nobody knew where, and leaving little trace behind! How the pounds went, and the hundreds went, and the thousands went—if he was fortunate enough to possess thousands to go—he may not recollect without wincing, to this hour. Mark Cray's thousands went. But ere they had come quite to an end, the Great Wheal Bang Company was in full operation in London, the shareholders had answered to their calls, and the money was flowing in.

No lack of money to be feared then. And the operations at the mine were conducted on a much grander scale than heretofore, and the returns were certain to be without parallel, and Mr. Barker was in a glow of triumph, and Mark Cray in a state of ecstatic delight, and the lucky shareholders leaped up sixteen scales in the ladder of society. How many set up carriages on the strength of their future riches it is beyond my power to tell. The money flowed down to the mine, and the works went on beautifully, and the specimens of ore that came up to town were said to be more valuable than any ore ever was before. As to Mr. Barker and Mark, their expenses were not deemed worthy of a thought: with all that money going out weekly for the mine, personal expenditure was but as a drop of water in the ocean, and of course it was unnecessary to think of limiting it. Mrs. Cray, with her vanity and her love of display, was in the seventh heaven; while Mark looked back to his prosy life at Hallingham and wondered how he had endured it. He wondered how any of the doctors left there endured it, and pitied them from his heart. The thousand a-year or so he once thought to enter upon as successor to Dr. Davenal was recollected with contempt now.

This much must be said for the Great Wheal Bang Company—that its projectors were at least honest in their belief of its genuineness. In that they differed from some other companies we have heard of, which have turned out to be nothing but a swindle—if you will excuse the word—from the earliest commencement, the very first dawning dream of their projectors. Mr. Barker was of that strangely sanguine nature which sees a fortune in the wildest scheme, and plunges head and heart and creed into the most improbable speculation: Mark, an utter tyro in mines and all that concerns them, including companies, saw only with Barker's eyes. When Mr. Barker assured the entranced shareholders that one hundred pounds put into the Great Wheal Bang would multiply tenfold and tenfold, he spoke only the sanguine belief of his heart. When Mark Cray declared to his brother Oswald that a thousand pounds embarked in it by him would make him a rich man for life, he asserted the honest truth according to his conviction. No wonder the two gentlemen-promoters were eloquent.

Mark had made several visits to the scene of the mines, and he came back each time with (if possible) renewed assurance of the brilliant future; with increased ardour. Had the Chancellor of the Exchequer obligingly made Mark an impromptu present of a hundred thousand pounds, Mark would have flung it broadcast into the mine, did the mine thirst for it. He did not understand these things in the least; and the perpetual bustle going on, the number of the miners, even the very money paid in wages and suchlike expenses, were to Mark only an earnest of the rich returns that were to come hereafter. Mark would go back to London in a glowing state, and send his friends the shareholders into a fever, longing to realise the prosperity that seemed so close at hand. The weekly reports overshadowed other weekly reports with envy, and created a furore in the speculating world. Some of the shareholders who understood mines, or thought they did, better than Mark, went down to the Principality, and examined into the state of things for themselves; they found them quite satisfactory, and came away as charmed as Mark. In point of fact, prospects did look well; the lead was of an unusually good quality, and there seemed no reason whatever to anticipate anything but success. Caroline had accompanied her husband once to the mines; but the stay there (putting prospects aside) did not please her: it was "rough," she told Mark, and it was very dull at the little inn; and she was glad to come away from it all ere the second day was over.

Perhaps the only person within the circle of Mark Cray's acquaintance not bitten by the Wheal Bang fever was Miss Davenal. Even Oswald Cray was to succumb at last. He would not become a shareholder; he was too cautious a man to enter upon possible future liabilities, the extent of which no human being could foretell: but he did feel inclined to put a thousand pounds into Mark's hands, and tell him to do the best with it. It may almost be said that Oswald was worried into doing this. Mark would not let him rest. At the onset of the affair, when the glorious prospects of the Wheal Bang were first astonishing the world, Mark had urged Oswald to become one of them; a director or at least a shareholder; but Oswald had turned a deaf ear. He felt greatly vexed at Mark's imprudence at abandoning Hallingham and his profession, leaving a certainty for an uncertainty: he felt more than vexed at the manner in which Mrs. Cray's money was disposed of, so entirely opposed to the dying injunction of Dr. Davenal. so opposed (Oswald deemed) to all wisdom and prudence; and he set his face resolutely against the Wheal Bang. But Oswald was but mortal. As the weeks and months went on, and the mines became to all appearance valuable, the company flourishing, and Mark, in conjunction with others, dinned for ever into his ear the fortune he might make at it, Oswald began to waver. He had a thousand pounds laid by, and he felt half inclined to risk it; Mark over-persuaded him; and his visit to the Messrs. Knollys's office the day he encountered Sara Davenal was for the purpose of making certain inquiries of those gentlemen relating to the Wheal Bang.

Not so with Miss Bettina Davenal She set her face resolutely against the Great Wheal Bang from the first, and nothing turned her. She had never forgiven Mark and his wife for quitting Hallingham, and her reproaches to them could not cease. The apparent prosperity of the Great Wheal Bang changed not her opinion in the least. Mark asked her once whether she would take shares in it, and produced a Wheal Bang prospectus to point to its merits. She angrily replied that she would as soon throw her money into the Thames, that it would not be a surer way of getting rid of it, and rang the bell for Mark and his prospectus to be shown out of her house.

Mark Cray sat in the board room at the city offices of the Great Wheal Bang. A noble room, the cloth on its long table of the freshest green and the finest texture. Mark leaned his elbow upon this cloth as he talked and laughed with some of the friends of the Great Wheal Bang, who were getting rich so easily. It was not a board day; but visitors were numerous at all times.

"I had a line from him this morning," said Mark, continuing the conversation. "Spirits? I should think he does write in spirits!—what are you talking of? They are getting up quantities of ore now. It will soon be ready for the market."

"And its quality does not deteriorate?" asked Mark's immediate listener, a middle-aged gentleman with wise-looking spectacles on his nose.

"Deteriorate!" repeated Mark. "But you shall see the letter." He began to turn over the pipers on the table, and the diamond ring on his little finger, a hundred-guinea investment of his, began to show out the colours of a prism in its glittering brilliancy.

"It is of no consequence," returned the gentleman, when Mark could not readily find it. "I can take your word. When does Barker come up again?"

"Today or tomorrow; I am not sure which. I should like you to have seen his letter, though it is but a line or two. The only motive for our fresh call upon the shareholders is to hasten the operations, and so speed the returns. With more capital afloat we can increase the workers at the mine, and bring the ore out more quickly."

"It was to have been in the market by this."

"One cannot calculate to a day. It won't be long now; and its richness, when it does come, will astonish the world. Do just as you like: take the shares or leave them. This gentleman would not have had them to dispose of but that he has urgent need of the money. He is over in Austria now, and has written to me: he is an old friend of mine."

"I'd not hesitate a moment to take them were it my own money; I wish I had more to embark in it. But this is money belonging to my wards; and their relatives are so anxious that I should choose a safe investment, one in which there can be no risk."

Mark Cray rose from his seat. The word "risk" offended his pride, and he could only wonder that any one could be idiot enough to use it in connection with the Great Wheal Bang Mine. But Mark had no need to solicit now the taking of shares: half London was ready to snap them up: and he was too great a man to permit his time to be wasted unnecessarily.

"Consider over it, if you please, until tomorrow morning, Mr. Gilham," he said, as he moved away. "You can see the secretary if you come in before ten. After that the shares will not be disposable."

There's no safer way to make a buyer eager, than for a seller to be indifferent; and Mr. Gilham and his spectacles went hastening after Mark, ready to close the bargain. But Mark was already the centre of an eager group, not to be got at again lightly. The next time Mr. Gilham caught sight of him, he was descending the wide staircase, surrounded as before by a crowd of attendant worshippers, who were unwilling to part with the great man and his widely-extending influence.

But great men must dine as well as small, and Mr. Cray was hastening home to that necessary meal. He extricated himself from his friends, and stepped into his cab that waited at the door: a favourite vehicle of Mark's, built under his own superintendence, in which he generally went to and fro morning and evening, driving his blood horse himself. Glancing at his watch as he dashed along Cheapside, he found it was considerably later than he had thought, and urged the horse to a quicker pace.

For Mr. and Mrs. Cray were expecting friends to dinner that evening. Dr. Ford of Hallingham and his two daughters were making a short stay in town, and had been invited by Mark and his wife—neither of them loth to show off their new grandeur, and to send it to be talked about in Hallingham.

Suddenly Mark threw the horse nearly on his haunches by the violence with which he pulled him up. Oswald Cray was on the pavement. He advanced to Mark at the latter's sign.

"Hare you decided about the thousand pounds, Oswald?"

"Partially. I went down to Knollys's this morning, and they recommend the thing strongly. But I have worked hard for my money, Mark, and don't care to lose it."

"Lose it!" scornfully returned Mark. "The Great Wheal Bang won't be a losing concern. Look here, Oswald! I have but one motive in pressing the matter upon you: this mine of wealth has come flowing into my hands, and I do consider it a great pity that you, my only brother, should not reap some benefit from it. Others, strangers, are making their thousands and thousands—or will make them; and it's nothing but wilful blindness for you to let it slip through your fingers. It's obstinate folly, Oswald. Give me the thousand pounds, and I'll soon make you ten thousand."

"The fact is, Mark, I cannot feel so positively sure of its turning out well as you do."

"Oswald, I tell you that it will. I and Barker have means of knowing facts connected with the mine that I don't speak of, even to you. As I assured you the other day, so I repeat it; your money cannot be lost. It is a perfectly sure and safe investment; I will answer for it with my life. Will you come home and dine with us?"

"I have dined."

"Dined!" echoed Mark, rather scornfully, for he was learning to despise any but the most fashionable hours—as many another newly-made great man has learnt before him. "Come round in the evening, then, and see old Ford of Hallingham. Barker will be there, I expect, and we can talk this over further."

Mark Cray touched his horse, and the cab and its freight bounded off. Mark did not draw rein again until Grosvenor Place was reached.

CHAPTER XLI

A SLIGHT CHECK

The house was blazing with light, every window bright with it. Mrs. Cray loved pomp and vanity in all their forms, and she generally caused her rooms to be lighted with the first glimmer of twilight. Mark Cray stepped into his handsome hall and was received by a couple of footmen. Flinging his hat to one, his gloves to another, he bounded upstairs to his dressing-room, conscious that he was keeping the dinner and his guests waiting.

Did Mark Cray ever cast a sigh of regret to the simple life at Hallingham, when he and his wife used to sit down to mutton cutlets and a pudding, and think the fare good enough? Did she regret it at any odd moment? Not yet. Dress and dinners, with expense of other sorts, bring a fascination with them all too enthralling to the senses. How they pall upon the wearied spirit in time, how they deaden the heart and debase the intellect, let those answer who have become their slaves; but Mark Cray and his wife had not reached that period of weariness yet. You may be very sure, knowing what you do know of the world and the generality of people who populate it, that Mr. and Mrs. Cray wanted not for what is called society. The great projector of the great Wheal Bang Company, holding in his own hands the power to make others rich, was not likely to lack adulation in his private capacity any more than in his public one, and he and his wife drank their fill of it. Mark's mind was shallow, and his head tolerably empty, but he was sufficiently attractive in manners to win his way in society, even without the adjunct just mentioned. Mark was looked upon as of good connections also; for it had somehow got reported that he was a nephew of the proud Baronet of Thorndyke. Perhaps it may be forgiven to poor empty-headed Mark that he held his tongue from contradicting it, and suffered the world to think he was of the family of that great man. As to Caroline, people were in love with her beauty and her youth; and the costly extravagances of the house in Grosvenor Place bore their own charm. Altogether, more guests crowded the doors of Mr. and Mrs. Cray than the doors could always hold. Many satellites of the great world, of a position far above the real one of Mark Cray and his wife, flocked to pay them court; and neither of them was wise enough to see how unsuitable are extremes, or to discern that the acquaintance would never have been condescended to but that Mark was the Great Wheal Bang's powerful chieftain. Therefore it was nothing unusual for Mark Cray to receive dinner guests at his board; on the contrary, it would have been a marked circumstance now, had he and his wife dined alone.

Mark washed his hands and hurried on his coat, and in a few minutes was at his dinner-table, his guests on either side of him. One guest at it Mark could only regard with astonishment, and that was Miss Davenal. Not that Miss Davenal was not fitted to grace a dinner-table; no lady more so at her age in the three kingdoms; but she had so resolutely abstained from honouring Mark's house with her presence that he had never expected to see her in it again. Caroline said she should invite her and Sara to meet their old friends the Fords, and Mark had laughed when he heard it. "She'll never come," he said; "you might as well invite the lioness from the Zoological Gardens." However, here she was: she had chosen to come. She sat on Mark's left hand, her delicate features quite beautiful in their refinement; Miss Ford was on his right, a shrinking little woman of forty years; Miss Mary Ford and Sara Davenal were lower down; and the physician, a short, red-faced, shrivelled man, who talked incessantly and wore nankeen pantaloons, was next to Caroline. "Put a knife and fork for Mr. Barker," Mark had said to his servants: but Mr. Barker had not made his appearance yet. Those were all the guests.

There is something false about Caroline today. Look at her dress! It is white watered silk, gleaming with richness, as the dewdrops are gleaming in the white crape flowers in her hair; and it, the white silk, is elaborately trimmed with black ruchings and ribbons. That black, put on by her maid, taking the girl a whole afternoon to do it, has been added with a motive. Caroline, in her evening dress, has long put off the mourning for her good uncle, her more than father, dead though he has been but four months yet; but she is today a little ashamed of her haste, and she has assumed these black ribbons before these

Hallingham friends and her aunt Bettina, to make believe that she still wears it. Her violet eyes are intensely bright, and her cheeks glow with their sweetest and softest carmine. Sara wears a black crape robe, a little edging of white net only on its low body and sleeves, and she wears no ornament, except the jet beads on her neck and arms. The two Miss Fords are in copper-coloured silks made high: when they saw Mrs. Cray's white silk, fit for the court of our gracious Queen, they felt uncomfortable, and attempted a sort of apology that they had brought no evening dress with them to town.

And the dinner is in accordance with Caroline's attire. Soup, and fish, and entrées, and roasts, and jellies, and sweets, and fal-lals; and more sorts of wine than the Miss Fords, simple and plain, could remember afterwards to count; and flowers, and plate, and servants in abundance: and grandeur enough altogether for the dining-room of England's Premier.

It was this state, this show, this expense, that so offended the good sense (very good always, though sometimes over severe) of Miss Bettina Davenal, and kept her aloof from Mr. and Mrs. Cray's house. If Mark really was making the vast amount of money (but it would have taken a wiser tongue than Mark's to convince her that that usually assumed fact was not a fallacy), then they ought to be putting it by, she argued: if they were not making it, if all this was but specious wealth, soon to pass away and leave only ashes and ruin behind it, then Mark and Caroline were fit only for a lunatic asylum. In any point of view, the luxurious appointments of the dinner she saw before her were entirely out of place for middle-class life: and Miss Bettina felt an irrepressible prevision that their folly would come home to them.

But she knew better than to mar the meeting with any unpleasant reproaches or forebodings then, and she was as cordial and chatty as her deafness allowed. It was a real pleasure to meet Hallingham friends, and Miss Bettina enjoyed herself more than she had ever done since the doctor's death.

The entertainment came to an end, and Caroline marshalled her guests to the glittering drawing-room: glittering with its mirrors, its chandeliers, and the many lights from its gilded girandoles. Dr. Ford and Mark followed shortly, and found them drinking coffee. Caroline and Sara were stealing a minute's private chat together: they had lived apart of late.

"How did you get my aunt to come?" Caroline was asking. "We thought she never intended to honour us here."

"She came of her own accord. I did not say a word to press it. I have been so vexed this afternoon, Caroline," resumed Sara, turning to a different subject. "My aunt has told me finally that she will not have Dick and Leo up for their holidays."

Caroline shrugged her pretty shoulders; very much as if Dick and Leo and their holidays were perfectly indifferent to her. "I don't think I should, in Aunt Bettina's place. Boys are dreadfully troublesome animals; and now that—that poor Uncle Richard is not here to keep them in order—" another shrug finished the sentence.

"Oh, but that is one reason why I so wish them to come," said Sara, her voice somewhat tremulous. "I don't expect that they can be had always; that would be unreasonable; but to stay at school just this first time after poor papa's death!—it will seem so hard to them. Caroline, could you not have them up?"

"I!" returned Caroline, amazed at the proposition.

"You have a large house and plenty of servants. It would be an act of real kindness."

"Good gracious, Sara! I'd not have them: I'd not be worried with those two boys for six weeks if you paid me in gold and diamonds. They—who's this?"

The door had opened, and one of the servants was waiting to make an announcement:

"Mr. Oswald Cray."

Caroline ran to meet him. He looked rather surprised at her attire, and began apologising in a laughing sort of way for his own morning-coat. He had expected to meet only Barker and Dr. Ford. A greeting to the Hallingham people, and he went up and held out his hand to Miss Davenal.

"You are a great stranger, Mr. Oswald Cray. I did not suppose that the formal call you made upon me when I settled in town three months ago was to be your only one."

"I am a sadly busy man," was his answer. "Offending I fear some of my best friends through not visiting them. But I can scarcely dare to call my time my own."

"Out of town, do you say? Well, that is an excuse of course Sara, here's Mr. Oswald Cray: you used to know him in Hallingham."

The blushes tingled on her cheek as Mr. Oswald Cray touched her hand. Tingled at the thought that it was not the first time they had met that day.

"What have you been doing with yourself, Oswald, since I saw you before dinner!" called out Mark, who was pointing out the beauty of the paintings on his walls to the Miss Fords.

"I have been to Pimlico since then."

"To Pimlico! Oh, I know: to that friend of yours; It strikes me you go there pretty often."

"As often as I can spare time for," returned Oswald.

Mark laughed. Had he possessed that refined regard for the feelings of others, never wanting in the true gentleman, he had not so spoken. "I know. But you need not be so close over it, Oswald. That Miss Allister is a nice girl, is she not?"

"Very," was the emphatic reply.

"One to be esteemed. Eh?"

"As few can be esteemed by me." Oswald spoke in his coldest, most uncompromising tone: his haughty face turned almost defiantly on Mark. He was the last man to brook this sort of speech, and in that moment he despised Mark. Sara had a book in her hand, and she never raised her drooping eyelids from it. What was it to her now whom he esteemed? But she heard: all too plainly.

There was a pause of silence; rather an unpleasant one. It was broken by Miss Mary Ford.

"I must not forget to ask after your old servant Watton, Miss Davenal. Does she like her place? I suppose you see her occasionally."

"Thank you, I don't like it at all," returned Miss Davenal, hearing wrongly, as usual. "What was Mark asking you, Mr. Oswald Cray?"

"Watton is quite well; I saw her this morning," interposed Sara, who perhaps did not care that Mark's choice of subject should again be brought forward. Mrs. Cray caught up the words.

"Saw Watton this morning, Sara! Where did you see her?"

And the very moment the unlucky admission had left Sara's lips she knew how thoughtless it was to have made it, and what an undesirable discussion it might involve.

"Where did you see Watton?" repeated Mrs. Cray.

"I had a little business that way, and called upon her," replied Sara. She was obliged to speak: there was no help for it; and all the room seemed to be listening to her answer, which she had not time to weigh.

"Business down that way!" echoed Caroline. "Why, it is in the City! What business could you have there?"

"Not much: nothing of moment to you, Caroline;" and Sara, in her dismay and fear, turned and began talking rapidly to old Dr. Ford.

"Aunt Bettina," called out Mrs. Cray, in a slow distinct voice, "what business took Sara to the City this morning? I thought only gentlemen went there."

Aunt Bettina heard, and lifted her hand in momentary petulance, as if the subject angered her.

"You must not ask me. Sara has her own secrets and goes her own ways since your uncle's death. I am not allowed to know them."

Sara looked up to reply, perhaps to defend herself; but she remembered what was at stake, and forced herself to silence. Better that the blame should lie upon her! She had caught a momentary glimpse of Mr. Oswald Cray: he was leaning against a table in the distance, his eyes fixed upon her, reading every change in her countenance; his own face stern and impassive.

What more would have been said or asked was interrupted by the entrance of another guest. A middle-sized man of thirty, with radish hair and whiskers, a free manner and voluble tongue. Mark started forward with a shout of welcome, and introduced him to the strangers. It was Mr. Barker.

"I have brought up the grandest news, Cray," he exclaimed, in a state of excitement. "There's another lode found."

"No!" echoed Mark, his eyes sparkling. "Another lode?"

"Dutton came upon it yesterday afternoon after I wrote those few lines to you. By Jove, gentlemen"—throwing his looks round the room—"I am afraid to calculate what will be the riches of this mine! Mark, old fellow, I hope our success won't drive us into Bedlam—as the case has been with some millionaires."

Miss Bettina, who had contrived to hear, cleared her throat. "It's a great deal more likely to drive you into the union, sir."

It was an unexpected a check to Mr. Barker's enthusiasm that he could only stare in amazement at Miss Bettina. He had not met her before. "Never mind her," said Mark, in an undertone, "its only old Bett. And she's as deaf as a post."

But Mr. Barker did mind. "Why, ma'am," said he, going close to her, "what do you mean?"

"I can't forget a good old proverb that I learnt in my young days, sir," was her answer: "one that I have seen exemplified times upon times in my course through life. 'He that would be rich in twelve months is generally a beggar in six.' I know what good newly-discovered mines are apt to bring, sir, however promising they may look." Mr. Barker fairly turned his back upon her; he believed she must be little better than a lunatic; and gave his attention to Mark and the more sensible portion of the company.

"The people are up in arms down about there," he said. "Lots of them who wrote for shares in the new allotment have not succeeded in getting any, and I thought they'd have torn me to pieces. I can't help it. It's a dear impossibility that the whole world can go in for being rich. If luck falls on one, it doesn't fall on another."

Dr. Ford, to whom Mr. Barker had seemed to appeal, nodded his head. "I hear great things of this mine, sir," said he.

"Great things!" repeated Mr. Barker, as if the words were not sufficiently expressive. "It is the very grandest thing that England has seen for many a day. The golden wealth of the Spanish Main is poor compared to it."

"I'm sure I hope it will answer."

"You—hope—it—will—answer!" echoed Mr. Barker, his red face going rather purple. "Why, sir, it has answered. It is answering. I could take my interest in it into the money market tomorrow, and sell it for half a million of money. Answer!"

Oswald Cray came nearer. "When shall you begin to realise?" he inquired.

"In about six weeks from this."

"Six weeks! Really to realise?"

"We might get some loads off before, if we chose, but we don't care to begin until the sales can go on uninterruptedly. The lead is coming up beautifully; vast quantities of it. You never saw such lead. It bangs all other in the locality into fits."

Mr. Barker in his joyous excitement was scarcely choice in his mode of speech. He was not particularly so at any time. He rubbed his hands—which looked as red as if they had been dining for ore—one against another.

"A fellow came up to the place—Lord What's-his-name's agent—and began handling the specimens. 'What sort of ore d'ye call this?' he asked. 'The best that ever was dug,' some of our men answered him. 'And so it is,' said he: 'we can't get such as this out of our pit.' No more they can: not an owner of 'em in all Wales."

"But you will not be selling freely in six weeks?" returned Oswald. "It is impossible."

"Impossible, is it?" retorted Mr. Barker. "It would be in most cases, I grant you; it's not in ours. You go and look at the thousands of men on the works. The Great Chwddyn mine doesn't deal in impossibilities."

"Would you be so good as tell me what you call that word, sir?" asked the physician, putting his hand to his ear. "We can't get at the pronunciation of it at Hallingham."

"And we can't here," returned easy Mr. Barker. "One calls it one thing and one another. As to trying to speak it like the natives, nobody can. We call it the Great Wheal Bang up here. Not that it's at all appropriate or correct to do so, but one can't be breaking one's teeth over the other. You see—Halloa! what's this? For me?"

One of Mark's servants had entered with a telegraphic dispatch. It was addressed to Mr. Barker.

"Your man has brought it round from Piccadilly, sir. He thought it might be of moment."

"Let's see. Where's it from?—Wales? Ay. Another lode discovered, I'll be bound!"

Mr. Barker carried the paper across the room, and opened it under the lights of a girandole. He stared at it more than read it; stared at the words as if unable to understand them: and a curious expression of puzzled bewilderment, half wonder, half dismay, struggled to his face. Mark Cray had come to his side, all eagerness; and Oswald was watching them from the distance.

"Is it another lode, Barker?"

"Hush! There has been a slight irruption of water," whispered Barker, thrusting the paper into his pocket. "Good heavens! that would floor us at once."

Mark Cray's mouth dropped. He stared as helplessly at Mr. Barker as the latter had stared at the dispatch. The sight of his face awoke Mr. Barker's caution.

"For goodness' sake, Cray, don't look like that! They'll see you, and suspect something. This must be kept dark, if possible. I daresay it's nothing. I'll go back again tonight."

He turned away with a beaming face to the company, laughing merrily, talking gaily. They might have well deemed that two fresh lodes had been discovered instead of one. Mark, not quite so quick in recovering his equanimity, stayed where he was before the girandole, looking in it in an absent sort of manner, and pushing his hair back mechanically. Perhaps this was the first time that even the possibility of failure had come close to Mark, face to face.

Barker was the first of the guests to retire, and Mark left the room with him. As the latter was returning to it he met his brother, who was also departing.

"Not going yet, Oswald? What a one you are!—Afraid of being in the streets late, it's my belief. I say! when am I to have the thousand pounds?"

"My mind is not quite made up yet," was the answer, a rather unexpected one to Mark's ears. "Mark, did Barker get any bad news tonight?"

"Bad news!" repeated Mark, as if quite at a loss to know what could be meant.

"By that dispatch from Wales?"

"Not at all," returned Mr. Mark, volubly. "He had forgotten to leave some instructions behind him, so they telegraphed. What put your head upon bad news?"

"Barker's countenance as he read the dispatch; and yours also when you joined him. You both looked as though some great calamity had occurred."

Mark laughed blithely. "Oswald, old fellow, you were always inclined to be fanciful. The mine is a glorious mine, and you'll be a blind booby if you don't secure some benefit in it. I'll answer for the safety of the investment with—with—my life," concluded Mark, speaking rather strongly in his loss for a simile. "Can't you rely upon me?"

O Mark Cray! His protestations of the "safety" were excusable before, when he believed what he said: but they were not now. Since that ominous message arrived his very heart had been quaking within him. In the few confidential words he had just exchanged with Barker on going out the latter had said: "We must get all the money we can, for we shall want it. Water, no matter how slight the irruption, plays the very deuce with the costs of a mine." And Mark Cray, to avert, or help to avert, or to conceal the calamity, was quite ready to sacrifice his own good faith and the money of his brother.

CHAPTER XLII

IN THE TEMPLE GARDENS

You have heard and read of those false promises that keep faith to the eye and break it to the spirit, bringing a flood-tide of anguish in their train. As such may be described the realisation of the long-deferred hope—the money—so anxiously expected by Sara Davenal. It came in due course, after a little more waiting; that is, the order to receive it was sent to her: but it did not bring pleasure with it. For the sales had not realised so much as was anticipated. Do they ever realise as much? Dr. Davenal had expected there would be about three thousand pounds: five hundred over and above the sum owing. But the money fell short by two hundred pounds even of this sum: and there was not enough to pay Mr. Alfred King.

O it was a great burthen to be thrown upon this girl in her early years, in her solitary loneliness! When the news came, and the small sum of money stared her in the face in figures all black and white, she looked around her in despondency. She felt that she had no friend, save God.

Feeling half-hopeless, Sara sat down and considered what was to be done. Two thousand three hundred pounds certainly were not two thousand five hundred, and she had little expectation that Mr. Alfred King would be satisfied with it. An ordinary creditor, whose debt was a legitimate one, would of course not remit two hundred pounds: but this debt was different, for she had every reason to believe it was no legitimate debt, but money paid to purchase silence. Then a voice whispered her they would be all the less likely to remit it; they would hold out for it to to the last farthing. Whose silence she could not tell. But for the mysterious hint of Mr. Alfred King that others were interested in this business she might have thought it was his alone. The disagreeable impression left upon her mind by that interview had not in the least worn away: she greatly disliked Mr. Alfred King; she very greatly disliked the thought of visiting him again.

"Mark must help me," she said. "He is rolling in wealth, and two hundred pounds will not be much to him. It will be my own money. His covenant with my dear papa was to pay me three hundred pounds yearly for five years, and he has not begun the payment yet." Quite true Mr. Mark Cray had not yet handed over a shilling of the covenant money. Miss Davenal had pressed for some of it at the time of Mark's quitting Hallingham, but Mark had declined. She had brought it under his notice since, and Mark had made excuses still. He was not bound to pay it until the expiry of the year subsequent to Dr. Davenal's death, he said, and it would be most convenient to him to pay it then. Too proud to press the matter further for her niece, Miss Davenal contented herself with a dignified silence: but she did wonder whether it was that Mark would not or could not pay it. If he could not, why then how hollow, how false was all the show and luxury they had entered on in Grosvenor Place! The real truth of the matter was, Mark's expenses of one kind or another were so great that he had no ready money to spare; on the contrary, he was often at positive fault for some. And Mark was not a willing paymaster at the best of times: these careless spendthrift men frequently are not.

Yet the Great Wheal Bang was flourishing: how flourishing its elated shareholders could tell you; and Oswald Cray, relying on the assurances of his brother, had embarked his thousand in it. That alarming dispatch, with its still more alarming news, had turned out to be more smoke than fire; and when Mr. Barker reached the mine, whither he had hurried with all speed, he found the danger over. There had been an irruption of water, but a very slight one; it did not transpire beyond the locality: and Barker and Mark kept the secret well from the shareholders.

Sara went to Mark. She told him, speaking very gravely, that she had urgent need of two hundred pounds to complete some arrangements of necessity left in her charge by her father. Mark's answer was that he could not help her then; that it was not in his power. Perhaps he could not. They had not yet begun to realise, for that untoward accident, slight as it was, had served to retard the works, and there was no lead yet in the market. A short while, Mark said, and she might come to him for two thousand, and welcome, if it would be of any service to her. Large promises! But Mark had always dealt in such.

Sara had nowhere else to turn to for money in the wide world. Her aunt she knew could not help her; Miss Davenal's income was of a certain extent only, and their living absorbed it. So she wrote to Mr. Alfred King, and he appointed a day to meet her in Essex Street.

Once more, once more, she had to go forth to the unpleasant interview. All was unpleasant connected with it; the object, the journey, the very house, and Mr. Alfred King himself: but she was obeying the command of her dead father, she was seeking to save the reputation, perhaps the life, of her living brother; and Sara Davenal was not one to shrink on her own account from responsibilities such as these.

But surely the spirit of mischief was in it all? It seemed like an evil fate upon her—at least, so she thought in her vexation. For on this day, as on the other, she encountered Mr. Oswald Cray.

Not at the offices, but at the gate of the Temple garden. It occurred in this way. As before, she found she had to wait a considerable time before she could see Alfred King, and she wandered into the quiet courts of the Temple, and came to the larger garden.

The gate-keeper would not admit her to it at first; she had not the entrée, he said; but she told him her case: that she was a stranger, and had to wait an hour and a half to keep an appointment at a solicitor's in Essex Street. Her sweet face and her plaintive tone—for the voice catches the mind's sorrow—won him over, and, though he grumbled a little, he let her enter. It was peaceful there; shut in from the world's turmoil: the grass was green, and the paths were smooth; and Sara sat on the bench alone, and watched the river steamers as they passed and repassed on the Thames.

It was in leaving the gardens that she encountered Mr. Oswald Cray. He had business that day with a barrister in chambers, and was passing the gate as she was leaving it. Sara shrank within the gate again, in the hope that he might not accost her.

It was a vain hope. Surprised to see her there, so far from home and alone, he inquired the reason in the moment's impulse. The crimson blush, called into her face at the meeting, faded to paleness as she answered: "An appointment." She could not say she was there for pleasure.

And, besides, that utter weariness of spirit, when we no longer struggle against fate, had grown to be hers. It seemed of little moment whether he knew her errand that day or not: a faintness of heart, not unlike despair, was weakening her energies.

"An appointment?" he repeated. "Not at the place where I saw you before? Not with Mr. Alfred King?"

"Yes, that is where I am going," she replied, feeling she could not battle against the questions. "I was to have seen Mr. Allred King at twelve; but I was late, and so I have to wait for him."

"But it is not expedient that you should go there," said Oswald.

"I must go there," she answered, all too energetically in her desperation. "Were the interview to lead to—to my death, and I knew that it would, I should go."

The words, so unlike her calm good sense; the tone so full of hopeless sorrow, told Oswald how full of grief must be the heart they came from. They had strolled, unconsciously perhaps, down the broad walk of the garden, and were now passing a bench. "Will you sit down for a minute," he asked, "while I say a few words to you?"

"Yes: if I have time. My appointment is for two o'clock, and I wish to be there rather before than after it."

He took out his watch and showed it to her. There was plenty of time to spare.

"Have you to keep these appointments often?"

"I never kept but the one you know of. I hope—I am not sure—but I hope that the one today will be all I shall have to keep. It is a singular chance—that you should meet me on both days!"

"I don't think anything in the world happens by chance," gravely observed Oswald. "Do you recollect the interview I had with you at your house, just after your father's death?" he resumed, after a pause.

Sara turned her face to him in her surprise. "O yes."

"And do you remember," he continued, his voice assuming its sincerest and tenderest tone, "what I said at that interview?—That nothing would give me so much pleasure as to be your friend, should you require one. Sara—forgive me if I go back for a moment to our old familiar forms of speech—let me prove myself one now!"

"In what manner?" she asked, after some moments of hesitation.

"If I am able to understand anything of this business you need one. You seem to stand alone in it; no one to counsel you, no one to help."

"It is true," she said, "I have to stand in it alone. I must stand in it alone."

"Suffer me to be, so far, your friend."

She faintly shook her head. "You could not be."

"It is true that—that—the period has not arrived, perhaps for either of us, when we had contemplated such a friendship might begin. But we must waive that: necessity alters cases. Sara, let me serve you! I ask it in the name of Dr. Davenal. Surely you can have no objection?"

Her eyes were swimming in tears as she looked straight before her on the gravel path. "In anything but this I should only be too thankful. Sometimes I feel that I am left without a friend in the wide world."

"Why not in this?"

"Because it is a matter that I may not confide to any one. It is"—she lowered her voice—"a secret."

"I will be true as steel. No matter what dishonour may be in it, it shall be held sacred within my breast; never betrayed, never spoken of. I judge that it is not a pleasant secret; therefore I use the word dishonour. It is more fitting that I should be engaged in this matter than you."

For a single moment the temptation came over her to tell him what it was: just as the temptation to tell him the secret connected with Lady Oswald's death had once momentarily assailed Dr. Davenal. But it passed away almost with the thought. She could not speak of her brother's fault; she could not. Neither might she delegate to another the last directions left to her by her father. Safely grasped in her hand she held those sealed papers left by Dr. Davenal; how could she transfer them even to Oswald Cray?

"I wish I could tell it you!" she said in a tone of pain. "But I cannot; it is not possible. You will have guessed that this is not my own secret. It is a charge that was left to me by my dear father when he was dying: and I am obliged to fulfil it. He had no one to leave it to but me."

"Your brother being away. I can understand so much. Suffer me to stand to you, in this, in your brother's place. I am sure Captain Davenal would wish it."

The faint colour of dread came into her cheeks as she thought how far he would be from wishing this discussed with Mr. Oswald Cray. "I can't tell it," she murmured.

Oswald turned his gaze upon her, his dark blue eyes never more earnest, more eager.

"Will you let me urge this according to the dictates of common-sense? Is it fit that you, being what you are, a lady—young, refined, inexperienced—should be dancing attendance at Jones and Green's offices; men who do not bear too good a reputation in the legal world, to meet principally Mr. Alfred King, a man who bears a worse?"

The crimson shone in her cheeks. Put in this way it was anything but pleasant to the refinement of which he spoke. "I know, I know," she said impulsively. "I felt terribly the going there the day you saw me; I feel it again now. But indeed I cannot help myself. It was a solemn charge left me by my father, and in going through with it I am but doing my duty. God is over me," she simply added. "I have had a great deal to try me, a great deal to bear! but I am striving to do right under Him."

Her lip quivered as she spoke, and she paused from emotion. It was too much for the stoic philosophy of Oswald Cray. All the old feelings pent up so long, buried only, not subdued, resumed their sway with uncontrollable force, like a torrent let loose down a mountain's side. He caught her hands in his; he bent his face near to hers, its whole expression one of the deepest love; his persuasive voice, trembling with agitation, was sunk to the softest whisper.

"Sara, my dearest, I still love you better than anything on earth. Heaven knows how I have striven to forget you since that cloud fell upon us. It has been of no use. Bereft of you, life is but one long dreary path, growing more cruelly monotonous day by day."

Her heart beat wildly, and for one brief interval a hope, sweeter than any earthly dream, stole into it like a golden ray of sunshine. Only for an instant: she knew that it was but so much deceit, for him as for her.

"Are there no means by which we may forget that cloud and return to the past?" he resumed; his voice hoarse with its emotion, and so low in tone that she could scarcely hear it. "Better to sacrifice a little prejudice than to pass a whole life in dissatisfied pain. Let the dishonour—pardon me for thus alluding to it—rest with the dead: perhaps it has been wrong from the first to make it our sorrow."

She looked at him, not quite understanding. He saw the doubt.

"Be my wife, Sara. I can then take these troubles upon me as my legal right. On my sacred word of honour, I will never cast a reproach to the past, so much as in thought. No! I will not let your hands go until you tell me by word of mouth what I know—that your heart is mine still; that we cannot be faithless one to the other."

She felt faint with the moment's pain. The dewdrops of emotion were gathering on her face, and he would not loose her hands that she might wipe them away.

"If we never were true to each other, let us be so now," he went on. "It is too solemn a moment for equivocation: it is no time for us to pretend ignorance of our mutual love."

It was indeed no time for equivocation or for doubt. Sara rose superior to it. A reticence that might have been observed at another time was forgotten now in her emotion and pain.

"I have not been faithless: perhaps I never shall be. But we can never be more to each other than we are now. The dishonour clings to me, and always will cling."

"Sara! don't I say that I will forget it?"

"No; I would never bring the possibility of—of—of—I think you do not understand," she broke off, lifting her white face to his. "It was not only dishonour."

"What else?"

"Crime." A change passed over his countenance as he raised his head, which had been bent to catch the word. Soon it brightened again. Never perhaps had his besetting sin been so quiescent: but pride, even such pride as Oswald Cray's, is a less strong passion than love.

"It was not your crime, Sara. And it has passed away."

"It has not passed."

"Not passed!"

"Not yet. There's danger still."

Oswald bit his lip. "Danger of what?"

"Of—of—exposure," she faintly said. "Do not force me to say more. Only believe one thing—that I can never be your wife. Do you think if there were no insuperable barrier that I should have made one?" she added, her face flushing a hot crimson. "Forgive me: I scarcely know what I say: but you wished that we should speak without reserve."

"Sara, let me fully understand. Do you imply that there exists any good and substantial reason still, call it insuperable barrier if you will, why you ought not to become my wife? Wait a moment. Before you give an answer remember that to my heart it is fraught with either life or death."

"I do not imply it; I fully state it. Oh, don't visit it upon me!" she exclaimed, as his face seemed to be assuming its old haughtiness. "It is not my fault. I did not work the disgrace."

"No," he answered, soothingly, "it is not your fault. Forgive me," he softly whispered. "The blow to me is heavy."

"It may pass for you. It will pass. You will form new friendships, new ties, and forget the old. Better that it should be so."

"But never a new love! Never one who will be to me what the other has been."

She rose from her seat. Oswald drew her down on it again.

"As I hinted just now, Sara, the time when we may mix freely as friends has not yet come; it would not do for either of us. But I must make a last appeal to you—suffer me to be your friend in this one strait. Is it not possible that I can act for you?"

"It is not possible. There are certain reasons why neither you nor anybody else can do this; and, putting these aside, there is the weighty one that it was the charge bequeathed to me, and to me alone, by my dying father. Thank you for all," she whispered, as she suddenly rose and held out her hand, her soft dark eyes speaking their thanks to his.

He rose also. He did not release her hand, but placed it within his arm to lead her up the solitary path. If those grave, middle-aged counsel, deep in their briefs behind the dusty windows opposite, had glanced out at the interview, it probably reminded them of their own sweet spring-time.

Sara withdrew her hand at the garden-gate, but he walked by her side through the courts to Essex Street. She halted there to say adieu.

"I suppose I must not ask to accompany you?"

She shook her head. "I must be alone."

"Fare you well then," he said. "May all good angels guard you!"

Mr. Alfred King was waiting for her. He was evidently not pleased at two hundred pounds of the sum being missing; but he turned it off upon the "other parties." They would not accept it, he said, unless paid in full; and he hinted at consequences to Captain Davenal. He would not sign the receipt; told Sara it was useless to unseal it; but he did write a receipt for the present cheque paid. Altogether, it was a less satisfactory interview than even the former one had been, and Sara quitted him with a sinking heart. She had not the remotest idea where to get the money; and a despairing foreboding was upon her that Edward must yet pay the sacrifice of his crime.

"How long will they wait?" she asked herself, as she went shivering up Essex Street. "Suppose they send me word that they will not wait?—that Edward—oh, if I had but the means to—"

"Well? Is the thing happily over? You said this might be the last interview." It was Oswald Cray. He had waited for her. Her mind was preoccupied with its fears, almost bewildered, and she scarcely knew what she answered.

"No! it is not happily over. It is all unhappy, and I am frightened. The money I took them was—was—" She broke off with a start. Recollection had come to her.

"Was what?" he asked.

"I think I forgot myself;" she murmured, as a burning flush dyed her face. "My mind is full of trouble. Pray, pardon me, Mr. Oswald Cray."

CHAPTER XLIII

AN IRRUPTION ON MARK CRAY

If anything could exceed the prosperity of the Great Wheal Bang Mine itself, it was the prosperity of those immediately connected with it. There was only one little drawback—ready money ran short. It had been short a long while, and the inconvenience was great in consequence; but the prolonged inconvenience was now approaching to such a height that even that sanguine spirit, Barker, even Mark Cray in his confiding carelessness, felt that something must be done to remedy it.

Of course the cause of this will be readily divined—that the Great Wheal Bang's ore was not yet in the market. The heat of summer had passed, September was in with its soft air and its cool breezes, and still that valuable ore had not begun to "realise." It was obstinate ore, and it persisted in giving the greatest possible trouble before it would come out of its mother earth, where it had been imbedded for ages and ages. Those who understood the matter best, and the process of working these mines, tedious at all times, did not consider that any time was being lost; and it is more than probable that the impatience of Barker and Mark Cray alone caused the delay to appear unduly long.

The money swallowed up by that mine was enormous, and Mark Cray got half-dismayed at odd moments. The shareholders were growing tired of the calls upon their pockets; yet they were on the whole confiding shareholders, believing implicitly in the mine and its final results. As a natural sequence, the mine's wants being so great, its mouth so greedy a one, Mark Cray and his friend could have the less money to play with on their own score: still they managed to secure a little for absolute personal wants, and tradespeople of all denominations were eager to supply anything and everything to the great men of the Great Wheal Bang. How entire was the confidence placed in the mine by these two masters of it may be seen from the fact of their depriving themselves of money to pour it into the ever-open chasm. They might so easily have diverted a little channel into their own pockets! True, it might not have been quite the honest thing to do, but in these matters few men are scrupulous. Mark had surreptitiously sent a few shares into the market and realised the proceeds; but he had done it with reluctance: he did not care to part with his shares; neither was it well that the Great Wheal Bang's shares should be afloat.

Standing at the window of their drawing-room on this balmy September afternoon were Mark Cray and his wife. The fashionable world were of course not in London, but Mr. and Mrs. Cray formed an exception—there is no rule without one, you know. Mark felt that he could not be absent from those attractive offices in the City, even for a day. It was well that one of them should be seen there, and Barker was everlastingly running down into Wales. "Never mind, Carine," he said to his wife. "We'll take it out next year: we'll have a three-months' autumn trip in Germany. The money will be rolling in upon us then, and I need not stick here to keep the shareholders in good humour, as I have to do now." Carine obediently acquiesced; and she did it with cheerfulness: she had not been sufficiently long in her new and luxurious home to care about leaving it.

But she solaced herself with all the gaiety that was obtainable within reach. Drives out of town by day, and the theatre at night, or some other amusement accessible in September. On this day they had been to a wedding at the house of some new friends at Richmond; and they had but now returned. If you look out you may see the fine carriage with its four grey horses just turning from the door, for Caroline, capricious Caroline, wayward and whimsical as a child, had stepped out of it undecided whether to go out again and drive in the Park before dinner. So she kept the carriage waiting until she was pleased to decide not to go.

"I am a little tired, Mark, and they'd be ever so long taking out those post-horses and putting in our own," she said to her husband. "We could never go in the Park with four horses and postboys wearing white favours. Empty as the drive is, we should have a crowd round us."

"Taking you for the bride; and a very pretty one!" returned Mark, gallantly.

Caroline laughed; a little all-conscious laugh of vanity. She laid her beautiful bonnet of real lace and marabouts—and for which the milliner would assuredly charge £10—on a side-table, and threw off her costly white lace mantle. The folds of her silk dress, its colour the delicate bloom of the spring lilac, rustled as she went back to the window.

"Only think, Mark, we have been married nearly a year! It will be a year next month." Mark stood with his face close to the window. He was looking at the trees in the Green Park, their leaves playing in the golden light of the setting sun. Caroline flirted a few drops on her handkerchief from the miniature essence-bottle dangling from her wrist, and raised it to her carmine cheeks. The day's excitement had brought to them that rich bloom so suspiciously beautiful.

"I declare there's Barker!" exclaimed Mark. "I thought he'd be in."

Mr. Barker was dashing up the street in a cab, as fast as the horse's legs would go. He had been at the offices all day, doing duty for Mark. He saw them at the window, and gave them a nod as he leaped out. Mark looked at his watch and found it wanted yet some time to dinner. They sat down now, all three together, leaving the window to take care of itself. There was always so much to say when Barker was there. He talked so fast and so untiringly; present doings and future prospects were so good; and Caroline was as much at home in it as they were. They had had a splendid day in the City, Barker said volubly, except for grumbling. A hundred, or so, groaning old disappointed fellows had been in, who wanted to embark in the Wheal Bang and make their fortunes, but there were no shares to be had for love or money, and they were fit to bite their fingers off. Altogether, nothing could be more smooth, more delightful than affairs, and Barker had received news from the mines that morning promising loads upon loads of ore in a month or so's time.

Mark rubbed his hands. "I say, Barker, what do you say to a quiet little dinner at Blackwall tomorrow?" cried he. "I and Carine are thinking of driving down. Will you come?"

"Don't mind if I do," returned Barker. "What, time?"

"Well, not very late. The evenings are not so light as they were. Suppose we say"—

Before the hour had left Mark's lips he was stopped by a commotion. A sound as of much talking and bumping of boxes in the hall below: of boxes that appeared to be coming into the house. Caroline went to the window and saw a cab drawn up to the door, a last trunk being taken off it, and three band-boxes in a row on the pavement.

"Why, who can it be?" she exclaimed.

The question was soon set at rest. A lady in fashionable half-mourning entered the room and clasped Mark round the neck. Three young ladies entered after her and clasped Mark also, all three at once, two by the arms, one by the coat-tails. Mr. Barker's red whiskers stood out in wonder at the sight, and Caroline's violet eyes opened to their utmost width.

"We thought we'd take you by surprise, darling," the elder lady was saying. "The girls declared it would be delightful. I couldn't afford any change for them this year, Mark, out of my poor means, and we determined to pay you a visit for a few days. And so we have come, and I hope you can take us in."

"Yes, but don't smother me, all of you at once," was poor Mark's answer. "I am glad to see you mother; and I am sure my wife—Caroline, you remember my mother and my sisters."

It was certainly an imposing number to take a house by storm, and there was vexation in Mark's eye as he looked deprecatingly at his wife. But Caroline rose superior to the emergency. She came forward prettily and gracefully, and welcomed them all with a cordial smile. Mrs. Cray the elder could not take her eyes from her face: she thought she had never seen one grown so lovely. She withdrew them at length and turned them on Mr. Barker.

But that gentleman scarcely needed an introduction. He was of that free and easy nature that makes itself at home without one; and in an incredibly short time, before indeed the strangers had taken their bonnets off, he was chattering to them as familiarly as though he had known them for years. They were rather pleasing girls, these sisters of Mark—Fanny, Margaret, and Nina: very accomplished, very useless, and bearing about them the tone of good society.

Leaving Mark to welcome them, we must turn for an instant to the house of Miss Davenal. Sara was at rest, for she had paid Mr. Alfred King. In her desperate need—it surely might be called such!—she wrote the facts of the case to Mr. Wheatley. Not telling him the details, not saying a word that might not have been disclosed to the whole body of police themselves, but simply stating to him that she had very urgent need of this two hundred pounds for her father's sake. The result was, that Mr. Wheatley sent her the money. But he was not a rich man, and he candidly told her he could not have done it but for the certainty there existed of its speedy return to him. Sara lost not a moment in seeking another and a final interview with Mr. Alfred King. The papers were given up to her, the receipt signed, all was done as specified by Dr. Davenal, and the affair and the danger to Edward were alike at an end. The horrible nightmare on Sara Davenal's days was lifted; the fear which had been making her old before her time was over. Her countenance lost its look of wearing pain, and she seemed like a child again in her freedom from care.

Yes, the dreadful nightmare was over, and Sara was at rest. In her immunity from pain, in her renewed happiness, it almost seemed as if the world might still have charms for her. You can look at her as she stands in the drawing-room by Miss Davenal's side. It is the same evening as the one spoken of above, when Mrs. Cray and her daughters made that irruption upon Mark. Sara is in evening dress—a black gauze, with a little white net quilling on the low body and sleeves. Her white cloak lies on the sofa, and she is drawing on some new lavender gloves. But look at her face! at her cheek's rich colour! at the sweet smile on the lips, at the bright eye! Is it the anticipated evening's enjoyment that is calling these forth? No, no; the pleasant signs spring from a heart at rest: a heart that had long been aching, worn, terrified with a secret care.

It was very rare indeed that Miss Davenal went out, but she had accepted an invitation for dinner that evening. She had a few friends in London, not new ones (of new ones she had made none); but old acquaintances of her earlier days. The friend she was going to this evening, Lady Reid, had been her schoolfellow at Hallingham; they had grown up together, and Bettina Davenal was her bridesmaid when she married young Lieutenant Reid, who had then his fortune to make. He made it out in India, and he came home a colonel and a K.C.B.; came home only to die, as is the case with too many who have spent their best days in the Indian empire. His widow lived at Brompton, and Miss Davenal and she liked nothing better than to spend an hour together and talk of the days when they were so young and hopeful. How different, how different to them was the world now! Could it be the same world? Many of you, my readers, have asked the very question.

Neal had gone to the livery stables to order round a carriage, for Miss Bettina had a horror of cabs, and had not put her foot inside one since the evening of her arrival in London. She stood in her rich black silk and her cap of that fine white lace called point d'Angleterre, glancing from the window and talking with Sara. They had had news from Bombay that afternoon from Edward. Great news! and perhaps Sara's cheeks owed some of their unusual colour to this.

Captain Davenal was married. He had fallen in love with a pretty girl in India, or she had fallen in love with him, and they were married. She was an only child, he wrote them word, and an heiress; her name Rose Reid, now Rose Davenal. Miss Davenal felt nearly sure it must be a niece of her old friend to whom she was that evening engaged. Lady Reid's late husband had a brother in the civil service at Bombay, reported to be a rich man, and it was probable this was his daughter.

"It is just like Edward," she said tartly to Sara, as she watched for the carriage. "To think that he should marry after a month or two's acquaintance! He can't have known her much longer."

"But he says she is so pretty, aunt; so lovable!" was Sara's pleading answer. "And—if she is an heiress, I am very glad for Edward's sake."

"Ah," grimly returned Miss Bettina, having as usual heard all awry, "that's it, no doubt, the money's sake. I don't forget a good old proverb: 'Marry in haste and repent at leisure!' Here comes the carriage."

They went down to it. Neal, all perfection as usual, assisted them in and took his place by the side of the driver. They were nearly at their journey's end when, in passing a row of houses, Sara, who happened to be looking out, saw Oswald Cray at one of the windows: and by his side a fair face half-hidden by the crimson curtain; the face of Jane Allister.

A mist gathered over her eyes and her heart. She looked out still, mechanically; she saw the name written up as they left the houses behind them, "Bangalore Terrace;" she answered her aunt's remarks as before; but the change within her was as if sunshine had given place to night.

Why, could she still be cherishing those past hopes? No; never for an instant. She knew that all was over between her and Oswald Cray; that he was entirely lost to her. But she could not put away from her the old feelings and the old love; she could not see him thus in familiar companionship with another without bitter pangs and wild emotion. Perhaps Jane Allister was to be his wife!

Neal left them at Lady Reid's, his orders being to return with the carriage a quarter before eleven. When he reached home it was dusk; and Dorcas, attired in her bonnet and shawl, came to him in the passage, and said she was going out to do a little shopping.

Neal watched her fairly off and then went indoors. He closed the shutters of the dining parlour, went up to the drawing-room, where he set the candle on the table, and closed those shutters also. He took a leisurely survey of the room, apparently searching for something, and reading, en passant, a note or two left upon the mantelpiece, and then he took his seat before Sara's desk.

That little episode, the spoiled lock of the doctor's desk, had taught him caution; he would not make the same mistake with this. Neal was an adept at his work: and, by the ingenious use of a penknife and a piece of wire, the desk was opened. It may be a question how long Neal had waited for this opportunity. Such a one had not occurred for months: his ladies out, and Dorcas out; and the house wrapped in the silence of night, and not likely to be invaded.

And now a word to my readers. Should there be any among you who may feel inclined to cavil at this description of Neal's treachery, deeming it improbable, let me tell you that it is but the simple truth—a recital of an episode in real life. The reading of the letters, the opening of the desks, the ferreting propensities, the treachery altogether, were practised by a retainer in a certain family, and the mischief wrought was incalculable. It separated those in spirit who had never been separated before; it gave rise to all sorts of misconception and ill-feeling; it caused animosity to prevail between relatives for years: and the worst was—the worst, the worst!—that some of those relatives were never reconciled again in this world, for before the truth came to light death had been busy. As Coleridge says,

"Whispering tongues can poison truth."

What Neal's motive was I cannot tell you. What the motive of that other one was, was as little to be traced. There was nothing to be gained by it, so far as could be seen. It may have been that the prying propensities were innate in both natures; the love of working mischief inherent in their hearts. Certainly it was the ruling passion of their lives. The most extraordinary inventions, the strangest stories, were related by the one: you will find, before you have done with the other, that they were not abjured by him.

The first letter Neal came to in the desk—at least, the first he opened—happened to be one from Mr. Wheatley. By that he learned that two hundred pounds had been lent to Sara in the summer for the "completion of the payment she spoke of." Coupled with his previously-acquired knowledge, Neal came to the conclusion that the trouble as regarded Captain Davenal was over, and the money paid. The precise nature of the trouble Neal had never succeeded in arriving at, but he did know that money had to be paid in secret on his account. The next letter he came upon was the one received from the Captain that day: and if Neal had hoped to find groans and trouble and difficulty in it, he was most completely disappointed. It was one of the sunniest letters ever read; it spoke of his girl-wife and his own happiness: not a breath was there in it of care in any shape. Neal was nonplussed: and the letters did not afford him pleasure.

"The thing all settled!—the money paid!" he repeated to himself, revolving the various items of news. "No wonder she has looked sprightly lately. Why, for months after the doctor's death she seemed fit to hang herself! I thought some change had come to her. And he is married, is he!—and has picked up an heiress! I don't like that. Some folks do have the luck of it in this world. It's a great shame! And she has no right to be happy, for I know she hates me. I know she suspects me, that's more. I'll try—I'll try and deal out a little small coin in exchange. There's always that other thing, thank goodness; the break with Mr. Oswald Cray. I wonder if she saw him this evening at that window? I did; and I saw the young lady too. I hope it's going to be a match, if only to serve out this one?"

With this charitable wish Mr. Neal resumed his research of the desk. But nothing more of particular moment turned up, and he soon made it fast again in his own artistic manner, which defied detection.

And when Dorcas came in she found Neal, his supper eaten stretched comfortably before the kitchen fire, taking a dose.

CHAPTER XLIV

WAS SHE NEVER TO BE AT PEACE?

News of an unpleasant nature was on its way to Miss Davenal and Sara; but they sat at breakfast unconscious of its nearness, waited upon by Neal the immaculate, in all confiding security, and entirely unsuspicious of that gentleman's desk researches of the previous evening. A letter came in; it was directed to Miss Davenal in the handwriting of Dr. Keen.

"What's a-gate now?" exclaimed Miss Davenal, as she opened it. For it was not very usual for the doctor to write in the middle of a quarter.

"Dear Madam,—

"I grieve much to have to inform you that an accident has happened to your nephew Leopold. It being a half-holiday yesterday afternoon (granted, according to annual custom, on the auspicious occasion of Mrs. Keen's birthday), the young gentlemen had leave accorded them to go into the fields and gather blackberries. Engaged in this (hitherto deemed harmless) recreation, Leopold unfortunately met with a fall. In stretching up to reach a high branch, he lost his balance, and fell from the top of a bank. I fear he may have been pushed, but the boys appear not to be quite clear upon the point. At any rate, he fell in some way with his arm doubled under him, and on examination it proved to be broken.

"Deeply sorry as I am to be obliged to impart to you this sad news, I can yet qualify it in some degree by stating that it is a simple fracture. It was at once set, and the surgeon assures me it will do as well as possible. Mrs. Keen bids me say that she does not think Master Leopold has appeared very strong of late; I have remarked myself that he looks delicate. Master Davenal, I am happy to say, is quite well, and gives us every satisfaction in his studies, in which he takes great pleasure.

"With very kind remembrances from Mrs. Keen to yourself and Miss Sara Davenal, and best compliments from myself,—I remain, dear Madam, faithfully yours, John Keen.

"Miss Davenal."

Miss Bettina gave the letter to her niece in an excess of vexation "If that mischievous Dick was not at the bottom of it, I shall wonder!" she exclaimed. "He pushed him off in his roughness. He is rough."

Sara gathered in the words of the letter in silence, with strained eyes and a beating heart.

"I'd have every blackberry-tree in the land rooted up, if I had my will," proceeded Miss Bettina. "Boys are as venturesome as monkeys when their mouths are in question. They don't care for their clothes or how they get torn; they don't care for their shirtfronts or how they get stained; they fight, and quarrel, and climb, and scratch their hands and faces with the thorns, and all for greediness—that they may fill themselves with those rubbishing berries. And now they have caused this mischief! The boy's arm may be weak for life. Yes, if I had the power, I'd destroy every blackberry-tree that grows. I should think D. Keen will interdict 'blackberrying' for the future."

"I wonder how it happened?" said Sara, musingly.

"So do I," said Miss Bettina, in a tart tone. "One would think the bank was as high as a house. They'd climb up a house, boys would, if they thought they should find blackberries growing upon its roof. Ah, never shall I forget—it has this moment recurred to my mind—Leo's father coming home in a sorry plight when he was a boy. He went blackberrying. He went without anybody's knowledge, too, and was absent for hours, and we grew alarmed at home, as was natural, for he was but a little fellow of eight. I remember my dear mother feared he had fallen into some pond, but we children thought Johnny had gone after the wild-beast caravan, which had been in the town exhibiting two bears and an elephant. He arrived at home at dusk; and I'm sure he looked more fit to belong to a caravan than to a gentleman's house. His knees were out of his trousers, and his brown-holland blouse was in flounces, and his shirt-frill had three hanging rents in it, and his hair and face and hands were crimson with the stains, causing my mother to cry out with fear at the first sight of him. To crown all, he had filled his new straw hat with the blackberries, and the juice was dropping through the crown! John does not forget that exploit, I know, to this day. Your grandpapa gave him a sound whipping and sent him to bed supperless; not so much for the plight he had put himself into as for roaming out alone and frightening my dear mother. Johnny was ill for three days afterwards with stomach-ache, from the quantity he had devoured. He remembers blackberrying, I know; and I should think Mr. Leo will, after this."

"I hope his arm will soon be well!"

"Dr. Keen might have mentioned what surgeon was attending to it! if Mark Cray had remained at Hallingham," continued Miss Bettina, very sharply—for it was impossible for her to speak of that exit of Mark's without sharpness—"he might have gone over by rail, and seen that it was being properly—What do you say, Neal?"

Miss Bettina's interruption was caused by the entrance of Neal. Mrs. Cray's maid had come round, and was waiting to speak to Miss Sara.

"Let her come in," said Miss Bettina.

The tone was as sharp a one as that just given to the absent Mark. Caroline's maid, a remarkably fashionable damsel, did not reign in the favour of Miss Bettina. She came in in obedience to orders; a pink gauze bonnet on the back of her head, and a pair of dirty and very tight straw-coloured gloves strained on her hands. Miss Bettina's countenance lost none of its severity as she surveyed her.

"What do you want, Long?"

"If you please, mem, my message is to Miss Sara Davenal," returned Long, pertly, for she did not like Miss Bettina any more than Miss Bettina liked her.

"Tell it, then. Miss Sara Davenal's there, you see." Long fairly turned her back on Miss Bettina as she delivered the message she was charged with. She explained that Mr. Cray's mother and sisters had arrived unexpectedly the previous night, and the object of her coming round now was, to ask if Miss Sara Davenal would go out with Mrs. Cray senior that morning.

"Arrived last night unexpectedly!" exclaimed Miss Bettina, who had been bending her ear. "How many of them?"

"Four," replied Long. "Mrs. Cray and three Miss Crays."

"It's well the house is large! I should not like to be taken by storm in that way."

"I suppose I can go, aunt?"

"I suppose you can't refuse. What's it for? Where is she going?"

"Where is Mrs. Cray going, do you know, Long?" asked Sara.

"I believe she's only going shopping, miss," answered the girl, who was always civil to Sara. "I heard her say she must get a bonnet, and other things, before she could appear in London. My mistress has promised to take the young ladies out, and she said perhaps you'd be so good as accompany Mrs. Cray senior, as she does not know London."

"I don't think I know it much better than she does," observed Sara, smiling. "But you can tell Mrs. Cray that I shall be happy to accompany her, and to render her any service that I can. Oh, and, Long, will you tell your mistress that we have received sad news from Dr. Keen," she resumed, as the maid was turning away. "Poor little Leopold has broken his arm."

"And that he did it scrambling after blackberries," indignantly added Miss Bettina.

The maid departed, saying that Mrs. Cray senior would be round in the course of the morning. Sara went up to the drawing-room, and opened her letter-case, which she used sometimes instead of her desk. Her first thought was to write a few words to poor Leo. But ere she began she leaned her aching brow upon her hand; the vision she had seen at the window of Bangalore Terrace, as they drove to Lady Reid's the previous evening, had left its sting upon her brain.

A slight tap at the door, and Neal came in. He could not but note the weary expression of her face as she looked up at him. He advanced to the table, some papers in his hand, and spoke in a low voice as if what he said was for her ear alone.

"The postman brought another letter, Miss Sara. It was enclosed in this envelope addressed to me by Master Richard. Perhaps you would like to see what he says." Neal was really honest in this. Possibly he saw no opportunity to be otherwise. Sara, in some curiosity, took the papers from Neal's hands. The whole lot was characteristic of Dick. The envelope was addressed "Mr. Neal, at Miss Davenal's. Private," the proper address of their residence being added. On opening it when delivered to him by the postman, Neal had found it to contain a sealed letter for Miss Sara Davenal and a scrap of paper evidently torn from a copy-book for himself. On the latter he read the following lines, and these he now showed to his young mistress.

"Dear Neal, give the note to my couzin Sara when nobodys buy and be sure dont let aunt bett see it or therell be a row, R. D."

"Oh, thank you, Neal," she said heartily. But as the man left the room and she broke the seal, a half-dread came over her of what it would contain.

"Dear Sara,—

"The most horrid catastrofy has hapened, leo's gone and broke his arm, and I want to tell you how it was done I must tell somebody or I shall burst, leo's a brave littel chap and kept his mouth shut when old Keen and the docter were asking questions and let him think it was through the blackberys, we had half holliday it was Mrs. Keens berthday and we went after the blackberys, this was yesterday afternoon, and about 6 of us, me and Jones and tom Keen and Halliday and leo and Thomson, if you want to know which of us it was, where separated from the rest and got into one of farmer clupp's feilds and what should we see but his poney trying to nible at the short grass, we set up a shout, which Halliday stoppt for fear of being heard, and caught him, and then there was a shindy as to which 3 of us should have first ride, for we were afraid thered not be time for the other three if the school came up, and the under master dogskin (thats our name for him hes a sneek) was with them, so to end the dispute we all 6 got on the poney and a stunning gallopp we had only it was rather close to sit, well leo was the hindmost and as he hadnt much beside the tail to sit on he fell off but he must be a great duff for he had held on all round the feild once, he says it was Jones moved and made him fall and tom Keen says hes sure it was, for Jones who has got the longest legs kept jogging them to make the poney go and he was next to leo and leo held on by him, I was first and guided the poney and in taking the sweep round at the turning leo shot off behind, his arm was doubled under him and a soft duffer of an arm it must be for it took and broke, we didnt know he was gone at first, Jones called out, young Davenal's off, but we thought nothing and galloped all round the feild again, he was lying there when we got back, and his face was white and we called to him and he never answered so we stopt the poney and went to him, Jones tried to pull him up and leo screamed, and halliday calls out Im blest if I dont think hes hurt, leo began saying he hoped he wasnt kill'd, you know what a regular little muff he is, we picked him up at last and when we saw his arm hang down we were frightened above a bit, well we didnt know what was to be done, we carried him into the next feild where the poney wasnt, for fear of anybody suspecting and just as we had laid him by the bank the rest of the fellows came down the lane and saw us and tom keen called out that davenal junior was hurt, with that they came up and Marsh (thats dogskin) looks up at the high bank above leo and sees the blackberys growing atop of it and sings out to leo, I know how this was done, you where on the top of that bank trying to get blackberys beyond your reach and you fell off it, well if you'll believe me sara we never told the story to say yes, only Jones said says he I'm sure I dont know sir how ever he managed to fall, and Marsh he thought he did fall off the bank and went off to take the news to Keen, and us 6 all thought what a jolly chance it was that we had happened to lay him down by the bank, and none of them ever saw the poney, leo was carried home and Mrs. Keen she came out with a face as white as his, tom how did it happen, says she laying hold of tom, and we got affraid again, for toms uncommon fond of his mother, but he didnt split, and then Keen came and the surjon came and Keen he says to leo how did you fall did any body push you off the bank, no sir says leo, and the surjon he asked how t was done, and leo shook like anything, and began to cry, afraid he should have to tell a story at last which he cant bare, he was shut up in a room then with the doctor and Keen and one or two more and we heard him cry out when they were setting his arm, but you know what a baby he is poor little chap and I wish with all my hart it had been me instead of him, the worst is I should have lost my share of the supper and a jolly good one they give us on her berthday every year, cakes and tarts and pidjon pies and lots of things and we have to dress for it and a heap of duffing girls come to it in white frocks but we dont mind em much, and dear sara thats the whole facts of how it came about and I couldn't write it truer if I were telling it to poor Uncle Richard himself, leos all jolly this morning and he is in bed and has got no lessons to do and he says I am to tell you that he'll never get on a poney with 6 again and Mrs. Keens very kind to him, and Miss Keen (shes the big one you know) is going to read him some storys, he says I am to tell you it doesn't hurt much and oh sara there's only one thing we are sorry for, that Uncle Richard isnt alive to cure him because hed have him home to Hallingham to do it and perhaps me as well and I should get a holliday from these horrid books, I shall send this to neal for fear of aunt bett, and mind you hide it, and dont let a sight of it reach her, we are aufully afraid of that about the poney getting to old keens ears for thered be the dickens to pay, yours affectionately

"Dick.

"p s leo sends his love and he hopes you wont be angry with him for breaking his arm and I am writing this after school at twelve instead of playing, Good buy."

Sara smiled, in spite of herself, as she folded up the letter. But she thought it rather a wonder there had not been a few broken legs among the "6," instead of one broken arm.

She got ready for Mrs. Cray, and went down to the dining-room. Miss Bettina was gone out then. She took up a book, but had not been looking at it many minutes when she saw Neal coming up the street talking to a young person whose condition in life it was rather difficult to guess. In these days of dress it is difficult. She had a pretty face, Sara could see that, though a veil covered it; her gown was one of those called a "washing silk"—and very much "washed out" it seemed to be; and a smart shawl, just flung on the shoulders, trailed on the ground behind. But for this trailing shawl and a sort of general untidiness, there would have been something superior about the girl. In the face she looked like a lady, and Sara had seen many a lady worse dressed.

Sara, behind the blind, could see them, but they could not see her. Neal stood a moment at the door, and then looked down over the railings of the area.

"Are the ladies out?" he asked.

"Yes," came back for answer in Dorcas's voice. The woman evidently did not know that Miss Sara had not accompanied her mistress.

"You can come in then," Sara distinctly heard Neal say to the lady—if lady she was. And he opened the door with his latch-key.

They stood talking in the passage for some little time in an undertone, and then Neal took her into the back room. It opened to the dining-room with folding-doors; but the doors were always kept closed: and indeed the back room was chiefly used as Neal's pantry. Sara, who at first had been doubtful whether it might not be a visitor to herself, came to the conclusion that it was only a visitor to Neal, and she resumed her reading.

But the voices grew rather louder; and the words "Captain Davenal" caused her to look up with a start. No wonder she should start at that name, remembering the past. A sudden fear same over her that something or other connected with that past was again threatening her brother.

She could not hear more, for the voices dropped again to their covert tone. Another minute, and Neal was conducting the stranger to the front door.

"We shall hear more by the next mail; but there's not the slightest doubt he's married," Sara heard him say as he passed the room. "The lady is an heiress: a Miss Reid."

"Well," cried the other voice, "I'll have satisfaction. I'll have it somehow. I don't care what punishment it brings him to, I'll have it."

The visitor went away. Neal closed the street-door upon her and turned to behold his young mistress at that of the dining-room, a scared look in her eyes, a white shade upon her face.

"Neal! what has that young "—Sara hesitated between the words person and lady, but chose the former—"person to do with Captain Davenal?"

She had spoken without reflection in her impulse; in her renewed fear, which she had deemed buried with the past. Neal for once in his life was confounded. He did not speak immediately; he was probably striving to recall what had been said, inconvenient for her to hear.

"Tell me at once, Neal; I insist on your speaking," she reiterated, attributing his hesitation to unwillingness to speak. "Indeed it is better that I should know it. What was she saying about my brother?"

That alarm of some nature had been aroused within her, that she was painfully anxious, and that the alarm and anxiety were connected with Captain Davenal, Neal could not fail to read. But his speech was certainly less ready than usual, for he still kept silence.

"I heard you tell her that Captain Davenal was married; that further news would be in by the next mail," pursued Sara, growing more inwardly perturbed with every moment. "What was it to her? Who is she? For what purpose did she come here? Neal, can't you answer me?" and her voice grew quite shrill with its alarm and pain.

"Miss Sara—if I hesitated to answer, it is that I do not like to speak," he said at length. "I tell the young woman she must be mistaken in what she says—that it can't be. But she won't hear me."

"What is it that she says? Have you seen her before today?"

"She has been here once or twice before. But for understanding that you and my mistress were out I should not have allowed her to come in this time. I am very sorry that it should have happened, miss."

"But what is it?" returned Sara, nearly wild with suspense. "What has she come for?"

"She has come to ask questions about Captain Davenal."

"But what about him? What is he to her?"

Neal coughed. He took out his handsome silk handkerchief—he always used very handsome ones—and wiped his mouth. Sara trembled. His manner was unpleasantly mysterious, and it seemed that she was on the verge of hearing something terrible.

"Does she know my brother?"

"She says she does. Miss Sara, I would have given a great deal to prevent this happening today. It will only worry you, and I daresay I could still have put her off and kept her quiet."

"Neal, tell me the worst," she cried, her voice and heart alike growing faint. "I must hear it now."

"Well, Miss Sara, she says she is the wife of Captain Davenal."

"She—says—she—is—the—wife—of—Captain Davenal!"

The words were echoed slowly in very astonishment, a pause between each. Vague as her fears had been they had not touched on this.

"It is what she says, Miss Sara. I told her it must be one of two things—either that she was deceiving me in saying it, or that she was herself deceived. But she insists upon it that she is his true and lawful wife; that she was married to him nearly twelve months before he went abroad. She says my late master, Dr. Davenal, knew of it."

Sara stared at Neal in a sort of helpless manner. Never for a moment did it occur to her to question the truth; her mind accepted it—a terrible calamity; worse, it seemed in this moment, than all that had gone before.

"She came here this morning in consequence of hearing of the Captain's marriage to Miss Reid. I acknowledged that news had come home to that effect. It would have been quite useless, you see, Miss Sara, to deny what's known publicly."

"Neal! Neal! you will not mention this?" came the feverish wish, the first uttered in her bewilderment. "You will guard it faithfully? We—I—some one must see what can be done."

"You may entirely depend on me, Miss Sara," replied Neal, speaking more impressively than was his wont—Neal the impassive. "Of course, miss, the chief thing will be to guard against exposure."

Sara turned into the dining-room, mind and body alike sinking. A sick, faint fear came over her that this must be the secret connected with her brother which had been disclosed that long past night to Dr. Davenal. Another moment, and she did not see how that could be. There would have been no crime in it: Captain Davenal was not married then. Her brain was in a chaos of perplexity, her mind agitated with doubt. If this young woman—lady—whatever she might be—was Edward's wife, how could he have married Rose Reid? Was it the money tempted him? Calm, self-controlled though she was usually, a groan of despair broke from her lips.

Neal in the back room thought she called him, and came round to the dining-room door. She looked up as he stood there and stared at him, just as though she had forgotten who he was.

"Did you call, Miss Sara?"

"I—I—I did not call. Neal—do you know—what the name is?—I mean—what it was?"

"Yes, miss, I know so much as that. Catherine Wentworth."

He retired, leaving Sara alone. Almost a rebellious thought was stealing over her—was she never to be at rest? Not at much rest just then certainly; for Mrs. Cray had driven to the door and was asking for her.

Sara tied her bonnet mechanically and went out. Mrs. Cray was seated in a fly. She would not alight then, she said: she had a great deal to do. Sara stepped in. Mrs. Cray was an imperious-looking woman, fair and pale, with a handsome face. Sara thought her over-dressed and very fidgety. They were not much acquainted when at Hallingham.

"I have nothing to wear," she said to Sara. "I want a host of things. A bonnet first. Mrs. Mark Cray has given me the address of a superior dressmaker. She is a little selfish, is she not?"

"Who is?" cried Sara, in answer to the sentence, which came out rather abruptly after the rest.

"Mrs. Mark Cray. To confess to you my opinion, I think she might have lent me the carriage this morning, instead of sending me out in a hired fly, and keeping the carriage for herself and the girls. It seems to be the way of the world nowadays—the young before the old. She is Mark's wife, and I am only his mother."

Whether Sara would have found a suitable answer is uncertain. Something outside completely took away all thoughts of it. They were at that moment passing the War Office; and, coming from it with an angry and determined look upon her pretty face, was the person whom she had just heard called Catherine Wentworth. Sara shrunk back in the cab's corner, dismay on her countenance, dismay in her heart. Had she already denounced Captain Davenal at headquarters?

From milliners to linen-drapers, from linen-drapers to dressmakers, one place after another continually, until Sara was tired to death, the day wore away. The afternoon was getting on when the last commission was done, and Mrs. Cray, who had put on the new bonnet just bought, had leisure to think of the horse and driver.

"Poor things, they must want some repose," she remarked, as she came out of the Pantheon. "Well, there's only one place more. Will you tell the man, my dear?" she added as she got in. "Parliament Street. You know the number, I suppose."

"What number?" inquired Sara. "Where to in Parliament Street?"

"To Mr. Oswald Cray's. Bracknell and Street, I think, is the name of the firm."

"There!" returned Sara in her discomposure. "I can't go there."

"Not go there! My dear, I must go there. Mr. Oswald Cray is my step-son. I shall call in for a minute to let him know I am in London."

Opposition would be worse than acquiescence. Besides, what could be her plea? Sara, all her pulses fluttering, spoke the address to the driver, and took her place in silence opposite Mrs. Cray.

CHAPTER XLV

MRS BENN'S WRONGS

"Then, Benn, I'll not have it done! You can't go."

"But I tell you I have got my orders. I am sent."

"And who gave you the orders, pray, Joe Benn? Who sent you?"

"Mr. Oswald Cray. And the best thing for you to do is to hold your tongue and take off that there guy of a bonnet, and hide your bare arms, and put on a apron that's clean, and otherwise make yourself decent, for you have got to do it. And when folks have got to do a thing, they may as well make up their minds to do it in the best way and readiest way they can."

Mr. Benn, in thus breathlessly telling his wife she had "got to do it," did not allude to the little items of personal embellishment he mentioned, but to something else which Mrs. Benn abhorred above all things—that of waiting on gentlemen. It happened now and then that a luncheon or other meal would be ordered at the offices in Parliament Street for some stranger or friend stopping in London, which meal Mrs. Benn had to prepare, and her husband to wait at. On this day Mr. Street had ordered mutton-chops to be ready for two o'clock, and the tray laid for three persons; and this it was that was discomposing Mrs. Benn. In the first place, it was one of those oft-recurring periodical battles of her life—a cleaning-day; in the next place, her husband had just given her the startling information that she would have to wait at the meal as well as to cook it. "And a fine object you be, to do it!" he had wound up with in a mutter to himself.

Certainly Mrs. Benn did not appear to particular advantage today, looking at her in an artistic point of view. You have had the pleasure of seeing her once before in the high costume donned for the occasion of those days specially marked in her calendar. I don't think there's much change. Her bonnet, black once, rusty brown now, is on, brim downwards, crown up, strings tied in a knot at the back; her apron is a piece of wrappering off a bale of goods, embellished with sundry holes and fastened round her with an iron skewer; and her gown, turned up under it, is pinned into a heap behind. She stands over the Dutch oven, her arms bare and black, and a fork in her hand; and ever and anon as she stoops to turn or touch the chops in the Dutch oven, the gathered gown sways itself up at the back, not unlike a sail. Mr. Benn is in his shirtsleeves, having taken off his coat to brush it, preparatory to going out.

"It's sure to be the case! I've marked it times and times again!" burst forth Mrs. Benn, trying to fling off a live coal which bad intruded itself into the Dutch oven. "If ever there's lunch or any bothering extra of that sort wanted, it's safe to be on my cleaning-day! Mr. Street have got no more consideration nor a stalking gander; and Mr. Oswald Cray have got as little. They might remember my cleaning-days, and spare a body on 'em."

"And a fine speech that is," said Mr. Benn, in a reprimanding tone. "You'd better not let it come anigh their ears. We are here, you and me, to do what work's required of us, at any hour, whether it's cooking or whether it's waiting, and your ord'nary work must give way when it's wanted to give it. They'd soon get other servants in our places."

"He comes to the top o' the stairs just as the clock was going one," observed Mrs. Benn, paying no more attention to the words of her husband than if she had been deaf. "'Are you there?' he calls out, and I looked up and see it was Mr. Street. 'Yes, sir,' says I, 'I be;' and I was in a cloud of dust at the moment fit to smother you, a doing out of that there wood and bottle cupboard. 'Oh,' says he 'some mutton-chops for two o'clock, and lay the tray for three. And do 'em well,' says he, 'and a dish of mashed potaters.' A nice thing that was for me to hear!—and to have to go out the figure I be, after chops, and to be hindered in my cleaning a good two hours! Ain't that enough, Joe Benn, without having to turn to and wait?"

"I can't help it," said Joe, civilly, as he put on his coat. "If I am ordered work out of doors I must go about it, just as you must the work in. Mr. Oswald Cray has sent me down to Limehouse, and I must be back before the office closes. Don't I tell you I can't even stop for my dinner?"

He went away without more words. He probably would have had a few sent after him, but for an unlucky catastrophe that occurred at the moment. The saucepan of potatoes fell on its side, and enveloped Mrs. Benn and the Dutch oven in a mass of steam. It took all that lady's best attention to remedy it; and when she looked up Mr. Benn was gone.

Very reluctantly indeed did she set about making herself presentable; but, as Benn had said, there was no help for it. She washed her face and hands, and turned down the gown, and drew down its sleeves, and put on a white apron, and replaced the choice bonnet with a clean cap, grumbling bitterly all the time. And at the appointed hour she took up the luncheon-tray.

Three gentlemen partook of the meal—Mr. Street, Oswald Cray and a well-known contractor, who had only that day arrived in London from Spain, and was going into the country to his works by a four o'clock train. They were discussing business while they ate.

A certain projected line of rail in Spain was being organised. Bracknell and Street were the engineers, and it was proposed that Mr. Oswald Cray should go out as superintendent. The details of the affair do not concern us; but it must be mentioned that the sojourn in Spain would be likely, from certain attendant circumstances, to prove of great advantage to Mr. Oswald Cray in a pecuniary point of view.

After the departure of the guest Mr. Street and Oswald remained together a few minutes talking. "You'll not think of declining it, of course, Cray?" remarked the latter. "I only wish I could go!"

"I don't see how you will manage without me here," remarked Oswald.

"We must manage in the best way we can. Bracknell must be with us more than he has been lately. Of course we could send somebody else to do the Spain business were it impossible that you could leave; but it is not impossible, and I speak in your interest when I say it is a chance you ought not to miss."

"True. I shall like to go, if home affairs can spare me. I suppose it will involve a stay there of two years?"

"Nearer three," remarked Mr. Street. "Then we will consider your going as settled; and things must be at once prepared at home contingent upon it."

"Yes," acquiesced Oswald. "Wait a moment," he added, as Mr. Street was turning away to descend. "I want to speak to you about Allister. I wish you would take him on again."

Mr. Street pursed his lips up. He had a round face and small light eyes, in which sat a hard look. Whether it was the hard look or not, I can't tell, or whether it was that the look was only the index of the nature—as it generally is—certain it was that Mr. Street was not liked in the house. Oswald knew the sign of the contracted lips.

"What is your objection?" he pursued. "Allister's quite well apparently, and—"

"Apparently! there it is," interrupted Mr. Street. "It's a great hindrance to business, these sickly clerks— well one day, ill the next; especially in such a house as ours. We have no time for it."

"Allister seems well. At one time I thought his lungs were fatally diseased, but I begin to believe I was entirely mistaken. It is nearly twelve months since the worst symptoms left him, and he seems now as strong as I am."

"Pooh!" said Mr. Street. "A warm climate, if he could get to it, might set him up; but in this place of change and fogs and damp, rely upon it he'll not keep well long."

Oswald was silent. So far as the warm climate went, he agreed with Mr. Street. Had Frank Allister the opportunity of going to one it might set him up for a long life.

"How has he lived?" asked Mr. Street. "He has no money."

"He has done work at home lately. We have furnished him with some to do; plans and estimates, and such like. He has had tracings also from another house or two."

"Is that sister of his with him still?"

"Yes. She is a faithful ally. She has taken a daily situation as companion to a blind lady. It all helps to bring grist to the mill. Allister is very anxious to come back, Mr. Street. I really see no reason why he should not. I am sure of one thing—that he is as capable of doing his work here now as any clerk we employ."

"Now. Will you guarantee that he shall continue capable of doing it?"

"I wish I could guarantee it."

"Of course. If wishes were horses—you know the old adage. Were I to take him on now, perhaps in winter he would get ill, and have to leave again. We can't afford those interruptions."

"I trust indeed he would not. He passed well through last winter; improving in it every day."

"Last winter was a mild one, except for a little extreme cold we had in November. Next winter may be a severe one. I tell you, Cray, there's only one safeguard for Allister; and that's a warmer climate. At any rate, a more settled one. Such is my opinion."

Oswald would not give in. "Considering that Allister is now in health and strength—"

"Strength for him," put in Mr. Street.

"Well, strength for him if you like to put it so. But I am sure you would be surprised to see how strong he does appear to be. Considering this, and that he believes himself to be permanently and radically cured, it will sound very hard to him if I tell him that we cannot take him back again."

"If your wish is to have him back—that is, if you make a personal matter of it—have him," said Mr. Street. "I see you want it."

"Yes, I do," said Oswald. "I wish him back, both as a matter of personal liking and that his services are efficient. This departure of mine for Spain will involve the taking on of at least one mon clerk. Let it be Allister."

"Have it as you like, then," said Mr. Street. "Let Allister come back at once. Tell him to come on Monday."

So it was settled. They went down talking together, and encountered Mrs. Benn on the lower passage with a hearth-broom in her hand.

"May I take the tray away, gentlemen?"

Oswald nodded, and the woman went upstairs, her face and her temper as crusty as they could be.

"I wonder the world's let go on!" she ejaculated, as she flung the broom on a chair and began to put the things together on the tray. "I wonder how they'd like to have a day's cleaning to do, and to be called off for three mortal hours in the midst of it? It's four o'clock if it's a minute, and I was stopped in my work at one; and if that's not three hours, I'd like to know what is. I've set to nothing since; how can I, dressed up to please them? and I'm sure—my! what cormorants!"

The subjoined sentence, given utterance to by Mrs. Benn in her surprise, had reference to the mutton-chop dish, on which her eyes had just rested. She stood a moment gazing at it, her hands uplifted.

"If they haven't gone and ate 'em all! Nine thick chops, and only the tails of two of 'em left! Well, I'd not own to such famine if I was gentlefolks. I sent 'em up for show—for I don't forget the trimming I got for skimping the number last time chops was ordered—never supposing they'd eat 'em. I meant two of them chops to come up again for Mr. Oswald Cray's dinner; they'd have done for him, warmed up. And now they're demolished!—and I must dance out again to that butcher's—and Benn a-wanting something with his tea, as he's sure to do, going out without his dinner!—and me with; all the lower part of the house to do yet!—and got my things to change again. It's a wonder the world do go on!"

She carried the tray down; but what with glasses and other things, she could not carry all at once, and had to make two journeys of it. It did not add to her geniality of mood. Arrived in the kitchen the second time, she took the things off the tray, folded the cloth carefully—for in such matters she was very particular—and laid it in the dresser-drawer. Then putting the other things in a stack to be washed by and by, she began to make preparations for resuming the interrupted work. As a preliminary to this, she slowly turned her gown up over the white apron, and looked round for the broom. After casting her eyes in all directions, and casting them in vain, recollection returned to her.

"Drat the broom! If I haven't gone and left it upstairs. I wish their luncheons and their bother was far enough!"

She turned down her gown again, possibly lest she might encounter either of her masters on the way, and proceeded up the kitchen stairs. The broom lay on the chair where she had flung it, in Oswald's sitting-room. As she took it up she espied some crumbs under the table, and stooped down to brush them carefully into her hand, grumbling all the while.

"It's just like 'em! dropping their crumbs down like so many children! The trouble I'd used to have with that when old Bracknell was here! He'd shake his table-napkin on the carpet, he would; and Benn, he'd come away and never—"

"Is this the room? Is he here?"

To be interrupted by those words in a female voice close to her elbow brought Mrs. Benn to her legs at once. A lady in a gay white bonnet and violet-tipped feathers, with other attire on the same grand corresponding scale, stood confronting her. Mrs. Benn could only stare in the first moment from consternation. And the lady stared too, first at the room, then at Mrs. Benn, waiting for her question to be answered.

"Is who here?" cried Mrs. Benn.

"Mr. Oswald Cray. We were ushered up here by a young man whom we saw in the passage. He said this was Mr. Oswald Cray's room, and he would send him to us. Is he well?"

Mrs. Benn naturally looked round for some one to whom the "we" could apply, and saw a young lady at the door. A sweet-looking young lady whose manner was timid and hesitating, as if she did not like to advance further into the room. You need not be told that it was Sara Davenal. She had wished to remain in the fly while Mrs. Cray came up; but Mrs. Cray had insisted on being accompanied by her indoors, and

Sara was obliged to yield, for she was unable to give any good reason against it. How could she hint at the relations which had once existed between her and Mr. Oswald Cray?—at the love that lingered still?

"He's as well as a body can be; leastways if his luncheon's anything to go by, which he have just eat," replied Mrs. Benn in answer to the question of the lady, whom she had not taken a fancy to, as she was permitting her tone to show. "Did you want him?"

"I have come to see him," was the answer. "He is my step-son, and we have not met for a good while."

Mrs. Benn's manner turned to a sudden thaw. In her crusty way she was fond of her master, Mr. Oswald Cray; and she thought she might as well be civil to the lady before her as his step-mother.

"Take a seat, ladies," she said, dusting two chairs with her white apron, and disposing herself to be cordial and confidential. Fate seemed to be against Mrs. Benn's cleaning that day, and we most of us resign ourselves to what can't be helped. This appearance of Mr. Oswald Cray's step-mother Mrs. Benn regarded as an era in that gentleman's life, for she could not remember that during his whole residence there any living relative had come to inquire after him, with the exception of his brother.

"His step-mother," cried she approvingly, as she stood behind a chair and rested her arms on the back of it, one hand grasping the brush. "And might your name be the same as his, ma'am—Mrs. Oswald Cray!" "I am Mrs. Cray," replied the lady, with emphasis on the one word, and an impulse to resent the familiarity. But she felt inclined to encourage the woman in her sociability, feeling a curiosity as to the everyday movements and doings of Mr. Oswald Cray.

Sara sat a little apart, near the centre table. Her cheek rested on her fingers, and her eyes were mechanically fixed on a small chart or plan, which lay at the end of the table opposite to where the luncheon-tray had been. Quite mechanically her thoughts were buried in the unhappy occurrence of that morning: the advent of the stranger at her house and the startling communication of Neal. The gossip of Mrs. Cray and the woman fell on her ear like the humming of gnats in summer; heard, but not heeded. Oswald did not appear; and Mrs. Cray, always restless, as Sara had that morning found out, started from her seat and said she should go to the rooms below in search of him.

Mrs. Benn had this peculiarity—and yet, I don't know that it can be called a peculiarity, since so far as my experience teaches me, it is characteristic of women in general—that however pressing might be her occupations, if once called off them and launched into the full tide of gossip, the urgent duties would give way, and the gossip be willingly pursued until night should fall and stop it. Mrs. Benn, deprived of her chief listener, the elder lady, turned her attention on the younger.

"Would you believe it, miss," she said, dropping her voice to a confidential tone, "his mother's coming here this afternoon bears out some words I said to my husband only a day or two ago, just as one's dreams gets bore out sometimes. I says to Benn, 'Mr. Oswald Cray's relations'll be up, now there's going to be the change.'"

"What change?" asked Sara.

"His marriage, miss."

Ah, she was all too awake to the present now. Her lips parted; her brow turned cold. "His marriage?"

"It can't be nothing else but his marriage," repeated Mrs. Benn. "Benn was waiting on him at dinner, and he told him there was perhaps going to be a change, that he wouldn't have him to wait on long, for he might be leaving. Joe Benn he comes down and repeats to me, all wondering, like the gaby he is, what his master meant by it. Why, his wedding of course, says I; it don't take a conjuror to tell that. Well, she's a nice young lady."

Sara had her hand raised to her face, apparently pushing back her braided hair. "Who is she?" came breathing from her lips; and she could hardly have helped asking it had it been to save her life.

"Well, it's Miss Allister, if it's anybody," returned Mrs. Benn, in apparent contradiction of what she had just asserted. "They are as thick as two peas, and I know he goes there a'most every evening."

Sara had heard enough. In her confusion of mind she had scarcely noted a change taking place in the room. With the last words Mrs. Benn and her brush glided away, and Oswald Cray had come in. Some one had told him that a lady was waiting for him in his room, but he was busy at his desk at the moment and waited to finish what he was about. Nothing could well exceed his surprise when he saw seated there Miss Sara Davenal.

Sara rose. She saw by his manner that he was ignorant of his stepmother's visit, and she felt a little embarrassed as she explained. "She had only come with Mrs. Cray; Mrs. Cray had just gone down in search of him."

Oswald supposed she alluded to his brother's wife, and made no answering comment. As he stood with Sara's hand in his in greeting, he noted how pale she was; for the startling communication of Mrs. Benn had scared the blood from her face. It was somewhat singular that this was the first time they had been alone together since that memorable day of meeting in the Temple gardens: they had met once or twice casually at Mark's in a full room, but not otherwise.

"Have you been well?" he asked. "You are not looking very strong."

"Oh, quite well, thank you."

Oswald hastened to ask a question that had long been on his mind. One that had troubled him perhaps more than he cared to acknowledge to himself: but he had not felt justified in seeking a special occasion to put it.

"Now that I have the opportunity, will you forgive me if I ask whether that unpleasant matter is settled that caused your visits to Essex Street? I still think you would have done wisely to confide it to me."

"It is quite settled," answered Sara, her tone full of satisfaction. "Settled and done with." Ah, poor thing, she forgot momentarily, as she spoke, the fresh grievance opened that morning, which was perhaps connected with it.

"I am glad of it," he heartily said. "I should not like to have gone away for an indefinite period knowing that you were in any dilemma, and no one perhaps to see you out of it. Friendship may still exist between us tacitly, if not yet actively," he continued in a low earnest tone. "Nothing else is left to us."

She thought he alluded to his marriage. She stood something like a statue, feeling cruelly wronged, but loving him beyond everything in life. Not wronged by him: it was fate that wronged her: he would have loved her still, had he dared, and she felt that he honoured her in all tenderness. She felt—and the hot crimson came dyeing her face at the thought—that he loved her better than that other one.

The rebellious tears welled up to her eyes, and she turned her face away. "Are you going to be absent long?" she asked, trying to speak indifferently.

"I think so. How long I cannot tell yet. I am going to Spain."

There was a pause of silence. Sara, with an air of unconcern, began putting straight the crape folds on her dress skirt. Oswald turned to the door.

"Where can Caroline be?" he exclaimed. "Did you say she had gone down in search of me?"

"Not Caroline. It is not Caroline. It is Mrs. Cray, Mark's mother. I came out with her to show her the way to different places, but I did not know she was going to bring me here."

"Mark's mother!" But ere Oswald could say more, Mrs. Cray appeared. She had found her way into Mr. Street's room downstairs, thinking it might be Oswald's, and had remained making acquaintance with that gentleman. Oswald Cray the rising engineer, and Oswald Cray the interloping little son in her husband's house, were essentially two people in the worldly mind of Mrs. Cray.

CHAPTER XLVI

AN UNWELCOME VISITOR

Mark Cray and his wife were attiring themselves by gas-light for some scene of evening gaiety. The past fortnight—for that period had elapsed since the arrival of Mrs. Cray in London—had brought nothing else but gaiety. Shopping in the morning, drives in the afternoon, whitebait dinners at Blackwell or Greenwich, dinners at Richmond, theatres in the evening, receptions at home, parties out; noise, bustle, whirl, and cost. Caroline loved the life; were it taken from her, she said randomly to Mrs. Cray one day, she could not survive, she should die of ennui; and the Miss Crays had never been so happy in their lives, or their mother either.

Their visit had come to an end now, and they had left for home that morning. Unwillingly, it is true, but Mrs. Cray had deemed it wise not to wear out their welcome. They were a large party; and she privately contemplated a longer visit in the spring, during the glories of the London season. Mark had treated them right regally, and had contrived to screw out from some impossible pocket a twenty-pound note, which he put into his mother's hands for the journey. "I shall be able to allow you and the girls something worth having next year, when the ore's in the market regularly," he said to her. Altogether, Mrs. Cray was well satisfied with her impromptu visit.

"I say, Carine," cried Mark, coming forth from his dressing-room, "what's gone with my diamond studs?"

"Where's the use of asking me?" was Carine's answer, who was turning herself slowly round before the large glass, to contemplate the effect of a new dress which her maid had just finished fixing upon her. "You must make haste, Mark, or we shall be late. The dinner's at seven, mind; and I know it does not want above a quarter."

"We shall get there in five minutes," carelessly answered Mark. "I can't find my diamond studs."

"I think they are in your dressing-case, sir," spoke up the maid. "I saw them there a day or two ago." Mark went back, and found he had overlooked them. He finished dressing himself, all but the coat, and came into his wife's room again.

"Carry, isn't it old what's-his-name's affair tonight in Kensington Gardens? We promised to go, didn't we?"

"Of course we did, Mark. I intend to go, too. He says it will be a charming party in spite of the world being out of town. We shall get away from the dinner by ten o'clock, I daresay. Shall I do?"

She was turning herself round before the glass, as before. Between two glasses, in fact, one in front, one behind. Her dress was some beautiful fabric, white and mauve; and her violet eyes and her glowing cheeks spoke all too plainly of her besetting vanity. Certainly, if vanity is ever pardonable, it was in Caroline Cray as she stood there, so radiant in her youth and beauty.

"Oh, you'll do," returned Mark, with scant gallantry; but his white necktie had been refractory, and he was resettling it again. At that moment he heard a knock at his dressing-room door.

"Who's there? Come in," he called out, stepping into his own room.

One of the men-servants entered and presented a card to him. Mark, whose hands were busy with his necktie, bent his head to read it as it lay on the silver waiter. "Mr. Brackenbury."

"Mr. Brackenbury!" repeated Mark to himself. "Who on earth's Mr. Brackenbury? I can't see anybody now," he said to the servant. "Tell him so. I am just going out."

"I told the gentleman you were on the point of going out with my mistress, sir, that the carriage was waiting at the door; but he insisted on coming in, and said you would be sure to see him."

"Who is it?" cried Caroline, stepping forward.

"Some Mr. Brackenbury. Don't know him from Adam. Go down, George, and say that I can not see him, or any one else, this evening."

"The idea of strangers intruding at this hour!" exclaimed Caroline. "Mark, I daresay it's somebody come to worry you to get them shares in the mine."

Mark made no reply. He was in enough "worry" just then over his necktie. "Bother the thing!" he cried, and pulled it off entirely with a jerk.

The servant came back again. He bore another card, a few lines added to it in pencil.

"I must and will see you. Denial is useless."

Mark Cray read the words twice over and decided to go down. They almost seemed to imply a threat, and he did not understand threats. Mr. Brackenbury had arrived in a Hansom cab, the horse reeking with the speed it had made; but Mark did not know that yet.

"I won't be a minute, Caroline. The fellow insists on seeing me. I'll just see what he wants."

Tying on a black necktie temporarily—the one he had taken off earlier—and putting on his morning coat as he descended the stairs, Mark entered the room where the visitor was waiting. And then Mark recognised Mr. Brackenbury as a gentleman who had recently purchased a few shares in the mine. Amidst the many, many shareholders, it was not surprising that Mark had forgotten the name of one of them. In point of fact these few shares had been Mark's own. Being excessively pressed for ready money he had ordered his broker to sell them out.

"Oh, Mr. Brackenbury!" said Mark, shaking hands with him in a cordial manner. "Do you know, your name had completely escaped my memory. I have not a moment to spare for you tonight. I am going out with my wife to dinner."

"Mr. Cray," said the visitor, a middle wed, solemn-looking man, "you must return me my two hundred pounds. I have come for it."

"Return you your two hundred pounds!" echoed Mark. "My good sir, I don't understand you. What two hundred pounds?"

"The two hundred pounds I paid for those shares. They were transferred from your name to mine; therefore I know they were your own."

"They were my own," said Mark. "What of that?"

"Well, I must have the money returned to me, and you can receive back the shares. I have brought them in my pocket. I am of a determined spirit, sir, and I will have it returned." Mark flew into a rage. He was a great man now, and great men do not take such words with impunity. "You can have your money back tomorrow," he said, with haughty contempt. "Take the shares to my broker—if you don't possess one of your own—and he will repurchase them of you."

"Ah," said Mr. Brackenbury. "But I want the money from you tonight. I want it now."

"Then you can't have it," returned Mark.

Mr. Brackenbury advanced—both of them were standing—and laid his finger on Mark's arm. "Mr. Cray, I have not come to you as an enemy; I don't wish to be one, and there's no occasion for unpleasantness between us. I want my money back, and I must have it—I must have it, understand, and tonight. After that, I will hold my tongue as long as it will serve you."

Was the man talking Greek? was he out of his mind? What did it mean? Mark's indignation began to lose itself in puzzled curiosity.

"I have had a private telegram tonight from the mine," resumed Mr. Brackenbury, dropping his voice to a cautious whisper. "Something is amiss with it. I jumped into a Hansom—"

"Something amiss with it!" interrupted Mark, cutting short the explanation, and his tone insensibly changing to one of dread; for that past summer's night which had brought the telegram to Mr. Barker recurred vividly to his mind. "Is it water?" he breathed.

Mr. Brackenbury nodded. "An irruption of water. I fear—you'll see, of course—but I fear the mine and its prosperity are at an end. Now, Mr. Cray, you repay me my money and I'll hold my tongue. If this does not get about—and it shall not through me—you'll have time to negotiate some of your shares in the market tomorrow morning, and put something in your pocket before the disaster gets wind. I only want to secure myself. Trifling as the sum of two hundred pounds may seem to you, its loss to me would be utter ruin."

Mark felt bewildered. "And if I do not give you the two hundred pounds tonight, what then!"

"Then I go out with the dawn of morning and publish the failure of the mine to the City. I'll publish it tonight. But you'll not drive me to that, Mr. Cray. I don't want to harm you; I have said it; but my money I must have. It would not be pleasant for me to proclaim that there has already been one irruption of water into the mine, which you and Barker kept secret. I happen to know so much; and that the shares were sold to me after it, as I daresay shares have been sold to others. Perhaps the public might look on that as a sort of fraud. I do; for I consider a mine never is safe, once the water has been in it."

Mark paused. "It is strange that news of this should have come to you tonight and not to me."

"Not at all," said Mr. Brackenbury. "I am having the mine watched. It is only lately that I heard about that first irruption of water: I did not like it; and as I happen to have a friend down there I got him to be on the look-out."

"Is it any one connected with the mine?" asked Mark, sharply.

"Yes, it is; no one else could do it. But that's of no consequence. I had a telegram from him tonight—"

"Will you let me see it!" interrupted Mark.

"I did not bring it with me. It told me that the water was flowing into the mine; flowing, mind; and it added these words. 'Not known here yet.' I infer, therefore, that the men had left the mine for the night, that the mischief will not be generally known there until the morning, and consequently cannot be known here. You will have time to save something."

Mark felt as if water were flowing over him. He stood there under the gas-burner—the servant had only lighted one—a picture of perplexity, his face blank, his hand running restlessly through his hair, after his old restless manner, the diamond studs in his shirt sparkling and gleaming. All this sounded as though some treason, some treachery, were at work. If this man could get news up, he and Barker ought to have got it.

A knock at the door. It opened about an inch, and Caroline's voice was heard.

"Mark, we must go. We are keeping the dinner waiting." And Mark was turning towards her, when Mr. Brackenbury silently caught him by the arm, and spoke in a whisper.

"No! Not until you have given me my money."

"Allow me to say a word to my wife," said Mark, haughtily. "I will return to you in an instant."

Caroline stood there with questioning eyes and a rebellious face. Mark shut the door while he spoke to her.

"You must go on alone, my dear. I can't come yet. I'll join you later in the evening."

"Mark! What's that for?"

"Hush! This gentleman has come up on business from the City, and I must attend to him," whispered Mark. "I'll get rid of him as soon as I can."

He was hurrying her out to the carriage as he spoke, and he placed her in it, she yielding to his strong will in her bewilderment. Once seated in it then she spoke.

"But, Mark, why should he come on business now? What is the business?"

"Oh, it has to do with the Great Wheal Bang," said Mark, carelessly. "It's all right; only I can't get away just at the minute. I won't be long. They are not to wait dinner, mind."

The carriage drove away, and Mark returned indoors. His unwelcome visitor stood in the same place, apparently not having stirred hand or foot.

"How am I to know whether this news you have brought it true?" was Mark's first question. And Mr. Brackenbury looked at him for a minute before replying to it.

"I don't altogether take you, Mr. Cray. You cannot think I should knowingly bring you a false report; my character is too well respected in the City for you to fear that; and you may rely upon it, unhappily, that there's no mistake in the tidings forwarded to me."

"Well—allowing that it shall prove to be true—why can't you take your shares into the market and realise tomorrow morning, as well as coming to me for the money tonight?"

"Because I am not sure that I could realise!" was the frank response. "I don't suppose the intelligence will be public by that time; I don't think it will; but I cannot answer for it that it won't. You must give me the money, Mr. Cray."

Mark took an instant's gloomy counsel with himself. Might he dare to defy this man, and refuse his demands He feared not. Mark was no more scrupulous than are some other shareholders we have read of; and the chance of realising something in the morning, to pit against the utter ruin that seemed to be impending was not to be forfeited rashly. But how was he to pay the money? He had not two hundred shillings in the house, let alone two hundred pounds.

"I can't give it you tonight," said Mark; "I have not got it to give."

"I must and will have it," was the resolute answer. "I daresay you can go out and get it somewhere: fifty people would be glad to lend you money. I shall stay here until I have it. And if you deem me scant of courtesy tonight, Mr. Cray, you may set it down to the sore feeling in my mind at the circumstances under which the shares were sold to me. I'd never have touched them had I suspected water had been already in the mine."

"That's talking nonsense," said Mark, in his irritation. "The mine was as sound and as safe after the water had been in it as it was before. It was nothing more than a threatening; nothing to hurt."

"A threatening—just so. Well, it is of no use to waste time squabbling over terms now. That will do no good."

Mr. Brackenbury was right. It certainly would do no good. Mark went out, leaving him there, for he refused to stir; and, not seeing a cab, ran full speed to Mr. Barker's lodgings in Piccadilly. A Hansom could not have gone quicker. It was not that he hoped Mr. Barker would supply the two hundred pounds; that gentleman was as short of ready cash as himself; but Mark was burning with impatience to impart the disastrous news, and to hear whether Barker had had intelligence of it.

Disappointment. When Mark, panting, breathless, excited, seized the bell of Mr. Barker's house and rang a peal that frightened the street, he was told that Mr. Barker was not within. He had gone out in the afternoon: the servant did not know where.

"Has any telegram come up from Wales tonight?" gasped Mark.

"Telegram, sir? No, sir; nothing at all has come tonight, neither letter nor anything."

"I'll be back in a short while," said Mark. "If Mr. Barker returns, tell him to wait in for me. It is of the very utmost importance that I should see him."

He turned away, jumped into a cab that was passing, and ordered it to drive to Parliament Street. The two hundred pounds he must get somehow, and he knew nobody he could apply to at the pinch, save Oswald.

Mark was not the only visitor to Oswald Cray that night. He had been sitting alone, after his dinner, very deep in deliberation, when Benn came up showing in a gentleman. It proved to be Henry Oswald.

They had not met since the funeral of Lady Oswald twelve months before, and at the first moment Oswald scarcely knew him. Henry Oswald was a cordial-mannered man. He had not inherited the cold heart and the haughty bearing so characteristic of the Oswalds of Thorndyke, and he grasped Oswald's hand warmly.

"I have been out of England nearly ever since we met, Oswald—I am sure you will let me call you so, we are near relatives—or I should have sought to improve the acquaintance begun at that short meeting. I want you to be friendly with me. I know how wrong has been the estrangement, and what cause you have to hate us; but surely you and I can afford to do away with the prejudice that has kept you from Thorndyke, and Thorndyke from you."

Oswald saw how genuine were the words, how earnest the wish imparted in them; and from that moment his "prejudice" went out of him, as far as Henry Oswald was concerned, and his eye lighted up with an earnest of the future friendship. He had liked Henry Oswald at that first meeting; he liked him still.

They sat together, talking of the days gone by, when they two were unconscious children. Of Oswald's mother; of the conduct of her family towards her; of the insensate folly—it was his son called it so—that still estranged Sir Philip from Oswald Cray. They talked freely and fully as though they had been intimate for years—far more confidentially than Oswald had ever talked to his half-brother.

"I shall be proud of your friendship, Oswald," cried the young man, warmly; "if that's not an ominous word for one of us. But I fancy you inherit the family failing far more than I. You will be one of the world's great men yet, making yourself a name that the best might envy."

Oswald laughed. "If the world envies those who work hard, then it may envy me."

"I can tell you what, Oswald, if work's not envied in these days, it is honoured. In the old days of darkness—I'm sure I can call them so, in comparison with these—it was such as I who were envied. The man born with a silver spoon in his mouth, who need do nothing his whole life long but sit down in idleness and enjoy his title and fortune, and be clothed in purple and fine linen, and fare sumptuously every day—he got the honour then. Now the man of industry and talent is bowed down to, he who labours onwards and upwards to use and improve the good gifts bestowed upon him by God. It may be wrong to say it, but I do say it in all sincerity, that I, Henry Oswald, born to my baronetcy, envy you, Oswald Cray, born to work."

From one subject they went to another. In talking of the Cray family, they spoke of Mark, and from Mark the transition to the Great Wheal Bang Company was easy. Henry Oswald had heard and read of its promise, and he now asked Oswald's opinion of its stability. He had a few hundreds to spare for he had not been an extravagant man, and felt inclined to embark them in the Great Wheal Bang. Oswald advised his doing so. He himself had embarked all his saved cash in it, a thousand pounds, and he thought he had done well.

"Then I'll see about it tomorrow," decided Henry Oswald; "and get it completed before I go down to Thorndyke."

He departed soon, for he was engaged out that evening, and Oswald resumed the train of thought which his entrance had interrupted. The deliberation it may be said. He was pondering a grave question: Should he not despatch Frank Allister to Spain in place of himself? Allister was equally capable; and two or three years' residence in that climate might renovate him for life. It would be a great sacrifice for him, Oswald; a sacrifice, in some degree, of name and fame, and of pecuniary benefit; but he was a conscientious man, very different from the generality of business men, who seek their own elevation, no matter who is left behind. Oswald as a child had learnt the good wholesome doctrine of doing to others as we would be done by: and he carried it out practically in life, content to leave the issue with God. How many of us can say as much?

A few minutes' earnest thought and he raised his head with a clear countenance. The decision was made.

"Allister shall go," he said, half-aloud. "Should he get ill again in this wretched climate next winter, and die, I should have it on my conscience for ever. It will be a sacrifice for me: but how can I put my advancement against his life? I ought not, and I will not."

The words had scarcely left his lips when Mark came in. Not Mark as we saw him just now, troubled, eager, panting; but Mark all coolness and smiles. A little hurried, perhaps, but that was nothing.

He had come to ask Oswald a favour. Would he accommodate him with a cheque for two hundred pounds until the banks opened in the morning? A gentleman, to whom was owing that sum on account of the Great Wheal Bang bad urgent need of it that very night, and had come bothering him, Mark, for it. If Oswald would accommodate him, he, Mark, should feel very much obliged, and would return it in the morning with many thanks.

"I have not got as much of my own," said Oswald.

"But you can give me a cheque of the firm's, can't you?" returned Mark, playing carelessly with his diamond studs.

Oswald did not much like this suggestion, and hesitated. Mark spoke again.

"It will be rendering me the greatest possible service, Oswald. The fellow has to leave town, or something, by one of the night trains. You shall have it back the first thing in the morning."

"You are sure that I shall, Mark?"

"Sure!" echoed Mark, opening his small grey eyes very wide in surprise. "Of course I am sure. Do you think I should forget to bring it you? Let me have it at once, there's a good brother. Carine will think I am never coming; we have to go to two parties tonight."

Oswald wrote the cheque and gave it him. It was a cheque of the firm: "Bracknell, Street, and Oswald Cray:" for Oswald's name appeared now.

And Mr. Mark carried it off with him. "There's a good brother," indeed! I wonder how he slept that night!

CHAPTER XLVII

COMMOTION

With the wing of the dawn—that is, with the wing of the dawn for business in London—Mark Cray was at the offices in the City. Barker was there before him, and started forward to meet him as he entered. Mark had not succeeded in seeing Barker the previous night.

"Cray, it's all up. I'm afraid it's all up."

"Have you heard from Wales?"

"I got a telegram this morning. There's an irruption of water, in earnest this time. It's flowing in like so many pumps. Look here."

Mark's hands shook as he laid hold of the telegram. "I wasn't in bed till three o'clock," said he, as if he would give an excuse for the signs of agitation. But though he tried to account for his shaking hands, he could not for his scared face.

Yes Mr. Barker was no doubt right: it was "all up" with the Great Wheal Bang. Mark and he stood alone over the table in the board-room: in consultation as to what they could do, and what they might do.

Might they dare—allowing that the public still reposed in happy security—to take some shares into the market, and secure themselves something out of the wreck? Barker was all for doing it; at any rate for trying it—"whether it would work," he said. Mark hung back in indecision: he thought there might be after-consequences. He told Barker the episode of Mr. Brackenbury's visit, and of his satisfying that gentleman with the cheque of Bracknell, Street, and Oswald Cray, which cheque was no doubt cashed by that time.

"Mean old idiot!" apostrophised Mr. Barker. "That's always the way with those petty people. They'll make more fuss over their paltry hundred pounds or two than others do over thousands. I'd not have paid him, Mark."

"I couldn't help it," said Mark. "You should have seen the work he made. Besides, if I had not, he'd have proclaimed the thing from one end of London to another."

"Well, about these shares," said Barker. "We must make as much as ever we can. Will you go, or shall I?"

"Perhaps it's known already," returned Mark, dubiously.

"Perhaps it isn't. Brackenbury gave you his word that he'd keep quiet, and who else is likely to know it? Letters can't get here till the afternoon post, and nobody at the mine would make it their business to telegraph up."

Mark stood in restless indecision. When annoyed, he was fidgety to a degree; could not be still. Perhaps he had inherited his mother's temperament He pushed back his hair incessantly; he fingered nervously the diamond studs in his shirt. Mark was not in the habit of wearing those studs by day, or the curiously fine embroidery they were adorning. Whether, in his confusion of faculties, he had put in the studs that morning, or had absently retired to rest in his shirt the previous night, studs and all, must be left to conjecture.

"Look here, Barker," said he. "If news had not come to us of the disaster, to you and to me, I'd willingly have taken every share we possess into the market, and got the money for them down, if I could. But the news has come: and I don't think it would do."

"Who's to know it has come?" asked Barker.

"Well, things do often come out, you know; they nearly always do; especially if they are not wanted to. Perhaps the telegraph office could be brought up to prove it, or something of that."

"Well?" said Barker.

"Well," repeated Mark. "It mightn't do."

"Oh, bother, Cray! We must do it. We must stand out through thick and thin afterwards that the message never reached us. I could; and you are safe, for you have not had one at all. Look at our position. We must realise. Of course we can't attempt to negotiate many shares; that would betray us; but a few we might, and must. We must, for our own sakes we can't stand naked, without a penny to fall back upon."

Mark still hesitated. "I'd have done it with all the pleasure in life but for this telegram," he reiterated. "For one thing, Oswald would never forgive me; my name's the same as his, you know; and I shall have to face him over this two hundred pounds: that will be bad enough. And there's my mother. And my wife, Barker; you forget her."

"I don't forget her. I am thinking of her," was Mr. Barker's answer. "It's for her sake, as much as ours, that you ought to secure a little ready money. You'll want it. I know that much, for I have been down in luck before."

Mark looked irresolute and pitiably gloomy. "I don't see my way clear," he resumed, after a pause. "Let's put the thing into plain black and white. I go out, and sell some shares, and get the money paid down for them, and pocket it. An hour afterwards the news spreads that the mine's destroyed, and the shares are consequently worthless. Well, Barker, my belief is that they could proceed against me criminally for disposing of those shares—"

"Not if you did not know the mine was wrong when you took them into the market."

"Nonsense," returned Mark, irritably, "they'd be sure to know it. I tell you it would be safe to come out by hook or by crook. They'd call it felony, or swindling, or some such ugly name. Do you suppose I'm going to put my head into that noose? I was born a gentleman."

"And do you suppose I wish either of us to do it?" retorted Barker. "I shouldn't be such a fool. I never go into a thing unless I know I can fight my way out of it. I shall take a few shares into the market, and feel my way. I shall sell them for money, if I can; and you shall share it, Mark. I suppose you won't object to that."

No, certainly, Mark would have no objection to that.

"I did not hear of the disaster until later, you know," said Barker, winking. "News of it came up to us by the afternoon post. If they do find out about the telegram, why, I never opened it. Nobody saw me open it," added Barker, with satisfaction. "I have had so many up from the mine at my lodgings that the servants sign and put them in my sitting-room as a matter of course. This one was put there this morning, and I found it when I came down, but nobody was in the room. Oh, it will be all right. And I say, Mark, if—"

Mr. Barker's smooth projects were stopped. Absorbed in their conversation, he and Mark had alike failed to notice a gradually gathering hum in the street outside. A very gentle, almost imperceptible hum at first, but increasing to a commotion now. With one bound they reached the window.

A concourse of people, their numbers being augmented every moment, had assembled beneath. They were waiting for the opening of the offices of the Great Wheal Bang at ten o'clock. And the hour was almost on the point of striking.

"It's all up," shouted Barker in Mark's ear. "The news is abroad, and they have heard of it. Look at their faces!"

The faces were worth looking at, though not as a pleasant sight. Anger, rage, disappointment, above all impatience, were depicted there. The impatience of a wolf waiting to spring upon its prey. One of the faces unluckily turned its gaze upwards and caught sight of Barker's. Barker saw it; he had not been quick enough in drawing away from the window.

"They'll not be kept out now, doors or no doors," said he quietly to Mark.

Mr. Barker was right. Ere the words had died away upon his lips a sound as if the walls of the house were being beaten in ensued. The bells commenced a perpetual peal the knocker knocked incessantly, the doors were pushed and kicked and thumped. In the midst of it rose the sound of human voices in a roar: disjointed words distinguishable amidst the tumult. "Let us in! Come out to us!"

Mr. Barker advanced to the stairs, and leaned over the balustrades. "Williams," he called out to an attendant official below, "you can open the doors. The gentlemen may come up."

It was curious to note the difference in the two men. Barker was as cool as a cucumber; self-possessed as ever he had been in his life; ready to make the best of everything, and quite equal to the emergency. Mark Cray, on the contrary, seemed to have parted alike with his wits and his nerves. Not more completely did he lose his presence of mind in that long past evening which had been so fatal to Lady Oswald. His hands shook as with terror; his faff was white as death.

"Will they pull us to pieces, Barker?"

"Pooh!" said Barker, with a laugh at the evident tremor. "What has taken you, Mark? Let them rave on a bit without answering, and they'll calm down. Put that in your pocket," he continued. "It will be a trifle to fall back upon."

He had touched the diamond ring that glittered on Mark Cray's finger. Mark obeyed like a child. He took it from his hand and thrust it into his waistcoat pocket; next he buttoned his coat, some vague feeling perhaps prompting him to hide the studs; but he did it all mechanically, as one not conscious of his actions. Terror was holding its sway over him.

"Why should they be excited against us? Heaven knows we have not intentionally wronged them."

"That's just the question I shall ask them myself when they are cool enough to listen to it," rejoined Barker with a gay air. "Now then comes the tug of war."

In they came, thick and threefold, dashing up the stairs and pouring into the room like so many bees. And then it was found that Mark's apprehensions had been somewhat premature. For these shareholders had come flowing to the offices not so much to abuse the projectors of the company as to inquire the true particulars of the disaster. The news had gone forth in a whisper—and to this hour neither Mark nor Barker knows how, or through whom, it had oozed out—but that whisper was vague and uncertain. Naturally those interested flew to the offices for better information. Was the damage of great extent? and would the mine and the company stand it?

Barker was of course all suavity. He treated the matter more as a joke than anything else, making light of it altogether. An irruption of water? well, perhaps a little drop had got in, but they must wait for the afternoon's post. It would be all right.

He looked round for Mark, hoping that gentleman's face would not arouse suspicion; but he could not see him. Mark, as Barker learnt afterwards, had contrived to escape from the room as the throng entered, and got into the street unnoticed, and leaped into a cab. Mark was beside himself that morning.

The unfortunate news spread from one end of London to the other. It was carried to Oswald Cray; but the day was advancing then. "The Great Wheal Bang Company had exploded, and there was a run upon the office." Oswald was startled; and betook himself at once to the premises, as the rest had done. On his way he called in upon Henry Oswald, and spoke a word of caution.

"It may be a false rumour," said he; "I hope it is. But don't do anything in the shares until you know."

A false rumour! When Oswald reached the offices he found it all too true a one. The secretary to the company, without meaning to do ill—indeed he had let it out in his lamentation—had unwittingly disclosed the fact of the previous irruption of water in the summer: and the excited crowd were going wild with anger. Many of them had bought their shares at a period subsequent to that.

Oswald heard this, and went to Mr. Barker in the board-room. That gentleman, rather heated certainly, but with unchanged suavity of demeanour, was still doing his best to reassure everybody. Oswald drew him aside.

"What a dreadful thing this is! What is the real truth of it?"

"Hush!" interrupted Mr. Barker. "No need to tell the worst to them. You are one of us. I'm afraid it is all up with the mine; but we will keep it from them as long as we can. Anyway, it's no fault of ours."

"What is it that they are saying about an irruption of water having occurred in the summer?"

"Well, so it did," answered Mr. Barker, whose past few hours' temporising with the crowd caused him perhaps to throw off reserve to Mr. Oswald Cray as a welcome relief. "But it wasn't much, that; and we succeeded in keeping it dark."

"Did Mark know of it?"

"Mark know of it!" rejoined Barker; "of course he knew of it. What should hinder him? Why, the telegram bringing the news was given me at Mark's house; and, by the way, you were present, I remember. It was the evening that old doctor in the yellow trousers was there, with his two frights of daughters."

The scene rose as in a mirror before Oswald's memory. Dr. Ford and his daughters, Miss Davenal and Sara, Caroline Cray in her silks and her beauty. He remembered the telegram, he remembered that it appeared to disturb both Barker and Mark; and he remembered Mark's denial to him that anything was amiss with the mine.

"I do recollect it," he said aloud. "It struck me—perhaps it was rather singular it should do so—that something was wrong. Mark declared to me that it was not so."

The words seemed to tickle Barker uncommonly.

"Ah," said he, laughing, "Mark told me of it, and how he turned you off the scent. You'd not have put your thousand into it, perhaps, had you known of the water."

"Perhaps not," quietly replied Oswald. "And my thousand was wanted, I suppose."

"Law! you don't know the money that's been wanted," was the response. "And that irruption of water, slight as it was, made the demand for it worse. The mine has sucked it in like a sponge."

Oswald made no answering remark. "I suppose this irruption is worse than that?" he presently observed.

"Indeed I fear this is another thing altogether—ruin. But we ion% know anything certain until the post comes in this afternoon. We have had no letter yet."

"How did the news of it come to you?"

"By telegram. But the first news came to Mark; in an odd manner, too. A curmudgeon of a shareholder, old Brackenbury, went up yesterday evening to Mark just as he was going out to dinner with his wife, and insisted upon his paltry money, only two hundred pounds, being returned to him. He was inclined to be nasty; and if Mark had not satisfied him he'd have gone over London proclaiming that the mine was overflowing with water. The odd thing is, who could have telegraphed the news to him. We must have a traitor in the camp. Mark told me—oh, ah," broke off Mr. Barker, interrupting himself as a recollection flashed upon him—"I think he got the two hundred from you."

"And Mark knew the mine was then ruined!" returned Oswald, drawing in his lips, but not losing his calm equanimity.

"Brackenbury said it was. He didn't know it otherwise. Brackenbury—Halloa! what's that?"

It was a shout in the street. A shout composed of roars, and hisses, and groans. Drawing up to the door of the offices was the handsome carriage of Mark Cray; and the crowd had turned their indignation upon it.

One look, one glimpse of the white and terror-stricken faces of its inmates, and Oswald Cray bounded down the stairs. They were the faces of Mrs. Cray and Sara Davenal.

What could have brought them there?

CHAPTER XLVIII

DAY-DREAMS RUDELY INTERRUPTED

Before a costly breakfast service of Sèvres porcelain, with its adjuncts of glittering silver, on the morning subsequent to the visit of Mr. Brackenbury, had sat Caroline Cray, in a charming morning robe of white muslin and blue ribbons, with what she would have called a coiffure, all blue ribbons and white lace, on her silky hair. A stranger, taking a bird's-eye view of the scene, of the elegant room, the expensive accessories, the recherché attire of its mistress, would have concluded that there was no lack of means, that the income supporting all this must at least be to the extent of some thousands a-year.

In truth Mark Cray and his wife were a practical illustration of that homely but expressive saying which must be so familiar to you all; they had begun at the wrong end of the ladder. When fortune has come; when it is actually realised, in the hands, then the top of the ladder, comprising its Sèvres porcelain and other costs in accordance, may be safe and consistent; but if we begin there without first climbing to it, too many of us have an inconvenient fashion of slipping down again. The furniture surrounding Caroline Cray was of the most beautiful design, the most costly nature; the lace on that morning-robe, on that pretty "coiffure," would make a hole in a £20 bank-note, the silver ornaments on the table were fit for the first palace in the land, and Mr. and Mrs. Cray had got these things about them—and a great deal more besides which I have not time to tell you of—anticipatory of the fortune that was to be theirs; not that already was. And now their footing on that high ladder was beginning to tremble: just as that of the milkmaid did when she sent the milk out of her milk-pails, and so destroyed her dreams.

Caroline sat at her late breakfast, toying with a fashionable newspaper—that is, one giving notice of the doings of the fashionable world—sipping her coffee, flirting with some delicate bits of buttered roll, casting frequent glances at the mirror opposite to her, in whose polished plate was reflected that pretty face, which in her pardonable vanity she believed had not its compeer. All unconscious was she of that turbulent scene then being enacted in the City; of the fact that her husband was at that moment finding his way to her in a cab, into which he had jumped to hide himself in abject fear and dismay. Caroline had slept sound and late after her night's gaiety, and awoke in the morning to find her husband had gone out.

The French clock behind her struck eleven, and she finished her breakfast quickly, and began thinking over her plans for the day. Some excursion into the country had been spoken of for the afternoon, and now Mark was gone she was at an uncertainty. Mrs. Cray tapped her pretty foot in petulance on the carpet, and felt exceedingly angry with the tiresome stranger who had disturbed her husband when he was dressing on the previous evening, and kept him from going out with her to dinner.

"How long did that gentleman stop here last night, George!" she suddenly asked of the servant who was removing the breakfast things. "Mr.—what was the name? Brackenbury, I think."

"He stopped a good while, ma'am. I think it was between nine and ten when he left."

"What a shame! Keeping Mr. Cray all that while. I wonder he stayed with him! I wouldn't. I'd make people come to me in business hours, if I were Mark."

She sat on, after the departure of the breakfast things, leaning back in an easy chair and turning carelessly the leaves of a new novel, those that would open, for she did not exert herself to cut them. A very listless mood was she in that morning, tired and out of sorts. By and by her maid came in to ask about some alteration that was to be made in a dress, and Caroline told her to bring the dress to her.

That a little aroused her. It was a beautiful evening dress of flowered silk, and she stood over the table where the maid laid it consulting with her about some change in the colour of the trimmings. Becoming absorbed in this, she scarcely noticed that some one had come into the hall and opened the door of the room. Some expression in the maid's countenance as she looked up caught her attention, and she turned quickly round.

Mark was there, glancing into the room. Mark with a white aspect and a scared dreamy look on his face. Before Caroline had time to question, in fact almost before she looked, he was gone and had closed the door again. So quiet had been the movement, so transient the vision, that Caroline spoke in her surprise.

"Was not that your master?"

"Yes, ma'am. Something was the matter, I think. He looked ill."

"I will go and see. Mind, Long, I'll decide upon pink. It is the prettiest colour."

"Very well, ma'am. As you please, of course. I only think pink won't go so well with the dress as violet."

"I tell you, Long, that violet will not light up. You know it won't, without my having to reiterate it over to you. No colour lights up so bad as violet. Pink: and let the ruchings be very full and handsome."

Speaking the last words in a peremptory tone, she went in search of Mark. He was standing upright in the dining-room, in the midst of its floor, looking more like a man lost than a man in his composed senses.

"Mark, what's the matter?"

He turned to his wife,—he had been undecided whether to tell her or not. It was a question he debated with himself on his way down: that is, it had been floating through his mind in a sort of undercurrent. To concentrate his thoughts deliberately upon one point sufficiently to debate it was that day beyond the power of Mark Cray.

Mark's true disposition was showing itself now. Vacillating and unstable by nature, utterly deficient in that moral courage which meets an evil when it comes, and looks it steadily in the face to see how it may be best dealt with, the blow of the morning had taken away what little sense Mark possessed. He was as a frightened child; a ship without a rudder; he was utterly unable to distinguish what his proper course ought to be: he did not know where to go or what to do; his chief thought was, to get away from the torrent that had broken loose. He must hide himself from the storm, but he could not face it.

When he jumped into the cab, and the driver had said, "Where to, sir?" he gave his home in Grosvenor Place in answer, simply because he could not think of another direction to give in that bewildering moment: so the cab drove on. But Mark did not want to go to Grosvenor Place. He had nothing to get from there: he had no business there, and a feeling came over him that he had rather not meet his wife just then. He wanted to hide himself and his bewildered mind and his scared face in some nook of remote shelter, far from the haunts of men, where that remorseless crowd, just escaped from, would not pounce upon him. Mark had not given himself time to ascertain that their disposition was pacificatory: he was wondering rather whether they had yet pulled the offices down. Neither Mark Cray nor Caroline was fitted to encounter the storms of life. So long as the sailing was smooth it was well; but when the waves arose, rough and turbulent, the one proved physically, the other morally, unable to breast them.

Mark stopped the cab as it was turning into Grosvenor Place; some vague feeling prompting him that it might be safer to steal quietly into his home than to dash up to it in a cab. The tidings had perhaps travelled far and wide, and people might be already there, as well as at the offices. Mark was half determined to make the best of his way at once to the scene of the Great Wheal Bang itself, the mine; and see with his own eyes whether things were so bad that they could not be mended. At least he should be away from his furious enemies in London. One more under the influence of reason than Mark Cray might have thought it well to ascertain whether those enemies were so furious, before running from them. When a man of no moral courage loses his presence of mind, he merits pity perhaps rather than condemnation.

"Mark, what's the matter?"

With her actual presence before him, with the pointed question on her lips, Mark Cray's indecision went completely out. He could no more have told her the truth at that moment, that the golden prospects so implicitly believed in had turned to ruin, and the offices yonder were being besieged by noisy shareholders, than he could have told it to the besiegers themselves.

"The matter?" repeated Mark, at a loss for any other answer.

"You look as if something were the matter, Mark. And what have you come back for?"

"Oh, I left some papers at home," answered Mark, speaking as carelessly as he could. "There's nothing the matter with me. The fellow drove fast, that's all. I gave him an extra sixpence."

Perhaps Caroline did not deem this communication particularly relevant to the subject. "What made you go away so early, Mark?" she asked. "You never settled anything about Hendon today."

"Well, I don't think I can go," said Mark. "I'll—I'll see later. Hark!"

Mark's "hark" was spoken in echo to a thundering knock at the door. A knock and a ring enough to shake the house down. He looked round at the walls for a moment as if he wanted to make a dash into them; he stepped towards the window, hesitated, and drew away again; finally he opened the door to escape, but too late, for voices were already in the hall. Caroline looked at her husband in wondering dismay.

"Mark, what has come to you?"

"Hush!" whispered Mark, the perspiration welling up to his forehead, as he bent his head to catch the sound from those voices. "Hark! hush!"

"Is Mr. Cray at home?"

"No, sir. He went to the City early this morning." How Mark Cray blessed his servant for the unconscious mistake, he alone could tell. The man had not seen his master come in, and had no idea he was in the house.

"Gone to the City, is he? Are you sure?"

"Quite sure, sir."

A pause. Mark's heart was beating.

"What time will he be home?"

"I don't know, sir."

Another pause. "I suppose Mr. Barker's not here?"

"Mr. Barker? O dear no, sir."

And that was followed by the closing of the hall-door. Mark Cray gave a great gasp of relief, and went upstairs to his own room.

He did not stay there above a minute. Caroline—she remembered it afterwards—heard a drawer or two opened and shut. She had been following him, but was momentarily detained by a question from her maid, who was coming out of the breakfast-room with the dress upon her arm. Caroline stopped while she answered it, and in going up the stairs she met Mark coming down.

"Who was that at the door, Mark? Did you think it was any one in particular?"

"I don't know who it was."

"You seemed alarmed. Or annoyed."

"Well," returned Mark, speaking rather fast, "and it is annoying to have business fellows corning after me to my house. Why can't they go to the offices?"

"To be sure," said Caroline, reassured. "I'd not see a soul here, if I were you."

He had been walking on towards the hall-door while he spoke. But ere he had well reached it, he turned, and drew his wife into one of the rooms.

"Look here, Caroline: I'm not sure but I shall have to go down to the mines tonight. If so, it is just possible I may not be able to come here first. So you won't be alarmed if you don't see me home."

"What a hurry you must be in!" exclaimed Caroline. "Not come home first!"

"But if I do go, mind, it will be on a little private matter that I don't want known," he continued, taking no notice of the remark. "So, if anybody should ask where I am, just answer that you can't tell, but that I shall be back in a day or two. Do you understand, Carine?"

"Quite well. But, Mark, you will come home first, won't you?"

"I only tell you this in case I don't come," he answered evasively. "I have a good deal to do today. Goodbye, Carine."

"But about Hendon?" she interrupted.

"Hendon? Oh, I am quite sure I shan't have time for Hendon today. If you don't like to go without me, we must put it off for a day or two." He stooped to kiss her. Opening the hall-door, he stood on the steps, looking right and left; carelessly, as it seemed; in reality, cautiously. Very timorous was Mark Cray in that hour; he did not like that people should have hunted him to his very home. Then he turned to the Victoria Station, perhaps as the nearest point of refuge. He would make his way to Wales, to the mine, as straightly and speedily as he could, consistent with precaution.

Mark had been gone the best part of an hour, and it was hard upon midday. His wife was just deliberating whether to go shopping in the afternoon, or make calls, or pay a visit to the empty park, or take a drive out of town; which way, in short, would be the least tedious of killing the precious time that God had given her, when she was aroused by a formidable summons at the door, and a noise as of many steps and voices besieging the hall.

What next took place Caroline never clearly remembered. Confused recollections remained to her afterwards of angry demands for Mr. Cray, of indignant denials to the servant's assertion that his master was in the City; the hubbub was great, the voices were threatening. Caroline's first surprise was superseded by indignation; and that in its turn gave place to alarm.

You all know what it is to pour oil upon a spark of fire previously ready to burst forth into a flame. When the Great Wheal Bang's shareholders had flocked to the Great Wheal Bang's offices that morning they were on the balance, as may be said, between war and peace; somewhat uncertain in their own minds whether to treat Mark Cray and Mr. Barker as unfortunate fellow-sufferers with themselves, or to expend upon them their wrongs and their wrath. That mistake of the Great Wheal Bang's secretary—as alluded to in the last chapter—turned the scale. In his dismay and confusion he inadvertently referred to the former irruption of water, and the unlucky disclosure maddened the throng. They forthwith looked upon themselves as dreadfully injured people; in fact they jumped to the conclusion that the Great Wheal Bang itself was little better than a swindle; so apt are we all to rush into extremes. Barker did what he could to stem the torrent; but the crowd vociferously demanded to see Mark Cray. It was he they had known mostly in the affair, for Barker was usually at the mine. And, not finding Mark answer to their demands, some of them tore off on the spur of the moment in Hansom cabs to his residence.

Caroline stood the very image of dismay. She did not show herself; she was too much alarmed; she peeped from the half-closed dining-room door and listened, just as Mark had done a short while before. Confused words of "water" and "mine" and "swindle" and "ruin" saluted her ears; and the demands for Mr. Cray became more threateningly imperative. Some movement of the door occurred; she staggered against it; and it was observed from the hall. Perhaps it was only natural to the belligerents to conclude that Mark Cray was there. They pressed forward to the room; but upon seeing that the lady was its only occupant, the young and lovely lady in her gala morning dress and the roses chased from her cheeks by fear, they drew back and clustered outside it.

"What is it you want!" gasped Caroline from her trembling lips.

One of the foremost answered her. He was a gentleman, and he raised his hat, and made his tone as courteous as his sense of injury allowed. They were very sorry to disturb her, but they must see Mr. Cray. They had come to see him and they would see him.

"I assure you that he is not here," said Caroline, her earnest voice carrying truth with it. "He has been gone some time."

"He was at the offices this morning, madam, and disappeared. We were told he had no doubt come home."

"It is true," she answered. "He went to the offices very early, and came home again about eleven o'clock for something he had forgotten, papers I think he said. He did not stay two minutes; he got them and went back again. What is it that is the matter?"

"Back to the offices?" they asked, disregarding the question.

"Yes, back to the offices. He said he must make haste, for he had a great deal to do today. I am sure you will find him there." She had no suspicion that she was asserting what was not true. Whether they believed it or not—though most of them did believe it—they had no resource but to act upon it. Filing out again, they jumped into the cabs, and rattled back at the rate of nine-and-twenty miles an hour.

Leaving Mrs. Cray in a grievous state of perplexity and of distress: for they had spoken of "ruin" as connected with the mine. She was one of those who cannot bear suspense: she had no patience; no endurance, not even for an hour. In a tumult of hurry and emotion, she had her carriage brought round, called for Sara Davenal, to whom, however, she did not tell what had taken place, and drove on to the City almost as fast as those cabs had driven, to get an explanation of Mark.

The cabs had arrived previously, and their occupants found they had been deceived. No Mark Cray was at the offices, or had been there since his first departure from them. They burst bounds, in tongue at any rate, and talked of warrants and prosecutions and various inconvenient things. Other shareholders joined in the general fury, and it may perhaps be excused to them that when the carriage of Mark Cray suddenly appeared in the general melée, they turned their rage upon it.

That is, they pressed round it and saluted it with reproaches not at all soft or complimentary. Possibly in the moment's blind anger they did not see that Mark himself was not its occupant. They were, on the whole, men who knew how to behave themselves, and would have desisted, perhaps apologised, when they had had time and calmness to see that only ladies were there: but that time was not allowed them.

One came, with his tall strong form, his pale, resolute, haughty face, and pushed them right and left, as he laid his hand on the carriage door.

"Are you men?" he asked. "Don't you see that you are terrifying these ladies? Stand back. I had thought—"

"Oh, Oswald, save us! save us!" came the interrupting cry, as Caroline Cray caught his hand. "What is it all? what has happened?"

He got her out of the carriage and into some adjacent offices, whose friendly doors were opened to them. Sara followed, unmolested, and Oswald went back to rescue, if might be, the carriage. But the gentlemen had been a little recalled to common-sense by the incident: and the carriage was no longer in danger. Smashing Mark Cray's carriage would not make good their losses, or bring forth him who was missing. Oswald returned to Mrs. Cray.

"It is all right again now," he said. "The carriage is waiting for you a little further off. Shall I take you to it?"

"But I want to go into the offices, Oswald," she feverishly rejoined. "I want to see Mark. I must see him."

"Mark is not at the offices. Neither would it be well that you should go there just now."

"Not at the offices! where is he then?"

"I don't know where he is. I should like to find him."

He spoke in a cold, proud, bitter tone, and it struck dismay to the heart of Mrs. Cray. Indeed Oswald's frame of mind was one of the most intense bitterness. He had been plausibly defrauded out of his money: his pride, his sensitive honour, his innate justice, had been wounded to the core. All this disgrace Mark Cray had been earning for himself; Mark, his half-brother!

"But I must see Mark," she reiterated in a helpless manner. "Don't you know where I can go to find him, Oswald?"

"I do not indeed."

"I want to know what has happened. I heard them speak of ruin; of water in the mine. Can you tell me?"

"News has come up that an irruption of water has taken place. I find it is not the first: but the other, they say, was not serious."

"And this is?"

"I fear so."

"But what right have those men to be so angry, so excited against Mark? He did not let the water in." Oswald made no answer. If Mark had treated those shareholders with the duplicity that he had treated him, they had certainly a very good right to be angry and excited.

Mrs. Cray turned towards the door in her restlessness to take a reconnoitring glimpse of the state of affairs outside. Mark might have come up! might be in the midst of the mob! Sara, who had waited for the opportunity, drew near to Oswald Cray, and spoke in a whisper.

"Is it ruin?"

"Irretrievable—as I believe," he answered, his voice unconsciously assuming a strange tenderness as he looked at her pale, sad face. "Ruin for Mark Cray, perhaps for many others." And the words fell like a shock of ice on her heart. What would become of the engagement that she had made to repay the two hundred pounds to Mr. Wheatley from the money owing her by Mark?

CHAPTER XLIX

THE EVENING OF THE BLOW

It was the peculiarity of Miss Bettina Davenal to be more especially deaf when suddenly surprised or annoyed. Possibly it is the same with other deaf people. Sara Davenal stood before her in her drawing-room striving to make her comprehend the state of affairs relative to the Great Wheal Bang; and not at first successfully. Miss Bettina had not understood why Mrs. Cray had driven round in hurried agitation that morning and carried off Sara by storm: Caroline would not explain why, and Sara could not. Sara had returned home now, willing to afford every explanation; indeed believing it to be her duty so to do; but Miss Bettina, offended at the morning's slight, was keeping her heart closed; and when that was shut, the ears would not open.

"What d'you say? You went up to the offices? I should like to know what took you and Caroline to the offices? Young ladies don't require to go to such places."

"She went to try to see Mark, aunt."

"Ugh!" growled Miss Bettina. "Mark told her, indeed! If Mark Cray told her to go down the mine amidst the lead, she'd do it. Doesn't he see enough of her at home?"

"She went to try to see Mark, Aunt Bettina," repeated Sara, more slowly. "I—I am afraid they are ruined."

"Serve them right," returned Miss Bettina, catching the last word, but attaching no importance to it.

"Some disastrous news has been received from Wales, from the mine. Caroline says a Mr. Brackenbury called in Grosvenor Place last night—"

"Mr. who?"

"Mr. Brackenbury. She did not know then why he called, but Mr. Oswald Cray has now told her that he brought the first news of it to Mark. It had come up to him by telegram."

Miss Bettina Davenal bent her ear. "He came up by telegram! What do you mean by that? Have they got a new invention that brings up people, pray? Why are you not more careful how you speak, Miss Sara Davenal?"

"I said the news came up by telegram, aunt. It came to Mr. Brackenbury; and that's why he called on Mark last night. At least so Mr. Oswald Cray told Caroline. Caroline had been surprised or annoyed at his visit; she did not understand it; and she mentioned it to Mr. Oswald Cray."

Miss Bettina lifted her hands helplessly. "What's any Mr. Brackenbury to me?—or Oswald Cray either? I want to know why Caroline took you to those offices today?"

"I am trying to tell you, aunt," said poor Sara. "Mark went up to the offices early this morning before Caroline was awake; he came home again about eleven, saying he had forgotten something, but Caroline thought his manner absent and strange. He left again, and soon after the house was invaded by quite a crowd of men, gentlemen, demanding to see him—"

"Had they got an organ with them?"

Miss Bettina's interruption took Sara rather aback. "An organ, aunt? I don't know what you mean."

"Not know what I mean!" was the wrathful answer. "Crowds don't collect round houses unless there's a cause; organs or monkeys, or some such nonsense. What did they collect there for?"

Sara bent her head lower and strove to speak with even more distinctness. "It was a crowd of gentlemen, aunt; gentlemen from the City; though perhaps I ought not to have said a crowd, but it was what Caroline called it to me. They came down in Hansom cabs, she said, and they were fierce in their demands to see Mark, and they'd hardly go away again, and they said the mine was ruined. Caroline was alarmed, and she went up herself to try to see Mark, but she did not like to go alone, and came round for me."

The words were as a hopeless jumble in Miss Bettina's ear; their sense nowhere. "I wish you'd be clear," she said, tartly. "If you want to tell me a thing, tell it in a straightforward manner. Why do you mix up crowds and organs with it?"

"Dear aunt, I never said a word about an organ. The—mine—is—ruined," she added, almost out of heart with her task.

"What's ruined?" shrieked Miss Bettina.

"The mine. The Great Wheal Bang." Miss Bettina heard this time. She had lived in expectation of the news ever since the Great Wheal Bang first jumped into existence. Nevertheless it scared her; and an expression of dismay sat on her refined features as she turned them on Sara with a questioning gaze.

"I believe the water has got in. They say it is utter ruin. And Mark Cray can't be found."

"What has Mark Cray found?"

"He can't be found, aunt. He was not at the offices when we got there, and the shareholders—as I suppose the people were—attacked the carriage: some of them have sunk a great deal of money in the mine. There was no real danger, of course; but Mr. Oswald Cray got us out of it."

Miss Bettina stared hopelessly. "Oswald Cray got you out of the mine! What are you talking of?"

"Out of the carriage, aunt; not out of the mine. That's in Wales."

"Do you suppose I thought it was in London?" retorted offended Miss Bettina. "You'll be obligingly informing me where London is next. Where is Mark Cray?"

"No one seems to know. His wife does not; except that he said to her he might have to go down to Wales this evening, and she was not to mention it. She is in great uncertainty and distress."

"What's she in?"

"Uncertainty, distress," repeated Sara. "She is as frightened as a child. I fear she will not be a good one to bear misfortune. I went home with her and remained some time; it was that made me so late. When I came away she was growing very angry with Mark: she says he ought to have told her of it this morning."

"And so he ought," said Miss Bettina. "Ah! I never cordially approved that match for Caroline, and the doctor knew it. She'll see what he's made of now. You say you came in contact with the shareholders: what did they say?"

Sara hesitated. "They were saying very disagreeable things, Aunt Bettina."

"That's not telling me what they said."

"They talked of deceit and—and swindling. They seem dreadfully bitter against Mark Cray."

"Dreadfully what against him?"

"Bitter."

"Oh," said Miss Bettina. "Mark Cray's a fool in more ways than one; but they should blame themselves, not him. Mark told them the mine was of gold, I daresay; but it was their fault if they believed it. A man might come to me and say, If you will give me a ten-pound note I'll bring it you back tomorrow doubled, and if I fell into the trap I ought not to turn my anger on him. Mark Cray believed in the mine: those schemers are so sanguine."

Sara bent her head until her lips almost touched her aunt's ear, and lowered her voice to a cautious tone: but somehow it was terribly distinct to Miss Bettina.

"Aunt, I fear it is not quite so straightforward as you think. There was an irruption of water in the summer—a slight one, I fancy—and Mark and Mr. Barker concealed it. It is this which makes the shareholders so angry, and, they say—they say they can prosecute him for it."

"Who said this?" asked Miss Bettina, after a pause.

"I can hardly tell who. We heard a great deal of talking altogether. One gentleman came up to Mr. Oswald Cray as he was taking us to the carriage again, and asked him if he was not Mark's brother. Oswald replied that he was Mark's half-brother; and then the gentleman said harsh things, and Oswald could not stop him, and could not get us by."

Miss Bettina poured forth question upon question. Incensed as she had been against Mark Cray and his wife for the past months, much as she had blamed their folly, sharp as were her prophecies of the final results, perhaps this was worse than she had bargained for. She had looked for ruin, but not for criminal disgrace.

"And Mark can't be found, you say?" she asked, her tone a shrill one.

"No."

She sat down to the dinner-table, for the day had gone on to evening, despatching Neal for a fly while she ate a bit, and then she went out, taking Sara. "Grosvenor Place," she said to Neal And that observant domestic knew by the compressed lips, the clasped hands, the rigid head, how inwardly flurried was his mistress.

They found Caroline in a state of emotion, bordering upon hysteria. Fear, anger, perplexity, and despair, succeeding each other so rapidly that her mood may have been said to savour of the whole at once. Poor Caroline Cray knew nothing of either endurance or reticence; her anger against Mark was great at the present moment, and she gave way to it loudly.

"Where is he?" was the first pointed question of Miss Davenal.

"I don't know where he is. He might have trusted me. It's not his fault if the water has come into the mine, and he had no cause to go away; but if he had gone, he might have taken me. Barker has been down here in a dreadful passion, and says Mark was not a good fellow to steal a march on him and leave him alone all day to fight the battle with the shareholders. A hundred people, about, have been here after Mark, and it's a shame that I should be left to hear all the remarks."

"Is Oswald Cray with you?" asked Miss Bettina.

"Oh, my goodness, I don't suppose he'll come here again," returned poor Caroline, half beside herself. "I thought him cold and queer in his manner today. Barker says he is vexed at losing his thousand pounds; and that Mark got two hundred more from him last night after he knew the mine had gone. Oswald said nothing to me, but of course he is incensed at it."

Miss Davenal had been listening with her hand to her ear, and she heard pretty well. "Do you know the particulars of the calamity?" she asked. "Is the mine irretrievably ruined!"

"I don't know anything, except that I'm fit to go mad," she answered, beginning to sob like a petulant child.

In that one first moment of the blow Miss Davenal was generous enough to spare reproaches for all the folly of the past, though she had plenty at her tongue's end. She had not sat down since she entered; she had stood rigid and upright; and when she went out to the fly she ordered it to Mr. Oswald Cray's.

"Tell the man to drive quickly," said Miss Bettina to Neal. "What do you say, Sara? Let you stop with Caroline? Caroline wants neither you nor me; I can see that. There'll be trouble over this."

Mrs. Cray had not chosen an inapt word when she said Oswald must be incensed against Mark. It was precisely Oswald's present state of feeling. He saw that the thousand pounds had been nothing but a stopgap; not drawn from him for his own good and benefit, as Mark so largely boasted, but for Mark's own necessities. And as to the two hundred pounds of the previous night, the money of the firm—Oswald did boil over at the thought of that. Oh, why could not Mark have been upright and open! why could he not have gone to Oswald with the truth upon his lip, and said, Let me have this two hundred pounds in my dire necessity, and I will repay you when I can! Oswald was not the brother to refuse him.

Oswald had had a battle with himself. When he returned home after that scene in the city, feeling that his money, the twelve hundred pounds, was irretrievably lost, he sat down and thought. Should he cancel the offer made to Frank Allister to go out to Spain, and take the appointment himself, as at first intended? Was he justified in foregoing it, under this unexpected loss? The same considerations swayed him now as previously; his own interest versus Frank's health, perhaps life; but how weighty a balance was now thrown into his own scale!

If ever Oswald had need of a better guidance than his own, he had need now. And he was conscious of it. He had many failings, as we all have; and his pride often stood in his way; but he had one great and good gift—a conscience that was ever prompting him on the upward way.

"No, I will not hesitate," he said to himself. "The necessity for Allister's going remains the same, and he shall go. I must overget this other loss as I best can, though it may be years first, but I'll not set my own interest against Allister's life."

And so Frank Allister and his sister received no countermand, and they proceeded to Mr. Oswald Cray's that evening, to talk over arrangements, as it had been decided they should; and they never knew the sacrifice that had been made for them, or had the least suspicion that Mr. Oswald Cray had yielded up the appointment.

When Miss Davenal and Sara arrived, Mrs. Benn received them. That errant husband of hers and valued servant of the firm, was out again. This was not Mrs. Benn's cleaning-day; but any little extra duty, though it was but the receiving a visitor at unusual hours, put her out excessively; and it was not usual for a levee of ladies to attend the house in an evening. She appeared at the door with the ordinary crusty face and a candle in her hand.

"Is Mr. Oswald Cray at home?" was Neal's demand.

"Yes, he is," returned Mrs. Benn, speaking as if the question injured her very much indeed.

Neal stepped back to the fly, and opened the door for the ladies to alight. Mrs. Benn stared at the proceedings with all her eyes.

"Well, if this don't bang everything!" she ejaculated, partly to herself, partly to the street. "If he was agoing to have a party tonight, he might have told me, I think. And that there Benn to go out, and never light the hall-lamp first! It cracks my arms to do it: a nasty, high, awk'ard thing! Will he be for ordering tea for 'em, I wonder I when there ain't nothing but a hot loaf in the house, and one pat o' but—"

"Show me to Mr. Oswald Cray's private rooms," came the interrupting voice of Miss Davenal, as she entered.

"This way," returned sulky Mrs. Benn; "there's one of them there already."

The "one of 'em" must have applied to the assumed evening party, for in the sitting-room sat Jane Allister. Her bonnet was off, her shawl was unpinned; her fair face was serene and contented, as though she were in her own home. Miss Davenal bowed stiffly in her surprise, and the rebellious jealousy rose up in Sara's heart.

"Is Mr. Oswald Cray not here?" asked Miss Davenal, halting on the threshold.

Jane Allister came forward with her good and candid face, and Miss Davenal's reserved tone relaxed. "Mr. Oswald Cray is downstairs with my brother and another gentleman. They are settling some business together; I don't think they will be long."

Miss Davenal did not hear, but Sara repeated the words to her. They sat down; and Miss Allister, finding the elder lady was deaf, took her seat by Sara.

"I came here tonight to settle particulars about our Spanish journey," explained Jane Allister, as if in apology for being found there. "I am going to live in Spain."

Sara heard it as one in a dream. Oswald Cray was going to Spain for a lengthened residence: he had told her so when she was in that room a fortnight ago. If Jane Allister was going with him, why then, it must be that they were going to be married immediately.

Her face flushed, her brow grew moist. In a sort of desperation, in her eager wish to know the worst at once, she turned to Jane Allister.

"Are you going with Mr. Oswald Cray?"

"I am going with my brother."

"With—your—brother! And not with Mr. Oswald Cray?"

"No, surely not. How could I go with Mr. Oswald Cray? It would not be proper," she simply added.

"I—I thought—I meant as his wife," said poor Sara, all confused in her heart sickness. "I beg your pardon."

"As his wife!—Mr. Oswald Cray's! Nay, but that is an unlikely thing to fancy. I am not suitable to Mr. Oswald Cray. Do you know him?

"O yes."

"Then you might have been sure he'd not cast his thoughts to a plain body like me. Why should he? I am not his equal in position. He has been a brother to Frank, and I reverence him beyond any one I know as a good and true friend. That's all."

Why did her heart give a great bound of hope at the words, when she knew—when she knew that he was lost to her? Oswald Cray came bounding up the stairs, but a mist had gathered before Sara's eyes, and she saw nothing clearly.

"Frank is waiting for you, Jane. He will not come upstairs again."

"Does he know about everything?"

"Everything, I think. We have discussed it all, and he will tell you. But he is coming again in the morning."

Oswald had spoken as he shook hands with Miss Davenal. Another moment and they were alone together: the young Scotch lady had left the room.

"Mr. Oswald Cray, you must tell me all you know of this unhappy business, from beginning to end," said Miss Davenal. "I have come to you for the information, and I beg you to conceal nothing. Is Mark Cray in danger?"

Oswald scarcely knew in what sense to take the word. He hesitated as he looked at Miss Davenal.

"How has it all come about? Let me hear the whole of it; the best and the worst. His wife professes to know nothing, and it was of no use my asking her. The water has got into the mine."

"It is said to be overflowing it; but particulars are not ascertained yet," replied Oswald, as he proceeded to speak of what he knew.

It was not much, for he was nearly as much in the dark as they were. Miss Davenal listened with compressed lips.

At the conclusion of the interview, Oswald took Miss Davenal out to the fly upon his arm, placed her in it, and turned to Sara.

"The last time I saw you I had a journey in my head," he said in a low tone; "I told you I was going to Spain."

"Yes."

"I am not going now. I have given up the idea. We shall send out a gentleman instead; my friend, Frank Allister. Goodnight; goodnight, Miss Davenal."

Severely upright in the carriage sat Miss Davenal, her countenance one picture of condemnation for the absent Mark. Only once did she open her lips to Sara opposite to her, and that was as the carriage turned out of the glare and gas of the more populous streets to the quiet one which contained their home.

"What would your brother Edward say to this, were he at home?"

What would he say to something else? As the carriage drew up to the door, a female figure was slowly pacing before it, as if in waiting. And Sara shrank into the remotest corner of the carriage with a shiver of dread, for she recognised her for the stranger. Catherine Wentworth.

CHAPTER L

HARD USAGE FOR DICK

Do you remember the severe weather of the Christmas of 1860? How for once we had an old-fashioned Christmas day, when the icicles hung bright and frozen from the trees and the ponds were alive with skaters, after the manner of the Christmases we read of, of the days gone by. It was indeed a bitter winter, that at the close of 1860, and an unusual number of the poor and friendless, the sick and ailing, passed from its biting sharpness to a better world.

In the mind of one it almost seemed as though he had held some mysterious prevision of it; and that was Oswald Cray. When deliberating, the previous autumn, whether he should go to Spain himself, times and again had the thought recurred to him—what if we have a sharp winter?—how will Allister weather it? And now that the sharp winter, more terribly sharp than even Oswald dreamt of, had indeed come, he was thankful to have sacrificed his own self-interest. In that more southern climate Allister would no feel the cold of this; and it almost seemed as if the thought alone brought to Oswald his reward.

"Isn't it stunning, Aunt Bett?"

You will probably recognise the words as likely to emanate from nobody's lips but Mr. Dick Davenal's. Mr. Dick had arrived for the holidays; rather against the inclination as well as the judgment of Miss Bettina, but she did not see her way in courtesy to exclude him. Leopold had been in town with her since October, she and Sara nursing him; so it would have been unkind to keep Dick at school alone for the holidays. Miss Bettina said London was a bad place for Dick; he would be getting into all sorts of mischief: perhaps get run over, perhaps get lost; it was uncertain what: but Sara, in her love for the boy, promised to keep him in order and out of harm. A rash undertaking.

What of the Great Wheal Bang? The Great Wheal Bang was gone for ever It had passed out ignobly, never probably to be heard of as a mine again, except in name at certain law courts, to which some of its angry shareholders persisted in bringing it. Mr. Barker was abroad, and did not come home to face the storm; it appeared there was no law to force him home, the matters of the Wheal Bang just escaped that; and he carried on a free-and-easy correspondence with some of the exasperated shareholders, who told him to his face in their answers that he deserved hanging.

And Mark Cray? Mark Cray was nowhere. The defunct company did their best to find him, but, try as they would, they could not discover his hiding-place. They assumed he was out of the country, most probably with Barker, and perhaps their home search was, through that very assumption, less minute than it might have been. A run from danger is always more formidable than a faced one; and if Mark Cray had only faced those shareholders he would no doubt have found their bite less hurtful than their bark. That they were loud and threatening and angry, was true; but Mark would have done well to meet the worst, and get it over. The luxurious house in Grosvenor Place had been long ago abandoned by Mark and his wife; and so temporarily had it been lived in, so fleeting had been the enjoyment of the carriages, the servants, the society, and all the rest of the accessories, that altogether that time seemed only like a dream.

"Isn't it stunning, Aunt Bett?"

Dick was standing at the dining-room window, his sparkling eyes devouring the ice in the streets, the tempting slides in the gutters. A young gentleman who was coming to the house with a small tray of meat upon his back had just gone down one beautifully, and Dick longed to be behind him. Leo stepped to the window to look, and thought he should like it too; but Leo was not in strong health, as Dick was.

"Isn't it what?" asked Aunt Bett, looking up quickly. "Raining?"

"Stunning," roared Dick.

"I wish you would learn to speak like a gentleman, Richard, and not use those expressions. If they do for school, they don't do for home."

"I have been oiling my skates this morning," continued Dick. "They are rather short, but they'll do."

"Oiling what?"

"My skates."

"What cakes?"

"Sk—a—tes, Aunt Bett. Everything will bear today."

"Nothing bears in London," said Miss Bettina. "You must not try it, Richard. A great many boys are drowned every winter in the Serpentine."

"What muffs they must be!" returned Dick; "Aunt Bett, the ponds would bear you if you'd put on a pair of skates and try. They'd bear me a hundred times over."

"Would they?" said Miss Bettina. She turned to Sara, who was busy at the table and pointed with her finger to indicate Dick.

"I will not have him to go into this danger. Do you hear, Sara? You undertook to keep him out of harm, if he came to us; so see to it. Perhaps the best plan will be to lock up his skates. I don't want to have him brought home drowned."

Dick was resentful. He might have broken into open rebellion but for fear of being sent back to enjoy his holidays at school. He sat in a sullen sort of mood, on the edge of a chair, his hands in his pockets clicking their contents about, and his boots beating time restlessly on the carpet.

"How it's all altered!" he exclaimed.

"How is what altered?" inquired Sara. They were alone then. Miss Bettina had gone from the room to give Leopold his eleven o'clock dose of strengthening medicine.

"Since Uncle Richard's time. Why, he bought me those very skates last winter, when that frost came in November. That is, he sent word to school that I might have them. And then we had no more ice at all! and Uncle Richard kept wishing through the holidays there might be some for us! He'd have let us skate."

Sara was silent. Things had indeed altered since then.

"It's an awful shame of Aunt Bett! The ice stunning thick, and a fellow can't enjoy it! Drowned! She might get drowned herself perhaps, but I shouldn't. Uncle Richard would have let us skate in Hallingham!" added Dick, excessively resentful. "He wanted us to skate."

"But I think it was a little different, Richard dear. Those ponds at Hallingham were not deep; and people do get drowned in the Serpentine. And there's nobody to go with you." Dick tossed his head. "Perhaps you think I want somebody! You had better send a nursemaid. Fine holidays these are!"

A few minutes more of sitting still and Dick could stand it no longer. He darted into the passage and snatched his cap. Sara, quick as he, caught him with the street-door in his hand.

"Dick, it must not be. You know I have answered for you to Aunt Bettina."

"All right, Sara. I'm not going near the Serpentine, or any other deep water."

"You promise?"

"Yes; on my honour. There! Why, I have not got my skates. I'm going up and down the street-slides; that's all. You can't expect me to sit twirling my thumbs all day in Aunt Bett's parlour, as Leo does."

She had no fear then. If Dick once gave his honour, or if put upon his honour, he could but be a loyal knight. Left to himself, no promise extracted from him, he would have decamped right off to the Serpentine, or to anything else mischievous and dangerous; but not now.

But Dick "took it out"—the words were his own—in street-slides. All the most attractive ruisseaux within a few miles of home Mr. Dick exercised his legs upon. It required a terrible amount of resolution to keep his promise not to "go near" the forbidden water; and how long Dick stood in envy, his nose frozen to the park railings as he watched the streams of people pouring towards the ice, he never knew. He was not in a good humour; the slides were very ignoble pastime indeed, only fit for street-boys; and he thought if there was one gentleman more ill-used than another that day in all Her Majesty's dominions, that one was himself.

Mr. Dick stopped out his own time. He knew that he would be expected home about one o'clock to have something to eat; but as nothing had been expressly said to him, he took rather a savage pleasure in letting them expect, punishing his hunger. He saw a man selling hot potatoes; and he bought three and ate them, skins and all. Dick was not in the least troubled with proud notions: Leo would have looked askance at the tempting edible, and passed on the other side; Dick danced round the man's machine while he feasted, in the face and eyes of the passers-by. If Miss Davenal had but seen him!

Altogether, what with the slides, the hot potatoes, and the temper, Mr. Richard Davenal remained out long after dark. When he began to think it might be as well to return home, and to feel as if fifteen wolves were inside him fighting for their dinner, he was in some obscure and remote region of Chelsea, where the population was more crowded than aristocratic, and the ice abundant. Happening to cast his eyes to a clock in a baker's shop he saw that it wanted but twenty-five minutes to six.

"My?" ejaculated Dick in his dismay. Miss Davenal's dinner-hour had been altered from six to five while the boys were with her, and Dick had certainly meant to be home to time. He had not thought it was so late as this. Dick's hair stood on end, and the wolves fought desperately.

"Suppose old Bett should say I shan't have any dinner?"

The shop next door to the baker's was a cook's shop—as they are called: and perhaps Dick's dreadful doubt caused him irresistibly to linger for a fond moment at the window and gaze at the attractions inside. Under Dick's very nose was a steaming mound of beef just out of the pot, some parsnips round it; other joints were there in plenty; peas-pudding, plum-pudding, sausages, and a whole host of things irresistible to a boy in Dick's famishing condition. He mechanically put his hand into his pocket, lest a stray sixpence might by some miracle be there. In vain. Dick Davenal was one who could not keep money for an hour, and his having sufficient to buy the potatoes was a fact notable.

Hurried as he was, he could not tear himself from the tempting shop. The shopman, in a white apron, a great carving-knife and fork in his hand, was cutting thin slices from a cold round of beef and placing them in the scale on a piece of white paper. The balance went down, and he rolled the paper round the meat and handed it to the customer waiting for it, a young woman—or rather lady, for she looked like one—who wore a black veil over her face. She gave him sixpence and some halfpence in return, but the man did not seem to like the sixpence; he held it close to the gas and then showed it to her, and she put her veil aside and bent her face nearer while she looked at it.

If ever Dick Davenal believed he was in a dream he believed so then. He rubbed his eyes; he rubbed his frozen nose; he stared through the intervening steam; and he pinched himself to see whether he was awake. For that face was the face of his cousin, Mrs. Cray.

Dick could not believe his senses. The shopman apparently decided that the sixpence was a good one, and put it in his till, and the lady had left the shop before Dick recovered his bewilderment. He had believed Mr. and Mrs. Cray were abroad. From a shrewd boy like Dick it had been impossible to guard the secret that something was wrong; besides, he had heard of the failure of the Great Wheal Bang, and that its promoters were away, abroad or somewhere.

But that was surely Caroline gone out of the shop with a paper of meat in her hand! Dick's spirit went down to zero. However he might condescend to the purchase of hot potatoes, and such like stray escapades, he did not like to see Caroline buy cooked meat and carry it away with her. Dick knew that something or other must be all wrong, and he suddenly felt as timid as Leo.

She crossed the road and went down a by-street, where the lights were scanty and the houses poor. Dick followed her. He saw how tightly her veil was drawn over her face; and she walked with her head down: it might be to keep out the cold, or it might be to avoid observation.

She turned into a house on the left-hand side whose door stood open; a shabby-looking house, but sufficiently large. Dick, hardly certain in his own mind yet, deliberated whether he should follow her and show himself: and when he at length went to the door nobody was in sight. He took courage and knocked; and a woman came out of the parlour on the right.

"Is Mrs. Cray here?" asked Dick.

"Mrs. who?"

"Mrs. Cray. She's just gone in."

"There's nobody here of that name. Who's Mrs. Cray? You have mistook the house, young man." Dick had his wits about him, as the saying runs, and they were sufficiently alert to prevent his insisting on the point of its being Mrs. Cray. "I'm sure I saw some lady come in," said he.

"Mrs. Mark came in a minute ago, for I met her in the passage. First floor if you want her."

"Can I go up?" asked Dick.

"That's as you please," returned the woman, who was crusty enough to be first cousin to Mrs. Benn. "The other lodgers in the house is nothing to me, who goes up to 'em or who doesn't."

She retreated inside the parlour and banged the door. Dick stumbled upstairs in the dark, the words "first floor" having guided him. Some light came in from a window on the landing, and he distinctly heard Caroline's voice in the front room. Dick-fashion, he burst in without knocking.

Caroline gave a short scream. She was untying her bonnet, and the paper of meat, slowly unfolding itself, lay on the table. It was a plain sitting-room carpeted with drugget, a large sofa covered with dark blue stuff seeming to take up one side of it. A white cloth was spread on part of the table, with some tea-cups and saucers, a loaf of bread, and a piece of butter.

"Caroline, I was sure it was you!" The first moment of surprise over, Caroline threw herself on a chair and burst into tears. Dick sat down opposite to her and stared round the room, staring off his bewilderment. Poor Dick was not possessed of any superfluous sentiment, and the sobs and emotion only made him feel awkward. The sight of a home face was too much for Mrs. Cray.

"Is Mark here?"

Dick asked presently.

"No." Dick glanced round again, but he could see no door except the one he had entered at.

"I'm sure I heard you talking to somebody, Caroline. It made me know which was the room."

"I was talking to myself. The words I said were, 'I hope Mark will not be long,' and I suppose I spoke them aloud."

A few final sobs, and the emotion passed. Dick was timid, almost nervous, and he never remembered to have been so in his life. A thought crossed the boy's mind of what his uncle Richard would say, could he see this curious state of things.

"Do you live here, Caroline!"

"Yes. We went away in the country for a little time at first; but it was so out of the way of hearing anything, so dull, so wretched, that we came back again. Mark thought it would be better to come pretty near to the old neighbourhood; that there was less chance of our being looked for there than elsewhere."

"You don't have all the house."

"All the house!" echoed Caroline. "We only have this room and the use of the kitchen, which I hardly ever go down to. That sofa is a bed," she added, pointing to it. "Mark draws it out at night."

Dick felt more at sea than ever. "Has Mark got no money?"

Caroline shook her head. "There's a little left; not much. We did not save a thing from Grosvenor Place. People came in and took possession while Mark was away, and I got frightened and left it. Afterwards, when my clothes were asked for, they sent me a boxful of the poorest I had, and said those were all. I don't know whether it was that they kept the best, or that the maid-servants helped themselves to them. Dick!" she passionately added, "I'd rather die than have to bear all this."

"Do you have to go out and buy the meat?" questioned Dick, unable to get the practical part he had seen out a his head.

"There's a boy that waits on the lodgers, the landlady's son, and he goes on errands sometimes. Mark thought we should be safer in a house like this, where there are different lodgers, and one does not interfere with the concerns of the others; that we should be less likely to attract notice. In truth we were afraid to venture on a better place where persons might recognise us."

"Afraid of what?" questioned Dick.

"I'm sure I hardly know," she answered. "Of his being arrested, I suppose."

"I say, does Sara know you are here?"

Caroline shook her head. "I have written her a note twice, saying we are safe; but Mark would not let me give the address. Aunt Bettina has shaken us off, there's no doubt; she'll never forgive Mark."

"Forgive him for what!"

"Oh, altogether," returned Caroline with a gesture of impatience. "There was the leaving Hallingham, and Sara's money, and other things."

"Where is Mark?" continued Dick.

"He won't be long. He strolls out a little after dark, but he does not care to venture abroad by daylight. And so, you are up for the holidays, I suppose?"

Dick nodded. "Aunt Bett wouldn't have us at midsummer. But Leo broke his arm, and he wasn't strong, and she sent for him; and then she said I might come up for Christmas, and we could both go back to school together. I say, wasn't it unkind of her not to have us in the summer? She said her house was small. Summer holidays are jollier than winter ones, especially when they don't let you go on the ice."

Did a remembrance cross Caroline of somebody else who would not have them in the summer?—whose house was not small? Probably not. Caroline had room only for her own griefs. Since the falling of the blow she had existed in a state of bewilderment. The change was so great, the order of things so completely altered, that at times she believed she must be in a prolonged dream, and should shortly wake up to reality. As one who has suddenly put ashore in a foreign country, where the land, the customs, the people, and the tongue, are all strange to him, and he can only accept them passively, yielding himself perforce to the necessity of circumstances, so it was with Caroline Cray. Believe me, I am telling you no untrue story.

"How you cough?" exclaimed Dick, as she was interrupted by a heavy fit of coughing, not for the first time.

"I caught a bad cold. It was very bad for a day or two, and I lay in bed. O Dick! I wonder if I shall ever have a bedroom again!"

"Couldn't you have a bedroom as well as this room?" sensibly answered Dick.

"There was only this room to let when we came here, and we thought it would do. It's tolerably good-looking you see, and we are more to ourselves. Every week, too, we are hoping to leave it."

"Where to go to?"

"I don't know. Mark says something will be sure to turn up."

"I say, do they know about this in Barbadoes?"

"Not from us. I daresay Aunt Bettina has taken care to tell them. Is she as deaf as ever, Dick?"

"She's deafer. And she's getting a regular old woman. What do you think? she'd not let me go out skating this morning, for fear—"

A gentleman entered, and cut Dick's revelations short. The boy looked at him in puzzled bewilderment, for he thought he knew him, and yet did not. It was a full minute before Dick recognised him for Mark Cray.

Formerly Mark had whiskers and no moustache; now he had a moustache and no whiskers, and his beard was growing, and his face looked longer. He had on blue spectacles too. Altogether, Dick was hardly certain yet.

Mark did not seem glad to see him. In manner he rather appeared to resent the accident which had discovered them to Dick, than to feel pleasure at it. Caroline put the slices of beef upon a dish, made the tea, and asked Dick to partake.

But Dick declined. And nobody, perhaps, would have given careless Dick credit for the true motive, or for the real self-denial that it was to a hungry boy. He had somehow drawn a conclusion that Mr. and Mrs. Cray had not too much meat for themselves, and he would not lessen it.

"I can't stay now," he said rising, "I shall have Aunt Bett at me as it is. Goodnight, Mr. Cray; goodnight, Caroline."

Mr. Cray followed him down the stairs. "You must be very cautious not to say that you found us here," he said. "Can we depend upon you?"

"As if you couldn't!" returned Dick. "I know! A fellow of ours at school has got a big brother, and he has to be in hiding nine months at least out of every year. I'll tell nobody but Sara." He vaulted off, or perhaps Mark Cray's injunction might have been extended to Sara in particular. When he reached home, Miss Bettina, who had believed nothing less but that he was drowned, and had sent Neal to a circuit of police-stations, met him in the corridor, followed by Sara and Leo.

"You ungrateful boy! Where have you been?"

"Don't, Aunt Bettina! No need to seize hold of me in that way. I have only been sliding. I haven't been to the water."

"You shall go back to school tomorrow," said Miss Bettina, as she turned into the dining-room.

Dick caught his cousin by the arm. "You be off after Aunt Bett, Leo; I want to speak to Sara. I say," he continued in a whisper, as Leo obeyed him, "I have seen Caroline and Mark Cray!"

"Nonsense, Dick! Why did you stay out so and frighten us?"

"I have. I should have been in earlier but for that. Frightened? How stupid you must all be! As if I couldn't take care of myself. I saw Carine in a beef and pudding shop, buying cold meat, and I watched where she went to, and I've been there for half an hour, and I saw Mark. He has shaved off his whiskers, and wears blue—"

"Hush!" breathed Sara, as Dorcas came up the stairs. "You must tell me later."

CHAPTER LI

The cold, bitter, biting winter passed away, and when the lovely spring came round again little trace was left of its effects, save in the remembrance of those in whose homes sickness, or privation, or death, had been busy.

Two of those visitations had been rife in the poor house of Caroline Cray: sickness and privation. Perhaps you noticed Caroline's reply to Dick's question of whether Mark had no money: there was a little left, she said, not much. Left from what? Dick did not ask.

If ever an unfortunate company had come to grief more completely than other unfortunate companies, it was surely that noted one, the Great Wheal Bang. Sympathising friends—Barker's and Mark's—were wont to assure those gentlemen that they had "managed wretchedly:" and if we may dare to assume that the reproach was levelled at the fact of having secured nothing for themselves, it was a right one. On the day that Mark Cray went up to the offices for the last time he had but a trifling sum of money about him: Caroline had even less in her own purse; and that was all. Barker's word of precaution had secured the diamond ring and studs, and these were converted into money, Mark and Barker equally dividing the spoil. Barker, with his share, took a little tour abroad while the cloud blew over; Mark, as you have seen, went into hiding, and lived upon his part as long as it held out.

Yes, it was an unhappy fact, very debasing indeed after all the glory of Grosvenor Place, lowering as you may feel it to be to this history, Mr. Mark Cray hid himself by day, and slipped out to take the air at dusk in a moustache and blue spectacles. Mark Cray could but be a coward in the hour of trial; he ran from the danger instead of facing it. Had Mark but looked the angry shareholders and the trouble in the face, he need not have been so very fearful; but to look a difficulty in the face was not in the nature of Mark Cray. He scarcely understood what he was afraid of; he did not know what they could do to him— whether imprison him, or make him a bankrupt, or what; and Mark would rather have jumped into the sea than ascertain. He was exactly like a child who runs away screaming from a dark closet, and dare not look to see whether cause for terror is there. Some of us, my friends, have been sadly frightened at shadows.

When this state of affairs was to end, and what was to get Mark out of his difficulty, he did not at present see. As long as the money lasted he was not unduly anxious. He had great faith in something "turning up," he had unlimited faith in Barker; and Barker's letters were pretty frequent, and in the highest degree cheering. Barker happened to have a cousin, about the nineteenth remove, settled at Honfleur, in Normandie, and Barker had steered for the same port, and seemed to be living at ease there. Towards the close of the winter he wrote word to Mark that he had something good in contemplation, connected with Paris, and if it came to anything Mark should share in it.

But when Mark's money was gone things changed. He grew restless and gloomy. He could not starve, he could not go to the workhouse: he must do something. Miss Bettina Davenal would not help them: she said she could not—perhaps with justice. Leopold Davenal had been an expense to her, and was still; he went back to school after the Christmas holidays with Dick, but he was not strong yet, and sundry expensive extras were provided for him out of her pocket. That was not much: but a heavier expense had fallen upon her: for she had repaid Mr. Wheatley the two hundred pounds borrowed by Sara. Sara had disclosed to her aunt the fact of borrowing it, and in her pride Miss Bettina had made a sacrifice and repaid the sum. She had none left to bestow on Mark; there was clearly no help to be had from her.

And Caroline? You can take a look at her as she sat in the sun, which was shining into the room this bright day in early April. Perhaps you remember a remark Dr. Davenal once made—that Caroline was not one, as he believed, to bear well the adversities of life. Dr. Davenal was quite right: neither physically nor mentally did they agree with poor Caroline.

I don't know whether anybody gets ill at once under a great shock. Caroline had not. When it fell upon her she was too stunned, too entirely surprised, to be anything but bewildered. It may be questioned if a change so sudden—from seemingly assured prosperity to hiding and disgrace and poverty—has ever fallen. You may feel inclined to question it in this instance; nevertheless, I repeat that I am telling you the simple truth. The reaction had come now, and Caroline Cray gave way sadly. Her cough, that Dick remarked upon, had got well; but she would lie back in her chair all day, and it seemed next to impossible to get her out of it.

But if the body was at rest the mind was only the more active. Caroline's hours, in point of fact, were pretty equally divided between outward complaining and inward lamentation. Such lamentation is nearly always rebellious, and so was hers. The blow had been so complete; the change was so very great! All that pomp and vanity, all the luxuries, the carelessness, the pleasure attendant on that one past sunshiny wave in life's current, to have given place to this! Perhaps the worst mortification, looking back, was that the play now seemed to have been so unreal; as if they had had no right to indulge in it, were such fools to have embarked in it, worse than fools to have believed in it. Mortified, fretful, miserable, Caroline Cray seemed to live but in repining and repentance. Mark was different He neither repined nor repented; he was always restless, always expecting something to turn up; and he would stalk up and down the room, giving tongue to all sorts of wild visions of what he would do were he but clear of the world and the Great Wheal Bang.

As he was doing now. While Caroline sat listless and inert in her chair, Mark was indulging a dream of the future, sanguine as a child. He had lately taken to consult the newspapers, and one tempting advertisement in particular had attracted him. Mark Cray was getting that experience which comes inevitably in a life of vicissitude; he had yet to learn how many of these advertisements are but traps for the unwary, how next to impossible to be the one successful applicant, if they are genuine. But ever and anon Mark's dream was brought unpleasantly to a break, as the recollection intruded itself that he was not a free man.

"You see, Carine, if I were but clear of that resentful company, there are a hundred good things to be picked up. I'm sure there's a dozen at least in the paper every day. That's a splendid thing, I know, that one advertisement of this morning; any fellow securing that—"

"Where's the use of talking of it?" interrupted Carine. "It all comes to nothing. You know you are not clear of the company."

She spoke in a fretful, peevish tone. Just at first, Mark's sanguine visions of rising again more gloriously than ever, like a phoenix from its ashes, had somewhat infected her, but she was learning what they were worth: as she had just said, "it all came to nothing." Utterly weary was her spirit. Hope deferred making the heart sick; but hope destroyed—and it had come to that with Caroline Cray—maketh it die.

Physical privation tells terribly on the mind as well as the body, and it was telling upon her. They were next door to starving. What made it worse for Caroline was, that hers was a constitution requiring the best of nourishment. The Davenals were a healthy family, but there had been a taint in her mother's blood. These physical privations would alone have made Caroline fretful: and she could not help it.

"I shall be clear of it soon," said Mark.

"But how?"

Even sanguine Mark could not detail the precise means by which the emancipation was to be accomplished. "Oh, somehow," said he, in his careless way. "The company must wind itself up."

"Why can't you apply to Oswald?"

He shook his head very decisively. "I can't face him. And if I did, he'd not assist me. He has lost too much, and is sure to bear malice."

"Are we to go on like this for ever?"

"I hope we shan't go on so for a month. I wish you'd not talk so, Caroline."

"How am I to talk? You have been saying the same all along?"

"Well it's of no good your looking on the dark side of things. You are always doing it now." Caroline was silent for a few moments, when she suddenly lifted up her hands, and her voice broke into a passionate wail.

"Oh, if that money had been but settled on me, as Uncle Richard wished! This must be a judgment upon us for defying his last commands."

"Rubbish!" said Mark.

"Are we to go out in the street and beg?" she plaintively asked.

"Are you going to be a child? One must get a rub or two through life; Caroline. Barker has been down upon his beam-ends five or six times, just as much as we are, but it has always come right again."

She relapsed into a fit of weeping; half her hours, abed and up, were so spent. Mark had ceased either to soothe or reproach; he had tried both, but ineffectually; and now was fain to let her weep simply because he was helpless to prevent it. Mark Cray could not be unkind; he was not that; but he was hardly the right sort of husband for adversity. Shallow-minded, shallow-hearted, possessed of no depth of feeling, there seemed something wanting in him now. He did his best to cheer his wife; but the result was not satisfactory.

The fits of weeping would sometimes go on to hysterics; sometimes stopped just short of it. As this one stopped. Caroline suddenly roused herself and looked round wearily at the mantelpiece, as if there were a timepiece there, perhaps in momentary forgetfulness. Grosvenor Place had been rich in such; elegant bijoux, worth no end of money.

"I wish Sara would come!"

"Sara?" repeated Mark, halting in his monotonous promenade.

"I wrote to her to come."

She spoke the words half defiantly. Sara, in consequence of the discovery of Mr. Dick Davenal, had come to see them once; but she was not encouraged to repeat the visit. Mark especially was against it. "If we have them coming here, we may get dropped upon," he had said to his wife; "it would never do." But poor Caroline, wearied out with the wretched loneliness that seemed to continue month after month, and to have no end, had at length written to her cousin.

"Why did you not tell me, Caroline?"

"You might have forbidden me."

"It's just what I should have done. We don't want her here. What good will she do?"

"What good will anything in the world do? I wish I was out of it!"

Mark Cray began to ask himself the question whether the expected visit could be stopped now. He had an intense dislike to meet Sara Davenal; we all shrink from meeting those whom we have injured directly or indirectly. But the question was set at rest by Sara's entrance, and Mark, after a short greeting, disappeared.

All Caroline did for the first quarter of an hour was to sob hysterically. Sara, in slighter mourning now, unfastened the white crape strings of her straw bonnet, and sat over her in dismay, her sweet face full of compassion for the change she saw.

"I want to know how it is all to end," were the first distinct words Caroline uttered. "Am I to stop here till I die?"

A question difficult for Sara to answer. "Is Mark doing nothing?" she asked.

"He is doing nothing. He can't do anything while that business of the Wheal Bang hangs over him. If that were settled, there are fifty things he might get into. And if it can't be settled, we may both of us as well die at once as be famished to death. For that's what it would come to. Those poor creatures that shut themselves up with the fumes of charcoal are not so much to blame, after all."

"Caroline!"

"Well, I mean it," returned Caroline, a sullen tone beginning to mingle with her sobs. "It is all very well for you to exclaim 'Caroline!' as if I were mad; but you don't know what sorrow is. Nobody does until poverty comes."

Sara thought that there were worse sorrows to be borne in the world than poverty. And she was right; bad as poverty, to those unaccustomed to it, undoubtedly is. "What can I do for you?" she gently asked.

"Here we are, buried alive, and nobody comes near us! Sara, if you only knew how I yearn for a home face!—how I lie and cry for it!"

"Mark—and you also—said I must not come, lest it might lead to discovery."

"Neither must you, I suppose. At least, not often. But sometimes I think it would be well if discovery happened. There'd be an end to this uncertainty at any rate. What is Mark to do if the thing can't get settled?"

She asked the question in strange earnestness, and Sara was struck with the yearning beauty of the lifted face, of the wasting form. The violet eyes were larger than of yore, the cheeks were of a delicate crimson, and the hands were long and white and thin.

"But can it not get settled?" returned Sara.

"We have nothing to eat, you know. That is, there's bread, and suchlike; but I can't eat it. Mark will dine on bread and cheese, or a thick slice of bread and butter; and he really does not seem to mind; but I can't. O Sara! if I could but have a good dinner!"

Sara caught up her breath. What comfort could she give?

"Sometimes, when I am sick with hunger I lie and imagine the dinners we used to sit down to in Grosvenor Place. I imagine it, you know; that they are before me now, and I am eating them. Turkey and bread sauce, or salmon and lobster sauce—it's nearly always substantial things I think of, I suppose because of my hunger—and I quite seem to taste them, to eat through a whole plateful Sara, it is true."

Sara Davenal had heard the doctor speak of some kinds of hunger as a disease, and could only suppose this must be one. "I wish—I wish I could help you," she murmured.

"You can't, I know. You have it not in your power, and Aunt Bettina won't; she's implacable. I did not send for you to ask it. But, Sara, there's Oswald Cray. If you would ask him perhaps he might do something for Mark."

The words startled her. "Ask Oswald Cray!"

"I think if he would listen to any one, it is you. I don't forget how fond he used to be of you in the days gone by. Indeed, I got to think—but I was wrong, I suppose, so let it pass. O Sara, you'll ask him for my sake! Don't abandon us quite. I think he might help Mark out of this difficulty. Perhaps he might see the company, and get them to be friendly with Mark; or perhaps he'd pay a few of Mark's pressing debts. It might not take much money?"

"But why cannot Mark ask him?"

"He won't. Mark would rather it came to the charcoal—not that anything of that sort would ever be in his line—than apply to Oswald. There was some trouble between them about the money Oswald put into the mine, and Mark has kept away from him since. That is just why I have sent for you. Mark will not apply to Oswald; no, not if it were to save him from prison; and I don't feel well enough to go, and my bonnet's shabby. O Sara, when a recollection comes over me—and it is always coming—of the nice clothes I had, and how foolishly they were abandoned, I feel fit to go mad. Anyway, unless a change takes place, I shan't want clothes long. Sara, surely you will do for us so trifling a thing as this!"

To pursue the interview would be waste of time. When Sara Davenal quitted her cousin it was with a given promise to see Oswald Cray. Very much indeed did she shrink from it; as much as she had shrunk from those interviews with Mr. Alfred King: but she saw no other means to help them; and in truth she did not anticipate much would come of this.

Money seemed to be wanted everywhere. Miss Bettina complained sadly of shortness; the repaid money to Mr. Wheatley had crippled her: and Captain Davenal's letters to Sara dwelt on his embarrassments. They told her privately how "hard up" he was, and in his random meaningless way said he should have to run away to Australia and dig for gold, unless some dropped shortly from the clouds. Captain Davenal's wife, as it turned out, was only an heiress in prospective; but he appeared excessively fond of her, anxious to supply her with every luxury: and we all know that a married captain's pay, without other means, does not accord with luxuries in India.

His wife! Over and over again Sara asked herself how it was possible Edward could have married her, how he could speak of her in the fond manner that he did, if there really existed that impediment. All the trouble and the care seemed to fall upon herself individually—upon her own hidden heart. So long as there existed a grain of doubt, she could not speak of this to Edward; and, besides, the letter might fall into the hands of his young wife.

Personally, Sara had not been annoyed by Catherine Wentworth. Occasionally through the winter and spring she had seen this young woman hovering outside waiting for Neal; twice she had come boldly to the house, knocked, and asked for him. Miss Bettina's keen eyes had seen her once. "Is it one of your nieces, Neal?" she graciously asked; "pray, invite her in." "Oh no, ma'am, she is no relative of mine," returned Neal, with pointed emphasis. Sara's breath had quickened at the colloquy, but it ended there. She was surprised at this immunity from personal annoyance, and wondered how long it would be hers.

It was a coincidence rather remarkable that Oswald Cray should be at the door when Sara returned home from the visit to Caroline. About once in three months he made a call of politeness on Miss Davenal. Sara met him turning away: Miss Davenal was out, and he had left his card. He would have passed her after shaking hands—his visit was not to her—but Sara detained him, her cheeks in a glow at having to do it.

"It is very strange," she exclaimed. "I was but now thinking how I could best get to see you. Do you mind coming in with me for five minutes?"

He returned with her, perhaps all too willingly. A great many of us are tempted to stray from the strict line of duty marked out in our own minds. Sara led the way to the drawing-room, and told him where she had been, and what Caroline said. The declining sun—for the afternoon was drawing towards its close—fell on Oswald as he sat listening to her. It was the same noble face that she had so loved to look upon—calm, still, good; but somehow all its youth seemed to have passed away. The eyes had a look of habitual sadness; some silver threads mingled with the dark chestnut hair. She simply repeated Mrs. Cray's words, almost as a child repeats a lesson; throwing no persuasive tone, no pleading of her own into it, for she felt that she had no right to do so.

"Did Mark Cray wish you to ask me this?" he inquired, as she ceased the tale.

"Not Mark; only Caroline. By what she said, I fancy Mark Cray feels—feels ashamed to ask you anything."

"And he well may," answered Oswald, the old look of pride unpleasingly crossing his face. "I could have borne almost anything from Mark better than deliberate deceit. I cannot, no I cannot forgive it."

Neither spoke for a few moments. Sara had untied her bonnet-strings, and sat with her face a little bent, the eyes raised straight to him in their simple trust. He had one glove off; it was a black one; and he was gently swaying it as his elbow rested on the arm of the chair.

"I cannot quite understand what it is that Mrs. Cray would ask me. She cannot seriously expect that I should pay Mark's debts. His personal debts alone would take, I imagine, a far deeper purse than mine. I am but making my way upwards, and Mark has taken care to put me back to an extent I shall not readily recover. Pay Marcus Cray's debts! It is not within my power, any more than it would be within my will."

Sara was silent, save for a glance. It said how foolish she herself had thought the demand.

"I very much fear that Mark Cray is one of those men who want others to 'pay their debts' throughout life," he resumed. "There are such. Were he free tomorrow he would be embarrassed again in a year. To assist such men is no charity."

"Do you think anything can be done to clear him of the company?"

"Not while he keeps aloof. Mark himself must know it to be impossible, or ought to know it. The only chance for these affairs to be wound up is for him and Barker to come forward."

"Yes, I thought so," she answered. "But—Caroline tells me—they are near upon starving!"

"More shame to Mark!" exclaimed Oswald. "I cannot describe to you how this affair has pained me. Mark is my father's son, and his disgrace seems to be reflected upon me. His hiding himself is the worst part of it all. While he does so he is only prolonging the trouble and the ill. Believe me, it would not be a kindness to help Mark. Let him come forward as a man and a gentleman ought; that would be the best help to him."

Sara felt that he was right; but she felt also that Mark would not come forward; and what was to be the ending?

"They are living in only one room; it is at—."

"Don't tell it me?" impulsively interrupted Oswald, something like anger in his tone. "I would not for the world be made cognisant of Marcus Cray's hiding-place. People have come to me for it times and again; and I am thankful to assure them in all truth that I know it not."

He rose, as if wishing to put an end to the subject, and held out his hand to Sara.

"At least you will forgive me for presuming to trouble you so far," she murmured. "I could not help it: Caroline besought me very piteously."

His dark blue eyes, so earnestly bent on her, gave sufficient answer, even without the pressure of the hand, the tender tone of the low words.

"You should not speak of it in that light. If you knew how great a pleasure it is to me for you to ask me anything! I had almost said it is the only one left to me in my matter-of-fact working life. You and I have none too much of such: it seems to me that we both have to suffer for the wrong-doing of others."

CHAPTER LII

SOMETHING "TURNED UP" AT LAST

You might have taken a picture of the group in Mark Cray's room today, if only by way of contrast to that of yesterday. The living figures were the same: Mark, his wife, and Sara Davenal; but the contrast lay in the expression, in the tone of feeling. Yesterday it had been nothing but gloom, depression, almost despair; today it was all hope and hilarity. The cloud had gone from the faces of Mark and his wife, to give place to almost triumphal gaiety. On Sara's there was a look of pleasure, mingled with perplexity, as if she would rejoice with them, but as yet scarcely understood what there was to rejoice at.

Poor Mark Cray! The very slightest straw of expectancy was sufficient to send his sanguine spirit into the clouds. All this change had been wrought by a letter from Barker, which the eleven o'clock post had brought. Barker, who was another of Mark's stamp, had suddenly discovered, or thought he had discovered, that an English doctor was wanted in Honfleur. He wrote over to Mark, strongly recommending him to come and establish himself, and to lose no time, lest the opening should be snapped up. "There's a goodish many English here," said the letter, "and not the ghost of an English doctor. If an English fellow gets ill he must die, unless he chooses to call in a French surgeon, and the chances are he'll bleed him to death. If you'll believe me, they bled a young English lady this week for measles! She seemed ill, and her friends called in a Monsieur Somebody, with a name as unpronounceable as that mine of ours, and he looked at her, and asked a few questions, said he thought she was sickening for some disorder or other, and therefore he'd bleed her. Well, he did bleed her, and ordered her some drink, called tissan, or some such name—I always shirked my French at school—which it's my belief is made of nothing but sugar and water. Bleeding for measles! The English say to me: 'What a boon it would be if we had a countryman established here as doctor!' So Mark, old fellow, I've thought of you; and my advice to you is, come and try it until something better turns up. I'm off to Paris shortly, but I'll stop here and welcome you first, if you decide to come. I know you hate your profession, and so do I, or I might try the opening myself; but if you don't mind taking it up as a temporary thing, I think you may manage to find enough practice to get along with. Living's cheap over here, and the scenery's lovely, though the town isn't much. Havre is only twenty minutes' distance by steamer; it's over the water—the manche, as they call it; and Harfleur lies by its side, nearer to us still. We have got an English church, you can tell Mrs. Cray, if she's particular upon the point; we had a splendid sermon last Sunday, preached by a stranger. Altogether, it seems to me to be worth your thinking of under present circumstances, and when the horizon has cleared a little, you can leave the place as readily as you come to it."

And this was the golden bait that had laid tempting hold on Mark. Perhaps to a man "under his present circumstances," as Mr. Barker put it, it did look favourable. Estimating things by comparison, it looked more than well. That one present room he was in, the dinnerless days, the blue spectacles, and all the rest of the little disagreeables you have heard hints of, were things to be flown from with the fleetest wings, if they could be exchanged for the position of a flourishing doctor in Honfleur. Mark was on his exalted ropes again, and his wife seemed to have thrown off her sorrow and her ailments.

The first consideration was money. This desirable place could not be reached without some. Even sanguine Mark allowed that. Just a little, to allow of their getting there, and a pound or so to pay for lodgings, and carry them on until his patients came in. He and his wife were deep in the difficulties of the matter when Sara interrupted them. She had come to tell Caroline of her ill-success with Oswald Cray.

But Caroline was in no mood to listen to aught that savoured of non-success, and Sara's news was overwhelmed with the other. Barker's letter was read to her, and Mark enlarged upon it in his sanguine strain.

"I knew something would turn up," said he. "Barker's a right good fellow not to keep it himself. Those continental towns are charming, if you can put up with the sameness: of course they get a little same after a time. Not all of them, though. We stopped three months in Boulogne once, before my father's death, and were sorry to come away from it. Only think how this will set Carine up, after all the late bother."

"I fear Honfleur is a small place to support a medical man," observed Sara, who could look at the proposal more dispassionately than the other two.

"It's a lovely place," fired Mark. "Barker says so. It's renowned in history. If the places he mentions are not of note, I'd like to know what are. History tells us that! Why, it was from Harfleur that the children of one of the kings set sail and were overtaken by a storm and drowned, and the poor old father never was seen to smile again. I'm sure I remember having to learn that in my history. Honfleur a small place! Not support a doctor! You must be saying it for the purpose, Sara!"

"Well, Mark, I don't think it is large; but what I meant was, support an English doctor. Are there enough English living there to do that?"

"Of course there are," returned Mark, whose sanguine mood resented nothing more than a check. "Would Barker say there was an opening if there wasn't?"

She could have retorted that Barker had no more judgment than Mark; but it was utterly useless, and she held her tongue. Besides, she did hope that Mark might pick up some practice, and any change seemed an improvement upon the present state of things.

It seemed that there was only Oswald to apply to in the difficulty, and Sara was asked to do it. She declined. Upon which Caroline, in a defiant spirit—for she was angry with her—said she would go to him herself.

She kept her resolution. At the dusk of evening, not before, Caroline Cray took her way to Parliament Street, her step quick, her mood defiant still; not defiant against anybody in particular, but against the whole world save herself and Mark.

But when she came in view of the house she slackened her pace, going on slowly and cautiously, as one who wishes to reconnoitre the ground beforehand. What was she afraid of? Of meeting any of the wrathful shareholders of the Great Wheal Bang? If so, it was surely a singular coincidence that one of them should at that very moment be at Oswald Cray's door.

He was being shown out by a lady in an inverted bonnet, if the term may be held applicable—brim downwards, crown upwards. Caroline recognised him at once as a Major Pratt, rather an extensive shareholder. Some acquaintanceship had sprung up between him and Mark, and the Major had dined twice in Grosvenor Place. Mrs. Cray shrank into the shade, and drew her veil tighter over her face. He passed without seeing her, and Mrs. Benn, after taking a look out up and down the street, gave the door a bang after him.

Suffering a few moments to elapse, Caroline went to the door and knocked at it. Mrs. Benn had just reached her kitchen, and it went very much against the grain of that amiable lady's temper to have to go up again. Flinging open the door, she confronted the applicant, opposition written in every line of her face, in every movement of her working arms, bared to the elbow.

"I want to see Mr. Oswald Cray."

"You want to see Mr. Oswald Cray!" repeated Mrs. Benn, the tight and disguising veil completing her ire. "Well, that's modest! When folks come here they ask if they can see him—and that's pretty bold for young women. What might you want, pray?"

"I want him," angrily returned Caroline. "Is he at home? If so, show me into his presence."

Something in the refinement of the voice, in its tone of command, struck on the ear of Mrs. Benn. But she was at warfare with the world that evening, and her prejudices were unconquerable.

"I don't know about that. The other night a lady walked herself here, as bold as could be, and said she wanted to see Mr. Oswald Cray; and when I let her go in, it turned out that she had got some smuggled cambric handkechers to sell, and she kept worriting of him to buy for five-and-twenty minutes. 'Mrs. Benn,' says he to me afterwards in his quiet way, 'I don't want them sort of people showed in to me.' But how be I to know one sort from—Oh, so it is you, is it, Joe Benn? I wonder you come home at all, I do! You have been two mortal half-hours gone, and nothing but visitors a-tramping in and out. Perhaps you'll attend to 'em."

Caroline turned instinctively to the respectable-looking man who approached the door. "I wish to see Mr. Oswald Cray. My business is of importance."

"Certainly, ma'am. Is Mr. Oswald Cray alone?" he asked of his wife.

"Yes, he is alone. And I should think he'd like to remain alone, if only for a moment's peace and quiet. He can't get no rest at his work, any more than I can at mine."

She stood before Oswald with her veil thrown back, her face working with emotion, her hands clasped. The table was between them. Benn had closed the door after showing her in, and Oswald, who was busy over some tracings, rose and stared in very astonishment. She gave a summary of her business in a rapid, breathless manner, as if fearing there would be no time left to tell it in. Mark had at length an opening of escape from the present misery, if he could only be helped to embrace it. A surgeon was wanted at Honfleur, and the place was offered to him.

Oswald pressed her to a chair, sat down, and questioned her.

"Why does not Mark come forward and show himself?" he presently asked.

"Come forward and show himself?" she repeated. "What, and get put into prison?"

"He must come, sooner or later. He cannot remain a proscribed man all his life. What end has he in view by remaining concealed? What does he promise himself by it?"

"I don't know."

"But Mark ought to know. He must be aware that there's an imperative necessity for his coming forward; that it is a thing there is no escaping. What does he wait for?"

"He says he wants the storm to blow over first."

"The storm will not blow over. Were Mark to hide himself for ten years, and then appear, it would only raise itself again. The very best thing that he can do is to appear and face it."

"Then he never will—at least, not yet awhile. And, Oswald, I don't think you are a brother if you can wish him to do it. But I did not come here to discuss that," she added. "I came to ask if you would lend me— me, not Mark—the trifle necessary to take us over the water. I will pay you back again if I have to save it up by sixpences."

She betrayed more restlessness of manner than Oswald had ever observed. Since her entrance she had been incessantly taking off and putting on the left-hand glove. He thought her changed. Her face looked worn, her eyes anxious.

"It would be doing you no kindness, Mrs. Cray. Believe me, the only plan open to Mark is to come forward and meet the company. His stopping away makes things worse. Major Pratt was here just before you came in, asking if I could give him news of Mark. I am tempted to wish often that I had no connection with him. Tell him to face this."

"I will not tell him," she answered, her cheeks crimson, her violet-blue eyes shining with a purple light. "If you will not advance me these poor few pounds that I plead to you for there'll be nothing for us but to lie down and die. I have not"—she paused, struggling with her emotion—"I have not had a proper meal these three months; I feel often sick with want. Sometimes I wish I was with Uncle Richard."

Oswald hesitated, whether to ring at once for refreshment or to wait until her emotion had spent itself. He compassionated her with his whole heart.

"What would ten or twenty pounds be to you?" she resumed. "Ten might take us there; twenty would seem like a fortune. Won't you give us a chance of life?"

"It is not the money I think of; it is not indeed, Mrs. Cray. But Mark ought not to go to Honfleur while these clouds are hanging over him."

"Let me have the money," she pleaded; "let me have it. I don't want you to give it me tonight, only to promise it to me. Uncle Richard would have done as much for you."

What was he to do? What would you have done, my reader? Upright, honourable just though he was, he did not resist those tearful eyes, those pleading hands, and he promised her the money that would carry Mark Cray farther and farther away from his creditors.

"And now what will you take?" he asked, ringing the bell.

"Nothing. I don't think I am as strong as I was; and in moments of excitement I feel unable to touch bit or drop. Wine? no, I am not strong, I say; I am not used to wine now; only half a glass of it, and I should hardly walk home." He did not intend that she should walk, he told her; and he induced her to take a very little wine, but she could not eat. Then he gave her his arm downstairs.

Mrs. Benn met them in the hall. Caroline hastily drew her veil over her face, but not before the woman had caught a glimpse of her features. Oswald let himself out at the door, and shut it after him, and Mrs. Benn backed against the wall to recover her amazement.

"Mrs. Cray!—his brother's wife! them that are in hiding! And the last time she was here it was in a coach and four, as may be said, with her feathers in her bonnet and her satins on her back! What a world this is for change—and work! Yes she have just gone out, that there lady, Joe Benn, and the master with her. And you not up to open the door!"

CHAPTER LIII

A NEW HOME

It was an exquisite scene; one of the very prettiest in Normandie. The old town, with its aged and irregular buildings rising one over the other like hanging gardens; the large expanse of water, clear as a sheet of glass, bright with the early sun, stretching out underneath as far as the eye could see; the hills on the right, with their clustering trees and their winding road, leading to the nestling houses in the village of St. Sauveur; Harfleur opposite, standing as a background to the plain of crystal, with its old castle (or what looks like one) conspicuous, and its gentle mounts green and picturesque; Havre lying next it almost side by side, with its immensity of buildings and its long harbour;—these were what may be called the prominent parts of the canvas, but were you looking at it you might find the minuter points of the filling-in even more interesting. The whole made a magnificent tableau, which, once seen, must rest upon the charmed mind for ever.

The Hôtel du Cheval Blanc, situated at one end of the town, was perhaps the best spot in all Honfleur for admiring this panorama—unless, indeed, you mounted the heights above. Standing in one of the end rooms of this hotel on the second floor, whose windows commanded two sides of view, the town and the water, was a gentleman whom you have met before. You could not have mistaken it for anything but a French room, with its bare floor, its tasty curtains, and its white-covered chairs. The tables had marble tops, hard and ugly, but the piano opposite to the fireplace was of tolerable tone.

It was the best of the two sitting-rooms in the hotel; better than the one on the first floor underneath, because these windows were low and cheerful, and those were high and grim. This room and a chamber into which it opened (whose intervening door could never be got to shut, and if shut couldn't be got to open) looked right over to Harfleur. For the matter of that the room opened into two chambers, but the one was closed up just now, and we have nothing to do with it. Like most French rooms, it seemed made up of doors and windows.

The gentleman standing at the window was Mark Cray. Resident at Honfleur more than a month now, this was the first time he had been called in to see a patient. A traveller had been taken ill at the Cheval Blanc in the middle of the night, had asked if there was an English doctor in the place, and Mark was summoned.

It was rather a serious case, and Mark had not left him yet. The door between the rooms was open, but Mark kept as still as a mouse; for the patient, he hoped, was dropping into a doze. Mark had occupation enough, looking out on the busy scene. It was high tide, and the harbour, close on which the hotel was built, was alive with bustle. Fishing-boats were making ready to go out; fishing-boats were tiding in, bearing their night's haul. The short pier underneath had quite a crowd on it for that early hour; women with shrill tongues, men with gruff ones, who were waiting to tow in a merchant vessel drawing near; idlers only looking on,—their babel of voices came right up to Mark, and had he been rather more familiar with the Norman tongue he might have known what all the gabbling was about. A quiet wedding-party, three men and three women, were taking a walk on the pier, two and two, after the performance of the early ceremony; or perhaps it had been performed the previous day, and this one was the continuance of the holiday,—one never knows; the gala caps on the women's heads—such caps as we may see in pictures—flapped out their extraordinary wings: a sober, middle-aged, well-conducted wedding-party of humble life. They probably came, Mark thought, from some few miles inland, where the water and the boats were not everyday objects, as at Honfleur, for their interest in these seemed intense. Every minute there was something new, as is sure to be the case with a full tide at early morning: now, an entanglement of boats at the entrance of the harbour; now, the snapping of a cord and deafening noise in consequence; and now a flat barge, heavily laden, went rounding off to the Seine, to toil up between its green banks as far as Rouen.

Suddenly a noise as of the waters being cut through arose, and Mark, who was watching the toiling barge and wondering what she was laden with, turned his head to the left. The steamer plying from Havre was coming in—had almost reached the port. She had made a fine passage that morning: not twenty-five minutes yet had passed since she steamed out of Havre. The coming in, and the going out again of these steamers, twice each way in the summer days, is the great event in Honfleur life.

In she came to the harbour, swiftly and steadily, rounded the point under the hotel windows, and moored herself in her place opposite the hotel entrance. Mark Cray changed his window now.

Quitting that at which he had been standing, he quietly opened the one which faced the town and inner harbour, and leaned out to watch the disembarking of the steamer's live freight.

"I wonder how many of them will be coming into the hotel to breakfast," he murmured. "I wish—"

What he was about to wish was never known. A voice from the inner room interrupted him. And it was not by any means a feeble voice, but rather a loud one.

"Mr. Cray!"

Mark hastened in. To his surprise he saw his patient, whom he had left in hope of sleep, out of bed and dressing himself. Mark, as medical attendant, made a strong remonstrance.

"I feel a great deal better," was the answer. "I can't lie any longer. Is not that the boat come in?"

"Yes," said Mark. "But—"

"Well, I told you I must go back by her to Havre, if I possibly could. Necessity has no choice."

Mark could only look his amazement. The boat would go out again almost directly, and the patient stood little chance of having time for breakfast. "You cannot go by this boat," he said. "There'll be another later in the day."

"I can't wait for that. I must be away from Havre by an early train."

"But I—I don't know that I can pronounce you out of danger," remonstrated Mark, hardly able yet to realise the fact that a gentleman, thought to be dying in the night, was dressing himself to go off by a steamer in the morning.

"I know these attacks of mine are bad—dangerous, I suppose, while they last; but once over, I am well, except for weakness. And the long and the short of it is, I must go to Havre by the return boat."

Mark Cray saw that further objection would be useless. The chamber-man (I can't help it if you object to the appellation; the hotel had no women servants) came in with warm water, and the traveller ordered a cup of coffee to be ready by the time he got down. Mark went back to the sitting-room. He would stay and see him on board.

The steamer's first bell had rung when the traveller came forth. Mark caught up his hat and gloves. "I hardly know what I am indebted to you," said the stranger, placing a thin piece of paper in his hand. "Perhaps that will cover it."

It was a hundred-franc note. Mark would have given it tack, badly though he wanted money. It was too much; altogether too much, he exclaimed.

"No," said the stranger. "I don't know what I should have done without you; and you have stayed with me the night. That's being attentive. I was taken ill once before in the night at an hotel in France, where there happened to be an English doctor in the town, and they got him to me. But he was gone again in an hour, and in fact seemed to, resent having been disturbed at all. I didn't pay him more than I was obliged."

"Ah, he had plenty of practice, perhaps," cried Mark, rather too impulsively. "But indeed this is paying me a great deal too much. I don't like to take it."

"Indeed it is not, and I hope you will accept my thanks with it," was the conclusive answer.

Mark Cray saw the traveller on board the boat, watched it move off, turn, and go steaming down the port And then he made the best of his way home, the hundred-franc note in his pocket seeming to be a very fairy of good fortune.

They had come to Honfleur the latter end of April; this was the beginning of June; and poor Mark had not found a single patient yet. Mr. Barker had been there to receive them on their arrival. How Barker contrived to live, or whence his funds came, Mark did not know, but he always seemed flourishing. There are some men who always do seem flourishing, whatever may be their ups and downs. Barker was in Paris now, apparently in high feather, his letters to Mark boasting that he was getting into "something good."

Mark ran all the way home; his lodgings were not far, near the ascent of the Mont Joli. Could scenery have supplied the place of meat and drink, then Mark Cray and his wife might have lived as epicures, for nothing could well be more grandly beautiful than the prospect seen from their windows. But, alas! something besides the eyes requires to be ministered to in this world of wants.

It was a small house with a garden before the door, and was tenanted by a widow lady and her servant. Mark and his wife occupied a small sitting-room in it and a bedchamber above; opening from the sitting-room was a little place about four feet square, which served for kitchen, and was let to them with the rooms. They waited on themselves; it is rare indeed that attendance is furnished with lodgings in France. But madame's servant was complaisant, and lighted their fire and did many other little things.

Caroline was in the bedroom, dressing, when Mark returned;—dressing in that listless, spiritless manner which argues badly for the hope and heart. It was a pity their expectations in regard to Honfleur had been so inordinately raised, for the disappointment was keen, and Caroline perhaps had not strength to do battle with it. She had pictured Honfleur (taking the impression from Barker's letters and Mark's sanguine assumptions) as a very haven of refuge; a panacea for their past woes, a place where the English patients, if not quite as plentiful as blackberries, would at least be sufficient to furnish them with funds to live in comfort. But it had altogether proved a fallacy. The English patients held aloof. In fact, there were no English patients, so far as they could make out. Nobody got ill; or, if they did get ill, they did not come to Mark Cray to be cured. Tribulation in the shape of petty embarrassment was coming upon them, and Caroline began to hate the place. She was weary, sick, sad; half dead with disappointment and ennui.

Unfortunately, there was becoming a reason to suspect that something was radically wrong with Caroline. Not that she thought it yet; still less Mark. Dr. Davenal had surmised that her constitution was unsound.

During the time of their sojourn at Chelsea, where Mr. Dick Davenal came so suddenly upon them, and Mark was accustomed to go out to take the air adorned with blue spectacles and a moustache, Caroline, in undressing herself one night, found—or fancied that she found—a small lump in her side, below the ribs. She thought nothing whatever about it, it was so very small; in fact, it slipped from her memory. Some time afterwards, however, she accidentally touched her side and felt the same lump there again. This was of course sufficient to assure her that it was not fancy, but still she attached no importance to it, and said nothing. But the lump did not go away; it seemed like a little kernel that could be moved bout with the finger; and in the week following their arrival at Honfleur she first spoke of it to Mark.

Mark did not pay much attention to it; that is, he did not think there was any cause to pay attention to it; it might proceed from cold, he said, or perhaps she had given herself a knock; he supposed it would go away again. But the lump did not go away, and Caroline had been complaining of it lately.

On this past night—or rather morning—when Mark was at the hotel with the patient to whom he was called, Caroline had been recreating her imagination with speculations upon what the lump was, and what it was likely to come to. Whether this caused her to be more sensitive to the lump than she had been before, or whether the lump was really beginning to make itself more troublesome, certain it was that her fears in regard to it were at length aroused, and she waited impatiently for the return of her husband.

"Mark, this lump gets larger and larger. I am certain of it."

It was her greeting to Mark when he entered and came up to the chamber. She turned her spiritless eyes upon him, and Mark might have noted the sad listlessness of the tone, but that it had become habitual. He made no reply. He was beginning himself to think that the lump got larger.

"And it pains me now,—a sort of dull aching. I wonder if it's coming to anything. Just feel it, Mark."

Mark Cray drew her light cotton dressing-gown tight across the place, and passed his fingers gently over and over it. He was not so utter a tyro in his profession as to be ignorant that the lump might mean mischief. Caroline, with most rapid quickness of apprehension, noted and did not like his silence.

"Mark! what is it? What's going to be the matter with me?"

"Nothing, I hope," replied Mark, speaking readily enough now. "It will go away, I daresay. Perhaps you have been fidgeting with it this morning."

"No, I have not done that. And if the lump meant to go away, why should it get larger? It does get larger, Mark. It seems to me that it has nearly doubled its size in the last week."

"I think it is a little larger," acknowledged Mark, feeling perhaps that he could not get out of the confession. "How long has it pained you?"

"I can't remember. The pain came on so imperceptibly that I hardly know when it first began. What is the lump, Mark?"

"I can't tell."

"You can't tell?"

"I can't tell yet. Sometimes lumps appear and go away again, and never come to anything."

"And if they do come to anything, what is it that they come to?"

"Oh, sometimes one thing and sometimes another," answered Mark lightly.

"Can't you tell me what the things are?" she rejoined, in a peevishly anxious tone.

"Well—boils for one thing; and tumours."

"And what becomes of these tumours?" she quickly rejoined, catching at the word.

"They have to be taken out.

"Is it very painful?"

"Law, no. The pain's a mere nothing."

"And cancers? How do they come?" proceeded Caroline after pause. "With a little lump at first, like this?"

"Cancers don't come there. You need not fear that it's a cancer. Carine, my dear, you must be nervous this morning."

She passed by the remark, hardly hearing it. "But Mark—you say you can't tell yet what it is."

"Neither can I. But I can tell what it is not. I'll get you a little ointment to rub on it, and I make no doubt it will go away."

Caroline was doing her hair at the moment. She had the brush in one hand, the hair in the other; and she paused just as she was, looking fixedly at her husband.

"Mark, if you don't know what it is, perhaps somebody else would know. I wish you'd let me show it to a doctor."

Mark laughed. He really believed she must be getting nervous about it, and perhaps deemed it would be the best plan to treat it lightly. "A French doctor Why, Carine, they are not worth a rush."

"I have heard Uncle Richard say the contrary," she persisted. "That the French, as surgeons, are clever men."

"He meant with the knife, I suppose. Well, Caroline, you can let a Frenchman see the lump if it will afford you any satisfaction. You don't ask me what has kept me out all these hours!" rejoined Mark, changing the topic. "I have had a patient at last."

"Yes, I suppose that. He was very ill, perhaps, and you had to remain with him."

She spoke in the wearied, inert tone that seems to betray an entire absence of interest. When the spirit has been borne down with long-continued disappointment, this weariness becomes a sort of disease. It was very prejudicial now, in a physical point of view, to Caroline Cray.

Mark took out the note. "See how well he paid me!" he cried, holding it to her. "I wish such patients would come to the Cheval Blanc every day!"

The sight aroused her from her apathy. "A hundred-franc note!" she exclaimed with dilating eyes. "O Mark! it is quite a godsend. I shall believe next in Sara Davenal's maxim: that help is sure to turn up in the time of need."

In the time of need! It was a time that had certainly come for them. The surplus of Oswald Cray's twenty pounds, remaining after the expenses of removal were paid, had come to an end, and neither Mark nor his wife had seen their way clear to go on for another week. It was in truth a godsend; more strictly so than Caroline, in her lightness, deemed.

But the money, welcome as it was, did not take the paramount place in her mind today that it might else have done. That was occupied by the lump. Caroline's fears in regard to it could not be allayed, and she insisted upon being taken to a doctor for his opinion, without any delay. Mark made inquiries, and found a Monsieur Le Bleu was considered to be a clever man. He proposed to ask him to call, but Caroline preferred to go to him, her reason being a somewhat whimsical one, as expressed to Mark: "If he has to come to me I shall think I am really ill." Accordingly they went that same afternoon, and the interview, what with Mark Cray's French and the doctor's English, was productive of some temporary difficulty.

They started after their early dinner. M. Le Bleu lived not very far from them, but in the heart of the town, and Mark began by calling him Mr. Blue, sans cérémonie. Mark had learned French at school, and therefore considered himself a French scholar. On the door was a brass plate—"M. Le Bleu, Médecin;" and a young woman in a red petticoat, grey stockings, and sabots, came to the door in answer to the ring.

"Is Mr. Blue at home?" demanded Mark. "Mossier Blue, chez elle?" continued he, tying to be more explanatory, in answer to the girl's puzzled stare.

"O Mark," whispered Caroline, her cheeks flaming at this specimen of French. "Monsieur Le Bleu, est-il chez lui?" she hastily said, turning to the servant.

Monsieur Le Bleu was "chez lui," the girl said to them, and they were admitted. A little middle-aged gentleman in spectacles with no beard or whiskers or moustache, or any other hair to speak of, for that on his head was as closely cut as it could be, short of being shaved, came forward. He asked what he could have the honour of doing for them.

"Speak English, Messeu?" began Mark. "Parle Anglishe?"

"Yas, sare," was the amiable response, as the doctor handed Caroline a seat. "I spack the Anglishe, moi."

"Oh then we shall get on," cried Mark. "Madame here, ma femme, it's for her. I don't think it's much, but she would come. That's my name"—handing in his card.

The Frenchman was a little puzzled by so much English all at once, and relieved himself by looking at the card.

"Ah, c'est ça, Meestare Cr—Cr—Craw," pronounced the doctor, arriving with satisfaction at the name after some stammering. "And Madame what has she?"

"Malade," briefly responded Mark. "Elle a une—une—lump—come in the—the (what's French for side, I wonder?) in the côté. Ici, Messeu," touching himself; "mais il est très petite encore; no larger than a—a—petite pois."

Clearly the gentleman did not understand. Mark had drawn him aside, so that they were speaking apart from Caroline.

"A-t'elle d'enfants, Madame?"

"Oh, oui, oui," responded Mark, at a venture, not catching a syllable of the question, the Frenchman seemed to speak so rapidly.

"Et combien? I ask, sare, how many; and the age of them; the age!" "Three-and-twenty. Vingt-trois."

"Vingt-trois!" echoed the doctor, pushing up his glasses. "Mais, n'est pas possible. I say it not possible, sare, that Madame have twenty-three children."

"Children!" shouted Mark, "I thought you said age. She has not any children; pas d'enfants, Messeu. She found of it before we quitted England—avant nous partons d'Angleterre."

Monsieur Le Bleu tried hard to understand. "Where you say it is, sare, the mal? Est-ce que c'est une blessure?"

"It's here," said Mark, touching him now. "It came of itself—venait tout seule, grande at first comme the tête of an épingle, not much more; à présent larger than a big pea—a petite pois."

The doctor's ear was strained, and a faint light broke upon it. He had enjoyed the pleasure of conversing with English patients before; in fact it was mostly from them that he was enabled to shine in the language.

"Ah, je vois. Pardon, sare, it not a blessure, it a—a—clou—a bouton? I ask, sare, is it a button?"

"It's a lump," returned Mark, staring very much. "A sort of a kernel, you know. Comprends, Messeu?" he questioned, in no hurry, perhaps, to make any worse suggestion.

The doctor gravely nodded; not caring to confess his ignorance. "When did he arrive, sare?"

"When did who arrive?"

"Him—the mal, sare."

"Oh, the lump. Several weeks back—quelques semaines, Messeu. Pas beaucoup de trouble avec; de pain! mais trouve nervous this morning, and—and—thought she'd like a doctor's opinion," concluded Mark, his French completely breaking down.

"Bon," said the surgeon, wishing Mark did not talk English quite so fast. "Madame has not consultayed a docteur donc, encore?"

"Only me," replied Mark. "I'm a doctor myself—docteur moi-même, Messeu."

"Ah, Monsieur est médecin lui-même," cried the doctor, making a succession of bows in his politeness. "That will facilitate our understandings, sare. Has Madame the good—the bonne santé de l'ordinaire?" he continued, coming to a breakdown himself.

"Santé de l'ordinaire!—I wonder what that is," debated Mark within himself. "Vin ordinaire means thin claret, I know. I no comprendre, Messeu," he confessed aloud. "Ma femme eats and drinks everything."

"Is Madame—je ne trouve pas le mot, moi—is she saine, I would ask?"

"San?" repeated the puzzled Mark. "Why, you never mean sane, surely!" he exclaimed in astonishment. "She's as sane as you or I. What on earth put that in your head, Messeu? she doesn't look mad, I hope!"

"I no say mad," disclaimed Messeu. "I ask if she—ah, voilà le mot, quel bonheur!—if she healthy?—if she partake of the good constitution?"

A recollection flashed across Mark Cray's memory of a doubt he had once heard drop from Dr. Davenal as to whether Caroline's constitution was a healthy one. "Elle a porté très bien," was his answer to Monsieur, plunging into his French again. "This mayn't be anything, you know, Messeu."

"I not like these boutons though, sare."

"Which buttons," demanded Mark.

"The buttons you do me the honour to consult for. Je ne les aime pas, soit clou, soit tumeur—n'importe pour l'espèce. In the place you indicate to me it is like to be a tumeur, and she is obstinate."

"Who is, Messeu?" asked Mark, in doubt whether the incomprehensible Frenchman did not allude to his wife's temper.

"She herself," lucidly explained Messeu. "I have held cases that would not terminate themselves at all by anyway, no not for the years."

"Oh, but this is not a case of that sort," said Mark, half resentfully. "A few simple remedies may disperse it."

"Yes, I hope," agreed the doctor. "I would demand of Monsieur if he has tried the sangsues?

"The what?" cried Mark, who had not the remotest idea what sort of a thing "sangsues" could be. "No, I have not tried it."

"J'aime assez la sangsue, moi. She is a useful beast, sare."

Mark nearly groaned, Whatever had "useful beasts" to do with this lump of Caroline's? Useful beasts? "Is it a camel you are talking of?" he asked.

"A camel!" repeated the doctor, staring at Mark. "Pardon, I no understand."

Mark was sure he didn't. "You spoke of useful beasts, Messeu?"

"Yas, they have moche virtue, the sangsues. They do good to Madame; they bite her well."

Mark was never more at sea in his life. Roaming away in search of camels, his home perceptions were perhaps a little obscured in that moment. Bite Madame? What on earth was "sonsues?"

"I speak of the little black beast that long when she full—" pointing to his finger. "You call them litch—litch—"

"Leeches!" interrupted Mark, with a laugh. "I could not understand, moi; Je pensé, Messeu, que vous—vous—speak of wild beasts."

"Yas," said the doctor complacently, "I thought you understand, sare."

"Bon pour Madame, vous dit, Messeu, the sonsues?"

"Je pense que oui. Mais—but I no say trop before the examen of Madame. I would see the hurt, me. I go to your house, sare, and meet Madame without her robe. I go tomorrow at four of the clock after twelve, if that will arrange you."

"So be it," returned Mark, when he had puzzled out the words "Je dis à ma femme que—que—it was of no use for her to call here, herself; you'd want to see her dishabillayed. Je vous merci, Messeu."

And when they were walking home Mark said to his wife how very glad he was to find he had kept up his French.

CHAPTER LIV

A BELL RINGING OUT AT MIDNIGHT

I wonder whether you remember that most charming weather we had in the October of that same year 1861. The first fortnight of the month was more lovely than can be imagined of October; it was brilliant and warm as summer.

Toiling up the ascent of the Côte de Grace went Mark Cray and his wife on one of these delightful days. The word toiling would be misapplied to you, I hope, for the way is gentle, the ascent easy; but it was toil now to Caroline Cray. The past three or four months had made a great change in her: health and spirits had alike sunk. As the lump got larger—we may as well call it by its familiar name—the body got weaker, and she felt the fatigue of walking now. Mark and the weather's unusual beauty had tempted her out, and they had taken the way through the town to the Côte de Grace.

Winding up the shady road—and the sun was too hot not to make the shade welcome—they gained the top. Caroline sat down at once on a bench that faced the sea: Mark stepped forward to the edge, dangerous enough if unprotected, and looked down. Was any panorama ever more beautiful? It happened to be full tide, as it was that morning when you saw him looking at it before—the same view, from the windows of the Cheval Blanc. But the same view, extended, enlarged, altogether grander, from the height on which he now stood.

Mark Cray took a glass from his pocket—it belonged to Monsieur Le Bleu, with whom they were now passably intimate—one of those small but effective telescopes rather rare to meet with. Adjusting its focus, he swept it round the horizon. He turned it to the right, and saw the women winding up the paths on their way from Honfleur market, their unbecoming borderless caps of everyday wear quite plain to him. Opposite was Harfleur, flickering in the light and shade; underneath him, beyond the cultivated precipice, were the walks by the sea—if you call it sea—the road winding on afar, the bathing establishment with its seats, and its linen spread out to dry. Havre itself looked rather cloudy from local smoke, but its entrance was beautifully clear, and Mark put up his glass again to gaze at it. Vessels, great and small, were rounding the point. A large steamer, which he recognised as the London boat, was turning into it, her steam so full, seemingly so close, that he might have fancied he heard its hiss. A fine sailing vessel was being towed out, to commence her long voyage; she looked like an Indiaman. The steamer plying between Havre and Trouville had reached its midway passage; a little funnelled boat was bearing swiftly on in the direction of Fiquefleur bay; an ugly, black-looking yacht had pointed its nose towards the dangerous bar of Quillebeuf; one of the everlasting flat barges was moving imperceptibly up the Seine; smaller boats and more picturesque were coquetting on the manche, and the Honfleur steamer was coming on quickly, leaving Havre far behind her. Mark extended the glass in the direction of the extreme left, and studied the vessels in the distance. Not a breath seemed to fill their sails. The blue and clear waters of the Seine were not calmer than that sometimes turbulent sea: river, manche, sea, were today still as a lake. A fair scene! none fairer throughout the department of the Calvados.

How familiar the scene had grown to Mark Cray he could tell you now. His days unfortunately were days of idleness, and he, had nothing to do but look at it from some point or other of the heights. Mark's fondly-anticipated patients had not come to him: whether the handful of English stationary at Honfleur preferred Monsieur Le Bleu or one of his compatriots to attend them, or whether they were so disobliging as to keep in perfect health, Mark Cray never clearly ascertained. All he could be sure of was, that he was not summoned. His professional services had been called into requisition but three times, including the stranger at the hotel who gave him the large fee. An English maid-servant had come to him once to have a tooth drawn; she could not speak French, she said, and did not like to go to a chemist's shop for it; Mark drew it, borrowing his friend Monsieur Le Bleu's pincers—or whatever you call the things—and charged her three francs. He said five at first; but she slightly reproached him, said she could have it done in a shop fer one and in fact had but three francs with her. So Mark took the three. The third time he was called in to a gentleman who said he had lived in Honfleur six years and had never been ill yet. He had now got an attack of what he called "La grippe," which Mark interpreted into the gripes, utterly unconscious that la grippe in French means influenza in English. The patient soon got well, despite a little wrong treatment at that; and Mark's remuneration was ten francs. That was all he had earned, this ten francs and the three for the tooth, besides the present made him at the hotel.

How were they to get along? How had they got along? They, poor sufferers, looking to the past, could hardly tell. Barker, who was in Paris still, full of wild hopes as usual, had sent Mark once a hundred-franc note in a letter and a promise of more; a little had come to Caroline from Barbadoes, for she had told of her woes; and so they existed somehow. Mark Cray was by no means one to sit down tamely and starve; any hopeless scheme rather than that; but Mark was caged, as it were, at Honfleur, and did not see how to get away from it, or where to travel to. Under happier auspices that "lump" might not have got so large as it was now getting: had that Great Wheal Bang mine only sent its ore to market instead of getting drowned it might never have shown itself at all; or, at least, not for years.

Mark Cray lowered the glass and turned to speak to his wife, who was seated but three or four yards behind him. Towards her left were those enclosed and accommodating gardens of entertainment, where you might order a dinner and eat it al fresco, or where you might take your own basket of provisions and they would bring you drink from the house, wine, milk, beer, lemonade, or coffee, at choice. Behind her, looking beyond, rose the little Chapelle de Nôtre-Dame-de-Grâce, on whose interior walls were recorded accounts of devoted pilgrims who had toiled on crutches up to the shrine, and whose faith Our Lady had rewarded by an instantaneous cure, whereupon they went down rejoicing, leaving their crutches behind them, a memento of the miracle. On the right was the small building called, surely by courtesy, the Observatoire, where innumerable wonders might be seen for two sous. And on the near plateau close around was many a bench similar to the one occupied by Mrs. Cray; the grass forming a carpet underfoot, the trees a shade overhead. A pleasant spot to rest in on a summer's day; a charming tableau to look upon in silence.

"Won't you come and have a look, Caroline I don't think I ever saw the atmosphere so clear on a brilliant day."

She only shook her head by way of answer: wearily, despondently.

"The boat's coming in," he resumed. "Two minutes more, and she'll pass us. You'll like to see her go by."

"I can't Mark. My side is paining me worse then ever. I must not walk up the hill again."

It was a very obstinate side, as M. Le Bleu would express it, a very persistent, provoking lump, and that renowned practitioner—who was really a skilful man, for all his obscure English—had formed his own opinion upon it. It baffled him and his remedies persistently. Even those highly-regarded bêtes, the sangsues, had tried their best to subdue it—and tried in vain. Evidently the effective remedy was not sangsues. The lump had had its own way all these months. It had been growing larger and larger, giving by degrees more and more pain. Monsieur Le Bleu had once hinted his doubts of a "tumeur fibreuse," and Mark had politely retorted that he was an idiot to fancy such things. What the end of it all was to be—of the disease, of the semi-starvation, of the next to impossibility to go on in Honfleur, and the equal impossibility to get away from it, of Mark Cray's little difficulty with England and the shareholders of the old company—would take a wiser head than either Caroline's or Mark's to tell.

This day has been noticed because it was a sort of turning-point in this persistent malady: not a turning for better but for worse. Whether the walk up the hill injured her—for perhaps she had grown really unfit for it—or whether the disease itself made a sudden leap onwards, certain it was that poor Mrs. Cray never went up the Côte de Grâce again. She walked home with Mark very slowly, and fainted when she got in. Mark did not like her look, and ran off for Monsieur Le Bleu. It was only the fatigue, she said to them: but the next morning she did not rise from her bed.

Several weeks dragged themselves slowly on, Caroline growing worse and weaker. An idea arose to her—it may have almost been called a morbid fancy—that if her uncle Richard were alive and at hand, her cure would be certain and speedy. From him it was natural perhaps that her hopes should stray to other English doctors; not young men such as Mark, but men of note, of experience, of known skill; and a full persuasion took possession of her mind that she had only to go to London to be made well. It grew too strong for any sort of counter-argument or resistance; it became a mania: to remain in Honfleur was to die; to go to England and the English faculty would be cure and life.

Mark would have gratified the wish had it been in his power, but how was he to find the money? But for Barker, they could not have gone on at all. He sent a trifle to Mark from time to time, and they managed to get along with it. Once, when they were at a very low ebb Mark had written a pitiful account of their state to his brother Oswald, and a ten-pound note came back again. Ah what a contrast was this to the prosperity that might have been theirs at Hallingham!

Winter had come now. December was in; its first days were rapidly passing; and so intense had grown Caroline's yearning for home that Monsieur Le Bleu himself said to keep her would be to kill her. "It would only be the passage-money, Mark," she reiterated ten times in a day. "I should go straight to Aunt Bettina's. Angry as she was with us for leaving Hallingham, she'd not refuse to take me in. Mark, Mark! only the passage-money!"

And Mark, thus piteously appealed to, began to think he must do something desperate to get the passage-money. Perhaps he would, if he had only known what. But while Mark was thinking of it help arrived, in the shape of a hundred-franc note from Barker. Things were beginning to look up with him he wrote. Perhaps he meant this as an earnest of it.

"Divide it, Mark," she said, with feverish cheeks. "I know how badly you want it here: but I want it badly too. I want help, I want medical skill; divide it between us: fifty francs will take me over."

And so it was done. How willingly Mark would have given her the whole!—but that was impossible. How willingly he would have gone with her to take care of her on the voyage!—but that was impossible. Mark Cray might not show his face in London. He took her as far as he could, and that was to Havre. On the morning after the arrival of Barker's letter and its inclosure they were off: and so great an effect had the knowledge that she was really going wrought on Caroline, that she seemed to have recovered health and strength in a manner little short of miraculous.

She walked down to the Honfleur boat; she would walk; she was quite well enough to walk, she said. As they turned out of the house the postman was approaching it, selecting a letter from his bundle.

"Pour Madame," he said, giving it to Mark.

It was from Sara: they could see that by the handwriting. Caroline thrust it into her pocket. There was not time for reading letters there; the bell of the starting boat had sounded over the town, and they and the man behind, who was wheeling Caroline's trunk on a barrow, had much ado to catch it. They read the letter going over. It was merely a friendly letter of news, the chief item, of which news was, that they were expecting Captain Davenal and his wife hourly from India.

"Then, Caroline, they won't be able to take you in," was Mark Cray's remark.

"Oh, yes, yes, it can be managed," was her answer, so feverishly and eagerly delivered that Mark suspected she feared he might wish to detain her; and he said no more.

But now, when they reached Havre, Mark discovered that he and Caroline between them had made a very stupid mistake as to the departure of the London boat. He afterwards found that they had inadvertently consulted the list of departures for November, instead of December. There was no London steamer departing from Havre that day.

They stood on what is called the English Quai, Caroline weak, sick, depressed. A check of this kind thrown upon one in her state of health is as very despair. Opposite to them was moored a small English steamer; a board upon her, or which was inscribed "for London," indicating her destination. "I could go by that," she said, feverishly; "Mark, I could go by that."

"I don't think it is a passenger boat," was Mark's reply.

They advanced to the edge of the quai and looked down. Two or three men, apparently English, were taking bales of goods on board by means of a crane. "Is this a passenger boat?" Mark asked them.

"No sir. She's for goods."

The answer was unmistakably English. A stout, middle-aged, respectable-looking man, who was seated across a bar, watching the men and smoking a pipe, looked up and inquired of Mark why he asked.

It was the master of the vessel. They got into conversation with him, and told him their dilemma. He was a kind-hearted man, and he offered to convey the lady to London if she could put up with the accommodation. She was quite welcome to go with them, free of expense, he said, and his wife had come the trip with him this time, so she'd not, as it were, be alone on board. How eagerly Mrs. Cray seized upon the offer, rather than go home again to wait a day or two for the regular boat, I'll leave you to judge.

She went at once on board, and the vessel got out of harbour in the course of the afternoon, the master saying they should make London on the afternoon of the following day. But there's no time to linger over this part, or to give any details of the voyage; it is enough to say that the passage, from unavoidable causes, was an unusually slow one, and they did not reach their destination in the Thames until late in the evening. It was a memorable day for us that; Saturday the 14th of December; a day of sadness irreparable for our land. Not quite yet, however, had the hour of calamity come; and the astounding grief, half paralysing England with its suddenness, had not fully broken upon it.

It was getting on for ten o'clock before Mrs. Cray was able to leave the steamer. To present herself, an unexpected intruder, at Miss Davenal's at midnight was not to be thought of. All the way over she had been revolving the news contained in Sara's letter, of which she had made so light to Mark: should Captain Davenal and his wife have arrived, she did not think there would be room for her; and the untoward lateness of the hour increased her difficulty.

There came a thought flashing into her mind, welcome as a ray of light. "I wonder if Watton could take me in for the night?"

Her kind friends, the captain and his wife—and very kind and hospitable they had been to her—had a cab called, and Mrs. Cray and her trunk were placed in it, a tide-waiter allowing the disembarkment. She was then driven to St. Paul's Churchyard.

Watton came out in a state of wonder. A lady in a cab inquiring for her! Perhaps it was not lessened when she recognised Mrs. Cray: but Mrs. Cray looking so awfully ill, so greatly changed! Watton, always of a demonstrative temper, could not conceal her shock of dismay; and perhaps the woman's words first imparted to Caroline a suspicion of what her real state might be. Always with Mark, he could not detect the ravages in her face as a stranger detected them; and the recent voyage of course added its evil effects to her looks.

"Watton, could you take me in for the night?"

She was too fatigued, too worn and ill to enter upon her demand with introductory circumlocution. Watton only stared in reply. This, coupled with Mrs. Cray's appearance, momentarily took her wits away.

"I could lie on a sofa, or on a blanket put down on the carpet, anywhere just for tonight. I don't like to go on so late to Aunt Bettina's; they do not expect me, and will have gone to bed. And you know what she is, Watton."

"To be sure I can take you in, Miss Caroline," returned Watton, recovering herself partially, and warming to the poor sick girl. "Thirty hours in a steamer! My goodness! And they are horrid things always. I crossed over to Jersey once in my young days, and I shall never forget it. Of course you can't go on to Pimlico tonight. Bring in the trunk, cabman."

The trunk was placed inside the passage, the man paid and dismissed, and Watton was closing the street-door, when it was pushed against. She flung it open with an impatient word, and a gentleman entered. Watton was taken by surprise. "I beg your pardon, sir, I'm sure. I thought it was the cabman wanting to stand out for another sixpence."

He passed her with a smile, glanced at Caroline and the trunk, and was making his way up the stairs, when she again addressed him.

"Is there any fresh news, sir?"

"Yes, and it is not good, Mrs. Watton," he replied, turning to speak. "Report says that a telegram has been received from Windsor, stating that there is no hope; that the Prince is rapidly sinking."

His voice was low, his manner subdued; and he raised his hat with unconscious reverence while he gave the answer. Watton lost her breath.

"It may not be true, sir! it may not be true!"

"I trust indeed it is not."

"But, sir, was there not hope this afternoon?"

"According to the report that reached us, there was. Could the Prince only bear up through this one night all would be well."

He passed up the stairs as he spoke. Watton led the way into a sitting-room at the back of the house, and Mrs. Cray followed her in perplexed silence, in eager curiosity, unable to understand the words she had heard.

That great and good Prince, whom England knew too little, and whom to know was to love, was indeed lying in extremis in the castle that had been his many years' home. On that calm, clear, soft December night, when the streets of London were alive with bustle and pleasure, there was a dying bed not many miles away from it, around whose hushed stillness knelt England's sovereign, England's royal children. The gracious and benignant Prince, the faithful consort, the loyal husband, the tender anxious father, was winging his flight away; sinking gradually but surely from those loving arms, those tearful eyes, those yearning prayers, which could not keep him.

London had been shocked that day. Not so shocked as she might have been; for perhaps not one living man within her walls realised to his mind the possibility of the worst. Death!—for him! It was impossible to contemplate it: and from the first duke in the land down to the little pauper boys who sold for a penny the newspapers containing the bulletins none did seriously fear it.

Mrs. Cray listened as one aroused out of a dream. The Prince ill!—ill unto danger! The Prince who had been associated in men's minds as one enshrined in a bright halo of prosperity, in the very sunshine of happiness!—who had looked down from his dizzy height on other men as if he stood above the world! It seemed incredible. Watton gave the details, so far as they were known to the general public; the few days' illness, the apprehensions excited on the Friday, the fluctuating accounts of that same day; the unfavourable news of the morning, the afternoon's opinion of the medical men at Windsor, that if the Prince could only bear up through that one night—the night now entered upon—all would be well. And now the latest tidings were that he was sinking!

Mrs. Cray forgot her own weakness, her fatigue, in these all-absorbing tidings. But it was as impossible for her to believe in the worst for him as it had been for the public. A few minutes of awestruck consternation, and hope reasserted its supremacy in her heart. Nay, not only hope, but a certainty that it "would be well." I honestly believe that such was the prevailing feeling in every breast. It was so hard, it was so hard to look upon the reverse side of the picture.

"We had heard nothing of this at Honfleur!"

"And we can't be said to have heard much of it here until today," was Watton's answer. "It has come upon us with startling suddenness. Oh, if we can but get better tidings in the morning!"

"We shall be sure to do that, Watton," said Caroline, in a low, hopeful tone. "Death surely could not come to him."

Watton made her some tea, and she sat over the fire in the sitting-room while she drank it. She could not eat: generally her appetite was good, but fatigue and excitement had taken it away tonight. She told of her residence in the French town, she hinted slightly at their want of success, and Watton looked grave as she spoke of her side.

"You think the London doctors can cure you, Miss Caroline?"—for the old name came far more familiar to Watton than the new one.

"I did think so," replied Caroline, feeling that the strong conviction of this, which had amounted to a disease in Honfleur, had in some unexplainable manner gone out of her. "I seem not to be sure of it, as I was before I came."

"And shall you make a long stay in London?"

"About a week. I have come for advice only, not to stay to be cured. Aunt Bettina's is no house for me; and perhaps I cannot even stay there at all. Captain Davenal and his wife may have arrived."

She heaved a sigh of weary despondency. Watton urged her to retire; but Caroline felt at rest in the easy chair, and still sat on. It was so long since she had seen a home face, or conversed with a home tongue.

"Who was that gentleman who passed us as I was coming in?" she asked, "he who spoke of the Prince?" And Watton replied that it was Mr. Comyng, a junior partner of the house, and the only one of the partners who resided there.

It wanted scarce a quarter to twelve when Caroline at length went upstairs to a very high bedroom. Whether it was Watton's room, or not Caroline did not know, but it had been made cheery. The curtains and bed were white and pleasant-looking, and a fire sparkled in the grate. Watton would have stayed with her to help her undress, but Caroline preferred to be alone.

When left to herself, she drew aside the window-curtains, and saw that the room faced the front: there stood old St Paul's, grim and formidable, and apparently so close to her that she might have fancied it within a leap. Letting the curtain remain open, she sat down at the fire, before which was drawn a chair as easy as the one downstairs.

She sat with her head pillowed on the high arm, gazing at the blaze, and musing over present events. Their strangely uncertain life at Honfleur, poor Mark's position and poverty, her own malady and the curious manner in which she had lost that eager faith in the result of her journey, her reception on the morrow by Miss Davenal—and with all these thoughts were mingled more prominently the tidings which had greeted her since her entrance.

Unconsciously to herself she dropped into a doze. It was a very foolish thing to do, of course, for she would have been much better in bed; but none of us are wise always. She dozed placidly; and the first thing that in the least aroused her, and that only partially, was the booming out in her ear of a deep-toned bell.

"St. Paul's clock striking twelve," was the supposition that crossed her mind in its state of semi-sleep. But ere many minutes had gone by she became alive to the fact that the striking did not cease, that the strokes of the bell were tolling out fast and loud as—as—a death-bell strikes out.

It has not been the fate of many to hear the bell of St. Paul's Cathedral strike out at midnight. Those who have will never forget it during life. Never, never, will it be forgotten by those few who heard it as it went booming into the air on that still December night, bearing forth its message of woe to the startled hearts of the metropolis.

For a brief moment Mrs. Cray wondered what was the matter. She sprang out of her chair and stood staring at the edifice, as if in mute inquiry of what it meant. And then—when she remembered what had been said that night—and the recollection flashed on her with that heart-sickness that generally accompanies some awful terror—she opened the window and leaned out.

Three or four persons were standing underneath, motionless, still as if they had collected there to gaze at the dark cathedral, to listen to the booming bell. "What is it?" she called out "What does it mean?"

Her voice, raised by excitement to unnatural strength and clearness, was heard distinctly. Those standing below looked up. In one of them she thought she recognised Mr. Comyng. He was standing bare-headed, his hat in his hand, and his solemn answer came up to her in the stillness of the night.

"Prince Albert's gone."

A moment of bewildering suspense, while the mind refused to admit the dreadful truth, and Caroline Cray turned sick and faint. And then the sobbing cry burst from her heart and lips—a cry that was to find its echo from thousands and thousands as the hours went on—

"Oh, the Queen! the Queen! May God help and support the Queen!"

CHAPTER LV

A DESOLATE NIGHT

Yes, he was gone. Great Britain rose on the Sunday morning to the news, for the telegraphs were at work, and the tidings were carried through the length and breadth of the land. And people did not believe it. It could not be! Why, it seemed but yesterday that he had come over in the flower of youth and promise to wed the fair young Queen! Dead! Prince Albert dead! None of you have forgotten the wide gap in the Litany that Sunday morning; the pale lips of the clergymen, compelled to make it; the quivering, breathless hearts that answered to it. But for the remembrance that God's ways are not as our ways, how many of those startled and grieved hearts would have felt tempted to question the why of the stroke, in their imperfect wisdom.

But to return to Caroline Cray, for the night was not yet over and the bell was ringing out. When the first immediate shock had passed, she quitted the window and leaned her head upon the counterpane. A solemn awe had laid hold of her, and she felt as she had never felt in all her life. Her whole soul seemed to go up in—may I dare to say?—heavenly commune. It was as if heaven had opened—had become very near. I may be mistaken, but I believe this same feeling was experienced by many in the first startling shock. This was so entirely unlike an ordinary death; even of one of our near and dear relatives. Heaven seemed no longer the far-off mysterious place she had been wont to regard it, but a home, a refuge, all near and real. It had opened and taken him in; in his early manhood; in his full usefulness; in England's need; when that wife and royal lady had learned to lean upon him; when his sons and his daughters were growing up around him, some of them at the moment in other lands, out of reach of the loving farewell of his aching heart! with his mission here—it so seemed—only half-fulfilled!—it had taken him in before his time, and gathered him to his rest. He did not seem to have gone entirely away; he was only hidden beyond reach and sight for a little while; that same refuge would open for her, Caroline, and others; a little earlier, a little later, and she and all would follow him. Heavy as the blow was in itself, incapable as she was of understanding it, it yet seemed an earnest of the overruling presence of the living God. Oh, what was the poor world in that night, with the strokes of the death-bell sounding in her ears, compared to that never-ending world above, that heritage on which he had entered!

Fatigue and emotion did their most on Mrs. Cray. In the morning she was unable to get up, and Watton wisely and kindly urged that she should not rise at all that day, but take a good rest, and go on to Miss Davenal's on the morrow. So she lay where she was, and listened to that gloomy death-bell, as it periodically gave forth its sound; and the bursts of tears, in her bodily weakness could not be suppressed, but came forth repeatedly to wet the pillow, as she thought of the widowed Queen, the fatherless children.

The day's rest did her a great deal of good, and she rose on the Monday renovated and refreshed. A wish had come over her that she could see a doctor and learn her fate before she went to her aunt Bettina's. She had not come to town with the intention of consulting any particular surgeon;—indeed she hardly knew the name of one from another. Watton, when sitting with her on the Sunday night, had spoken of a noted surgeon living in Westminster, and Caroline remembered then to have heard Dr. Davenal speak of his skill: and she determined to go to him.

She went up in an early omnibus through the mourning streets. The bells were tolling, the shutters were partially closed, men and women stood in groups to converse, sadness pervading every countenance. The surgeon, Mr. Welch, was at home, but she had to wait her turn to be admitted to him.

He was not in the least like Monsieur Le Bleu, except in one little matter—he wore spectacles. A silent man, who looked more than talked; he bade Mrs. Cray tell her case to him from beginning to end in the best manner she was able, and he never took his spectacles from her face while she was doing so.

What she said necessitated an examination of the side. It could be but a slight one there, dressed as she was, but the surgeon appeared to form a pretty rapid opinion. She inquired whether it was curable, and he replied that he could not say upon so superficial an examination, but he would see her at home, if she would tell him where she lived. In her reply, when she said she had no home in London, it escaped her that her husband was a medical man living in France.

"What part of it?" he inquired.

"At Honfleur."

"Honfleur!" echoed the surgeon in an accent of surprise. "Is there sufficient practice to employ an English medical man at Honfleur? I should not have thought it. I was there a year or two ago."

The consciousness of the truth of what the "practice" was dyed her cheeks with their carmine flush. Her eyelids drooped, her trembling fingers entwined themselves convulsively one within the other, as if there were some sad tale to tell. Her bonnet was untied, and its rich white strings (for Watton had affixed these new ones, and taken off the dirty ones) fell on her velvet cloak, nearly the only good relic left of other days. That grave gentleman of sixty, seated opposite to her, thought he had never seen so lovely a face, with its fragile features, its delicate bloom, and its shrinking expression.

She raised her dark blue violet eyes, their lashes wet. Misfortune had brought to her a strange humility. "There's not much practice yet, sir. It may come with time."

He thought he could discern the whole case. It is that of some who go abroad; a struggle for existence, anxiety of mind and body, privation, and the latent constitutional weakness showing itself at last.

One single word of confidential sympathy, and Caroline burst into tears. Her spirits that morning were strangely low, and she had no power to struggle against emotion.

"I beg your pardon," she murmured apologetically when she could speak. "The fatigue of the long journey—the universal gloom around—I shall be better in a minute."

"Now tell me all about it," said Mr. Welch in a kind tone, when she had recovered. "There's an old saying, you know: 'Tell your whole case to your lawyer and your doctor,' and it is a good injunction. I like my patients to treat me as a friend. I suppose; the practice in Honfleur is worth about five francs every three months, and that you have suffered physically in consequence. Don't hesitate to speak: I can shake hands with your husband: when I was first in practice I had hardly bread to eat."

It was so exceedingly like the real fact, "about five francs every three months," and his manner and tone were so entirely kind and sympathising, that Mrs. Cray made no pretence of denial. The practice was really not enough to starve upon, she acknowledged: none of the English residents at Honfleur ever got ill.

"But why did your husband settle there? Was it his first essay?—his start in life?"

"O no. He was in practice at Hallingham before that, in partnership with Dr. Davenal."

"With Dr. Davenal!"

The repetition of the name, the astonished tone, recalled Mrs. Cray to a sense of her inadvertence. The admission had slipped from her carelessly, in the thoughtlessness of the moment. Mr. Welch saw that there was something behind, and he kept his inquiring eyes fixed upon her. She felt obliged to give some sort of explanation.

"After Dr. Davenal's death my husband gave up the medical profession, and embarked in something else. He thought he should like it better. But it—it—failed: And he went to Honfleur."

Her confusion—which she could not hide—was very palpable: it was confusion as well as distress. All in a moment the name, Cray, struck upon a chord in the surgeon's memory. It was his custom to take down the names of his patients ere he entered upon their cases, and he looked again at the memorandum-book before him. "Cray."

"Your husband is not the Mr. Cray who was connected with the Great Chwddyn Mine!" he exclaimed. "Marcus Cray?"

She was startled to tremor. There was no cause for it, of course the fact of its being known that she was Mark's wife could not result in their taking him. But these unpleasant recognitions do bring a fear with them, startling as it is vague.

"Don't be alarmed," said the surgeon kindly, discerning the exact state of the case. "I do not wish ill to your husband. I was no shareholder in the company. Not but that I felt an inclination for a dip into it, and might have had it, had the thing gone on."

"It was not Mr. Cray's fault," she gasped. "He would have kept the water out had it been in his power: its coming in ruined him. I cannot see—I have never been able to see—why everybody should be so much against him."

"I cannot understand why he need keep away," was the answering remark.

He looked at her inquiringly as he spoke. She shook her head in a helpless sort of manner: she had never clearly understood it either.

"Ah well; I see you don't know much; you young wives rarely do. Did you know Dr. Davenal?"

"He was my uncle," she said. "He brought me up. I was Miss Caroline Davenal."

Another moment of surprise for Mr. Welch. It seemed so impossible for a niece of the good and flourishing physician-surgeon to be so reduced, as he suspected she was—almost homeless, friendless, penniless.

She was struggling with her tears again. With the acknowledgment her memory had gone back to the old home, the old days. She had scarcely believed then there was such a thing as care in the world; now—?

"You will tell me the truth about myself," she said, recovering composure. "I came to England to learn it. Pray don't deceive me. I am a doctor's wife you know, and can bear these shocks," she added, with a poor attempt at a smile. "Besides, I seem to know the fate that is in store for me: since Saturday night I have not felt that I should get well."

There was one moment of hesitation—of indecision. Caroline caught at it all too readily. "I see," she said, "there is no hope."

"I said nothing of the sort," he returned.

"But I am sure you think that there is not. Mr. Cray thought there might be an operation: the French doctor said no."

"I cannot tell you anything decisive now. I will come to you if you will tell me where."

She gave him Miss Davenal's address. "I am so sorry to trouble you; I did not think of that. A few days and I shall go back to France."

"No," replied the surgeon. "You must not think of going back. It would not do."

"But I came. And it has not hurt me."

"You must not return."

He spoke in a tone so quietly grave that Caroline did not like it. Could it be that he knew she would be unable to go back? What would become of Mark? what would become of her? But she could not take up his time longer then.

"Is this right?" she asked timidly, as she laid a sovereign and a shilling on the table.

"It's quite wrong," said he. "Doctors don't prey upon one another. My dear lady, do you think I should take money from Dr. Davenal's niece?—or your husband's wife? Anything that I can possibly do for you I shall be most happy to do—and I am glad you happened to come to me."

She went out of the house. Why it should have been she could not tell, for certainly Mr. Welch's words had not induced it, but the conviction of a fatal termination, which had but dawned upon her before, had taken firm possession of her now. Lost in thought as she walked, she missed the turning by which she had gained the surgeon's house, and, found herself at last in a labyrinth, far away from omnibuses and anything else available.

One directed her this way; one directed her that. Weary, faint, unfit to move another step, she found herself at last in a street whose aspect seemed more familiar; but not until she caught sight of a door-plate, "Bracknell, Street, and Oswald Cray," did she recognise it to be Parliament Street.

The temptation to go in and ask to be allowed to rest was strong upon her, but she did not like to do so, and walked on, longing to sit down on every door-step. A little way further and she met Oswald Cray.

When the physical strength has been taxed beyond its power, especially in a peculiar case such as hers, any little break to it of mental excitement either renovates it for the moment or destroys it utterly. It was the latter case with Caroline.

"Mrs. Cray!" exclaimed Oswald, in surprise. "I did not know you were in London."

She caught hold of something in her faintness. Whether pillar, railings, post, she could not have told. Her brow grew moist, her lips white. Oswald hastened to support her.

"I have lost my way," she gasped, leaning heavily upon him. "I missed it when I came out of the surgeon's, Mr. Welch. I came over from Honfleur on Saturday, Oswald; I came to consult an English doctor. I am dying."

"Dying!" repeated Oswald. "No, no, it is only a little faintness."

"Not this. I shall be better of this directly. It is my side. I'll tell you about it when the faintness has passed. I thought there was no hope for me. I know it now."

He was leading her gently, by slow steps, towards the house. "How is Mark? Is he here too?" he asked.

"Not Mark. He cannot come, you know."

"Is he getting on?"

"Oh, Oswald! getting on! There's no practice; and we have not a penny-piece; and—I—I am dying. Oh, if I had not to die abroad! If Mark could but come to me."

"Where are you staying?" he asked after a pause.

"Watton gave me shelter. It was late when the boat got up, too late to go on to my aunt Bettina's, and I called at Watton's, and asked her to take me in. Oswald!—Oswald!—"

"What?" he asked, for she had dropped her voice, and her utterance seemed to be impeded by emotion.

"I heard the bell toll out for Prince Albert! I was close to it!"

"Ah!"

"Oswald! can you realise the fact that he is dead?"

"Not yet; scarcely yet. It is difficult to believe that he is taken, while we are left. It seems to us, in our finite notions, that there's hardly a man in the realm but could have been better spared. But God knows best."

His tone of pain had changed to reverence. There was no more said until they reached his door. He assisted her upstairs to the old sitting-room, the same sitting-room, with the same plans and charts and signs of work on its table. Oswald was a full partner now. Industry—trustful, patient, persevering, fair-dealing industry—had met with its reward. Did you ever know it fail? I never did.

Mr. Bracknell had virtually retired from the firm, leaving most of its profit to Mr. Street and Oswald Cray. Had Miss Sara Davenal been the daughter of the still-living and flourishing physician, on whom not a cloud rested, as was the case in the years gone by, Oswald could have asked for her hand now, and given her a home that even he would have deemed worthy of her.

Not having her, however, or any other lady, as a wife in prospective, he was content to let the home remain in abeyance, and lived in the old rooms, putting up with the comforts and agreeables Mrs. Benn chose to provide for him. The first thing Caroline did, on being placed on an easy chair, was to faint away. It was the only time she had fainted since the day in October when she walked to the Côte de Grâce. Mark Cray gave fatigue the benefit of the blame then, and it was probably due to the same cause now. When Mrs. Benn came up in answer to Oswald's summons, nothing could well exceed her amazement at seeing a lifeless lady lying in the chair, her bonnet hanging at the back by its strings, her gloves on the ground, and Mr. Oswald Cray rubbing her unconscious hands.

The first thought that occurred to Mrs. Benn was one of wonder how she got there: the second, that it was some stranger who had come to the offices on business, and had been taken ill.

"She's married, at any rate," remarked that lady, as she took up the left hand to chafe it. "But nobody would say so to look in her face. She's like a girl."

"Don't you know her?" returned Oswald, glancing at the woman. "It is Mrs. Cray; my brother's wife."

Mrs. Benn gave a shriek in her surprise. "Her! Why, sir, how she's altered! She looks fit—"

"Hush!" was his interrupting caution, for Caroline began to revive. "Can't we improvise a sofa or mattress, or something of that sort, to place her on?"

CHAPTER LVI

In the same house at Pimlico, and in the same attire as of yore, save that the deeper mourning had been exchanged for rich silks, and the black ribbons on the real guipure caps for white or grey, sat Miss Bettina Davenal. She was not altered. She had the same stately presence, the same pale, refined features; she was of a stamp that changes little, and never seems to grow old. Sara had changed more than her aunt, and the earnest, sweet expression, always characteristic of her face, was mingled now with habitual sadness. She wore a robe of soft grey cashmere, its white collar tied with ribbon, and bows of the same ornamenting the lace sleeves shading her delicate wrists.

Miss Bettina stood, grandly courteous; Sara's cheeks were flushed, and she played with a key which had happened to be in her hand as she rose. Oswald Cray had come in unexpectedly, and was telling the story of Caroline; telling it rapidly, before he took the chair offered him. What with the extraordinary nature of the news, and Miss Bettina's inaptitude for hearing, it was a difficult business as usual.

"Come over from Honfleur in a goods-boat, and it didn't get here?" exclaimed Miss Bettina, commenting on what she did hear—for Oswald repeated the particulars Caroline had disclosed to him on her revival. "And where do you say she's lying, sir?"

"In my sitting-room in Parliament Street."

"The boat is?" questioned Miss Bettina, looking at Oswald keenly, as if she thought he had lost his senses. "I beg your pardon Mr. Oswald Cray, I must have misunderstood."

"Caroline is lying there, not the boat. I fear she is very ill. She looks so; and she says she is suffering from some fatal complaint."

"Fatal mistake! I should think so," returned Miss Bettina. "If ever a man made that, it was Mark Cray when he threw up Hallingham. But what's she come for? And why did she go to you instead of to me?"

But Sara had drawn near to Oswald. She had heard the explanation aright, and the words "fatal complaint" frightened her. "Do you know what it is?" she asked. "Is she very ill?"

"She is so ill, if her looks may be trusted, that I should think she cannot live long," he answered. "I came down to you at once. Something must be done with her; we cannot let her go back to Watton's. If you are unable to receive her, I will get a lodging—"

"But we are not unable to receive her," interrupted Sara. "Of course we are not. My aunt—"

"Caroline doubted whether you had room. She has just told me you were expecting Captain Davenal and his wife."

"We are looking for their arrival daily. Perhaps the ship may be in today. But they will not stay with us: Lady Reid expects them there. Did you not know Edward was coming?" she continued, quitting for a moment the subject of Caroline. "His wife's father is dead, and business is bringing them home. She has come into a large fortune."

"Will you let me understand what this matter is?" interposed Miss Bettina.

It recalled them to the present. But to make Miss Bettina understand—or rather hear—was a work not speedily accomplished. She even was aware of it herself.

"I am not myself today, sir," she said to Oswald Cray. "I have not been myself since yesterday morning. When the tidings were brought to me that—that it was all over with that good Prince—I felt as I had never felt in my life before. It is not a common death, Mr. Oswald Cray, or a common loss, even had we been prepared for it. But we were not prepared. That Royal Lady and her children were not prepared; and we can but pray God, who tempers the wind to the shorn lamb, to love and help them."

"Amen!" responded the heart of Oswald.

When there was a real necessity for Miss Bettina Davenal's relenting in her severity, she did relent. She returned with Mr. Oswald Cray, and Sara went with them. On her way she spoke to him about the rise in his prospects, a rumour of which she had heard from Neal.

"Is it true?" she asked, bending forward to catch his answer, as he sat opposite to her in the carriage.

"It is true that my share has been considerably increased. Mr. Bracknell has retired."

"I suppose you will take a house now?"

"I think not," said Oswald. "Single men don't care to set up a house of their own."

"What men don't?"

"Unmarried men."

"Oh," said Miss Bettina. "Do you never intend to marry?"

Oswald laughed. "I have no time to think about it, Miss Bettina."

Miss Bettina did not catch the answer. "Some time ago we had reason given us to think that you were about to marry. Did you change your mind?"

It was a home question. Oswald could have joked it off but for that gentle, conscious, Dent face in the opposite corner. "We have to give up all kinds of fond dreams and visions, you know, Miss Bettina. Youth is very apt to indulge in such: and they mostly turn out vain."

"Turned out vain, did she? I must say I did not think she was in a position worthy of you."

Oswald opened his eyes. "Of whom are you speaking, Miss Davenal?"

"Of you. I was not speaking of any one else."

"But the lady? You alluded to a lady."

"Oh, the lady. You don't want me to tell you her name. You know it well enough. That young Scotch lady whose brother was ill."

He breathed with a feeling of relief. A fear had come over him that his dearest feelings had been exposed to Miss Davenal—perhaps to others. Sara's colour heightened, and she raised her eyes momentarily. They met Oswald's: and she was vexed with herself.

"I shall most likely live a bachelor all my days, Miss Davenal. I believe I shall."

"More unwise of you, Mr. Oswald Cray! Bachelors are to be pitied. They never get a cup of decent tea or a button on their shirts."

"I am independent of buttons; I have set up studs. See," he continued, showing his wrists. "And tea I don't particularly care for."

Miss Bettina thought he was serious. "You'd be happier as a married man, with somebody to take care of your comforts. It is so different with women; they are happiest single—at least, such is my belief—and their comforts are in their own hands."

"The difficulty is to find somebody suitable, Miss Bettina. Especially to us busy men, who have no time to look out."

"True," she answered. But whether she heard or not was another matter. "What's Mark Cray about?" she presently asked, somewhat abruptly. "Doing any more harm?"

"I hear he is not doing any good. There's no practice in Honfleur."

"No politics?"

"Practice."

"Nobody in their senses would have thought there was. Perhaps he expects to get up a mining scheme there, and dazzle the French."

"If he is to do any good for himself, he must come over and get clear of the mining scheme here," observed Oswald.

Miss Davenal nodded her head and drew in her lips. It was not often that she condescended to make the slightest allusion to Mark Cray.

Mrs. Cray was asleep when they entered. She lay on the couch hastily improvised for her, dressed, and covered with a warm counterpane. One hand was under her wan cheek, the other lay outside, white, attenuate, cold. Miss Bettina Davenal took one look; one look only with those keen eyes of hers. It was quite enough, and an exclamation of dismay broke from her lips. Caroline opened her eyes and gazed around in bewilderment.

"Aunt Bettina! Have they brought you to see me? Will you take me in for a day or two until I can go back?"

"I have come for you," said Miss Bettina.

Until I can go back! Poor thing! what had she to go back to? A lodging in a foreign land that they might be turned from at any hour, for the rent could not be paid up; scanty nourishment, care, trouble, almost despair. Only Mark to lean upon, with his wavering instability: his vague chatter of the something that was to "turn up." Better depend upon a reed than upon Mark Cray.

Sara Davenal had drawn back for a moment, that the shock on her own face might be subdued before presenting it to Caroline. Oswald passed round to her.

"Is she dying?" came the frightened whisper.

"Do not be alarmed," he answered. "She looked worse than this when I first brought her in. She has had a good deal of excitement and fatigue these last few days, and that tells upon her appearance."

"Yes—but—do you know there's a look in her face that puts me in mind of papa's. Of papa's as it was the night he died."

It was not often that Sara gave way to emotion. The moisture had gathered on her brow, and her hands were trembling. Oswald gently laid his hand upon her shoulder.

"You are not going to faint, surely, Sara!"

"No, no "—and the slightest possible smile parted her trembling lips. "I used to think I was very brave, but lately—at times—I have found myself a coward. I seem to become afraid at trifles," she continued in a dreamy tone, as if debating the question with herself why it should be so.

"Where's Sara? I thought I saw her."

Sara moved forward at the words. She suppressed all sign of emotion as she stooped over her cousin. Caroline was the one to show it now. She burst into tears and sobbed hysterically.

"If Uncle Richard were but alive! He could cure me."

"Don't, Caroline, don't distress yourself. There are doctors as clever as papa was."

"I kept thinking"—she turned her colourless face to Sara as she spoke—"I kept thinking at Honfleur of Uncle Richard; that if the old days could come back again, and I were at home with him at Hallingham in the old house as it used to be, I should be well soon. The thought kept haunting me. And, Sara, I am sure if my uncle were alive he could cure me. I shall never believe otherwise."

She paused. Sara knew not what reply to make. Miss Davenal did not catch the words, and Oswald leaned on the back of a chair in silence, only looking at her as she lay.

"Why should this conviction have haunted me? Uncle Richard was gone. Mark kept dinning in my ears that there were other doctors as good as Dr. Davenal, and at last I grew to think so too, because they were English. So I came over; I should have had a fever or died if I had not come; and now I see how foolish the hope was, for they can't cure me. Nobody could do it but Uncle Richard."

Miss Bettina had been bending her ear close to the invalid, and caught the sense of the words. "Why do you think nobody can cure you?"

"I feel that they can't. No: Uncle Richard's gone, and there's no chance for me."

They got her ready, Oswald helped her down to the carriage, and she was conveyed home. The only home she would henceforth know in this world. Dorcas stood in the passage, and looked on askance as she entered the house. That the blooming young bride whom she had received into the Abbey at Hallingham little more than two short years before!

Sara gave up her room to her as the most commodious one in the house, herself taking the chamber at the back of it, which had been occasionally occupied by Dick and Leo. Caroline looked round the room as she lay in bed, a curious, inquiring sort of gaze in her eyes.

"Have I been in this room before?" she suddenly asked.

She had never been in it. Her visits to Miss Bettina's, during the prosperity in Grosvenor Place, were not sufficiently familiar to allow of her entering the bedrooms. Sara told her she had never yet been in it.

"I seem to know it all; I seem to have seen it before. I suppose it's a sign that I shall die in it."

She spoke dreamily, alluding to a foolish superstition that she had heard in her childhood, and probably had never thought of since. It was not a very promising beginning.

Miss Davenal wrote a line to Mr. Welch, the surgeon, and he called in the evening. Caroline was better then, calm and cheerful. Her spirits had revived in a wonderful manner; but it was in her nature to be subject to these sudden fluctuations.

"Shall I get well?" she asked, when his examination was over.

"I will do what I can for you. The pain I think can be very considerably alleviated."

It was not a satisfactory answer. To most ears it might have savoured of considerate evasion, but it did not to Caroline's. "Must there be an operation?" she resumed.

"No."

She looked up at him from the depths of her violet eyes, pausing before she spoke again. "Monsieur Le Bleu said there must be an operation, if it could be performed. If, he said; he did not seem sure. It was the only chance, he said."

The surgeon met the remark jokingly. "Monsieur Le Bleu's very clever—as he no doubt thinks. I will see you again tomorrow, Mrs. Cray."

"But—stay a moment. Tell me at least by which day I shall be ready to go back. You can put me in the proper way of treatment, and I will pursue it over there."

"Not by any day. You must not think of returning to France."

She looked puzzled: there was a wild expression in her eyes. "Do you mean that I shall not be able to return at all?"

"Yes, I do. I say that you must not venture upon the shores of France again. We can't think of trusting you to the care of that clever French doctor, you know."

And before Caroline had recovered her surprise sufficiently to rejoin, Mr. Welch had left the chamber and was down in the drawing-room with Miss Davenal. She bent her head as she waited for his opinion.

"Do you wish for the truth, ma'am?" he asked.

"Wish for what?" repeated Miss Bettina, putting her hand to her ear.

"The truth."

"Do I wish for the truth?" she retorted, affronted at the question. "Sir, I am the daughter of one surgeon and the sister of another; I don't know to whom the truth may be told if not to me. It is necessary that I should know it."

Mr. Welch gave her the truth: that there was no hope whatever. At least, what he said was equivalent to that.

"And the operation that she talks of?"

"It cannot be performed. The case is not an ordinary one."

Miss Bettina was for a minute silent. "My brother, Dr. Davenal, always said Caroline had no constitution."

"Dr. Davenal was right," returned the surgeon. "Mrs. Cray is one—if I may form a judgment upon so short an acquaintance—who could never, even under the most auspicious surroundings, have lived to grow old."

"I remember a remark he made to me after Caroline's marriage with Mark Cray was fixed—that it was well she should marry a doctor, for she'd need watching. A fine doctor, indeed!" continued Miss Bettina, irascibly, as she recalled Mark's later career. "If my poor brother had but known! I suppose it is all this disgrace that has brought it on!"

"It may have hastened it," said the surgeon. "But this, or some other disease, would inevitably have developed itself sooner or later. The germs were within her."

"And now what can be done for her?"

"Nothing in the world can be done for her, as regards a cure. We must try and alleviate the pain. That she will now grow worse rapidly there's not a doubt. Miss Davenal, she must be kept tranquil."

It was all very well for Mr. Welch to say she must be kept tranquil; but Caroline Cray was one who had had an absolute spirit of her own all her life, and an excitable one. When Miss Bettina went up to her room after the departure of the surgeon she found her in a wild state. Her cheeks were crimson with incipient fever, her eyes glistening. Sara, terrified, was holding her down in bed: begging her to be reasonable.

"I want to go back at once, Aunt Bettina," she exclaimed, throwing out her arms in a sort of frenzy. "He says I can't go back to France, but I will go. What does he know about it, I wonder? I was well enough to come, and I am well enough to go back! Be quiet, Sara! Why do you wish to prevent my speaking? You'll send me back today, won't you, Aunt Bettina?"

"I'll send for a strait waistcoat and put you into that," shrilly cried Miss Bettina in her vexation. "This is a repetition of the childishness of the old days."

"I won't be separated from Mark. Though he has been mistaken and imprudent, he is still my husband. It's a shame that Mr. Welch should want to keep me here! Don't you be so cruel as to side with him, Aunt Bettina."

For once in her life Miss Bettina Davenal lent herself to an evasive compromise. She promised Caroline that she should go back when she was a little stronger, perhaps in two or three days, she said. And it had the desired effect. It soothed away the invalid's dangerous excitement, and she turned round on her pillow and went to sleep quietly.

But as the days went on, and the disease—as the surgeon had foretold—rapidly developed itself, it became plain to Mrs. Cray herself that returning to France was out of the question. And then her tone changed. She no longer prayed in impatient words to be sent: she bewailed in impassioned tones that she must die away from her husband. One day, towards the end of December, it almost seemed that her brain was slightly affected, perhaps from weakness. She started suddenly from the sofa in the drawing-room, where she was reclining, and seized hold of the hands of her aunt in a wild manner.

"O Aunt Bettina! Aunt Bettina! if I had not to go over there to die!"

"Over where?" cried Miss Bettina. "What are you talking of, child?"

"There. Honfleur. If I had not to go! If I could but stop in my own land, among you to the last! It may not be for long!"

Miss Bettina, what with the suddenness of the attack and her own deafness, was bewildered. "I don't hear," she helplessly said.

"They have got two cemeteries, but I'd not like to lie in either," went on Caroline. "Mark won't stop in the town for ever, and there'd be nobody to look at my grave. Aunt, aunt, I can't go over there to die!"

"But you are not going there," returned Miss Bettina, catching the sense of the words. "You must be dreaming, Caroline. You are not going back to Honfleur."

"I must go. I can't die away from Mark. Aunt, listen!" she passionately continued, clasping the wrist of Miss Bettina until that lady felt the pain. "It is one of two things: either I must go to Honfleur, or Mark must come here. I cannot die away from him."

The cry was reiterated until it grew into a wail of agony. She was suffering herself to fall into that excess of nervous agitation so difficult to soothe, so pernicious to the sick frame. Sara came in alarmed, and learned the nature of the excitement. She leaned over the sofa with a soothing whisper.

"Dear Carine! only be quiet: only be comforted! We will manage to get Mark here."

The low tone, the gentle words, seemed partially to allay the storm of the working brain. Caroline turned to Sara.

"What do you say you'll do?"

"Get Mark over to London."

She thought for a moment, and then shook her head and spoke wearily, a wailing plaint in her tone.

"You will never get him over. He is not to be got over. I know Mark better than you, Sara. So long as that miserable Wheal Bang hangs over his head he will not set his foot on English ground. I have heard him say so times upon times since he left these shores, and he will not break his word. He is afraid, you see. O Aunt Bettina!" throwing up her arms again in renewed excitement—"what an awful mistake it was!"

"What was a mistake?" returned Miss Bettina, catching the last word and no other.

"What!" echoed the unhappy invalid in irritation. "The quitting Hallingham; the past altogether. It was giving up the substance for the shadow. If we had but listened to you! If Mark had never heard of the Great Wheal Bang!"

Oh, those ifs, those ifs! how they haunt us through life! How many of us are perpetually giving up the substance for the shadow!

CHAPTER LVII

DREADFUL TREACHERY

Mr. Mark Cray stood on the little bit of low stony ground that bordered the coast at Honfleur, just outside the entrance of the harbour. Mr. Mark was kicking pebbles into the water. Being in a remarkably miserable and indecisive state of mind, having nothing on earth to do, he had strolled out of his lodgings anywhere that his legs chose to carry him; and there he was, looking into the water on that gloomy winter's evening.

But pray don't fear that he had any ulterior designs of making himself better acquainted with its chilly depths. Men in the extremity of despair have been known to entertain such; Mark Cray never would have dreamt of it. There was an elasticity in Mark's spirit, a shallowness of feeling quite incompatible with that sad state of mind hinted at, and the most prominent question pervading Mark, even now was, how long it would be before something "turned up."

Not but that Mark Cray was miserable enough; in a bodily sense, however, rather than a mental. It was not an agreeable state of things by any means to have no money to go on with; to be wanting it in a hundred odd ways; to be told that if he did not pay up at his lodgings that week he must turn out of them—and the French have an inconvenient way of not allowing you to evade such mandates. It was not pleasant to be reduced to a meal or so a day, and that not a sumptuous one; it was not convenient to be restricted to the pair of boots he had on, and to know that the soles were letting in the wet; it was not cheery to be out of charcoal for the cooking réchauds, or to have but a shovelful of coals left for the parlour; moreover and above all, it was most especially annoying and unbearable not to have had the money to pay for a letter that morning, and which, in consequence of that failure, the inexorable postman had carried away with him.

Mrs. Cray's assertion—that her husband never would be got over to London so long as the formidable Wheal Bang threatened danger—proved to be a correct one. Mark had declined the invitation to go. News had been conveyed to him in an unmistakably impressive manner of the state his wife was in, and an urgent mandate sent that he should join her. Oswald only waited his consent to forward him funds for the journey; and poor Caroline hinted in a few private lines that he could choose a steamer which would not make the port of London until after dark, and could wear his spectacles in landing. All in vain. Mark Cray had somehow contrived to acquire a wholesome terror of the British shores, and to them he would not be enticed.

But—has it ever struck you in your passage through life how wonderfully things work round? Caroline Cray was dying; was wanting her husband to be by her side and see the last of her, as it was only right and natural she should; but he—looking at things as he looked at them—was debarred from going to her; it was—judging as he judged—a simple impossibility that he should go. And this great barrier was turning her mind to frenzy, was making a havoc of her dying hours, and increasing her bodily sufferings in an alarming degree.

It did seem an impossibility. If Mark Cray refused to venture to his own land so long as the Wheal Bang held its rod over him, it was next door to certain that he could not come at all. The Wheal Bang's shareholders would not relax their threats except on the payment of certain claims, and who would be sufficiently philanthropic to pay them? Nobody in the wide world. So there appeared to be no hope of Mark's return; and the knowledge that there was not was entirely taking from Caroline Cray that tranquillity of mind and body which ought if possible to attend the last passage to the tomb: nay, it was keeping her in a state of excitement that was pitiable for herself and for all who beheld her. "If Mark could but come!" was the incessant cry night and day. "I can't die unless Mark comes."

You have heard that beautiful phrase, "Man's extremity is God's opportunity," and though it may strike you as almost irreverent to introduce any matter connected with Mark Cray as an exemplification of it, what came to pass was surely very like a proof of the truth of that phrase. Poor, erring, shallow-pated Mark! even he was remembered, neglectful as he had been of the Great Remembrancer.

While Caroline was lifting her hands to heaven with a vain cry in which there was no trust; while it seemed to all that there was no human feasibility of bringing Mark to England, that feat was accomplished in the easiest and most unexpected manner. Is it too much to say that a Higher Power was at work in answer to that poor woman's despairing cry?—though the human agencies employed were of the least exalted.

Mr. Barker, who was doing something grand and good (good in his sense) in Paris, found it necessary for his own plans to pay a visit to London. And when there, he, to use his own phrase got "dropped upon;" in other words he fell into the still outstretched hands of the Great Wheal Bang. That it was unexpected to himself there's no doubt; for he was one of those men who believe implicitly in their own luck. Once in the mesh, Barker resolved to make the best of it. He had done nothing wrong, nothing that he could be punished for, and he carelessly told them that his only motive in not surrendering beforehand was the bother of having the accounts to go over. Perhaps it really was so.

Mr. Barker's usual luck attended him now. After he was arrested and had been kept in durance for four days, the shareholders released him. The very shareholders themselves released him; the wronged, imitated, angry shareholders! Surely there was some charm in Barker's tongue! He talked them over to the most miraculous degree; and they took him out of prison, somebody going bail for the single debt on which he had been taken. Now that the thing had come to a crisis Barker was as eager as they were to get it to a settlement, and he went to work with a will. A settlement, however, could not be come to without the presence of Mark Cray; Mark and Barker were both made bankrupts, and it was necessary that Mark should come over—or else never come over any shore. So Barker wrote for him.

We left Mark standing on the water's edge. He was all unconscious of these doings at home which so nearly affected him; and he stood there speculating as to what news the letter, refused to him in the morning, contained. By some mischance Barker had neglected fully to prepay it; he had put on a fourpenny stamp, but the letter turned out to be over weight by a hair's breadth, and of course the Honfleur postal authorities declined to give it up.

"What he's doing in London puzzles me," cogitated Mark,—for he had recognised the writing on the letter as Barker's. "He told me he should not show himself there until the bother was over. What took him there now, I wonder?"

He stopped to single out a particularly shiny stone imbedded in the mud, lifted it up with his toe, and kicked it into the water. A little shrimping-boat was making towards him, for it was low tide, laden with its spoils of the day. But it was not very near yet.

"It's well that she should have gone over as she did," he resumed, his thoughts reverting to his wife. "Heaven knows I should like to be with her; but she has all she wants there, and here she'd have nothing. I wish I could be with her! As to their saying—that Welch, or whatever his name is: I don't remember any great light of that name—that she's incurable, I don't believe it. That old Blue said the same, or wanted to say it—such jargon as the fellow talked to be sure!—but Blue's nothing better than an old woman. By the way, I wonder how long Blue intends to stop away! It's fine for these French fellows, taking a holiday when they choose, and leaving their patients to a confrère! I wish he had left me the confrère on the occasion, t'would have been a few francs, at any rate, in my pocket. The French wouldn't have had that, I suppose! their envious laws won't permit an Englishman to practice on them. Oh, if some rich countryman of one's own would but get ill!"

Mark Cray strolled a few steps either way, and halted again in the same place as before; he kicked six stones into the water, one after the other, the seventh was an obstinate one, and would not come out. Dull and dreary did the waves look that evening, under the grey and leaden sky. That's speaking rather metaphorically, you know, for in point of fact there are no waves off Honfleur, except in the stormiest of weather.

That Mark Cray's condition was a forlorn one nobody can dispute. He had no friends or acquaintance in the town; a latent, ever-present consciousness of their straits, their position and its secrets, had caused him and his wife to abstain from making any, And one or two English residents who had shown themselves disposed to be friendly were repulsed at the onset. Not a single person within reach could Mark Cray apply to with the slightest justifiable plea of acquaintanceship and say, Lend me sixteen sous; that I may pay for a letter! Even Monsieur Le Bleu, as you have gathered from his soliloquy, was away. But Mark wished much to get that letter, and he was thinking how he could get it at this very moment as he looked out across the water to the opposite coast, to the dark cloud that hung over Harfleur.

"'Twould be of no use going to the post-office unless I took the money," he soliloquised. "They'd never let me have it without. Stingy old frogs! What's sixteen sous that they can't trust a fellow? Help must come to me soon from some quarter or other; things can't stand in their present plight. That very, letter may have money in it."

Grumbling, however, would not bring him the letter, neither would kicking pebbles into the manche: Mr. Mark Cray grew tired of his pastime, and turned finally away from it. He sauntered through the waste ground underneath the side windows of the hotel, his ears nearly deafened by the noise of the rough boys who were quarrelling in groups over their marbles, made a détour across the bridge, glanced askance at the slip of building grandly designated Bureau des Postes, and turned off towards his home. It was a soft, calm evening in January, gloomy enough overhead, but in the west the sky was clearing, and a solitary star came peeping out, imbedded like a diamond in its grey setting. To a mind less matter-of-fact than Mark Cray's that star might have seemed as a ray of hope; an earnest that skies do not remain gloomy for ever.

Mark turned in at his little garden, and was about to ring gingerly at the house door; as one, not upon the most cordial terms with a frowning landlady, likes to ring; when a voice in the road greeted him.

"Bon soir!"

"Ben soir," returned Mark, supposing it was but the courteous salutation of some chance passer-by, and not troubling himself to turn his head.

"Et madame? quelles nouvelles avez-vous d'elle?"

Mark wheeled round. It was Monsieur Le Bleu.

Mark Cray extended his hand, and his face lighted up. In his desolation even this French doctor was inexpressively welcome.

"I didn't know you were back, Mr. Blue: savais pas que vous retournez, messeu," added he, taking his customary plunge into the mysteries of French.

"I come from return this after-midday," said the surgeon. "I ask, sare, if you have the news from madame?"

"She's worse, and can't come back," said Mark. "Plus malade. Not to be cured at all, they say, which I don't believe; pas croyable; messeu. I don't believe the English médecin understands the case. Non! jamais."

"Do I not say two—three—four months ago, me? I know she not curable I feel sure what it was. You call it 'lump' and 'bouton'—bah! C'est une tumeur fibreuse. I say to you, mon ami, you—tiens! c'est le facteur!"

For the facteur had come up at an irregular hour, and this it was which had caused Monsieur Le Bleu's remark of surprise. The bureau des postes had despatched him to offer the letter a second time to Mark.

"Has monsieur got the money now?" he demanded in quick French, which was a vast deal more intelligible to his French auditor than his English one. "If not, our bureau won't be at the pains to offer the letter a third time, and monsieur must get the letter from the bureau himself if he wants it."

What with the amount of French all at once and the embarrassment of the situation, Mark Cray devoutly wished the postman underneath the waters of the manche. That functionary, however, stood his ground where he was, and apparently had no intention of leaving it. He bent over the gate, the letter in his outstretched hand. Monsieur Le Bleu looked on him with some interest, curious to know why the letter had been refused. He inquired why of Mark, and Mark muttered some unintelligible words in answer, speaking in French so excessively obscure that the surgeon could not understand a syllable.

So he turned for information to the facteur. "Did Monsieur dispute the charge?" he asked.

"Not at all," replied the man. "It was not a dispute as to charge. The English Monsieur had no money. It was a double letter: sixteen sous."

"Ah, no change," said Monsieur Le Bleu, with a delicacy that many might have envied, as he turned his eyes from Mark Cray's downcast face. "It's a general complaint. I never knew the small change so scarce as it is: one can get nothing but gold. Hold, I'll take the letter from you, facteur, and monsieur can repay me when he gets change."

The surgeon handed the sixteen sous to the postman, and gave the letter to Mark. Mark spoke some obscure words about repaying him on the morrow, and broke the seal.

There was still light enough to see, though very obscurely, and Mark Cray's dazed eyes fell on a bank-note for £5. The surgeon had bade him goodnight, and was walking away with the postman: Mark Cray was only half-conscious of their departure. Debt did not affect Mark as it does those ultra-sensitive spirits who can but sink under its ills: nevertheless, he did feel as if an overwhelming weight had been taken from him.

He rang at the bell, loudly now, feeling not so afraid of madame, should she answer it. And he lighted his little lamp and read the letter. Read it almost in disbelief, half doubting whether its good news could indeed be true. For Mr. Barker had written all couleur de rose: and a very deep rose, too.

The Wheal Bang had come to its senses, and the worry was over. He, Barker, was upon confidential terms with all the shareholders, shook hands with them individually thrice a-day. There would be no fuss, no bother; the affairs were being wound up in the most amicable manner, and Mark had better come over without an hour's delay, and help. The sooner they got it done, the sooner they should be free to turn their attention to other matters, and he, Barker, had a glorious thing on hand just now, safe to realise three thousand a-year.

Such were the chief contents of the letter. Whether Barker believed in them fully himself, or whether he had dashed on a little extra colouring as to the simplification of affairs relative to the Great Wheal Bang, cannot be told. It may be that he feared hesitation still on the part of Mark Cray, and wished to get him at once over. In point of fact, Mark's presence was absolutely necessary to the winding-up.

Mark yielded without the slightest hesitation. If Mark Cray had confidence in any one living being, it was Barker. He forthwith set about the arrangements for his departure. It would take more than the five-pound note to clear all that he owed in Honfleur; so he paid madame, and one or two trifles that might have proved productive of a little inconvenience at the time of starting, and got away quietly by the boat to Havre, and thence to London.

But, oh! the treachery of man! When the steamer reached the metropolis, Mark Cray walked boldly ashore in the full glare of day, never so much as shading his eyes from the sun with those charming blue spectacles you have heard of, never shrinking from the gaze of any mortal Londoner. Mark's confidence in the good-fellowship of the Wheal Bang's shareholders was restored, his trust in Barker implicit: if he felt a little timid on any score, it was connected with his clothes, which certainly did not give out quite so elegant a gloss as when they were spick and span new. Mark stood on the quay, after landing, and looked round for Barker, whom he had expected would be there to meet him.

"Cab, sir?"

"No," said Mark.

"I'll wait here a minute or two," decided Mark to himself. "Barker's sure to come. I wrote him word what time we might expect to be in—though we are shamefully late. He can't have been and gone again!"

Somebody came up and touched him on the shoulder. "Mr. Marcus Cray, I believe?"

Mark turned quickly. "Well?" said he to the intruder, a shabby-looking man.

"You are my prisoner, sir."

"What?" cried Mark.

"You are my prisoner, sir," repeated the stranger, making a sign to another man to come closer.

Mark howled and kicked, and for a moment actually fought with his assailants. It was of course a senseless thing to do; but the shock was so sudden. He had felt himself as secure, stepping on those shores, as any grand foreign ambassador could have felt; and now to find himself treacherously pounced upon in this way was beyond everything bitter. No wonder that for the minute Mark was mad.

"It can't be!" he shrieked; "you have no warrant for this. I am free as air; they wrote me word I was."

"Would you like a cab, sir?" inquired the official civilly, but not deigning to answer. "You can have one if you like. Call one, Jim."

A cab was called; the prisoner was helped into it and driven away—he was too bewildered to know where.

And that's how Mr. Mark Cray was welcomed to London. His rage was great, his sense of injury dreadful.

"Only let me come across Barker!" he foamed. "He shall suffer for this. A man ought to be hung for such treachery."

Mark Cray was, so far, mistaken. Barker was as innocent in the arrest as he was. An accident had prevented his going down to meet the Havre steamer.

CHAPTER LVIII

THE GALLANT CAPTAIN HOME AGAIN

Captain Davenal and his wife had been expected in England in December—as you have heard; but the time went on, and February was at its close before they arrived. They had been compelled to land at the Cape in consequence of the illness of Mrs. Davenal, and had to remain there some time. She had come into a very large fortune on the death of her father; a considerable portion of it was settled upon her, and the rest, a munificent sum, lapsed to her husband. So Captain Edward Davenal was once more at his ease in this world of changes.

Gay, handsome, free, sunny, it might have been thought that not an hour's care had ever been upon him. No allusion to a certain dark episode of the past escaped his lips when he and his sister met: there were no signs that he so much as remembered such a trouble had ever been. They were the present guests of Lady Reid, and would remain so for a short time: It was Captain Davenal's intention to take a furnished house for a term. His leave of absence was for two years; but they did not care to be stationary in London the whole of the period. Sara was charmed with his wife: a gentle, yielding, pretty thing, looking so young as to be a girl still, and dividing her love between her husband and infant son, a fine young gentleman born at the Cape. A dread fear assailed Sara Davenal's heart as she looked upon her; for that curious matter, touching the young woman who claimed to be connected with Captain Davenal, had never been cleared up. Not since the previous December had Sara once observed her approach the house: but she had twice seen her in conversation with Neal at the end of the street, the last time being the very day of the arrival of Captain Davenal. It was altogether strange in Sara's opinion if the young woman fancied she really had a legal claim of the nature she mentioned on Captain Davenal, why had she not asserted it openly? If she had no such claim, if she were an impostor, for what purpose had she put the claim forth? There had been no demand for silence-money; no attempt at extortion. However it might be, Sara's duty was plain, now Captain Davenal had arrived—to acquaint him with the circumstances.

"I have some papers to give you," Sara whispered to her brother at Lady Reid's, the night of his arrival there.

"Papers? O yes, I suppose so. I shall be with you tomorrow."

So he had not quite forgotten the affair. On the conclusion of the matter with Mr. Alfred King Sara had sealed up certain papers and receipts according to the written directions of Dr. Davenal; and these she waited to put into her brother's hand.

Mrs. Cray was with them still. She had taken to her bedroom entirely now, and was gradually dying. Mark was with her. His difficulty with the Great Wheal Bang's shareholders, and particularly with that one cautious shareholder who had saluted Mark so unpolitely on his landing from Havre, was virtually over: Mark enjoyed liberty of person again, and things were in process of adjustment. Miss Davenal so far overcame her repugnance to Mark as to allow him to be in her house, but it was only in consideration of Caroline's dying state. They could do nothing for her. They painted her clothes with iodine as she lay on the sofa day after day before the chamber fire; it was the only thing that brought any alleviation to the pain.

It happened that Captain Davenal's first visit to the house was paid at an opportune moment, in so far as that his interview with his sister was free from fear of interruption. Miss Davenal had gone to Lady Reid's, to see and welcome the travellers. Neal was in attendance upon her, and Caroline was asleep. Mark Cray was in the City; he had to go there frequently, in connection with the winding-up of the company of the Great Wheal Bang.

Captain Davenal came in, all joyous carelessness, telling Dorcas, who admitted him, that she looked younger and handsomer than ever: and poor Dorcas—who was not young at all, and had never been handsome in her life—felt set up in vanity for a month to come. Sara was in the drawing-room. It was the first time of their being alone, and Captain Davenal held her before him and scanned her face.

"What has made you get so thin?"

"Am I thin?" she returned.

"Dreadfully so. I have been telling Dorcas that she's handsomer than ever, but I can't say the same of you. What is the cause, Sara?"

"I think people do get thin in London," she replied with some evasion. "But let me be rid of my charge, Edward."

She went to her bedroom and brought down Dr. Davenal's desk. To Edward's surprise he saw that it was bound round with a broad tape and sealed. When Sara had placed the papers in the desk, received from Mr. Alfred King, she had immediately sealed up the desk in this manner; a precaution against its being opened.

"What's that for?" exclaimed Captain Davenal, in his quick way, as he recognised the desk and to whom it had belonged. "Did my father leave it so?"

Sara replied by telling him her suspicions of the desk's having been opened; and that she had deemed it well to secure it against any future inroads when once these papers were inclosed in it.

"But who would touch the desk?" he asked. "For what purpose? Was young Dick at home at the time?"

"Dick was not at home. But Dick would not touch a desk. I would not answer for Dick where a jam cupboard is concerned; but in anything of consequence Dick's as honourable as the day. I suspected Neal, Edward."

"Neal!"

"I did. I feel half-ashamed to say so. Do you remember telling me that papa had a suspicion or doubt whether Neal had not visited some of his letters?"

"I remember it. I thought my father was wrong. Neal! Why, Sara, I'd as soon suspect myself."

"Well, I can only tell you the truth—that when I found cause to fear this desk had been surreptitiously opened, my doubts turned to Neal. You see, we have no one about us but him and Dorcas; and Dorcas I am certain is trustworthy. But I admit that it was in consequence of what you told me that I cast any doubt on Neal. However it may have been, I deemed it well to secure the desk afterwards."

She had been opening the desk as she spoke, and she took from it a sealed packet and handed it to Captain Davenal. He opened it at once; glanced over its contents, two or three papers, one by one, and slightly drew in his lips.

"What a shame!" he burst forth.

She did not like to ask questions. She only looked at him.

"That they should have bled my father in this manner. Scoundrels! I was away, therefore the game was in their own hands. Did you read these papers, Sara?"

"I was obliged to read them; to see that they tallied with copies that papa had left. He left written instructions that I should do so."

"To whom was this money paid?"

"To Mr. Alfred King. Don't you see the receipts?"

"I'd walk ten miles before breakfast any morning to see the fellow hung. It's what he'll come to."

"He told me that he and you had once been friends," she said in a half-whisper.

"And so we were. I believed in the fellow: I had no suspicion that he was a villain, and I let him draw me into things from which I could not extricate myself. I was a fool; and I had to pay for it."

In Sara's inmost heart there arose unbidden a rebellious thought: that others had had to pay for it; not Captain Davenal.

"Did it affect my father's health, this business?" he inquired in a low tone.

"I fear it did," she replied, feeling that she could not avoid the confession. "I am sure it affected him mentally. There was a great change in him from that night."

Captain Davenal folded the papers slowly, and pushed them into his waistcoat pocket in his usual careless fashion. "What a fool I was!" he muttered; "and what a rogue was that other!"

"Are they safe there, Edward?"

"Safe enough until I get home. They will be burnt then, except this final receipt. Oh, if my father had but lived! I could at least have repaid him his pecuniary lose. It took all he left behind him I suppose, to satisfy it?"

"Yes; all."

"He told me he feared it would, or nearly all, in the letter he wrote me when he was dying. Did things realise well?"

"No, very badly. There was not enough to satisfy the claim by two hundred pounds. Finally, Aunt Bettina advanced that."

"Does she know of this?" he exclaimed, in a startled tone.

"No, I kept it from her. It was difficult to do, but I contrived it."

"You were a brave girl, my sister! I don't know who would have acted as you have! All this trouble upon you, and never to worry me with it in your letters!—never to ask me for money to help in the need!"

"I thought you had none to give," she simply said.

"True enough: I had none; but most sisters would have asked for it. I shall repay at once Aunt Bettina; I shall repay, more gradually, to you the half of what my father possessed before this trouble was brought by me upon him. What do you say?—my wife's money? Tush, child! Do you know the amount of the fortune we have come into? It will be but a drop of water in the ocean of that amount. If I did not repay it to you, she would."

Sara looked up.

"My wife knows all. I told her every word."

"O Edward! Before your marriage!"

"Not before. I suppose I ought to have done so, but it would have taken a greater amount of moral courage than I possessed. I couldn't risk the losing her. I told her, partially, a short time after our marriage: the full particulars I did not give her until last night."

Last night! Sara was surprised.

"She fell in love with you yesterday, Sara, and I thought well to let her know what you really were—how true you had been to me."

Sara was silent. It was in her nature to be true; and, as she believed, it was in her nature to be able to suffer.

"There were times when I felt tempted to wish I had stayed at home and battled with it," resumed Captain Davenal, after a pause. "But in that case the scandal would probably have gone forth to the world. As it was, no living being knew of it, save you and my father."

"And Mr. Alfred King," she said. Another name also occurred to her, but she did not mention it—that of Oswald Cray.

"Alfred King? Sara, my dear, I don't care to enter into particulars with you, but he was with me in the mess; more morally guilty, though less legally so, than I was. He has never told it, I can answer for, for his own sake."

"He always spoke to me of being only a sort of agent in the affair," she said. "He intimated that the money was due to other parties."

"Was due from himself, then. But it is over and done with: let it drop. And now, Sara, you must allow me to ask you a personal question: are you still engaged to Oswald Cray?"

The demand was so unexpected, the subject so painful, that Sara felt the life-blood leave her heart for her face. "I am not engaged to Oswald Cray," she said in a low tone. "I—I cannot say that I ever was engaged to him."

A pause. "But—surely there was some attachment?"

"A little: in the old days. It is very long ago now. How did you know of it?"

"Oswald Cray himself told me. It was the evening we went up to town together after Caroline's wedding. He knew I was going out immediately with the regiment, and he gave me a hint of how it was between you. Only a hint; nothing more. I suppose—I suppose," more slowly added Captain Davenal, "that this miserable business of mine broke it off. I conclude that when Oswald found at my father's death that you had no money he declined the compact. It's the way of the world."

"Not so. No. I do not think money or the want of it, would have any influence on Oswald Cray. In this case it certainly had not. We had parted before papa died."

"What then was the cause, Sara?"

Should she tell him?—that it was his conduct broke it off? Better not, perhaps; it could do no earthly good and would be only adding pain to pain.

"It is a thing of the past now, Edward; let it remain so. The cause that parted us was one that could not be got over. We are friends still, though we do not often meet. More than that we can never be."

Captain Davenal was sorry to hear it. Thoughtless and imprudent as he was by nature himself, he could not but be aware of the value of Oswald Cray. Such a man would make the happiness—and guard it—of any woman.

"I think I had better mention one fact to you, Edward," she resumed, after some moments given to the matter in her own mind. "You have been assuming that no one was cognisant of that business of yours, except papa, myself, and Mr. Alfred King; but—"

"No other living soul was cognisant of it," interrupted Captain Davenal. "My father's promptitude stopped it."

"Oswald Cray knew of it."

"Impossible!" he said, recovering from a pause of surprise.

"He did indeed. I am not sure that he knew the exact particulars, but he knew a very great deal. I believe—I fancy—that he had gathered even a worse impression of it than the case actually warranted."

Captain Davenal was incredulous. "From whom did he learn it?"

"I cannot tell you. I have always feared that, as he knew it, it must have been known to others."

"I tell you, Sara, that beyond you and my father, and King, nobody in the world knew of it. You are under some mistake. Oswald Cray could not have known of it."

"Nay then, Edward, as it has come so far I will tell you the truth. Oswald Cray did know of it, and it was that, and nothing else, that caused us to part. He—he thought, after that, that I was no fit wife for him," she added in a low tone of pain. "And in truth I was not."

A pause of distress. "Unfit as my sister?"

"Yes. I suppose he feared that the crime might at any time be disclosed to the world."

"But how could he have known it?" reiterated Captain Davenal, the one surprise overwhelming every other emotion in his mind. "King I know would not tell; for his own sake he dared not: and we may be very sure my father did not. He sacrificed himself to retain it a secret."

"That Oswald Cray knew of it I can assure you," she repeated. "He must have known of it as soon—or almost as soon—as we did. From that night that you came down to Hallingham in secret his behaviour changed; and a little later, when a sort of explanation took place between us, he spoke to me of what had come to his knowledge. I know no more."

"Well, it is beyond my comprehension," said Captain Davenal; "it passes belief. Good Heavens! if Oswald Cray knew it, where's my security that others do not? I must look into this."

He was about to go off in impulsive haste, probably to seek Oswald Cray, but Sara detained him. The uncertain doubt, the dread lying most heavy on her heart, was not spoken yet.

"Don't go, Edward. You will regard me as a bird of ill-omen, I fear, but I have something to say to you on a subject as unpleasant as this, though of a totally different nature."

"No crime, I hope," he remarked in a joking tone, as he reseated himself. It was utterly impossible for Edward Davenal to remain sober and serious long.

"It would be a crime—if it were true."

"Well, say on, Sara: I am all attention. I have been guilty of a thousand and one acts of folly in my life; never but of one crime. And that I was drawn into."

Captain Davenal did right to bid her "say on," for she seemed to have no inclination to say anything; or else to be uncertain in what words to clothe it. It was a decidedly unpleasant topic, and her colour went and came.

"I would not mention it, Edward, if I were not obliged; if I did not fear consequences for you now you have come home," she begun. "It has been weighing me down a long, long while, and I have had to bear it, saying nothing—"

"Has some private debt turned up against me?" he cried hastily. "I thought I had not one out in the European world. I'll settle it tomorrow, Sara, whatever it may be."

"It is not debt at all. It is—"

Sara stopped, partly with emotion, partly from her excessive reluctance to approach the topic. Should it prove to be altogether some mistake, a feeling of shame would rest upon her for having whispered it.

"It's what? Why don't you go on?"

"I must go on if I am to tell you," she resumed, rallying her courage. "Did you ever, before you went out—marry anybody?"

"Did I—what?" he returned, looking up with an exceedingly amused expression on his face.

"O Edward, you heard."

"If I heard I did not understand. What do you mean? Why do you ask me so foolish a question?"

"You have not answered it," she continued in a low voice.

Captain Davenal noted for the first time the changing hue of her face, the troubled eye, the shrinking, timid manner. His mood changed to seriousness.

"Sara, what do you mean? Did I marry anybody before I went out, you ask? I neither married anybody, nor promised marriage. I—Halloa! you don't mean that I am about to have a breach of promise brought against me?"

The notion was so amusing to Captain Davenal that he burst into a laugh. Sara shook her head; and when his laugh had subsided she bent her cheek upon her hand, and related to him, calmly and quietly, what had occurred. The Captain was excessively amused: he could not be brought to regard the tale in any other light than as a joke.

"What do you say the lady's name was? Catherine what?"

"Catherine Wentworth."

"Catherine Wentworth?" he deliberated. "I never heard the name before in my life; never knew any one bearing it. Why, Sara, you do not mean to say this has seriously troubled you?"

"It has very seriously troubled me. At times, what with one dread and another, I seemed to have more upon me than I could bear. I had no one to whom I could tell the trouble and the doubt: I dared not write it to you, lest your wife should get hold of the letter."

"And if she had? What then?"

"If she had?" repeated Sara. "Do you forget the charge?"

"It's too laughable for me to forget it. Rose would have laughed at it with me. Sara, my dear, rely upon it this has arisen from some queer mistake."

His open countenance, the utter absence of all symptom of fear, the cool manner in which he treated it, caused Sara to breathe a sigh of relief. Half her doubts had vanished.

"The strange thing is, why she should make the charge—why she should say she was your wife. It was not done to extort money, for she has never asked for a farthing. She said papa knew of the marriage."

"Did she?" was the retort, delivered lightly. "Did she tell all this to you?"

"Not to me. I have never spoken to her; I told you so. What I have learnt, I learnt through Neal."

Captain Davenal paused in reflection. "Who knows but that gentleman may be at the bottom of it?" he said at length. "If he opens desks—I don't say he does, I say if he does—he might get up this tale."

"And his motive?" returned Sara, not agreeing with the proposition.

"Nay, I don't know."

"But Neal did not come forward with the tale. It was in consequence of what I accidentally heard her say that I questioned Neal; and I must do him the justice to declare that it was with very great reluctance he would answer me. I heard Neal tell her, apparently in answer to a question, that there was no doubt

Captain Davenal was married; that he had married a Miss Reid, an heiress. She replied that she would have satisfaction, no matter what punishment it brought him (you) to."

"And Neal afterwards assured you that she was Captain Davenal's wife?"

"Neal assured me that she said she was. Neal himself said he did not believe her to be so; he thought there must be some mistake. She declared she had been married to you nearly a twelvemonth before you quitted Europe, and that Dr. Davenal knew of it."

"The story-telling little hussy!"

"Edward, I confess to you that I never so much as thought of its not being true in that first moment! I think fear must have taken possession of me and overpowered my judgment."

"You should have written to me, Sara."

"I have told you why I did not: lest the letter should fall into the hands of your wife. And I believe that a dread of its truth made me shrink from approaching it. That very same day I saw the young person come out of the War Office. I did not know, and don't know, whether it is the proper place to lodge complaints against officers, but I supposed she had been to lodge one against you."

"And you have seen her here since, at the house?"

"Occasionally. She has never been troublesome. She has come, apparently, to say a word or two to Neal. I have never questioned him upon the visits: I have dreaded the subject too much. Only yesterday I saw Neal speaking with her at the corner of the street."

"Well, Sara, I shall sift this."

She lifted her head. "Yes?"

"I shall. It would not have been pleasant had the rumour reached the ears of my wife."

He walked to the window and stood there a moment or two, a flush upon his face, a frown upon his brow. When he turned round again he was laughing.

"Did Aunt Bett hear of this!"

"O no."

"She'd have taken it for granted it was true. Had anybody told her in the old days that I had married sixteen wives, and then set the town on fire with a lighted torch, Aunt Bett would have believed it of me. But, Sara, I am surprised at you."

She glanced at him with a faint smile: not liking to say that the dreadful business, the secret of that past night, which had no doubt helped to send Dr. Davenal to his grave, had, at the time, somewhat shaken her faith in her gallant brother. But for that terrible blow, she had never given a moment's credit to this.

CHAPTER LIX

THE SERGEANT-MAJOR'S WIFE

Captain Davenal had made light of the matter to his sister. Knowing how unfounded was the charge, the whole thing struck him as being so absurd, so improbable, that his mind could but receive it as a jest. Nevertheless, upon reflection, he saw that it might prove a subject of serious annoyance: such charges, especially if maliciously made and well planned, sometimes cost a world of trouble in their refutation.

He had said it was his intention to sift it. Sara suggested that he should do what she had shrunk from doing—question Neal. Captain Davenal hesitated. If there were any foundation for his suspicion that Mr. Neal might have had something to do with making the charge, it would not perhaps be policy to speak to that gentleman in the present stage of the affair. Better try by some other means to find out who the young woman was, and all about her. It is true that without the help of Neal Captain Davenal did not see his way clear to accomplish this: to seek for an unknown young woman in London, one to whom he had no clue, was something equivalent to that traditional search, the hunting for a needle in a bottle of hay.

"I wonder if Dorcas could tell us anything about her?" he exclaimed, ringing the bell upon impulse, as he did most things. And when Dorcas appeared in answer to it, he plunged into a sea of questions that had only the effect of bewildering her.

"You must know her, Dorcas," interposed Sara. "It is a young woman, rather nice-looking, who has come here occasionally to see Neal. She generally wears large shawls that trail on the ground. Captain Davenal has a reason for wishing to know who she is."

"You must mean Mrs. Wentworth, Miss Sara."

"Mrs. Wentworth! Is that her name?" repeated Sara, feeling a sort of relief that the servant had not said Mrs. Davenal.

"That's her name, Miss. She is an officer's wife, and is in some trouble about him. I believe Neal is her uncle."

Sara looked up. "Neal told my aunt that the young person was not his niece."

"Well, I don't know," said Dorcas; "I think she is his niece: at any rate, I have heard her call him uncle. I heard her call him wide no longer ago than last night, Miss Sara."

"Where was that?" interposed Captain Davenal.

"It was here, sir. She called to see Neal. I was passing downstairs at the time from Mrs. Cray's room, and it seemed to me that there was some dispute occurring between them. She asked Neal to tell her where Captain Davenal was staying, and Neal refused. He said she should not go troubling Captain Davenal."

A pause from all. Sara's face grew troubled again.

"What did she want with me?" asked the captain.

"I don't know, sir," replied Dorcas. "I only heard that much in passing. I was carrying Mrs. Cray's tea-tray down."

"Do you know where she lives, this Mrs. Wentworth?"

"Not at all, sir. I have never known that."

"Edward, she is evidently looking out for you!" exclaimed Sara, as Dorcas retired.

"I hope and trust she is, and that she'll speedily find me," was the retort of Captain Davenal. "Nothing should I like better than to find her. I have a great mind to ask Neal openly what it all is, and insist upon an answer."

There was no opportunity for further conversation then. Mark Cray came in. Captain Davenal did not think him improved in anyway. There was less of openness in his manner than formerly, and he rather appeared to evade Captain Davenal, quitting his presence as soon as he conveniently could. The next to enter was Miss Bettina. It was the first time she had met her nephew, and she was disposed to be cordial. Miss Bettina had gone forth that morning to visit his young wife, entertaining a secret prejudice against her, and she returned home liking her. The little baby had been named Richard, too, and that gratified her.

A short while later, and Captain Davenal and his sister stood in the presence of this very young woman, Catherine Wentworth. In a room in Lady Reid's house, when they reached it—for Sara walked home with him—she was waiting. She had gone there inquiring for Captain Davenal, and upon being told Captain Davenal was out, she asked to be allowed to wait for him.

The sequel of this episode is so very matter-of-fact, so devoid of romance, that some of you, my readers, may think it might have been as well never to have introduced it. But in that case what would become of the closing history of Neal? It was quite necessary, if that gentleman was to have a faithful biographer.

Sara Davenal sat, the white strings of her bonnet untied, wiping the drops of moisture from her relieved brow. So intense was the relief that when the first few moments of thankfulness were past, she looked back with a feeling of anger that her mind's peace, for long long months, should have been disturbed so unnecessarily.

They were talking fast, this young woman and Captain Davenal. She had gone to Miss Davenal's house over and over again to inquire after him; she had handed Neal more than one letter to forward to him to India; she had been at the house the previous night, demanding to know where the captain was staying, and saying that she would see him; and she had this morning found out his address at Lady Reid's, and had waited until he came in.

But all for an innocent and legitimate purpose. Mrs. Wentworth—and she was Mrs. Wentworth—had never seen Captain Davenal in her life before; had never pretended that she had; she was only seeking him now to get from him some information of her real husband, Sergeant-Major Wentworth, of Captain Davenal's regiment.

One train of thought leads to another. Captain Davenal remembered now to have heard that the sergeant-major, a very respectable man, had voluntarily separated himself from his wife, and left her behind him in England when their regiment sailed for India, in consequence of some misconduct on her part. He stood there face to face with the young woman, trying to reconcile this plain statement of facts with the account of past assertions related to him by Sara.

"You are Sergeant-Major Wentworth's wife, you say," observed Captain Davenal, regarding her narrowly, watching every word that fell from her lips. If there had been any conspiracy between her and Neal to undermine his sister's peace, he felt that he should like to punish both of them. Sara had had enough of real troubles to bear, without having false ones brought upon her.

"Yes, I am," she replied. She had a wonderfully pretty face, now that it could be seen without her veil, and her manners were pleasing—nay, ladylike. But still there was the look of general untidiness about her that Sara had noticed before, though she did not wear a shawl today, but a black cloth mantle, cut in the mode.

"May I ask if you ever allowed it to be understood that you were anybody else's wife?" rejoined Captain Davenal, putting the question in the most convenient form he could, and in a half-jesting tone.

"Anybody else's wife?" she repeated, as if not understanding.

"Ay; mine, for instance?"

"Why, of course I never did. I don't know what you mean, sir."

"Does Neal know you are Sergeant-Major Wentworth's wife?"

"O dear, yes. I have done nothing a long while but beseech of him to write to you, sir, and ask if you would speak in my behalf to Wentworth, and make him allow me more, or else let me go out to him in India."

Sara interposed. It might not be wise in her, but she could not help herself: "I once accidentally heard a conversation of yours with Neal. You were speaking of this gentleman, Captain Davenal; it was the very day that we had heard news of his marriage with Miss Reid. I remember you said something to the effect that you would have satisfaction, cost what punishment it would to him. Did you allude to your husband?"

"Yes, I did," the girl replied. "And I hope he will be punished yet. I remember the time too. I had had a letter that morning from one of the women who went with the regiment, a soldier's wife. She spoke of my husband in it in a way that vexed me; and she said, amidst other news, that their Captain—Captain Davenal—had just got married. The letter put me up to think that perhaps Captain Davenal could do some good for me with my husband, and I came off at once to Neal and asked him. Neal said he should not trouble Captain Davenal with anything of the sort; and the answer made me angry, and I reminded Mr. Neal that I could say one or two things about him that might not be pleasant if I chose to be ill-natured; and at last he promised to send a letter for me to Captain Davenal, enclosed in one from himself, if I liked to write and state the case. I remember quite well saying that I would have satisfaction somehow, no matter what the punishment to Wentworth. Did my letters ever reach you, sir? I wrote two or three."

"Never."

"Like enough Neal never sent them," she exclaimed with an angry toss. "He said he did; and I have been always asking him whether he received no answer for me."

"Is Neal your uncle, Mrs. Wentworth?"

"I call him so sometimes, sir, when I want to be pleasant with him, but in point of fact he is no real relation. My step-mother is his sister; and that makes him a sort of uncle-in-law."

"And you have not—excuse my pressing the question, Mrs. Wentworth, but I have a reason for it—given Neal reason to suppose that you were ever married to any one except Sergeant-Major Wentworth?" resumed Captain Davenal.

"Never in my life, sir," she replied, and her accent of truth was unmistakable. "Say to Neal that I was married to anybody else! What for? It would be childish to say it; he knows quite well that I was married to Serjeant Wentworth. He was not serjeant-major then."

The falsehood then had been Neal's! Captain Davenal glanced at Sara. But the sergeant's wife spoke again.

"Could you interest yourself for me with Wentworth, sir?"

"Ah, I don't know. It is a ticklish thing, you see, to interfere between man and wife," added the captain, a jesting smile upon his lips. "What is your grievance against Wentworth?"

Mrs. Wentworth entered on her grievances; a whole catalogue. She required that her husband should send for her to be with him in India, or else that he should make her a better allowance, so that she could live "as a lady." She knew he got plenty of prize-money she said, for she had been told so; and she finished up with stating that she had been to the War Office, and to half-a-dozen other offices to complain of him, and could get no redress.

"Well," said Captain Davenal, "I'll tell you what I'll do: will write to your husband—a man for whom I have great respect,—and inquire his version of the quarrel between you. We should always hear both sides of a question, you know, Mrs. Wentworth. When I get his answer, you shall hear from me. To be candid with you, I must say that I don't think Wentworth is one to allow of much interference. He has good judgment, and he likes to exercise it. But I will write to him."

"And you'll promise to see me again, sir, in spite of Neal? What his objection was, I don't know, but he did all he could to prevent my seeing you."

"I don't think you need fear Neal's prevention for the future in regard to seeing me," said Captain Davenal, in a significant tone, as he civilly bowed out Mrs. Wentworth.

"Well, Sara, and what do you think of Neal now?"

"I can't understand it; I can't understand why he should have said it, or what his motive was," slowly replied Sara. "Oh, if he only knew the cruel days and nights it caused me to pass. Shall you tell Aunt Bettina of Neal's falsity?"

"Tell her!" repeated Captain Davenal. "Do you think I can allow her and you to be any longer under the same roof with a villain such as Neal?"

CHAPTER LX

LIGHT

Not to Miss Bettina, however, did Captain Davenal at once take his way, but to Parliament Street. The revelation of Sara that morning—that the one dark episode in his own past history had been known to Oswald Cray—was troubling Edward Davenal's mind far more than any sense of the inconvenience wrought by Mr. Neal.

They stood together in Oswald's sitting-room, the doors closed. A few words of greeting on both sides, and then the captain plunged wholesale, without any ceremony or preparation, into the object which had brought him.

"I have come to ask you a question," he began, dropping his voice to a confidential whisper. "How did you become acquainted with that miserable business of mine?"

"With what miserable business?" returned Oswald, in surprise.

"Don't you recall what I mean? That affair that swamped me. Or, I'm sure I may better say, swamped my father. The—the—those bills, you know."

Oswald did not know in the least. And said so.

"Hang it, Cray," exclaimed the captain, "why force a man to speak out? Those forged bills that I put into circulation, and couldn't get back again."

"I protest I do not know what you are talking of," returned Oswald. "I don't understand what it is you would ask me."

"I only ask how you became acquainted with the affair."

"I never was acquainted with the affair: with any affair such as you allude to," persisted Oswald. "I am not acquainted with it now."

"Do you mean to say that you did not become cognisant of that dreadful trouble I got into before leaving England?—The signing of those bills?"

"I never heard of it in my life. I never heard, or knew, that you were in any trouble whatever."

Captain Davenal sat staring at Oswald. How reconcile this denial with Sara's positive assurance of an hour ago? "You are telling me truth?" he cried, with a perplexed air.

"Entire truth," said Oswald. "Why should I not?"

"What then could Sara mean?" debated Captain Davenal aloud. "She tells me that you did know of it."

"Sara tells you so?"

"She does. She says that—I don't see that I need scruple to speak," broke off Captain Davenal, "it's all over and done with, I suppose—Sara says it was your knowledge of the affair that caused the breaking off of the engagement between yourself and her."

Oswald Cray was silent. A doubt crossed him of whether the gallant captain could have received some sabre-cut or sunstroke in India which had affected his brain. Captain Davenal noted his puzzled look, and strove to be more explanatory.

"When you and I were returning to town from Hallingham the night of Caroline's wedding, you hinted that there existed an attachment or engagement between you and Sara. For the first time I spoke of this to Sara this morning. She admitted that something of the kind had existed, but said it was over; and I saw that the subject was painful—one she wished to avoid. So I dropped it. Afterwards, in speaking of this worse business of mine, I observed that it had been known to three people only: my father, Alfred King, and Sara; but Sara interrupted me, saying that it was known to Oswald Cray. I disputed the fact; I said it could not have been known to you, but she persisted in her assertion, and finally confessed that it was in consequence of its coming to your knowledge that you broke off the engagement to her, deeming she was not worthy, as my sister, to become your wife. Pardon me yet a moment while I state that I am not here to question the decision; I don't wish to enter upon it at all, except to say that many would have done as you did, after what I, her brother, had been guilty of. All that is apart from the business, and I am only telling you how it came out. Sara assures me that it was the sole cause of breaking off the engagement, and that you must have known of it almost as soon as—as my father knew. Now, I want you to tell me, Mr. Oswald Cray, how and whence that affair came to your knowledge. Have I made myself clear?"

"Perfectly clear, so far as explanation goes; but it is nothing but obscurity to me, for all that. In the first place, allow me to repeat to you that I never knew before now that you were in any trouble whatever. This is my first intimation of it."

"And was it not that knowledge that caused you and Sara to part?"

"It was not. How could it have been when I assure you I did not possess the knowledge? A—a great trouble, of which I would prefer not to speak, did lead to the parting, but it was entirely unconnected with you."

"Well, this is Greek," returned Captain Davenal. "There was no other trouble connected with the family, except mine. I suppose you mean that it was connected with them?"

"Yes."

"With which of them? There was no scapegoat in it except me."

"It was connected with Dr. Davenal," said Oswald reluctantly. "I cannot say more."

"With my father? Nonsense, if you mean anything wrong. A more upright man never breathed. Fancy him sending forth bad bills!"

"I could not fancy him doing so," replied Oswald. "The matter had nothing to do with money."

"I'll lay all I am worth it had to do with me, with my business," impulsively spoke Captain Davenal. "I will tell you how it was—"

"Nay, it is not worth while," was Oswald Cray's interruption, as he thought how very different a thing was Lady Oswald's unhappy death from the topics under discussion. "Believe me, you had not, and could not have had, anything to do with the real question."

"But I'll tell you, now I have begun. I and my choice friend, as I thought him then,"—Captain Davenal spoke with scornful bitterness,—"got into an awful mess together, and could not get out of it. No matter whether it was gambling or horse-racing, or what not; money we were compelled to have. King assured me on his honour that in three weeks' time he should be in the possession of several thousand pounds, if we could only stave off exposure until then, and in an evil hour I yielded to his persuasion and wrote my father's name. The suggestion was King's, the persuasion was King's, the full assurance that all would be well was King's. I don't say this in extenuation of myself; the guilt and madness of yielding were all mine. Well, the days went on, and when the time came, and the thing was on the point of exploding, King had not got the thousands he had counted on: moreover, I found that his expectation of getting them had been from the first very vague indeed, and we had a desperate quarrel. The sneak turned round; threatened me with exposure, with ruin, and I had to go down and confess the truth to my father. He saved me—saved me at the sacrifice of all he had, and, I fear, of his life."

There was a pause. Oswald had grown strangely interested. Captain Davenal continued.

"I shall never forget the effect it had upon him—never, never. I speak only of the hour of the communication; I never saw him after that. I told him there might be trouble with these bills, to get them at all; that even with the money in hand to redeem them I was not sure the consequences could be averted from me. I saw the change pass over his face; the grey, scared look; and it did not quit it again."

"Where did you see him?"

"At Hallingham. I went down at some peril, after leave had been refused me at headquarters, getting to Hallingham about eleven o'clock on a Sunday night. I stayed an hour or so with my father in his study, and then went back to the station again, for I had to be at my post on duty the following morning. No one at home knew of my visit. I tapped at my father's study window and he let me in. Before I left, I asked to see Sara. I knew quite well, though they did not, that I should not go down again, and I did not care to leave for years without saying a word to her, so my father fetched her down from her room. We did not tell her the particulars, only that I had been doing something wrong, was in danger, and that my visit to Hallingham must be kept quiet. My poor father! I remember his asking in a burst of feeling what he had done that all this trouble should fall upon him. Another great trouble had befallen him that night in the death of Lady Oswald."

"Yes?" said Oswald with a calm manner but a beating heart. His thoughts were in that long past night, and Neal's description of it.

"It was very dreadful," resumed Captain Davenal, alluding to the matter of Lady Oswald. "My father was sadly cut up. Mark Cray had killed her through administering the chloroform."

Oswald felt his heart stand still, his face flush with a burning heat. He moved nearer to Captain Davenal: but his voice was quiet still.

"Did you say Mark administered the chloroform?"

"It was Mark. Yes. My father said he had especially forbidden Mark Cray to give her chloroform. Mark in the course of the day had proposed doing it, but the doctor warned him that chloroform would not do for Lady Oswald. When all was ready, he (my father) had to carry Lady Oswald's maid from the chamber in a fainting-fit, and when he got back to it he found Mark had administered the chloroform, which he had taken with him to the house surreptitiously, and was commencing the operation. The doctor said he could not make out Mark Cray that night. He was beginning the operation in so unskilful, so unsurgeon-like a manner, that my father had to push him away as he would have pushed a child, and perform it himself. But they could not recover Lady Oswald."

Oswald made no remark. He felt as one stunned.

"It struck me as being a most shocking thing," continued Captain Davenal. "I remarked to my father that it seemed like murder, and he said Yes, he supposed the world would call it such."

"But why did not Dr. Davenal declare the truth—that it was Mark who had given the chloroform?" interrupted Oswald. "Why suffer himself to rest under the imputation?"

"What imputation? There was no imputation to lie under. All the world supposed the chloroform had been rightly and properly administered, according to the best judgment of both of them."

True; true. Oswald Cray had been speaking in accordance with his own private knowledge, not with publicly-known facts.

"My father kept the secret for Mark Cray's sake. If it went forth to the world, he said it would blight Mark's professional career for life. He told me the facts, but he intended to keep them from all others, and he warned me not to divulge them. I never did. I am not sure that I should feel justified in telling even you now, but that Mark is no longer in his profession. My poor father made the remark that they were two heavy secrets for his breast to keep, mine and Mark Cray's."

The murmur of the words fell upon Oswald's ear, but he was as one who heard them not. A weighty amount of self-reproach was rising up within him. Captain Davenal talked on, and then hastened away, for he had Mr. Neal to settle with yet, leaving Oswald alone.

The scales, so long obscuring Oswald Cray's eyes, had fallen from them, and he saw the past in its true colours. The one wondering question that seemed to press upon him now was, how he could ever have doubted Dr. Davenal. Above his own self-reproach; above the bitter feeling of repentance for the wrong he had dealt out to her whom he best loved on earth; above his regrets for the late years wasted in a miserable illusion; was his remorse for having so misjudged that good man, misjudged him even to his grave. He saw it all now: how, when he questioned Dr. Davenal about his motives for administering the fatal medicine, he had taken the odium upon himself for Mark's sake: not even to him, his brother, would he, in his loving-kindness, betray Mark.

Never had the pride, the self-esteem, of Oswald Cray received a blow like unto this. He had plumed himself on his superiority; he had cast off Dr. Davenal as one unworthy of him; he had dared, in his self-sufficiency, to cast off Sara. Her father was a man of suspicion, and therefore she was no fit mate for him! Whereas, Oswald now learnt that it was his own brother who was the offender: Dr. Davenal and his daughter were the victims. The full value, the Christian conduct of that good man was patent to him now; the patient endurance of Sara became clear to him.

He lifted his hat and wiped the moisture from his brow, as he walked through the streets, all these considerations doing battle in his brain. The winter's day was cold, but Oswald's brow was hot; hot with inward fever. He was on his way to Miss Davenal's, to seek a conference with his half-brother: there were one or two questions he would put to him. He had taken his hat and come out the moment Captain Davenal left him: business and all else gave way before this.

CHAPTER LXI

THE BARGAIN SEALED

Mark Cray sat in his wife's sick-room. Mark Cray found it (between ourselves) rather tiresome to sit in his wife's sick-room: and Mark was very apt to doze asleep at his post. Mark was asleep now. He was dreaming a charming dream of greatness—in which some grand scheme of Barker's had succeeded, and he and that gentleman were sailing about the atmosphere in a triumphal car of gold, looking down with complacency on the poor toiling mortals in the world below—when Dorcas came in with a whisper, and aroused him. Mr. Oswald Cray was in the dining-parlour waiting to see him, she said: and Mark, after a stare at the girl, descended, pushing back his clustering hair, which had disarranged itself in his sleep.

Oswald was standing near the fire. He turned to Mark and spoke in a quiet tone.

"I have a question to ask you, Mark. It relates to the past. Who—"

"Oh, never mind the past," interrupted Mark, with a half-testy, half-careless sort of manner. "I'm sure there's enough worry in the present without going back to that of the past. I wish that horrid mine had been sunk a thousand fathoms deep before I had had anything to do with it. I daresay I shall pay you back some time!"

"It is not about the mine I wish to speak to you, or of payment either," calmly rejoined Oswald. "But, Mark, I want the truth from you—the truth, mind—upon another subject. It was you, was it not, who gave the chloroform to Lady Oswald?"

Mark made no reply, either truthful or otherwise. The question was so exceedingly unlike any he had expected that he only stared.

"It was supposed, I know, at the time to have been administered by Dr. Davenal. But I have reason to believe that it was administered by yourself during his temporary absence from the chamber, and against his sanction. Was it so, Mark?"

"I suppose you heard this from the doctor himself at the time?" was Mark Cray's remark. "I remember you were worriting over it."

"I beg you to answer my question, Mark. What you say shall go no further."

"Well, yes, it was so," said Mark; "though I'm sure I can't think why you want to bring up the thing now. I did give her the chloroform, but I gave it for the best. As I was to perform the operation I thought I had a right to exercise my own judgment, which was opposed to the doctor's. I was very sorry for the result, but I did it for the best."

"I wish you had told me the truth at the time, Mark. You suffered me to believe that the chloroform was given by Dr. Davenal."

"And what difference did it make to you which of us gave it?" was Mark Cray's reply, not an unnatural one. "You may guess that it was a thing I did not care to speak of. So long as it was assumed we gave the chloroform conjointly, in accordance with ordinary practice and our best judgment, nobody could say a word; but if it had been disclosed that I gave it by myself, on my own responsibility and against the doctor's opinion, I should have had the whole town carping at me."

Oswald had nothing further to say. He could not tell the bitter truth—that this miserable misapprehension had wrecked his hopes of happiness, had been making an ice-bolt of his heart in the intervening years.

Mark escaped, and returned to his wife's room, there to endeavour to drop into his golden dreams again, from which he seemed to have been aroused for no earthly use whatever. And Oswald stayed on in the hope of seeing Sara.

Not only in the dining-parlour of Miss Davenal's house was there a conference being held at that hour, but also in the drawing-room above: and but for the all-absorbing nature of his own thoughts Oswald Cray had not failed to hear the sounds. Captain Davenal had got Neal there, before his aunt. And Mr. Neal was slipping out of all accusations as smoothly as an eel.

The group was noticeable. Miss Davenal in her chair, upright and angry, only partially understanding the cause of the commotion; Captain Davenal standing, open and impetuous, talking very fast; Neal full of repose and self-possession, all his wits in full play; and Sara sitting apart in silence, her cheek bent upon her hand. Captain Davenal charged Neal with treachery, general and particular. Neal had his plausible answer ready to meet it all.

The interview was drawing to an end, and little satisfaction had been derived from it. Poor Miss Davenal's ears were in a mazed condition: desks, letters, inventions to Sara touching a Mrs. Wentworth, and a hundred other charges, jumbling hopelessly upon them, nothing being clear. Neal denied everything.

"You did tell Miss Sara Davenal that the young woman was my wife," cried Captain Davenal, indignantly.

"I beg your pardon, sir," said Neal, respectfully. "I said I felt quite sure she was not; that there must be some mistake. Miss Sara perhaps will remember that such was my opinion."

"At any rate, you said the young woman made the charge," persisted Captain Davenal, irritated at the assured coolness.

"I did, sir. I understood the young woman to make it. She—"

"But she never did make it," interrupted Captain Davenal.

Neal shrugged his shoulders in submissive superciliousness, meant for Mrs. Wentworth. "It may suit the young woman's purpose to say so now, sir. I fear she is not very strict in her adherence to truth; but she certainly did make it at the time. However, sir, I am quite willing to take the blame upon myself, to allow that I misunderstood her."

"Why, you have not the face to tell me that you have gone on believing it?"

"O dear no, sir. I was very soon afterwards convinced that the thing was a mistake altogether."

"And pray, why had you not the honesty to say so to Miss Sara Davenal?"

"I'm sure I should have been happy to say so, sir, had I possessed the least idea that it would have been welcome. But after the first blush, the matter appeared to be so very absurd that I never supposed Miss Sara would give to it a second thought. If my silence has caused any uneasiness, I can only say how deeply I regret it."

"Who is the young woman?" helplessly cried Miss Bettina. "And pray, Neal, how came it, if you had anything of the sort to say, that you did not say it to me? I am the proper person to hear these things; a young lady is not."

Neal advanced a step to his mistress and spoke in his low clear tone. "It was not my intention to speak to Miss Sara Davenal at all, ma'am, or to you either; I should not have thought of doing such a thing; but I could not help myself when Miss Sara questioned me upon the point."

All that was reasonable and feasible, and Miss Davenal nodded her head in approbation; but her nephew the captain got in a passion, and insisted that he should be discharged there and then.

Neal was quite ready to go, he said, civilly courteous, if his mistress saw fit to inflict upon him so severe a step. He was unconscious of having done anything to merit it. Perhaps she would be pleased to particularise his offence.

"He is a villain, aunt," broke forth the captain intemperately, before Miss Bettina could speak. "I believe he has been one ever since my father took him into the house. He has opened letters and unlocked desks, and altogether played the part of deceit. He shall go."

Neal interrupted, humbly begging the captain's pardon. He could most truthfully assure his mistress that he had done nothing of the sort; he had never opened a letter in the house, except his own; had never touched a desk, but to dust it. If Captain Davenal could mention any other distinct charge, he should be glad, as it would allow him an opportunity of refutation. No. His conscience acquitted him. He should quit the house, if he did have to quit it, with a clear character, and he thought his mistress would acknowledge that he deserved one. In the one little point concerning Mrs. Wentworth he might have been in error: first, in too readily giving ear to what she said; next, in not having spoken to Miss Sara to set the doubt at rest in her mind. They were mistakes certainly, and he greatly regretted them.

"Neal," said the captain, too hot-headed to maintain his dignity, "I'd a hundred times rather be an open villain than a sneak. Why, you know you have been nothing but a spy from the very moment you entered the house. Aunt Bettina, listen! Before the regiment went away I got into a little trouble, upon which I found it necessary to consult my father, and I went—"

"A little what?" asked Miss Bettina.

"Trouble. A little difficulty."

"Oh, ah, yes," said Miss Bettina. "You were always getting into it."

"Not such as that," thought the captain. "Well, I had to go down to Hallingham," he continued aloud, as he bent to her. "I did not care that any of you should know it, and I got down one night unexpected by my father. I was with him in his study for some time, and went back so as to be at duty the next morning. Would you believe"—pointing his finger at Neal—"that yon honest fellow was a spy upon the interview?"

Mr. Neal was a little taken by surprise, and Sara looked up astonished. But the man was not one to lose his impassability.

"He was at the window, looking and listening: not, I believe, that he could see and hear very much. And he afterwards went abroad and told of the interview: told that his master had a secret visitor at night. You little thought, Mr. Neal, that the visitor was myself, or that I should ever bring it home to you."

Neal, all unconscious innocence, gazed straight forward into Captain Davenal's face. "I have not the least idea what it is that you are speaking of, sir. My recollection does not serve me upon the point."

"O yes, it does," said Captain Davenal. "A subtle nature such as yours cannot forget so easily. Happily he to whom you carried the tale of the evening was a trustworthy man: he kept his own counsel, and told you Dr. Davenal's visitors were no business of his or of yours. I speak of Mr. Oswald Cray."

"Mr. Oswald Cray!" repeated Neal, plunging into reflection. "On my honour, sir, I have not the least idea of what it is you mean. A visitor at night to my late master in his study? Stay, I do remember something of it. I—yes—I was outside, taking a mouthful of fresh air preparatory to retiring to rest, and I saw some one—a stranger I took him to be—come stealthily in at the gate, and he was afterwards shut in with my master. I'm sure sir, I beg your pardon, even at this distance of time, if I was mistaken. I feared he might be a suspicious character, and I think I did go to the window, anxious for my master's personal safety. I could not have supposed it was you, sir."

Was it possible to take Neal at a disadvantage? It did not seem so.

"And it was anxiety for your master's personal safety that caused you afterwards to recount this to Mr. Oswald Cray? Eh?"

"Does Mr. Oswald Cray say I recounted it to him, sir?" inquired Neal, probably not feeling sure of his ground just here.

"That's my business," said Captain Davenal, while Sara looked round at Neal. "You did recount it to him."

"All I can say, sir, is, that if I did, I must have had some good motive in it. I cannot charge my memory after this lapse of time. Were I in any anxiety touching my master, Mr. Oswald Cray was probably the gentleman I should carry it to, seeing he was a friend of the family. I have—I think—some faint remembrance that I did speak to Mr. Oswald Cray of that mysterious visitor," slowly added Neal, looking fixedly up in the air, as if he were tying to descry the sun through a fog. "It's very likely that I did, sir, not being at ease myself upon the point."

Captain Davenal was losing patience. It seemed impossible to bring anything home to Neal with any sort of satisfaction. At the close of the captain's interview with Oswald Cray, the latter had mentioned—but not in any ill-feeling to Neal—that that functionary had spoken to him of the night interview at Dr. Davenal's; had said he was outside the window at the time. Oswald had not said more; he deemed it well not to do so; but Captain Davenal had become at once convinced that it was but one of Neal's prying tricks. He turned to Miss Davenal.

"Aunt Bettina, this is waste of time. In nearly the last interview I ever had with my father he told me he had doubts of Neal. He feared the man was carrying on a game of deceit. I know he has been doing it all along. Will you discharge him?"

"I can't understand it at all," returned Miss Bettina.

"I'll enlighten you one of these days, when you are not very deaf, and we can have a quiet half-hour together. Sara, what do you say?"

Sara rose from her seat, her cheek flushing, her voice firm. "Neal must leave, Aunt Bettina," she said, bending down to the deaf ear. "Edward is quite right."

Miss Bettina looked at them all in succession. Had she believed the accusations she would have discharged Neal on the spot, but she doubted them. She had thought there was not so faithful a servant in the world. And he looked so immaculate as he stood there!

"I don't go out of the house this night until he has left it, Aunt Bettina," resumed the captain.

"This night!" echoed Miss Bettina, catching the words. "I can't let Neal go without warning, leaving us without a servant. Who is to wait upon us?"

"You shall have my servant, aunt; one I have brought home with me—"

"No," said Miss Bettina, resolute in the cause of justice. "Neal, I will not part with you in that hasty manner. I cannot judge yet between you and Captain Davenal. That you must leave is obvious; but you shall have the proper month's warning."

Neal stepped up, all suavity. "I beg your pardon, ma'am; you are very kind, but I could not think of remaining a day to cause unpleasantness in the family. I had better go at once. I have my feelings, ma'am, although I am but a dependant. My conscience tells me that I have served you faithfully."

"I think you have, Neal."

"I have indeed, ma'am, and I hope it will be remembered in my character."

"Don't send to me for one," impetuously broke out Captain Davenal. "And now, Neal, the sooner you are out of the house the better. I shall keep my word: to see you away from it ere I quit it myself."

Neal bowed; he could but be ever the respectful servant: and retired. Miss Davenal was bewildered. What with parting with Neal, what with being left with nobody to replace him, she could not gather her senses. Captain Davenal sat down. First of all promising her that the servant he spoke of should be in the house before night, to remain with her until she was suited with one, he next began to enlarge upon Neal's delinquencies, and try to make her comprehend them.

Sara silently left the room. It was altogether a painful subject, and she did not care to hear more of it now. She went down into the dining-parlour, her movements slow and quiet; since Mrs. Cray's increased danger noise had been avoided in the house as much as possible. Some one was standing up by the mantelpiece, his back towards her; in the dusk of the room—for evening was drawing on—Sara took it to be Mark; and yet she thought she had heard Mark's step in his wife's chamber now, as she came downstairs. This gentleman was taller, too! He turned suddenly round, and the fire threw its light on the face of Oswald Cray.

She stood a moment in surprise, and then went up to him, holding out her hand as to any ordinary visitor, and saying a word of apology that he should have been left there unannounced. A strange expression, an expression of deprecation, almost of humility, sat on his features, and he did not touch the offered hand.

"I waited to see you," he said. "I came here to see Mark, who has been with me."

He stopped suddenly. His manner, his looks, were altogether strange. Sara thought something must have happened.

"What is the matter?" she asked. "You look as if you had some great care upon you."

"And so I have. That care that arises from shame and repentance; from finding that we have been upon the mistaken road of wrong; been treading it for years."

She sat down, quietly, timidly, looking to him for an elucidation, half-frightened at his emotion.

"I wish to have an explanation with you, Sara. I want—if it be possible—forgiveness. And I don't know how to enter upon the one or to sue for the other."

She had rarely seen him otherwise than calmly self-possessed. Generally, especially of late years, he was cold almost to a fault. And now he was as one blazing with an inward fire: his lips were scarlet, his brow was flushed, his voice quite hoarse with emotion.

"In the years gone by, I—I—threw you up, Sara. While I loved you better than anything on earth, knowing that you were the only one upon it who could ever awaken the passion within me, did I live to centuries, I voluntarily resigned you. That night in the Abbey graveyard at Hallingham, when we accidentally met—you have not forgotten it—I told you that I could not marry you; that you were not fit to be my wife—Hush! it was equivalent to it Sara, how can I stand now before you and confess that I was altogether under an error; that in my pride, my blindness, I had taken up a false view of things, and was acting upon it? Can you see my shame, my repentance, as I say it to you?"

"I don't understand you," she gasped, utterly bewildered.

"Will you so far pardon me—will you so far trust me after all that has occurred—as to give me this one single word of explanation? To whom did you attribute the cause of my acting in the way I did? Whose ill-conduct was it, as you supposed, that had raised the barrier between us?"

She hesitated, not perhaps caring to reply.

"I have had an interview today with Captain Davenal," he resumed, in a low tone. "He has given me the details of the unhappy business he was drawn into—the forged bills: I am, so far, in his entire confidence. Will that help you to answer me?"

"It was that," she said.

"That alone?"

"That alone. There was nothing else."

"Well, Sara, can you believe me when I tell you that I never heard of that business until today?—That Captain Davenal had nothing whatever to do with my course of action?"

Indeed she looked as though she could not believe him. What else then? she asked. Who had? Under what impression had he acted?

"Ah, there lies my shame! Sara, I dared—I dared to attribute ill-conduct to another," he cried with emotion. "In my pride and folly, in my mind's delusion, I presumed to set myself up for a judge over one who in goodness might have crushed me to nothing. I shall never get over the remorse during life."

"You—did not—attribute ill-conduct of any sort to me?" she said with white lips.

"To you! To you whom I have ever believed to be one of the best and truest women upon earth!—whom I have regarded through it all with an amount of respect unutterable! No, no. But the question serves me right."

She laid her hands one over the other as she sat, striving to keep her feelings under control. Praise from him was all too sweet yet.

"O do me justice so far, Sara! While I gave you up I knew that to my heart and judgment none were like unto you for goodness: I knew that if my obstinate pride, my spirit of self-sufficiency, did but allow me to marry you, you would be the greatest treasure man ever took to himself. Can you tolerate me while I dare openly to say these things?—can you believe that I am pouring them forth in my humiliation? I have loved you deeply and fervently; I shall love you always; but even that love has scarcely equalled my admiration and my respect."

"But who else, then, could have had any counteracting influence?" she returned, after a while.

"I dare not tell you."

"There was only Edward. I had no other brother. No one else could have done anything to bring shame upon—oh, surely you cannot mean papa!" she broke off, the improbable idea flashing over her.

"Don't ask me, Sara! In mercy to myself."

"Papa who was so good?" she reiterated, paying no heed to his words in her wonder. "He was so just, so kind, so honourable! I think if ever there was a good man on earth who tried to do as God would have him, it was papa. It is impossible you could suspect anything wrong in him!"

"My object in waiting to see you this evening was, first, to make my confession; secondly, to ask you to be more just, more merciful than I have been, and to forgive me," he rejoined in a low tone. "I must add another petition yet, Sara; that you would generously allow this one point to remain as it is between us."

"But I think you ought to tell me," she urged. "Did you indeed suspect papa?"

"Yes."

"But of what?"

"Ah, don't press me further, Sara, for I cannot tell you. A singular accident led me to doubt Dr. Davenal's conduct—honour—I hardly know what to call it—and there followed on this a chain of circumstances so apparently corroborative of the doubt that I thought I had no resource but to believe. I believed, and I acted upon the belief: I judged him harshly; I treated him coldly; I gave up you, my dearest hope and object in life; and this day only have my eyes been opened, and to my shame I learn that the whole thing, as regarded him, was a delusion. Will you—will you generously let my confession rest here?"

"Papa would not have done as Edward did," she whispered.

"No, no, it was not anything of that nature. Money and money matters had nothing to do with it. It was an entirely different thing. I am so ashamed of myself that I cannot bear to speak of this further. Surely I have said enough. It was a mistake, a misapprehension altogether: and the greatest act of kindness you can do me now is to let it rest here."

She sat gazing at him with questioning eyes, nearly lost in wonder.

"Yes, the impression under which I acted was a false one. There existed no cause whatever for my estranging myself from you. But for my own unpardonable credulity I need never have given you up: and the past years of anguish—and I know they have been full of anguish to both of us—ought not to have had place. I was misled by an unfortunate chain of events: and nothing remains to me but shame and repentance."

There ensued a silence. Sara was standing on the hearth-rug now, and he took his elbow from the mantelpiece, where it had been resting, and moved a step towards her.

"Can I ever hope for your forgiveness?"

"It seems to me that I have nothing to forgive," she answered, in a low voice. "If circumstances misled you, you could not be blamed for acting upon them, according to your belief."

"Sara!"—he laid his hand upon her shoulder, and his voice shook with the intensity of its emotion— "may I dare to hope that you will let me in my future life strive to atone for this?"

"How atone for it?" she faltered.

"Will you generously look over the past folly?—will you suffer it to be between us as it used to be?—will you be my wife at last?"

She trembled as she stood, the conscious light of love mantling in her cheek and in her drooping eye. Mr. Oswald Cray held her before him, waiting and watching for the answer, his lips parted with suspense.

"My brother's crime remains still," she whispered. "A memento of the past."

"Your brother's crime! Should you be punished for that?—for him? And what of my brother?" he continued, the revelation of the day imparting to his tone a whole world of remorse, of self-condemning repentance. "What disgrace has not my brother brought to me? O Sara; should the ill wrought by these ties part us? It never ought to have done so. Let us stand alone, henceforth, you and I, independent of the world! Don't try me too greatly! don't punish me, as in justice you might!"

For a moment her eyes looked straight into his with a loving, earnest glance, and then dropped again. "I will be your wife, Oswald," she simply said. "I have never tried to forget you, for I knew I could not."

And as if relief from the tension of suspense were too great for entire silence, a faint sound of emotion broke from Oswald Cray. And he bent to take from her lips that kiss, left upon them so long ago in the garden-parlour of the old house at Hallingham.

CHAPTER LXII

"FINANCE," THIS TIME

An afternoon in March. The sun was drawing towards its setting amidst gorgeous clouds, and the red light, illumining the western sky, threw its rays into an invalid's chamber, and lighted it up with a warm hue.

Something else was drawing towards its setting; and that was the feeble life of the chamber's chief occupant. It was a good-sized pleasant room: the bed at the end farthest from the window; the middle space devoted to the comfort of the invalid, a table with some books upon its handsome cover, a sofa, easy chairs, velvet footstools, and a few pretty ornaments to amuse the eye.

On the sofa, by the side of the fire, a coverlid of the lightest and softest texture thrown gently over her, lay the invalid, her hands white and attenuated, her face drawn and wan. But there was a strange beauty in the face yet; in the eyes with their violet depths, in the exquisite features shaded by the mass of silky hair. You do not fail to recognise Mrs. Cray. Just now the eyes were closed, and she was dozing peacefully.

At the opposite end of the hearth-rug, sitting restlessly in an easy chair, was Mark. Of late Mark had been rather prone to be as still and idle as his wife: the inert life wearied him, it chafed its spirit; but there was no escape from it at present, and Mark Cray had perforce resigned himself to it, as an imprisoned bird resigns itself in time to its cage. Mark's future prospects were uncommonly vague: in fact they were as yet bounded by the old expectation-anchor, the "something" that was to "turn up." Any time in the past few weeks his wife's death might have been expected, and Mark had yielded to the idleness of the circumstances, and been tranquil. Mr. Barker was away in Paris, and did not write; the Wheal Bang affairs were going on to a comfortable conclusion, and Mark was letting the future take care of itself. Strolling out for short walks; giving a quarter of an hour to the "Times;" wandering for a few minutes into the sitting-rooms and the presence of Miss Bettina, and lounging back in the easy chairs by the side of his wife—thus had Mark's recent days been passed.

But on this afternoon all was changed, and Mark's forced quiescence had given place to a fidgety restlessness, very characteristic of the old times. The post had just brought a letter from Mr. Barker— some accident or contrary weather having delayed the arrival of the French mail—and Mark Cray upon reading it felt exalted into the seventh heaven.

Barker had succeeded! He had brought out a company in Paris connected with finance; the great work he had been striving for so long. In three weeks' time from that date it would all be in full operation, and if Mrs. Cray were sufficiently well to be left, and Mark came over to Paris, he could instantly step into a post in the Company at a salary of eight hundred a-year to begin with. In about six months' time, according to moderate computation, the thing would be in full swing, and the profits inaugurated certainly at not less than six thousand per annum; the half of which splendid income should be Mark's. Such was Mr. Barker's news.

Can you wonder at Mark's restlessness? At his brightened eye, his flushed face, as he sits there in the chair, bolt upright, his hand raised incessantly to push back his hair? He glances across at Caroline—

whom he really loves very much still—and thinks what a pity it is that all this good fortune should have delayed itself until now. Had it come too late for her? Mark Cray in his sanguine fashion actually asks himself the question, medical man though he is. For the last two or three days Caroline had seemed so much better! only on this very morning she had told Mark she felt as if she were getting well again.

Mark moved his restless legs and contrived to knock down the fire-shovel. The noise awoke Caroline. She stirred, and turned her opening eyes on her husband.

"What was that? Did anybody come in, Mark?"

"I threw over one of the fire-irons. I am sorry it disturbed you. They are always sticking out, tiresome things! It's not a proper fender for a bedroom. Caroline, I have had a letter from Barker," he continued, rising in excitement and standing before her on the hearth-rug. "It's the most glorious news! The thing's realised at last."

"What thing?" asked Caroline, feebly, after a pause of bewilderment.

"The thing he has had on hand so long, the great scheme he has been working for. O Carine, I wish you could get better! There's eight hundred a year waiting for me in Paris; and there'll be an income of at least three thousand before six months are over. Three thousand for my share, you know. I'm sure you would like living in Paris."

She did not answer. Nothing was heard save the quick gasps of the panting breath, the result of excessive weakness, or—of—something else coming very near. Mark was struck with some change in her aspect, and bent down to her.

"Don't you feel so well, Carine?"

"I—feel—weary," was all she answered, her voice ominously low.

"Where's Sara, I wonder?" said Mark. "I'll go and send her to you. You want some beef-tea, or something, I daresay."

Mark went down the stairs, meeting Sara on them. In the drawing-room, with Miss Bettina, was Oswald Cray, who had just come in. He was a frequent visitor now.

The half-brothers shook hands, coldly enough. They were civil to each other always, but there could never be cordiality between them. Not because of the past; but because they were so essentially different in mind, in judgment, and in conduct.

"My luck has turned at last, Oswald," exclaimed Mark impulsively.

"In what way?" asked Oswald, who was leaning over the back of a chair while he talked to Miss Bettina.

"I have just had a letter from Barker," answered Mark, running his hand through his hair with his restless fingers. "I told you what a great scheme he had got on hand in Paris, but you turned the cold shoulder on it. Well, it's bearing fruit at last."

"Oh," said Oswald, evincing a desire, if his tone and manner might be judged by, to turn the cold shoulder on it still, metaphorically speaking. "How is your wife this afternoon?" he continued, passing to a different subject.

"She has been so much better the last few days that one might almost be tempted to hope she'd get well again," rejoined Mark, volubly. "She seems tired now—low, I thought. Sara's just gone up to her. What a shame it is that things turn out so cross-grained and contrary!"

The concluding sentence, delivered with marked acumen, reached the ear of Miss Bettina. She looked up from her knitting to scan Mark.

"If Barker's luck had only been realised six months ago, what a thing it would have been!" he went on. "Caroline might have got better, instead of worse. In the enjoyment of luxuries in a home of her own, renewed wealth and position in prospective, with the pure air of the balmy French capital, there's no knowing what benefit she might not have derived. And now it comes too late! I shall ever regret it for her sake."

"Regret what?" sharply interposed Miss Bettina.

Mark replied by giving a summary of Barker's luck. Miss Bettina paused, knitting-needles in hand, her keen grey eyes fixed on Mark, as she tried to understand him.

"Barker in luck!" she repeated, catching some of the words and the general sense. "Has he come into an estate in the moon? Don't be a simpleton, Mark Cray."

Mark Cray felt exasperated. Nothing angered him so much as for people to pretend to see these enchanting prospects with different eyes from his own. He had always been convinced it was done only to vex him. Poor Mark! He turned to Oswald, and began expatiating upon the good fortune that was drawing so near; and Oswald saw that it was of no use to try to stop him. The fever-mania had again taken hold of Mark.

"What is the scheme, do you say?" asked Oswald, just as he would have asked anything of a child; and perhaps it was not altogether his fault that a sound of mockery was discernible in his tone.

"It's connected with finance."

"Oh!" said Oswald.

"It is the grandest thing that has been brought before the public for many a year," continued Mark, his voice impressive, his light eyes sparkling. "The very greatest—"

"Grander than the Great Wheal Bang?" inopportunely interposed Miss Bettina, Mark's earnest tones having enabled her to hear better than usual.

"A hundred times grander," returned Mark, his mind too completely absorbed in the contemplation of the grandeur to detect the irony. "That is, better, you know, Miss Bettina. The mine was very good; but of course there was a risk attending that, from water or other causes, and the result unfortunately realised it. This is different. Once the company is formed, and the shares are taken, it can't fail. Barker and I went through the thing together over and over again when he was in London; we had it all down before us in black and white. We allowed for every possible risk and contingency, and we proved that the thing could not fail, if once organised."

Oswald listened quietly. Miss Bettina had lost the thread again.

"The job was to organise the thing," resumed Mark. "It could not be done without money, and Barker—to speak the truth—found a difficulty in getting that. The money market was tight here, and men don't care to speculate when money's not plentiful. He also required the co-operation of some French capitalist, who would put his name to it—some good man on the Bourse, and that was hard to get. Those Frenchmen are all so narrow-minded, fight so shy. He knows two or three good Englishmen in Paris who were willing to go into it, and who helped Barker immensely with advice and introductions, and that; but they had no funds at command. However, it's all accomplished now. Barker has fought his way through impediments, and surmounted them. The company's formed, the preliminary arrangements are successfully carried out, and fortune is at hand."

"What's at hand?" asked Miss Bettina.

"Fortune," repeated Mark. "I shall take one of those nice little boxes in the Champs Elysées. Some of them are charming. Or perhaps only part of one if—if Carine—O dear! it is hard for her that this luck did not fall in a year ago! I wonder," broke off Mark, passing to another phase of his future visions, "I wonder whether, if it were possible to get Caroline over to Paris now, the change might benefit her?"

"You think of residing in Paris?" said Oswald.

"Of course I do. Paris will be the centre of operations. Barker wants me over there at once; and the minute I join him I begin to draw at the rate of eight hundred a-year. Just to go on with, you know, until the money falls in."

"Mark," said Oswald, after a pause, "will it be of any use my saying a word of warning to you?"

"On what subject?" returned Mark, looking up with surprise.

"On this subject. It seems to me that you are falling into another delusion; that the—"

"No, it will not be of any use," burst forth Mark in strange excitement "I might have known beforehand that you'd turn out my enemy upon the point. If gold and diamonds were dropping down in a shower from the skies you'd not stretch forth your hand to catch them. There's a mist before your eyes, Oswald, that prevents you seeing these things in their proper aspect."

He began to pace the room as he spoke, chafing considerably Why was it that these little hints of warning awoke the irritation of Mark's spirit? Could there be an undercurrent of doubt in his mind whether Oswald was right and he wrong? However it might be, one thing was certain—that no warning, let it come from whom it would, could do any good with Mark.

As he turned to face them again, Sara entered. An expression of alarm was on her face, and she closed the door before speaking. She had come to say that Caroline appeared worse; altogether different from usual.

Mark ran up the stairs; Miss Bettina put down her knitting to follow. Sara turned to Oswald Cray.

"She knows you are here, Oswald, and would like to see you. She wants to bid you goodbye. I think her saying that alarmed me more than anything."

Caroline was on the sofa as before. Very quiet, save for her panting breath. Her white hands lay listless, her face, dreadfully worn though it was, was calm, tranquil. She looked at them one by one, and slightly raised her hand as Oswald entered. He bent down to her, taking it in his.

"Thank you for all," she whispered.

The change in her countenance struck them. It so far frightened Mark as to take from him his self-possession. He pushed Oswald away.

"O Carine, what is it? You cannot be going to die! You must not die, now that all this good luck is coming upon me!"

She glanced up at him, her eyes wide open, as if she scarcely understood.

"There's the most beautiful home getting ready for you in Paris Carine," he resumed, his voice sounding as if he were on the verge of tears. "We'll live in the Champ Elysées; it is the loveliest spot, and you can't fail to grow better there, if we can only get your disease to turn. O Carine! don't leave me just when I am able to surround you with wealth and luxury again! This will be a greater and a surer thing than the Great Wheal Bang."

"Don't, Mark! I am going to a better home."

"But I can't let you go until I have atoned for the past! I—"

"Hush, hush!" she interrupted. "O Mark! if you only knew how welcome it is to me! I am going to be at peace after all the turmoil. I am going to rest."

"Do you want to go?" pursued Mark, half-resentfully. "Don't you care to get well?"

"I have not cared to get well since I came to England. That is, I have not thought I should," she returned between the gasps of her laboured breath. "When I heard the bell toll out for Prince Albert, I asked who was I that I should be spared when he was taken? The next world has seemed very near to me since then. As if the doors of it had been brought down to earth, and stood always open."

That the death of the Prince, brought so palpably, as may be said, before her, had taken a great hold on the mind of Mrs. Cray there was no doubt. Several times during her later weeks of illness she had alluded to it. Her principal feeling in relation to it appeared to be that of gratitude. Not gratitude for his death; there was only sorrow for that; but for the strange impression it had left upon her own mind, the vista of the Hereafter. For the good and great prince to be taken suddenly from the earthly duties so much needing him was only an earnest, had one been wanting, that he had entered upon a better and higher sphere. It seemed that he had but been removed a step; a step on the road towards heaven; and it most certainly in a measure had the effect of reconciling her to her own removal, of tranquillising her weary heart, of bringing her thoughts and feelings into that state most fitting to prepare for it. Often and often had she awoke from a deep sleep, starting suddenly up and calling out, "I thought I heard St. Paul's bell again?"

"I wish the Great Wheal Bang had been in the sea!" gloomily exclaimed Mark Cray, who was no more calculated for a scene such as this than a child, and had little more control over his tongue. "But for that mine turning out as it did your illness might never have come on."

"Don't regret it, Mark," she feebly said. "God's hand was in it all. I look back and trace it. But for the trouble brought to me then, I might never have been reconciled to go. It is so merciful! God has weaned me from the world before removing me from it."

Mark Cray drew a little back and stood gazing at his wife a gloomy helpless sort of expression on his countenance as his right hand nervously pushed back his hair. Oswald was at the head of the sofa, Sara near to him, and Miss Bettina was at the far end of the room, looking after some comforting medicine drops. Thus there was a clear space before the sofa, and the red light from the fire played on Caroline's wasted features. That she was dying—dying suddenly, as may be said—there could be no doubt.

"If things had not turned out so crossly!" began Mark again. "I knew I should redeem the misfortunes of that Wheal Bang. I always told you I should extricate myself, Caroline."

"We shall all be extricated from our misfortunes here," came from her dying lips. "A few years more or less of toil, and strife, and daily care, and then redemption comes. Not the redemption that we work. O Mark, if you could see things as I now see them! When we are on the threshold of the next world our eyes are opened to the poor value of this. Its worst cares have been but petty trials, its greatest heartache was not worth the pang. They were but hillocks that we had to pass in our journey upwards, and God was always leading us. If we could but trust to Him! If we did but learn to resign our hands implicitly to his and be led as little children!"

Mark Cray felt somewhat awed. He began to doubt whether it were exactly the time and place to pour forth regrets after the misfortunes of the Great Wheal Bang, or enlarge on the future glories opening to him in the French capital.

"It is so much better for me to be at rest! God is taking me to the place where change and sickness cannot enter. I shall see Uncle Richard: I shall see poor Richard who went before him: I shall see papa and mamma, whom I have nearly forgotten. We all go, some sooner, some later. This world lasts but a little minute; that one is the home, the gathering-place. Mark, dear Mark! the troubles here are of so little moment; they are only trifling hindrances through which we must bear on to Eternity. Oh, trust God! They are all sent by him."

There occurred an interruption. Mr. Welch, who had not been able to call before that day, came in, and the solemn feeling that had been stealing over those in the chamber gave place to the ordinary routine of everyday event.

"Before the morning," the surgeon said when he left, in answer to a grave question put to him by Miss Bettina.

CHAPTER LXIII

SIX MONTHS LATER

The first scenes of this story were laid in Hallingham, and it is only well that it should close there. Well or not, it cannot be helped; for the chief personages you have met in its course were now gathered in that town.

Caroline died in March, and this was the beginning of October; so you see several months have gone on in the year. The cold ungenial summer of 1862 had come to an end, and the Great Exhibition, characteristic of the year, was drawing to an end also. Ah! how we plan, and plot, and work, and a higher hand mars it! A higher wisdom than ours looks on, and overrules, and changes all things! The one brave, earnest spirit, who had worked with all the energy of his true heart to bring about and perfect that exhibition, was alone not spared to see its fruition. Was there a single heart, of all the multitudes that flocked to it, that was not weighed down with a latent sense of the something wanting, and of the exhibition's failure?—of its failure in a general point of view, and of our own short-seeing helplessness? The gilt had been taken off the gingerbread.

In the Abbey at Hallingham, settled in it, as she hoped, for life, was Miss Bettina. With the death of Mrs. Cray all necessity for Miss Davenal's remaining in London had ceased. In point of fact, it may be said to have ceased from the time Mark Cray and his wife went into Normandie; but she had stayed on. Very much disliking London, Miss Davenal made arrangements for leaving it as soon as she could do so with convenience, and in June had come back to Hallingham. Some difficulty arose about a residence; Miss Davenal was not one who could be put anywhere. She possessed some houses of her own in the town, good ones, but they were let. Oswald Cray it was who directed her attention to the Abbey. It had never been occupied since Mark's short tenancy of it; and at last, after some few alterations had been made in it, to the increase of its indoor comfort, Miss Davenal took it on a lease and entered into possession.

So far as human foresight may anticipate in this world of changes, she had settled down for life. The great barn of a drawing-room had been made into two apartments—handsome both, and of good proportions; the one was the drawing-room still, the other was Miss Davenal's bedchamber. A quiet, tranquil life she might expect to live here with her two handmaidens, Watton and Dorcas.

For Watton had settled down also after her rovings, and come back to Hallingham. Watton had not lightly or capriciously resigned her superior situation in London; but ever since the past winter, Watton had been ailing. She tried three or four doctors; she took, as she said, quarts of physic; but Watton could not get strong. There was no particular disorder, and she came at length to the conclusion that it must be London that disagreed with her; and she gave notice co quit her place. So she was installed once more upper maid to Miss Davenal, and seemed since the change to have got well all one way.

She would have more to do than she had in the old days at the doctor's, for there was no Neal now. Miss Davenal declined to try another manservant, probably from a conviction that she should never replace the services of that finished and invaluable domestic. Miss Davenal was by no means convinced of the treachery attributed to him by Captain Davenal, and at odd moments was apt to look upon the charge as emanating solely from the gallant captain's fanciful imagination.

Neal himself was flourishing. Considering the precaution he took to keep himself right with the world, there was not much probability that he would ever be otherwise. Neal had entered on a situation with one of her Majesty's ministers; his lordship's own personal attendant. It was to be hoped there'd be no opportunity afforded him of getting at any of the state secrets! Ah, how many of these rogues are there, besides Neal, filling confidential posts in the world! Will it be so to the end of their career? Will it be so with Neal? I sometimes wonder.

The Abbey was gay just now, in this same month of October, for Miss Davenal was entertaining a party in it. Sara had left it a fortnight past with Oswald Cray; and Captain Davenal, who had come down to give her away, had remained since, with his wife, on a visit to Miss Davenal. He called her Aunt Bett still: but she was more cordial with him than she used to be, for she had learnt really to love the sweet young wife. She was in the habit of assuring him that Rose was a greater treasure than he deserved; and in that he did not contradict her.

Two other visitors at the abbey were Dick and Leo. Poor Leo could not recover his health; Mrs. Keen grew timid about him, and it was decided that he should go back to his native place, Barbadoes, for a short while, and see what that would do. His father and mother felt persuaded it would effect wonders, and of course they thought nobody could take care of him as they could; so Leo was on the point of sailing. Mr. Dick, tolerated in the capacity of visitor as a necessary evil for his brother's sake, had come home to Sara's wedding, and was allowed to remain still, to see the last of Leo. Dick found the Michaelmas holidays delightful. What with getting inside the jam-closets, and making raids on sundry neighbouring gardens where the pears and apples grew too abundantly, and teasing Captain Davenal's son and heir—a noisy young gentleman, who promised to be another wicked Dick—and taking stealthy rides on the tops of the railway engines (lying out all tempting on the opposite side to the pears and apples) Mr. Dick found the time pass charmingly. Captain Davenal took him out shooting now and then, by way of a treat. One day that the captain was otherwise engaged, the gun disappeared, and Dick also; and Miss Bettina went all but into a real fit, expecting nothing less than to see him brought home with his head shot off. Dick, however, reappeared with his head on, and a pheasant and a partridge in his hand, which he had shot and brought home in open triumph, defying the game-laws. Miss Bettina wondered how long it would be before Dick came to the gallows.

There was one more visitor at the Abbey. And that was Mark Cray. Mark, however, had been there but for a day or two, not for the wedding. He had come to bear off Leo Davenal: for the compagnon de voyage and protector of Leo to the West Indies was to be no other than Mark.

Mark Cray was down in feather. Dreadfully so. After his wife's death Mark had made his way to Paris, to enter upon the brilliant career he supposed to be in readiness for him. Not quite ready, however, he found when he got there; some trifling preliminaries had to be completed yet. Mark thought nothing of the check: he was sanguine: Barker was sanguine; it was only a little delay: and Mark amused himself most agreeably, looking at the houses in the Champs Elysées, against the time came that he should require to fix upon one.

Mark's friends in England heard nothing of him until the middle of the summer; and then Mark himself appeared among them uncommonly crestfallen. That something was wrong, appeared evident. Mark gave little explanation, but news was gathered from other sources. It appeared that Mr. Barker's grand project, with "finance" for its basis, had come to grief. At the very hour of its (expected) fruition the thing had in some ingenious manner dropped through, and thereby entailed some temporary inconvenience, not to say embarrassment, on its two warm supporters, Barker and Mark. Of course it was entirely undeserved; a most cruel stroke of adverse, ill-natured fate; but nevertheless both of them had to bow to it. Mark Cray came over to England; and Barker was compelled to go into ignoble hiding, nobody but himself knew where, while he smoothed his ruffled plumes, and gathered his forces for a fresh campaign.

Reposing in quiet was all very well for Barker, who appeared to have some perpetual fund to draw upon somewhere: though, in point of fact, the man had not a penny in the world, and how he managed to get along in his tumbles down from luck, he alone could tell: but it was not well for Mark Cray. Mark had not the plead genius of Barker—or whatever you may please to call it—the talent of extracting funds from some quarter or other for daily wants. If Mark was not "in luck," Mark stood a chance of starving. When Mark went back to London he had no home, no money, it may be said no friends; and, but for his meeting Captain Davenal one day accidentally, Mark could not, that he saw, have gone on at all. Later, some real luck did come to Mark. His late wife's friends—who had never been made acquainted with the grand expectations of the great Paris scheme—wrote to tell Mark that through the unexpected death of one of the medical men in Barbadoes, an excellent practice might be secured by him if he chose to go out and step into it.

Be you very sure, Mark Cray did not hesitate. Hating the profession though he did, feeling an innate conviction within himself that he was ill-qualified for it, he yet decided to embrace it again as his calling and occupation in life. When it comes to starving with a man, there's not much choice. So the decision was made, and Mark Cray was going out immediately to Barbadoes, and was to take charge of Leopold Davenal.

Once before you saw Miss Davenal waiting in that Abbey for the return of a bridegroom and bride from their wedding-tour. She was so waiting in like manner now. Oswald Cray and his wife had stopped at Thorndyke for a day or two on their return, as they were now about to stop at Hallingham, on their way to their new home in London.

Not as the guests of Sir Philip Oswald. Sir Philip had gone to that place where visiting is not; and Sir Henry was the master of Thorndyke. He had wanted Oswald and Sara to stay the whole of their holiday there; but they had preferred a greater change.

Miss Davenal sat in her drawing-room. The October sun was getting low, but still the expected guests had not arrived. Near to Miss Davenal, nursing a dancing baby that would not be coaxed to stillness, was a pretty, gentle woman—Mrs. Davenal. Leo stood at the window, looking out, and Mark Cray sat in a distant chair, restless, and pushing back his hair as usual. Mark did not altogether relish the expected presence of his half-brother but there was no help for it. They had not met since Mark went off to Paris in the spring, largely telling Oswald that his debt to him would be paid with interest ere the year was out.

"Is not that a carriage, Leo?"

"No, Aunt Bettina, it's a baker's cart going by."

Miss Davenal caught enough of the reply to know that it was not what she asked after. "Where's Richard?" she presently said.

"I saw him over there on an engine just now," was Leo's answer, pointing towards the station.

"He'll be brought home on one some day, blown up. Rose, my dear, that baby is tiring you. Let Leo ring for the nurse."

Mrs. Davenal laughed, and was about to say that the baby did not tire her and she would rather keep him, when Dick burst in.

"It's coming down the road; it will be here in a minute. Look, Aunt Bett!"

He dashed across the room to the window as he spoke. Example is contagious, and they all followed him. One of the Thorndyke carriages was drawing up to the door. Excitable Dick quitted the window and flew down again.

They were soon in the room. Sara, with her sweet face at rest now, and Oswald behind her. A few moments given to greeting, and Sara had taken the baby, and Oswald was shaking hands with his brother.

"I had no idea we should find you here, Mark."

Mark answered something which nobody could catch, and Captain Davenal came in.

"Is Henry Oswald with you?"

"No," said Oswald. "He will be in Hallingham tomorrow. He sadly wanted us to stay longer with him, Miss Bettina, and go on straight to London from Thorndyke. What would you have said to that?"

"Thank you," said Miss Davenal, hearing it was impossible to say what. "I shall be happy to see him."

"Have you seen your old friends, Mark?" asked Oswald; "have you been out much?"

"I have not been out at all, and I have seen none of them," responded Mark, gloomily. "I don't want to see them."

"How's Mr. Barker? Have you heard from him lately?"

"I heard the day before I came here," replied Mark, a shade of brightness rising to his countenance. "Barker has all the luck of it in this world. He is in something good again."

"Again!" repeated Oswald, suppressing his strong inclination to laugh.

"So he writes me word. It's something he has taken in hand and is going to perfect. If it comes to anything I shall return from Barbadoes and join him."

"Oh," said Oswald. "Well, Mark, I hope you will have a pleasant voyage out there, and that you will find your journey all you can wish."

Dinner would soon be ready, and Sara was shown to her room. It overlooked the Abbey graveyard. She took off her bonnet and stood there, lost in many reminiscences of the past, in the changes that time had wrought, in the uncertain contemplation of the future. What would be poor Mark Cray's future? Would he abide at Barbadoes, applying himself as well as his abilities allowed him to the pursuit of his legitimate profession?—or would his unstable, weak mind be dazzled with these illegitimate and delusive speculations to the end, until they engulfed him?

How strangely, how wonderfully had they been brought through changes and their accompanying trials! In this very room, where she now stood, Oswald had been born. The poor little boy, sent adrift as may be said without a home, motherless, as good as fatherless, had worked out his own way in the world, striving always to make a friend of God. Ah, when did it ever fail? It is the only sure help in life.

And what had her own later troubles been; her cares, anxieties, sorrows? Looking back, Sara saw great cause to reproach herself: why had she so given way to despair? It is true that she had never, in a certain sense, a degree, lost her trust in God: but she had not believed there could be this bright ending. A little ray of the setting sun was reflected on the tombstone formerly noticed; it fell on the significant inscription, "Buried in misery." Sara wondered whether he, the unhappy tenant, had never learned to abide in God.

So absorbed was she in thought that she did not notice any one had come into the room, until a hand was laid upon her shoulder. It was her husband's. He put some letters down in the broad, old-fashioned window-seat.

"They have been sent on to me here from the office," he explained, as Sara glanced at them. "Business letters, all. In one there's a bit of gossip, though: in Allister's."

"Is one of them from Allister?"

"Yes. Jane's going to be married. They have met with some Scotch gentleman out there, an old acquaintance of Jane's, and things are settled. Frank says his tongue is broad Scotch, and he can't understand half he says. Jane does, however, so it's all right."

A smile played upon Sara lips, as she thought of the past jealousy. She might tell her husband of it some time. "Does Mr. Allister keep well!" she asked.

"He has been quite well ever since he went there: he says very strong. I hope it has set him up for life. What were you thinking of so deeply, Sara, that you did not hear me come in?"

"At the moment, I was thinking of that evening when you and I met there, in the graveyard," she answered, pointing down to it. "What a miserable evening it was!"

"Don't dwell on it, love. I cannot, without a pang of shame."

"Nay, but it is pleasant to look back upon it now, Oswald. It is pleasant to contrast that time with this."

He shook his head with a sort of shiver, and relapsed into silence, his hand thrown round her.

"Oswald," she resumed in a low tone, "won't you tell me what your suspicion was?"

"I will tell you some time, Sara; not now. Oh, my wife, my wife, how much is there in the past for many of us to repent of!" he continued in what seemed an uncontrollable impulse. "And it is only through God's mercy that we do repent."

She laid her head upon his shoulder and let it rest there. Its safe abiding-place, so long as the world, for them, should last.

Only through God's mercy. My friends, may it be shed on us all throughout our pilgrimage in this chequered life, and ever abide with us unto the end! Fare you well.

MRS HENRY WOOD (aka ELLEN WOOD) – A CONCISE BIBLIOGRAPHY

Danesbury House (1860)
East Lynne (1861)
The Elchester College Boys (1861)
A Life's Secret (1862)
Mrs. Halliburton's Troubles (1862)
The Channings (1862)
The Foggy Night at Offord: A Christmas Gift for the Lancashire Fund (1863)
The Shadow of Ashlydyat (1863)
Verner's Pride (1863)
Lord Oakburn's Daughters (1864)
Oswald Cray (1864)
Trevlyn Hold; or, Squire Trevlyn's Heir (1864)
William Allair; or, Running away to Sea (1864)
Mildred Arkell: A Novel (1865)
The Argosy (1865)
Elster's Folly: A Novel (1866)
St. Martin's Eve: A Novel (1866)
Lady Adelaide's Oath (1867)
Orville College: A Story (1867)
The Ghost of the Hollow Field (1867)
Anne Hereford: A Novel (1868)
Castle Wafer; or, The Plain Gold Ring (1868)
The Red Court Farm: A Novel (1868)
Roland Yorke: A Novel (1869)
Bessy Rane: A Novel (1870)
George Canterbury's Will (1870)
Dene Hollow (1871)
Within the Maze: A Novel (1872)
The Master of Greylands (1872)
Johnny Ludlow (1874)
Bessy Wells (1875)
Told in the Twilight: Containing 'Parkwater' and nine short stories (1875)
Adam Grainger: A Tale (1876)
Edina (1876)

Our Children (1876)
Parkwater: With four other tales (1876)
Pomeroy Abbey (1878)
Lady Adelaide (1879)
Johnny Ludlow, Second Series (1880)
A Tale of Sin and Other Tales (1881)
Court Netherleigh: A Novel (1881)
About Ourselves (1883)
Johnny Ludlow. Third Series (1885)
Lady Grace and Other Stories (1887)
The Story of Charles Strange (1888)
Featherston's Story. A Tale by Johnny Ludlow (1889)
The Unholy Wish and Other Stories (1890)
The House of Halliwell. A Novel (1890)
Ashley and Other Stories (1897)
Victor Serenus (1898)
Johnny Ludlow. Fifth series (1899)
Johnny Ludlow. Sixth series (1899)

Translations
Les Channing. Traduit de l'Anglais par Mme Abric-Encontre (1864)
Les Filles de Lord Oakburn: Roman traduit de l'anglais par L. Bochet (1876)
La Gloire des Verner: Roman traduit de l'anglais par L. de L'Estrive (1878)
Le Serment de Lady Adelaïde: Roman traduit de l'anglais par Léon Bochet (1878)

www.ingramcontent.com/pod-product-compliance
Lightning Source LLC
Chambersburg PA
CBHW060217030726
47499CB00004B/1082